Praise for *Ancient Evenings*

"Mailer's Egypt is a haunting and magical place, primeval, mysterious. The reader wallows in the scope, depth, the sheer magnitude and—yes—the fertility of his imagination."
—*The Washington Post Book World*

"[*Ancient Evenings*] makes a miraculous present out of age-deep memories, bringing to life the rhythms, the images, the sensuousness of a lost time."
—*The New York Times*

"Astounding, beautifully written . . . A leap of imagination that crosses three millennia to Pharaonic Egypt and returns that land's essences . . . the perfumes of its queens . . . the putrescences of the Nile . . . war, magic, the gods, death, reincarnation . . . lusts, ambitions, jealousies, betrayals . . . There is more to admire and enjoy in these pages than in ten ordinary novels."
—*USA Today*

"Pulses with life, richness, power and daring . . . Within this complex, often violent . . . story, the glory and brutality of ancient Egypt unfolds. Mailer's portrait of Ramses II gives fascinating life to the stone images, and his accounts of the field and the palace are moving, fascinating and often uproariously funny."
—*The Philadelphia Inquirer*

"Sensuous, superbly written . . . A symphony of spirit and earth, of smoldering sex and slumbering tombs . . . Mailer enchants and transports across a gulf of centuries and civilizations, yet the fears and lusts he irradiates with his gifts are unchanged millennia later."
—*Cosmopolitan*

"*Ancient Evenings* is like no book Norman Mailer has written. It is lush, sensuous, sexual beyond gender. A progressive revelation of mysteries, sacred and profane."

—*Vogue*

"Literally exhilarating . . . He has written a novel like no other . . . a new and permanent contribution to the possibilities of fiction and our communal efforts at self-discovery."

—*New Republic*

By Norman Mailer

Ancient Evenings

Ancient Evenings

A Novel

Norman Mailer

RANDOM HOUSE TRADE PAPERBACKS

NEW YORK

To my daughters, to my sons, and to Norris

I believe in the practice and philosophy of what we have agreed to call magic, in what I must call the evocation of spirits, though I do not know what they are, in the power of creating magical illusions, in the visions of truth in the depths of the mind when the eyes are closed; and I believe . . . that the borders of our mind are ever shifting, and that many minds can flow into one another, as it were, and create or reveal a single mind, a single energy . . . and that our memories are part of one great memory, the memory of Nature herself.

W. B. Yeats, *Ideas of Good and Evil*

Contents

I

The Book of One Man Dead

Crude thoughts and fierce forces are my state. I do not know who I am. Nor what I was. I cannot hear a sound. Pain is near that will be like no pain felt before.

Is this the fear that holds the universe? Is pain the fundament? All the rivers veins of pain? The oceans my mind awash? I have a thirst like the heat of earth on fire. Mountains writhe. I see waves of flame. Washes, flashes, waves of flame.

Thirst is in the rivers of the body. The rivers burn but do not move. Flesh—is it flesh?—lies beneath some heated stone. Lava rises in burned-out fields.

Where, in what cavern, have such disruptions taken place? Volcanic lips give fire, wells bubble. Bone lies like rubble upon the wound.

Is one human? Or merely alive? Like a blade of grass equal to all existence in the moment it is torn? Yes. If pain is fundament, then a blade of grass can know all there is.

A burning number came before me. The flame showed an edge as unflickering as a knife, and I passed into that fiery sign. In fire I began to stream through the clear and blazing existence of the number 2.

Pain entered on a pulse. Each rest between each pang was not enough—oh, the twisting of hope, the tearing of fiber. My organs had surely distorted, yes, and the shriek of bone when it cracked. Doors opened into blasts.

Pain took abode in the most brilliant light. I was exposed to burning rock. Demonic, the heat of the sun, and blood boiling in the veins. Would it never be blood again? The current of the highest fires told me then—by the intensity itself—that I would not be destroyed. There had to be some existence on the other side. So I let go of my powers as they charred in my heart. These dying powers might yet give life to other parts of me. For I could see a thread quivering in the darkness, a tendril alive in the smoked-up carbon of my meats, fine as the most exquisite nerve, and through each pain, I looked for this filament in every refinement of anguish, until pain itself took on such radiance that I knew a revelation. The filament was not one thread, but two, wound about each other in immaculate delicacy. They twisted together during the most intolerable spasms, yet were quick to draw apart at the first relief, and with such subtlety of movement that I was certain I witnessed the life of my soul (seen at last!) dancing like a dust-tail above the flame.

Then all was lost again. My bowels quaked with oceanic disruption, ready to jettison whole fats, sweetmeats and gravies of the old pleasure-soaked flesh, frantic as a traitor springing his leaks under torture. I would give up anything to ride lighter in the next wave of odium, and in the darkness of waves of flesh smacking raw waters of sound, I labored.

I could not bury myself in such sulphurs. It was not the fumes, but the terror of suffocation; not death by fire, but the soil burying me. It was the clay! A vision came forward of clay sealing the nostrils and the mouth, my ears, and into the sockets of my eyes—I had lost all vision of the double filament. There was only myself in these buried caves and the hammering of my gut. Yet if I were to be buried in the murk of these screaming scalding wastes, I had gained a vision with which to torment myself. For I comprehended the beauty of my soul at just the moment I could not reach its use. I would perish with such ideas even as I gained them!

A moment of peace arrived then in this storm and tumult of the pipes. I knew the solemn desolation of the subsided center of the hurricane, and in that calm I saw with sorrow that I might now be wise without a life on which to work my wisdom. For I had a view of old dialogues. Once I had lived like master and slave—now both were lost to each new seizure—oh, the lost dialogue that had never taken place between the bravest part of me and the rest. The coward had been the master. Something came apart then in the long aisles of my pride, and I had a view into the fundament of pain, the view as beautiful as it was narrow. But now the mills of vituperation were turning again. Like a serpent whose insides have blown apart, I gave up, sued for peace, and gave birth to my bloody clotting history of coiled and twisted eviscerate. Some totality of me went out of my belly, and I saw the burning figure of the 2 dissolve in flame. I would be no longer what I had been. My soul felt pained, humbled, furious at loss, and still arrogant as beauty itself. For the pain had ceased and I was new. I had a body again.

One

The darkness was deep. Yet I had no doubt. I was in an underground chamber ten paces in length by half in width, and I even knew (just as quickly as a bat) that the room was all but empty. Stone was the surface of the walls and the floor. As if I could see with my fingers, I had only to wave an arm to feel the size of the space beyond my reach. It was exactly so remarkable as to hear voices by the hairs of one's nose. For that matter, I could smell the scent of stone. Say that an absence was in the air, some hollow that dwelt within another hollow. Now I was aware of a granite coffer near to me, as aware, indeed, of its presence as if my body had walked within—it was huge enough to be my bed! But a step away, as if on guard, were some aged droppings on the floor, pellets from a small fierce animal who had managed like myself to find its way here, and left its deposit and gone. For there was no skeleton to speak of the beast. Just the scent of some old urine-cursed dung— But where was the passage by which the animal could have entered? I breathed in the horror that comes when the air is close with an animal's mean excrement. That has its own message to give!

Yet, I could also recognize a pure bouquet of fresh night air that had chosen to enter this chamber. Had it come from a shaft in the rock used by the cat?

In the dark, between two blocks of stone, my fingers soon found a niche not much greater in width than a man's head. Still, by its fresh breath, it must lead outside. The air that arrived through the shaft was only a whisper, not strong enough to stir one hair on a feather, but it offered the cool of the desert when the sun has been down for much of the night. Toward that cool murmur, I stretched, and to my surprise was able to follow my arm up the niche. It was a long shaft between great blocks of stone, and in places seemed no wider than my head, but it went in a straight line at a steep angle upward, a filthy trip. The dead shells of countless beetles cluttered my way. Ants went by my skin. Rats piped in high terror. Still, I climbed with no panic, only in surprise at the narrow dimensions of this passage. Surely I was not able to make my way through—it was hardly larger than the burrow of a snake—yet I might as well have been without shoulders or hips. Cunning was in my touch as if, like a snake, there was no fear of being caught in the passage ahead. I was capable of becoming narrower. But that is no better than to say I traveled with my thoughts through the long narrow shaft, my body sufficiently supple to obey—a most peculiar sensation. I felt altogether alive. The whisper of the air before me had phosphorescence. Particles of light glowed in my nose and throat. I was more alive than I could ever remember and yet felt no yoke of muscle and bone. It was as if I had been reduced to the size of a small boy.

When I lay at last near the mouth of the passage, my view was of the sky at the end of the shaft and moonlight slanted over the edge. As I rested, the moon passed full into view and anointed me. From orchards in the distance came a scent of date and fig trees, and the clear refreshment of the vines. The air on this night gave intimations to me of gardens where once I made love. I knew again the smell of rose and jasmine. Far below, by the riverbank, the palms by the shore would be black in outline against the silver water of the river.

So I came out at last from the end of the shaft in that great hill of stone. I stuck my head and shoulders into the open night, pulled through my legs, and gasped. Beneath the light of the moon was a long white slope of stone with the earth far below, but out there on the plateau of the desert, mute as a mountain of silver, there at the end of my gaze, was a Pyramid. Beyond it, another. Nearer to me, all but covered in sand, was a stone lion with the head of a man. I was perched on the slope of the Great Pyramid! I had just been—it could be nowhere else—in the burial chamber of the Pharaoh Khufu.

Harsh as the sound of a man's snore was the name of Khufu. He was gone a thousand years, and more. Yet, at the thought of having been in His tomb, my body was too weak to move. The sarcophagus of Khufu had been empty. His tomb had been found and robbed!

I thought my heart would strike its last sound. My stomach had never felt so pure a slop of cowardice. Yet I was a man of valor, as I seemed to remember, perhaps a soldier, renowned for something— so, I could swear—all the same, I could not move a step. In shame I shivered beneath the moon. There I was, on the slope of our greatest Pyramid, moonlight on my head and heart, the statue of the immense lion below, and the Pyramids of the Pharaoh Khaef-ra and the Pharaoh Men-kau-ra to the south. To the east, I saw the moon on the Nile and far to the south, I even saw the last of the lights in the lamps of Memphi where mistresses were waiting for me. Or were they waiting for another by now? I was so reduced as to think it did not matter. Had I ever had a thought like this before?—I, whose first fear used to be that I was too ready to kill any man who looked at my woman? How exhausted I felt. Was this the price I paid for entering the tomb of Khufu? In gloom, I began to make my way down, sliding from crack to crack in the limestone, and knew some foul change had taken place in me already. My memory, which had given every promise (in the first glow of moonlight) that it would return, was still a sludge. Now the air was heavy with the odor of mud. That was the aroma of these lands, mud and barley, sweat and husbandry. By noon tomorrow, the riverbank would be an oven of moldering reeds. Domestic animals would leave their gifts on the mud of the bank—sheep and pigs, goats, asses, oxen, dogs and cats, even the foul odor of the goose, a filthy bird. I thought of tombs, and of friends in tombs. Like the plucking of a heavy string came a first intimation of sorrow.

Two

I was in the most peculiar situation. I still did not know who I was, nor how old I might be. Was I mature and powerful, or young and in the beginning of my strength? It hardly seemed to matter. I shrugged, and began to walk, taking, for whatever reason, a path through the Necropolis, and as I meandered, I began to explain to myself what I saw, or so I would put it, for I felt in the oddest position, and like a stranger to my own everyday knowledge.

Before me, I must say, was no more to see than the straight streets of this cemetery in the moonlight, a view without great charm, unless there is charm to be found in high value. Cubit for cubit, the city of the dead had the dearest plots in all of Memphi, or at least that is what I certainly remember.

Wandering down the alleys of our monotonous Necropolis, sauntering past the shuttered door of one tomb, then another, I began—for no reason I could give—to think of a friend who had died recently, the dearest of my friends, this memory seemed to say, and the most absurd and violent death. Now, I had no more than to wonder whether his tomb was anywhere near about, and was visited with more recollections. My friend, I was ready to think, came from a powerful family. His father, if I could recall, had once served as Overseer of the Cosmetic Box—I would die, I thought, before lusting after such titles myself. Still, that was not a career to be sneered at altogether. Our Ramses, if I remembered correctly, was as vain as a beautiful girl, and detested any flaw in His appearance.

Of course, with such a father, my friend (whose name, I fear, still eluded me) was certainly wealthy and noble. Poor entombed bugger! He must be, at the least, a descendant of the great Ramses, yes, the one, I could recall, who died something like a hundred years ago, our own Ramses the Second. He had ended as a very old man with a great many wives and more than a hundred recorded sons and fifty daughters. They produced ancestors in such numbers that today you cannot begin to estimate how many officers and priests are Ramessides by at least half of their line. For truth, hardly a rich woman in Memphi or Thebes will fail to offer one bona-fide cheek of her buttocks, royal as the Pharaohs, and she will not fail to let you know. To be descended from Ramses the Second may not be exceptional, but it is indispensable—at least if she wants a family plot in the Necropolis. Then, she had better be, at least by half, a Ramesside. In fact, you cannot even buy a tomb in the Western Shade if you are not, and that is only the first requirement in such commerce among Memphi matrons. There are not enough plots. So they go to great lengths. For instance, the mother of my dead friend, the matron Hathfertiti, was always prepared to trade. If the price was good enough, the sarcophagus of an ancestor could be transferred to an inferior tomb, or even shipped downriver to another necropolis. Of course one had to ask: Who was the deceased? How substantial was his curse? That was the unspoken part of the transaction—you had to be ready to take on a few malevolent oaths. But some were ready to welcome them if they were terrible enough to bring the price down. For example, Hathfertiti had been bold enough to sell the tomb of her dead grandfather. Concerning this dead relative, her husband's grandfather (who happened incidentally to be her own grandfather since she was certainly her husband's sister) it was told to the buyer that old man Menenhetet had been the kindest and most benign of men. His vice was that he could not harm his enemies. His curse need hardly be feared. What torture of the truth! In secret, it was whispered that Menenhetet had been known to eat fried scorpions with bat dung—just so great was his need to protect himself against the curses of the powerful. He had had a mighty life, I seemed to remember.

Now the buyer to whom Hathfertiti was selling this plot, an ambitious little official, was not untypical. He knew the best protection against any evil spell was for a petty Ramesside like himself to own a fine tomb. So long as he had none to offer his family, every visit of his wife and daughters to the better homes of Memphi was bound to fail. They simply had no position in the ranks of the dead. So they were living already with a curse—they were snubbed. For what is a curse but an unfair theft of strength? (Whatever is attempted in the way of improving your position brings back less than the effort exerted.) This Ramesside's wife and daughters began to weep so often that he was ready to take his chances with the wrath of the dead grandfather. Maybe if he knew more about the old man, Menenhetet, he would have waited, but he felt the awe of acquiring a possession that is beyond one's means but absolutely fashionable.

My recollections of these transactions seem to have had a purpose. Now I remember my friend's name! It is Menenhetet the Second. (The name is, by the way, a typical example of family affectation— Menenhetet the Second—as though his mother were a queen.) Yet I do not know if he was so royal as that. All I remember is that he was a hellion among us, his friends, and on certain nights was so full of wild impulses that he could have summoned demons. I think some of us began to regret the nickname, Ka, that we gave him. It seemed clever at the time, since it not only means *twice* (for Menenhetet Two) but is also our good Egyptian name for your Double when you are dead, and the Double has a changeable personality, it is said. So it fit him. With our friend Ka, you could never know when he would take on a lion, but then he also liked to swear vile things against the Gods and that left us uneasy. There was not much piety among us, far from it, and part of our pride was to be man enough to take the name of a God in vain, but Ka went too far. We did not like to share his blasphe-

mies when they were uttered, after all, for no better reason than ungovernable rage at his mother. For when Hathfertiti sold the tomb of
Menenhetet the First to the petty Ramesside, Ka soon learned that it
had been his tomb as well. At least by the terms of the will of his
great-grandfather, Menenhetet the First.

Now, standing in the moonlight of the Necropolis, full of a sorrow I could hardly comprehend for the death of Menenhetet the Second, I do not know if I was there when Hathfertiti spoke to him
about the tomb—although I would suppose that Ka was left nothing.
All the same, the details are not clear to me. It is better to state that
this is what I seem to recall. Should we say I was like a boat poling my
way into the harbor through the openings of a fog? Now, even as I
took stock of my position here on one of the meanest alleys of the
Necropolis, I had the impression that I was not far from the cheap
plot Hathfertiti had had to purchase in a great hurry after his sudden
death. Recollections came again of a pious funeral but a mean tomb.
Into my ear now came the sound of Hathfertiti's voice telling all who
would listen that Ka's desire was to be on the lowest edge of the Western Shade. That was a scandal. As everyone knew, Hathfertiti was
simply too stingy to pay the price for a decent chamber. Still, Hathfertiti kept to the same sad tale: Meni had kept having a dream, she
said, that he must rest at first in a mean abode. But when he was ready
to move, she would receive a message in her sleep. Then she would
shift him to a fine property. All this was uttered in such loud lamentation that those who heard her were repelled. It was no part of our
etiquette, after all, to encourage any of the seven souls, shades, and
spirits of a dead man to pay visits back to the living. The aim, suppos-
edly, of a funeral is to send all seven off with comfort to the Land of
the Dead. So we had a natural fear of a man who had gone out vio-
lently. His ghost could keep up an obstreperous relation to his family.
It is precisely at such funerals that the bereaved must take great pains
to placate the dead man rather than scorn him. It was foolhardy, in
that case, for Hathfertiti to avow that she would soon shift her son's
coffin to her best crypt. Everyone knew she was keeping that tomb

for herself. We even wondered if her real intent might be to goad our Menenhetet Two into the tormented journeys of a ghost! Worse! The funeral might have been lavish, but the tomb itself was so mean that grave robbers would hardly fear to break it open. (The curse that robbers take on themselves at the door of a poor tomb is, after all, rarely forceful. That is because the greater malevolence is between the poor departed and the relatives who left him so poor!) One had to wonder then if Hathfertiti was making certain that the vault of her son would be defiled.

I had come to the head of the alley that led to Meni's vault, and from there had a view. Many of these tombs were no larger than shepherds' huts (although only in the Necropolis do you find such huts of marble) but each roof was a miniature pyramid with a hole on the steep front. By that alone you could know you were in the Necropolis since the hole was the window for the Ba. If every dead man had a Double and we knew it as his Ka, he also had his own intimate little soul, the Ba, the most intimate of the seven powers and spirits. This Ba had the body of a bird and the face of the deceased. That was the reason I remembered now for the arched little window in these steep little pyramids. An exit for the Ba. Yes, it was coming back to me. Of course! Any bird I could see in a tower window here would be the Ba of whoever was in the sarcophagus below. For which common bird was likely to come near when Necropolis ghosts were about? And I shivered. Necropolis ghosts were hideous—all those unappeased officials and unrewarded warriors, priests unjustly punished and noblemen betrayed by near relatives, or, even more common, the ghost of robbers killed in the act of violating a tomb. Worst of all, the victims of the robbers—all those mummies whose wrappings had been violated while the thieves poked about for jewels. Such mummies proved to smell the worst. Think of what vengeful corruption has to be present in any well-wrapped corpse that succumbs eventually to rot, after rot has been prevented. That has to double the effect. Whatever!

I now met a ghost. He was not three doors from Meni's tomb, and

I must say he had a malignity to leave me faint. Close to the worst kind, he was recognizable by his rags as a grave robber. He was also proprietor of a stench beyond measure. It now descended on me.

In the moonlight, I saw a wretch with no hands and a leper's nose collapsed into three tatters. A misery, that nose, a mockery of the triple phallus of Osiris, Lord of the Dead, yet a nose still able to twitch beneath his wild yellow eyes. He was certainly a full ghost. I could see him as clearly as my hand, yet I could see through him.

"For whom do you look?" he cried out, and his breath, if it had consisted of dead crabs rotting in the worst mud of the Nile, would have been a fragrance compared to the horrors that lived on his wind.

I merely lifted my hand to drive him away. He scuttled backward.

"Do not go into the tomb of Menenhetet One," he said.

He should have terrified me but did not. I could not understand why. If he had failed to retreat and I had been obliged to drive him away, it might have been worse than plunging my fist into a thigh gone on gangrene. He was a pale of repulsion into which you did not dare advance. Yet he was afraid of me. He would not approach any closer.

All the same, I had hardly escaped without cost. His words entered my head with his reek. I did not know what he meant. Had Menenhetet One also been moved into this cheap tomb bought for Menenhetet Two? Was that a new event? Or was I in the wrong street? But if my memory had a foundation, this was the narrow alley to which the mourners had marched on that high sun-filled day when prize white oxen with their horns gilded gold and their white flanks decorated in green and scarlet paint had pulled the golden sledge of Meni Two to his last appalling home. Was this ghost attempting to mislead me?

"Do not enter the tomb of Menenhetet One," he intoned again. "Too much disturbance will result."

That he, this invader of graves, was now ready to warn others, made me laugh. In the moonlight, my merriment must, however, have stirred the shadows, for the ghost recoiled. "There is more I could tell you," he blurted out, "but I cannot bear your stench," and he was gone. The subtlest punishment he had suffered was to think his own odor came from others. So he would go blundering through every encounter.

Now, right on his disappearance, I saw the Ba of Meni Two. It appeared at the window. The Ba was not even the size of a hawk, and its face was as small as a newborn child, yet it was Meni's face, the most handsome I had ever seen on a man. Now reduced, his features were exquisite, as if an infant had been born with the intelligence of a full-grown adult. What a face! If it now gazed on me, it looked away immediately. Then the Ba of Menenhetet Two opened its wings and with a doleful sound, ugly as a crow in its full funds of pessimism, cawed once, cawed twice, and flew away. Depressed by such indifference to me, I moved to the door of the tomb.

As I stood in the portal, I was drenched in the most sudden and lamentable sorrow, huge and simpleminded, as though his own grief came to me from my dead friend Meni. I sighed. My last memory of this place was the slattern appearance of the entrance, and that had not changed. I remember thinking it would be easy to violate, and once again I felt that sense of accommodation which allowed me earlier this night to pass out of the narrow shaft from Khufu's chamber. Now, my finger flowed, or so it felt, into the grooves of the wooden keyhole. When I turned my hand, the prong rose, and with it, the bolt.

I stepped into the tomb. It made me aware of my skin as if a fingernail had touched my scalp. A cat's tongue could have been scraping the soles of my feet. They tingled. I had a frightful sense of disorder and stink. The moon was shining through the open door, and by that light I could see that any offerings of food which had been left were long ago gorged by robbers. Valuables were broken or gone. The thieves' passion to besmirch was evident all over the place. What an outpouring of the coffers of the gut! Full payment! I was in a fury. The slovenliness of the caretakers! In that instant, my eye saw a charred stick in a bronze sconce on the wall and on the full rise of my rage I glared at it so fiercely that I was hardly surprised when smoke unfolded, the charcoal at the tip began to gleam, and the torch was lit.

I had heard of priests who could concentrate their wrath enough to start a fire by the light of their eye, but rarely believed such tales. Now, it seemed, if anything, more natural than striking sparks on dried wood.

What a waste! Floods of future chaos lived in the discontents of these unruly thieves. Beware of those who live at the bottom of the kingdom! They had smashed as much as they had stolen. It obliged me to think of how exquisite Meni's apartment had been in the last years of his life, and, on the instant, I could recollect Hathfertiti sobbing even as she tried to consult me on which of his alabaster vases and collarplates, his bracelets and jeweled girdles were to be buried with him. Should she inter his long box of ebony or his chest of redwood, his blond wig, his white wig, his red, his green, his silver, or his black wig, his cosmetic case, his linen loincloths, his full linen skirts, even his ebony bed (which I knew she was desperate to keep for herself, and did). Then, how to choose among the weapons, the gilt bow and gold-painted arrows, the spear with the jewels in the shaft—were all these delightful items to accompany him to the tomb? In the middle of such reveries, she would cry out, "Poor Meni!" and added pious lamentations that would have sounded absurd in any voice less deep than her own. "The fruit of my eye has been eaten," she would scream at the white walls in this serene wing of their villa, his superb wing, his eye for the finest works he could afford never more evident than by his absence, and she, a picture! debauched by her sense of loss, her heart twisted by the obligation to bury so many of these jeweled prizes and golden beauties. She wept over his baby chair, a masterpiece of bronze with gold foil laid in, wept so long she kept it. Even his knives, his palette box, and brushes she could hardly bear to entomb, while his axe blade—a treasure from the reign of Thutmose the Third with a hollow grillwork within the blade to depict a wild dog eating a gazelle from behind—well, Hathfertiti's nose began to bleed before she could recognize that this, having been a gift to her son, could not be taken back. Of course, this enabled her to keep other objects, particularly his crown of feathers, his leopard skin, and his scarab of green onyx with all six of the beetle's legs in gold. Be certain that whichever part of Meni's collection was finally sent to the tomb turned out to be the true ratio between Hathfertiti's greed (eight parts) and Hathfertiti's belief in the power of an after-world (five parts). But then she would never allow herself to succumb altogether to greed. That could leave a hole through which demons would pour. Once, she had even given me a lecture on Maat, predictably the most pious sermon you could receive. For Maat was rightthinking, and never cheating one's neighbor. Maat was the virtue of balance, yes, Hathfertiti in the midst of the roaring waters of her greed could still speak respectfully of Maat. Without it, what is there she would not have kept for herself?

Yet with the torch in my hand, I would never accuse Hathfertiti of any excess of right-thinking. Witness the scatter on the floor! At the least, she had given a welcome to robbers who had no sense of Maat at all. Their urine was on the food, and do not speak of what was caked on the gold plates they left behind.

The next room proved worse. The burial chamber had not even been dug beneath, but was merely a continuation of this room. There was no more for partition than a wall of mud-brick. Cheap! There was no barrier to passing from the offering chamber right into the burial chamber. Still, I hesitated. I did not want to go in.

The air was different as I crossed the second threshold. There was the faintest suggestion of an odor so fearful I came to a stop. My torch was not steady and shook with twice the upheaval I expected. Of course. Not one sarcophagus but two. Both smashed. The outer coffins had their covers thrown into a corner. The lid of each inner coffin was also torn off. And the mummy cases, now exposed, revealed the thefts. Wherever a gem had been plucked, the high patina of the surface was marred with a small crater of plaster. All the collars and amulets were gone. Of course. And the painted face and chest of Meni (the portrait as beautiful as he had once been beautiful) was scarred. Three vertical slashes distorted the nose. Some crude attempt had been made to knife through the wrappings on the chest.

Such damage was small compared to the feet! The robbers had started to undo the windings there. A hopeless tatter of linen wrap-

pings covered the floor, some in bandages of endless length, others in
squares and scraps. A litter underfoot. An animal might have been
collecting materials for a nest. Even the bones of a chicken. The robbers had eaten in here. If my nose was true, they had not dared to
defecate as well, not in here with the wrapped bodies! Still, the origin
of that faint but unsettling odor was clear. One of the exposed feet
was beginning to molder.

In a corner, the other sarcophagus was equally disturbed. It could
belong only to Menenhetet One. He had been moved here by Hathfertiti in time to be violated. My legs, however, were not about to
take me in his direction. No. I did not dare to go near the mummy of
the great-grandfather.

Near to me, however, was Meni, his feet uncovered and his tomb
despoiled. The food for his Ka had been gobbled by the thieves. That
infuriated me. I could see his aura well, and its three bands of light
were of a pale violet hue as near to invisible as three ridges of hills
behind one another on a misty evening.

I did not like to look at it. There was every message to be read in
the color of an aura. Hathfertiti in a rage had an unmistakable separation of orange, blood-red, and brown, whereas the former Pharaoh,
they said, had an aura of pure white, pure silver, and gold. This pale
violet light about my friend's wrapped body spoke, however, of exhaustion, as if what little was left of him might be trying to maintain
some calm among many horrors. Be it said, the first of these had to be
the presence of the other sarcophagus. At the thought of looking at
the great-grandfather's remains, I put my torch down in confusion.
Immediately, it went out. I had a sense of how much strength must be
used by Meni Two merely to withstand the presence of the other.

Yet now this oppression seemed to ease. I do not know if it was
due to my effort—suddenly, I felt very tired—but in any case, Meni's
aura brightened. The air eased. I felt an impulse to study what was left
of his poor foot.

That was the worst choice I could have made. In the hole at the toe
was a feast of worms. In those pullulations who could know how
much of his foot was gone? The aura was absent here. Near the toes,

no glow was left but for the faint pale-green light that rose from the body of the maggots themselves.

Then, as I watched, the aura swelled again. I saw a snake crawl into the doorway of the burial chamber. Seizing the torch, I struck one overhead blow at its head, then another, and caught it. The body whipped in a final dance. Right after the last quiver, my torch began to burn. Nor did I hesitate to carry the light back with me. I had an impulse to look again at the worms.

But studying the cavity of Meni's foot, that white and feeding mill, I was aware suddenly of a bruise on the ball of my own foot. To what length must friendship be pursued that I must now limp in company with my old companion? A detestation rose in me against the corruption of his body. I was ready to put my torch to the hole in his foot, fry his worms, seal the putrefying flesh. In fact, I started to do so, but drew back from the fear I might suffer a scorched foot myself. Now I was hungry, suddenly and maniacally hungry. I clamped my jaws against the beginning of this prodigious desire for it would have had me sniffing like a dog at the Canopic jars beside the coffin, those four jars of the Sons of Horus each the size of a fat cat, but the carved head of Hep, the ape, held the carefully wrapped small intestines of the dead man, and the jar watched over by Tuamutef, the jackal, could offer the same for the heart and the lungs, while Amset, with the head of a man, now owned the stomach and large intestines, even as Qebhsenuf, the hawk, carried the liver and the gall bladder. To my horror, thoughts of a broth to be boiled out of these preserved organs would not leave my head, no matter how I drew back from so hideous a temptation. On the other hand, I had to satisfy my hunger. I could hardly leave the tomb, cross the Necropolis, walk all the way to the Nile, then find a food shop with a fire and some old witch to feed me, no, not at this hour. Food had to be found here. Near to panic from the onslaught of such obscene desires, I found myself on my knees and I was praying. The wonder was that I remembered. But, oh, those worms in the unwrapped and swarming hole of the foot. They provided the prayer.

"When the soul has departed," I said softly, the light from my

torch casting shadows on the ceiling, "a man sees corruption. He becomes a brother to decay and he sinks into a myriad of worms, he
becomes nothing but worms. . . .

"Homage to Thee, Divine Father Osiris. Thou did not wither,
Thou did not rot, Thou did not turn into worms. So will my members have being everlasting. I shall not decay, I shall not rot, I shall not
putrefy, and I shall not see corruption."

My eyes were closed. I looked within myself deep into the darkness of the blackest earth I had ever seen, black as the Land of Kemt,
our Egypt, and in that blackness I heard my words reverberate, as in
the tolling of a large bell at the tithe-taker's gate below Memphi, and
knew these words had a buoyancy greater than the ascension of
prayers on odors of incense. The echo reverberating in the closed
darkness of my eyes, I could contain my hunger no longer, and held
up my arm with all five fingers extended as if to say, "With these five
fingers, I would eat," and turned in a circle, committing myself to
Gods or demons I did not know.

In reply, five scorpions came in file out of the hawk-faced jar of
Qebhsenuf, God of the West, the liver, and the gall bladder, and
crossed the floor from the bier of Menenhetet One up to the hole in
the wrappings of Menenhetet Two. There, they began, I assume—
for I was not ready to look—to devour the worms. Did they go on to
the flesh of Two? I do not know, but my sore foot burned with the
fiery spice of a nest of ants.

Three

As if to mock me for my desperation in this dreadful place, I thought of an evening in Memphi full of food and wine and the sweetest conversation. I did not know if it was a day ago, or a year, but I was visiting with a priest at his sister's house, and in that month—what a lively month for me!—I had been the sister's lover. The priest—did I remember him truly as a priest?—had been (like many another good brother) her lover for years. How we talked. We discussed every subject but which one of us should make love to the sister.

She was, of course, excited by our appearance together—did she not have every right to be? When he left the room, she whispered for me to wait and watch her brother and herself. A girl from a good family! At just the right moment, she said, she would put herself into position above him. She hoped I would be ready then to mount her. She promised to be able to receive us both. What a wife she would make! Since I had already had her by other mouths, so to speak, I was pleased at what she planned to save for me—this lady's buttocks were the equal of a panther (a plump panther). But then if you were lucky, you could get a sniff of the sea by any of her ports. Or catch the worst swamp. She could give you the sweet and subtle stink that was in the best of the mud—the smell of Egypt, I swear—or be as fragrant as a young plant. A lady with gifts enough for both of us, and I did as she said that night, and soon proved to the priest that the living could find their double as quick as the dead (because he soon lost all sense of who was more of a woman, his sister or himself—except that he alone was completely shaved of hair—a way to learn where we were in the middle of this embrace).

Glimpsing such memories, however, certainly made my hunger worse. Like a wound that throbs, its fury was now increasing with every breath. It was not love I wanted to make, but food I needed to gorge upon.

I had to be in some fatal fever—it was certain I had never felt a hunger like this before. My stomach felt drawn down a long dark hall and pictures of food danced before me. I thought of that instant at the Beginning when the God Temu created all of existence with one word. The kingdom of silence had come to life in the gathering of sound from the heart of Temu.

Ergo, I raised my arm once more, fingers pointing to the unseen sky above this ceiling, and I said, "Let there be food."

But there was nothing. Only a small whimper reverberated into the empty space. I was faint with the emptiness of the effort. My fever burned. Before my closed eyes, I saw a small oasis. Was deliverance being offered? I trudged through the litter on the floor, as if crossing an imaginary desert—how real it was: the sand stung my nostrils! Now I was in the corner, and by the light of my torch, saw lovely paintings on the sides of Meni's broken coffin. They were portraits of food. All the rich food that the Ka of Meni Two might request when hungry was there, a dinner for a dozen friends with tables and bowls, vessels and jars, vases and animal joints, thighs hanging from hooks, all painted on the wall of this broken coffin. What a masterpiece of offerings! Domestic fowl and winged wild game I could see, ducks and geese, partridge and quail, tame meats and meats of the wild bull and wild boar, loaves of bread and cakes, figs and wine and beer and green onions and pomegranates and grapes, melons and the fruit of the lotus.

It was painful to look. I did not dare to search my mind for the words of power (which I must once have learned) that could now bring to me a portion of this painted food, bring it out where I might sup upon it, no, the food painted here was for Meni Two, a resource to be used by him if his other gifts of game and fruit were stolen.

Then I had the thought of betraying Meni, and was surprised to realize—given my damnable and fragmentary memory—that he must be a true friend to me. For I discovered that I had no wish to raid this store of painted provisions; on the contrary, my voracity seemed quieted by my scruple. As I stared at the painted food, hunger softened into that more agreeable state when appetite is about to be satisfied. Lo! With no effort at all, my jaws were working, and a piece of duck, or so it tasted (neatly broiled upon well-managed embers) was in my mouth, and juices—no longer was I ravenous—of its meat ran agreeably down the empty corridor to my stomach. I was even tempted to take the food away from my lips and look at it, but curiosity was no folly to be tolerated by the satisfaction of a moment like this. Besides I was overcome by the generosity of my friend Meni. He must have taken full recognition of his own need for food, yet had given me some (by way I suppose of his influence in the Land of the Dead).

More food came, flavors in plenty, ox-meat and goose, figs and bread, one taste of each. It was amazing how little food was required to satisfy what had been such a huge hunger. In my stomach, for instance, was the sensation of a full tankard of beer I had not knowingly swallowed. But I felt so nice as to be mildly drunk, and even burped (with a taste of copper from the tankard) and found myself saying the end of the prayer that accompanies the petition for food. So heavy was the desire for sleep that like a child I complained aloud because there was no place on the floor to lie down in all the distasteful litter of these wrappings. It was then I reasoned that if Meni were kind enough to offer me food intended for his Ka, he would hardly mind if I slept by his side, and so I put my torch in a sconce, and got up next to his mummy case, not even worried (thus deep were my limbs already out on slumber) that my foot lay near his foot and scorpions were nesting in the exposed hole. But I was settling in and had time once to burp and think that the meat I had eaten while good was hardly from the kitchens of the Pharaoh for it smacked of the garlic cheap restaurants were ever ready to employ. Then, on the edge of the world of sleep which began so near and went so far away, I thought of Meni and his kind heart and his love for me, and sorrow powerful as a river of tears flooded my heart. Slowly, hearing my own sigh, I returned to sleep, and he, in the deepest communion of friendship, from the domain of the grave, received me. And we went out together, he in the Land of the Dead, and I, by my half in the land of the living, and I knew that I must be feeling all that he had felt in the hour of his death.

Four

Within such sleep, I believe I journeyed through the shade that passes over the heart when the eyes close for the last time, and the seven souls and spirits make ready to return to heaven or go down to the underworld.

Cold fires washed behind my sightless eyes as they prepared to leave. Nor did they take sudden flight, but departed with the decorum of a council of priests, all but one, the Ren, one's Secret Name, who left at once, even as a falling star might drop through the sky. That is as it must be, I concluded. For the Ren did not belong to the man, but came out of the Celestial Waters to enter an infant in the hour of his birth and might not stir again until it was time to go back. While the Secret Name must have some effect on one's character, it was certainly the most remote of our seven lights.

I passed then through a darkness. The Name was gone, and I knew the Sekhem was next. A gift of the sun, it was our Power, it moved our limbs, and I felt it begin to lift from me.

With its absence, my body grew still. I knew the passing of this Sekhem and it was like the sunset on the Nile that comes with the priest's horn. The Sekhem was lost with the Ren, and I was dead, and my breath went out on the last glory of the sunset. The clouds in such a sky gave their carmine light. But with evening, dark clouds remained in view, as though to speak of storms before morning. For the Sekhem would have to ask its dire question. Like the Name, it had been a gift of the Celestial Waters, yet unlike the Ren, it would, as it left, be stronger or weaker than when it first entered me. So this was the question: "Some succeed in using Me well. Can you make that claim?" That was the question of the Sekhem, and in that silence, my limbs stiffened, and the last of the power to give some final shake of the skin gripped itself and was done. Extinction might have been complete but for the knowledge that I was awake. I waited. In such a darkness, void of light, no move in the wind, no breath to stir a thought, the inquiry of the Sekhem persisted. Had I used it well? And time went by without measure. Was it an hour, or a week before the light of the moon rose in the interior of my body? A bird with luminous wings flew in front of that full moon, and its head was as radiant as a point of light. That bird must be the Khu—this sweet bird of the night—a creature of divine intelligence loaned to us just so much as the Ren or the Sekhem. Yes, the Khu was a light in your mind while you lived, but in death, it must return to heaven. For the Khu was also eternal. Out of the hovering of its wings, there came to me a feeling, yes, of such tenderness as I had never known for any human, nor received in return—some sorrowful understanding of me was in the hovering of the Khu. Now I knew it was an Angel, and not like the Power and the Name. For the return of my Khu to heaven would be neither effortless nor unhindered. Even as I watched, it was clear that one of its wings was injured. Of course! An Angel could not feel such concern for me without sharing a few of my injuries and blows. Just as such understanding returned to me, however, so must the Khu have come to recognize its other duties because the bird began to ascend, limping through the sky on its bad wing until it passed beyond the moon, and the moon passed behind a cloud. I was alone again. Three of my seven lights had certainly departed. The Name, the Power, and the Angel, and they would never die. But what of the other souls and lights, my Ba, my Ka, and my Khaibit? They were not nearly so immortal. Indeed, they might never survive the perils of the Land of the Dead, and so could come to know a second death. There was gloom within my body after this thought came to me, and I waited with the most anxious longing for the appearance of the Ba. Yet, it gave no sign it was ready to show. But the Ba, I remembered, could be seen as the mistress of your heart and might or might not decide to speak to you, just as the heart cannot always forgive. The Ba could have flown away already—some hearts are treacherous, some can endure no suffering. Then, I wondered how long I must wait before seeing my Double, but if I recalled, the Ka was not supposed to appear before the seventy days of embalming were done. At last, I was obliged to remember the sixth of the seven lights and shadows. It was the Khaibit. The Khaibit was my Shadow, imperfect as the treacheries of my memory—such was the Khaibit—my memory! But I made a count. Ren, Sekhem, and Khu, the Ba, the Ka, and the Khaibit. The Name, the Power, and the Angel, my Heart, my Double, and my Shadow. What could be the seventh? I had almost forgotten the seventh. That was Sekhu, the one poor spirit who would reside in my wrapped body after all the others were gone—the Remains!—no more than a reflection of strength, like pools on the beach as a tide recedes. Why, the Remains had no more memory, and no less, than the last light of evening recollects the sun.

With that thought, I must have swooned for I entered a domain separated from light and sound. It is possible I was away on travels because the passage of time was what I knew least of all. I waited.

Five

A hook went into my nose, battered through the gate at the roof of the nostril, and plunged into my brain. Pieces, gobbets, and whole parts of the dead flesh of my mind were now brought out through one aperture of my nose, then the other.

Yet for all it hurt, I could have been made of small rocks and roots. I ached no more than the earth when a weed is pulled and comes up with its hairs tearing away from the clods of the soil. Pain is present, but as the small cry of the uprooted plant. So did the hooks, narrow in their curve, go up the nose, enter the head, and poke like blind fingers in a burrow to catch stuffs of the brain and pull them away. Now I felt like a rock wall at the base of which rakes are ripping, and was warm curiously as though sunlight were baking, but it was only the breath of the first embalmer, hot with wine and figs—how clear was the sense of smell!

Still, an enigma remained. How could my mind continue to think while they pulled my brain apart? They were certainly scooping chunks of material as lively as dry sponge through the dry tunnels of my nose, and I realized—for there was a flash in my cranium when the hook first entered—that one of my lights in the Land of the Dead had certainly stirred. Was it the Ba, the Khaibit or the Ka that was now helping me to think? And I gagged as a particularly caustic drug, some wretched mixture of lime and ash, was poured in by the embalmers to dissolve whatever might still be stuck to the inside of my skull.

How long they worked I do not know, how long they allowed that liquid to dwell in the vault of my emptied head is but one more question. From time to time they lifted my feet, held me upside down, then set me back. Once they even turned me on my stomach to slosh the fluids, and let the caustic eat out my eyes. Two flowers could have been plucked when those eyes were gone.

At night my body would go cold; by midday it was close to warm. Of course I could not see, but I could smell, and got to know the embalmers. One wore perfume yet his body always carried the unmistakable pungency of a cat in heat; the other was a heavy fellow with a heavy odor not altogether bad—he was the one with breath of wine and figs. He smelled as well of fields and mud, and rich food was usually in him—a meat-eater, his sweat was strong yet not unpleasant—something loyal came out of the gravies of his flesh. Because I could smell them as they approached, I knew it was daylight so soon as the embalmers arrived, and I could count the hours. (Their scent altered with the heat of the air in this place.) From midday to three, every redolence, good and bad, of the hot banks of the Nile was also near. After a time I came to realize I must be in a tent. There was often the crack of sailcloth flapping overhead, and gusts would clap at my hair, a sensation as definite in impression as a hoof stepping on grass. My hearing had begun to return but by a curious route. For I had no interest in what was said. I was aware of the voices of others, but felt no desire to comprehend the words. They were not even like the cry of animals so much as the lolling of surf or the skittering of wind. Yet my mind felt capable of surpassing clarity.

Once I think Hathfertiti came to visit, or since it is likely the tent was on family grounds, it is possible she strolled through the gardens and stopped to look in. Certainly I caught her scent. It was Hathfer-titi, certain enough; she gave one sob, as if belief in the mortal end of her son had finally come, and left immediately.

Somewhere in those first few days they made an incision in the side of my belly with a sharp flint knife—I know how sharp for even with the few senses my Remains could still employ, a sense of sharpness went through me like a plow breaking ground, but sharper, as if I were a snake cut in two by a chariot wheel, and then began the most detailed searching. It is hard to describe, for it did not hurt, but I was ready in those hours to think of the inside of my torso as common to a forest in a grove, and one by one trees were removed, their roots disturbing veins of rock, their leaves murmuring. I had dreams of cities drifting down the Nile like floating islands. Yet when the work was done, I felt larger, as if my senses now lived in a larger space. Was it that my heart and lungs had been placed in one jar, and my stomach and small intestines in another? Leave it that my organs were spread out in different places, floating in different fluids and spices, yet still existing about me, a village. Eventually, their allegiance would be lost. Wrapped and placed in the Canopic jars, what they knew of my life would then be offered to their own God.

How I brooded over what those Gods would know of me once my organs were in Their jars. Qebhsenuf would dwell in my liver and know of all the days when my liver's juices had been brave; as well would Qebhsenuf know of the hours when the liver, like me, lived in the fog of a long fear. A simple example, the liver, but more agreeable to contemplate than my lungs. For, with all they knew of my passions would they still be loyal once they moved into the jar of the jackal Tuamutef, and lived in the domain of that scavenger? I did not know. So long, at least, as my organs remained unwrapped, and therefore in a manner still belonged to me, I could understand how once em-balmed, and in their jar, I would lose them. No matter how scattered my parts might be over all the tables of this tent, there still remained the sense of family among us—the vessel of my empty corpse com-fortably surrounded by old fleshly islands of endeavor, these lungs, liver, stomach and big and little guts all attached to the same memories of my life (if with their own separate and fiercely prejudiced view—how different, after all, had my life seemed to my liver and to my heart). So, not at all, therefore, was this embalming tent as I had expected, no, no bloody abattoir like a butcher's stall, more like an herb kitchen. Certainly the odors encouraged the same long flights of fancy you could find in a spice shop. Merely figure the vertigos of my nose when the empty cavity of my body (so much emptier than the belly of a woman who has just given birth) was now washed, soothed and stimulated, cleansed, peppered, herbified, and left with a resonance through which no hint of the body's corruption could breathe. They scoured the bloody inside with palm wine, and left the memories of my flesh in ferment. They pounded in spices and peppers, and rare sage from the limestone foundations to the West; then came leaves of thyme and the honey of bees who had fed on thyme, the oil of orange was rubbed into the cavity of the ribs, and the oil of lemon balmed the inside of my lower back to free it of the stubborn redolence of the viscera. Cedar chips, essence of jasmine, and branchlets of myrrh were crushed—I could hear the cries of the plants being broken more clearly than the sound of human voices. The myrrh even made its clarion call. A powerful aromatic (as powerful in the kingdom of herbs as the Pharaoh's voice) was the myrrh laid into the open shell of my body. Next came cinnamon leaves, stem, and cinnamon bark to sweeten the myrrh. Like rare powders added to the sweetmeats in the stuffing of a pigeon, were these bewildering atmospheres they laid into me. Dizzy was I with their beauty. When done, they sewed up the long cut in the side of my body, and I seemed to rise through high vales of fever while something of memory, intoxicated by these tendrils of the earth, began to dance and the oldest of my friends was young while the children of my mistresses grew old. I was like a royal barge lifted into the air under the ministrations of a rare Vizier.

Cleaned, stuffed, and trussed, I was deposited in a bath of natron—that salt which dries the meat to stone—and there I lay with weights to keep me down. Slowly, over the endless days that followed, as the waters of my own body were given up to the thirst of the salt (which

drank at my flesh like caravans arriving at an oasis) so all moisture,
with its insatiable desire to liquefy my meats, had to leave my limbs.
Bathed in natron, I became hard as the wood of a hull, then hard as
the rock of the earth, and felt the last of me depart to join my Ka, my
Ba, and my fearsome Khaibit. And the shell of my body entered the
stone of ten thousand years. If there was nothing I could smell any
longer (no more than a stone can be aware of a scent), still the hardened flesh of my body became like one of those spiraled chambers of
the sea that are thrown up on the beach, yet contain the roar of waters
when you hold them to your ear. I became not unlike that roar of
waters, for I was close to hearing old voices that passed across the
sands—if now I could not smell, I could certainly hear—and like the
dolphin whose ears are reputed able to pick up echoes from the other
end of the sea, so I sank into the bath of natron, and my body passed
farther and farther away. Like a stone washed by fog, baked by sun,
and given the flavor of the water on the bank, I was entering that
universe of the dumb where it was part of our gift to hear the story
told by every wind to every stone.

Yet even as I was carried on these voyages with Meni (his lacquered
case wet with my breath—so close did I hold him) I must have stirred
in sleep, or gone through a space in the travels of sleep, for two clouds
appeared to meet. Could it have been the touch of these clouds that
rocked my sleep? I felt my body descend, breath by breath, into the
case of the mummy, yes, sink into it as if the hard case were only a soft
and receiving earth, yes, was melded into the case of the mummy, and
my memory was one with Meni again. Once more I felt the ministrations of the embalmers, and lived through the hours when they
washed the natron from my hardened body with the liquor of a vase
that held no less than ten perfumes, "O sweet-smelling soul of the
Great God," they intoned, "You contain such a sweet odor that Your
face will never change or perish," words I did not hear, but their cadence had been heard before, I understood what was said, and never
had to sniff the unguent with which they rubbed my skin and smeared
my feet, laid my back in holy oil, and gilded my nails and my toes.
They laid special bandages upon my head, put the bandage of Nekheb

on my brow, and Hathor for my face, Thoth was the bandage over my ears, and folded pieces within the mouth and a cloth over the chin and back of the neck, twenty-two pieces to the right of my face were laid in, and twenty-two to the left. They offered up prayers that I might be able to see and hear in the Land of the Dead, and they rubbed my calves and thighs with blackstone oil and holy oil. My toes were wrapped in linen whose every piece had a drawing of the jackal, and my hands were bandaged in another linen on which were images of Isis and Hep and Ra and Amset. Ebony gum-water was washed over me. They laid in amulets as they wrapped, figures of turquoise and gold, of silver and lapis-lazuli, crystal and carnelian, and a ring was slipped over one gold-painted finger, its seal filled with a drop of each of the thirty-six substances of the embalmer. Then they laid on flowers of the *ankham* plant, and widths and windings of linen, narrow strips longer than the length of a royal barge, and folded linens to fill my cavities. In company with Meni I breathed the embalming resin that would seal the cloth to my pores of stone. I heard the sound of prayers, and the soft breath of the artists as they painted my burial case and sang to one another in the hot tent beneath the moving sun, and on a day I came to know at last the sounds of paving stones thundering beneath a sledge while I was dragged with all the weight of my case to the tomb where I would be put away in my enclosing coffins, and I could hear the quiet sobbing of the women, delicate as the far-off cry of gulls and the invocation of the priest: "The God Horus advances with His Ka." The coffin case bumped on the steps of the tomb. Then hours passed—was it hours?—in a ceremony I could neither hear nor smell, but for the grating of vessels of food and the knocking of small instruments and the sound of liquors being poured upon the floor, but that resounded through the stone of me like an underground river in a cavernous fall, and then the blow of a rock fell on my head and was followed by the grinding of chains, but it was only the scratch of an instrument upon my face. Then I felt a great force opening my stone jaws, and many words flowed into my mouth. I heard a roaring of the waters of my conception, and sobs of heartbreak—my own? I did not know. Rivers of air came to me like a new life—and the forgotten first instant of death also came and was gone as quickly. Then was my Ka born, which is to say I was born again, and was it a day, a year, or not for the passing of ten Kings? But I was up and myself again apart from Meni and his poor body in the coffin.

Yes, I was separate, I was aware of myself, but I was ready to weep. For now I knew why Meni was my dearest friend and his death an agony to me, yes, my dim memory of his life was now nothing but the dim memory of my own life. For now I knew who I was, and that was no better than a ghost in a panic for food. I was nothing but the poor Ka of Menenhetet Two. And if the first gift to the dead was that they could add the name of the Lord to their own name, then I was the Ka of poor helpless Osiris Menenhetet Two, yes, the Ka, the most improperly buried and fearful Ka who now must live in this violated tomb, oh, where was I now that I knew where I was? And the thought of the Land of the Dead opened to me with all the recognition that I was but a seventh part of what had been once the lights, faculties, and powers of a living soul, once my living soul. Now I was no more than the Double of the dead man, and what was left of him was no more than the corpse of his badly wrapped body, and me.

Six

So, I could appreciate why I had no memory. If I was the Double of Menenhetet the Second, as brave and petty as the original, I could still remember no more of him than was needed to give a proper expression to his features. A Double, like a mirror, has no memory. I could only think of him as a friend, my closest friend! No wonder I wished to lie next to his mummy case.

Yet if my recollections could offer no more feeling than is provided by a long scar on the skin, nonetheless I was myself. My face could still give others every delight. Had I ever made love to Hathfertiti? How could I know? But I felt no embarrassment to be thinking so of my mother—a mirror hardly had a mother. Why should I not be the coldest element of Meni's heart? Yet, standing in the litter of his—my—violated tomb, I knew that the balance to these loveless thoughts was the rage I felt for Hathfertiti. At this instant, I could have killed her. For soon, I must leave this place, soon, if I dared, I would have to take the road through the western desert that led to the Duad and the Land of the Dead—did it really exist, as the priests said, with monsters and boiling lakes? How could I endure the trials when I could not remember my deeds and so would hardly be able to explain them? A fear of dying came over me for the first time, the true fear—I understood that I could cease. To die in the Land of the Dead, to perish with one's Ka, was to die forever. The second death was the final death. Oh, how rank were my circumstances. How unjust! Hathfertiti had done so little for my tomb!

In this rage, I was hardly able to breathe. Anger was too powerful an emotion for the delicate lungs of the Ka. The Ka was reputed to be short of breath. That was why a sail was supposed to be painted on one wall of the tomb—it might encourage the breath of the Ka to return. But here, on these walls, was no painted sail. Suffocated by my fury I did try, nonetheless, to bring before me the image of one, and succeeded in stirring a breeze to titillate the hairs in the nostrils of my nose—how could I be dead if the hairs of my nose were so keen? Yet in taking this clear breath, the fear of dying a second time came over me with force equal to my rage. For Hathfertiti's oversights would cost much. Where was the painted portrait to show me standing near water? What would I drink? Like an omen came a dry spot, fierce as a boil, to the back of my throat.

Nor had any of the four doors of the winds been drawn on the sides of my coffin. Of course I could not breathe easily if such an insult had been given to the winds. Curious mother! She had also neglected to prepare a box with my navel string. So, too, had I lost one more route through the Land of the Dead.

Here was another oversight. So soon as I examined the rolls of papyrus packed in my coffin with me, I could recognize that the texts of important prayers were missing. I was amazed at how many I could remember: the Chapter-of-not-dying-a-second-time, the Chapter-of-not-allowing-the-soul-of-a-man-to-be-shut-in, the Chapter-of-not-allowing-a-man-to-decay-in-his-tomb. I was beginning to feel an anger so large and so fortifying that my rage was calm. I felt a great desire to summon Hathfertiti.

As if to search for a sign, I knelt. Under the litter of linen, I discovered a dead beetle, yes, the dung beetle there before me. Just as it used its hind legs to push a ball of dung many times larger than itself up into a safe hole where this dung could feed its eggs, so did the priests used to tell us how Khepera, looking like a giant beetle, carried the Boat of Ra across the sky every day, rowing with His six legs through the heavens. That was a common explanation popular for children and peasants. I, however, had no need of such stories. I could believe that if a Great God chose to hide in a beetle, it was because Gods liked to conceal themselves in curious places. That was the first law of great secrets. Therefore I ate each of the dead beetle's wings just as slowly as my palate could bear. The dry membranes cut like little knives, and the head, although I chewed it carefully, turned out to be only a small dry grit, but I confess that as I swallowed, I tried to picture the head of Hathfertiti. Calling upon no incantations, but most certainly filled with contempt for the iniquity of my mother, I said, "Great Khepera of the heavens, let justice prevail. Present me with the living Hathfertiti." Through my closed eyes, I felt a sudden light and there was the muted sound of thunder through my feet. But when I lifted my head, it was not Hathfertiti I saw. Before me, instead, was the gaunt body of the Ka of old Menenhetet One. I cannot say I liked the way my great-grandfather looked at me.

Seven

He was dressed like a High Priest and for all I knew he was a High Priest. His head was shaved and he seemed to inhabit the air of his own presence, as if each morning his body was sanctified. Yet he looked like no High Priest I had ever seen. He was too dirty and very old. Ashen was the color of his white linen robes and the dust of years had beaten into the cloth. Ashen was the color of his skin, even darker than his garments, but rubbed in the same dust, and the toes of his bare feet looked like fingers of stone. His bracelets had turned to shades of green. The corrosion of his anklets was black. Only his eyes were bright. His pupils were as expressionless as the painted look of a fish or a snake, but the whites were like limestone in the light of the moon. By the light of my torch, it was only the white of his eyes that enabled me to be certain he was not a statue, for he remained motionless on a chair beside his coffin, and could have passed in age for a hundred years old, a thousand years old, if not for the fierce light of those eyes.

I felt a return of the oppression I knew when looking at his coffin. He was so old! One could not even describe his features for lack of knowing where the nose reached the flesh of the cheeks. Just that wrinkled were the terraces of his skin. He seemed close to lacking existence altogether, yet made me so uneasy by his presence, that I thought to rid myself of him. Quickly. As if he were some noxious insect. So I took a step to the Canopic jar nearest to his coffin—it was Tuamutef—and twisted its lid. The top came off easily. The jar was empty. No wrapping of the heart and lungs was in the vase of the jackal. I turned to Amset. Also empty.

"I have eaten them," said Menenhetet One.

Had the thin air of his throat not been warmed by the sun since the day he died? The echo of a cold cavern was in his voice.

"Why," I was about to ask, "why, great-grandfather, have you eaten your own blessing?" but the impertinence of the question was pulled from my mouth before I could ask it. I had never known such an experience. It was as if a rude hand reached into my throat deep enough for me to gag, seized my tongue, and shucked it from the root to the tip.

It was then I felt a fear clear as the finest moments of my mind. For I was dead, so I understood once more (again as if for the first time) and being dead, might now be obliged to meet every terror I had fled while living. Of these terrors could it be said that my ancestor, Menenhetet, might prove the first? For I could certainly recall how often we talked of him in my family and always as a man of unspeakable strength and sinister habits.

Now, as I stared at him, he spoke. "What," he asked, "are your sentiments?"

"My sentiments?"

"Now that we are together."

"I hope," I said, "that we will begin to know each other."

"At last."

The same keen air was in my lungs that I had known in the tomb of Khufu. The best of myself must have come back to me for I felt the curious exhilaration, even the certainty, that I was meeting my enemy. Was I meeting the enemy of my life—now that I was dead? But speak not of death. It was without meaning to me. I had never felt more vital. It was as if I had decided on some terrible day to make an end of myself and had walked to the edge of a cliff, looked down into the gorge, knew I would certainly step into the space before me and in one fall be dead. At such a moment I might know fear in every drop of my blood, yet the future would feel as alive as lightning. Just now I had that sense. It was the happiness of being next to my fear, yet separate from it, so that I could be free at last to know all the ways I had failed to live my life, all the boredom I had swallowed, and each foul sentiment of wasted flesh. It was as if I had spent my days beneath a curse, and the sign of it—despite every lively pandemonium of gambling and debauch—was the state of immutable monotony that dwelt in my heart. The sense of being dead while alive—from what could it have come but a curse? I had an inkling then of the force of the desire to die when that is the only way to encounter one's demon. No wonder I stood before him in an apprehension as invigorating as the iciest water of a well. For on how many lovely evenings in how many lovely gardens had I told funny stories about the filthy habits of the first holder of my name? How we cried with laughter at tales of his calculation, his cunning, his sacrilegious feasts of bat dung.

But now, as if he had heard my thought, he stood up for the first time, not a big man nor so small as he had first appeared, and dusty as the loneliest roads of the desert.

"Those stories," he murmured, "left my name repulsive," and by the air of self-possession with which he said this, I began to wonder whether I was most certainly his moral superior. That he was the guide to my final destruction, I did not cease to believe, but that he might also have a high purpose now occurred to me. If, in these curious intoxications of knowing I was dead, I had begun to feel as splendid as a hero, still I could not remember my heroism. Nonetheless, I had hardly doubted that my purposes (if I could ever find them) would be noble. Now, I was not as confident.

"Do you think," he asked, "I am handsome? Or ugly?"

"Are you not too old to be either?"

"It is the only answer." He laughed. In mockery of me, his finger idled from side to side. "Well, you are dead," he said, "and certainly in danger of expiring a second time. Then you will be gone forever.

Goodbye, sweet lad. Your face was more beautiful than your heart."
Abruptly, he gave an old man's snigger, unspeakably lewd. "Are you
content to let me be your guide in Khert-Neter?" he asked.

"Do I have a choice?"

"The navel string is already prepared. The portrait of Meni standing in the water has been commissioned to an artist most esteemed in
the circle of my friends, and he will also do a painting of the sails that
will catch the breath of evening in the delicate lungs of my son." His
voice had taken on the self-indulgence of Hathfertiti's voice, her arch
pleasure in hearing the full sounds of herself. "Of course I've had so
much to do that the work never gets begun. I hear the tomb is a mess
and all broken into and shit upon. Poor Meni. How, I wonder, are he
and Old Guano getting along?"

I laughed. I had rarely heard such mimicry. If once I mocked the
Gods, and fornicated with priests, it was never with ease equal to this.
I was beginning to see the stimulations of my condition: to be dead
yet more alive than before—that was as intoxicating as a night when
you are ready for anything.

"Tell me of Khert-Neter," I said in a merry tone, as if asking for
another drink.

The old ravaged face, wrinkled as the shell of a turtle who has
walked through fire, now showed a High Priest's love of ceremony.
"Strengthen my breath," he said in his cavernous voice.

A transformation came to him with these words, however. The
dirt about his body began to look like silver dust, and his right arm
was raised toward the heavens. His eyes stayed in solemn contemplation of the ground. Yet, next, he winked at me. I was shocked. He
seemed to delight in flinging my thoughts about in all directions. "We
need," he said, "to prepare you. After all, you have forgotten what
you know. That is common to the Ka. It keeps a poor memory of our
most sacred customs."

But his shifts gave me no time to recover my wit. Now he spoke in
ceremonious tones again. "O Lord Osiris," he began, and touched his
forefingers to his thumbs as though to form two eyes: "I have passed
over rivers of fire and through geysers of boiling water. I have entered

the dark night of the Land of the Dead and gone through the seven halls and mansions of Sekhet-Aaru. I have learned the names of the Gods at the door to each hall. Hear of the difficulty of this beautiful young man whose Ka would accompany me. How can he obtain the patience to learn the names of the three guards at the door to each hall when his memory is infirm? Know the hazards. The Doorkeeper at the Fourth Hall is named Khesefherashtkheru, and the Herald who examines those who die in the night only replies to the sound of Neteqaherkhesefatu. And these are but two of the twenty-one names which the Ka of this boy must learn if he is to pass through the gates of Sekhet-Aaru." My great-grandfather paused, as if to contemplate those names. "Yes," he said in a voice of much resonance, "I, who am Osiris Menenhetet One, have survived Your judgment, Lord Osiris, so give ear to my prayer that You spare the Ka of this young man from such fires, for he is no other than the splendid Osiris Menenhetet Two, my great-grandson, son of my granddaughter, the Lady Hath-fertiti, who was my concubine in life and kept in carnal knowledge of me through the years of my death, may the scorpions continue to serve me."

I was bewildered. The prayer was devout, yet not like any I knew, and I was much confused by the remarks he had just made about my mother.

"I could tell you more," he said. "I can say the prayers for repulsing the serpent and spearing the crocodile. I can give you the wings of a hawk so you may fly above your foes. Or show you how to drink the ale in the body of the God Ptah. I can reveal the gates to the Field of Reeds and teach you to come forth from the fishing net. Yes, I will do all this if I am your guide."

I was drowsy before the need to sleep. That ancient subterranean voice invoked so many names. I might mock those names, but to call upon such a host in so short a time left me weak. Now I realized that the strength of my Ka seemed as short-lived as the confidence of a child to stay on its feet when first it learns to walk. I had an impulse to prostrate myself before him.

Yet he was never more repulsive. I could dine in every royal garden

of the Nile with the tales I might tell if I survived this night. He was
ludicrous in the extreme, this dusty old man with his deep cold voice,
lonely as the loon, and yet imbued with confidence—figure the ab-
surdity of his speech when he broke wind from his buttocks with
every God he named, a cacophony of claps, pips, pops, poops, bel-
lows, and on-booming farts, and all—by the look of his expression—
of the most delicious obscenity. He gave a little aristocratic greeting
of his wrist to each monster, divinity, or ogre he invoked, as though
he contained carnal knowledge of them all and so could drop salutes
of thunder from the ramparts of his old canal. The tomb stank; once
from the litter of all those spoiled wrappings, and now from the
storm of his speech with all the sulphurs of his breath and the break-
winds of his body.

"Do you know anything that is true of my life?" he asked.

I replied, "You tortured prisoners, prayed to the filthiest Gods, and
feasted on substances no one could tolerate."

"I prayed to Gods Whose powers were so fearsome that others
shunned Their works. And ate many a forbidden substance. The secrets of the universe are there. Do you think I became Overseer of the
Lord God Osiris by daring too little?"

"I have no trust," I said, "in the idea that you are the Overseer of
Osiris. I witness no superiority to your knowledge." But the remark
was too bold. I shivered even as I spoke.

He smiled as if our conversation had passed wholly into his domain. "What do you witness?" he remarked. "You do not know the
story of Osiris. You do not even remember what you were taught by
the priests."

I nodded unhappily. I did not. I could think of tales I had been told
in my childhood about Isis and Osiris and others of those Gods from
Whom we all began, but now, as if the depths of such stories were as
lost and far apart from me as the wrappings of my organs in their
Canopic jars, I sighed and felt as hollow within as a cave. While I
could not say why I thought this was so, it seemed to me as if nothing
could be more important than to know these Gods well, as if, indeed,
They could fill all that was empty in my marrow and so serve as true

guides to the treacheries I would yet have to face in the Land of the
Dead. For now I remembered an old saying: Death is more treacherous than life!

When Menenhetet, however, nodded back at me in mockery of
my need, I felt obliged—in some last rally of my pride—to speak my
most determined criticism. "I cannot believe you are an emissary of
Osiris," I told him. "Your stench would repel the nostrils of the
God."

Menenhetet One gave a sad smile. "I have the power to offer any
smell you desire." And in the silence that followed, he was clean as
perfume and sweet as grass. I bowed my head. Osiris, most beautiful
of the Gods, must have concern for me if His Overseer was Menenhetet One. What an appeal to my vanity was such a thought.

Therefore, I asked my great-grandfather if he would tell the story
of Osiris and of all the Gods Who lived at the beginning of our land,
and to prove I was sincere, I moved across to sit by him. He smiled,
but did not welcome me in any other way. Instead, he reached into a
fold of his long dusty skirt and, one by one, removed a number of
scorpions, each of which he held in turn with a practiced and tender
hand. One scorpion he placed upon the lid of each eye, two at the
gates of his nostrils, one for each of his ears, and he laid the last scorpion on his lower lip, seven scorpions for the seven orifices of his
head. Then he gave one more nod, grave as a stone.

"In the beginning," he said, "before our earth was here and the
Gods were not born, before there was a river or a Land of the Dead,
and you could see no sky, it is still true that Amon the Hidden rested
within His invisible splendor." Here, Menenhetet raised a hand as if
to remind me of the elegant gesture the High Priest would use in the
Temple when I was a child.

"Yes, it is from Amon that we know our beginning. He withdrew
from the Hidden to come forth as Temu, and it was Temu Who made
the first sound. That was a cry for light." The solemnity of the priests
by whom I had been instructed in my childhood was upon me, and
my limbs had no power. "The cry of Temu," Menenhetet said, "quivered across the body of His Wife, Who was Nut, and She became our

Celestial Waters. Temu spoke in so great a voice that the first wave stirred in Her, and these Celestial Waters brought forth the light. So was Ra born out of the first wave of the waters. Out of the great calm of the Celestial Waters was born the fiery wave of Ra, and He lifted Himself into the heaven and became the sun even as Temu disappeared back into the body of His Wife, and was Amon again." Menenhetet exhaled his breath. "That is the beginning," he said.

I was feeling the same respect I used to know when priests spoke of the first sound and the first light. "I will listen," I told him.

So soon as I uttered these words, however, he removed the scorpions, replaced them in the fold of the skirt from which he had brought them forth, and began to talk in another tone of voice, as if the solemnity of what was said in the Land of the Dead could not endure more than one part in seven against our most solemn hours in life. For now, with hardly a warning, he became most disrespectful of the Gods, even scandalous in what he had to say as if They were all his brothers in a large and disreputable family. With all I had heard of his capacity for sacrilege, I could still not believe how obscene the story of Osiris soon became.

Nor was I prepared for how long it would take. Before we were done I would be obliged to know Them well.

II

The Book of the Gods

The Flock of the Gods

One

Like an old man whose throat is a pot of phlegm, Menenhetet began to cackle at these foul jokes awaiting us. "Put a divine lady before Ra," he said, "or a slippery old sow—it was all equal to Him. He liked them all. His only problem was to find a wife cool enough to bear His heat. So He settled on the Goddess of the sky." Menenhetet began to choke in laughter once more. "Ra could change the shape of His prick to any of the forty-two animals: ram, ox, hippo, lion—just pick the beast!—but He once made the mistake of telling Nut that He did not like to make love to a cow. So She chose to live in the body of one. It is always that way with marriage." He nodded. "Whenever She could, Nut rushed down to the mud-baths with Geb. What a wallow! Revenge is never so dear to a woman as when her perfidies go right up her husband's nose. Ra was so infuriated that for the next five nights, five children were put into Her womb. Ra and Geo were on Her so constantly that the earth steamed and the sky was covered with fog."

Now Menenhetet ceased talking. A sadness came upon his face, as if the matters of which he would next speak could not be called amusing. "Now, whether," he said, "these five offspring were fathered by Ra (whose children They were immediately declared to be) or belonged to Geb, will never be known, but by one or the other, Nut gave birth in the first hour to Osiris, and in the second, Horus was delivered; on the third, Set burst out of His mother's side, thereby creating a rent in the sky through which lightning could strike. Isis came out in a dew of moisture, and Nephthys, born last, was given the Secret Name of Victory for She was the most beautiful. She would yet marry Her brother Set, even as Isis was wed to Osiris (although it is said of Isis and Osiris that They were already in love with one another within the womb). Under such circumstances, how can one ask who was half sister and brother?"

Here his voice came so close to my ear that I did not know any longer how his knowledge was imparted. When I closed my eyes, the story even seemed to belong for a little while to me, and, indeed, I could hear the voice of Ra.

"I look upon My children," He shouted, "and do not know if They are Mine, or crawling things from the caverns of Geb. I am damaged even as I damn Them, for I cannot say whether I curse Them unfairly, or not enough."

The three brothers, Horus, Osiris, and Set, and the sisters Isis and Nephthys lived in a house full of bad omens. Even as children, They played at treachery and dreamed of murder. The curse of Ra passed into the marriage of Isis and Osiris, and the marriage of Set and Nephthys.

Yet what a difference between them. Isis loved Osiris and found Him more attractive than Herself, whereas Nephthys was miserable. Set's body scorched Her belly. Under the fire of His temper, She felt the stones of the desert. "How can My name be Victory," asked Nephthys, "if My womb burns when He enters Me?" But Osiris was as cool as the shade of an oasis. His fingers were tender when He passed a dish. There came a night when Nephthys betrayed Her husband with Osiris.

Now, Set had a plant which bloomed each night on His return, yet this evening the plant was limp.

"Lift your face," said Set, "for I am here."

In response, the plant fell dead. Now Set knew that Nephthys was with Osiris, and when She came back, He could see that the night with His brother had been more beautiful to Her than any hour with Him. Then, Nephthys confessed that She had conceived, but with a joy in Her voice He never heard before. The hatred of Set began to grow upon this shame. He fornicated with Nephthys every night, and the thought of Osiris whipped His hips to a gallop. He worked so hard to crush the creation in Her belly that the mother began to feel loathing for what She carried. In the hour of birth, Nephthys wept, and could not look at the baby's face. Conceived in beauty, the creature came out as misshapen as the depredations of Her womb. A face of mean ferocity was presented, and it gave off a low odor—Anubis, the God with the head of a jackal, had been born. Nephthys carried this Anubis to the desert, and exposed Him. But Her sister, Isis, was determined that the infant should not be lost. If Anubis was the proof of Her husband's most treacherous hour, still Isis knew that the infant should not be lost.

Menenhetet now said aloud, "Whoever is born out of treachery must not be slain against his will."

"Why would that be true?" I asked.

"Because demons are conceived when people die in rage."

I did not like what he said. In what manner had my own end come? To hide my uneasiness, I told him, "You are reputed to have killed every slave who would not work."

"That was in the gold mines, and I did not kill them. They died of overwork. Besides I never said I did not wish to deliver demons," replied Menenhetet One, and shivered. Like the sound of water readying to boil were the whispers of his voice. Yet I still saw all he had to tell, and most clearly. So I knew that Isis, hunting with dogs offered the scent of linen stained with the birth, soon found the baby. Menenhetet One sniffed at his finger, and a scent of sour blood passed over to me. He merely smiled at this passing display of his powers.

"Isis," he said, "trained the child to be Her guard. Now, Anubis is the jackal who holds the scales of judgment. Before Him, the dead must appear. Have you forgotten that as well?" When I made no sign, he nodded. "In one pan is placed the dead man's heart, on the other is laid the feather of truth, and woe to the dead if the scales do not balance. Anubis can judge such things. His first day had no more promise of long life than is given to a feather. You may come before Anubis yet." Menenhetet smiled, but when I offered nothing, he merely shrugged, and took up his account again. "Contemplate the murderous rage of Set," he said. "His wife's bastard was still alive. Set swore a vengeance that would never weaken no matter how many years He had to wait, and they were many. For Osiris was not only the first King of Egypt, but the greatest. He had taught us how to grow wheat, and make beer from barley, how to cultivate corn, raise good grapes and ferment good wine. He even taught us how to ferment the fermentation and find the seven powers and spirits of the soul in a cup of kolobi. But then, Osiris began to travel over the Very Green to pass on this knowledge to more ignorant lands and it proved foolhardy. He was so worshipped at every court that by the time of His return to Egypt, He had become too aware of His beauty.

"In the first month of His homecoming, Set invited Him to a great feast, and excited the vanity of Osiris by telling Him of a magnificent chest that He had built to fit the body of the God closest to Temu.

"Set called for the chest to be brought, and commanded the seventy-two Gods of His Court to lay within it one by one. The box fit none of Them. Nor did it match the proportions of Set. At last it became the turn of Osiris, and He was a perfect fit. 'You are so beautiful,' said Set, as His brother lay down. Then He slammed the cover. Seven of His warriors sealed it with molten metal.

"Now they carried the chest to the Nile and lay it on the water. It floated away on an afternoon when the sun was in the sign of the scorpion. And Osiris was gone.

"When Isis heard of this, She let out a cry that became part of the shriek men utter when they behold their own wound, and She began to search for the coffin in the marshes of the Delta and in the swamps."

And I, as if suffering an equal blow, now moved and sat with the side of my face against the cool wood of poor Meni's burial case, poor Meni indeed! Who, but myself! As Menenhetet One continued to tell his story, I think I must have crawled out along a branch of sleep and fallen from there into another sleep since I only came back into the passage of his voice after the coffin of Osiris had floated all the way down the waters of the Nile and was out at sea on a voyage to Byblos by the shores of Lebanon. There I heard the smack of the last wave as the box was lifted by a swell into the branches of a little evergreen growing out of the rocks on the beach. Yet that poor shrub, twisted by every wind, began to thrive as soon as Osiris came to it, and its trunk grew right around the coffin and rose to prodigious height until the King of Byblos saw it and thereupon had the tree cut down and made into the central pillar of his new palace.

To this shore came Isis, led by Her seven scorpions, and when She arrived at the court of Byblos, and the Queen received Her, Isis smelled of a fragrance sweeter than any garden.

To this Queen, Astarte, the first measure of rank was superb appearance. She only wished those as lovely as herself to come near. Therefore, she welcomed Isis; indeed, they cherished each other so tenderly that Isis could even ask the Queen to beg the King to cut down the pillar, and thereby free Her husband from the coffin. It was a monumental request. The greatest room in Byblos would be destroyed. From the day, however, that he had felled the tree to build the chamber, this King, Melkarth, had become secretly fearful of the silence in his palace. So he agreed.

When the chest was opened, however, Osiris was found in a dreadful state. His face was covered by worms. Isis let out a cry of lamentation, and so loud was the clamor of Her voice that the youngest child of Melkarth died in fright. Blood poured from his ears.

The death was not wholly lamentable to the King. He was far from convinced of the paternity of this son for he had been stricken with impotence as soon as the magnificent tree was down. Now, he felt desire for his wife come back, and he took the Queen to his rooms, and tried to be happy, but could not. He feared to enjoy himself so soon after such a death. It might cost another. But then Melkarth realized that he trusted none of his sons, and was therefore ready, on Isis' departure, to lend Her the oldest of his boys to serve as crew.

Her ship had hardly gone from sight of land before ministrations were begun over the body in the coffin. Loosing the seven scorpions from the hem of Her skirt, She instructed them to devour the worms that lived on the face and limbs of Osiris. The scorpions worked with all the speed of the wind in the sails, and were as round as pigeon's eggs before evening. Now, Isis crushed these sluggish bodies to make an unguent, and thereby cast off all protection such scorpions could provide—indeed, even as She killed them, She knew they would send a message to their brothers: "Beware of Isis!"—yet She was determined to repair the beauty of Osiris. The oil for such a restoration could be found only in the bellies of these scorpions full of worms. So, She rubbed this unguent upon Her legs and belly. Having stripped Her skirt for this purpose, She thereby aroused the poor Prince of Byblos until his seed was on the deck. This, She also added to Her skin (for the Prince was favored with the features of his mother) and then washed Osiris in the salve by laying Her body upon Her dead husband and, by this, so excited the return of His seven scattered lights that He came back from all the swamps, harbors, mountains and seas of His death to the home of His body. In this hour, young again, and beautiful, lying on His back, He discharged His seed up into Isis, and it was the first time a Goddess ever dared to sit upon a God. The Prince of Byblos, spying on this copulation, was struck with such a look of malevolence from Isis that he died on the spot and fell into the sea, and Horus, the other brother of Osiris, also died at that instant (breaking His back in a fall from a horse) whereupon Horus, the child of Isis and Osiris, was conceived in the same moment, but He came out with a weakness in His legs. Since Gods do not often die, Horus, the newborn, was a transformation of Horus, the brother, and it is certain the child grew quickly and was a full-grown man in fourteen years. But they were to be hard years. Isis knew that Ra and Set were waiting for Her.

When She came back to Egypt, Isis looked, therefore, to hide the chest containing Her husband. Yet it was not easy to find a place. For the coffin had to rest where the direct rays of Ra could fall upon it. The Sun could only send a curse upon Gods Who tried to hide from

Him. Osiris would be safe from Ra's wrath, if His coffin were not buried. Therefore, Isis chose a shallow lake in the swamps of the Delta, and fixed the box with stones so that it would not float away from the papyrus plants surrounding it; yet, with the lid removed, Osiris could lay open to Ra for His blessing.

Still, Isis felt far from secure. Since Ra could always lay a curse when He went behind a cloud, She had had, at considerable cost, to make Her peace with the scorpions. She took a vow to protect their safety for all their lives to come. It was necessary. She had need of them. Scorpions were that rare species for whom the rays of the Sun are an irritant. So, when the Sun hid itself, they were quick to come out of the ground and wait by the coffin of Osiris. All through the day, therefore, whether in sun or by the vigilance of the scorpions in the gloom, the body of Osiris was guarded. And at night, in the darkest hour of the night when Ra wandered through the underworld, in that wholly dark hour when the scorpions began to sleep, then Isis was confident Set could not find His brother in such a swamp. Besides, Anubis reigned in this hour of greatest darkness, and He was loyal to Isis—which is to say, true so long as He could be. The powers of Anubis might be steadfast in the dark, but loyalty paled just before the dawn when He knew the hour of the jackal, and would wander off.

Now, for months, Set had slept by day and ridden by night, but to no purpose until He convinced Ra to ask the Moon to travel for all of one night into the dawn.

So Set obtained a few more hours of moonlight. But He still had to find the swamp where His brother was hidden. Therefore, He called upon every memory. That was equal to saying His pride had to writhe again in all the shame of the cuckold. Yet if He was obliged to think of Nephthys with Osiris, it was but a step from there to see Osiris in the embrace of Isis, and that made it possible for Set to enter the thoughts of Isis. So, on this night, when the sun was down, Set offered His breath to the evening sky and to the dark ridges of the earth (His mother and father, no less!) and turned slowly until His thoughts could look into Isis where She lived in the town of Buto.

Motionless as a hunter, Set waited until the moment when the depth of early night was lit by the moon rising over the swamp. Then, into His mind, at the moment it came into Isis' mind, arrived the image of the grove where Osiris was hidden. Set spurred His horse, and charged up and down the swamp in search of that view until in a fever of sweat, laved in His own coating of mud, there in the last of the moonlight in the hour of the jackal, He found the open chest unguarded, the scorpions sleeping, and Anubis gone. In this pale hour before dawn, Set lifted His sword and butchered the dead body of His brother, hacking free the heart, the backbone and the neck, the head and legs and arms, Osiris' stomach, His intestines, His chest, His liver, even His gall bladder, His buttocks! Set would certainly have amputated the genitals if He had not stopped to make a count and discovered He had fourteen pieces already, a number twice seven, thereby a formidable doubling of bad luck to His enemies. But then His frustration was great because He could not mutilate His brother further, and His blood raged until He raised His sword and chopped off His own thumb. And left it in the mouth of Osiris. With His horse, He carried the coffin and the fourteen pieces back to camp, then sent His men to deliver the chest to the camp of Isis. Now He got ready to travel up the Nile. Employing a galley of the most powerful oarsmen in the kingdom, His boat would sail, He knew, and be rowed faster, than Isis could ever follow, and on this journey He would bury the parts of Osiris in different places. But first, in all the vigors of His victory, He chose to go down the separate mouths of the Delta and leave the lower limbs at Bubastis and Busiris (which is why the hieroglyph of the letter B is a drawing of a leg) and He even left one arm at Baloman for good measure, the other at Buto where Isis lived, stopping there long enough to rape Her favorite handmaiden and strew two more pieces in the swamp. Isis was helpless in this hour.

Set then left parts of Osiris at Athribis and Heliopolis and the head at Memphi, gave burial to one section of the body at Fayum, then further up the Nile to Siut, Abydos and Dendera, and feeling safe at last, trusted His men to row the long distance with the last piece up the river to Yeb. And if these men had walked, it would have taken thirty days and thirty days again. But they stopped to celebrate, and so it took twice as long.

Now, Isis lost all desire to move from Her bed. Her breast had no milk. Near to human was Isis in the depth of Her unhappiness. Set had overcome Her magic. Certainly, Her most intimate forces gave no intimation of return. In this sad time, Her thoughts drew tears whose fall gave birth to rain—a last gift of the sweet powers in the body of Osiris scattered now from the marshes of the Delta to the waters of the First Cataract.

I do not know if it was this unfamiliar sound of rain in our Egyptian air, but a haze drifted over my thoughts and I could see these Gods no longer. It was startling to recognize Menenhetet as he looked at me out of the blazing white of his eyes. "We come," he said, "to the activities of Maat. Without Her, all might be lost for Isis."

Two

"Yes," he said, "Maat is so devoted to the smallest measure of balance, that She chose a feather for Her face. To think that She is the daughter of Ra!" Again, I was confounded by the phenomenon of his laughter. It was as if the greed of the worst beggars passed through him, some sewage of mean human tide. Yet he seemed altogether oblivious to the blow this gave his dignity. "Yes," said Menenhetet, "Maat is the most innocuous of Ra's fornications. In fact, She was conceived by a little bird who (after all the quick and timid trips of her life) became, for once, intoxicated by the warmth of the air. Soaring on a current, this downy fluff rose to the arms of Ra, up, up, in a trance, and immediately expired—what a copulation! The mother was roasted to a crisp, and the child drifted down to us as a feather, a genius of balance between heartfelt attraction and clear immolation." He gave another disturbing laugh. "Now that same feather is used by Anubis to weigh the moral worth of the heart of each dead person." He shrugged again. "Of all of His children, Maat is the only one who has no guts to lose, so She is fearless. She was the only divinity brave enough to scold Ra about His favors to Set, and did no less than tell Her Father: 'It is dangerous to protect a victor from the curses of those He defeated. Such a God will prosper too easily, and the world will tip.'

" 'Do not speak of balance,' Ra told Her. 'I ride in a golden ship by day, but am obliged to travel through the Duad by dark and give battle to the serpent. If I ever lose, the world will not see My light again.' "

Menenhetet gave vent to his laugh. "I can assure you, Maat was not about to tell Ra that the perils of the serpent were small."

And again, as if the story pulled on me like a stream of passing spirits, the sights in my mind began to stir. I could see that Ra no longer fought alone, and many Gods and Goddesses were by His side to trap the serpent. Indeed, Ra had to do no more than chop Aapep into pieces. All the same, the labor made Him breathe heavily. Ra was growing old.

Maat, rebuked by Her Father, began to watch the habits of His pilot-fish. For these two creatures, named Abtu and Ant, would serve as His eyes when it came to navigating the perils of the Duad. Each night, swimming to either side of Ra's boat, they guided the entourage past fires, boiling pits, and stench. By day, however, the fish, justifiably fatigued, chose to become two short pieces of rope, and they would sun themselves on the banks of the Nile. There they basked, two bights of bleached hemp, so short that no passing fisherman would think of splicing them to a larger rope. Maat, now traveling in Her natural condition—a feather in the wind—soared along the riverbank until She passed over the pilot-fish.

Hovering in place, She succeeded in putting Abtu and Ant into shadow. Deprived of the light of Ra, their ability to reason was confused, and so they quit the shore for the water, but the shadow of a serpent now flickered on the surface. They were not aware it was the feather twisting its supple spine above the river to cast patches of shade below. So, they chased the shadow of that serpent down the current until Maat led them to the pelvis of Osiris stuffed in the stump of an uprooted palm, a place that Maat knew well. (She had been present as the spirit of balance when Set on the last stroke cut off His own thumb instead.) Now, Abtu leaped on the phallus of Osiris, bit it off, choked it down, and danced in frenzy through the water. His skin was luminous; he felt composed of light. A terror! Where to hide? In panic, both fish rushed to the shore to reassume their existence as pieces of dull hemp, yet when Abtu turned back into a rope, he was whiter than the moon, and Ant had to cover him with mud until it was time to swim off to the Duad once more. In the dark, however, he gleamed. He would call attention to them all. In fury, Ra lifted him from the water and swallowed him. Ant was left to serve as the pilot, but since he could not keep the boat off the rocks on his blind side, the bark shuddered and scraped from every blow, and, the phallus of Osiris sticking in His stomach, Ra soon grew ill.

The balance shifted. Since the God's member proved indigestible, Ra began to feel most uncomfortable, and allowed the sky to cloud. Isis stirred in Her bed and listened to the gulls. Their cawing went on through gray and hazy days. Other birds came to tell how the noble horse on which Set hunted in the swamp had shied from a fallen tree, and broke his leg. The good luck of Set might have shattered.

Isis dared to remember the hour when She and Osiris gave conception to Horus. Even as the Prince of Byblos fell backward once more into the sea, so did a message come from the Ka of Osiris. Isis must arm Herself with the Secret Name of Ra. She began to listen to the gossip of the Gods.

Now, She heard that Ra was old and His bones had changed from gold to silver as His limbs grew stiff. He dribbled when He spoke. His seven emissions fell constantly to the earth, and the paths were covered with His earwax and His sweat, His urine, His turd, His snot, His semen and saliva.

Isis contemplated how to use these leavings. The full bowel of the sun certainly reeked of wealth. Yet, how could She know which monsters of the sulphurous night might also be set free? That was power too much. Isis needed the Secret Name, no more. Why conclude that Ra excreted His Secret Name each day?

So, too, did She avoid sweat. In His perspiration might be the honor of His name, but such sweat also gave off the odor of every animal He became while making love. And *their* Secret Names. An abundance and a confusion.

Nor did She think to look for His seed. The Secret Names of future sons and daughters would be in that seed, but not His own. So did She also pass over the snot and the earwax. Ra hardly listened to what others said, so in His earwax was much stupidity, while the nose was a poor place to conceal the Name when every wind would sniff it out. Only urine and saliva were left: a choice of the sour waters of His blood, or the well of His mouth. Each had a clear attachment to the Name. Like a great river (that carries off many a secret from the land) was Ra's urine. But those waters went back to the Celestial Waters. Nut would certainly be displeased if Isis tried to steal a Secret Name from Her. Therefore, Isis chose saliva. It was the spirit of Ra's speech. At the center of His speech must be the Name. Therefore, She took up moist dust near a spot where the old God, walking on His path, had drooled, and She worked this moist dust into clay, and added to it an old powder made of the semen of Set (which She had kept from the skirt of the handmaiden Set had raped). There could be no better way to fortify a poison than to mix the leavings of one's enemies. So Isis shaped this mortar from the spit of Ra and the semen of Set and molded it into the form of a snake, and anointed its fangs (which came from the cuttings of Her fingernails) with the poison of scorpions. Then Isis said to these fangs, "Go out. Discover in your enemy what is most different from yourself. Attack Him there. Loose your sting!" The venom of Isis' heart flowed from Her eye, and every carnal memory of Ra was in it. For with no innocence had She studied the seven varieties of His emission. His scent had been left on Her. Despite Her adoration of Osiris, which was like the tenderness of the sky as evening fell on the oasis and animals stood next to one another, Isis could never prevent one outrageous desire. It was the thrill to Her belly at the sight of Ra. So She had indulged one secret hour with Her father. How the death of Osiris brought back the burden of Her old deception. She had never told Her husband, and Osiris, therefore, had believed Himself too well beloved. Knowing too little of the powers of other Gods, He had entered Set's coffin too carelessly. To Her own rage at Ra was added, therefore, the turmoil of Her own deception. With what a spell did Isis leave the serpent on the path!

Ra passed through the cool fields of heaven pouting and dribbling as He took His short walk in the dawn. On this route had Isis set Her snake. As the old God approached (His belly still churning on the indigestible phallus) the snake leaped through the distance within itself from the inert clay to the vital curse, and lanced its fang into the God. And the poison said: "Burn, Ra, as flame licks at Your loins. Freeze in the chill of Your golden eye as the light leaves. A poison has been made that will find Your last extremity!"

And the Sun-God felt the presence of all He was not. It crept across Him and His limbs began to struggle, and heat became His torture. He staggered and His will had fear of all that was strange in His flesh. His skin lost its hue and He was pale as platinum, pale as the silver of His bones. The old age of Ra turned in His mouth, and His lips made Him spit on the earth. The poison came into His flesh even as the Nile spreads over the fields. "What has stung Me?" He cried out. "It is something I do not know and have never made." And He gave the great cry of bewilderment all men have since uttered to themselves at the moment death is on them. "Come here, Gods and Goddesses," He cried out, "all You Who were formed from Me!"

The air altered. Light and dark flowed, colors engulfed other colors. Gods and Goddesses manifested Themselves from the four pillars of the sky, up from the river, and across from the winds of the desert. The waters of the Duad boiled.

Ra said: "At dawn, I was passing through the kingdom of Egypt for I wanted to see what I had made, and a serpent bit me. I feel colder than water and more inflamed than the fire. My legs sweat, My body shakes, My eyes are weak. Water pours from My face as in the time of flood. Agonies have entered."

In the pall that followed, dark as the blood that dries on sand after a war has passed, Isis spoke. For that first instant, the Gods snickered: They all knew of Isis' humiliation by Set. There was, however, no uncertainty in Her tone. "Great Ra," She said, "You have been poisoned by an art devoted to Your death."

"I cannot die," said Ra. "I am the First, and the Son of the First."

"You will die," said Isis, "unless You reveal Your Secret Name. He who is able to reveal His Name will live."

"I will not tell My Secret Name," said Ra. "If I am gone, the earth bursts, and the heavens are lost with the earth. For I have created the heavens and the secret of the horizon."

She came forward. Step by step, She entered the aura of Ra. Now, She whispered into His ear. Her voice quivered through His flesh.

He tried to stand to His full height, but was bent over in wretchedness.

"I cannot die," said Ra. "My Father gave a Secret Name in fire, My Mother annealed It in the waters. They hid My Name when I was born. No word can have power over Me so long as My Name remains unknown."

"The poison," said Isis, "will reach to the last corner of Your flesh. The semen of Set is in that poison and He knows no fear at searching You."

"I will reveal My Secret Name to *all*," said Ra. A cry came up from the Gods, then a silence. But Isis knew that Ra would lie. In the past, His eyes would always show His earnest heart when He spoke with no truth.

"My names," said Ra, His mouth so tight with pain that His jaw could hardly move, "My names are without end. My forms are the form of all things. Every God has His existence in Me."

"Do not die, Great Ra," cried the Gods. But They did not know if They wished for His life or His death. They did not know what They desired—a fearful day for the Gods.

"My name," shouted Ra, "is Maker-of-Heaven-and-Earth.

"I am He-Who-links-the-mountains-together.

"I am He-Who-caused-the-great-flood.

"I am He-Who-made-the-joys-of-love.

"I am He-Who-made-the-horizon.

"I am the Being-Who-opens-His-eyes-and-light-comes.

"I am the Being-Who-closes-His-eyes-and-it-is-dark.

"I am He-Whom-the-Gods-know-not."

He stumbled and almost fell. Isis said: "There is no mention of the Secret Name. Soon You will be consumed by the poison. Declare the Name." As She spoke, the Gods gave a murmur. She was more splendid than Ra. Side by side, They stood together, and She was more splendid.

"I am He-Who-creates-the-fire-of-life," said Ra.

"I am He-Who-is-Khepera-in-the-morning, Ra-at-noon, and Temu-in-the-evening."

"I am He-Who . . ." His voice failed. Poison was climbing the cataracts of His blood, and the seas were His mind on fire. The glare of heat was in all of existence. Consumed by heat, He tore off His clothing.

"Search Me," Ra cried out.

In view of the Gods, Isis came forward, took off Her robes and lay upon Him. From within His belly, the phallus of Osiris gave life to the stick of His old loins and He came forth into Isis with the Secret Name (and all of the semen of Set that He had swallowed with the poison, and this act loosed the most terrible lightning ever seen in the skies of Egypt—thus was Set first made lord of lightning and thunder) and so did Ra pass His Secret Name over into the belly of Isis. It entered on a quiet voice that told Her: "Temu is One, the Celestial Waters are Two, and Ra, child of Temu and Nut, is Three. So His Secret Name is Three. Roar, Isis, like a lion that we may hear the sound of 'r' in all the tongues. For the roar of the sun is the light of earth. And the heir of Ra shall be as the light of the mind, which is death. Hail, Osiris, Lord of the Land of the Dead. Rise, Isis, who holds the Secret Name of Ra. You are all that is and has been, and all that will be and is."

Three

Isis rose, and the foam of the old man drained from Her legs. She said, "Spew, poison, spew! Out of Me! Out of Ra! Ra lives, and the poison dies." Then She put on the great golden robe Ra had left on the floor. The robe was filthy, but sediments and waters washed from it as if by rain, and Isis stood in glory. The Gods applauded. They were terrified. Some remembered old calumnies upon Isis. (Still the prettiest of Them was already trying to capture Her eye.) But a stranger came forward from the back of Their ranks holding a robe to cover Ra. The stranger's hair was white, yet His face was young and more beautiful than any other. It was the Ka of Osiris.

He stood beside Isis and held Her hand. At that instant, His body became lost in Hers. His flesh was so transparent that Osiris disappeared into Her. To Ra, She said, in the voice of Osiris, "Old God, when there is need for gentle days, You may bring sugar to the fruit trees, and encouragement to the crops of the fields. But when You enter the Duad by night, You will wear My winding sheet. Now will My son, Horus, be the golden eye of the day, and the silver eye of the moon. In the Duad will I rule over the dead, and through My wife,

Isis, will I rule over the crops of the Nile. Go forth, to perform Your duties." As He separated from Isis, Osiris became visible again. Holding His body but the width of a finger apart from Her body (for whenever They touched, His presence flowed forth into Her again) He ordered the Gods to return to Their places, and dream of no new power. The master of the future was here, and Osiris opened His loincloth to reveal that if His phallus had been devoured by Abtu, and the fish in turn swallowed by Ra, now He, Osiris, had become the devourer of He who devoured Him. In consequence, His phallus had three limbs. One for Ptah, the master builder, stood forth like a post and glowed hot as metal in the forge. Another was massive, motionless, and dark as Seker, knobbed like a root from the depths of the earth. Last, all but transparent, was the phallus of Osiris Himself, and it arched like a rainbow after His wanderings through the air, the surf, and the mist, a luminous phallus for the Lord of the Mind, Osiris, God of the Resurrection.

At this sight, Ra vomited. Yet nothing came out of His belly. The once indigestible phallus was certainly gone, and He could only slink away.

When Isis and Osiris were alone, however, Their conversation was less majestic. "It is part," said Osiris, "of the difficulties of Our position that We cannot even touch each other, or I will disappear again. So We won't touch. For then We cannot talk, and there is much to tell You. I know more about the Duad than You would care to hear." He gave a tender smile, and added in His lightest, most agreeable voice, "As a young Prince, I could never listen to any wretch whose tale would bore Me. Now I spend My years taking account of the endless justifications of the dead. Their piety is insatiable. 'Was it your fault, or the fault of your wife?' I ask some absolute wretch, and his answer invariably is that 'It would take the Lord Osiris to know.'"

"Yes, You must be weary," answered Isis in a small voice. The coolness of His greeting was certainly a distance away from Their last embrace off the coast of Byblos.

"I can only say," said Osiris, "that I have had to wander through varieties of existence I would not describe." He yawned.

A look of revulsion came over Her face. His breath, while not corrupt, had the smell of the void. She felt Her powers disappearing into this emptiness. Smiling wisely, He drew farther away, and gave a sad smile. "Yes, We must talk," He said. "Our position is most vulnerable. We must talk quickly. Therefore, I will pass over the abominable pleasures You took with Ra. Even if that cost My life."

"I will pass over Your day with Nephthys."

Osiris nodded. "It does not matter what We have done. I cannot reign by Your side until You put together what has been laid asunder fourteen times."

"The search should not be difficult," said Isis. "I have more power than ever before."

"No," said Osiris, "there is always one more power to need." Again, He smiled sadly. "All of Me must be found and properly embalmed in fourteen years."

"What if it takes longer?"

"You will inherit the woes of Set. Choose between lightning and thunder."

So Isis went back to the Nile, and Osiris, in full possession of the voids of the dead, ruled in Her place. Heaven was a muted region and entertainments were few. Affairs proceeded beneath a quiet sky. Ra merely nodded His head to old admirers as He took each daily ride, and Isis, on any convocation of the Gods, would sit at a distance from Osiris. Her beauty began to be lost.

To Find each piece of the body of Osiris proved difficult. In the first year, She found nothing, nor in the second, nor third. In three years, nothing. With Anubis, She hunted through far-off regions, but the dogs She employed were of no use. Having the wisdom of a jackal, Anubis could certainly teach His hounds to search for the faintest traces of a scent, but there was no odor to the dead man. Even His loincloth offered no more than a hint of the thighs of Isis—sufficient for the dogs to come near to attacking Her.

So, They found nothing. Perhaps it was in the balance of Maat not to be able to locate more than one piece each year. Since Set had already strewn three in Buto before the gates of Her camp, why assume, asked Isis, that They would come upon the fourth until the fourth year was begun?

Anubis asked what She had done with the First three pieces, and when She replied that She laid them in a bed of natron, Isis began to brood upon Her own remark. While the eleven unfound pieces could have decomposed long ago, still She must proceed as if they existed. Why not expect, therefore, that each fragment had been wise enough to float toward a marsh where salt would abound? So in each region She could limit Their search to the pools, beds, bends, and swamps of natron.

Yet even if They looked for damp flats full of embalmer's salt, the dogs were still without a scent. Anubis mixed herbs that might suggest the presence of Osiris, but they did not guide the dogs. He came at last to propose that the child, Horus, conceived from a dead God, might have something of His Father's odor, that is to say, His lack of it. "I do not know if hounds can bear such emptiness," was Isis' reply. Nonetheless, She took Her skirt and gave it to Horus for play. He chewed on it, rolled His body in the wrappings, and returned a torn garment. Having put it on, Isis then anointed Herself with mandrake, and fortified it with myrrh so that the mandrake would grow aromatic while She slept and travel out to the lost parts of Osiris.

At dawn, Anubis passed the cloth to the dogs. The hounds went through convulsions which left them so acute in the nose that each year of the remaining years, a part of Osiris' body was found quickly. But then not all the credit need be given to the dogs. The head of Osiris, the first piece found, still had the thumb of Set in its mouth, and Isis was able to use that thumb to guide Her boat. By the rudder of Set, therefore, or the nose of the dogs, it never took more than a week, and the remainder of the year could be devoted to building a tomb.

Of course, it was not easy to find priests for such a task. Many were afraid of Set. But when She encountered a promising fellow, Isis would tell him: "We will take this Divine part, and add to it a body of wax. You are the only one to know that here rests only a fourteenth part of Osiris. Yet the part will be as the whole, and you will be the

High Priest in this nome of Egypt." Then She would seal the pact with a kiss. Isis always detested that small embrace. Divinity passed out of Her lips and into the priest's mouth even as his will was surrendered to Her. Thereafter, he obeyed all instructions. Yet She lamented that the lips of fourteen such men, mortal and monotonous, must She know upon Her mouth before the fourteen tombs could be built. A trace of these priests, born of fourteen more or less ordinary women, would yet add their depredations to Her features. Her only consolation was that each priest had been deceived. For the part of Osiris that She gave them was also made of wax. The pieces of the true body were locked in a chest of natron, and on such a throne She sat while sailing up the Nile, or drifting down.

On the first day of the fourteenth year, Isis, Anubis, and the hounds found the last soaking stump of Osiris in the steaming salts of Yeb, and the sun went through an eclipse. Isis trembled from a sudden fear of all the worlds to come. The leg stood up in Her grasp as if its will were to walk. Then it fell from Her hand, and in the instant of its fall, She had a vision of wars to ensue between Horus and Set. Horror was still upon Her house. Isis, however, walked through the salts to Her papyrus bark, and laid in the leg with the other pieces. She wrapped the body, and in the evening, called for Her sister Nephthys and Maat and Thoth. Together, with Horus, They slaughtered a bull to mark the end of the curse of Set.

Now, Horus, Who was fourteen, and heavy in the chest and thin in His legs, opened the eyes and mouth of Osiris, which was the First time the Ceremony of the Opening of the Mouth was ever performed, and Horus said, "Let the Ka of Osiris come forth from the eyes and mouth of His new abode." And the Ka of Osiris joined Them, and His odor had the fragrance of the finest gardens of Egypt, and They ate well that night. In the morning, They departed toward heaven, for Osiris was full of concern at the storm-wracked sky. There had been lightning and thunder toward dawn. "We were just in time," He said.

Four

"If you think," said Menenhetet One, "to enter mysteries, you have not begun. The story I have offered is no more than a ripple of light on water. While all is true, still there is a secret behind every secret I offered. I, as an example, was one of the fourteen priests Isis kissed. If it was a thousand years ago, still it gave me courage to explore into many matters that are forbidden."

We sat there in silence, my mind now shamefully aware of the handicap of my imperfect memory, as if like a cripple with one arm and one leg, I tried to put a saddle on a horse. I could not comprehend his life. Did he lie? Had he ever been a priest kissed by Isis? And was he ever a General who won so many battles that he could live on the gifts given him by the Pharaoh? I seemed to remember that as so. But indeed which Pharaoh could it be? Deep as my anger for Hathfertiti was the desire to see her, if only to ask after these simple matters. Why could I not remember stories about my great-grandfather? Once again I knew a sense of oppression.

He sat back in his chair and I could notice for the first time—it was in fact the first time my fear of him had diminished sufficiently to look at anything but his eyes—that the legs of his chair were of

gold and had been cast as the forelegs and hind legs of a lion. Menenhetet now had the expression of a lion—he was indeed as dignified
as an old General who lives in the recollection of old exploits. "Yes,"
he said, "a man can feel accomplishment if he begins as the son of a
whore, yet so distinguishes himself as to rise to command the Gold
Rank of Ra, the Horses of Set, the Hidden of Amon, and the Foundry
of Ptah. Those four great divisions were at one time under my command. Yet I began in the ranks. The child of a whore is favored, after
all, with knowledge others do not have. His mother being familiar
with many embraces, so my sword was always ready for the flash
of the other sword. I had a quick eye and I learned to think in ways
that others do not. I had been, after all, one of the lovers of my
mother."

"And of my mother."

He cackled. He winked. The palm of one hand was now clapped to
his brow, and the other grasped himself by the scrotum. Crude was
the move and a huge humor to him: "As above, so below," he choked.

I found myself as repelled by his sudden shifts as I was confused.
In the elegant surface of his manners was a crack through which
would ooze from time to time the worst putrescence of an old man's
thoughts.

"Yes," he said, "I was the lover of your mother. And your mother
was sweeter than my mother." His merriment washed through my
dignity. We laughed together. I was horrified at how little character
was possessed by my Ka. I might as well be an uprooted weed blown
about by every desert wind.

"Did you really become one of the fourteen priests of Isis?" I could
not help but ask. "Or did you lie to me?"

"I lied to you. The traveler from distant places is an everlasting
liar." He smiled. "I was not one of the original fourteen priests of Isis
any more than my mother was a whore—in truth she was only a peasant. Yet I did not lie to you altogether. The life of the dead is maintained by a careful repetition of their history. So, each year, on the
banks of the Duad, Isis passes among us, selects from our ranks fourteen men who used to be priests, and repeats the kiss that founded

Her husband's temples. I am always selected, but that is because She appeared to me in a spell when I was still alive, and embraced me."

He gave an elegant, aristocratic and utterly exhausted flutter of his fingers as if the hand that once carried the heaviest sword would not have the vitality now to pick the stem of a flower. "The Gods," he said wearily, "are capable of anything. They do everything." And in sudden wrath, he added, "That is why They have real need of Maat. If not for Maat, there would be no end to the destruction They cause. Nor the wild passions They strew when They turn into animals. The abominable situation is that Their transformations depend on shit, blood-sacrifice, and fucking, and They respect none of it. They do not appreciate how magic is obedient to the deepest principle."

When I could only mutter that I did not understand what he said, he looked at me and declared, "In its true exchange, one cannot gain a great deal unless one is willing to dare losing all. That is how the loveliest plunder is found. You do not buy a few words of power, say them over a colored powder, sprinkle it on the sand and ask for the dancing girl to come to your hut tonight. The girl may certainly arrive, and she will dance on your doorstep, but if you have no true power yourself then she will also leave behind an inflammation on the head of your penis, and eggs of vermin in the hairs of your thighs. One has to pay a price for magic. Put the colored powder on the sand, but also take a vow to draw your sword next day at the first insult, and obey that vow whether the dancing girl brings poverty or pleasure. That is the obligation. Look for the risk. We must obey it every time. There is no credit to be drawn from the virtue of one's past."

"Not even once?"

"Not in magic. In piety, but not in magic. Look to the example of Isis. She was a noble woman by every measure, a loyal wife, a brave soldier, practiced at magic, supreme in Her will. Yet at the end (and it is at the end of each trial of magic that the worst ambush waits) She betrayed Her family."

"But She did not."

"Let me tell you again. There is the magic we invoke, and the magic that calls upon us. Do you recall that Isis dropped the fourteenth piece of the body of Osiris in the salts of Yeb, and saw battles to come between Horus and Set? That was a warning to find a proper sacrifice or there would be no peace. She heard Her own voice tell Her to slaughter a bull, but as She killed the beast, Her voice also told Her that the sacrifice was not great enough to compensate for the evil powers of Set. She must add the blood of a more painful loss. She must cut off Her own head, and replace it with the bull's face." Menenhetet now giggled. When I asked him why he laughed, he remarked, "I am thinking of the fearsome creature who hides in the little feather of Maat. She carries the principle of balance to the point of torture. Naturally, Isis protested. I can promise you that She did not fail to recite the virtues of the fourteen years of Her wanderings. Indeed, She was so eloquent in presenting Her achievements of the past as safeguards for the present that Maat actually reduced Her demand. It would now be sufficient for Isis to lay Her forehead on the hairy ridge between the horns of the bull. In time, over months to come, She would certainly develop horns, and Her features would grow to look like a cow.

"Isis said no. After fourteen years in the company of Anubis, she was weary of the ugliness one feels when obliged to look every day at a dull face. The vanity of Isis in this hour was greater than Her loyalty to Horus. So, She would only offer the simple sacrifice of the bull, and when the funeral was done, and Osiris rose, They returned across the storms to the new court of the Ka of Osiris where They would raise Their son to confront Set in the wars to come.

"Now, since Set's powers had been reduced, the heat of His wrath no longer scorched the earth. After the yearly flood, Egypt flowered into so many oases that they grew together into forests, and Horus, conceived on the open sea, prospered in this damp climate, and grew powerful in His ungainly way. If His shoulders took on the strength of a bear, He moved nonetheless like an ape. Bent over weak legs, His sense of well-being was strong only in the trees, or down by the exhalations of the swamp. Yet, even at such agreeable times, He did not smile. For as He grew, Horus directed every thought toward the increase of His strength. Laughter, for instance, He did not permit

Himself. It relaxed His muscles, and thereby allowed too much force to return to the earth."

Here, my great-grandfather's voice came nearer to me, and we traveled together in the thoughts of Horus as He brooded on the weakness of His lower limbs, and listened to the talk of war. If many thought the battle should take place between Osiris and Set, the Gods, after some debate, concluded that Osiris was too valuable to be lost. The Ka, being only one of the seven souls and spirits of the living, is outnumbered by just such a proportion of seven to one for any test of might.

Of course, some Gods argued there should be no contest at all because Set was unworthy. He looked like a brigand. He had grown heavy, and His red hair and red face were choleric. His skin was the color of a boil, His beard the hue of dark blood. There were ulcers on His face and hands, and veins in the bulb of His nose. His strength was fearsome, but as foul as His sweat was His breath since He drank nothing but wine that came from profane grapes. Indeed, He cultivated vines grown from the blood of thieves so foolhardy as to have robbed a temple, after which the thieves were devoured by a herd of lions at their own oasis. Now, when Set drank of this vine grown from ground moist with thieves' blood, His breathing had the sounds of a storm. He ate the meat of the wild boar and left its juice on His fingers in order that His hands should never slip from a weapon. He lived in old skins whose scent was so repulsive that His servants deserted Him one by one to swear loyalty to Horus. Even His favorite mistress, Puanit, got up from His body one night, washed in the Nile, and set out for the camp of Horus. Set, on awakening, went to follow her, but became so drunk He fell asleep in the mud and returned home looking filthier than ever (as if Geb had been indeed His father). Word came back of Puanit's exploits among Horus' men, and Set was now ridiculed by His few remaining servants. Puanit described the boils on His bottom as fiercer than the sores of His face. She spoke of His testicles as slack, and only referred to Set by the contemptible name, Smu. All the while she made every attempt to seduce Horus, even declaring herself ready to lick His feet. The God's toes, she promised, would be more nimble for the approaching battle.

Set started a fire of dead vines from the grove of His profane grapes, and took the flame into His lungs. Then He blew this fire over the wine, and was thereby intoxicated to a degree greater than He had known before. In the force of this drunkenness, He was ready for war, and left to seek Horus.

There, in the other camp, Osiris was asking His son, as He asked each morning, "What is the most noble act You can perform?"

"It is," said Horus, "to avenge My Father and Mother for the evil done to Them."

Then Osiris took Horus through exercises to strengthen His legs. Horus attempted, for example, to strangle an animal between His thighs (although so far He had done no better than to wrench the neck of a calf).

On this morning, Osiris asked a new question. "Which animal is the most useful for combat?"

"A horse," said Horus.

"Why not a lion?" asked Osiris.

"If I needed assistance, I would think of a lion, but I want an animal to carry Me in pursuit of Set once He runs away."

"You are ready," said Osiris. "Before this, there was little question in My mind about the outcome, but now I know My Son will be Lord of the Living." And He promised a horse if the need should arise for pursuit. Then Osiris told Him to wait for Set in the open plain outside the walls of Memphi and try to lure Him into the swamp where neither would have footing. That way, the contest could depend on the strength of Their arms. In a great atmosphere of confidence, Horus went off to meet His uncle. At the last moment, Isis even gave Him the withered thumb of Set She had used to guide Her through the swamp. This thumb, She informed Her son, could extricate Him from one great trial, so He must wait to use it wisely.

Menenhetet looked at me, however, as if dissatisfied.

"What is wrong," he asked, "with the training of Horus?"

"In it, I don't find," I replied, "any of the divine intelligence of Osiris."

"It is not present," agreed Menenhetet. "Osiris doesn't seem vengeful. Secretly, I will tell you that He is not fond of Horus. The boy is void of charm.

"Moreover, Isis is bored these days. She speaks fiercely to the youngest Gods. (Revered by everyone as the noblest wife of all, the pleasures of flirtation are closed.) While She thinks Her son is a dank and solemn monotony of strength, She must pretend to enthusiasm for His mission.

"Horus, in His turn, is ignorant of His parents' feelings. His life is so empty of interest that He knows only that He has not much desire to become Lord of the Living. When His exercise is done, His mind is empty.

"Yet, in the camp of Horus, not one servant or warrior dares to speak of disaster. The most obvious difficulties won't be discussed. Horus, for example, is utterly innocent of the sentiments of real combat. He does not know how panic can swallow the mind when facing a deadly man. He has not seen the eye of that opponent! Besides, the camp has been disrupted by Puanit. If, in preparation for battle, there is any mood worse than false confidence, it is carnal mischief. The most sensible exercise for Horus is to concentrate upon His legs. Instead, He is twitching with unaccustomed pleasure at the thought His toes might soon be licked.

"Well, They meet on the field Osiris has suggested, in what are now the gardens about the Temple of Ptah, but then it was only the edge of an unnamed marsh, and the followers of Horus and the few remaining servants of Set came together and formed a great circle about the two warriors. Thoth, Osiris, Isis, Nephthys, and four other Gods appeared to serve as judges.

"In that circle all waited, and Horus stared at Set across a distance of twenty paces. A silence descended into the grove, and it lasted until the moment Horus could not bear to wait longer, and took out His sword, a sound of withdrawal as noisy in this quiet as a snake crossing a bed of shells, and Set's breath was as hoarse in reply as if combat had commenced. Yet when He removed His sword from the scabbard it was with the quick and whistling sound of a blade well drawn, and They moved then toward each other, but slowly, the air filled with caution." Here my great-grandfather extended an arm as if to share this combat with me, and again I could see what he saw.

Now Horus and Set came into reach. When each slammed a sword against the other's blade, the advantage was to Horus. His arms were stronger—that was clear from the shock to both—and His hands were fast. The smell of Set grew rank with the sweat of twice-fortified wine. Aware that the power He took from His grapes might soon evaporate, He went on attack, looking to confuse Horus with rapid moves from side to side, but His attack was soon worn out by these exertions. Set drew back a step. Each tried to stir, each man searched for breath. Each was wondering whether the other was as quickly used-up as Himself. Now, They continued by the quiver of an elbow, or the inclination of a knee, just out of distance of each other.

Horus began to feel as if Set's exhaustion was greater than His own. Were Set's responses as slow as they seemed? Horus flung His shield. Sudden as that. There was Set without a sword. And His skin was close to the purple of old meat. He took a step backward, then another, and in that instant Horus lunged to take Him through the heart, a clumsy move. A warrior as old as Set was not to be finished so simply. He ducked under, caught Horus by a leg, and gave a twist to drop Him. Then Set smashed His shield into Horus' unprotected face. The blow shattered the nose of the boy, and drove His teeth through His lips. His sword leaped out of His hand. Set kicked it away, whereupon Horus seized the shield of Set, hurled it, and missed. Now, both were unarmed.

Horus' face was like the disembowelment you see on a battlefield. Still He came forward to close with Set. But the older man stepped back and took off His breastplate so that He might be more comfortable when grappling. Horus did the same. In another minute, both were naked. Since each, for His separate reasons, wished to fight in the marsh, They were soon off the field and into the swamp. But as They entered the mud, Set turned to all who were watching and revealed a mighty erection. It stood out like a branch strong enough for a man to climb upon. Even the followers of Horus offered up their approbation, for it was a mark of great merit to have an erection in combat. That spoke of true bravery since combat was obviously His desire.

To show agreement, Menenhetet now separated his robes to show his own phallus. I might as well have been struck with the shield of Set. For Menenhetet presented a stout knob and shaft. I pretended not to notice, but began to feel as fatigued as if I were in combat myself, and my lungs and liver shook, a curious remark if my Ka (like any other) was without the substance of liver and lungs, but then I realized that my Canopic jars were vibrating at my feet.

"You are nearer to a comprehension of Khert-Neter," murmured my great-grandfather, and covered his thighs.

"Contemplate the shame for Horus," he said. "Having been shown once to the Gods with His smashed face, He was now twice exposed. His lower powers were puny. 'Look upon the future God of the Living,' cried Set and threw a handful of mud into Horus' face. Blinded, Horus in a vertigo of elbows and knees went tumbling over a stump into the swamp water. Immediately, Set pushed Horus' head and shoulders into the muck. Now, the boy's arms had to be used to keep His nose above the water. His weak legs were up behind Him on the stump. Down between His buttocks rammed the hard phallus of Set, and ohhhh," said Menenhetet, "what an entrance! Lava was ready to boil. The Nile prepared to froth. Isis turned paler than Her bark of papyrus, and Osiris became transparent again. A scream went up from Horus like the wail of a mortal boy, while Set was throbbing with pride. As He held the separate cheeks in His separate hands, He singed the boy's shoulders with the fire of His breath, and made ready to take entrance. No God dared to speak if Horus was to be cleaved. For this wasn't a buggery like the sports of your boyhood where one coward inches up the lost resistance of another. Here was one of the Great Gods entering that male womb where time is buried."

"Womb . . . ?" I stammered.

"In Khert-Neter," said Menenhetet, "there is a river of feces deep as a pit. Across it, the dead must swim. The Ka of all but the wisest, most prepared, or most courageous, will expire in that river, weeping for their mother. They have forgotten how they came out of her. Between piss and shit are we born, and in water do we die the first time, slipping off to death on the release of our waters. But the second death is in the full pits of the Duad. Do I sit before you and fart? Do you smell every odor of the constipated, the gluttonous, the sulphurous, the caustic, the fermentative, the infectious, the rotten, the corrupt, the putrescent? It is because I had to swim the river of feces, and succeeded in crossing only at a great price. The spirit of human excrement is now in the breath of my Ka, which is to say, in my emotions, and in my irregular courtesy. Small wonder that every disproportion is also in my manner, yes, every happiness that was interrupted, every injustice to an honest endeavor, as well as all the squandered seeds of tender love that found no root, and this is not even to speak of energetic lust when it has no place to go but to the coils of one's digestion (although much of such lust turns to piss) enough! You have no gift for your trip to Khert-Neter if you do not comprehend that shame and waste may be buried in shit, but so is many a rich and tender sentiment as well. How then can this cauldron of emotion be no more than a burial chamber? Is it not also part of the womb of all that is yet to come? Is not part of time reborn, by necessity, in shit? Where else can be found those unresolved passions which—frustrated, unworked, or, by their stench, maniacal—must now labor twice as hard to germinate the future?"

He had never been this eloquent, nor as elegant in his appearance. I could no longer see the dust of his pores in the glow these words gave to his skin. Out of the lines of his wrinkles came a play of light. Yet the finer he looked, the more I was ready to distrust him. His language had too powerful an effect on me. I was now aroused and by the sweetest turnings of sex; my belly was as sentimental as a flower, and my buttocks in honey—I had never felt so agreeable before. Was this the power and pleasure of a woman? Whatever had become of my pride in a phallus as dependable as my arm? To go soft before these hymns to the sinuosities of shit! It used to be legitimate, if a filthy

habit, to jam the force of one's own cock into the ass of any friend (or
enemy) weak enough to take it, a way of measuring ourselves, but
nonetheless! every mark of a noble Egyptian was his detestation of
such dirt. The smell of the mud was too close to our lives—our white
linen spoke of the distance we maintained from such subjects, the
whiter the better. So were our walls white, and the complexion of
our Gods when we painted Them. So were our noses most distinguished when they turned up nicely. Yet here was Menenhetet seduc-
ing my attention with the glories of this repulsive topic.

"You are dead," he said, "and the first shock is that your mind will
now seek to appreciate what formerly it despised. If I have survived it
is because I overcame all sense of abhorrence in swimming the Duad."
He was now so gentle that into my sweet arousal came an unexpected
tenderness for Menenhetet, the first I had felt. That gave a sense of
rest. I needed to like someone other than myself! But as if my great-
grandfather had no need of my good feelings, he went back without
warning to his account of Set's attempt to bugger Horus.

"Did He succeed?" asked Menenhetet. And replied, "Not at this
time, not here. Horus still owned, we must remember, the old thumb
of Set that Isis tied into the thick hair of His head. Now, head down,
the bolt of Set riding on His sphincter, He knew that if He did not
escape, the Land of the Dead might yet be carved out of His bowels.
So, He reached up a hand, tore out a gout of hair to free the thumb,
and waved it in the air. Set's erection was lost. Abruptly Set's penis
was as small as His amputated thumb, and Horus, in a tempest (at
last!) of godly fury at what almost had been done to Him, seized the
testicles of Set with such force that the calm of the heavens was forever disturbed. The sudden noise of a squall is equal to the fury with
which Set struck back at Horus' brow, and the young man's face was
soon hideous, His eyes half uprooted. He looked like a hippopotamus.

"On this moment, they entered a new form of battle. While transformations are common in godly war, and the Gods seek to be artful
in Their choice, still, They must also be ready to take up the form of

any beast They come, willy-nilly, to resemble. So, when Set tore the eyes of Horus half out of His head and gave Him the expression of a hippopotamus, Horus was obliged to turn into that unfamiliar creature.

"They fought then in a bog, hippopotamus against hippopotamus, with grunts, hoarse slaverings, and atrocious roars, Their limbs so short and sturdy that when each got a leg of the other in His throat, the spectacle became as obscene as the sight of hogs suckling in a trough.

"Yet the judges were not disgusted. This part of the battle was expected to thrash in the mires, and gather up the repulsions of the atmosphere, drain the swamps, and flush the filth of the Nile. It would have been a great purification if it had gone on, but Set called a halt. The slime of Their bodies had begun to excite Him. He was losing ferocity too quickly. Set had assumed that Horus, being younger, would be rendered anxious by such slippery contact, but to Horus, this steaming intimacy was gloomy. He wanted His teeth in Set— none of this slithering of torsos—He strained for that luminous instant when the rage of your effort can taste the blood of the other. His lower teeth protruded, His nostrils drew together, His skin in repudiation of such oily struggle grew bristles. His lower teeth were like tusks. He had changed into a wild boar.

"Applause came to Him from the Gods Who watched. It was daring to choose the animal most like Set, and brilliant to select such a transformation now rather than to let Set choose it for the end. Horus could hardly have done better. Was there another hour of His life when He was more of a wild boar? He and Set came charging out of the marsh and ran up and down the field, slashing into each other's flanks, biting ferociously, sobbing and shrieking, carving wounds into one another until a spray of blood flew off each time They came together with a crash.

"To the surprise of most, the advantage was turning to Horus. A God, like a man, is never stronger than in the hour He discovers His valor. Horus was delivered of oppression—He was no longer afraid to fight. What uproar in Himself! He even enjoyed the intoxication of the pain. Each time Set's teeth tore His hide, He roared with new ferocity, His torn eyes pulled back into the knotty little sockets of the boar, while two gems of fire looked out. His broken nose was like a red and bleeding mouth, and the teeth that cut through His lips glistened in a collar of spikes. Set fled. To the jeers of the onlookers He retreated far enough to gain time for the last transformation. When He turned back to the field, it was as a black bear. Such a choice was difficult to comprehend since Horus had more of the natural build of such an animal, but the pain of Set's wounds was great enough to look for the thickest hide, and He buried Himself in the meats and folds and near-to-impenetrable substance of a bear. There, He undertook His defense.

"This strife between the bears went on for a day, and then a night, and before They were done, it was three days and three nights. Horus held Set in a captive grip and made Him undergo a long and stubborn torment as He was bled of the great power of a bear. To sustain Himself in this pain, He had no more to call upon than the endless bitterness of His life, and it provided the fortitude not to surrender. It even enabled Him to withstand the exultation of Horus Who passed through all the intoxications of victory except victory itself, and so was exhausted finally of all enthusiasm, and merely lay with the bulk of His bear body upon the bear's body of Set, and kept His teeth in the neck of Set until all the illumination He had tasted in His enemy's blood was consumed and Horus lay at last with His caked face in the matted fur of the other.

"On the morning of the fourth day, declared victor by the judges, He had ropes brought to Him, and in a creaking voice ordered His assistants to pinion Set's limbs to stakes, and when they were finished, Set lay on His back, body lashed, looking at the sky. Slowly, like the change of light over the hours of the day, so did Set come back into the form of a wounded man lying near death on the field, but Horus was taken up on the shoulders of His friends and carried away to the river where They washed His wounds and cleaned the ravages of His face. Slowly, He, too, gave up the body of the bear. Then Horus slept for a day and a night in the joy of knowing that Set would not escape since guards trusted by Isis were in watch over Him."

And as if his words could be my words, my great-grandfather now became silent. His story, however, did not cease. Indeed, I do not think it lost one thought.

Five

Horus slept well. It was a night for celebration, and the Gods cheered every appearance of Isis and Osiris. For the first time in years, the Lord of the Dead offered the touch of two fingers to His wife's elbow (an old gesture to tell of carnal desire in the midst of formal ceremony) but Isis felt a foreboding that had little to do with pleasure. "Do You know," said Osiris, "the boy was better than I expected," and decided one virtue of this victory was that it enabled Him to feel love for His son.

"I am worried Set will escape," Isis answered, and later, when They tried to sleep, She was restless and went off to walk in the night, while Osiris tried to meditate on the source of Her uneasiness. He saw the face of His first son, Anubis, and sighed as quietly as a leaf listening to the approach of a light wind. In that sigh was the recognition by Osiris that His mind might be as pure as silver, and luminous as the moon, but His talents for divination could never be applied to any matter concerning Set. He had lost that power on the night He made love to Nephthys. One did not torture the feelings of a brother without disturbing every composure of the deep.

Now, when Isis reached the field where Set was pinioned in His bonds, She dismissed the guard and sat in the moonlight. Set made no sign at Her appearance. Exhaustion hung in tatters on His presence. So it was not easy to tell Him of His crimes nor the grim years He had caused. Instead, Isis found Herself brooding over the young and naked body of Her sister Nephthys next to the body of Osiris and felt Herself shaking with surprising rage. "I suffer," Isis said to Herself, "for all those who are deadened by evil copulations," and She could feel no wrath at Her brother, only the strength of the silence between Them. Now, She heard Set say, "Sister, cut My bonds."

She nodded. She felt meek. Beneath the light of the moon, Isis cut the ropes from Set, and He rose slowly from the ground, and, looking at Her, made the curious and childlike move of putting His thumb into His mouth. Sparks flew from His fingers and She saw His strength return. Then Set saluted and walked away.

Now, Isis knew a little of what She had done. By this unforeseen generosity to Set, She had begun to pay for ignoring the sacrifice suggested by Maat. So, She could not return to Osiris, but wandered through the night, and did not care what happened to Her. And in the morning, awakening with bad thoughts of His mother, Horus crossed the field to find that His uncle was gone.

Poor Horus. Until this battle, His emotions had tasted no better than the food of peasants who toil in caves: roots, grubs, and smoked beetles were the nourishment of His heart. Now, He had been to the feast of His own triumph. He was a man whose temper blazes for the first time in righteousness. "Where is My mother?" He roared in a voice to recall the worst voice of Set, and who did not hear? Nor did He have any trouble in finding Her. The eyes of those who had seen Isis pass, looked away. He could determine the direction She had taken by observing the back of everyone's head, and in the woods, He soon found Her.

"Who has released My enemy?" He asked.

Then Isis was afraid, yet She answered, "Do not speak in such a tone to Your mother."

He heard the fear She hoped to conceal, and, on the instant, raised His sword, and cut off Her head. "Now that I am victorious, I will never hesitate again," He started to say, but burst into tears instead, and wept with more grief than He had ever known. Picking up the head of His mother, Horus ran into the wilderness.

On the instant, what was left of Isis turned into a statue of flint. In such a headless state would She remain.

It is possible Osiris never knew a greater test of His understanding. While He could perceive His wife's act as a godly response to some warp in the order of things, it could not be said He felt forgiveness toward Horus. I was right, thought Osiris, not to trust My Son. What savage temper! Conceived out of the chill of My corpse, He is wild as a weed. "The future Lord of the Living is wild as a weed," repeated Osiris, and He was not given to repetition. But He did not know what to do. Hideous was the prospect of being wed forever to a headless statue. Indeed, how could one avenge such a wife? Yet, He could not leave Horus unpunished. That would invite chaos. So, Osiris gave word that His Son must be pursued.

Set was the first to take up the chase. He went out as a middle-aged warrior hardly healed from His wounds. He had, however, regained confidence. For when Isis cut His bonds, He felt as if a great power was released from Her and given to Him, and He prayed for noble and exalted strength. To the Hidden One, He said: "Monarch of the Invisible, allow Me a magnification of this great power that Isis releases (by betraying Her Son). Let lightning be as five hands where once it was five fingers." The heavens answered in a quiet voice, "Put the thumb that still belongs to You in Your mouth," and Set did as He was told, and felt balm come into His wounds, and His eight free fingers gave off sparks. So He was confident when He went out to look for Horus.

There was no battle, however. Set came upon a youth who sat in the stupor of grief. Set did not waste the opportunity. Immediately, He plucked out Horus' eyes (and indeed they were still weak from the wounds of the war). As Horus ran about in a circle (for blindness came upon Him in a whirlpool of pain) a stroke of lightning more deranging than the fall of a great stone shivered the earth, and the blood-red sockets of Horus' face showed as green as the brilliance of grass. Set felt a fear of the force given to Him by His prayer, and gave up all attempt to kill Horus. Instead, He grasped the head of Isis and ran away. Horus, seeking to pursue, stumbled off a cliff at the edge of the wood, and wandered in blindness through the desert.

By then, Set was far off. Having been granted this success, Set was not free of the awe He felt before these new powers. So, He took the eyes of Horus from the pouch in which He kept them, and planted those eyes in the ground, and even as He watched, they grew and became the lotus, which plant had never been seen before (and this lotus was soon to proliferate and become the royal plant of the Pharaohs). Watching, Set was tempted, however, to desecrate the head of His sister. The voice that had told Him to suck His thumb was now mocking Him. "You are too kind to Your enemies," said that voice. "Do not weaken what lives in the roots of Your temper. Befoul Her. Pollute Her flesh." From His anus to His navel, Set was one godly churn. The head of His phallus was a plum ready to burst. Lust was the purest impulse He knew—to paint semen on another. But in fear, He forced Himself away, and in a convulsion, masturbated over a field of lettuce. "Oh," murmured the voice, "You have made a mistake."

Set did not listen. What masturbator does? Chilled, subdued, He quit those silent bespattered vegetables, and came back to Memphi, but on every day that followed, His hunger to gorge on lettuce had become as great as His taste for meat.

So soon as He returned, Set presented the head of His sister to Her statue. Isis did not trust the gift. Mute, and incarcerated in stone, still She could feel that the head was contaminated. Thoth, Who had been serving as Her doctor, while other Gods were off in search of Horus, was also dubious. Thoth, with His thin arms and baboon face, might be the least virile of the Gods—He was married to Maat!—but He was also the Chief of Scribes and the Lord of Words. Of course, He would be the one to know how to speak to a statue. Having been alone with Isis for many hours, He began to put His hands on the flint with subtle strokes. So Isis began to converse. When it came to such matters, Thoth had the finest ears. After He laid a finger on the stone, He knew how to receive the reply. (It was in the quality of the silence.

But how many have ears to distinguish between one silence and another?)

Since the statue of Isis was without eyes to weep, tears could only flow from Her breast. That is to say, moisture appeared at each nipple. Thoth placed His hands there. During this vigil, He had grown familiar with Her shape, and if He knew nothing of the smoothness of Isis' skin (which once was finer than the patina of marble) Thoth's fingers enjoyed the rough flint. Like many a scribe to follow, He was not comfortable with the undulations of women. Irritation was more stimulating to His mind. Whenever some fires of incense were lit, His lungs would look for the harshest smoke—a small damage to the flesh improved His ability to think. Just so, His fingers even showed a blister here and there where they had fretted too long at the stone.

While holding Her, Thoth would often place His forehead against Her thigh. He would ponder what He wanted to ask, and try to compose the question with such purity of mind that the thought could reach into the mute recesses of the flint. Then, Isis would sooner or later reply. Not, however, by words. Pictures would come instead into His mind, misty at first, but sometimes this fog would dissipate, and Thoth would see Her response in an unmistakably clear image.

Now when He inquired if She would like the head returned to Her body, the flint presented no more than a muddy river to His mind, too muddy, that is, for vision until Thoth was given one wholly unpleasant view of the buttocks of Set in the midst of defecation. The flint had given its opinion of the head.

This vehemence left Thoth unsettled. Still, He tried to let His next thoughts flow quietly. He suggested that while She might no longer desire Her own face, still the heads of many birds, animals, insects, or flowers might be satisfactory.

Her reply made Him wait, but at last He was encouraged to wander in His mind down a jungle trail. Thoth, too sedentary for long marches, watched in wonder while strange animals and birds flashed in front of His closed eyes. He had never seen land so green, nor hills so steep. Huge insects crawled into his vision, and leaves of papyrus waved. Then He saw the horns of a gazelle, then a cobra. Now a herd of cows came forth to graze, and as He moved toward this herd, only one cow remained in sight. He could see nothing but the cow's head, lovely and soft was this cow's head, then Thoth heard the first sound ever to issue from stone. A ruminative voice full of the flavor of grass came forth, and as He opened His eyes, the flint was returning to flesh and Isis was before Him in all the beauty of Her own body, younger by years after this incarceration in stone. No longer headless, She had the small and comfortable horns of a fine cow. And the new name of Isis was Hathor.

Thoth could not keep from touching Her. If He was never guilty of excessive fornication—dry as the feather of Maat had been His small itch—still He was now as unstrung as a cat in heat. So, Hathor, in recompense for His long labors, allowed Him to rub against Her. The touch of real flesh put a rent, however, in His sluices, and He spewed all over Her flank. She was kind, and wiped His face, offered one kiss of a massively lolling tongue, and departed in search of Her son.

It proved no long search. The sound of Horus' cries reverberated through the desert. Blind, bewildered, His heart bruised, He lay near a grove by a spring and moaned in a voice that seemed small to Himself, yet it was so pure in its burden that His mother could hear it from many hills away. And when She finally reached His sightless body, She had a seizure of pity as if Her blood had passed through His sorrow.

Horus was surrounded by a field of lotus. It had flowered out of the first lotus that grew from His eyes, and a gazelle was feeding on the leaves. Isis, without hesitation, took milk from this gazelle. The animal never retreated as the Goddess approached for Isis was in the head of Hathor, and when did a gazelle have fear of a cow? Indeed, the animal barely knew she was being milked. She assumed this strange cow merely wished to pay homage, and did not know, poor cow, how to begin. Now, discovering that nothing was desired of her but milk, the gazelle (none so secretly vain as the gazelle) stamped her front paws on Hathor's breast, then, in a panic at her daring, rushed off. Hathor went up to Horus, and licked His face, washing gazelle's milk over those outraged sockets where His vision had been. Delicately, She uncovered His loincloth so that the breeze which rose from the spring might soothe His parts, even as the milk gave balm to His empty sockets, and indeed this tender wind on His loins offered peace to the harsh blood-crusted void above His nose. Horus, receiving these caresses, felt seeds beginning to germinate where once His eyes had been. He wondered if flowers could grow from His brow, and reached up to touch the petals, but, instead—through a waterfall of blood and tears and pearly milk—saw His own two hands, and cried aloud, "My mother has forgiven Me." In the next instant, He saw the sad, luminous eyes of Hathor, and smelled Her great tongue with its odor of earth and grass licking at His brows. Then He could only say, "How can I forgive Myself?"

She put a finger on His brow to convey the answer: Whatever He prized most had to be offered to His father. And Horus wondered what He could give up.

Even as He asked Himself, He looked out on the desert and it was uncommonly beautiful. The rocks were the color of rose, and the sands a powder of gold. Wherever light gleamed on stone, He saw gems. Beholding a vision of such generosity, Horus no longer debated. "O Father," He said, and His desire was to utter each word with dignity, "I, Horus, Your Son, have been returned My eyes in order that I may offer them to You."

The new vision of Horus fell into darkness, and the loss reverberated like boulders crashing in a gorge. When He opened His eyes once again, His sight was restored, but there was all the difference in His view. To His left eye, each color was still resplendent. Yet His right eye saw the depth of gray in every stone. When both eyes looked out together, the world did not appear beautiful nor hideous, but well-balanced. So He could see Isis in all the loveliness of Her body and the shock of Her broad cow's head.

"Let Us go back," She said sadly, and They returned holding each other's hand.

"I can tell you," said Menenhetet in a sharp turn of voice, "that as soon as They entered the walls of Memphi, Horus' eyes were put to a new test, and His simplicity of mind to a greater one. Osiris had decided that Horus and Set must stand before Him."

Six

"It is the passion of Osiris," Menenhetet remarked, "to conquer chaos. That is why in Khert-Neter, He is quick to extinguish the mediocre. It is important that only the Ka of the finest should survive in the Land of the Dead. Otherwise, the human stock that heaven takes into itself would not be rich in courage, pleasure, beauty, and wisdom. Ruthless selection becomes, thereby, the kindness of good husbandry. On the consequence, Osiris is never merciful for too little. Yet He will always be lenient when it is a matter of forming agreement among Gods. Since They are eternal, great chaos can boil up out of prolonged dispute. So Osiris looks to make peace among Them. Maybe that is why He forgave so much when Set and Horus appeared before His tribunal." Menenhetet now inclined his head as if to return me to the illusion that I could hear the story without listening to his voice.

"Both of You," said Osiris to His brother and His son, "have fought with courage and suffered much. Horus lost the vision to look on His life, and Set lost the eye of His loins. Out of the mercy of this Court which seeks for harmony among Gods, Set has been given back His loins, and Horus His eyes. Go now, both of You, and feast together. Those who have fought with the ferocity of gladiators should know one another as friends. Share in the virtues of Your battle. Discover the power of peace. Go in peace."

The Gods cheered. Horus looked with His rich eye upon Set, and saw the passion that may be found in a red complexion. He thought His uncle splendid. He could have employed His other eye, but for fear it would reveal such unpleasant sides of the uncle that He would wish to disobey His Father, Horus contented Himself with the fair view of both eyes and they saw much suffering. In His gentlest and most courteous voice, therefore, Horus asked Set to come to His camp.

"No, nephew," said Set, "there We will be surrounded, and never speak alone. Come to My camp. I am deserted, and You will spare Me the company of silence."

Affected by these sad words, Horus departed with Set, and They walked side by side down all the distance to the uncle's camp, and Set slaughtered one of His captive boars and They roasted the carcass into the evening, drinking Their meat down with wine pressed from the grapes that grew in the blood of the devoured thieves. By the campfire, They paid great compliments back and forth, and spoke of the other's great skill in combat. Finally, Set made a speech to the spirit of wine. "Some," He said, "crush the grape with a wine-press, but I want my slaves to step on the grapes with their feet. For nobody has more desire to travel than a slave, and this wish gives flight to the spirit of the grape." He raised His glass. "My wine will make You ready to do what You have never done," and Horus applauded, and They drank a final toast, and fell asleep by the fire.

Out of this slumber, Set came awake with the memory of His erection on the first day of battle, and He fondled His nephew's scrotum and tickled His backbone, and swore He would try to proceed no further. False vow. There is no rest at this place. Set remembered how His phallus had been ready to enter the bowels of His nephew, and that pumped Him up with the sweetest stinks, and He was full of greed.

Horus tried to stay asleep. The drops of gazelle's milk that He had swallowed had put Him into the happiest tolerance and bliss, just the state in which to receive a few caresses. He was certainly getting ready to learn how much of Himself could be entered by another. What a nice balance that would give to the fires of His victory.

Set, however, was shaking to find Himself so close to the flesh of the son of Osiris. Set was squalling like a boar. The smell of the boy's cheeks had Him wild. A spew of curses on the milk of Isis and the crotch of Osiris came out of His mouth with such a caterwauling of dead thieves' screams that Horus saw before Him the sad eyes of Isis in the head of Hathor and freed His sphincter, and caught the semen in His hand, while Set, with a blind cry of exultation, crashed into sleep and the deepest snore.

Horus, befuddled from drinking thieves' wine on top of gazelle's milk, forgot at once what had happened. Much too generously had Isis bathed His eyes. The milk left Him with every docility of a fool. He went wandering out of Set's camp with His wet hand held before Him as if pearls had collected there, and moonlight was on His face. He had not gone a hundred steps before He met His mother.

Isis had been waiting all night at the outskirts of Set's camp. She knew the weakness of Her husband when it came to understanding His brother. Bathing the moonlight with Her silent prayers, She had been sending Her words of power into the swamp to roll like mist over Set.

"But how little," said Menenhetet, "can magic offer when the heart of the magician is heavy with fear? It is the first paradox of magic, and the worst, that it is always least available when we are most desperate. On this night, Isis was working within a cow's head not yet familiar to Herself. How could She measure the potency of a curse when instead of widening a delicate nostril, She now had to revolve a nose as large as a snout? With such unfamiliar instruments, the question is whether She was able to affect anything that night, at least until the moment She did. But, finally, She did. How else account for Set's stupidity in so exploding, oink, oink," said Menenhetet, "that He fell asleep without knowing His semen was left in the enemy's hand. Can you believe it? He dreamed that His seed was taking knowledge, drop by drop, of the secret turns of Horus' bowels. I can promise you that Set snored with raucous expectation of orgies of possession in years to come. He was certain that Horus could now keep no secret imparted to Him by Osiris. Sweet dreams!" said Menenhetet. "Isis took one look at the hand of Her son, and exclaimed, 'The seed of Set is as dense as milk of silver,' and all of Set that had collected in the palm of Horus now was heavy, and brilliant like the moon. That liquid silver became our first ball of mercury, no more (and no less!) than a distillation of the seed of Set. Isis, now in full recovery of Her wisdom, encouraged Horus to throw this gout of mercury into the swamp even if every weed in the marsh must turn poisonous. On the consequence, our native Egyptians, eating the meat of beasts who graze upon these weeds, have turned as spineless as mercury in their will, and so we are reduced from a great nation into one without character, yes, every ejaculation of our Gods that is not left in the body of another is the birth of a new disease. Much of Maat resides in this stern principle. Otherwise, Gods could sow Their seed everywhere."

He took a breath and smiled. "Be certain that when Horus threw the milk of silver into the swamp, it took the skin of His hand along. Isis gave Him a new palm, however, by rubbing the sore flesh of His fingers in the liquor of Her thighs and that proved as beneficent as the milk of the gazelle—although we will not pause over such a caress. Indeed, I mention the gesture only to assure you that Horus was so excited by the velvet of His new skin that He promptly ejaculated into it, and such an outpouring, as He was told at once by His mother, would prove precious in a little while."

Menenhetet nodded, even as I watched Isis lead Horus back to the camp of Set. Passing His snoring body, full of its harsh and carnal dreams, They wandered into the garden where lettuce now grew in abundance. Horus assured Her that during the feast of wild boar, Set had often stuffed just such a head of lettuce into His throat, and half-choking, eyes bulging, jaws near dislocated, had crushed the leaves, and swallowed it whole. ("No one," said Horus, "can eat lettuce in a manner equal to Set.") Now, at a sign from Isis, He cast the semen in His hand all over this field and it fell in many threads, and subtle sounds were uttered, altogether a curious music. Those long liquid strings shook with the life of the living, which is to say, all the shock of wars to come, even the sounds of horns and trumpets not yet blown. A sigh of music also came to Isis and Horus out on the edge of the field, but it was only the subtle murmur raised by the legs of an army of spiders who left the garden after the intrusion of Horus' threads upon their webs. How the moonlight glittered. On the way home, Isis sang lullabies to Horus. "His development to manhood," said Menenhetet, "has obviously been uneven, but two events occurred by morning. Set awakened and gobbled more lettuce, and Horus became Isis' lover."

When he saw how much interest arose in me at this remark, my great-grandfather held up his hand. "Of this affair, I will say a little, but only when we are done. For now it is enough to know that Horus was wise by morning, and Set stirred in His bed with all the pride of one who has made a conquest the night before. On His loins, He could smell the shame of Horus' cheeks, and it mixed nicely with His own pride. So Set made great plans. Before Ra had even risen into the full height of noon, Set called the Gods together.

"Assembled in haste, and curious in the extreme, They heard a powerful speech. Set had put on robes of red, brighter than His skin, and in a voice of fire, He said, 'On the day that Horus and I made battle, victory should have been Mine. His head was in the mud. But by the use of My lost thumb, He slipped out of My grip—a trick taught by His mother. He has blood like the milk of His mother. From that moment, no test was left but theft. You saw it. Yesterday, His Father—who pretends to be My judge—commanded Us to go away and feast. We did. Now, I tell You, I am the victor. For in the night, I rode in glory upon His back, and I was as large as the tree that grows from the nut. The flood that rose out of My loins was emptied into the contemptible backhole of the boy Horus standing here beside Me. May I say He bleated like a sheep and cooed like a pigeon. He was My possession. So I say: Do not make Him the Lord of the Living, or I will steal a secret each time I enter His bowels. It is better when great powers are given to the strong. Let Horus serve as My assistant. His hips are weak.'

"Set expected Horus to attack, and was ready. But Horus only threw back His head and laughed. To the judges, He said, 'I have listened with a good and happy heart. My uncle is a thin little man with a loud voice. He squawks like a bird. He lies. It is I who had the onus of traveling up His withered crack, and I did it for nothing better to do. Try for all of one night, My judges, to listen to My uncle's farts. I confess that I would have done better to hurl a spear into a swamp. Old men are dirty.'

"How much Horus had learned in His night with Isis! The oil of Her thighs must have offered more than the milk of the gazelle. Set had no recourse. He drew His sword. Horus, nimbly, darted away, and at a sign from Osiris, the warriors of the court held Set.

"In a bright, clear voice, Horus said, 'Let the Gods summon Our seed from last night. Let the seed tell Who speaks the truth.' Assent came from Set as quickly as from the others, and Thoth was ordered to stand between the disputants. 'Put Your hand upon the buttocks of Horus,' Osiris commanded, 'and ask the voice that is in the semen of Set to declare itself.' Osiris' own voice was not confident. He doubted His son.

" 'I speak,' said Thoth, 'to this seed of Set. Tell Us where you are. Speak from the place where you find yourself.' In the distance, out of the swamps, came a loud and heavy croaking of mercury. The full pestilence of the weeds was in the air, and the Gods murmured that the semen of Set—foul stuff!—must have been ejaculated into the swamp.

"Then Thoth put His hand on the hips of Set, that is, so far as He dared, for Set was shaking with rage, but Thoth proceeded to make the same speech to the semen of Horus. Would it appear? A voice flew right out of Set's buttocks. It was a full, sweet-smelling wind, and it said, 'I am the transformation of the seed of Horus.' This wind smelled sweet as lettuce. The Gods roared. For They knew Horus had buggered Set.

"It would not have been over, and Set might have plotted another revenge, but on His return to camp, He found out He was pregnant. A God may conceive a child by His mouth, or His anus, but if we know it was here by way of the mouth, Set did not. A miserable pregnancy! The creature was born half-man, half-woman, and soon died in the suffocations of attempting to make love to Itself. Set still serves as the Lord of Lightning and the God of Thunder, but He is bewildered, a heavy and near-motionless God who cannot be certain whether He told the truth, or was, indeed, buggered. So He is now mad. It is more difficult for a God to know peace of mind than a man." Menenhetet sighed. With a sense of movement as deliberate and concentrated as an old hag untying a cloth of many knots, he rose, move by move, flexing one joint into another through a series of gestures forward and back until he was standing on his feet. "Are you ready?" he asked.

"You still have not spoken of the affair of Isis and Horus."

"Nor should I. They remain among the most powerful of Them."

"Yet I must know more. What if I encounter a God in the Land of the Dead?"

"You will not. They live in the summits. You do not know a God until you have seen a great mountain." He sighed again. "Let me say that Isis and Horus had a long affair. It still continues. I whisper to you that cohabiting with Her son keeps the form of fidelity to Osiris. So He is calm, and blesses Them. Her act does not strip Him of honor, but maintains the stability of Their family. And the affair has given Horus much wisdom which He needs as Lord of the Living. It has also given Isis more satisfaction than a Goddess with the head of a cow can rightfully expect when She copulates with a hawk. For it is the shape of that fierce bird Horus has chosen for Himself. Now, He need never fear His weak legs, and every Pharaoh worships His wings.

I can say that the God Horus, fully grown, is not at all like the boy, and has become as great as His Father. Such is the extent of the knowledge He has received from Isis."

Now, my great-grandfather beckoned to me. "It is time to begin our travels in Khert-Neter," he said. "Are you ready?"

I felt a childish fear of every force beyond the door of this tomb. Yet there was nothing to do but nod.

When we went out into the night, Menenhetet clapped his hands. Doubtless he wanted to signify the end of one spell and the commencement of another. I waited, but only the stench from his breath was remarkable. We were back in our alley of the Necropolis.

III

The Book of the Child

One

Our way brought us back to the Pyramid of Khufu. It was hard to pretend I felt calm. My fear of all that was yet to come now lay on me like a slab of stone, and the sight of the Great Pyramid did not reduce my turmoil. With each of Menenhetet's steps I felt more woe for he walked ahead of me with the quick pace of someone trying to escape a bad odor, and I remembered the grave robber who fled as I approached the door to my tomb. He had loathed my breath even as I had detested his—a sign the wretch was in another realm than my own. But if this were true, what conclusion should I draw about Menenhetet and myself?

Could he be my Khaibit? That was a thought to leave its echo! My Shadow? Who could be more at odds than the Khaibit and the Ka? The Ka might be one's last poor means of continuing to exist, but it could not bear the weight of much memory. The Khaibit, however, knew all that had happened to you. So it could distort what the Ka did remember. An instrument for evil!

This conviction that Menenhetet was my Shadow came on me with such force that I was about to ask, "Are you the Khaibit of Menenhetet Two?" but did not from the fear that he would only confuse

me further by some such remark as, "No, you are the Ka of Menenhetet One and I am the Khaibit."

So I did not speak, and only continued to travel behind him at his
quick rate. It must be said he moved like my guide, his white robe
wrapped about him in disdain for casual contact with beggars or bats,
yes, everything in his posture spoke of a servant who leads his guest,
and will not suffer any distracting encounter. Even as we emerged
from the Necropolis, a man was standing at the gate with his palm
open, a beggar's palm with no fingers. Not missing a stride, Menenhetet struck him a sharp slap on the arm to make it clear no approach
would be tolerated. Indeed, the man flinched as we passed, and I realized I must look like a noble to him.

But then I had not contemplated my clothes until now. When had
I first come to wear these clean white pleats, this jeweled breastplate?
A memory returned of a promenade taken by the banks of the Nile,
and multitudes bowing before me. The picture was so clear as for me
to believe it, and my pleasure was not unlike the satisfaction I had just
known before the respect of the beggar. Warmed by such tokens, my
mood took a quick turn for the worse, however, so soon as I began to
ponder my great-grandfather's remarks about Horus and Set, for I
had to suppose that Menenhetet, given the occasion, would try—put
no fine word on it—to bugger me. The quiet arrogance of the old
man that he could bring off such a feat was curious. I did not know
whether to think of him as laughable. After all, the muscles of my
hips spoke of pride—nothing was broken in *my* back. Even as we
walked, I felt quietly of my arms and legs and was reassured. My
means might be one-seventh of what once it had been, but I still did
not see how that foul old man could be the first to take carnal ownership of me. I was remembering how my friends and myself used to
think of ourselves as virgin to other men until some fellow was brave
enough to grab us from the rear. Of course, once your body was broken into by another, that was a true turning. An aristocrat would
allow himself to be used in such a way but once, as if, truth, we had
one royal flower to offer. We were determined that no one we did not
admire in every way could even begin our seduction. Some of us

went on in such chastity for years. That could become a vice. One might grow into a spinster who has waited too long and so is vulnerable to any passing lout. The balance of Maat is in the choice.

Now I wondered if I had been one of those who waited too long. What a horror if Menenhetet One became the first. No, not conceivable, I thought, not as I watched him walk before me in a flapping old man's step, his head covered against a chill although it was a warm night. Nonetheless, he did not move altogether like an old man.

I was uneasy. We were now near the foot of the Pyramid of Khufu, and as though my reluctance to go on was evident, Menenhetet came to rest and began to speak again, although I could hardly listen. His breath was so mingled with mine. I do not know what he sniffed in my throat, but I thought I had stepped into the scalding odor of urine. It was like a cave of bats—a fair guide to the corruptions of the Duad. Yet in the act of suffering his fumes, so was I delivered of the worst of them. His breath was now endurable, and not much worse than old garlic and old teeth.

"The common entrance to the Duad," he said, as he shivered in the warm moonlight, "is far beyond the First Cataract—a long journey, and not the route for us. We will go in by way of a cave that can be found in the sky."

I would never have understood this last remark if the Pyramid had not been there before us, but in the moonlight these limestone slopes were gleaming bright as marble, and their shadows looked dark as velvet. I remembered the chamber of Khufu in the center of this Great Pyramid. Was that a cave in the sky by which I had once been ready to enter the Duad, and by myself? Had I taken the wrong turning? But I had no taste for such questions.

Menenhetet was speaking, meanwhile, about matters so trivial I hardly listened. It was something about a Hebrew slave he had kept, and curious customs among the Hebrews. "They are demented," said Menenhetet, "and happy to remain shepherds. They do best when talking to themselves in the hills. Nonetheless, I have observed that barbaric people, like beasts, live closer than we do to their Gods. As an example," he said, and in truth his voice was calming the weakness of my body, "I remember the odd language of this Hebrew slave. At first I thought it a dialect spoken by an imbecile since he did not seem to have any notion of yesterday or tomorrow in anything he said. Yet he must have had a hundred words for *cut,* and used one for slicing reeds, another for meat, or fowl, and separate kinds of fruit, not to speak of chopping down a tree, or cutting off a hand, not stupid at all when you think that everything we cut has its spirit severed most abruptly. A good word does well to propitiate the pain. No, we would not," mused Menenhetet, "wish to dispatch each of our enemies with the same cry. So, the variety of these words led me to study that shepherd's language, and I began to see enigmas in his tongue. The Hebrews, I discovered, live with what is before them at every instant—their words reflect such a simple condition. 'I eat,' they say. Simple! But when they wish to speak of what is not before them now, why then you cannot tell (unless you know the trick of the language) whether they are speaking of what is past, or what is yet to come. It seems the same in the way they say it. They tell you, for example, 'I ate,' and you won't know whether they have finished the meal or are going to eat in a while, not unless you listen so carefully as to realize they actually said, '*And* I ate.' That means: they *will* eat. They know how peculiar time can be! And on their thick tongues! Conceive of it! How can we be certain that what we say we will do tomorrow has not in truth taken place yesterday, although we cannot quite remember since it was in a dream. So do not," said Menenhetet, touching me gently by the shoulder, "feel too weak before what is to come. It could have happened to you already. Yes, dear son of my dear grand-daughter, Hathfertiti, your terror may have more dignity than you know. It might belong to the remorse of your past rather than tell you of some unendurable torture to come."

Then, indeed, I felt relief. His long speech had managed to calm me, and again I felt something like good feeling for the old man at this unexpected turn of kindness.

Now, as the moon passed over the peak of the Pyramid of Khufu, Menenhetet raised his hand delicately, and I gasped at the beauty of that white light which came down upon us from the triangular slope.

Menenhetet spoke in the quietest voice, as if the smallest quiver of his throat might distort the purity of the light: "This divine Pyramid," he whispered, "is the exact equal of the First Hill that Temu brought up from the Celestial Waters. So it is the tomb to contain all other tombs. By entry into this Pyramid, you will descend into the currents of the Duad."

And as I looked at the great slope before us, smooth as a sheet of papyrus in the moonlight and large to my eyes as the expanses of the desert, so did I wonder how we might ever enter. The joinings of each great block of limestone must be narrower than the space between two fingers when squeezed together. But I had not long to wait. Menenhetet walked the last hundred steps to the base, and there he threw back his head and uttered a cry I had never heard before, not the long warble of a bird nor any mysterious grunt out of a beast, but a voice as shrill in its center as the piping of a bat, and a slab of stone on the slope above us revolved in its socket like a door.

"It is time," he said to me, and began with surprising nimbleness to mount the slope. I followed, expecting my breath to be locked with anguish; yet, I felt no fear. But then a child knows less awe before the rising of the sun than does a man. Was I entering at the moment when death could feel most natural to me? I know that as we went through the opening into the Pyramid, a change came upon the air. If I had been blind, my ears would have told me that I was passing into another domain. I listened to a delicate silence, close to the unheard quivering of a small bird's wings. The hush of every temple was in the weight of this silence, and the lost echo of each animal sacrificed on the altar stone. I knew again the haze that rises from the dying beast, the drip of its blood bringing peace to the same air that has just been stricken by the murder of the animal. If we had wounded the stone by our entrance, the echo of our footsteps in these vaults would quiet all disorder.

Down we went along a promenade in the dark, down some low tunnel that made us stoop, and before us was the scuttling of rats, and a scattering of insects, while bats flew so near I all but heard the menace of their brain.

Yet these disturbances also ceased. There came, as we walked, a sense of calm heavy as the oily swell of the Nile on the flood, and I began to have an expectation of larger space opening before me, and, indeed, in the next ten steps, we entered a tall and narrow gallery. By the pipings of the bats, I supposed its ceiling must have been thirty feet above, and the gallery was dark. All the same, I could feel light about me. I did not see a thing, but the interior of my mind was so full of light I could recall how, on a given day in my childhood, I had passed once down the Nile with my parents in a barge under a sky of sunlight so brilliant that my thoughts felt exposed to the sun, as if all of me was in a golden barge afloat in a golden light. My father and mother were taking me to visit the Pharaoh, and I was so alive with the pleasure of my limbs that I even remember the color of saffron in the gown I wore. On that morning there would be sights to disrupt the eye and savage your nose—the corpse of a dog was rotting on the riverbank—but the day was begun in splendor, and each push of the boatman's pole restored my calm even as the sound of our steps in the tunnel now overcame the rustlings of the insects and the bats.

At this moment, Menenhetet took my hand, and I noticed that my great-grandfather's breath was perfumed; the air he exhaled from his lungs must share the intoxication of my interior light. Some of the calm of that morning remained in the warmth of his palm as if we were sharing the loyalty of family flesh, but soon, given the narrowness of the passage which made walking side by side awkward, he had to withdraw his hand. As I went on in this darkness, bathed in light behind my eyes, I seemed to pass through vales of heat and cold, the air collecting in chill pods like the void of a tomb; yet another five steps, and I was back in the balmy Egyptian night breathing the warm perfume I had first taken in on my great-grandfather's breath, a scent that did not seem to come from him so much as from the stone itself, until I began to feel as if we were not on our way up a steep narrow ramp so much as winding our passage from tent to tent or a mysterious bazaar, and in each tent lived a presence pure to itself. One had only to offer attention, and into one's thoughts wisdom would seep as naturally as the infusion of an herb in water will set free its essence.

Within the intoxication of this light, and the gatherings of aroma, I began to feel as if I did not move with my body, but glided along in a bark. I could still reach out an arm on either side, and the walls of the gallery were there to touch, yet I felt closer to the Nile on that one golden day I could remember of my boyhood, or, rather, as if much confused, like the Hebrew who could not separate what was to come from all that he might dream, I felt as if the river was washing along the floor, and the walls were riverbanks, and I was on the Nile once more, even as on that day of brilliant sunlight I had rested on cushions of a yellow cloth brighter than the saffron of my garment. A silver filigree in the cushion still tickled intimately against my seat, so that, unseen by my parents, I was trying to rub the tender skin of my cheeks against those tendrils of silver thread—a sweet pleasure, for I was no more than six.

My parents were speaking. What they said left their lips with many a twist (since now I remember how deceitful they were often to one another) and the curve of their words must have traveled with us on the serpentine of the Nile awash in golden light upon the brown waters of the river, and we passed by green and mud-gold banks, even the gold inlay on the cedar wood of the fine seats of our barge still journeyed with me in the curve of their words and my mother was speaking, I remember, of a sacred bull (and I was hearing her voice even now as I stood with my hands on the wall of this stone gallery as near to me as a palm tree one could reach on the bank) and her voice was no ordinary voice, but full of the command of every sensuous instinct, deep as the voice of a man but full of tender and mysterious resonance. She had only to hum a note with that voice, say no more than "The crook and the flail of the Pharaoh Ptah-nem-hotep," and my belly felt as dusky as the colors of a dark rose.

My father rarely replied to what she said. Speech between himself and my mother was not their common practice, and they were now together for excellent but separate reasons—they were each paying a call on this same Ptah-nem-hotep, our own Ramses Nine, my father on a trip that took place nearly every day, and my mother on a rare visit, although I did not know as I thought of it now why she did not,

given her beauty, visit with the Pharaoh more often. But the cynicism
of this thought—so far from the understanding of a boy of six—
proved enough to dispel the memory. My mind was brought back to
our ascent up the gallery, and I ceased to live on that morning and no
longer floated within it.

Menenhetet now led me to an alcove by one of the walls. Since I
still felt, in some measure, the sensation of being on a boat, it was not
unlike floating into a harbor on a dark night. The presence of light in
my body was certainly gone. Then I gave an exclamation. In front of
me was water at the level of my waist. I could see a star within this
water—had the floor become my sky? I felt a clear thrill as if I were
falling into depths yet would never smash; the thrill ceased, and I realized I was looking into a large bowl of water, and the star was a reflection. The heavens were beyond, still beyond!—Menenhetet had
only led me to a place in the Pyramid where a shaft came down to us
at a sharp angle from the sky. When I now peered upward I could see
the star in the aperture at the top. Even as I looked, it moved away
from the center. In the interval I had studied it, this star had traveled
enough to shift its position a palm's width in the water. How remarkable that Menenhetet could lead me to the reflection at the instant its
light lived in the center of the bowl.

"That star has not been seen in this place for three hundred and
seventy-two years," he told me now. "We have a night for wonders
between us all," and for some reason this pious thought put a stimulation on my loins, and a curl of the happiest anticipation commenced
at the root of my spine and curled upward like incense. An incantation came to me, from where, I do not know, but I said aloud: "The
Pharaoh takes the blood of His beloved, and He plants therewith by
the light of the sun.

"What grows from the earth," I heard myself say, "is the blessed
plant of papyrus, and beneath the hands of men it becomes a field for
scribes. And they plant their messages on this field. All the plants of
the papyrus dwell in the clamor of all the writings that will ride upon
that field like chariots, yet the field remembers a riverbank and every
bud is like the lips of a mouth and every leaf a tongue of honey."

I saw the Nile again, and the heats were rising off the indolence of the river.

This incantation, out of impulses as curious as I had ever known, for I had never heard the words before, produced a power sufficient to draw back into me the golden light of the Nile. Then I said, "Papyrus is a plant abhorred by crocodiles," and had one moment of childish joy merry as the desire long ago to sprinkle flowers with the golden waters of my urine, and clear as that day, I also saw the flutter of a tiny spurwing as she nibbled at river worms embedded in the mouth of a crocodile, yes, saw that armored beast on the muddy banks, its mouth open in good-humored languor at the cleaning of its teeth by the spurwing, an improbable couple, but domesticity was in the fanning of her wings and the sleepy grunts of the great lizard. Some boatmen were singing on the Nile, "Oh, papyrus is a plant abhorred by crocodiles," and nodded as they rowed upstream. Our boatmen, reduced by the heat to no more than a breechcloth to cover the purse of their penis and testicles, pushed against the long poles guiding us downstream, and the marvelous tickling in the skin of my seat began again, and I, in my turn, pushed against the silver filigree of the cushion. "Mud," said my mother then, "is in my nostrils and my pores," and she turned the fine curve of her nostril to the sight of a chariot, a horse, and a rider galloping in the heat of the day and in the dust of the road beside the riverbank, and I had then, as a child of six, even while full of delight at the passing of the charioteer, a clear glimpse forward into myself at twenty-one, as if I was not only the child but could see the life I was yet to live.

As I stared at that star which hovered in the mirror of the water, the sentiment became so real that the past came back to me as if I were truly six, and yet could see myself at twenty-one, and I was again with that priest at his sister's house and saw a view of the Nile from her window and heard the sounds of river water stroking the bank even as the body of the priest gave intent slaps against her flesh.

I, next to Menenhetet, looking down through the darkness at the star, was overcome with the force of two such memories, myself at six, myself at twenty-one, and felt faint. It was then that my great-

grandfather took my hand again. A vine grew foliage in my belly,
curled along my limbs, and flowed out of my hand into the knuckles
and thumb of Menenhetet, and my mind turned back to that gilded
barge that drew my mother, my father, and myself down the Nile so
that I understood at last why our Egyptian word for the eye is most
certainly the same as our word for love and both are identical to our
word for tomb. Whether love or the depth of mood which arose from
such a tomb, the sensation that came from his fingers was certainly
carrying me along the river, and belonged more to the brilliance of
that long-departed day than to this niche off a pitch-black gallery in
the depths of the Pyramid of Khufu.

Then, with a twist to my memory as simple as pulling a lemon
from a tree, so did I discover that Menenhetet was on the barge, and
that was most certainly at odds with what I could remember. Yet I
had only to give up the feeling—it was no longer a certainty—that
Menenhetet had died in the year before I was born, and he was, yes,
on the boat, and speaking to my mother. If I had seen the barge at first
with my father and mother next to me, and with clarity more vivid
than a temple painting, now I saw Menenhetet as well. He, too, sat
beside me and his hair showed the silver of a virile maturity while the
lines on his face had not yet become a myriad of wrinkles, terraces,
and webs, but exhibited, instead, that look of character supported by
triumph which comes to powerful men when they are sixty and still
strong.

Yet to see him with us was to give me as well some confusion as to
where we were on the river. I knew we were on our way to visit the
Pharaoh but now I could not understand why we did not travel up the
river when my parents' villa had its grounds located a long walk
downstream from the Palace. Yet now we were going with the current, no sails set, and no oarsmen at work.

There was only the boatman we called Stinking Body at the bow
with his long pole to fend us off the bars, and Head-on-Backwards at
the helm (that Head-on-Backwards who was also called Eater-of-
Shadows for whenever we sailed upstream to the south, the tiller was
in the shade of the sail). But now we were drifting down into the

brunt of that prevailing breeze that came up out of the Delta, a wind strong enough to let us sail without oars upstream against the current. Today, however, we drifted down, lazily, Neha-Hau in the bow and Unem-Khaibitu, the Eater-of-Shadows, in the stern, while the rest of the crew—Bone-Smasher, White-Teeth, Eater-of-Blood and He-of-the-Nose—a tremendous nose—were lolling against the gunwales, an easy day for them.

I was thinking that boatmen had ugly faces when at rest. If obliged to row upstream under the worst of conditions (when the river was in flood and they were working too hard to sing in unison) then the sound of their breath came close to the anguish of weeping, and they had the maniacal expression of horses in a frightened gallop, such an intensity of expression, such torture in the effort, that they could not be wholly ugly. At rest, however, their faces usually looked swollen. Nobody knew why rivermen when ashore were always in more fights than any other kind of laborer in Memphi, unless it was that they drank more beer, but it was true. Most of them had faces which looked as if a lion had been chewing on their cheeks. Besides, there was the whip. That was forever laying the welt of new scars over the old ones on their shoulders. Now and again it flicked around their neck to reach their face. As a result, half the boatmen were blind in an eye. (If blinded in both, they went to other labor.)

Set-Qesu, the head boatman, not named Bone-Smasher for too little, was the one to apply the whip. When the winds were strong, my great-grandfather would on occasion take the lash. He could make the tip dance, crack it around a man's waist and flick his navel, or if an oarsman ever stopped to scratch himself, sting the boatman's armpit with such precision that a few hairs would fly off. Unfortunately, there was every reason to scratch. Where was the boatman without his lice?

That bothered my mother considerably. She had a detestation of body-insects so intense that she could lose her composure at mention of them. While this was hardly an unusual attitude for a young matron of Memphi (since many in their fear of infestations would crop their heads and wear wigs for every public appearance) my mother was proud of her hair. It was vigorous and dark, and had a wave that curled with the sinuosity of the snake. So she preferred to keep it long and live in fear of head-lice. Indeed, there had been an episode just the night before. But now as I recollected, so was it also clear why we did not row upstream toward the Pharaoh's Palace, but rather drifted down. My mother, my father, and I had spent last night with Menenhetet who lived up the river south of Memphi in a great house one hundred paces in width, an equal number in depth, and three stories high. It was said he had fifty rooms, and I knew he had a roof garden with awnings made of the material of tents, for there was a view from that roof at evening when the sun filled the river with a million red and dancing fish, and the desert to the east turned to indigo, even as the sandstone hills to the west became pink and carmine and orange and glowing gold, like the blood-fire of an oven as the sun went into the hills.

My great-grandfather spoke to me at that moment—a rare occasion. I was used to relatives and servants recognizing that I was not an ordinary child, indeed I could even feel again the sweet purity of the admiration I used to evoke in men and women to whom I spoke, for they were usually delighting in how adult I was for six. Menenhetet, however, had never indicated I was of any interest to him. Yet, now, he put a hand on my waist and drew me forward.

"Have you looked at the colors on the palette of the scribe?"

I nodded. "They are black and red." When I saw the light in his eye, I added, "They are like the sky at evening and the sky at night."

"Yes," he said, "that is one reason they are black and red. Can you give me another?"

"Our deserts are red, but the best earth is black once the flood has passed."

"Excellent. Can you offer another reason?"

"I can think of none."

He took out a small jeweled knife and put the point to my finger. A drop of blood came forth. I would have cried out, but something in his expression kept me still. "That is the first color to remember," he told me, "just as black is the last." He said no more, merely patted me,

and left, but, later, I heard him chatting with Hathfertiti and he mentioned my name. I could tell by my mother's low sensual laugh that
his words were kind. She always took physical pleasure in a good reference to me as though her own body were being admired, and if I
happened to be in her sight, a musk of affection would come from
her. Under that loving look, my body felt bathed in flowers. I had
learned to gather such love as if it were a perfume equal to the breath
of recollection. Nothing was more beautiful to me as a child than this
power of memory. Fortified by the pleasure my mother took in me,
each sight I recollected came back with luster. I could look at the red
hills across the river on this sunset and have dreams of the wonders of
the desert as I fell asleep, and the silver water of an oasis.

Tonight, since there was almost no wind, the torches at the corners
of the roof were lit and a servant stood by each torch with a pot of
water. That was my great-grandfather taking his enjoyment of the
fire in face of the ever-present danger of the servant falling asleep and
a wind springing up. Every few years a great wooden house would
burn that way. On the consequence, the torches were a luxury: one
needed good servants to guard such fires. Of course, the torches did
give a light that was more exciting than our candles.

By one of the torches, a woman was dancing. She moved with
slow undulations of her body as lascivious as the curve of Hathfertiti's hair, and the sistrum with its singing wires was played by a dwarf
wearing nothing but a gold purse and a few bracelets on his stunted
biceps. He played with a tiny man's frenzy and her hips quivered to
the sound he made.

In fact, Menenhetet's little orchestra brought a stir to the guests
when they appeared. The harper, the cymbal player, the piper, and
the drummer were all dwarfs, no taller than myself, and all exceptionally skillful except for the one who played the harp since his arms
were too short and therefore left his longer runs full of peril.

They also spoke in strange languages, being descended from prisoners captured in old wars with the Kings of Arvad, Carchemish, and
Egerath, and their voices together with their little faces roused a stir
of applause for everything they played. It was all received with exag-

gerations of attention from Menenhetet's guests, who were priests and judges, rich merchants and neighboring nobles from the best temples and good society of the land just south of Memphi, prosperous people certainly, but not so prosperous that they did not feel honored to be asked to my great-grandfather's house and honored again by being invited up to his roof garden, although I heard a few murmur in disappointment this night that the most illustrious guests were not so celebrated as expected, and no one, but for my father, was a high official from the Palace.

All the same, Menenhetet's reputation was renowned from the Delta to the First Cataract. Even my nurse used to giggle lasciviously at the mention of his name, and the gossip I heard among the guests (for I was considered too young to comprehend their jokes) concerned which women had already had an affair with Menenhetet as opposed to those he was considering. It must have been a disappointing evening for the wives (and a relief to more than one husband) that he spent most of his time sitting next to my mother. I stayed away. Sometimes, when they were near one another, I could feel a force so powerful I would not dare to walk between them, as if to interrupt their mood could strike you to the ground.

This evening, Menenhetet did not leave her side. They sat unmoving through the music. My father could hardly decide where to go. Sitting near them, he was not given much for his attempts at conversation, and when, on the confidence of his own fine features, he proceeded to charm one wife or another, the attempt soon ran out. For nothing came back to him from Hathfertiti—she sat side by side with Menenhetet in a silence that spoke of their attention for one another. Hathfertiti held a tuft of black hair in her fingers, and with it she stroked the black curls of her head. The tuft, taken from the tail of a sacred bull, prevented the onset of gray hair, and my mother continued this ritual with self-absorption, as if these intent caresses to herself would increase her inestimable value.

After the music was done, a few guests began to leave. Here, anyone could have recognized how immense was the reputation of my great-grandfather since he did not even speak to them as they approached his chair, knelt, and touched their foreheads to the floor. Only a Pharaoh, a Vizier, a High Priest, or one of the most honored Generals of the nation would act in such a fashion. Indeed, Menenhetet presented his indifference to the departure of his guests with such a natural concentration upon his own thoughts, so equal in gravity to Hathfertiti's immersion in the stroking of the bull's hair upon her head, that the guests moved away without a sign, and yet were not displeased, but rather, looked honored that they had been allowed to stand before him, as if now they could hear the echo of his great feats in the boredom he showed in the presence of those he had invited. Standing in silence before his silence, so they could feel steeped in tales of his wickedness and knowledge of magic, and indeed these feelings came over them with such power that it left me feeling most alive until I could as well have existed in two abodes of time. I was not only standing in a corner of the roof garden near the slaves who guarded the torches, but was returned as well to the black alcove in the Pyramid with the light of the star on the water, able to know from this memory of childhood that my guide for the Land of the Dead had been a man of great esteem when he was among the living. And learning this, I was carried along on that stream of sensation which came to my hand from his bent fingers, and leaned forward, and to my great surprise gave him a kiss, there in the darkness, on his withered lips.

They opened like the dirty skin of an apricot just pulled from a dusty tree, and I felt the ripe warm flesh of a mouth so rich with sensuous promise that the kiss even lingered on the air after I drew back, and by that movement must have turned in my mind to Menenhetet and my mother sitting together on the roof garden in carnal silence.

I do not know how long it was before they were alone, but now the guests were gone, and my father had departed as well—where to, seemed hardly to my mother's concern—and even I was gone so far as anyone might know, for I had wandered to the other side of the roof, and, in fascination, was looking down on the last of the guests strolling through the avenue of flowers in the long garden below. The moon had risen and by its light the water in the wading pool was so brilliant that I could nearly see the captive fish. The servants of Me-nenhetet had searched the marshes and swamps with their nets that afternoon to find the most brilliant examples of the sun and the moon in gold and silver fingerlings.

My great-grandfather's gardens were much talked about in Mem-phi. But for the estates of the Pharaoh, there may not have been an-other superior to it. The pool was renowned for the work of the craftsmen who had laid out decorations in tile that looked like flowers but were composed of rare stones—garnet and amethyst, carnelian, turquoise, lapis-lazuli and onyx were some. I knew their value when the servants who guarded the pool looked back at me with the eyes of falcons: they were responsible that none of the gems came loose from their setting or were stolen. Such a loss would have been worth one of their hands.

In fact, there were white wooden posts in the fields of vegetables beyond the avenue of flowers, and you could find more than one withered hand nailed to a post, or even showing the white of the bone next to the white of the post. They made an atrocious sight at the head of these fields of wheat and barley and lentils, these plots of onions and garlic, cucumber and watermelon, but the fields pros-pered. There was a gaiety in the fields like the prosperity of Gods, as if the marrow of merriment came up from divine bellies, up through the earth.

That afternoon I had wandered past the lanes and arbors of my great-grandfather down to the ferns and eel-ridden marshes at the rear of his lands. His high ground was an island now in the flood, and the marshes looked like lakes with no trail through them, so I came back by way of the vineyards and picked the grapes and wandered through arbors of oranges and figs, past lemon trees and olive trees, acacia and sycamore, and ate a pomegranate and spit out the seeds still thinking of the dry bloodied hand nailed to the post and wanted to splash in the pool again and piss my own water onto the gold and sil-ver fish—excitement came to me at the thought they would drink my offering. Or did such excitement rise from the barnyard cries of sheep and goats that came to me like the groaning of a stone hinge in a large

door? It was a sound to match the heat of the day and the fermentation of food, and it gave pleasure to my thighs. I lived in moldering
smells on a slow and heavy wind from the livestock sheds, an unpleasant odor and yet not all unpleasant. I felt drawn by the heat in this
afternoon to a full taste of the feast beneath my feet—as if the Gods,
now merry, were at a banquet in the earth below. Even the braying of
the donkeys and the cries of the hens became part of this heavy marrow of the air. Later in the night, watching my mother and Menenhetet on the roof, there was less mystery to me at the force between
them. Indeed those buddings I had felt in my heart and my thighs had
all come together this afternoon and I had felt my first transformation
that was like the Gods'. For in that hour, wandering down the avenue
of flowers, such was the magic in the groupings of geranium and violet, of dahlias, irises, and wondrous flowers whose names I did not
know, all burgeoning like a garden in me, that I was overpowered at
last by the smell of flowers. As I breathed their perfume, so did other
flowers open petals in my flesh, and a green stem rose from the center
of my hips to my navel. I was inhaling musk into my heart and the
power of the earth rose up once in my belly, and fell back again like
another body coming alive within my body, and rose once more, and
I was wet all over and in some river rich and white, like a cream in the
heat, and did not know where the blooms of these flowers ended, and
I began.

Now, as I looked over the gardens and saw the light of the moon
on the pool, and the lanes that led to the servant and slave houses, saw
the glow of fire to melt the pitch in the boat builder's shop where
workmen for some reason were still busy this night, as I looked on the
very last of the guests sauntering down the lanes and disappearing in
the turns of a clever maze, so I also knew what was now passing between my mother and her grandfather, and I shivered at the mad cry
of a monkey who called out from his cage in a near-human if sadly
demented voice. How the moon was shining. In the heat, it seemed as
heavy as the earth beneath my toes this afternoon. A gazelle gave its
small cry.

Some fear was arising in Hathfertiti, some gathering of apprehension she could not locate. Even as the monkey gave his cry at the on-coming shift in the air, I felt a bolt of terror fly from my mother to me just before she screamed. Not aware that I was near, her horror was pure in its panic—I do not think I had ever heard my mother scream before. Then she began to weep like a child. "Take it off. Take it off me," she begged, and grasped Menenhetet's hand, pulling his fingers to her head, while whimpering with fury at the unmistakable knowl-edge that something was certainly crawling in the luxuriant bush of her coiffure.

He found the louse in an instant, cracked it between his thumbnails in another, while Hathfertiti was racing her fingers through her hair, crying out with a frantic petulance, "Are there more? Will you look?"

He soothed her as if she were an animal in fright, stroking her hair like a mane, holding her chin, murmuring to her in a language of meaningless words so soft they could have served for the intimate babble a man gives his horse or his dog, and she calmed a little as he drew her to the light of a torch, ignoring the servants still there, one to each torch, standing unmoving through the night—no reason why Menenhetet would have hesitated to do anything in front of them, but now, by the flare of the torch, he searched her scalp and assured Hathfertiti it was clean. At last, she calmed and he led her back to their couch.

"Are you sure there was only one?" she asked.

He smiled. The wickedness of his smile was complete. Now Me-nenhetet kissed her, but so adroitly, with such a lingering intimation that she leaned toward him for another. "Not yet," he told her and gave one more of his little smiles so that I could not know if he re-ferred to the insects or the kiss. I felt again a bolt of terror spring from her to me. But then I was already frightened. I did not wish to listen to what they might say next. I knew it would be close to what I could hear on many a night in the voice of my nurse with either of her two friends, the Nubian slave who worked in the stables, and the Hebrew slave from the metal shops who sharpened the knives and the swords. One or other was always with her in the room next to mine at night, and from there came the sounds of the barnyard and the birds' cries of the marsh and the swamp. My nurse and her companion grunted each night like pigs or roared like lions, and sometimes they came forth with high whinnying sounds full of every muscle in their belly. Through all of my father's estate would such cries come up in the night, the long sighs of one couple seeming to start the growl of another only to bring forth a third roaring with pleasure, thereby encouraging the animals to join with their barks and screams and lowing sounds.

Now, my mother stood up and would have left Menenhetet, but she looked instead into his eyes and their expressions were locked again. They did not speak, but the power of the attraction which had kept them looking into one another's eyes for all of an evening was here again, as if each pressed with the power of his will against the other, and I felt ill. Except I was not sick so much as thrown about by two winds that came howling at that instant over all of my childhood, and I heard him say to her, although indeed I do not know if it was his voice that entered my ear or his thought (for just as some are deaf, so had they begun to say of me that I was the opposite of those who cannot hear since even what was unsaid could come into my mind). Whether he spoke it, therefore, or thought it only to himself, I certainly heard my great-grandfather say, "Your best opportunity with the Pharaoh is tomorrow."

My mother replied, "What if I find what I want and you do not?"

"Then you must remain loyal to me," said my great-grandfather.

I did not dare to look and it was just as well, since even as my eyes were closing, so did Menenhetet push my mother to her knees before his short white skirt. I felt the force of their thoughts like one chariot running full amok into another, and again I saw into his mind. She must have seen it too, for all strength broke in her, and she cried out. My great-grandfather said, "Set's cock is in your mouth."

I had a true sense of poison then, like a vindictiveness brooding in the intestines of the wind, and do not know if I swooned but I was living in darkness, not six, nor twelve, not twenty-one, nor even dead—was I dead?—but in the alcove off the grand gallery of the Pyramid, Menenhetet's cock was certainly in my mouth. My jaws froze. I felt helpless in every muscle, and a rage at the core of my will. I had only to bite and he, too, would scream. I knew at that instant I was equal to my mother, and could not separate myself from her, could not say I was Menenhetet Two, the young and noble warrior, too soon dead, and feeling no fall from the heights of my own pride, for the mouth which sucked on him was not my own mouth but my mother's in all the windings of her thought and the currents of her senses, and I knew the cock of Set as she knew it on the roof garden of my great-grandfather's house above the banks of the Nile and his flesh was hot as the smelting pits of a sulphur mine to scorch the flesh of her palate. My mind resting in hers, so was my mouth living in her mouth, and I tasted a curse deep as the virulence in the seed of Set, and Menenhetet's hand was still holding mine, while the fingers of his other hand clasped the back of my head. Through my mother's ears I could hear the unspoken voice of my great-grandfather as he had spoken once to her while her mouth was engorged, and with a throbbing upon her face (my face) like the quivering of lightning in the heavy load of a murderous sky, so did something come up out of the bile of existence, some noxious marrow of the corruptions of the dead, and Menenhetet came forth into her mouth, so into my mouth, out of the loins of the dead Menenhetet, in the alcove of the Pyramid where I knelt so did his discharge come like a bolt and by the light of its flash I knew how he held her head on the garden of that roof, the iron of his last shuddering pulse dripping its salt onto the back of her tongue, and those thoughts passing from his head into hers, so was a cock withdrawn from my mouth in the dark, and I in the Land of the Dead began to feel a little happy expectation for what might be waiting next, even as Hathfertiti, lips bruised and perfumes turned by the onslaught of his carnal aroma, had a happiness nonetheless in her limbs and a scent of a rose in the finest folds of her meat since she, too, had an expectation now for the morning. On that thought, there still on my knees, I was transported with her, as by one breath of my mind, to the golden light of our trip downriver in all the splendid anticipation of an audience with our Pharaoh, Ramses Nine, while I dreamed of Him in all the morning effulgence of the Nile.

Two

Just as we can stare into the depth of a golden goblet and find the reverberation of a thought in the last drop, so did I comprehend that the last treasure of this day on the river would be found in the private rooms of the Pharaoh. Sitting on my cushion of silver filigree, the cheeks of my buttocks in subtle tumult, I curved my body into the soft reception of Hathfertiti's arm, and felt new heats in my thighs to bring back the memory of my mother and Menenhetet from the night before. What a transformation! Last night I had nearly cried out with my mother. Today I sat in the boat lulled with heat.

Of course, I had had an unexpected reward. For Menenhetet had gone on to make love to my mother. Or, as I saw it then, he moved with her in an act I could not recognize as grappling or a dance, nor yet as prayer, and it even looked at moments like the couplings of animals except that they did not present the stupid look that animals offer when they are joined.

About the time they were licking at each other with many an aristocratic growl, more like birds than hogs, I slipped away in a quandary of heat and humiliation, descended the stairs, found the room with my bed, and being obliged to sob at the thought of my mother

naked with my great-grandfather, was for the first time pacified in a
special way by my nurse, Eyaseyab. The part of my body that grew
between my legs, fierce until then only with the need to urinate, was
christened Sweet Finger by her in the dark, and Eyaseyab put her Syrian lips on it and gave me sensations I would not otherwise have
known. Even this morning when I looked across the water at her (for
Eyaseyab was in the barge that followed with the servants) I would
bring my hand to my nose and it would still smell of her mouth, a
nice round odor of onions, oil and fish (since my palm had certainly
held onto Sweet Finger long after Eyaseyab was gone) and so her lips
left a pull on my memory equal to the lap of soft waves on our hull as
barges rowed by in the other direction, and I laughed, to the astonishment of the others, when my father, hoping to enter the mood of
his wife and her great-grandfather, if by no more than the bite of his
teeth on the silence, now was heard to say, "This year, we're well rid
of the stink."

"No, its odor is fascinating, I confess," said Menenhetet after the
pause that followed my laughter.

"Well, I find it curious," said my mother, "on occasion."

And I was reminded of them licking each other. Of course, nothing was equal to our river when it began to rise and each old slime on
the flats began to stir with its last odors as the water reached higher
into the caked mud and old reeds while feasts of insects floated down
on the foliage—a terrible smell for a week as if our earth was shuck-
ing its filthiest skin, each village, now an island with its own high
ground offering the new stench of sheep and cattle pressed together
for these few weeks close enough to sleep in the huts of their peasant
masters, an atrocious condition but for nights of full moon when the
villages would look like dark islands on a silver lake, and the poorest
boat, not big enough for two men, just a tying and twisting of long
dry reeds coated with pitch would appear as elegant in such light as
the skiffs of papyrus on which my great-grandfather, my father, and
their friends would now and then embark on a hunt.

But on this fine morning when my father made his comment, the
stench was gone, and the river was no longer green from the first

sludge of the fields but high and red with the mud of the earth it had washed from cliffs upriver—a golden-red usually near to brown in color except on this exceptional morning when the sun was so brilliant that the gleam coming off the river was equal to a hundred suns, an emblazoning of gold upon red waters that lit up every passing bark until the meanest barge full of cabbages or jugs of oil, pots of grain, or near awash with a load of fine stone shimmered nonetheless in the light like a royal galley, and I remember one scow floating down beside us, its decks heaped with bales of papyrus that looked as white in their reflection as the best of treated linen. Try then to look into the blinding light that came from the gold and silver hull of a state barge of the King being rowed upstream with a group of royal officials to take on Pharaoh's duties in towns to the South. They stood beside a huge altar of gold in the stern, larger than five men kneeling side by side, a gift no doubt from Ramses Nine to one of His temples, and the officials cheered as they saw the pennants on the golden falcon in the bow of Menenhetet's ship and we nodded in our turn to the coiled cobras of gold on the raised cabin of this state barge. The royal ship was rowed by sixty oarsmen (for there was no wind) thirty in a row on either side, and with the speed they raised, no breeze could have taken them upriver as quickly. Their mast stood alone, its great red mainsail furled, the mast straight as Sweet Finger last night, but covered with gold: there was not anything on the boat that did not shine of gold or silver but for the straw matting on the decks, and the carved purple bulwarks of the oarlocks and the rail. In pace with its progress, a troop of charioteers guarded the treasures of the barge by marching down the road that led along the higher bank of the river, and an infantry of archers jogged with them in a trot to keep even with the pace of the oarsmen, their equipment jiggling, then a squadron of lances with colored flags and plumed Babylonian horses I saw, and two-man chariots. Purple, orange, red, and a yellow as saffron as the color of my own robes, were on the plumes and ribbons of the horses, and the painted medallions of the chariots. Naked children ran after them for as long as they could keep up—naked but for a bracelet or an armband. I saw a few stare at my yellow robes in awe, and when one boy my age looked at me, and I at him across the water, he bowed and kissed the ground. Meanwhile, every sound was going back and forth between the soldiers and the women they passed, a merriment as happy as the washing of the river, and greetings and even applause kept passing between our boat and the soldiers as though today were a festival, and open salutations were permitted. Just before we drew away from them around a bend in the river, so we came on some blacks by the bank playing tambourines in such a frenzy that my mother murmured, "The passing of the Pharaoh's barge is what has excited them so." Two beautiful black girls were also in this frolic, and squealed with delight when one of the mercenaries, a Mede with amazing blond hair, took off his helmet and bowed flirtatiously as his chariot pulled by. Even the harper on our boat, a sour priest who wore a leopard skin (of which he was very proud) over the white linen of his ceremonial dress, condescended to pluck a string of his lyre, and the Negroes whistled at the clarity of the tone. Red as the mud of the banks were the dates ripening on the trees, and I thought the state barge looked like the golden bark of Ra being rowed across the sky even as it went by the bend in the glare of the sun. It was the grandest sight I had ever seen on the river, but I was to witness a greater one in the next hour when we came to the outskirts of Memphi.

For an obelisk of black marble, as long as the sixty paces of the wading pool in my great-grandfather's garden, was being carried on the longest barge I had ever seen, and it was drawn by leather ropes, thick as a man's arm, that were tied to eighteen smaller boats built only for towing, and therefore so narrow that they could hold no cargo but their own oarsmen pulling in two rows of fifteen men side by side. How great must have been the burden of that black marble obelisk with its golden tip! I remember Bone-Smasher and Eater-of-Shadows, seeing such an armada of oarsmen, stood up in our boat as though they were dogs trained for fights to the death, and were measuring the heat it would put on their seven souls and spirits to row the obelisk up the river. The long cry of that labor came across the water—a cry which did not come to an end. The separation between the eighteen boats was wide enough for each sound to reach us by a separate route, and so it was like the overlapping frenzy of a myriad of birds when their feeding is disturbed. For that matter, the true sound of birds could also have been in those cries since the armada had certainly attracted them. Hawks, herons and crows, turkey vultures and hoopoes kept to a circle above, as if at any moment one of the oarsmen would collapse and be thrown overboard, and behind the great barge carrying the obelisk, kingfishers glided over the water and dove in frequently for the catch. Something in its deep wake drew the fish—maybe it was no more than the unusual wash. Not many a boat went up the Nile opening such waves. Even while we watched, one kingfisher was sucked under by the curl and came up drowned. A vulture leaped away with that death, its cruel wings giving off an exuberance like the spring of a good sword in the bright morning air.

On the bank, laid out on mats, catfish were drying in the sun with a net stretched over them on poles to protect the catch from the birds, and a boy balanced himself on top of one of the poles and kept trying to hit the larger hawks with a stick. A hare, cut off in the flood from the safety of the desert, came wandering by; the boy threw his stick at the hare, missed, and fell off his perch, so producing a merry laugh from Hathfertiti.

We were coming to the temples for Baal and Astarte at the outskirts of Memphi, foreign temples put up by Syrians and other such people from the East, and I heard my parents speak of how they were not impressive as buildings. Although new, they were only made of wood and the paint was peeling. Their foundations were dirty with river mud. Indeed, they were surrounded by all the confusion of the foreign quarter with its miserable little houses, crooked streets narrower than the lanes of the Necropolis, and one-room hovels of unbaked brick so poor they had been built to share a common wall and leaned on each other. A dissatisfaction came into our mood at this sight, as if even the water reflected the squalor, and our priest in the leopard-skin cape made a point of spitting over the side as we passed the temples, for which act Menenhetet reached over and pinched his cheek as though to mock the fellow for the solemnity of his aversion. The priest returned a sickly smile and promptly bowed his shaved head to the floor. Menenhetet languidly removed a sandal, and offered his foot for the priest to kiss, which set my buttocks tingling once more, for the priest—slyly I thought—slipped his tongue like a snake in and out of Menenhetet's toes.

"Play on the strings," said Menenhetet, withdrawing his leg, and the priest reached for the harp, and began to play a song about a white palette that asked to be loved by its red and black cakes of ink, a silly song and hardly to the taste of my parents and great-grandfather although I enjoyed it for I was still thinking of the look on the priest's face when he bent over my great-grandfather's toes—it had been so much like the happy snarl of a dog going at meat. My father, however, looked irritated as if the abominations of pride in that priest had been no more agreeable to witness than Menenhetet's complacency before such caresses. If no one could make love to him without such abasement, where did that leave my mother?—leave it that my father detested chaos, filth, and inelegance. Not for too little was he the Overseer of the Cosmetic Box. Even as we were drifting past that abysmal foreign quarter, so blatant in its wretchedness as to destroy all good mood in someone like himself, my father said: "It's not worth the burning."

"Well," said Hathfertiti, "there could be a nicer approach to the city. Can't they move these people inland?"

"Too swampy back there," said Menenhetet.

"Why not up the hill?" asked Hathfertiti, pointing to a cliff that must have been a half-hour's walk from the river.

It was a hill I knew, and liked. Some servants had taken me there on a long walk, and those cliffs had bees' nests high in the hollows of their rock. The boys who lived in the hovels here on the river used to climb halfway up the cliff, dare the bees, collect the honey, and descend. The servants with me laughed at how they had to suffer bee-stings on the way down with the honey, but from my protected place, flanked by two servants, I thought the boys were remarkable. So I listened carefully to talk of moving the foreign quarter onto the hill.

"It can't be done," said Menenhetet. "That is exactly where Nine talks of building the new fort."

"I still don't see," Hathfertiti remarked, "why they can't move these people—the fort will never get put up."

"You have a mind for military matters," remarked my great-grandfather.

I was merely hoping they would not build the fort too quickly so that some day, when old enough, I would also be brave enough to go up those cliffs for honey, and I thought of how little I knew of the manner in which such boys lived, poor boys who worked for their fathers in the fields near the river, and shivered so much at the picture that my mother drew me into the perfumed and wondrously delicate pillows of her scented breast and belly, and whispered, "The child dare not be ill again," and my father looked gloomy. For when I was ill, he had to pay attention to Hathfertiti's woes.

"No, the boy will be all right," said my father.

My great-grandfather gave me a look out of his large pale-gray eyes which in this bright light were like clear sky, and asked, "What is the color of your blood?"

I knew he was thinking of our last conversation, so I answered, "As red as it was last night."

He nodded. "And the sun?"

"The sun is golden, but we call it yellow."

"He is truly intelligent," breathed Hathfertiti.

"And the sky," said my great-grandfather, "is blue."

"Yes, it is blue."

"Explain then, if you can, the origin of such other colors as brown, orange, green and purple."

"Orange is the marriage of blood and the sun. So it is the color of fire." My mother had told me that. She now added, "Green is the color of grass."

But I was annoyed. I had been ready to give the explanation myself. "Yes, grass," I said, "is green, even as the sky is blue, and the sun is yellow."

Menenhetet did not smile. "Speak of the origin of the color of brown," he said.

I nodded. I did not feel at all like a child. Menenhetet's thoughts lived so clearly with mine that I had only to take a breath and I could feel the power of his mind.

"Brown," I said, "is like the river. In the beginning, the Red Nile was a river of blood in the sky."

"Now, the child will certainly catch fever," Hathfertiti murmured.

"Nonsense," said Menenhetet.

"May the child not be ill," said my father.

I had certainly stopped shivering and my body felt lucid. "Is purple a mixture of blood and sky?" I asked Menenhetet.

"Of course," he replied. "That is why it is also the color of madness." He nodded. "Just as rich earth is brown since all colors go back to it. Just so," he said with an evil addition, "is your ca-ca brown."

I laughed with delight.

"But what makes the color of white?" I asked.

"The child is not stupid," he murmured. He took me by the chin. "You are yet too young," he said, "to comprehend the color of white. That is the most mysterious of hues." He frowned at the look of disappointment on my face. "Think for now," he said, "of white as the color of stone, for that is where the Gods take Their rest."

"Is this why temples are made of marble?"

"Doubtless," he said, and remarked to my mother, "an exceptional wit. It convinces me that our blood is brilliant." He could not, however, keep from smiling. "Of course, given the intertwinings of the Ramses, it is a wonder we have any sense at all."

My father was in misery. "I implore you. Do not say such things," he murmured as if even the small scratch of those sounds on his ear would leave telltale marks of disloyalty to the Pharaoh upon his face.

The slow drift of our boat had stimulated the merchants of the foreign quarter, and a dozen came out to us in skiffs of every cheap description—some not better than a wooden case lashed to papyrus reeds. One was on a raft with two logs for pontoons, and others rowed up in small wooden scows. They bore down full of cargo for sale; some, for example, with vases of oil—lamp oil, castor-oil, oil of sesame; one idiot selling bowls of flax and barley actually tried to interest my mother in his bargains: "Exceptional fair price!" he kept

calling out in atrocious Egyptian and became so persistent he almost
lost his balance, for Bone-Smasher, wielding one of the long oars,
kept swinging it through the air at him (although as casually as raising
an arm in greeting) but the barley-man kept his boat just beyond the
end of the oar-blade, until, perceiving at last from the indifference of
my mother that he could yell his wares for hours and shift no affection
in her to flax or barley, he bowed with courtesy and turned away to
give space to another. They all came near: boats with every kind of
fruit and spice, boats with raw clay to sell, and milk, and henna, and
one with turfs of dung that stank so bad my mother cried out in annoyance and Bone-Smasher almost fell in the fury with which he laid
down his oar, took up his river pole and shoved the other prow
away—indeed he left a hole in the dung boat, right through the dried
reeds. Another came by with wigs, and Hathfertiti allowed it to come
close, studied a few heads of hair across a little water—I know she was
afraid of picking up lice and looked only for purposes of comparison
to her own wigs, then waved the craft away. A skiff came by with two
pigs for sale. At the look in Bone-Smasher's eye it backed water
quickly. Pig was not to be offered to us. Another boat had geese and
cranes, ducks and hens. We were not buying. A scow with two
wooden cages showed a hyena and a gazelle.

"Is the hyena male or female?" my father asked of Eater-of-
Shadows, who repeated the question to the boatman, and when the
answer was given by way of making a circle with fingers and thumb,
my father shook his head. "The Pharaoh has a female hyena already. I
thought if there were a male . . ."

"Has Ptah-nem-hotep succeeded in domesticating His hyena?"
asked my great-grandfather.

"The Pharaoh performs wonders in taming animals," said my father with implacable piety. "I have seen Him walk the hyena on a
leash."

My great-grandfather was reputed to have wrestled with a lion,
but he merely smiled, and looked up at a covey of quail flying over
our boat, their wings beating as fast as the tongues of hummingbirds.

A little scow, brightly painted, came by. Its merchant was its only sailor: a young man dressed in a white skirt, his body well-painted in red ochre. He made an agreeable appearance, and Bone-Smasher, at a sign from Menenhetet, allowed him to draw near. He was selling cosmetics, but his oils, almond and sesame with perfume added, were of low quality. Since my mother did not wish to disappoint his attractive face, as if such cruelty might reduce the beauty of her own features, she settled at last on some Asiatic pomade, a peculiar mixture that the young merchant assured her—speaking with his head down and through the intermediary of our boatman—was of his own invention and used on his own hair. Since that was as dark as a black olive and as lustrous as its oil, Hathfertiti asked by way of Eater-of-Shadows if oil from black olives was the base of his cosmetic, and when he said yes, she was able also to analyze the odor. "You have used oil of dates for fragrance," she said.

"The Princess is wise," he replied.

"But that is not all of your concoction?"

"Great Princess, there is one hair of a black dog, fierce as a wolf, in the bottom of the vase, and if the hair is not removed, so will the strength of your own hair not leave," he managed with considerable stammering to assure Eater-of-Shadows. I was giggling because the young merchant did not look at my mother but spoke to ugly-faced Eater-of-Shadows (who had an enormous nose) as if *he* were the Great Princess.

"I thank you for protecting the strength of my hair," said Hathfertiti, "but there is a strange odor in your mixture as well."

"It is the ground powder of horses' hooves," said the young man.

"Horses' hooves," said Eater-of-Shadows.

"Horses' hooves," said Hathfertiti, and after a pause laughed merrily.

"Hooves for the roots of your hair, Princess, and the health of your scalp."

She purchased the oil, and my father gave a small ring worth five copper utnu in payment. The young man bowed in recognition that he had not been obliged to haggle for his price, and when we drifted away, he continued to look in our direction with such admiration as to wish to remain with us forever.

My great-grandfather grunted. "A pretty boy," he said.

"Looks full of the love of his mother," said my father.

Menenhetet nodded. For once, he found agreement with my father. "I would advise him to stay out of the army."

My father guffawed. It was a coarse sound to come out of his elegance, but the thought of the young merchant rudely used by the troops made him laugh, and most suddenly.

"I don't believe," said Hathfertiti, "that I will use his oil for my hair. But it will go well on my breasts."

"Bound to," said Menenhetet. "All those horses' hooves."

My father guffawed again, and Menenhetet offered a warm and malicious look.

Around the bend we left the foreign quarter. Now, the white walls of Memphi were shining on the bank. We floated past the marble splendor of the Temple of Ptah and its sacred gardens, but only a few priests in white were to be seen on the paths. Then, the Temple of Hathor appeared around another bend.

Here, if my mother had had her way, would the town of Memphi have made its first appearance. These temples and parks told of the magnificence of our city. The serpentine wall was as delightful to the eye as a necklace of white stones, and behind was a view of high columns on two successive hills with a garden between. That was the last fine space we were to see. The river spread out around the next bend until it was as wide as a lake, and to the left was all of Memphi before our eyes, the harbor, the stone wharves for unloading cargo, the shipyards, the jetties, the causeways, the canals, the granaries, and every crowded house on every rise of ground, yes, there was our white city so recently red with dust in the dry season, now a bit muddy. It hardly mattered. Coming around this last bend was like entering the gates. Before I could even pick out the faces of workers on the docks, or soldiers guarding the marketplace, not yet close to the clamor of the shops or the cries of traffic on the avenue, I still knew the air on the river was different and full of messages. How splendid the city looked in this sunlight. Even the dust of the quarries shimmered. The water pails of a thousand shadufs kept rising and falling at the end of their poles, lifting water into sluices above them that passed the water to other shadufs on up to higher sluices until there was water for the fountains of the city in every square. Were there a thousand—or was it five thousand slaves?—cranking the long poles of these shadufs to raise our water? I know as we looked from our boat across that hot shimmering river, I could hear shadufs creaking near and far, and the sun blazed like a sword each time water splashed into a higher sluice.

In the basin of the harbor of Memphi, we came to a mammoth eddy between the jetty and the docks. Our boatmen unlashed their oars and began to row us by a short route through a canal that went behind a long promontory of the harbor. That way, to my pleasure, took us through a part of the city I did not often see, and I passed close to temples built—as my mother exclaimed—"a thousand years ago." They now sat in the depression of old damp holes. These temples were made of stone and therefore had endured after the wooden buildings that once swarmed around them had collapsed, and the brick buildings (molded from mud and straw) had washed away in one or another of our terrible rainstorms, the kind that came once every fifty years. My mother told me of how she saw such a storm when she was a child, and the roofs of palm thatch in poor houses came apart like old wet cloth. So the houses around these old temples kept being rebuilt until the new on top of the old reached to half the height of the temples, and left them in damp hollows, dark old gray stone, mournful as hippopotami fallen into pits. Around them, on each side of the canal, was all the din of the workshops, and our local markets. Quickly, for the boatmen rowed hard through many a smell of sawdust, and leather, manure, rotting papyrus and stone dust that blew over the canal from the masons' shops, past every whiff of bleaches that scored my nose, we went by the woodworking shops, and matting shops, past the sandalmakers, and a shop for the repair of harness and chariots, went by a forge, and a stable, and the linen factories of the weavers, past the embalmers, the shops of the undertakers and coffin-makers, past a woman at a loom working in the open air at the front of her shop not five feet from the edge of the canal, and next to her a currier was scraping the skin of a leopard, an awful odor coming up from the big dead cat to make my mother gag. Farther along we came to the back of a furniture shop and I saw two workers carry out a chest of ebony inlaid in silver, beautiful enough for the Pharaoh. It was being placed now, even as we went by, on a barge, and White-Teeth, the handsomest of our boatmen, called out, "Is that for Two-Gates?" and the worker on the dock replied, "It goes south, to the estate of the Great Menenhetet," which left a ripple of laughter on our gilded barge and even the oarsmen dared to join, for at that moment it was as if all of us on the boat belonged to the same family.

At the end of this short canal, as we came back to the harbor, the shops of the perfumers sweetened the air, and there were larger markets, and a school for priests, one long low building with white wooden pillars. Just past was a wig shop, and I saw one for a small boy, a beautiful blue, and would have asked my mother to get it for me as a gift, but the boatmen were rowing hard, and I felt an uneasiness in our boat, and recognized then that my great relatives were thinking of how soon they would see the Pharaoh.

At the end of the canal where we joined the river again, there was a plaza, and it was filled with every kind of priest and noble, soldier, boatman, and foreign trader, artisan, peasant, slave, water-carrier, caravan-hand, donkey-driver, and many women of all kinds, even a few ladies. To look at all these people from our boat never failed to please me. I felt so safe. It was another matter to walk through them. Then Eyaseyab was full of fear because every drunken soldier and vendor stared at her thighs (and I, walking beside her, at just such a height, had to look into their eyes). On the water, however, I could feel more cheerful. Each wine-shop and beer-house had its colored awning up, drumming and flapping like sails in the breeze off the harbor, and I could see people waiting in front of one, famous for its roast goose, to take home a cooked bird.

On the far side of the plaza, near the streets and the canals behind, in an open space guarded on three sides by newly built high walls and

on the fourth by a line of soldiers with their arms linked was a new
open-air shop set up by an edict of the Pharaoh. It had caused more
talk in Memphi—at least to measure by the amount of conversation
in my family—than any of His decisions in some time. For at this
shop, some of the silver ingots His boats brought back from Tyre, and
even a fair amount of the gold His caravans returned from the Granite
Mountains near the Red Sea, were now being fashioned by royal arti-
sans into amulets, breast pieces, gold collars, bracelets, scarabs, uraei,
even gold and silver shabti, while jewelry and such other foreign
treasures as scented woods and gums, coral and amber, linens and
glasswork and embroideries were for sale to the few people on this
plaza who could afford the price. Everyone who could not pressed
nonetheless against the line of soldiers for a look. Until now, such
ornaments had always been made in the shops of the Palace, within
the workrooms of the Temple of Ptah, or on estates as large as Menenhetet's. So eager was the crowd, therefore, to see these treasures
being worked upon by the Royal Craftsmen that some knelt to have a
peek between the guards' legs, and groans of admiration went up
whenever a foreign trader or some wealthy local official was admitted
through the line of soldiers, for he would be able to touch the objects
themselves. And each night, to prevent theft, the products, the tools,
and even the precious dusts of the metalwork were gathered up in
velvets, locked in boxes and carried away under guard to a royal vault.
Next morning they were returned to the plaza again.

Now, as if the gleam of such valuables at the end of the plaza
brought a glimpse of the end of our journey, the boatmen began
to lean on their oars, full strength coming from Stinking-Body
and White-Teeth, Eater-of-Blood, Eater-of-Shadows, Head-on-
Backwards and He-of-the-Nose—they all began to weigh on their
oars, and Bone-Smasher called the cadence. Our heavy barge picked
up the current as we came out of the eddy and our prow lifted in the
water and the river began to sing with the speed of our effort as we
came around the last point past the plaza and saw in full display along
the curve of the next bank, the limestone walls of Two-Gates which

rose as high as the three stories of Menenhetet's house. Sentries stood on the parapets above.

Before our boat was even tied to the mooring, a suite of sedan-chair carriers resting in the shadow of the wall came running toward us across a long open marble plaza down to the stone steps by the river. "Have use of our services, Great Lord," their leader called to Menenhetet. At a signal, the others knelt, bowed, and struck their heads to the marble floor.

"Who has need of your poor chairs?" said my great-grandfather. "The legs of my family are young."

"O, my Lord, there is great weight in every step that takes you nearer to His Presence."

"I cannot bear to think of the woe my body would put on your crooked back," replied Menenhetet.

"Great Lord, the chair weighs less when a noble lord like you is in it. Look, I lay my face on the seat before you sit down," said the leader, and was immediately copied by the other bearers who embraced the seat of their sedan chairs.

"And do you still kiss it after you are done carrying me?"

"Then I must kiss it twice," said the bearer.

"For your courtesy," said Menenhetet, "take us through the Red Gate, and to the end of the courtyard." And my mother, my father, my great-grandfather and myself all sat down in separate chairs and were lifted and carried across the marble plaza between the river and the walls of the Palace.

But even as we came nearer, we saw frightful sights. By the wall was a wretch with his neck manacled to a collar, then chained to a post. His hands must have been cut off but a few hours ago and the stumps of his forearms were bound with leather thongs to keep him from bleeding to death, yet his blood still dripped on the stone.

Leaning forward in his chair, Menenhetet asked, "What did you steal?"

"He—the-Great-God-Nine-among-us—is kind to let me live, because I stole too much," the wretch replied. It was not easy to hear him. As the price for an old crime—lying to a judge might be the reason—he had had his lips cut off. Now, his grin was like the exposed teeth of a skull.

Next to him stood a woman leashed to another post. In her arms was a blue baby. My mother looked away, but my great-grandfather asked, "How did you kill your child?"

"By suffocation."

"Was there food enough?"

"There was food enough," said the woman, "but the child's wailing left no breath in the house."

"When will you be released?"

"In another night."

"May your punishment prove too heavy."

Before us, were two great rectangular doors in the wall, side by side: a red granite gate with a papyrus plant cut into it for the Land of the North, and a limestone gate of white with a lily engraved above the door for the Land of the South. Now, a trumpet sounded. The huge red granite door began to open. "Enter Great Lord and General Menenhetet. Enter the honored family of Menenhetet," a herald cried out, and then intoned: "Here, in the Year Seven, under the Majesty of the King of the South and the North, the Beautiful Ka of Ra, Beloved of Amon, Son of the Sun, Si-Ra Ramses the Ninth, Horus-the-strong-bull-Who-lives-in-the-truth, welcomes you here."

"We enter in honor to His Life-Health-Strength, our Pharaoh, the good Ptah-nem-hotep," said Menenhetet, and turned to Bone-Smasher who had been walking on guard beside the sedan chair. "An extra ration of bread and beer for your men and their oars," he said as we were carried into the Palace ground. Geese were flying overhead, and pigeons scattered before us. Three hawks—I counted them— watched from a perch on the parapet.

Three

The longest courtyard I had ever seen was before us. If a grown man took a stone and hurled it as far as he could, picked up the stone and hurled it again, he would not have reached the middle.

Nor was it a handsome place. There were no pools nor statues, and the road of paved stones down the middle by which the sedan-chair carriers brought us was no wider than would be needed for four chariots abreast. On either side, an open red-clay square stretched to the walls, and I remember my mother speaking of how the Pharaoh paraded thousands of troops on this hot ground. Then, even as I looked across the space, a portal opened in a low barracks at the other end of the courtyard, and a company of Sherdens in heavy blue capes marched out to practice maneuvers. In the other corner of the courtyard were armories, and storehouses and sentry boxes, and even a huge cauldron of soup on a great fire, the smell of its broth passing to us across the clay.

As if Menenhetet's entrance had stirred activity, I could see targets of straw being set up against the wall to the side of the barracks, and archers were flexing their bows. A troop of chariots began to form

and reform their lines. From four files of seven they would elongate
into two files of fourteen, then wheeling, shift into two ranks of
fourteen, then extend into one long and near-to-perfect line of
twenty-eight chariots galloping on the instant across the field, no
wheel ever more than a few fingers ahead of another. On a sharp cry,
they came to a sudden stop, dust rolling off like a wave toward the
river wall, and it may have been fortunate for their captain that the
cloud did not come near us, since Hathfertiti turned with annoyance
in her chair, and said to my great-grandfather, "Promise we do not
stay here watching them."

He shrugged, but I saw his eye reach to the captain of these charioteers across the distance of the parade ground, and in response, that
man raised both forearms in salute, and came galloping toward us, the
soldier by his side trying to maneuver his leather shield against imaginary arrows, a set of gestures that took up all his balance, while the
captain of the charioteers, having wrapped his reins around his waist,
was now turning the horses to left or right by leaning from side to
side. Pressing backward, he would slow them; coming forward, he let
them gallop, swaying his body to make the horses wheel, stop, turn,
or charge, and if one could not foretell what his next maneuver would
be, all were nonetheless smooth. Meanwhile, his arms free, he un-
sheathed his bow, and put an arrow in it. When the captain swept
around us in a flourish, that gave my father a stir.

"Fool," he shouted. To which Hathfertiti gave a chill laugh. "I
think he's charming," she said.

"If the horse tripped, he could send the arrow in our direction,"
said my father.

The captain, having circled away from us, returned in a leisurely
trot, came to a halt, leaped out of his vehicle and touched his forehead
to the dust. He and Menenhetet began to speak to each other in a
strange language, strange as the language of the Sherdens I soon
guessed, and after a minute or two—with a last phrase in Egyptian:
"As you say, General"—the soldier raised his arm in salute, smiled at
all of us, at my mother most particularly, remounted, and walked off
slowly with his horse in order not to raise the dust.

"I told him I'd watch maneuvers later," said my great-grandfather.

"Thank you," said Hathfertiti.

Now we came to a smaller gate. A sentry let us through without a word. We had reached another courtyard.

"It is splendid how they use their reins," said Hathfertiti.

"But it is our grandfather who developed the style," said my father.

"Not really," she exclaimed.

"Certainly," said Menenhetet. "In the years before the Battle of Kadesh. That is why we triumphed on that day."

He said this with such pleasure that my mother could not resist saying, "I thought Ramses the Second was the victor at Kadesh, not your charioteers."

"The Pharaoh always wins the battle," said Menenhetet.

We were passing through another courtyard, immense perhaps as the first, but I did not know how large since it was divided by walls of trees into more than a few courts and enclosures. Wading pools were surrounded by gardens. To our left was a brightly painted wooden building, and I could see women pass from time to time along its covered balcony on the second story, while a murmur of curious laughter came back to us from their sight of Hathfertiti. We were carried now to a white wooden wall on which were painted enormous portraits of a hawk, a scorpion, a bee, a lotus, and a papyrus plant, all so lifelike that I was afraid to pass through, indeed I trembled at the nearness of the scorpion.

We dismounted from the sedan chairs, and the bearers, after a nod from Menenhetet, gave a quick kiss to the seat (whose leather was marked with nothing less than the hieroglyph—⊗—which represents the Land of the Dead). My father, having handed the sedan-chair leader a copper utnu, and the officer at the door having recognized us—I could see by the look of relief on his face that he had been expecting his distinguished guest for half the morning—we passed with many a bow by the attendants into the green and verdant garden of the Pharaoh's Court of Honor. There, trees with fruit I had never seen before grew at the edge of an oblong pool whose tiles were covered with gold.

"When these trees were young," my mother whispered to me, "their feet were set in pots, and they were put on boats and carried across many a storm until they reached our land."

"How does it look?" I asked, "where the river comes to the open waters?"

"There are more birds," she said, "than you have ever seen."

I was thinking of the squalling of those birds above that wet land, and how different they must be from the birds of this garden. Here, one flamingo had colors orange and pink and gold, and there was a black ibis, and plovers that raced from branch to branch showing feathers as brilliant as the tail of an ostrich. I remember when I was two, and still new to the thought of expressing myself, I had asked my mother why we put the heads of birds on so many of our Gods. (Having seen, long before I could read, how many of the sacred sticks our scribes drew on papyrus were of birds, I had assumed such hieroglyphs were given to us by the Gods as pictures of Themselves.) My mother had smiled then. "The child asks questions that bring peace to my mind," she said, "I feel the feather when he speaks." That was a reference to Maat I would understand only later—we had a saying that the edge of a feather was the closest you could come to touching the truth. Then, out of whatever composure my thought had given her, my mother said, "Birds are most respected—they fly."

Fly they did, and in this grove, they whipped and laced from branch to branch, and seemed to dart in delight at the reflection of themselves in the gold tile of the pool where their colors flew along the shallow bottom like rainbow-colored fish, yet even in their gaiety that rollicked through the shade of these foreign trees, I could hear the distant echo of panic. The sounds of these birds were stranger to me than the grunts of animals hard at work, for in those, at least, I could hear the sound of the earth—I suppose I mean to speak of that unheard sound that connects one's feet to the earth. Birds, however, always twittered of some unrest that was in the agitation of their flesh forever fearful of our ground, no, the earth was not a place where a bird could rest.

Nonetheless, this garden—after the glare of the courtyard—was a grove. Every smell of loam, and some I never smelled before, was in my nose, damp and mysterious as the cool I once discovered at the edge of a cave, and in this air, I felt the nearness of the Pharaoh. At the end of our walk, near to obscured by the foliage, was a small wooden villa painted in every bright color of the flowers of the garden, a peculiar building, on stilts perhaps, yet, like a house, built around all four sides of a patio, so that, walking beneath, we passed into deep shadow, then came out of the shadow to a place in the open center where the sun was shining.

I had always dreamed that the Pharaoh would rest on a throne at the end of a great hall, and visitors would approach by crawling forward on their knees, and indeed Menenhetet had told us how Ramses Two used to give vast audiences at festival time in the middle of an immense place in the old city of Thebes, but then, even as I was trying to think of how large that could have been—was it larger than where we had seen the charioteers at their drill?—we entered the patio and I felt the Pharaoh, or certainly felt His force as the sun blinded my eyes on our sudden emergence into its glare. A weight came down upon the back of my head heavy as the sun, and before I knew it, had me prostrating myself on the ground in the way I had been instructed, my hips in the air, my knees and face to the earth— was there a smell of incense to this sacred earth?—and had no idea whether it was a force from the Pharaoh on the balcony above that had laid me low, or only the hand of my father kneeling next to me on the one side and my mother on the other. In front of us, honored by his rank, Menenhetet had merely lowered himself to one knee.

In a moment, my mother and father rose with Menenhetet, their knees still to the ground, their arms extended—a position natural to my father (I could feel his happiness) and demeaning to my mother (I could sense now she detested it) but I, to my surprise, did not wish to move, as if, with mouth and nose pressed into the grit of the dirt, and my eyes not a finger's width above, I felt the heavy peace of that great circle in which we revolve before we sleep. Not daring to look up at the Pharaoh (Who had, by His Presence, forced my mouth to kiss the ground) I did not know if the weight on my back still came from His eyes, the full heat of the sun, or both (and very much the same) since I had been told from the day I heard the name, Son of the Sun, that no man on earth was nearer to Ra than our Monarch, Si-Ra Ramses Ninth in all of His great titles: Nefer-Ka-Ra Setpenere Ramses Kham-uese Meriamon (for Ptah-nem-hotep was only the name of His boyhood by which old friends and high officials could call Him).

Then, I do not know whether I passed through vertigo or bliss, but circles of color vibrated right up from the earth into my eyes, and I felt another force summoning me to rise until I lifted my eyes high enough to look up to the balcony for the face of the Pharaoh.

He was seated between two columns, and leaned with His elbows upon a gold railing protected by a red embroidered cushion. I could see no more of His body than a collar of gold that covered His chest, and above was His great Double-Crown, high and full as two sails, and with the small jeweled body of a gold snake above His right eye. It was more like looking at a large shield than at a man, the tall white crown of the Pharaoh forming the upper arch, and His collar, the lower. Or, so I might have thought but for His beautiful face between. He had eyes that were very large, and the black lines of the cosmetic made them more prominent. As my mother had told me, His eyes were famous for change of color: now bright and clear as the sky, they would yet reflect the dark of a moonless night. He had a long sad nose, not at all like other noses. It was very thin, and His nostrils were narrow as a cat's. As He turned His head I could see that the shape of this nose was curious, for the curve, by one view, gave to His elegant and aquiline face a fine scimitar, but from the other side, looked as mournful as a drop of water about to fall from a down-turned leaf. Beneath that narrow nose was a beautiful mouth, full and splendidly curved, and it lived in intimacy with the nose above, a most peculiar way to describe it, except it made me think of my nurse Eyaseyab standing next to me, since we did not look the least alike, and she was a slave, although I was never so comfortable as when I found myself with her, short fat Eyaseyab. As I looked at His mouth and nose, I could also see my nose against the thick skirt of Eyaseyab's upper thigh, and recollected the smell of earth and fish and riverbank that came off her. That seemed kin to the care with which Ptah-nem-hotep's narrow nostrils seemed to curl in the breath that came from His mouth, and I felt a strong desire to kiss Him. I wished to bury my sweet mouth—everyone assured me my mouth was sweet—on the lips of the Son of Ra, and this desire having come to me, gave permission to the next desire—and I saw myself straining at the tip of my toes to kiss the divine finger between the legs of the Pharaoh, an impulse I could hardly take in before my next thought was to do the same to my great-grandfather. There, beneath the spell of the Pharaoh's nose, as bewitching to me as the powdered navel of my mother, I had a vision of myself in the future, and I was a young man in a dark room within a dark mountain, there on my knees before the Ka of my great-grandfather, and I do not know if all I now saw at the age of six was only a gift given back to me from the Ka of myself remembering, at last, a day of my life, or whether I was not, in truth, on the patio of Ptah-nem-hotep (for so I called Him at once in my heart as if we were old friends) and therefore I was more alive here than in my Ka on its knees at the tomb of Khufu. Then—as if I rose from a night of awful dreams into the day—I became certain I was alive and six years old when, still kneeling with my arms before me, I looked up again to the face of the Pharaoh, and He spoke in a clear and ringing voice of the most distinguished tones, indeed a voice—I most certainly heard it—that, phrase for phrase, was equal to my great-grandfather at teasing a truth with quiet mockery.

"Menenhetet," said the Pharaoh, "can it be a small motive that encourages you to honor My invitation?"

"Matters of the greatest concern for myself would seem of small import to Your Majesty," said Menenhetet in a voice that floated forth like a leaf laid on water.

"You could not have a small reason. Only a modest explanation," said our Pharaoh, and pleased with this answer, added, "Rise, great Menenhetet. Take your family and join Me here." He patted the cushion beside Him.

An attendant led us to a painted stairway, and from there it was ten steps to the balcony. Ptah-nem-hotep embraced my great-grandfather and kissed my mother on the cheek. She bowed and kissed His toe, but demurely, like a cat, and my father, solemnly—he was received solemnly—knelt and gave an embrace to the other toe. "Tell me the name of Hathfertiti's son," said Ptah-nem-hotep.

"It is Menenhetet the Second," said Hathfertiti.

"Menenhetet-Ka," said the Pharaoh. "An ogre's name for a lovely face." He looked at me carefully and gave an exclamation. "Only the beauty of Hathfertiti could give birth to so perfect a face."

"Do not stand unmoving, my son," said my father.

"Yes," said Ptah-nem-hotep tenderly, "you had better kiss My foot."

So I knelt, and saw that His toenails were painted blue, and His foot, when I kissed it, was perfumed, and like my mother's scent, gave the odor of a dark red rose, or that I thought was the odor of His foot until I realized the floor had been washed in perfume. Kissing the space between the big toe and the next, my nose was pinched for an instant—the Pharaoh's toes were fingering me—and I felt a flash of pain, not pain so much as a white light within my body, a light that must have come from the Pharaoh; its intensity made me feel like a flower plucked up from its roots—did a flower see this same white light? As if I lived again in more than one place at once, so did I know what it would be like to come forth into a woman, my flesh embla-zoned in the white light of the God who came to meet me.

Much stimulated by this power of living in two houses, my tongue began to lick the crotch of the Pharaoh's foot, and I came away with more than an odor of rose. The faintest smell of earth and river and fish, all kin to the smell between Eyaseyab's thighs, was also there, and even a remote hint of the fierce manly odor of urine that could often reek from the height above Menenhetet's knees. I even felt full of the same kind of bemusement I used to know when smelling my wet fingers after tickling a little saliva over Sweet Finger or my hips and my navel. Living in the pocket of these odors, I felt the power once more of the Pharaoh's presence and understood, as if never before instructed, that the Pharaoh was indeed the nearest of men to the

Gods, yet I also knew He was a man who smelled a little like a woman, and His smells were near my own.

I looked up, bowed my head, withdrew two steps upon my knees, and stood slowly. The Pharaoh did not take His eyes from me. "Your boy is extraordinary," He said to Hathfertiti, "and has a sweet mouth. He will yet prove a scandal with his tongue." Turning His look from myself to my great-grandfather in a movement just so full of the gravity of His mind as the change in mood of the sky when the sun is covered slowly by a cloud, He said to Menenhetet, "You will do well to increase every strength in this boy that sits below his mouth."

"That may be the search of all men," said my great-grandfather.

"For Pharaohs as well," said Ptah-nem-hotep.

My great-grandfather responded with a most unexpected speech. "O You Who live in the night, yet shine upon us in the day; Who are wise as the earth and as the river; You of the Two Great Houses, intimate of Set and Horus, You Who speak to the living and the dead, ask of Your servant, Menenhetet, any small question he can attempt to answer, but do not ask him to ponder whether a Pharaoh has need of strength in those mysterious regions that lie above the thigh and beneath the navel."

He said all this with such an absence of fear and such cold prowess that he separated himself from the pious sound of his praise. He had shown me once how a captured officer might hand over his sword while feeling contempt for the General to whom he surrendered—it was the only time he ever played such a game with me—and I was wondering if he showed contempt for the Pharaoh now by the words of his speech.

"Tell Me, lovely Hathfertiti," said our Ramses Nine, "does he speak of Me in this fashion when I am not with you?"

"He lives," said my mother, "for word of Your smile and mention of Your approval."

"Tell Me, great General," the Pharaoh went on, with only a shrug of His fine shoulder for Hathfertiti's reply (which had been too quick) "is this the manner in which you once spoke to My great ancestor?"

Menenhetet bowed. "It was a young voice then. I have an old one now."

"Besides, the ancestor was a great Pharaoh," Ptah-nem-hotep said.

"The difference," said Menenhetet, "between Ramses the Second and Ramses the Ninth is as the difference between Great Gods."

"Of which Great Gods do you speak?"

"If I dare to name Them . . ."

"I give you permission."

"Ramses the Second was called Horus-the-strong-bull-Who-loves-the-truth. Yet He would remind me more of the Great God Set." Menenhetet took a pause for the effect of such boldness to be appreciated, and added, "Even as you, great Ninth of the Ramses, encourage me to invoke the presence of He Who is without compare, and is Osiris."

Menenhetet had made a splendid remark. Ptah-nem-hotep gave a rich laugh, almost as rich in the sound of its pleasure as the amusement I would sometimes hear in my mother's voice, and I wondered then if Ptah-nem-hotep could also groan with the same profundity of expression as Hathfertiti.

"They speak usually of Ptah, not Osiris," He said. "I am most delighted you are here." At an inclination of His head, servants brought cushions, and He beckoned for us to sit beside Him, even sharing the space on His own large cushion with my great-grandfather who, indeed, was embraced and kissed grudgingly on the mouth as soon as he sat down, after which Ptah-nem-hotep all but inquired of the taste left on His lips by a turn of tongue to the corner of His beautiful mouth. The Pharaoh, now inclining Himself to Hathfertiti, said, "While the servants anoint us, I will go on with this day's work. I have audiences yet to give but must tell you that they can prove tedious. Would you prefer to be taken to your rooms?"

"I would like to listen as the problems of the Two-Kingdoms are presented to Your wisdom."

"It will be a pleasure to have you at My side," He whispered to her, and my father immediately gave a signal. A few servants came up with alabaster bowls of scented water that they set at the feet of Ptah-nem-hotep, Menenhetet, my mother and myself. It was then the Pharaoh indicated a fifth cushion for my father. "You need not oversee the eunuchs, Nef-khep-aukhem," the Pharaoh told him.

My father had a spark in his eye at this mention of himself. It suggested he was not always given such a gift as to hear his full name. "Good and Great God," he replied, "I breathe the spirit of Your divine kindness but cannot rest upon my cushion for fear the eunuchs will commit an unpardonable error."

While my father did not often explain much of himself to me, once, unforgettably, I was told how his work as Overseer of the Cosmetic Box and Pencil could on occasion be as important as the post of the Vizier. For whenever times of trouble came to the Two-Lands, then the bearing of the Pharaoh, that is to say, His body, the clothing He wore, and the cosmetics put upon His face, was vital to the good fortune of Egypt. Any gesture that the Pharaoh might make on such a day could shift the course of battles in distant places. The perfection of His eyes, painted pale-green and black, could give magnitude to each inclination of His head. When the Pharaoh was seated on His throne (which always faced the river) He had only to incline the royal neck to right or to left and a breeze would begin in the Upper or Lower Kingdom. So did He need no more than to turn the handle of His crook, and benedictions could be sent to shepherds in valleys we did not see, even as the smallest shake of His flail would inspire field-overseers to whip their labor-gangs. His sunshade, made from an ostrich tail, promoted the health of flowers; the great necklace that covered His chest was the golden ear of the Sun; and His crown of feathers (when He chose to wear it) gave joy or solemnity to the song of birds. My mother had frowned as my father instructed me in these stories. "Why don't you tell the boy that it is only the ancient Kings Who could put on a leopard's tail and stir the animals in the jungle. Our Ptah-nem-hotep does not possess such power."

But even as a child, I could see that my father, despite his desire for perfect decorum, was most practical. "The Pharaoh," he answered, "would have infinite power if He were not constantly attacked by other powers who are also infinite."

"Why," she asked, "is He attacked?"

"Because of the weakness of the Pharaohs Who came before Him." He looked back at me. "For this reason, it is more important than ever that any ornament which touches His body be without flaw, or His power is weakened further."

I thought there had to be some error in my father's argument. Certainly, he was not always to be found in the presence of the Pharaoh. He was often at home. So he could hardly oversee every last cosmetic. Wondering about this, I saw that my father now stood to the side and did not really interfere with the work of the eunuchs who had come in with all the friendliness of puppies and all the grace of dancing girls while two of them began (humming little tunes and smiling at us) to wash Ptah-nem-hotep's feet with great playfulness, as if indeed like puppies they had something of a right to nip and gnaw on His ankles. Three others served Menenhetet, my mother, and myself. With a considerable amount of merriment, their teeth shining, they tickled the soles of our feet and wiggled their fingers like minnows between our toes, only to scourge the dead skin from our heels with their blunt fingernails.

After a while, they finished with our feet and began to massage our legs. They were handsome men and probably had been chosen from the same village in Nubia or Kush for they were all about the same size, and of the same deep black, and their resemblance to one another was increased by the shining ivory pin that passed through their nose, each pin set at the same angle to their mouth as if they had all been born with one decoration from one womb.

They knew their work and, with or without my father, would hardly make an error. Soon they were massaging not only our legs, but our necks and shoulders, and the eunuch serving Hathfertiti began to rub an oil in exquisite circles around her navel to which she gave unabashed grunts of pleasure, curiously clear and loud as if such a forceful sound was certainly part of a noblewoman's etiquette.

"I must purchase this eunuch from You," she said to Ptah-nem-hotep, Who smiled agreeably. "Are they not delightful?" He asked, and looked at the dark bodies of these five slaves with the same love I had seen my great-grandfather give to a team of matched horses or twin white bulls, and indeed, since the slaves wore nothing, one could see not only their plump and muscular haunches, but the shiny stump where their testicles had been and this gave them a nice resemblance to geldings.

Ptah-nem-hotep remarked, "You cannot imagine what joy these boys bring to My harem. If I were still a very young man, I might suffer a lover's jealousy at the thought of what their hands can give to My little queens, but fortunately, I am sensible and appreciate that the eunuch is a blessing for a Prince. No woman can soothe a man as well, nor massage him into the same peace," Ptah-nem-hotep sighed. "Yes, they even pacify the animals."

"They sound," said Menenhetet, "more agreeable than the Gods."

"They are certainly," said Ptah-nem-hotep, "less wicked."

Menenhetet nodded profoundly.

Hathfertiti said, "It is only in Your presence, Twice-Great-House, that I can listen to such conversation without trembling." But her words were too flattering. Ptah-nem-hotep replied, "Even as a slave may relieve the boredom of his master by teasing him, so may we speak lightly of the Gods," but now He looked captured by boredom.

My father chose this moment to say, "To be in the presence of the Twice-Great-House is to live without fear," except he looked not at all free of fear as he said it, for at just this moment, a servant came in to present a cooling drink, and Ptah-nem-hotep, making a gesture of annoyance, waved it away. "You and Hathfertiti," He remarked to my father, "certainly speak like brother and sister," and His enormous eyes lifted in the gentlest curve of surprise as if He could not comprehend how a Princess like my mother, so perfect in her manner (except for her occasional descent into piety) was not only married, but half sister, to a man so common in his birth as my father. I winced with certainty that the Pharaoh was thinking this, but knew whether He did or not that I would still think it because my mother had told me this was the first cause of shame in our family.

Yet, with an obvious concern for His guests—as if His mood might also wither if conversation did not improve—our Pharaoh now turned to my mother and said, "Do you favor the shade of blue in the wig I am wearing?" and asked the question with enough force in His voice to strike a spark of fire in her, so that she replied, "It is not as blue as the sky," at which they both laughed. My father gave a hurried signal to his assistant, the Overseer of the Royal Wig, who promptly came in with a large silver platter on which rested two black wigs, one straight, one with curls, and two new blue wigs, of which one was curled. I was cheered by the gaiety shown now by my mother and Ptah-nem-hotep. If the warmth of the Pharaoh's greeting had been put into misery by just one of her remarks, it had now been restored by way of what she last said, as if it were natural for Him to balance the gloom with which He responded to a flaw in manners by quickness to applaud any exhibition of skillful speech, even an acceptable—that is, very small—insult, at least when the mood, like a soup, was in need of some stirring.

Now He picked up a wig with straight fine hair and held it aloft for examination. "Nothing," He said sadly, "will come close to the blue of the sky. The best of pigments are ugly next to the hue I would like to place on My head, but cannot find."

"The child may have Your answer," murmured Menenhetet.

"You must be as clever as you are beautiful," said Ptah-nem-hotep to me.

My head was empty except for the powerful impulse to say yes. So I nodded.

"Do you know the source of blue dye?" He asked.

I would not have to wander far for an answer. It came to me by way of my great-grandfather. My mind felt like a bowl of water, and the least movement in Menenhetet's thought rippled through it.

"Why, Divine Double-House, the berry that is blue is the source of the liquid dye." My tongue felt empty after the remark, and I waited for what might come next.

"Excellent," said Ptah-nem-hotep. "Now tell me of a light-blue dye that is not a liquid but a powder. Where could you find its root?"

"Good and Great God," I said, "it is not in a root but in the salts of copper that such a powder can be found."

"He speaks as well as yourself," said the Pharaoh.

"He is my second house," said Menenhetet.

"Explain to me, little Meni, why My wig can never reveal the same blue as the sky."

"The color of the wig, Good and Great God, comes from the earth. Whereas the blue of the sky is composed of air."

"Then I will never find the blue I desire?" He asked. His voice was full of a sympathetic mockery that drew me near to Him. Even as I answered, "Never," I went on to add as easily, "Never, Great Pharaoh, until You find a bird with feathers as blue as the air."

Menenhetet struck his thigh in surprise. "The boy hears only the best voices," he said.

"He hears more than one voice," said Ptah-nem-hotep, and flicked my great-grandfather with His flail. "It's splendid you are here," He said. "And you," He said, now touching Hathfertiti with the same flail.

She responded with her best smile. "Never have I seen You looking more handsome," she told Him.

"I confess," said Ptah-nem-hotep, "that I am like a dead fellow, well wrapped. I am bored."

"That cannot be so," said Hathfertiti, "when Your eyes are like the lion, and Your voice is the companion of the air."

"My nostrils smell everything," He said, "including the oppression of every breath I take." He sighed. "When alone, I utter bird cries in order to amuse Myself." He gave a sharp little hoot in imitation of a bird protecting her nest. "Does that amuse you?" He asked. "Sometimes I think it is only by amusing others that I escape for an instant from the smell of everything. Here, little boy, little Meni-Ka, would you like to hear a dog speak in our tongue, not his?"

I nodded. At the simple look of amusement on my face, Ptah-nem-hotep added, "Even your great-grandfather cannot make a dog speak."

He gave a special clap to His hands, and called out. "Tet-tut!"

I heard a dog stirring beneath the house, then moving slowly up the stairs to the balcony with steps that, for an animal, were as full of decorum as two servants ascending on four well-trained feet.

A silver greyhound came into view. He had a most intent and serious expression.

"Tet-tut," said the Pharaoh quietly, "you may sit down."

The dog obeyed with no sign of agitation.

"I will introduce all of you," said Ptah-nem-hotep. "After I speak your name, please Me to keep thinking of it." He then proceeded to point out each of us to the animal. "All right, Tet-tut," said Ptah-nem-hotep. "Go to Hathfertiti." When the dog took a step forward and hesitated, He repeated, "Yes, My darling, go to the Lady Hathfertiti."

Tet-tut looked at my mother, then approached her. Before she could applaud this effort, Ptah-nem-hotep said, "Go to Menenhetet."

The dog backed away from Hathfertiti, turned once in a circle, and walked directly to my great-grandfather. When he was within two feet of him, he knelt, put his long muzzle to the floor, and began to moan.

"Are you afraid of this man?" asked the Pharaoh.

Tet-tut gave a long whimper eloquent as the stirring of flesh in a wound. *Tyiu, tyiuu,* was something like the sound he made.

"Do you hear?" asked Ptah-nem-hotep. "He is saying 'yes.'"

"I would complain of a lack of exactitude," said Menenhetet.

"Tu, tu," said Ptah-nem-hotep to Tet-tut, "say 'tooooo,' not 'tyoo.' Toooo!"

Tet-tut rolled on his back.

"You're a scamp," said Ptah-nem-hotep. "Go to the boy."

The dog looked about.

"To the boy. To Meni-Ka."

Now, he came to me. We looked into each other's eyes, and I began to weep. I had not been in the least prepared for this—I thought I would laugh—but sorrow seemed to come right out of Tet-tut's heart and into mine as directly as someone might pour water from a

jar, no, that is not so, it was more like the kiss Eyaseyab would give my
mouth when her day had been unhappy. On such an embrace I would
feel myself living in all the sad stories of the servant quarter. A mel-
ancholy now came to me from the dog just so complete as the woe I
felt when Eyaseyab told me about her relatives who worked in a
quarry and had to load great slabs of granite on sledges and pull them
up ramps with ropes. Sometimes, while working, they were whipped
until they dropped because the overseer had had too much to drink
the night before and was angry in the sun. Therefore, on the night
Eyaseyab told me about her relatives, I lived in the sorrow of her
voice. She had a heavy voice full of burden, yet it was not poor, for it
spoke of the enjoyment in her muscles when she lay down to rest. She
grieved for the men and women of her family she had known in her
childhood and told me they visited her at night in the depth of her
heart, not as in a dream where she might be afraid of them, but more
as if she were able to think of them when evening came, even if she
had not seen them in years, and she believed they must be sending her
the messages of their twisted bones because pains that felt like tortured strings came into her limbs then and told her of their lives just
as a bow can send an arrow flying.

I do not know what I remembered of her stories, nor how much
came to me from the dog, but it was more sadness than I could understand. The sorrow in Tet-tut's eyes was like the look I had seen in the
expression of many an intelligent slave. Worse. It was as if the dog's
eyes spoke of something he wanted to accomplish but never would.

So I wept. I could hardly believe the loudness of my clamor. I
squalled. The dog had managed to tell me of a terrible fright in a far-
off place and I was more afraid than I had ever been, as if I might not
live like a slave but still knew the fear that sooner or later I, too, would
know a life I did not want, and be powerless to go where I wished,
and this feeling was great enough to set me shaking with a force that
shattered the steadiness of the light. Then it was as if I lived in the
sun, and in the dark, but quickly, in the tremors, as if I were blinking.
Yet my eyes stayed wide open. I saw two existences at once: myself at

six debauched into tears, and myself in the dark, weeping in shame as I gorged on Menenhetet's cock, the tears so powerful my nostrils poured two rivers all over the old man's phenomenon of a grand member, yes, at six had a sight of myself debased in the Land of the Dead when I was twenty-one, and then Hathfertiti caught me up and shook me and suffocated me in an embrace, and removed me from the sight of the Pharaoh.

Four

By the way I was carried, I could feel her fury. My stomach was on her shoulder, and my head below her breast. The ground rose toward me and dropped away on every step as if I were swinging upside-down. But I was so scalded with fright that I might as well have been a small beast just dropped into boiling water, my life screaming out of me even as my flesh was being cooked. When we came to a stop and she set me down, I thought for a moment I had died—we were standing in a room so beautiful I did not know at first if we were in a house, a garden, or a pond.

Trees surrounded me. They were painted on every wall. I stood upon a watery marsh-grass floor, a golden marsh grass, and painted fish were swimming between the painted blades of grass. Above, stars were shining out of a painted evening sky, and in the red light of the western wall, the sun was setting, even as it had set last night to the west of my great-grandfather's roof, only now the view was of the Pyramids, and they were red as the meat of the pomegranate in this light, sitting on the painted plain of Jizeh between two of the four golden trees that held up the corners of this room. Doves and butterflies hovered in the steaming air, lapwings and green siskins flew in and out of the horns of oxen in the swamp reeds on the wall, water-lilies bloomed beneath my feet, and blue lotus almost concealed the rat who was stealing eggs from a crocodile's nest. In the midst of my weeping I began to laugh at the expression on the crocodile's face.

Now my mother put an arm around my waist and asked me to look at her, but I was staring at the ivory leg of the couch on which she sat. It was like the limb and hoof of an ox, or would have been if the hoof did not rest upon the polished floor instead of sinking into it, although as I continued to stare, the glaze was so high on the painted water that I could see my own reflection and my mother's which gave, therefore, the look of light on water after all.

We stood among all the birds and animals who lived in the paint and I could even see flies and scorpions placed by the artist in the roots of the grass through which the fish were swimming. I smiled finally at my mother.

"I'm ready to go back," I said.

She looked at me, and asked, "Do you like this room?"

I nodded.

"It is my favorite room," she said. "I used to play here when I was a child."

"I think I would like to play here," I said.

"In this room I learned that I was supposed to marry the Pharaoh."

I could see my mother on a throne beside Ptah-nem-hotep and they were both wearing blue wigs. A boy with a face different from mine played between them.

"If you had married Him," I said, "I wouldn't be here."

My mother's deep black eyes stared for a long while into my eyes. "You would still be my son," she said. Now she put me on her thigh and I felt myself sink very slowly into the flesh of her lap, a tender settling that did not seem to stop even when her flesh gave way no more; the reverberation of this delicious sensation went out like the last remembrance of evening and now I lived with bliss to equal the desolation I had known while staring into the face of the dog. How I loved the red light of the Pyramids as they reflected on the marsh-green polish of the floor.

"Yes, I was supposed to have married the Pharaoh. Would you have liked Him for a father? Is that why you began to cry?"

I lied. "I do not know why the dog made me sad," I told her.

"I think it is because you could have been a Prince."

"I do not think so."

"I was supposed to be the first wife of the Pharaoh."

"But you married my father instead."

"Yes."

"Why did you do that?"

Hathfertiti, as if aware of my power to visit—I never knew when—into the thoughts of others, now seemed to have no thoughts at all.

"Yes, you married my father, and I am his son, and now I'm happy you took me to this room." I did not know really what I was saying, except I knew I had somehow been sly enough to say what would encourage her to tell me more.

"You are not your father's son," she said, and her eyes looked for an instant into her own terror, so she added, "that is, you are, but you are not," and I knew she had thought of Menenhetet. "It does not matter," she went on, "whose son you are, since I called for you. I prayed for you to come forth, and in truth I will never again be so splendid as I was in the hour when all that was inside me called for you." She held my face in her palms, and her hands were so alive that I felt as though I lay in bed between two lovely bodies. "You came forth into my belief that I would give birth to a Pharaoh, and that is a belief I have continued to have even after I married your father."

"Do you still have such a belief?"

"I don't know. You have never been like other children. When I am alone with you, I do not feel a large difference in age between us. And when we are not together, I often think of what you say. Sometimes I believe thoughts come to you from other people's thoughts. Indeed, you see into the mind of others. You are most noble in such powers. Yet I do not think you will ever be a Pharaoh. In my dreams, I do not see the Double-Crown on you."

"What do you see for me?"

I had never been more sensitive to each wind that stirred in her mind, and so I saw again the black speck of the body louse that had frightened her, and I knew her fear. A worm might just as well have crawled over my own throat.

That, however, was only one of the two houses of my mother. The blood of a warrior like my great-grandfather must have inhabited the other, because when she looked at me again her eyes were as flat as an officer measuring the value of a captive. "Why did you begin to cry?" she asked. "Did the dog's eyes speak of a poor future?"

"They spoke to me of shame," I said, and thought of my mother and Menenhetet in their embrace on the roof garden. I must have sent my thoughts to her for the blood came to my mother's cheeks and she was angry.

"Do not speak of shame," she said, "after you have embarrassed me with the Pharaoh." I felt a flare of the fury with which she had picked me up and taken me from the room. "I do not think you will become a Pharaoh, for the same reason that the dog made you cry. You have the courage of a dog."

We spoke often to each other in this manner—one cruelty to pay for another. I enjoyed such contests. I was better at them than Hathfertiti.

"Oh," I said, "I did not cry for lack of courage but for simple misery that my father commands no respect. If, as you say, he is my father."

She slapped my face. Furious tears rolled down my cheeks. They must have cut into her sight like a hard stone scratching a softer one, for the flat look in her eyes, dull as black rock when she was angry, now cracked, and I saw the same sorrow in her that I had known when looking into the eyes of the dog. Something of the unspoken misery of my mother's life was in her expression. "Why," I asked, "did you not become the first wife of the Pharaoh?"

Again she did not answer me. Instead, she said, "I married your father because he was my half brother," and that was a useless reply considering how a good number of royal marriages (if not to speak of half the marriages of the poor) were between brother and sister, or half brother with half sister. It was not an answer at all. But I was still able to see in my mother's mind how my father looked when he was young, and to my surprise he was strong in face and even a little crude—not crude, yet young and smug and cruel in a way that many women might like. Today, he was different. His face was pinched. The air that came into his nostrils was finer but meaner than when he was young—only seven or eight years ago!—and I wondered if such a change was connected to the whispered hints with which I had lived for years while present at many an angry silence between my mother, my father, and my great-grandfather. Some discomfort often passed between them as if all were suffering the same indigestible meal. Afterward, coaxing my mother to tell me more, bullying her thoughts and pursuing them, I was finally informed of the family shame: The daughter of Menenhetet, my mother's own mother, Ast-en-Ra, had been married to a legitimate younger brother of Ramses III, but after this Prince's death and my mother's birth (in the same month) Ast-en-Ra next married a very wealthy man who came from a peasant family in the worst quarter of Memphi. As a boy, he had worked as a cleaner of latrines. That was the shame. He soon rose so high as to become a brothel-keeper (for by his reputation in bed he was near to the God Geb!) and on these profits succeeded in making a fortune. My grandmother, Ast-en-Ra, had married him, I was told, to avenge herself on Menenhetet, who treated her as his mistress from the time she was twelve, but ignored her once she married the Prince. In retaliation—so my mother insisted—Ast-en-Ra chose the man whose success would offend my great-grandfather most. Menenhetet only spoke of this second husband as Fekh-futi. It was our commonest expression for Shit-Collector, and my mother giggled as she told me, "Oh, Menenhetet was so jealous. He hated to hear that his daughter had married the most fabulous lover in Memphi. That's why he detested your father from the day he was born."

"Did you?"

"No, I liked him. He was my little brother and I adored him." A memory leaped from her head most naturally into mine and so I knew that she had seduced my father when he was six and she was eight.

But, as if aware again of this power in me to visit the thoughts of others, my mother now closed her mind—I could almost see it close—and for all I knew had no further thoughts at all, certainly none I could pursue.

Yet this clear picture I had of the naked child who would become my mother holding the naked body of the child who was not yet my father pressed against the memory of my mother and Menenhetet last night, and I knew for the first time why we speak of two houses of the mind. But such a thought was too large for my head, and I soon gave it up and felt a sweet relaxation, a nicety of pleasure in my limbs, as though something valuable had eluded me but would yet come back. It was then I knew that I wanted to rest among these painted walls where the breath of evening was forever the color of rose in the expectant air.

"Shall we go back now?" asked my mother.

"You go," I told her. "I would like to sleep in this room where you played when you were young." Events that never happened in my sight stirred about me, as if memories like birds from far away could light in your own nest. I thought of the wonder of Eyaseyab's lips on Sweet Finger, and clouds of honeyed feeling rose from me again.

"All right," my mother said, "I will leave you here. But you must not stray. I will be with the Pharaoh and your great-grandfather in the place where you saw too much in the eye of the dog." She shivered at the recollection. "So soon as you are tired of being alone, I want you to sit with us and give attention to what He says in His audiences. Many problems of government are considered there." She sighed. "He listens to the most tedious difficulties and sometimes solves them, although He is not, dear man, a practical heart." I noticed she spoke as if she were married to Him on this day at least, and remembered her saying to my great-grandfather, "What if only one of us comes back with what we want?" Now she smiled at me as she went out, a dazzling smile to leave me full of the most generous warmth, and I was alone then, and comfortable, and lay on that couch whose ivory legs were like the limb and hoof of an ox, while the rose-colored lights of evening never moved through all of the afternoon.

After a while I was not asleep but afloat in the place where one is so close to sleep that the two houses of the mind become like two boats that slip away from one another across the waters. I felt then how much of my existence might not be my own but still I felt no woe, no sense certainly that I was in any way not a true child of six, yes, I felt this with such confidence that I was happy and fell asleep. Or, let me say, I ceased to know where I wandered. My ships drifted away from one another and I lay there in the long false evening of that painted room.

Five

I awoke in a stillness so profound that I could picture the birds on the marble steps of the landing before Two-Gates, and could even feel one colored feather twitching delicately over another across all the distance of the three great courtyards that separated me from the river. I began then to have the most unusual experience although it was without peril and came as no surprise to me. It was just that—my mother having told me not to stray—I was nonetheless able to go off like two people in separate directions. My mind most certainly was now inclined on the one hand to leave the Palace altogether and follow our boatman, Bone-Smasher, as he went drinking through the marketplace of Memphi, yet by the other hand, I also sat in attendance on the Pharaoh and listened to how He disposed of the problems of government. Meanwhile, my body never moved. I obeyed my mother and did not stir from the couch. It was just that in a bewilderment of senses sweet as the pleasure older people must take in wine, so did I go off into the mind of the boatman we called Set-Qesu, and he was living in all the fury of his name, its sound on the ear just like its meaning. We called him Bone-Smasher but that was polite; his true name was Ass-Bone, a bugger of such

dimensions, said the other boatmen, that Set-Qesu could pulverize
the bone in your back.

I do not know why I followed, but I lived nearer to him than if I
sat by his side, and felt as if I knew his thoughts, not intimately—I did
not hear words go through his head, and maybe few words did—but
I could feel the anger in his chest, raw as the lungs of a lion, and his
sour stomach was souring mine. I felt as if I had been rolled up in a
rug full of old spit and old retchings while red ants explored my skin,
but that could have been the shock I suffered at daring to venture so
close. What I felt next was fatigue, a bitter ache in every nerve I knew,
more painful and certainly heavier than any tiredness I had known
before, and I heard Bone-Smasher growl to the people drinking near
him, "Had us up for the night fixing his boat, then pulling on the oars
today."

"No, he didn't," said a man waving a jug of perfumed beer, the
smell at once sour, bitter, and much too sweet from the perfume.
"You drifted down the river today."

"You don't drift, man, not in *his* boat. Every curl in the current is a
peril."

"Just drifting," said the man with the perfumed beer.

"Keep your rotten eye out of my face," Bone-Smasher told him.
The man talking, big as Bone-Smasher, had only one eye and it was
full of pus and inflamed. But looking around the bar, even in the dim
light of this dirty beer-house where there were no windows and the
only opening was the door, I could count the faces and most were
blind in an eye, maybe it was fifteen out of twenty. I did not know if
I had ever seen so many before. Among our servants, and certainly
among the servants of the Pharaoh, a half-blind man or woman was
kept only if they were old and trusted—who wanted to look upon a
wrinkled eye-socket every day? Whereas, here, I felt as if all our desert sand and all the dung of our animals, not to speak of the terrible
glare of the sunlight, had been rubbing on the lids of our people from
the hour they were born. I looked with discomfort at a drunk who
had fallen on his face and was lying in a corner of this bar, his forehead
ground into all the old filth of bread crust, onion rottings, spilled

beer, spilled wine, sputum, puke, and even a little mud where a puddle of beer had softened the dirt floor—deep in the litter of that corner, the drunk snored.

"Drifting," said the man with the pus-filled eye, "is drifting."

"Open your mouth again," Bone-Smasher told him, "and I'll stick my thumb in your other eye." I was close enough to live in the pleasure of his thoughts, and his fatigue was gone. He was breathing in all the enjoyment of a rage that filled his head with a red light. The red rim of the eye before him turned pale, then red as blood, and the other man's skin went from dark to the pale-white of a fish's belly, then as dark again as the purple of Bone-Smasher's rage (for it was not the colors of the man's skin which were changing but the sights in Bone-Smasher's head). He was looking at the other drunk's lips—so soon as they said one more word, Bone-Smasher would be on him. He could feel how his thumb would gouge the eye. It would pop in its socket like the pulp of a peach squeezed through its skin.

The girl who brought the drinks was standing before him, however. "Oh, let it be a good day, Set-Qesu," she said. "Drink until you are happy."

"Bring me eighteen cups of wine," he said, and smiled, and I could feel his drunkenness—I knew the dizziness passing over my head was the power of drunkenness for I had tasted wine, and it made me drunk, though not like this; the walls of the barroom were ready to fall on him should he stand up. To his surprise more than mine, he looked at the barmaid, and said, "Your dress is a beautiful white. How do you keep it so clean?"

"By staying out of reach of people with dirty hands," she cried out and skipped away.

"Come back," he bawled. "I want the wine from Mareotis."

"I'll be back."

"And a loaf of your filthy bread."

I had a glimpse then of the simple white dress being pulled from her body, saw his big hands in the cheeks of her buttocks and pulling them apart, saw her body wide open like a carcass in a butcher shop, except she was neither wounded nor bleeding, only twisting her limbs with his, and pleasure on her face. Then he was sitting on her head with his breechclout off, a club of a phallus between his legs, and with it he beat on her breasts. I knew it was only something to see within his head, for the girl had gone to the long table where the jars of wine were kept, and was now bringing one back, a flat loaf of bread under her arm. "This is the wine from Buto," she said.

"The wine from Buto stinks," he said.

He did not sit down. Still swaying, so that I could have been perched like a mouse on the back of his neck—yes I saw these events with all the wonder of a mouse—I also saw the walls swaying. Taking the wine she brought, he pulled a stopper of hard wax out of the jug, poured wine into his cup, swallowed it, poured another. The drink went down with the taste of blood.

"It smells in here," he said.

"Pay me, Set," she murmured, "and the air outside will feel good."

"It's hot outside and stinks in here." He was furious, but had forgotten why. From his breechclout, from a fold in the hairy skin of his testicles, his fingers running under the cloth and over his short hairs just long enough for the girl's mouth to quiver (he did not know, nor did I, whether her lips trembled or he only thought they moved at the feel of his finger on himself) he brought out from that fold of his flesh one of his copper coins, in weight a quarter of an utnu, heavier than both of my testicles together, and waved it under her nose with a gesture he might have borrowed from his Lord, Menenhetet, so resourceful was its mixture of contempt at the reek of this bar, and pride in the luxury of the manner by which he had plucked it forth. "I'll marry you someday," said Bone-Smasher and began to roll toward the door, the brown earth of the floor equal to the dark-brown of the Nile in late afternoon. Feeling the floor flow toward him like a slow-moving stream, he had a great need to pass water himself, and the size of that desire left me and Sweet Finger obliged to share the pressure on his scrotum and it hurt me more than a door closing on my foot. I wondered that he did not roar. He turned around, however, wheeling as ponderously as a barge coming about in the river, and went up to the drunk with one red eye.

"You don't drift down the great river," he said, and belching up a bile of spiced beer, palm brandy, and the last belts of the wine of Buto, added, "There are currents that turn in a circle and holes to suck you in." He was about to add that there were rocks you could not see when the water was high so you had to remember where they were or they'd stove you in, but the drunk with his lonely eye merely beamed and gave a foolish look, and waved his forefinger. "You drift," he said as if the profundity of every wise thought was here.

Bone-Smasher pulled his cloth to the side and disgorged urine all over the man. Laughter went through the bar until Bone-Smasher was done. The drunk merely collected humiliation, then simpered, sat down and began to sleep. Bone-Smasher turned. He was happy for a moment. The loaf of bread under his arm, he started for the door. No one said a word until he was almost clear, but the smell of his urine followed him strong as the hot water of a horse on straw. A babble began in the depth of the bar as he went out and built in its bravery as it passed by all the poor tradespeople and apprentices and workmen until they were throwing half-eaten onions at him and crusts of bread (but from a distance) and he staggered into the street with the majestic balance of his heavily stupefied head going around the thought of re-turning to knock a head or two together. The last words he heard through the door were the clear threat of someone saying, "Your Lord Menenhetet will hear of this." Then he was alone on the street (and only myself to follow his breathing) and his lungs were gasping in as much strain as if he had been pulling on the oars for hours, breathing in fear and some ecstasy of the fear itself. Menenhetet had had him whipped near to death on one occasion and the sensations were the most unforgettable of his life, and, aware once more of him-self on the street, children hooting at him, men and women giving him a good space, only one young fellow big as himself, standing in the middle of the dark and narrow street with the walls four stories high, he and the other approaching slowly—they would have to fight if they touched—that confidence turning to caution as they came near each other's rage. They passed, both men shamed by the failure to touch. Set, feeling tired, sat down in a small plaza by a shaduf where women were gathering water with their pails, and reached into his loaf of bread, broke out three fingers' worth, began to chew.

My mother always told me I had a mouth of little pearls, and it is certain I never tasted bread like this. It felt as rough on the tongue as bran, and before he had taken three bites, his jaws ground down on a whole grain the size of a pea and it chipped his tooth, or what was left of the stump of that tooth, cracking it hard enough to drive a spear through his drunkenness. He cried out from the sudden pains in his mouth, for they went reverberating back through all the years his teeth had been broken down by grit and pebbles and sand and whole grain and flakes of stone from the grinding wheel. He saw his mother working into flour a fistful of wheat she had scattered on a hollowed-out slab outside the door of the house where he grew up, and maybe it was the smell of the bread he held to his nose now, the same sour urine in the pores of the bread, but he was back in the work of his childhood getting all the dung, manure, paste and shit of all the donkeys, chickens, goats, cows, dogs and sheep, all of that old pungence lived in his nose, balls and turds and flops for his mother to shape into bricks and dry in the sun. That was the stuff with which they baked the bread when they could not find wood, and there was never enough wood. By the smell of the stuff he now ate, his nose must be traveling through the anus of a goat, and he whimpered again from the throbbing in his newly cracked stump of a tooth, the whimpering as agreeable to him as the ebbing of a wound on its way to heal, and he stood up smiling or glaring (as the mood took him) at whichever woman happened to be passing through this little square, her eggs and live chickens for sale, one girl with a goose flapping under her arm, another woman with a ream of linen she had woven, the color so white it blazed the sun back into his eyes, and he had a long stumbling recovery as he bounced on his feet from step to step down a road that led to the great square of the market, the sun overhead as cruel as a body sleeping next to him with baleful breath. He traveled with his eyes closed, and the sun's rays searing the red irritated rim of his eyes. There were some who said all the Gods could live in one God, and He was the Sun. If this was true, then He was angry now.

The Gods were in the shit, Bone-Smasher said to himself, smelling the old dung in the bread, and he chose to glare at one lovely lady passing by in a transparent dress. She had long dyed-blue hair oiled, then wound at the bottom around little balls of wax. She was wearing bracelets and beads, and had pinned a flower just above her ear. He stared as she walked around him, stared at what he could see of the shadow of her pubic hair, stared at the faint and intricate tattoo on her chin, hoping he would see the insignia of a whore and could go along to her brothel, but she was gone while he debated, and I felt a stirring in his groin different from the urge to urinate, this felt more like the earth beneath a large rock when the rock is being lifted.

"Strength and booze," he called after her, "strength and booze," and when she did not reply, and what he could see of her buttocks through the transparent dress was also about to disappear, he began to laugh (which hurt his tooth) and shouted, "A word to the wise is a stick on a dumb ass," a saying that came from Menenhetet who would use it when he whipped the boatmen. Bone-Smasher had taken it up to whip other boatmen, his mind now in the glue of these drunken thoughts because of the peculiarity that stick and word had exactly the same sound. He had never noticed that before. *Medu* was the word for word and *medu* was the word for stick. In the middle of burping, he suddenly felt splendid. Putting your stick up a woman was the same as giving her the word, yes, language was like a box he had once seen with another box inside it. He could feel his cock right now, and it had an eye for dark places. "The Gods are in the shit," he shouted, and fell on his face.

Naked boys were going by and naked little girls. All the children of the quarter were going by, some in no more than a bracelet to show they might be naked but not altogether poor, and they went by in a circle around Bone-Smasher's revolving brain. He lay on the street, and a naked boy with a thick tress of hair covering his ear now stopped, looked carefully at Bone-Smasher and, giggling a little, tried to urinate on his foot. But it was only a few drops. Bone-Smasher stirred, the boy's drops pinched off, and the boatman was dreaming again.

Donkeys passed by with loads of straw—he looked at them from the ground, one eye open. Large-horned oxen, driven back from the market, crowded through the plaza, and walked around him. Fishermen passed with baskets of fish, and a baker with loaves. The pastry, meat, fruit, shoes, corn, sandals, onions, and wheat, the beads and perfume and oil, the honey and the sleeping mats, bronze razors, pick-axes, baskets of corn and a brace of ducks, a vendor with leather bottles for wine passed him on their way to the market or back from it. The smell of dates and spices, honey and almonds and pistachio came out of a store to his back, and now another store opened on this little plaza, and a cook and two waiters began the evening meal. Around the turn in the street from the plaza where the great square opened were a number of other food-shops I had visited with Eyaseyab and I remembered the smell of roasting goose and the stews they would make from the gravy in the sauce pans. Once, with her, I had spent part of a morning watching them chop the vegetables—she liked the cook!—now I was next to dreaming with Bone-Smasher of the joy of buying cooked food in one of these places and taking it home. That was prosperity, thought Bone-Smasher in the repose of his sleep on the street, and he dreamed of expensive shoemakers who offered sandals with turned-up points, and of the goldsmith who made earrings and bracelets from African ingots. There was one necklace of electrum with lapis-lazuli from Elam. Bone-Smasher had heard that Elam was at the end of the world, and he wanted the necklace: The boat of his mind sailed out for Elam across the deserts to the East, and all the while blacksmiths and stonemasons were closing their shops and carpenters were walking home through the little plaza, and the shoemaker, the potter, the barber, the dyer stinking of carrion scraped from the hides. Slaves and merchants and foreign traders went by, and fine ladies carried in fine chairs. Two boys began to fight over a fall of manure steaming still from one of the horses in a chariot team that swerved at the last to avoid Bone-Smasher's head. The boys put down their collection baskets and were wrestling on the stones of the street until one could hold the other long enough with one hand to scoop up the horse-balls with the other, and Bone-

Smasher stirred, opened his eyes, saw the fights of his own childhood, and got up to stagger into the fires of the market at evening, scowling at all the blacks and Hebrews he saw milling in the great plaza, and as he moved on, so did I move away and withdraw my thoughts from Bone-Smasher in much the way that later, when old enough to make love to a woman, I would after a time take my leave of her with the satisfaction that I had gone into her body so well I had not known by the end where her belly ended and mine began, a pleasure to lose oneself that well. I also remember that when I would *withdraw*, yes, slowly take back my phallus to myself, be in myself again and no other, so just in such a fashion now did I withdraw my thoughts from all of Bone-Smasher's feelings and return to that rose-colored room of the Pharaoh as happy as if I had made love. It was then I became aware that the other house of my brain must have been living with the Pharaoh through the audiences He was now giving, for I awoke with a sentiment of much intimacy toward Him, the Pharaoh's feelings so sinuous and close to all I had been taught, that I felt much nearer to Him than to the boatman. In truth, the understanding that the Pharaoh was almost my father gave even more pleasure to joining Him—like the conclusion of a jump that proves to be safe.

Yet all the greater was the disappointment. For now I discovered that the interior of His person was much less agreeable to me than the first wonder I knew at kissing His toe. He was feeling no more at this instant than a cramp in His belly from a turn of His digestion, just the moderate pain of a man who is used to ignoring for all of a morning or afternoon the complaints of his body. That was His first sentiment, and, on the instant, it taught me what it was like to be a grown man with duties. There was so much sourness of spirit—as if His interior tasted like a lemon! Now I knew the bleak face of His unspoken feelings, and it was as grim as the weather when the sky turned dark with dust. In such storms, the air was cold, and that wind which we say is as mean as evil (which, for fact, is its name, the Khamsin—Evil!) blew steadily across the desert and howled down the narrow streets of Memphi leaving billows of sand in front of every door. Ptah-nem-hotep's thoughts were like the misery of sand stinging the skin, and I recognized to my own misery (after the sweet and natural fall of my mind into His) that His duty was like the weight of a dead man on one's back. Nothing warm was left in His heart, unless it was a desire for the moment when He could find repose in the calm of evening. Like an echo that is lost but for the remnant that lingers in one's reverie, so did I feel the last sensuous beauty of His heart seem to expire in all the solemnities of listening to the one man whom I had heard my parents speak of as often as Himself, the High Priest Khem-Usha of the High Temple of Amon at Thebes (who was also acting in these troubled days as our Vizier). Yet with all such power, this Khem-Usha still chose to speak up to the balcony from the floor of the Councillors below.

The Pharaoh had to force Himself to listen, and did. He felt that an audience with Him must be injured if He did not offer the finest attention. So, Ptah-nem-hotep listened to each word spoken by Khem-Usha. That was the cause of His pain. I, who now dwelt like a bird in a corner of His Double-Crown, felt the weight of the High Priest on the Pharaoh's fine ear.

Khem-Usha had a voice to command courtesy, as slow and deep as the echo of temple chambers, indeed only a voice as deep and hollow as his own could intone the gravest prayers. There was a power in the deliberation of Khem-Usha's voice that could overcome any mood contradictory to his own. Moreover, one's gaze could never slip away for long from the shining prominence of his shaven skull, and so could not avoid the solemnity of his large black eyes beneath their black brows.

Ptah-nem-hotep sat with His fingertips together, His arms on the red velvet of that railing from which He looked down on the Lords and Priests and Councillors and Royal Overseers who had come to this audience. Gathered in orderly files below were some ten or twelve men, standing, kneeling, or with their faces to the dirt as mine had been earlier. On the balcony Hathfertiti, Menenhetet, and Nef-khepaukhem sat in attendance around the Pharaoh, and they were also listening to Khem-Usha. He spoke as if each full sound he uttered was equal to the presence of a new statue in one's courtyard.

"O rising Sun, Who lightens the world with Your beauty," said Khem-Usha to Ptah-nem-hotep, "You drive away the darkness of Egypt.

"Your rays penetrate into all lands.

"There is no place deprived of Your beauty.

"Your words rule the destinies of all lands.

"You hear all that is said.

"Your eye is more brilliant than any star of heaven."

"In the name," thought Ptah-nem-hotep, listening to the sounds of movement in His stomach and bowel, "in the name of that river of food and drink which moves in Me, why must I listen to a psalm first offered to the Pharaoh Merneptah more than eighty years ago?" but He inclined His head to Khem-Usha as though the words were for Himself alone.

Now the Councillors who had been prostrating their faces in the dirt, rose to a kneeling position, and those who were standing, knelt. Only Khem-Usha was erect. He spoke, and the others answered in unison.

"Yours is the resemblance to Ra," they cried aloud.

"Every word that issues from Your mouth is like the words of Horus of the sunrise, and Horus of the sunset.

"Your lips measure words more truly than the finest balance of Maat.

"Who can be perfect like You?"

I could feel satisfaction arise in Ptah-nem-hotep sweet as honey itself, but then as if the taste were too agreeable, He thought: "I respond to words composed for another King. I am no stronger than Tet-tut who rolls on his back when praise begins." He gave a small cold smile to His audience. His head felt heavy from the Double-Crown.

"No monument is built," chanted the Councillors, "without Your knowledge. You are the supreme commander.

"If You say to the Celestial Waters, 'Come to the mountain,' the Waters will flow at Your word.

"For You are Ra.

"You are the great beetle Khepera.

"Your tongue is the sanctuary of truth.

"A God sits upon Your lips.

"You are eternal."

Khem-Usha knelt, then prostrated his forehead to the ground. The other Councillors touched their foreheads to the ground. My parents and Menenhetet, because they were sitting in royal armchairs, had only to bow their heads.

I could feel a power arise in the body of Ptah-nem-hotep during the recitation of these last words that He drew in from the devotion of those who were below. But I could also taste the bitterness of His tongue.

"Your last praises," He said to Khem-Usha, "are rich and wise and may even be appropriate, since they appear on the stone put up by My ancestor, the Strong-bull-Who-loves-the-truth, Great Ramses the Second. He had such words inscribed on a pillar along the road that leads to the mines of Etbaya."

Khem-Usha replied: "Your eyes read all the inscriptions, Great-loving-partner-of-the-truth."

"Last year at this time, you addressed Me in these same texts written for Merneptah and Ramses Two. I praised you then for your selection."

Khem-Usha replied: "Your ancestors are Great Gods, even as You will sit, Great Two-House, in such a place, equal in elevation to the praises given Your great ancestors."

Ptah-nem-hotep applied the tip of His forefinger to the end of His long and delicate nose, and I could feel His breath stirring. "To give Me words written for great ancestors only confers honor and strength," He said, "if the gift can fit the box." From the balcony, He stared down upon Khem-Usha, but the dark eyes of the High Priest did not weaken beneath his black brows; indeed, they stared back.

"For many years," said Khem-Usha, "I have dwelt in the language of prayer, but I do not know if my heart understands the balance of Your words, O Great Two-House."

"We seem to invoke the name of Maat," Ptah-nem-hotep replied.

"Is it agreeable to Her balance that praises for a brave man are laid upon the head of a prudent man? My ancestor Ramses the Second may not be happy to find the magnificence of His feats compared to the prudence of My judgments. Khem-Usha—this is the Day of the Pig."

"That is my knowledge, Great Lord."

"If we do not offer the truth to each other on the Day of the Pig, we will not come near to justice on other days."

A speech was now uttered in the Pharaoh's heart. Words as alert as soldiers on parade passed through His chest but none was said aloud. Only I could hear His thoughts. "Other Kings led their troops at the age of ten, but when I was that age, Khem-Usha, you led Me in a naked dance and we fell at the end all full of sweat in each other's arms and wrestled until I do not remember how much of the domain of your body was in My nose. Ramses Two tamed a lion and won the Battle of Kadesh, and Egypt was renowned from Syria to Punt—I have yet to lead an army into battle. I hear only from Generals who lose battles for Me. When Ramses Two was fifty, there was not a beauty in Memphi or Thebes who had not felt His heat on her mouth; I have a harem I do not visit, yet laughter issues from it. Half of My charioteers do not dare to meet My eye. This is the Day of the Pig when no custom is so valuable as to speak the truth. So I would beg of you, Khem-Usha, do not mock Me with the feats of the Great Ramses, dead for these ninety years, but let us speak of My true qualities which are prudence, wit, and the power to receive in calm the worst of bad news. Let us ask if such is worthy of a Pharaoh."

The passions of His heart, however, were to be whipped and whipped again until perfect obedience was kept. Aloud, He said to Khem-Usha: "Let Me accept your good wishes as they are expressed in the poets' great praise for My ancestors, Ramses the Second and Merneptah. Let your selection be well taken. I have enjoyed it. I would also have you know that here to celebrate with me on the Day of the Pig is the Great Lord Menenhetet, once General of the Armies of Amon, Ra, Ptah and Set, and," said Ptah-nem-hotep with a tender smile for Khem-Usha, "he is the last remaining survivor of the Battle of Kadesh and thereby, one must suppose, is a very wise man with much knowledge of Egypt."

"So far as I know," said Menenhetet with an easy smile and the powerful look of a virile man of sixty, "I am the only eye that still sees that battle."

Now the Councillors could be seen to whisper again. The Battle of Kadesh, the greatest battle of them all, had indeed been fought one hundred and fifty years ago in the early years of the reign of Ramses II, and that Pharaoh had kept His Double-Crown for sixty-five years before Merneptah followed and Amenmeses and Siptah and Seti II and a Syrian usurper for a few years—I could feel the amusement of Ptah-nem-hotep's mind as He observed the reckonings of His Councillors—yes, there had been Set-nakht, and Ramses III, Ramses IV, Ramses V, Ramses VI, Ramses VII, Ramses VIII and Ptah-nem-hotep Himself, our own Ramses IX, all of thirteen Pharaohs in the one hundred and fifty years that had passed since the Battle of Kadesh.

The Councillors lifted their foreheads and saluted Menenhetet. "Good," said Ptah-nem-hotep to Himself, "now they are wondering if I will make him My Vizier instead of Khem-Usha."

He had no more than finished this thought when I was brought back to myself on the couch in the rose-colored room. Hathfertiti was caressing me on the cheek. "Come," she said, "it is time for you to return to the patio." She smiled. "I would like you to see the awe with which they regard your great-grandfather."

"I did not know," I said to her out of all the surrender of this sleep that had been like a life, no, two lives—was it three if I counted myself?—"I did not know that Menenhetet was born one hundred and eighty years ago."

For certain, Hathfertiti gave me a look. Then she touched my forehead with reverence. "Come," she said, when she had control of her voice again, "I suppose it is time to tell you a little more of the truth. You see, it is possible that your great-grandfather has been born four times."

Six

When I did not know how to reply, she smiled tenderly. "Do not fear," she said, "your wisdom is equal to a boy of fifteen, and sometimes you understand matters that are beyond the grasp of a man, but then I think you have such powers because you were conceived at the time of a great event." She paused as though the sound of such words could injure the stillness of the air and added, "Let us say of what was almost a great event."

"Almost?" I asked.

"It did not quite take place."

As she said this, her fingertips passed around my forehead in a circle and I saw Menenhetet's face appear in the center of her thoughts, his features as twisted as a rag squeezed out of its last moisture—a frightening sight to have of my great-grandfather, but I knew what she meant. Menenhetet had come near to death on the day I was conceived.

She spoke, however, of other things. "I have known," she said, "that at times you enter the mind of those who are with you, but I did not know you could hear voices from another room."

"Not until this hour," I said.

"After I left you here?"

"Yes," I said. "I think it is because of the room. Because"—and I did not understand why I added this—"because of the loveliness of this room," but then I was learning what I meant by my words even as I spoke, indeed, I was recognizing that I could only learn what I knew as my voice passed into the air. For then I could feel the change I had made in what was before me, and thereby know the truth or error of what had just been said. So did I know at this moment that the loveliness of the room was like the bending of a fine bow and that was why my thoughts had flown so far.

"Yes, it may be time," said my mother, "to tell you of secrets I wanted to keep until you were older. But if you can hear others from so far away, what hope have I to hide my thoughts! I cannot."

"You can," I said. "Sometimes you choose to do that."

"At a price to myself," murmured my mother, and drew her fingertips to her eyes with a gesture so attractive that we both began to laugh for we both knew she had an image of wrinkles beginning in the corners of her eyes if she tried to squeeze back her thoughts from me. "Oh, you are a darling," she murmured, and kissed me carefully in order not to disturb the cosmetic on her lips. Her mouth had a flavor sweet as the heat of the air when bees are drowsy, and it may have been that I had risen too quickly from my curious sleep, but her lips laid a powerful languor over me. Then I felt a curl, some velvet and voluptuous turn beneath my navel, and I lived in my mother's memory of an afternoon and night when Menenhetet and then my father had made love to her, yes, both men in this room, one for all of the late afternoon (no matter how the walls were painted red for evening), and one for the muted red walls of this same room, seen later by the flame of a candle, and although Eyaseyab's full lips upon Sweet Finger had left many intimations of sensuous hours to come, still how could I commence to understand what went on in Hathfertiti's luxurious bed if I had not been inflamed by the sweet kiss of my mother's honeyed mouth? So I knew that the day in which I had been conceived might be one of the most remarkable of her life. Then, as if this languor she laid upon me left her less able to protect her own thoughts, so did I also acquire the knowledge that on the day of my conception, on that late afternoon, Menenhetet had made love to my mother, in a manner he had made love but three times before. At once, my mother tried to chase these pictures from her brain just so quickly as she thought them, but I had a true glimpse, as clean to the sight as the white of a stalk of grass when the root is pulled from the ground, yes, as intimate to my ear as the sibilance of that stalk surrendering its life in earth, the first light on the white root like a knife in the flank—so sudden is the pain of the grass—so did I come into the deepest secret of my family. For my mother's mind offered it up without a word, although her lips certainly trembled as these confessions poured from her mind. I learned—and all at once!—that my great-grandfather had the power to escape his death in a way no other may have ever done. For he had been able, during an embrace, to ride his heart right over the last ridge and breathe his last thought as he passed into the womb of the woman and thereby could begin a new life, a true continuation of himself; his body died, but not the memory of his life. Soon, he would show fabulous powers in childhood. So I understood why my mother could no longer keep such knowledge from me. I, too, showed such powers!

What a disturbance did this confession produce in me! I felt as if, on a bolt of terror, I had jumped across the lip of one life into another. What a tumult of confusion! When Hathfertiti, by way of these unsprung thoughts, began to reveal how Menenhetet had made love to her in this hour, the foam and disorder of her mind was like a great rush of waves in my mind, and my thoughts did not know how to stay afloat against the current of such uproar in her, no, what did I know of how to make love!

Of course, I was in a flood of two confusions—one from myself and the other from my mother—hers whether to tell me more; mine to grasp at what I had just been told. For if Menenhetet could die, yet become himself once more, so did I wonder if I was supposed to have been the fifth appearance—could it be said?—of Menenhetet the First. Or was I intended to become Menenhetet the Second, his true son, not his own continuation? Might I, either way, have been given his power to father oneself?

That opened an immensity in my heart: I was given a glimpse of ambition in myself more fierce than fires of flaming oil. So I understood the woe that made me weep when I looked into the eye of the dog. For Tet-tut must have seen me dead at twenty-one. Then I thought of my poor Ka in the alcove at the center of the Great Pyramid—that same Pyramid I could now see painted on the rose wall of this room!—who was that young man there on his knees, mouth open to the force of another's will? I looked at my mother in this confusion. Why had Menenhetet not entered his death at the moment he was ready?

I felt doors open in her mind. Again I saw the tortured face of Menenhetet in the center of a pool and was pulled through the mills of her thoughts in that moment when she felt death commencing in his heart. She was ready to catch his child with an exultation fierce as the roar of existence itself, all luminous with the vision of his death coming forth into the life she would bear for him, her great lover Menenhetet soon to become her child, but at that instant, he did not come forth, and lay instead on her body, half-dead for many minutes.

When, later, he withdrew, he said with a smile, "I do not know why I changed my mind." He even put a finger to her chin and murmured, "On another occasion." And departed from the body of his granddaughter, departed from that place where he had been ready to send his death, and I, comprehending this, could hardly know how much of me was similar to him—I knew only that I was kin to my great-grandfather in a hundred ways I could not name, my powers first, and remembered my mother saying, "Nef-khep-aukhem is your father and yet he is not." So I had a hint of the toils of her body on that long day when I was conceived. For she must have been so certain a child would come to her by Menenhetet that what she would contribute herself was swimming already in her blood. Yet it was my father who must have put the seed into her that evening. I had a view of a night full of fevers as my father and mother rode from the bed to the floor and back again, my father slamming upon her skin with such savagery and such wild gusto—so much did he hate her, and adore her—that she was ablaze with a lust coming right out of the smelting of all contempt. My father's lack of every quality a brave noble might possess made her desire him even more for his sly smells. At his best, he was something between a dog and a horse to her, there to enjoy and send back to his stall, as in fact she had enjoyed him from the time he was six and she was eight—used him for what he was, a younger brother. She could hardly endure his airs, his vanities, his weaknesses, his few brutal strengths. Yet the hair between her legs would stir when her brother was in the room. I was learning more about my father and my mother than she had ever wanted me to learn—I felt it now through Hathfertiti's efforts to close her mind from mine. But I was forcing her—as if this was the only seduction I could perform—to strip away each thought. So did I penetrate into one more secret she might have wanted me not to find, and I could tell by the spasm in my chest, yes, the thrill and nausea of this recognition, that what I was about to learn was, by the first hand, awful, and next that I was jealous. If for the first time, I was nonetheless jealous. For I realized that my father was powerfully attractive to my mother because of his father, Shit-Collector. Now, I understood, as if engraved in the stone of my heart, that my mother had grown up in the shade of her mother's desire for Fekh-futi—that uncontrollable desire!—and although I did not know how Fekh-futi looked, still my imagination insisted that he was one of the boys I had seen in my sleep this afternoon when I lived within Bone-Smasher's eyes—and I saw those boys in the alley fighting again for the balls of manure. So could I see Fekh-futi fighting other boys for every piece of dung he could find in the city until he was enthroned on a heap, and ordering about the whores in his brothels as they went by with their transparent dresses and long blue wigs—I did not know if these were my thoughts now, or my mother's, but I would certainly have been disgusted if not also near some old thrill as though I were two years old once more and still learning how not to soil myself (although mightily tempted).

Was it the pain of discovering my mother's appetite for Fekh-futi?

At this point, I realized that I had certainly lost her. Hathfertiti's mind was closed.

She took me by the arm then. "It is time to return to the Pharaoh," she said, and quick as that, as if I had just entered this rose-colored room for one glance, we departed and walked along that courtyard across which she had carried me an hour or two ago, screaming and upside-down.

Seven

What I had just learned was bound to affect me forever, yet the subject was so strange I might as well have awakened from a dream. Maybe that is why my confusion began to clear on our return to the Pharaoh's balcony. There, everything was much as I had left it. While Menenhetet was now sitting on the other side of Ptah-nem-hotep, so, too, had my picture of where I had expected him to be also shifted. There was nothing to startle my eye.

Below, on the patio, a Councillor was speaking of work in the quarries. I could see by the look on my father's face that these were not matters of grave importance. I had often heard my mother say that my father never had a thought of his own, and so his face could reflect everyone else's. I know I did not understand what she meant until the day she told him that his manners were superb because he was never bothered by the manners he had been born with—instead, he imitated the best manners he saw. That was a true description of my father. The angle at which one nobleman might cock his wrist quickly became—if my father thought it just—his own turn of wrist. So did he copy the delicate touch by which Ptah-nem-hotep brought a finger to the side of His nose when He was contemplating which fine remark to make, but then my father would even imitate the irony with which my great-grandfather might bow his head to indicate that he did not agree with what you just said.

I do not mean to say that my father acted foolishly. Today he had most certainly been ill-at-ease while attempting to serve the Pharaoh with my mother looking on, but on calmer occasions he would appear, to those who did not know him well, as a distinguished nobleman. The white of his linen was never soiled, and the charcoal with which he painted his eyes rarely smudged. His jewelry did not miss a stone. Since gems and beads were always falling out as their fastenings loosened, not even my mother could present so impeccable an appearance as my father.

In Court, his manner, which is to say, his fine collection of manners, served him well. Because I heard much talk of it in my family, I knew that it was necessary for the Pharaoh to have a man nearby who could make clear, by no more than the change of expression on his face, whether the matter directed to His attention had been proposed in suitable language. What a look of exasperation would come upon my father's face if the poor official speaking from the patio below had a hoarseness of throat, a stammer, or an inability to keep from repeating his facts. So it was not difficult to understand that my father was of good service to Ptah-nem-hotep. Certainly my father's expressions kept me most aware of the Pharaoh's immaculate sensitivity—how could that not be so when my father's face showed pain at every improper sound and thereby caused me to feel how delicate were the Pharaoh's ears. Any sudden interruption of mood made Him wince within as at the wanton collapse of the walls of a fine building. Now I knew why He had kept listening to Khem-Usha although He detested what was being said. Khem-Usha's solemn voice might be as oppressive to the mind of the Pharaoh as the slow insertion of clay in His nostrils, but Khem-Usha never altered his tones, so no matter what other pains he might inflict, his voice would not irritate the Pharaoh's ear.

The man speaking at this moment, however, was another matter. I could see by the encouragement in my father's eyes that Ptah-nem-hotep was not without sympathy for the fellow or his office. That the Pharaoh was also confident of His ability to offer good advice in this case could be told by the light but haughty touch of my father's finger to the side of his nose. His skill was to detect each change in the Pharaoh's attitude, and reflect that back to the Court. So he was as quick to each whim of Ptah-nem-hotep as I to the readiness of my mother to let me come into her thoughts—I could see by the look of strain across my father's brow that the official below, while personally inoffensive, even, in modest measure, estimable to Ptah-nem-hotep, had a voice, all the same, to bother His ears.

On the other hand, my father's face was full of patience which told me much about the Pharaoh. The man now speaking had generations of quarrymen in his voice, all with the same powerful back and legs. It was a throat to declare that the man who spoke was sober and knew what he knew. So his speech in the main was agreeable and tasted of bread and soup and the strength of family flesh. Of course, it also had the sound of stones pounding on other stones. His brain, as a result, was sluggish—thoughts did not come to him quickly. His tongue, like a crushed and crippled leg, never knew when it would stumble; his mind, forever short of breath, would sometimes heave and fail to move. To the Pharaoh's ear these lapses were as disturbing as the clatter of a stick smashing a jar.

Part of the difficulty was that the quarryman did not know how to read. So he had memorized the names of the men on the labor gang, the number of their injuries, their wages, the accounts for food—he was correct, but he was slow. Besides, this recital was hardly necessary. A scribe stood beside him with a roll of papyrus, and nodded his head in confirmation at each number recited by the manager of the quarries.

I wondered why the scribe did not read from the papyrus himself, but it was obvious, by the attention Ptah-nem-hotep was giving to the quarry official, that the bearing of the man and his ability to remember accounts could tell much about his honesty.

My mother's mind, when I tried to enter it again, was closed to me, or should I say closed to all I would wish to ask. With her skill—was

it equal to mine?—of knowing what was in *my* thoughts, she had
chosen to give *all* her attention to that poor quarry official. So, by
placing myself in her mind, I was given over to nothing better than an
admirable introduction to the difficulties of mining rock. She took
the numbers offered by this chief workingman and tried to see what
his men were doing. Yet, by the time it passed from her head to mine,
my toes were wriggling. Nonetheless, by such a roundabout method
of instruction, I came to understand why the Pharaoh listened so
carefully, and by a worthy and most serious effort I passed beyond my
boredom and came to recognize that this crude official, Rut-sekh, was
respected, even as his father and grandfather before him. They had all
been Overseers at the great quarries to the east of Memphi where,
shortly after the Ascension of Ramses IX to the Throne, a road was
begun across the desert to a great sea called Red, the Red Sea. Since
we were now in the Seventh Year of the Reign, I decided that the
road was as old as I was, at least if you counted the months I had lived
within my mother. So this increased my interest. I now began to comprehend that the problems on this road were curious. Ptah-nem-
hotep wanted to keep it a royal road, that is, wide enough for two
royal carts to pass in opposite directions, which meant a breadth of
eight horses. While such a width would be nothing grand in Memphi
where the Avenue of Ramses II offered a breadth of twenty horses
from the marketplace to the Temple of Ptah, still, the Road of Ramses IX would find difficulty as it went through the mountains. Given
the steep slopes, great rocks that could have been used for monuments
tumbled into the ravines below. In one place, said Rock-Cutter, they
had lost a week trying to raise a large block high enough to insert a
sledge beneath. Rock-Cutter confessed that the sledge, once inserted,
had collapsed from the weight, and tilted the rock toward the ravine.
After much consideration, they had to push it over. No sound, he
confessed, was so filled with the thunder of the Gods as the echoes of
that stone falling.

"It was a great loss, my Pharaoh," stated Rut-sekh, "yet I did not
know another way. One hundred eighteen men had been employed
in just that place for seven days and could not proceed farther without

removing the stone. During this delay, there was an expenditure of ten bags of grain, two large amphorae of oil, three amphorae of honey, twenty-two small bags of onions, five hundred forty-one loaves of bread, four amphorae of the wine of Buto . . ." His forehead creased with each figure recited, as if each item had been sniffed for rot, hefted for weight, and tasted for value. My father nodded gravely to indicate that Ptah-nem-hotep respected the honesty of Rock-Cutter at confessing to such mistakes.

"It is to your honor," the Pharaoh now said, "that you present the unfinished aspects of your task as quickly as the well-faced. The virtue of your character is as fresh to Me as the virtuous odor of the pine trees in My innermost courtyard."

"He will," went a thought from my mother's mind to me, clear as if she had said it aloud, "He will now certainly begin to brag about His imported pine trees."

"In the first year of My Reign," said Ptah-nem-hotep, "I had twenty-one young pines from the mountains of Syria brought across the sea to be planted in My innermost courtyard. There, fourteen now stand, still alive, although it was said that all would perish in a season. They are trees of the mountain and cold air, but they have a spirit of honest virtue, like your own, Rut-sekh, that speaks of clear mornings and hard work—yes, I will let you smell the fragrance of their virtue when the road is done."

"I am honored," said Rock-Cutter, looking at his feet. He seemed more than a little confused at the interruption of his recital. For the facts he had memorized must have been coming forward in his brain like oxen, one by one, each carrying a measured load, and whipped just often enough to keep from stopping.

"Yes," said Ptah-nem-hotep, "it is honest to confess one's errors. With other officials"—He swept the courtyard with His look— "I must find My way. To listen to their presentation, nothing is wrong, nothing will ever be wrong. Yet all is wrong. Yes," said Ptah-nem-hotep.

Rock-Cutter bowed again.

"Nonetheless," said our Pharaoh, "progress on the road is slow, injuries are numerous, and the losses in the labor force are discouraging."

"Yes, my Lord. Many of my men have gone blind."

"Is it from dust, or from splinters of stone?"

"It is the second, Great Two-House."

"When you gave your last report to Me in the month of Pharmuti, I recall that we talked about the scraping of the rocks. I asked you then to employ cedar chips to make the coals."

"I obeyed You, My Lord."

I do not know if I would have been able to understand what they now said, but by way of my mother's thoughts, I was able to see a thick bed of stone on which were laid hot coals in a narrow channel. When the bed had taken the heat of the coals, water was poured on. I listened to the hiss of steam, and saw the wet ash wiped away. A myriad of cracks were left in the groove, numerous as the cracks in clay when the flood is gone and the sun bakes the earth. I saw men chipping at these cracks with copper chisels and wooden mallets. After they were done, the channel, wide as a man's hand, had been deepened by the thickness of a finger. That was half a morning's work for two men. They would do it until the channel was deep enough to split the rock, sometimes, cubits deep.

I had already been taught to make measurements by these cubits, and was told the size had first been taken from the tip of Ramses II's middle finger to His elbow. I went around telling everyone that I measured more than two cubits tall—two cubits, one hand, two fingers—large for a child my age, was it not? and kept doing it until my mother told me to cease. Two cubits was nothing, she let me know, next to a man of four cubits. She had even seen a giant of five cubits. I ceased then to be concerned with this measure. But such talk now between the Pharaoh and Rock-Cutter refreshed my mother's memory of a cubit and she began to think about a great Pharaoh, tall and beautiful and vastly more like a God than Ptah-nem-hotep. I knew this could be no other than Ramses II but my mother saw Him as if He were alive before us, His arm extended and prayers said by the priests as the measurement was taken by the Royal String of the Royal

Scribe. This was my mother's offering to me of how the cubit had first been measured, but she was so full of pleasure, the late afternoon sun on the balcony now shining on her thighs, that she took her own measure of the cubit, and held the Royal String herself. Lo, the mighty phallus of Ramses II was equal to half the length, but since she saw Him, equal to Himself, before a mirror, the two phalluses, nose to nose, were the perfect royal measure if you took it from the root of one set of testicles over completely to the other. Then my mother left off thinking of cubits. She had just recognized that my mind was again in hers. I, in my turn, realized why she could never do arithmetic. She was not certain whether to be pleased at our closeness, or appalled at the rush of my education, but she smiled at me, and most tenderly (a naughty smile) and opening her mind to me again as easily as she might open her arms, so I rushed into the trap of her amusement for she now saw it as her motherly duty to instruct me in sad thoughts. I was therefore now obliged to contemplate all the poor stone-cutters who were going blind from the dust that flew out of pounding one stone upon another while dressing the face of an extracted rock. I saw some with red-rimmed eyes and others with blood from open cuts above their brows. One danced in pain, a stone splinter sticking to his eyeball, an atrocious set of sights until I realized my mother had put them together for me, and I was seeing, all at once, the quarry injuries of a full year.

Now, my mother, as if to make amends for her scandalous thoughts about the length of the cubit of Ramses II, began to listen again to Ptah-nem-hotep. He wished to know the time it took to make a channel in stone when cedar chips were used for the coals, as compared to how long it required when chips from date-palm, sycamore, tamarisk or acacia were employed. So he questioned Rut-sekh closely.

Rut-sekh assured our Pharaoh that he had put three of his best men on the cut while using the cedar chips. It still had taken fourteen days for a cut two cubits long and four deep to be accomplished by this gang. That had only been one day less than a cut of equal size done with sycamore chips whose coals had already been found superior to acacia, date-palm or tamarisk.

"If your fastest gang," said Ptah-nem-hotep, "is only one day faster than your average gang, the fires of cedar can hardly be more effective than the fires of sycamore."

Rut-sekh touched his forehead to the ground.

"Yet your first reports," said Ptah-nem-hotep, "told of cracks made by coals of cedar that were half a finger deeper than the hottest embers of sycamore."

"That is still true, Great Two-House."

"Then why is the job not done faster?"

As if the intimate discussion of these matters allowed Rut-sekh to forget to whom he spoke, he shrugged. It was the gesture of one workingman speaking to another, and only a momentary flaw in the immense respect he showed the Pharaoh, but, by the measure of disgust on my father's face, Rock-Cutter might as well have allowed an indiscreet sound to come popping out of his buttocks.

The Overseer must have taken in my father's face for he touched his forehead quickly to the ground, and said in sorrow, "My Pharaoh, I thought it would be quicker."

Then all was silent. Ptah-nem-hotep's lips pressed against one another but He said nothing. In the silence, I could smell the smoke of cedar chips, and understood that I was in Rock-Cutter's thoughts—by way of my mother or myself I hardly knew, but I was in his thoughts—except he hardly had them, it was more as if he moved from odor to odor when he was not ruminating over his figures to the Pharaoh. Then his head was like a shaduf—lifting a pail of water in one sturdy movement, emptying it, repeating the work. Now, with the memory of the smoke in his nostrils, he said, "Great Two-House, it was faster with the cedar, but the men made more mistakes." Rock-Cutter sighed.

"We had more injuries when working with the cedar. The men said it was cursed."

"How did you reply?"

"I whipped them."

"Now you are here before Me. You may speak the truth. Your Pharaoh is blind and dumb if none speak the truth."

"I would speak it, Great Two-House."

"Do. Even liars do well to speak the truth on the Day of the Pig."

"Great Two-House, I whipped my men with a heart so full I became afraid of the pains in my chest."

"Why did you feel such clamor?"

"Because, my Pharaoh, I could not disagree with my men. The odor of the smoke was strange."

Ptah-nem-hotep nodded. "Cedar comes from the shores of Byblos where the coffin of Osiris came to rest in such a tree."

"Yes, my Lord," said Rock-Cutter.

"If cedar was once the home of the Great God Osiris, the chips of the tree can never be cursed."

"Yes, my Lord." Rock-Cutter stood there. "It is the Day of the Pig, Great Two-House," he said at last.

"Speak the truth."

"My men do not often talk of the God Osiris. For us, it is better to go to the Temple of Amon." Rock-Cutter bowed his head once more to the dust.

"Don't you know," said Ptah-nem-hotep, "that Osiris is the God who will judge you in the Land of the Dead?"

Rock-Cutter shook his head. "I am only an Overseer. It is not for me to journey through the Land of the Dead."

"But you are a Royal Overseer. You may travel with your Pharaoh." Ptah-nem-hotep turned to my father. "Can there be many Royal Overseers," He asked, "who do not understand this value of the office?"

"Not many, Great Ptah-nem-hotep," said my father.

"One is too many," said the Pharaoh, and gave back His attention to Rut-sekh. "The honor that I offer," He said, "incites the light of no gratitude in your eyes."

"Great Two-House, I know that I will never be a voyager in the Land of the Dead."

"Is it because you cannot afford to be buried properly?" asked Ptah-nem-hotep. "Do not despair. Poorer men than you have become wealthy in My service."

"When I die, I shall be dead, Great God."

"How do you know?" asked Ptah-nem-hotep.

"I hear it in the sound one stone makes when it pounds against another."

Ptah-nem-hotep said, "That is an interesting remark." Abruptly, He yawned.

In the Court, everyone immediately yawned.

"We will not use the cedar chips," the Pharaoh said. "Their fires are hotter, their cracks go deeper, it is even a wood blessed by Osiris, but to a simple mind the fire is strange."

"It may go easier, Great Two-House," said Rut-sekh, "if my men work with smoke to which they are accustomed."

Ptah-nem-hotep nodded. Rut-sekh was dismissed with a small movement of His hand.

Other officials came in, to be followed by others. I could not give my attention to all they said, and soon could not give any attention. My mother frowned when I would scratch my navel, or rub my toes on the tiles of the floor, but then she was small help. Her mind had become as empty as mine and drifted like a boat of reeds. I began to wish I were back in the rose room where I could enter again into the mind of my Pharaoh. Here, not five cubits from His throne, I could not follow His words nor know His thoughts. Memories came to me of the banquet my family would enjoy with Ptah-nem-hotep that evening, a curious way to express it, but I did not feel as if I looked forward to the Night of the Pig so much as that it had already taken place and I need only remember what I must have already forgotten. Going forth in one life was much like recollecting another. Thinking of that, then thinking of nothing at all, I listened while officials came and went and spoke of many matters.

Of course, I could not follow all that was said. One official reported on the condition of the dikes around Busiris in the Delta and another spoke of work on the dams. A third told of the draining of the lakes, and the difficulties of drying and salting the mud eels found on the bottom. I drifted back to the wonders of that golden morning so long ago, yet just this morning, when I had seen a few fishing boats with their catch hanging on ropes that ran from the top of the mast to the prow and stern. They had gutted their fish and hung them up like clothes to dry. We came close to one such craft and the odor was clean and stinking at once, as if the blood of the river, which is to say the blood of the fish, had been washed in the sun, and that took me so far away from the Pharaoh and His serious concerns that I did not listen to the report on work in the mines nor to the Pharaoh's recommendation for using the horn of a gazelle as a socket superior to ivory for the spindle of a rock drill—I could not follow that either—and by way of my mother's drowsy opinion, thought little of a General of the Armies whose face was covered with scars and open ulcers. He was a tall fierce-looking man, but had only defeats to report and spoke of towns on the borders of Lower Egypt being burned by Syrian raiders.

"Do I never hear talk of victory?" asked the Pharaoh, and the General began to shake from the onslaught of a fever he had caught in his campaigns—I do not think it was fear he felt so much as a great chill, but he could not stop shivering.

There was a long inquiry by Ptah-nem-hotep into the ownership of the banks of an irrigation canal where two adjoining estates were in dispute over the amounts of water to be removed from the canal. This soon turned into another dispute between the same noblemen about the shifting of boundary stones. Accounts were brought by Royal Officials against merchants accused of mixing sand in the Palace flour, and one official read out from a list the names of ships that must be declared lost at sea. No word had been received from them in three years.

I amused myself by trying to come near my mother's mind once more. I do not know if it was my thoughts, or her thoughts, but I had started to think of the strangeness of fire, and wondered if in the flame lived the voice of all that was burning, that is not only the material which burned but the thoughts of the Gods Who lived in that country. At this instant, I felt the Pharaoh looking at me, opened my eyes and realized I had been passing through His thoughts. For the look in our eyes belonged to each of us, and we were in this way equal, and brothers.

I realized that I had certainly been asleep. The officials were gone, evening had come to the patio, and the Pharaoh was smiling. "Come, little Prince," He said, "it is time for us to eat," and He took me by the hand, while I felt the fatigue of His blood for all the long work of this afternoon.

Eight

On our walk through the gardens to the chamber where we would dine with the Pharaoh, my mother began to think of a conversation she did not wish to recall. Yet, once commenced, there was nothing but to remember all of it. How could one not? A few days ago, my father, knowing how the news would chew on my mother's heart, had told her the Pharaoh said that Menenhetet ate the dung of bats. To which my mother replied, "He takes it as a medicine," only to hear my father reply, "No, it is not so. He takes it for the contentment of his palate. The Pharaoh heard it most reliably from Khem-Usha. It was a long time ago but He cannot get it out of His mind. I think that is why there has been no invitation to Menenhetet for so long a time."

"Nor have I been invited," my mother could not restrain herself from saying.

"He would hardly think of you," said my father, "without remembering Menenhetet."

More recently, my father had begun to speak of Ptah-nem-hotep's interest in pigs. He talked about them constantly. "Did you know,"

Ptah-nem-hotep would say, "if a nobleman touches pig, he must go into the river immediately, and with his clothes on, no matter how good they are. That's to wash off the taint."

"I have, Good and Great God, never touched the beast," said Nef-khep-aukhem. "I have heard that leprosy may be caused by drinking pig's milk."

"No one I know has tried it," said Ptah-nem-hotep. He added: "Of course, it's not the sort of thing that would give your relative, Menenhetet, much pause." Which my father made a point of telling my mother.

Two days later, Ptah-nem-hotep was bemused again by the pig. "I spoke to Khem-Usha," He told Nef-khep-aukhem. "As I suspected, it is true. Swineherds, on pain of the removal of their nose, are forbidden from entering any temple. 'How would you know,' I asked Khem-Usha, 'if they came in disguise?' 'We would know,' he told Me. There is a priest for you. It is the perfect remark for a High Priest."

At this point, Ptah-nem-hotep took off His wig, handed it to Nef-khep-aukhem, inclined His head to receive another, studied the polished surface of His bronze mirror (or such, at least, was the view my mother imagined) and then said to my father, "I'm going to celebrate the Feast of the Pig this year." At the look in my father's face, He added, "Yes, we will eat of pig's flesh, you and Me, just like every other Egyptian at the fires in the markets guzzling on fat and tasty pieces, and, yes"—He paused—"I've not had your family here in a long time. Let's have a small dinner that night. Tell Menenhetet"—here, Ptah-nem-hotep gave His delicious smile—"to bring one of his bats."

"It would give me greater happiness, Good God, if it were You to tell him."

Ptah-nem-hotep smiled. "There'll be surprises. I wish to delight your wife and child on the Night of the Pig."

I did not know what to expect. When my parents or my great-grandfather gave a feast we had many musicians who not only played at harps and lyres but knew guitars and the cithara and the barbiton, and after the banquet would come many surprises. Jugglers would appear, acrobats, and wrestlers. Skilled slaves would throw knives at painted wooden blocks, and once, my great-grandfather even brought his guests down to the river and there, by his embankment, boatmen decorated with colored ribbons and wearing feather headdresses had used their oars like poles to try to knock each other into the water, a dangerous sport, I heard the guests whisper. In the excitement a good boatman could be drowned. None perished that night, and my great-grandfather had salts sprinkled on the torches so that we stood among fires of green and scarlet and in the midst of purple flames while the din rolled back across the water. That had been a great feast.

Tonight would not be the same. My mother said we would be only five for dinner. Still, the thought she passed to me was clear: Our Pharaoh, having given many lavish parties, would find more amusement in our small evening where we might linger over the exquisite refinement and brilliance of His conversation. I could already hear her speaking like this to friends in days to come. Yet, by the light in her eye, gleaming with marvels of anticipation, I knew she did not lie. The Feast of the Pig, no matter what my father had told her, was going to be wondrous.

It was. On this night I learned almost as soon as we began that I would eat food I never tasted before and hear conversation on topics unfamiliar to me. Indeed, I soon learned something on the secrets of purple contained in the snail, as well as how to put a letter in a dead person's hand, and was given hints of the virtues of cannibalism. And much else. And much else again.

As the dinner went on, and one strange food followed another into my stomach, my spirits played through perfumed fires, and my thoughts became inflamed. What my mother had told me about the hour I was made might as well have become a seed growing in the silence of my heart. The cheeks of my face were red, the conversation of my parents—was I to look to Menenhetet or Nef-khep-aukhem as my father?—squirmed in my stomach like sun-heated snakes, and I was feeling that wild merriment peculiar to childhood when every moment can bring a new, incalculable pleasure or, as easily, a clap of disaster. Since I could not begin to cry out with the uproar I would have liked to put forth, stimulation built fever upon fever in me, and passed from hardly tasting the food to moments when I was trembling to recover from all the directions in which my senses were scattered by each flavor.

We reclined by a low table of ebony on which were golden plates so thin they weighed less than my mother's alabaster, and the room was like a forest on fire and lit by so many great candles it brought us near to feeling the presence of the sun in the middle of the night; yet we were only inside a chamber of wood panels of a grain like the fur of a leopard, and I noticed that the Pharaoh, having changed His costume to another of pleated white linen that left His chest bare but for one shoulder, wore less ornament than any of us, indeed He wore no decoration except a leopard's tail attached to the rear of His skirt. He would reach about from time to time and catch the stem of this tail by His hand in order to thump the tip on the table, as though to indicate His excitement at something my mother or Menenhetet had said, and once, in the high vigor of amusement with which He did this, having struck the tail several times on the table and flung it back with a whoop—for He seemed in as much of a fever of laughter as myself— He succeeded in lashing that leopard's tail up into the middle of a great ostrich fan on a stand behind His seat, and the fan tottered and would have fallen if a servant had not caught it.

There were two behind each of us, and five or more for the Pharaoh, and their murmur, "Life, Health, Strength," to every service they gave, whether to fill a goblet, remove a plate, serve a new plate, or present us with a little more of the same dish, became so constant and reassuring as the sound of crickets in my family's garden. Again I knew that all was safe, as at home, where I had come to know that I could sleep so long as the ringing of insects did not cease, for their onslaught upon the silence was nonetheless a sign that nothing was worse than it had been the night before, and therefore the power of sleep which hovered in the darkness could settle down again on me. So did I enjoy the constant smacking of servants' lips, as if they would like to put themselves into the gusto of the flavors.

There were snails to begin, not larger than any I had seen before, but with a sauce of onion and garlic and some green herb so aromatic that I could smell the perfume of the Pharaoh's pines. I felt the herb ooze up my nose and leave the inside of my head agog with hollows, but then that was to be expected: my mother had told me that the name for all such herbs was *ooze-up*, even as frying onions could be called *ooze-out* when the smell traveled from room to room, and red-pepper was *ooze-spice* to some and *ooze-in* to others.

I liked the snails. We ate them on little pointed sticks of ivory with a tiny ruby on the end shaped like a Pharaoh's hat, and, cut with five small lines into the thin and precious stick, were two eyes, two nostrils, and a curved line for the mouth that did not look unlike the face of Ptah-nem-hotep if His face had been very thin, a jest I realized, a comic face for the Pharaoh. Seeing my surprise, He said, "These are used only for the Feast of the Pig. Tonight, you may laugh at Me. Tonight is your night."

"My night?" I felt bold enough to answer.

"On the night of the Feast of the Pig, the youngest child of the Princes comes first. Speak when you wish, dear child."

I giggled. The meal was only begun but the ooze-up had cleared my head until I felt as old and wise as my great-grandfather, a great empty wise head was what I felt between my ears, and the touch of the toothpick entering the shell and piercing the flesh of the snail made me feel like a warrior stepping forward into a cave where fires were burning and the meat of the beast waited for the flash of my spear.

"Do you like these snails?" asked Ptah-nem-hotep, and Night of the Pig or no, my parents replied instantly, both at once, to assure the Good God that never had they tasted meat of the shell so succulent. To which, Ptah-nem-hotep replied that the snails in the oval pond at the end of the Ramses II Promenade in the Long Garden were carefully sheltered by date-palms on one side from the sun, yet the pond was open at night to the moon, and thereby were the snails bathed in moonlight. Perhaps that is why they were eminently flavorful.

"Yes, they are so good, I would think your servants might steal them," said my great-grandfather, even as a few more were laid on his plate.

Ptah-nem-hotep shook His head. "The penalties are severe. Once, a maid took a few, and My father had one of her nipples cut off."

On any other night, my mother could probably not have spoken, but now she gasped. "Surely, You wouldn't do the same?"

"I detest the thought, but expect I would have to enforce such punishment."

"For one snail?" Hathfertiti persisted.

"I was a child at the time," said Ptah-nem-hotep, "yet I have not forgotten how My father opened His palm to show Me the punishment. She was a young girl, and her nipple was no larger than my little fingernail. I was ready to blubber in misery, but My father merely flicked it off His finger into the pond. Later, He told Me such severe justice had been required to remove the pall of theft from the place. Otherwise, the snails could have sickened. As you see, they're robust little creatures today, and oh, the lovely flavor of oil and onions and ooze-up. I sometimes think I can't have enough, but then I'm just a poor fellow on the Night of the Pig." He gave a merry laugh that made His fine curved lips look as alive for an instant as the flash of a horse galloping by. Or, was it a hawk coming down in a swoop? Animal and bird both raced through my head on the ooze-up. I tried to look at my mother but my eyes turned away from the boldness of the look she gave back into His eyes. If Ptah-nem-hotep carried no jewelry this night, my mother did not come near to doing the same. While she wore only a saffron-colored gown with no pleats and only one strap so that her right breast, the larger and more beautiful, was exposed, and had colored her nipple red, a rose-red from a rare scarlet dye, of a madder root I think, to match the narrow cloth of madder-red she wore about her throat in the style of a girl of the markets, she also wore a ring on every one of her nobly provocative fingers, and a light gold crown in the shape of a snake curled around her head with two green gems for eyes. How beautiful did that look against her black hair and her dark oiled shoulders. Now she turned her dark eyes on the Pharaoh.

Receiving the full bounty of her look, Ptah-nem-hotep seemed pleased. "Men-ka, My pet," He said to me, "do you know the first duty of a host?"

"How could Men-ka know?" protested my mother, but I noticed she took the Pharaoh's name for me, even though my pet name, until this moment, had always been Meni.

"Men-ka," said Ptah-nem-hotep, "the duty of a host is to amuse one's guests. So I wish to entertain you with an explanation of each dish set before us." He pointed to the empty shells in my plate. "As for example, these little palaces."

I nodded comfortably. I did not know what He meant, but it was the Night of the Pig, and everything made sense.

"You are a deliriously intelligent boy," He said. "Now follow Me with care, or I will cut off your nose." My father laughed at this re-mark. It was the first sound any of us had heard from him.

"Yes," said the Pharaoh, "I will cut off your nose and give it to your mother's husband."

My father laughed prodigiously.

"Do you like the color of purple?" Ptah-nem-hotep asked of me. I nodded again.

"It is the color worn by the Kings of Syria and the Hittite Kings, and some of the Hebrews, and many of the Assyrians. In Egypt we think they are absurd in their passion for this color. There is even one town they fight over all the time. That is because the only good pur-ple dye comes from there. Do you believe this?"

I nodded.

"It is the town of Tyre, and famous for a spiny snail. The inside of the shell has a purple that makes a superb dye when crumbled into powder. In Tyre, therefore, everybody collects snails. Little girls, and men half as old as your great-grandfather which is very old indeed, and midgets and giants all collect snails. They bring them in, and they crush them, and they pay no attention to the snail meat."

"Why not?" I asked.

"I don't know. Maybe they are tired of the taste. I suspect it is because it takes so long to pluck the meat out of each shell and the dye is worth much more. They are too rich and greedy in Tyre, you see, to take the time. They just squash the snails between stones, and wash them, and squash them again, until the purple begins to run. That purple settles in the vats and still has slimy little bits of snail left in it."

My mother gave vent to one of her sounds of disgust.

"Yes, it is revolting," said the Pharaoh. "Yet they extract a purple that brings ecstasies to the eyes of Eastern Monarchs. They call it royal purple. That is the color of Kings, they say in the East, but we are wiser and know it is the color of madmen." The Pharaoh roared in delight and thumped the leopard tail. "Bring on the next dish," He said.

His eyes were full of lights at the surprise in my face when only one servant came back bringing two metal bars, not as long as my hand, not as wide as two of my fingers, nor as thick as one, and Ptah-nem-hotep set them apart on a lovely alabaster plate.

"Look at this," said Ptah-nem-hotep. "It is black-copper-from-heaven." He handed the plate to my great-grandfather.

Menenhetet's dignity was too perfect, however, to allow him to serve his own curiosity. Quietly, he passed the plate to me.

"Let the boy have it first," he said.

"You do not know the pleasure you will miss," remarked Ptah-nem-hotep.

I, on my side, did not know how to touch this black-copper-from-heaven. Was it warm or cold? My fingers flickered up to the surface of one bar, danced away—it felt like any other metal, red copper for example. I lifted the bar and laid it down. It was heavier than copper, and somehow I knew it was harder. I slid it about on the plate.

"Try both bars," said Menenhetet.

"Why do you tell him that?" asked Ptah-nem-hotep.

"If all that my Pharaoh wishes to show us can be found in one bar, He would not have them bring us two."

Ptah-nem-hotep nodded in approval, and I felt enough courage to pick up each piece by my separate hands. Then I smelled the first bar. It had a cold odor that came from far away. As I brought the other up to my cheek, I felt again this cold stirring into the breath I took through my nostrils. Some life like none I had known before began to tremble in the metal. It was as if I listened to the quivering of a heart in each piece. That life was in the tips of these small bars of metal as they came near my nostrils, and then I cried out in fright and in joy, for I heard the Gods speak. Their silent command must have been uttered since the two pieces of black-copper-from-heaven pulled my hands together, and met with a click. They were married, and now stuck to each other although there was nothing to keep them together that I could see.

My father took both from me on the instant, then was obliged to surrender his prize to Menenhetet. Hathfertiti cried out with delight as she watched. "You are a magician," she murmured to Ptah-nem-hotep.

"I do nothing," He said. "The magic is in the metal itself."

"But where does black-copper-from-heaven come from?" she asked.

"A shepherd saw a ball of fire fall through the sky. It lay in the desert like a dead horse. He found it too heavy to move, but there were ragged pieces he could break off. These bars have been made from those pieces. Who knows what speaks in them?"

"Can You silence their force?" asked Menenhetet.

"For a time. These bars had to be heated in order to be beaten into shape. Then they were inert. But when an unshaped piece of black-copper-from-heaven which came from the same ball of fire was laid next to our bar, and the two were kept together, why, like members of a family, they must have prayed in the same direction. I can tell you that the bar gained such life from the rough piece it can now give life to other pieces that have been beaten."

They went on speaking of these peculiarities of black copper. Ptah-nem-hotep told how a drop of water, left on the bar, dried with an orange-red spot. The water had not turned to blood, however. It was rather that the surface of the black copper changed into a weak red copper powder that could be scraped from the bar. Who could comprehend why the Gods desired that?

I ceased to listen. I had heard about the Gods every day of my life and had seen Them everywhere—in the tail of a cat for instance, since only a cat can listen with her tail. I saw a God in the eye of a horse when it galloped by, and the same God was in every beetle, for their movements were faster than my thoughts. There was certainly a God in any cow. Where else could one come close to such a powerful knowledge of peace? There were Gods in flowers, in trees, and the Gods could always be found in statues for Their strength could rest in the stone. There was even a God in the wild boar. I could feel the God Set and know proper respect for His wrath when I smelled the wild boar in its cage. Such Gods were, however, not so frightening to me as this black-copper-from-heaven which moved past my nose. I had come near a God—or was it two Gods?—Who lived between the flash of lightning and the silence before thunder, and I was not at ease. My stomach still shivered from the touch of one metal on the other, yet I felt hungry.

Now, the servants returned with a small purple fruit for each of us. That is, I thought it was a fruit, but as it was set down in its small golden bowl I saw it was cabbage instead, a purple cabbage—I did not know there were such—and it smelled very sour.

"Beware of the vinegar," said Ptah-nem-hotep. "That is sour enough to give wrinkles to the mouth, but perfect for clearing your thoughts of the ooze-up." He raised His cabbage and took a bite as from a pomegranate. "A dreadful food," He commented.

"Why do you serve it?" asked Hathfertiti.

"Pigs thrive on cabbage. I thought we should acquaint ourselves with the habits of the friend we shall soon meet." Now He played with a few leaves. "Actually," He said, "this is superior vinegar and made from the best of My wine. I like a good vinegar, don't you?"

"Yes," said my father.

"No," said Hathfertiti.

"Small reason for you to like it," Ptah-nem-hotep stated. "Vinegar appeals to those who are full of pity for themselves."

"How can that be so?" asked my mother.

"It speaks of its disappointments. Just think of some poor wine that nobody drinks. It is obliged to sit in its jar until boredom makes it sour. What fury I taste in such vinegar."

"You have a fine palate," remarked my great-grandfather.

"An exceptional palate. I have a talent for eating, no, not for eating, for tasting. Here, take this cabbage away. It's sluttish."

"You are in an exceptional spirit tonight," said Hathfertiti.

"I am like this once a year."

"Once a year," said my father devoutly.

"Do you enjoy the vinegar?" asked Ptah-nem-hotep.

"It is powerful, but true to Your description," said my father.

I had not liked the cabbage and did not eat from it; and liked the next dish less, for it was quail and uncooked. The skin had been removed, and the bird seasoned, then the skin put on again as a blouse, but when I ate it—perhaps it was the salt, a garlic salt with a fierce ooze-in from another spice—the cold life not yet cooked out of the bird managed to fly up one nostril and out the other. I had to close my eyes. Then I could see twenty quail, like twenty black dots in a cloud who became twenty white dots in a cave, now they were black again. I began to laugh at the thought my nose wanted to pee, then I sneezed.

The roe of fish came next, served on a plate with a curious egg whose shell was not speckled but white, and my mother cried out, "Is this the egg from the bird of Babylon?"

"Most certainly it is," said Ptah-nem-hotep.

"The bird that does not fly?" asked my father.

"Yes. The Babylonian bird that does not like water and does not fly."

"What does it do?" asked my mother.

"It makes noise, and is stupid, filthy, and useless, but for its eggs."

"Are they as good as duck eggs?"

"Only if you are from Babylon," said Ptah-nem-hotep and everyone laughed. He told us then of how He had had these creatures brought to Him by ship. A tame bird, He kept repeating, but they made such a din of cackling and strutting and crying out that the oarsmen thought the birds were calling to their Babylonian Gods. So the crew was ready to slaughter their cargo at the first sign of a storm. "Fortunately, no big winds came. Now, I have the birds in a corner of My garden, and they take to the soil of Egypt. They multiply. Soon I will be able to send you some. In fact—I whisper to you—I like these filthy little cacklers. Their eggs seem good for My thoughts."

I was feeling gloomy, however. The heat of the great candles, the war of spices in my nose, my chest, and my belly, and the sad salty taste of the roe sat in me with sorrow. I did not know what to make of the egg from Babylon. It was raw and yellow in the yolk, not green, and it had a taste like cheese and wet walls and sulphur and flour-paste and I even thought it smelled a little like ca-ca on certain mornings, yet even as I could like such a smell on one day or another—if it came from me—so did I like the egg. It was as yellow as the Pharaoh's own butter that the servants were passing out now on sweet little cakes of the finest flour.

Still, the combination of fish eggs and bird eggs had certainly affected my mother for she began to talk to Ptah-nem-hotep of the day of my birth as if I were not there, speaking of how she had kept my birth back by holding her knees together, and said this with her bare breast leaning toward the Pharaoh. "I would not have him born," she said, "until the lucky hour was there. I did not want Meni, my Men-ka, to see the day until the sun was at its height and yellow as this egg," but when the Pharaoh merely nodded, and did not seem wholly rescued from the boredom that surrounded Him (the way death is always near a man who is wasting) my mother pushed away her roe and cried out, "You don't mean to tell me that these red little jellies might all have become fish."

"All," said my father. "There are always enough fish in the sea."

There was now a pause, not so much for the rebuke to my mother, as for the solemnity of my father's remark. We had eight or ten sayings such as "one thread saves seven stitches," "right-thinking is the husband of right-doing," or "enough fish in the sea," as my father had just observed. Such comments never asked for a reply, and so there was now, as I said, a pause, but it did not seem to leave any animosity against my father. It was as if everyone knew that he must have stopped the conversation for a reason. Since he thought only of the Pharaoh's wishes and knew them even as they were forming, everyone assumed, including the Pharaoh, that our Good God must have some desire to pause. In truth, He did.

"It is time," Ptah-nem-hotep said, "for *rep* and *repi,*" and to the laughter of everyone, He stood up, and left the room. I knew my parents were shocked. *Repi* had been the word taught to me as a polite way of announcing that I must urinate. But, *rep,* at least in the way Ptah-nem-hotep had spoken it, could only suggest an ugly beast breathing hot wind in every direction. In truth, *rep* was our most awful word for ca-ca, and the two together, *rep* and *repi,* were so terrible that no one, not even the Pharaoh, would care to say it on any night other than the Feast of the Pig. I suppose it was His way of reminding us that on this night not only could we speak of matters considered improper on all other nights, but indeed, were supposed to.

Once Ptah-nem-hotep had left, however, we were on guard against the servants for we could feel their ears come alive. Hathfertiti became conspicuously silent, and Menenhetet and Nef-khep-aukhem had a conversation about the best kind of throwing-stick to take out in the swamps for ducks. But their talk lapsed. I could hear my mother whisper to my father.

"Is He never like this on other nights?"

My father looked up from the last of his conversation with Menenhetet and shook his head.

Now, a dark and bearded Syrian in a heavy woolen ill-smelling garment was allowed to enter and he bowed profoundly before each of us, and poured out a liquid from a heavy vat barrel he carried in his arms, his own body reeking of the beer he served. So soon as he had filled our mugs, he was gone, but I could see the servants found the smell of his wet beer, old body-oil, sweat and damp wool altogether ferocious. The beer, however, to my parents' surprise, was exceptionally good, or, at least, so they declared, since they would not let me drink any. Then Ptah-nem-hotep returned, and related to us, as if there had been nothing exceptional in His departure, a charming story about the brewer.

"One night, I told Overseer of the Royal Kitchen to bring Me the best beer in Memphi, and next day he groveled on the floor at what he had to confess, but it seems our best brewer in all of this city is a filthy fellow named Ravah, the same one you saw, and he declared he would not send his beer to Twin-Gates unless he could accompany it. 'Didn't you flog the fool?' I asked. 'I did,' Overseer told me, 'and Ravah poured his beer on the ground. I could beat him half to death, he said, but there would be no beer unless he could serve the Pharaoh himself.' Well, it made Me curious. I told Overseer to bring the fool. Had to keep him at a distance because of his stench, but what a beer! Ravah claims it is his vat that makes it special, and I must say the drink gets better all the time. He says that since I have been sharing his beer, the cracks in his vat have more power than ever to flavor well. 'Joy-Bringer' he calls his filthy stuff, but it is good."

"He speaks of You, Divine Two-House, as sharing his beer?" asked my mother.

"Yes. Ravah says the power of the brew is promiscuous, and must be shared by all. That is the center of its strength. Do you know, I believe him? I sip this stuff and feel close to My people. I never feel that while sipping Unguent of the Heart"—he pointed to one amphora of wine—"or"—pointing to another—"Cellared in this Preserve. No," said Ptah-nem-hotep sadly, "then I feel close only to the priests."

"I do not know how you can speak that way," my mother said to Him in an intimate voice, as if at last, comfortable with her new manners on the Night of the Pig, she could scold Him just so naturally as if they had been married for ten years or more. "You are renowned for the quality of Your wine." Here she smiled a little drunkenly, as if she knew she was going to reveal her pet name for my father— "Why our good friend, Nef, has eyes as dull as muddy water when he speaks to me. But when he speaks of You"—she paused as if taking a dare with herself—"his eyes look like diamonds."

She gave a hiccup without covering her mouth, an act she would never have allowed on other nights, and said, "You may adore the snail, but I adore the Night of the Pig. You see, I think there is pig enough in each of us to make one feast a year. Of course," she smiled deliciously, "on this night we have a fear that restrains us. We fear we are nothing but pigs, whereas You are a God as well, Great-are-Your-Two-Houses-of-the-Pig!"

I felt an immense commotion in my ears, yet not a sound was uttered. The attention of the servants was equal to the silence of fish after one of their number has been pulled from the sea. My father's mouth did not close: so I had the first look of my life at the full size of his tongue—he had an immense tongue! Even Menenhetet stirred in disbelief. "You may not speak that way," he said sharply to Hath-fertiti.

Ptah-nem-hotep, however, saluted her with the last of His beer. "I have been called Two-Lions, Two-Trees, and once I was called Two-Divine-Hippopotami. I have been termed Son of Horus and Son of Set, as well as Prince of Isis and Osiris, I have even been named as heir to Thoth and Anubis, but, never, dear company, has anyone had the wit to think of My Double-House as the Pig-Sty of the North and the Pig-Sty of the South. I must only ask: where is the pig? You can bring it to us," He said over His shoulder to the servants, and gave back my mother something of the same delicious smile she had offered to Him. Yet each of His cheeks had a touch of red no larger than the pinch of a cruel finger, a red just so bright as blood in a boil beneath the skin, and anger rocked through the air. I felt as if the space between them had a red hue different from the air between others. The power of my mother and Menenhetet to glare at each other out of the very depths of their blood was equaled now as my mother stared into the face of the Pharaoh. While the heat of the great candles in the room became greater, the flame rose and my mother and Ptah-nem-hotep sat motionless.

Then she looked away. "Not even on the Night of the Pig may a woman gaze into the eyes of the Good God."

"Look into them," cried Ptah-nem-hotep. "On this night, the God is gone."

To me, He seemed at this instant more like a God than He had appeared all day. When my mother did not reply, He made a harsh and barking sound of triumph. "This is a marvelous night," He said, and took up His leopard's tail to hold the tip before His nose. "The tail of the leopard," He added, "was worn first by My great ancestor, Khufu, who taught the people of Egypt how to raise the weight of great stone. To the Pyramids!" and He pounded His tail on the table, as if pulling into Himself the strength of the stones. I thought I had never seen Him look so alive.

Nor so attractive to my mother. I knew jealousy again. Like a lover climbing a wall, so did my thoughts climb my mother's dark hair, my jealousy taking me through all of her reluctance to let me in—but then she could hardly keep me out. She was in more of a hurry to protect herself from the desire of the Pharaoh to enter.

She had cause not to let Him know what she thought. Intimate as I expected to be, I was not prepared to feel so quickly the carnal breath of her true mind, and knew in an instant why she had spoken— incredible still was the ring of those sounds in my memory: Two-Houses-of-the-Pig!—but then the words, high on the wave of the last swallow of Joy-Bringer, had only broken out of a sudden disturbance between her legs. My mind being in her mind, my body was in her body, and my legs among hers—so did I know that she had one thumping exchange of meat with Ravah in the passing of her thoughts. That way, I learned again what I had known before: not only servants like Eyaseyab, but ladies like my mother could take Sweet Finger in their mouth, except that Ravah did not have a Sweet Finger, for by way of my mother I saw a warty club, heavy-veined as a forearm, and as red in color as the spots on Ptah-nem-hotep's cheeks. She was still thinking of her mouth on Ravah, her nostrils breathing in his pubic hair, her head overtaken by old sweat, old beer and Syrian wool while through her thoughts went Ptah-nem-hotep's words on cabbage—"sluttish!"—and she shivered in recollection, and saw the genitals of other men as well, Bone-Smasher for the first, even as she had glimpsed his groin through the parting of his breechcloth on the boat that morning, and I knew Ravah was a handle to the jug, no

more, of her great recollection of Fekh-futi and how as a child, tickled at every recollection that his name was Shit-Collector, she used to
sit on his lap and try to catch a whiff of the old trade—gardens being
the root and breath of childhood pleasures. She had a moment when
she passed through an orgy of embraces, taken by every hole in her
body, a roar of sensations bloody as meat, and so she had cried the
words aloud (furious at Ptah-nem-hotep for allowing the beer of
Ravah to be laid on her tongue) had then, yes, indeed, said, or so I
heard it now: "Great Double Pig-Sty."

Yes, I had much to learn about my mother. If I could feel the Pharaoh's pleasure that Hathfertiti had cast down her eyes after trying to
stare into His, I also knew His anger at what she had said, and so must
she, for now, as if His only wish were for the pleasures of quiet conversation to absorb His new pleasures and calm His anger, so she said
in her very best voice, "Were You only jesting when You spoke of
wine as inferior to beer?"

"Oh, not inferior," said Ptah-nem-hotep, "but priestly. I'm too
much of a priest Myself, you see."

"Not at all," said my mother.

"Your kindness is voluptuous," said Ptah-nem-hotep. He reached
forward and touched the tip of His middle finger to the tip of her bare
breast. "Here comes the entertainment," He said cheerfully.

Nine

A beautiful girl, nude but for a girdle around her hips, entered with a three-stringed lyre. Taking no pause, she began to play a love song.

> *"How beautiful is my prince*
> *"How beautiful is his destiny."*

Ptah-nem-hotep gave her no attention, other than to tap the table in time to the music. An Ethiopian with a bony body, and a flute longer than I was tall, came in behind the girl and began to play as well. While the girl sang, three other girls started to dance. Like the lute player, they were naked but for the girdle that concealed the hair at the head of their thighs. I could not keep from looking at their navels and the beauty of their exposed breasts. How bright were their black eyes in the brilliant reflection of the great candles. The lute-player sang:

> *"Place sweet oils and good odors in my head*
> *"Lay flowers on my limbs*

"*Kiss the body of your sister*
"*For she lives in your heart*
"*Let the walls fall down.*"

"Let the walls fall down," sang Hathfertiti in refrain, and patted the buttock of the servant nearest her, even as the girl was laying flower petals around my mother's plate. "You are darling," said my mother to her, and the girl, reaching into a basket she carried at her hip, passed over to my mother a ball of wax with a delightful smell—roses and lotuses were in its perfume.

I began to understand that we were all to be covered with wreaths of lotus flowers, and that petals of roses would surround our new plates of alabaster, large and clear and milky-white, and I also understood that all of this, the girls, the flowers, the songs, and the intimacies of the servants—"You are so beautiful," whispered the serving girl to my mother even as her hip was being caressed, while my serving girl whispered to me, "You are not old enough to know where I could kiss you!"—yes, these agreeable conversations (which I had heard at more than one feast) were not unusual, but tonight they offered a fine fever at just the moment when the pig was brought out to us by two black eunuchs, nude but for their cloths. Yet, tonight, these breechclouts had been studded with precious stones that could come only from the Pharaoh's linen. The male servants carried the body on a great black serving dish and set it in the center of our table in the midst of a quick movement by the dancing girls that had much beating of feet, much undulating of their bellies, and a scintillating play of notes from the three-string lyre, the sounds coming in all the quick multitude of some altercation between the birds in the Pharaoh's garden. I was now aware of animals crying out all over the place, a dog first.

Here was the pig. I was not ready for the sight. He looked alive and fierce and like a man. I had seen wild boars in their cage, and they were ugly and full of spiky hair matted with filth and litter. Their snouts made me think of the stumps of thieves' arms after the hands had been cut off or would have, if not for the two holes of the nostrils, as dull and stubborn as any two holes you could poke in the mud with your fingers. This pig, however, had had his hair shaved off, no, he was peeled, I saw, as I looked at him, and his under-skin, now nicely cooked, was pink. His two fangs were covered with gold leaf, his paws had been manicured, then fixed with silver leaf, his nose had been scraped, and painted pink, the buds of white flowers were in his nostrils, a pomegranate in his mouth, and the servants, revolving the platter to show all sides of this decorated beast to all of us, I was given a view of the spiral of his tail, yet before I could demonstrate my cleverness by commenting that the spiral reminded me of the snail, I was treated to another surprise: a small roll of papyrus had been inserted into the pig's well-scrubbed anus.

"It is for you to pluck it forth," said Ptah-nem-hotep to Hathfertiti. With a sweet wash of giggles from the servants, full of the delight that they were witnessing the rarest of sights, Hathfertiti gave a kiss to her left hand, and with a flick of her fingertips plucked the papyrus from its place.

"What does it say?" asked Ptah-nem-hotep.

"I promise to read it before the meal is done," Hathfertiti answered with a droll look, as though to give the papyrus time to breathe.

"No, read it now," said our Pharaoh.

So she broke its seal of perfumed wax, unrolled it, gasped with delight as a ruby scarab fell into her plate—then touched it for luck to the tip of her nipple before she set it down. She read to all of us: "Just a slave on the Night of the Pig, but may you seek My freedom," to which my father and Menenhetet laughed. Ptah-nem-hotep and Hathfertiti did not. They stared back and forth with a tenderness so agreeable I wished to sit between them. It was as if there could be no end to the fascinating conversations they might have. All the while, my father looked on with pride, a happy, even a boyish look on his face as if by these attentions given to his wife, he was receiving an honor he had not wholly earned, while my great-grandfather kept a firm smile on his face until the corners of his mouth looked like two short fenceposts, and contented himself by rotating the great round black plate on which the pig rested, as though in this animal there were other messages to read.

That also gave me an opportunity to study our roasted monster, who looked like a pink hippopotamus just born, or some swollen dwarf, or now, turned so his head was toward me, looked human for certain, a priest, I thought to myself. I also began to giggle, for although dead, the pig-eye near me was open and almost transparent. It was like looking into a murky hall of marble, then worse—somewhere in the hall of marble, a beast stirred. Maybe it was the light of the candles reflecting from those pale dead green eyes, maybe the frozen straining gusto with which the jaws bit on the pomegranate, or even the voracious thrust of the nose, as if that painted snout were capable of breathing in not only the worst but the most powerful of smells— at any rate something in the immense calm and greed of this dead pig made me think of the High Priest Khem-Usha. I felt most peculiar, not a doubt.

"Cut the creature, and serve us," said Ptah-nem-hotep.

I could hardly swallow at first. My throat was numb with awe. The others, however, would show many expressions. My father, after the first bite, had an absurd glint in his eye as if he were trapped between pleasure and exposure—I had seen that look on his face once when I came into his room with my mother, for at that moment, he had his hands on a servant, one to the front, one to the rear, and both below her navel. In turn, my mother now showed a troubled expression as if fearful of dire consequences in all the comforts she tasted. Then I was so bold as to look at my Pharaoh, and He betrayed something like disappointment as if expecting a good deal more from the meat on His tongue. The music was playing loudly, but He silenced it. The dancers left, as did the lyre player, and the black slave with the long flute.

My great-grandfather had another expression altogether. He chewed the food slowly in his strong teeth, strong even for a man of sixty—I did not dare to think of one hundred and eighty!—and, as always, he took the measure of what he did, eating with strong regu-

lar motions of his jaws that produced the same soothing effect upon
me as the rocking of my cradle and thereby brought back the kindness
that lives in sleep side by side with the most terrible dreams. So I felt
lulled by the way he ate as if no force could shift the center of his
heart. That encouraged me to take a bite of my own food, but I almost gagged. For the meat was fat and soft and surprisingly intimate
in its taste—something like the confidence of Eyaseyab's tongue was
in my mouth. The pig knew me better than I knew the pig!

I wanted more at once, more of this low and fatty meat, and recollected by way of a little shiver how I had felt once when tasting an
atrocious medicine, its ingredients all secret—the worst taste and
smell of anything I had ever known, and it made me vomit endlessly.
I had nonetheless known in the peace that followed a smell that lived
in my nostrils, soft and warm and sly, even a little dirty, but it was like
the taste of the pig in my mouth now, and so I felt as if I were in communion with the Gods of wet corn, spoiled barley, moldering weeds,
even the odor of roses when they are dead was near to me as I ate the
pig and so I wondered if the pig was an animal not as alive as other
animals or at least lived closer to death, or to say what I really thought,
was stuck in its shit.

"Chew more slowly," said my mother.

Now, with the redolence of my nose, I watched and admired the
delicacy with which the Pharaoh ate, and took instruction from His
movements on how to use my hands. His fingers flew over the food
like birds' tongues, and when He chose to pick up a piece of meat
before Him, it was with one light precise pointing of His fingers. "I
think," He said, "we have had enough of this creature." One of the
servants made a sign. "Yes," Ptah-nem-hotep declared, "it has the
most contrary taste, Horus found the pig an abomination, and Set, of
course, adored it. I find Myself ripped in two by such disagreement
among our Lords."

Now, black servants came in to remove our alabaster plates and
what was left of the pig; I became intrigued with the deft fingers of
these servants and the humor of their movements. It was then I recollected how furious our Syrian servants had become when my father

acquired six black slaves trained for use at the table. It meant—even then I understood the importance—that my mother and father were now at a level of splendor equal to the Pharaoh's near family, a few high Officials, and two or three of our outstanding Generals. We could afford Syrians to bring the food, and blacks to take it away.

By way of my mother's teachings, I knew of course that the right hand was to be treated like a temple. (Indeed, as she said with a pout, I would never see a drawing of a noble Egyptian whose right hand crossed his body—that was only for workers and wrestlers.) No, the right hand was reserved for bearing arms and touching food, and therefore was to be washed in oil of lotus before every meal, whereas the left hand could perform those tasks we would not wish others to observe, particularly the wiping of oneself, in which practice I was not to linger. So I could see that this separation we made between servants who brought food and removed it was connected to the right and left hand. I knew our blacks were not happy in their share of the task. Often I would hear arguments with the Syrians, although such dispute could come to no more than grumbling since, sooner or later, the Overseer of the Kitchen would shrug and say, "It is the Master's orders." Still, I used to think the blacks were remarkable for the depth of the bad mood they could present, and sometimes I would even decide that the poorest black servant had more ability to call upon the foul humor of his Gods than anyone but Menenhetet, Khem-Usha, or my mother (who was kin to both in the power of her worst temper).

Tonight, however, the blacks were surprisingly cheerful, and soon burst into giggles. At one moment, I knew no reason for their mirth; at the next instant, I could have told it all. The Pharaoh was eating the very last of His pig using His left hand. How the blacks smirked.

"They love pig," He cried aloud as they left the room. "They love pig in the lands south of us," and He laughed and added, "yes, the blacker the skin, the sweeter is the taste of the pork, they say," and He looked around the table. "Tell me stories about black people," He demanded abruptly, "for I am fascinated with them. Their customs offer light." He thumped His tail for emphasis, as if to tell us that the time had most certainly come to entertain Him, and for this I was prepared since my mother had already informed me that when the Pharaoh wished to be amused, we should be ready with our stories. They must gleam like swords or be as beautiful as the flowers of the garden.

"I have heard," said my father, "that when an agreement is made on the exchange of property between black chieftains, one spits in the other's mouth, bows, opens his mouth and receives the other's spit in return. That is how they make the bargain legal."

"Can you see?" asked the Pharaoh, "Khem-Usha and I in such a practice?"

He was certainly in a most peculiar mood, in misery, yet most excited. While no one spoke, the air was full of conversation, or so it felt. My thoughts were drawn to His thoughts, and never did I enter more easily into His mind. But He had only one word in His head: Poison!

He looked at us, and shook His head. "Let us," He said, "speak of poison." He smiled at my great-grandfather. "Tell Me, learned Menenhetet, of its nature."

My great-grandfather smiled carefully. "It is a purity that does not cease," he said to the surprise of all of us. Until now he had returned few attempts to bring him into the conversation.

"I like," said our Pharaoh, "the manner in which you bring clarity to difficult matters. The purity-that-does-not-cease. Could one describe love in such a manner?"

"I could," said Menenhetet. "I have often thought that poison and love may come from the same place."

"Your remark is malignant," said Hathfertiti.

"Not at all," said Ptah-nem-hotep. "There is something poisonous about the act of love."

"The pig has put You, Good and Great God, into a foul mood," said my mother.

"Oh, not foul," said Ptah-nem-hotep, "poisonous!" He thumped His tail once more, one sharp thump to reward the precision of His humor. "Yes," He said, "poison is everything that we are not."

"Remarkable," murmured Menenhetet. "I must say Your mind is remarkable."

"A compliment," said the Pharaoh. "A true compliment from the old dog. Listen to Me, you ancient man, you've known them all, known My ancestors better than anyone, so tell us, was there one whose mind proved better than your humble Ptah-nem-hotep's?"

"None quicker," said Menenhetet.

"But stronger in mind?"

"My King of Upper Egypt and my King of Lower Egypt is the strongest in mind," said Menenhetet through the thinnest lips his mouth could form.

"Oh, let us talk of something else," said the Good God. "Let us"— He looked about—"speak of moon-blood."

"But that's awful," said my mother.

"Have you heard the views of black people on such a matter?" He asked.

It was obvious she did not wish to accept the subject. "I think children know little of the views and habits of people who live in the lands to the south," she said with a nod of her head at me.

Eyaseyab having slept with no clothing in my room on many a night, there was little about the occurrence of moon-blood I had yet to learn. Once a month, as regularly as the first passing of the full moon, she would come to bed for a few days with a girdle around her hips, and an odor, no matter how often she bathed, which made me think, if I awakened suddenly, that the river had made a turn in the night and was flowing past our room. I did not dislike the odor so much as I was curious about it. For I had heard the children of our servants whisper to me that all women during the fourteen days of the coming of the moon and the fourteen days of its going were (at one time or another) deep in moon-blood, and some women were even steadfast on such a course, and always of the same day.

I had asked if this were also true for my mother, and my playmate, the son of the blacksmith in our stables, acted as if he were in much trouble, for he dropped to his knees and kissed my toe—a disagreeable sensation since his lips were as chapped and rough (from the glare

of his father's fires) as a lizard's skin. Then he told me that my mother
was the relative of a Goddess and so could not have moon-blood. I
nodded, as if both of us knew this for certain, but in fact I was puz-
zled since I was always hugging my mother's hips and burying my
nose above her knees, higher and higher above her knees as I grew
older, and I never knew such happiness as then. Certainly, my mother
smelled of the best oil from the petals of the lotus, but she had other
odors as well, and now and again, faint as the scent of one departed
fish, there was a hint of the climate of Eyaseyab on the fifteenth night
of the moon when I felt as if I lived in those lands I had never seen to
the south where all the blacks were born and trees half as high as the
Great Pyramid of Khufu grew foliage to cover the sky while the
plants grew in such heat one could not breathe next to them—so
would I feel on the fifteenth night of the moon if Eyaseyab was in
pain, and I wondered how its light could lay such a wound upon
women.

It can be seen that the conversation from which my mother wished
to shield me could hardly be new to my ears, and Ptah-nem-hotep
not only chose to ignore her protest, but gave a smile to me. "Remarkable children must never be protected from what we say," He
said, and added, "don't you think?" to which I replied with a nod, as
if the thought were between the two of us. In fact I agreed. I always
felt as if something dreadful would happen if I could not hear every
word at every feast.

"I had a black slave," said Ptah-nem-hotep, "who told Me that in
the village of his grandfather, they did not allow women full of
moon-blood near the cattle. I cannot tell you how dangerous they
believe a woman to be at such a time. If she touches one of her husband's weapons, he is convinced he will find himself dead in the next
battle."

"They are barbarians," said my mother.

"I'm not so certain," said Ptah-nem-hotep. "There is much to
learn from them."

"Even their temples are made of mud. They do not know how to
cut a piece of stone. Nor how to write," my mother said. "Did You

ever notice how a slave acts when a scribe is at his palette? He whimpers like a monkey and breaks into a sweat."

"Yes," said Ptah-nem-hotep, "but they know of matters we do not know." He paused. "From Memphi, should I wish to send a message to Thebes, how quickly could I get it there?"

"Why, by horse," said my father, "if there are changes of horse, and the riders are fresh and do not sleep, it could be done in two days and two nights."

"More like three days," said the Pharaoh. "But no matter. Further to the south, beyond Kush and Nubia, the same message can be passed through the jungles and from the summit of one great hill to the peak of the next mountain, and down through the great bush of the valleys across the rivers—all of this has been described to Me—yes, across distances equal to the seven days of drifting and rowing down the Nile from Thebes to Memphi, or the two or three days by horse, yes, across all of such distance can the black people send a message in no more than the time it takes for our sun to pass from overhead in the middle of the day to its setting in the West by evening. That is how fast the black people may send a message over such a distance and without roads or trails. I do not call that barbaric."

"How do they do it?" asked my mother.

"By their drums," said Ptah-nem-hotep. "They do not know how to write, nor do they know the secrets and skills of our temples."

"Nor our tombs," said Menenhetet.

"No, not the cunning work of our tombs. But the black people know how to speak with their drums, and very well. They send messages rapidly."

"They are barbarians," said my mother. "We do better. We pluck a silent thought from the air."

"Yes," said my father. "Our Divine Two-House hears many such thoughts."

"My messages are usually incorrect," Ptah-nem-hotep answered. He began to laugh with sufficient force to thump His tail, yet, so soon as He was done, His face became curious and cruel. "At this moment, for instance, a butcher from the market of Ptah has killed his wife in a drunken fit—I see it clearly. Even as he is waiting for his neighbors to seize him, he appeals to Me for mercy. I hear him, but I choose to ignore his voice. He is guilty and a brute. The coarseness of his thought displeases Me."

"Yet, You have heard him?" asked Hathfertiti.

"Tomorrow, if I make inquiries, I will discover that a murder did take place, but not near the market of Ptah. Rather it was in the poor quarter behind the wall back of the Avenue of Amon. The murderer was a brick-maker, I will discover, not a butcher, and it was his brother he killed, not his wife. Or maybe it was his mother. You see, I receive thoughts from My people, but at what a great rate. And in such a din! If I open My ears!" He proceeded to open His eyes instead with a look of pain as if all His senses, ears first, had been assaulted by a clap of sound. "No, I do not often care to listen with all that is best in Me. It is too exhausting. Thoughts, after all, do not travel like arrows, but flutter like feathers, and come up one side or the other. So, I respect the blacks and their drums. They speak clearly to each other across great distances."

My mother said, "I, too, have a story on how to send a message. It concerns a woman who was married to an Egyptian officer, but she is now dead. He is alive and wishes to pass on a few words to her." I heard something delicious in my mother's voice. "One needs more than drums for that," she said.

She was terribly pleased with herself, as if she had learned at last how to make Ptah-nem-hotep—even in His drear mood!—follow her inclination.

"Go on," He said.

"The officer is in love with a charming woman. Yet he feels cursed. His dead wife will not forgive him. At night, in the arms of his new beloved, his member will not stay firm."

"Poor cursed fellow," said Ptah-nem-hotep.

"I expect the same would happen to me," said my father.

"It could never, old friend Nef," said my mother.

"Do go on," said Ptah-nem-hotep.

"Like most army officers," my mother said, "he can't stand priests. Yet he is desperate. So this officer goes to the High Priest."

"Do you know the officer?"

"I cannot say."

Ptah-nem-hotep began to laugh with true pleasure. "If you were a Queen, I would not know what to believe."

"You would never be bored," said my mother.

"Nor could I run My affairs properly."

"I would try to be good for such a reason alone," said Hathfertiti, "that the people of Egypt not suffer."

"Your wife is charming," the Pharaoh said to my father.

"She is blessed by Your presence," said Nef-khep-aukhem.

"Hathfertiti," our Pharaoh said, "what did the High Priest advise the officer?"

"He said to write a letter to the departed wife, and put it in the hand of any good person who had just died."

"Well, what happened?"

"The letter was sent in just such fashion, and the dead woman stopped haunting her husband. His member is firm once more."

"Only with great difficulty can a live woman forgive a man," Ptah-nem-hotep remarked. "I should think a dead woman cannot. Tell me what the officer wrote. It must have been a remarkable letter."

"I do not know what was in the letter."

"That is not enough for Me," said Ptah-nem-hotep. "What would you have said?" He asked Nef-khep-aukhem.

Now, I was amazed by my father. "I would have written to my dead wife that I miss her very much," he said. "Then I would declare that I feel close to her when I make love to other women. 'For I do not think of the other woman then,' I would say, 'only of you. Therefore, restore my strength. Let it come forth that I may be near you.'"

"I think we can appreciate such a speech more than the dead," said my great-grandfather.

"Why, what would you have told her?" asked Hathfertiti.

"I would speak to her as to a subordinate. The dead do not share our strength, you see. They are to us as one part in seven. So their curses can be blown away. We need only concentrate on the one part in seven. That is, after all, why few of us look forward to dying. In my letter, therefore, I would list the amulets I could employ against her, and the prayers purchased for me in the Temple. That should be enough to frighten her."

"Cold treatment of a dead mate," said Ptah-nem-hotep.

"I do not think we should allow anyone to weaken our member," said Menenhetet.

We were silent after this remark.

"You do not ask me what I would have written," said Hathfertiti.

"I am afraid to," said Ptah-nem-hotep.

"I will tell You later," my mother said. "The moment has passed." She paused, and looked at me, and for the first time I felt the point of her cruelty. "Ask my son," she said. "He has been listening."

"I would," I said, "I could write . . ." I did not know how to finish. Something of the same woe that came over me when I looked into the eyes of the dog was in my heart again, and finally I said, "It may be the most terrible story I ever heard," and I began, not to weep— I was determined not to weep before the servants—but I sat with my head down and the tears rolling over my face.

For I heard my mother's thought. I heard the letter she would write. "If you do not restore my strength, I will kill our child," was what she would have said.

In the time that passed, conversations did not take place, but their silence rose and fell. In this uncertainty, much bruised by the cruelty of the letter my mother would have written, I tried to enter her mind again in the hope she would treat me more tenderly, but was given instead the peculiar sensation of looking out on everyone in this room from the eyes of the Pharaoh. Thereby I saw my mother, my father, Menenhetet, and even myself from the Pharaoh's seat. That seemed natural, if most peculiar, and I realized that in trying to slip into my mother's head, I had entered—with obvious success!—into the Pharaoh's thoughts. It could only be due to my mother making her own attempt—at the same moment!—to pass into Ptah-nem-hotep's

mind. And succeeding! Looking out through His eyes, it was not hard
to comprehend that my mother's powers were hardly smaller than my
own.

Next instant, this peculiar, agreeable and natural sensation was
gone. Like the noble who touched pig, I was dipped into the river of
the Pharaoh's misery. Indeed, it was not misery He felt but an emotion for which I hardly knew the word, kin to the feeling I could fear
on awakening that a wretched event was certain to occur in the day to
come. So did I feel the meat of the pig rest like wax in the Pharaoh's
chest—not even to His stomach had the food descended—and some
oppression in this room weighed upon Him, some woe before the
presence of all things to come, as if indeed He could only keep all
troubles from Himself until His strength was gone. Feeling as if I had
entered a cave where every hue was dark as the purple dye that came
from the snails of Tyre, so did I also have the incomparable experience of studying my mother, my father and my great-grandfather
through the Pharaoh's eyes, and my family was not as I knew them,
indeed their expressions were not the same to Him as to me. Por-
trayed on my father's face was a fine cunning I would never have supposed him to have, and Menenhetet showed an obduracy as merciless
as the power of stone to crush one's flesh. Indeed, no matter how little
my great-grandfather had said at dinner, the man Ptah-nem-hotep
saw was more mysterious than stone, a boulder, in truth, that might
shatter in a great fall to reveal at its center a gem—or would it be a live
scorpion? With just such awe and just such doubt did Ptah-nem-
hotep look at Menenhetet.

As for my mother, but for the story she had just told, I would not
have recognized her. She looked more beautiful and more murderous
than my mother. As for myself, looking on myself through His eyes,
I was startled not by my good features but because I was the brightest
little animal I had ever seen, and more alive than I could ever suppose.
Yet my face knew such sorrow and horror! I had not expected that.
Nor was I ready for the love I felt in the Pharaoh's heart when He
looked at me. Nor for the sudden extinction of such love beneath the

awful oppression of the pig's meat in His belly, and I, on this shift of attention, was put back into myself as abruptly as I had left.

Ptah-nem-hotep began to speak. Like an oarsman whose instinct was quick, He began to talk of matters that could carry me away from such turbulence. The servants began to put out the great candles one by one, and the Pharaoh had time to say many things between the closing of one candle's flame and the long guttering of another. As we descended into darkness, I felt the room become like a cave.

He commenced by remarking that my mother's story had an echo of our great kingdom and made Him think of times that had passed. For while my mother, He said, had only spoken of people dwelling among us, or not long dead, yet He found sentiments of such intensity, particularly on the part of the dead wife, reminded Him of the great ancestors who had built the Pyramids.

I could hardly believe it was the voice of Ptah-nem-hotep. He spoke in the solemn measure of Khem-Usha, a slow voice to make me impatient if it were not that the spell of these long sonorous remarks most certainly calmed the uproar of my emotions. After a while, I even began to count how many voices had come out of our Pharaoh on this evening, some shrill, some deep, others coarse, or quick. I had heard reflections, in no more than the turn of a word, of accents that belonged to Bone-Smasher or Ravah, plus hints of a voice from many a province—I could recognize how fit it was that our Good God could, like a God, carry more than one man's voice. All the same, I had no expectation He might also speak like Khem-Usha. It was then I realized that Ptah-nem-hotep could not listen to a voice He did not like without feeling a desire to purge all reverberations of that sound. So we heard the tones of the High Priest, but so skillfully that Khem-Usha, wherever he was, must now feel a disturbance of his august calm, and be drawn like a piece of black-copper-from-heaven toward the imitation of himself by the Pharaoh.

In such a voice, Ptah-nem-hotep told the story. "Of My ancestor, Khufu," He began, "it is said that His eye rested on every stone in the Great Pyramid as it was set in place. It is also said that He dismissed

His little queens of the harem and kept only one wife. To Her, Neter-Khent, He gave the same loyalty as to His own person. For in fidelity, He believed, was His power. Sharing His body with one woman, and no other, would give Khufu the goodness of two noble souls, each with its seven parts. Thereby, They would not merely add their force to one another, but multiply it. Khufu, on the consequence, possessed seven times seven manifestations of strength.

"That," said Ptah-nem-hotep, "is the strength we have forsaken. We do not have the desire to build one Great Pyramid. We spend our lives on a hundred matters. We even conclude that we have chosen wisely. For how can there be a greater risk than to trust someone completely? Khufu may have been seven-by-seven times stronger than any other Pharaoh, but so, too, was His terror of losing His strength. Because of this, He could not go forth from His Palace without fearing that Ra would enter His wife's body, and steal His power. Khufu even built a tomb in the very center of the Pyramid so that the light of Ra could never reach Him. He also left words with His guards that if He should be killed on a visit to the works, Neter-Khent was to be stoned to death. He grew so distrustful of Her fidelity that soon He began to suspect His officers. At last He issued one order. No one in Memphi was to make love without His permission. The populace were obliged to obey. Which common man could trust his neighbors when every sound is heard on the street, and who could depend on the loyalty of his servants to be discreet? All, rich or poor, were obliged to be celibate. This mighty Emperor, His tomb greater than a mountain, commanded the loins of men and the womb of women." Ptah-nem-hotep coughed delicately into His hand. "So, even as Khufu was on His deathbed, He believed that He would never die since He was now wholly a God."

Ptah-nem-hotep paused and looked at each of us in turn, even giving me a full share of His eyes, as if my attention were as valuable as the others'. "I have looked for the wisdom," He said, "and have come to the conclusion that a Pharaoh being in part a man, and, in part a God, must never err too much to one side, or madness becomes His only choice. Khufu erred by seeking all the powers of a God. Whereas I may be seeking too few."

Now the Pharaoh was silent. He moved His lips as if to speak to us again, hesitated, and was truly silent. I knew a change in the evening was on us. All that had been strange yet harmonious, full of little terrors and odd delights, would now be disturbed. Waves were rolling across my thoughts from all directions. Indeed, in the next instant, without a servant to announce him, Khem-Usha came in.

Ten

If I had not seen him before, I would still have known that he must be not only the Vizier but the High Priest as well. For he entered with enough assurance to have been a great foreign Prince. I, who shared with the Pharaoh a breath that only the birds may know, which is that our wings—if we had had wings—would quiver at every shift in the air, knew my Monarch's bad mood had been as well placed as the hinge of a door.

The High Priest passed by me like a Royal Barge. I could have been no more than a raft of papyrus undulating in his wake. He was not a man of great size, but his head was huge, and his shaven scalp, being anointed with oil, made me most aware of how his head gleamed. He was also dressed in a short skirt that showed his heavy thighs, and his shoulders were covered with a wide cape of a sort I soon learned—since my mother's first greeting to the High Priest was to inquire about it—had been worn on rare occasions by the priests of olden times. It put me even more in awe of him than before.

"There may be food from the beast left for you," said our Pharaoh.

"I have had my evening meal," replied Khem-Usha in his slow, deep voice. Then, he added, "I do not observe the Night of the Pig."

Ptah-nem-hotep said: "Let us pray no Gods are insulted by such restraint."

"I do not consider my abstention an insult to any God." His manner suggested that he could annul sacrilege by the correct tones of his voice, and as if to show his displeasure, he did not sit down when our Pharaoh pointed to a seat, but instead said in his deep voice, "I would ask for an audience with Your Ear."

"It is the Night of the Pig. You may speak before all of us."

Khem-Usha was again silent.

"Our little feast has been altered," said the Pharaoh, "by your desire to visit. Yet you do not wish to sit with us. You have something to tell Me, therefore, and it is miserable. Khem-Usha, I was enjoying a merry evening. Do you often see Me when I am merry? No, you may agree with Me, you do not. Thereby, the people of Egypt suffer, don't they? For people can only play when the Gods are merry. You know that?"

Khem-Usha nodded, but with a look of weary patience.

"Tell me, has the King of Byblos killed the Egyptian envoys he is holding?"

"No," said the High Priest, "I did not come to speak of the King of Byblos."

"Nor is it about the Prince in Elam who imprisoned the chieftain favorable to Our interest?"

"It is not," said Khem-Usha.

"Then, I would ask you, Khem-Usha. What new and unhappy matters are before Us?"

"The Chief Scribe of the Vizier's office in Memphi just came to me with a message from the Chief Scribe in Thebes. It arrived by courier this evening. It tells me that two days ago, the metalworkers and the carpenters of the Necropolis of Thebes went on strike."

"Two days ago. Then why could this not wait for morning?"

Where others would have knelt at the rebuke, or even tapped their head seven times to the ground, Khem-Usha merely pursed his lips. "Divine Two-House," he said, "I came to see You tonight because the situation is onerous, and I am much occupied tomorrow. We must discuss it now."

"Yes," said Ptah-nem-hotep, "you have chosen the only moment that is possible." He was pleased by the droll look with which my mother supported His remark.

"It could be said," Khem-Usha stated, "that these Necropolis workers have been treated with much consideration. For two months no heavy work has been laid out for them. Yet these seventy light days of labor were credited to their account for the standard ration. Despite our generosity, they have still gone on strike."

"Khem-Usha, have they been given the ration, or merely credited?"

"The payments were ordered but delayed. All through Phamenoth, the corn, I am afraid, has been a week late. During Pharmuti, the oil and beer have been forthcoming, but, unhappily, not the corn." He paused. "And a shortage of beans. Then the fish could only be given half-ration. So they went on strike."

"How can your Officials allow such short measure?" Ptah-nem-hotep asked.

Now Khem-Usha looked as if there had been good reason why he wished to be alone with the Pharaoh. "The Chief of the Metalworkers and Carpenters in the City of the Dead at Thebes," he said, "is Nam-Shem. He was selected by You. If You recall, Great Two-House, I asked You not to choose our petty Officials. The sympathies of Your godly nature allow You to see the gifts of our people more quickly than their deceits. Nam-Shem owes more than a few gamblers and pimps. So he has sold fifty sacks of corn that belong to the Necropolis workers, and much else. When they did not receive their ration this week, they went on strike."

"Get the food to them," Ptah-nem-hotep said, "from your temple supplies."

Khem-Usha shook his head. "I fear," he said finally, "that is not a wise solution."

"One hundred and eighty-five thousand sacks of corn went to the Temple of Amon last year from the Royal Treasury," Ptah-nem-hotep replied. "Why do you begrudge fifty sacks to these workers?"

"They are well paid," said Khem-Usha. "My priests are not."

Ptah-nem-hotep looked at my great-grandfather, and repeated, "My priests are not!" Then He began to speak with a mockery in His voice that would have proved withering to any man who was less composed than Khem-Usha. "Do you know," He said, "in thirty-one years of His Reign, My Father gave more than one hundred thousand slaves to the temples, half a million head of cattle, and over one million plots of ground. Not to mention His little gifts. One million charms, amulets, and scarabs. Twenty million bouquets of flowers. Six million loaves of bread! I go over His records—I would not believe the amounts if I did not know that I, year by year, have been paying out nearly as much to Khem-Usha and his temples, and our Royal Treasury is not nearly so rich. Perhaps our festivals do not bring the river to the right height. Too much or too little—usually too little. Either I am not near enough to Amon, or you, Khem-Usha, do not say the prayers well enough. In any case, we are certainly low on grain. All the same, I do not know how you can begrudge fifty sacks of corn. My Father gave the temples half a million fish in thirty years and two million jars of incense, honey, and oil. A great Pharaoh was My Father, Ramses the Third, but not great enough to say no to the demands of the Temple on the Treasury. And I am only in His shadow. All the same, I tell you, Khem-Usha, give the Necropolis workers their share of grain. Put that situation in order. If I have made a mistake with Nam-Shem, do not take pride in it."

"I must do as You say," said Khem-Usha, "but I will also remark that Your gift will encourage these workers to strike again, and for less."

"Put the situation in order," Ptah-nem-hotep repeated.

Khem-Usha's face was without expression. He answered, "It has been, Divine Two-House, another occasion to live in the subtlety of Your heart. Yet, before I go, I must still ask for an audience alone. There is another matter, and I can speak of it before no one."

"As I have said, it is the Night of the Pig. So, tell it to all."

Khem-Usha, in disobedience of the Pharaoh, bent forward, however, and whispered into His ear. Then they looked into each other's eyes. I felt something in my balance waver. Ptah-nem-hotep said, "Yes, perhaps I will walk with you through the garden," and with a quick smile in our direction for so suddenly removing Himself, left with His High Priest and Vizier.

Eleven

While He was gone, my parents did not speak. Nor did Menenhetet utter a sound. A torpor came over me, full of the taste of the pig.

Stuffed, and a little confused by what had just taken place, I felt close to sleep. Like a bruise whose pain turns at last into tenderness, I was ready to forgive my mother. Maybe it was the golden light of the last candles reflecting in my gold goblet, but I soon began to mystify myself with the loveliness of the thought that the light in this room once lived in an abode of honey. For my mother had told me that the wax to make these candles came from the beehives of the Pharaoh. By such a light, I looked again at my parents, especially at the beauty of my mother, and thought I had never witnessed as many faces within her as I glimpsed tonight. Steeped in their thoughts, my heart now felt as mellow as any fifty-year-old, and I was so filled with cynicism (the first time ever to feel such superiority!) that I had to smile at how my mother, when at home, showed little of whatever tact she had offered tonight. Alone among us, she would display no respect nor patience when speaking to my father. Whatever was her own mood became the mood of our house. Her bad humors, quite the equal, as I say, of any black servant, used to leave me with the feeling that the day had grown intolerably hot. I used to believe she had the power to affect our weather; after long burning afternoons, her bad humor, if atrocious enough, was ready to spoil the sunset, and I remember suffocating evenings when the last clouds were black over the western hills.

When Menenhetet was present, however, another side of my mother would come forth. She could look as demure then, as a girl of eighteen, and I did not feel like her son so much as her younger brother, both of us there to worship Menenhetet, or so I used to think until the glimpse of them together last night which, if taken with her boldness tonight, made me think with some fear: "She has given everything to raising me. But now she wants more for herself."

I was also aware that our Pharaoh had been gone too long. My family was stirring uneasily. Just before the sight of His empty seat would most definitely spoil the pleasure of the evening, He came back. But in a peculiar state. I felt much unhappiness in Him, yet He was bright in His manner and even more feverish than before.

At once, He made a sign with His hand to the servants, and four Syrians brought us gifts.

A headrest of silver was given to my father, and Menenhetet received a small doll, carved in ivory, of a man dressed in fine linen. When one pressed the hips of this gift, as my great-grandfather soon did, a pale yellow phallus stood up, at which my father giggled uncontrollably for it had a red painted tip.

My mother was presented a grasshopper made of colored glass, and the head, which had two small rubies for eyes, was removable. Now, the loveliest odor of perfume wafted forth.

"Do not open it," said Ptah-nem-hotep, "for soon we will leave this room. Save it, I implore you, to sweeten the air of the next. Oh, dear, the boy," He said and made a gesture with His hand as if He had forgotten me, but of course He hadn't, and the servants brought out a fine small box in which rested the two pieces of black-copper-from-heaven. I was so delighted I forgot everything at once in playing with my bars and their pull seemed more mysterious than before, indeed when I closed my eyes, I could no longer know for certain what was up and down, so strangely were my hands drawn about. Ptah-nem-hotep looked then at my great-grandfather and said, "Explain this wonder to Me."

"I have seen nothing like it before," said Menenhetet. "This is not a piece of amber to draw to itself a few snips of cloth. Nor is it the charm of one eye upon another. This attraction has true weight."

"Would you suppose," asked our Pharaoh, "that there is desire in one piece of metal for the other?"

"I would say it is more than desire, and like a bend in the nature of things."

I could hear the curiosity in Ptah-nem-hotep's voice when He replied: "Where would you find this bend? In the river? In the sky?"

"I would be so bold as to speak of a bend in the passage of time," my great-grandfather murmured.

"I do not know what you mean. One could speak as easily of a knot or a cramp. Perhaps, dear doctor, you mean an inflammation of time?"

I wished to cry out to the Pharaoh, "Do not mock my great-grandfather or harm will come to all of us," but I did not dare.

Menenhetet, however, was as powerful as stone in the force of his silence. Only when all of us were looking at him, would he speak. "I wonder if such attraction is not a summons from the past that calls upon the future?"

Ptah-nem-hotep touched His tail most delicately to the table. "Fine," He said, "Wonderful. Each of us must know one eye of Horus. Between us, we ought to find the truth. For I would say: all-that-is-yet-to-come may be weighing upon what-has-passed." He nodded, He exhaled His breath, and stood up. We stood up. Our feast was over.

The servants led us out of the dining room, up some marble stairs, across many fountains and palms to a covered patio on which were sofas to recline. At the commencement of our view stood pillars of marble as noble as any on the facade of a temple, and beyond were the buildings of the Palace and many courtyards and gardens and walls, even a view of the river. I was so intent on what could be glimpsed in the distance that I hardly noticed how the servants had begun to bring in, one by one, a number of small covered boxes, set on stands, and the Pharaoh nodded as each was set in place. I had learned enough about Ptah-nem-hotep to know that a marvel you could encounter only in His Presence was soon to be revealed.

As the last torch was extinguished, each of the eight blacks came to stand by one of the hooded cages. In the darkness, we were unable to see each other's faces. Now, Ptah-nem-hotep clicked His tongue, and on that sound, the hoods were removed.

The darkness began to glow. Slowly we could see what He had prepared. Each cage was covered with a transparent linen. From the interior, behind each veil, appeared the lights of little stars who flitted back and forth, a myriad of lights in every cage. We gasped in pleasure, then applauded. What untold difficulty to capture so many hundreds of fireflies! How soft were the features of my mother by such a light, and, oh, the wealth of her love. We sat in a darkness lit by golden stars.

Twelve

 "By the light of these fireflies," said my mother, "what is Your request?"

"But I have none," said Ptah-nem-hotep.

"In our family," replied my mother, "we look to return a delight for a delight. What would You desire of us? It is Yours." I could not bear the boldness in her eyes as she looked at Him.

"I can think of many pleasures," said Ptah-nem-hotep, but He laughed as if to turn her away. "Let Me content Myself with expressing one desire. I would say I have contemplated it for years." As if, on reflection, this was certainly true, He nodded, and said, "The light of these mites makes Me think of the campfires of ancient armies." There was a quick exclamation from my father at the charm of this thought. Ptah-nem-hotep nodded again. "Yes," He went on, "I would ask of the General, your own grandfather Menenhetet who has much impressed Me with his thoughts on time, that he tell us the story of the Battle of Kadesh."

"I do not know," said Menenhetet slowly, "when last I have spoken of that day."

"I can only inform you," said Ptah-nem-hotep, "that I see this bat-

tle often. The heroism of My ancestor, Ramses the Second, appears in
My dreams. So, I say, should you wish to return a delight for a delight, yes, tell Me of the Battle of Kadesh."

My great-grandfather took a pause, and bowed. "As Hathfertiti
says, it is the custom of our family." He looked no happier, however,
than a thundercloud.

When he did not say another word, my mother's voice came forth.
"Speak of the battle," she said, and there was an annoyance in her
tone as if Menenhetet would spoil much if he did not take care.

Then we were all silent before the current of ill-will in my great-
grandfather. His face had the unspoken clamor of the sky before a
storm, and I could feel the force of this bad feeling pass directly into
my mother. Ugly as I knew his thoughts would be, I was not prepared
for such bitterness. "The degenerate who sups on bat shit has been
invited to spill a few secrets," were the unspoken words that went
from my great-grandfather to my mother.

"Know that I take pleasure to see you in My house," said Ptah-
nem-hotep into the silence.

Menenhetet bowed again.

"I can speak," he said, "in four voices. I can address You as the
young peasant who became a charioteer and rose to be General-of-
All-the-Armies, commanding the Divisions of Amon, Ra, Ptah, and
Set during the reign of Ramses the Second; I can inform you how in
my second life I was the youngest High Priest of Thebes during the
old age of the same Ramses the Second. Equally, I can speak of the
third Menenhetet, who became the wealthiest of the wealthy. Born
in the reign of Merneptah, he lived through Siptah, Seti the Second,
and other such Pharaohs as Setnacht. Now, if You desire, I can speak
as I am here, *Your* Menenhetet, a nobleman, a General, and later a
doctor of renown. I can tell, should You wish to hear, of the plot
against Your Father, or of the brief and miserable thrones of Ramses
the Fourth, Ramses the Fifth, Ramses the Sixth, Ramses the Seventh,
and Ramses the Eighth, who have all been lost to us in twenty-five
years, even as Your Majesty may reign longer than all of Them together."

I had often been told that the greatest mark of respect a man could give himself was to speak in a full voice on the worth of his rank and achievements. But my great-grandfather's speech was so short, it seemed rude, and then he startled us even more by his next words. They departed from every custom on how to address the Pharaoh. He now said: "Twice-Divine House, You speak of being happy to see me. This is, however, the Night of the Pig. So I will dare to say that until tonight, You have not invited me to Your Court in the seven years of Your Reign. Yet, now, You inform me that Your finest pleasure would be to hear an account of Your ancestor, Ramses the Second, at the Battle of Kadesh. My tongue is sour in my teeth. I waited for seven years with more in my heart than any man in Your realm. My ruler never called on me."

Hathfertiti made a choked sound.

A clear tone came, however, into our Pharaoh's voice, as if at last He had before Him a man who spoke his thoughts. "Say more," He commanded.

"Good and Great God, You will abhor what I say."

"I wish to hear it."

"Of those in Your Court who laugh at me, You are the first."

"I am not."

"Not tonight."

"No, it is true, I do not laugh at you tonight. I have laughed at you on other evenings."

"The echoes," said Menenhetet, "of such good humor have come back to me."

Ptah-nem-hotep nodded. "I know no one in My Court," he said, "who does not in some manner respect you. They certainly fear you. Nonetheless, you are the source of much derision. Do you have no idea why this is so?"

"I would like to hear Your voice give me the reason."

"The secret habits of our esteemed Menenhetet have been described as disagreeable."

"They are revolting," my great-grandfather replied. "I am known as the degenerate who sups on bat shit."

"There," said my mother, "he has spoken it aloud."

"Bats," said Menenhetet, "are filthy creatures, hysterical as monkeys, restless as vermin."

"Who can disagree?" said our Pharaoh. "It may be easier to speak of you with derision than comprehend your habit."

They looked at one another in the silence of men who have been saying too much.

"Do you do this," asked the Pharaoh, "in the practice of magic?"

Menenhetet nodded. "I wished to use what was learned in other lives."

"And did you succeed?"

"There was a time when I could not give up the pursuit of curious questions. So I refused to draw back from the voice that told of revelations to be found in the unspeakable odium of bats."

"You went forward?"

"For a few weeks, many years ago, I pursued the question, yes. I supped once, then twice on that loathsome paste. It offends me now to speak of it, but I found it necessary then, and I was given the answer I was looking for. It was smaller than I hoped, and that should have been the end of it, but the trusted servant who aided me in the preparation of the ceremony saw fit to tell one friend. No man can be trusted altogether. By the next night, all of Memphi was agog. I do not think there was a noble lad who did not hear of it. I, who wished to use what I had learned . . ."

"To what purpose?"

"To enrich," said Menenhetet, "the marrow of our failing lands." When our Pharaoh looked at him in some surprise, my great-grandfather held up his hand as if he were for a moment our Monarch. "I do not speak," he said, "of prayers that ask the river to rise to a good height. That is for priests. I speak of matters I do not wish to explain. It would take a knowledge of my four lives to begin to comprehend certain ceremonies"—here, at the look of displeasure on Ptah-nem-hotep's mouth, as cruel in its curve as the edge of a sword (so that I realized at once and forever how the desire to torture others came quickest to our Pharaoh when His curiosity was aroused, then balked) my great-grandfather shifted in the confidence of his manner long enough to say, "A man who would deal in strange ceremonies, and employ words of power, finds that he must address himself to one God more than others. To that God is sent not only the large part of his rituals, but his thoughts. So I sought to be the agent of Osiris, since He has spoken to me in the Land of the Dead. Only He, I believed, could enrich the marrow of our failing lands."

Now, no one was able to say a word, and the dignity of my great-grandfather was like the composure of a statue.

Who but Ptah-nem-hotep could enter such a silence? "I," He said, "am the Pharaoh Who reminds you most of Osiris?"

"Yes," my great-grandfather replied, "I would say it is so." He was watching the light of our Pharaoh's eyes (for even in the soft glow of the fireflies, a light was there to see).

"That is interesting. Please go on. I would like to hear of the injuries done to you by My Court."

"I do not wish to complain in Your Presence, but I will say that the little treachery of my servant went far. The desired effect of the ceremonies I undertook was undone by the derision of Your nobles. To my intolerable shame, I knew much but could do little."

"A magician," said Ptah-nem-hotep, "ought to be able to overcome much ridicule."

"The Gods listen to mean thoughts. They are obliged to. None of us is without magic when we speak to the Gods in a dream."

"Yet no more than one faithless servant, you say, is the reason for these terrible stories."

"I would not make that claim," said Menenhetet. "I have done many things of which pious people—and those who are less than pious—would not approve. But in the public mind, two foul suppers equal all the rest. It is a great pity. There is so much I would teach."

"Yes, I believe that. You may have been much slandered. Although I wonder. Is it," asked Ptah-nem-hotep, "no more than these stories about the bats that stick to you, or is it—and I will be as frank as the license of this night—is it not the subject of excrement itself that captures your thoughts? I have heard it said that as a doctor, your cures were extreme."

"I have led," said Menenhetet, "by my own understanding of such matters, an upright life. I have no fear of any subject, not when I can speak to a Pharaoh as wise in His understanding as Yourself. No," he said, "no, I feel no shame in telling of these mysteries. It is others who cannot bear to listen."

"I know I cannot," Hathfertiti told him. "The evening will be marred." She said it in so strong a voice that my great-grandfather looked at her with all the force of his eyes, and the strength of his will went back and forth with hers until she could stare at my great-grandfather no longer. It was his hour.

"If you would speak," said Ptah-nem-hotep.

"I will," said Menenhetet, and inclined his head to Hathfertiti. "We do not know," he said, "how such thoughts came to Egypt, but for a long time we have concocted our medicines of monkeys' dung, the pellets of snakes, goat balls, the manure of horses, cow flop, bird droppings, even the matter of our own honey-pots." He paused. "There came a time when I was obliged to ponder the qualities of the food we eat. Not only do we take our strength from it, but what we cannot use, or what we do not wish to use, is cast out. Excrement is full of all that is too despicable for us, but it also may contain all that we cannot afford to take into ourselves—all that is too rich, too courageous, or too proud for our bearing. If this is the Night of the Pig, then I say to You that more honesty, generosity, and loyalty to Your service is going to be found in the turds of Your nobles, grand ladies, and Your High Priest, than comes from the words in their mouths. For whichever food will nourish hypocrisy is quickly absorbed by Your royal friends, but every virtue You might wish them to guard for You is passed through."

"Well said," said Ptah-nem-hotep. "None of this is wholly strange to My ear." Indeed, His voice was so thin that He must have shared some of my great-grandfather's bitterness. There, in the lovely light of the fireflies, He argued, however, with the question. "Can you,"

He asked, "ignore the wisdom of the common people? They certainly regard clean linen as a sign of rank. Whoever is immaculate can take a stick to a fellow who is filthy. We even speak of a man we do not respect as equal to dung. Yet, your logic intrigues Me all the same. I cannot dispute it instantly. It is so curious. If our excrement carries away not only the worst of us but also the best, how could you find any virtue in the bowels of a man of noble character? By your argument, the meanest poisons ought to come out of him first. In that case, is the reverse not also true? Doesn't the poor man offer gold by way of his rear end? Why has the common wisdom of Egypt not brought everyone rushing to the meanest latrines of the foulest beggars? Think what wealth, bravery and generosity has to be found in the evacuations of such wretches."

Now, Hathfertiti roared with laughter.

My great-grandfather was, however, undisturbed. "Yes," he said, "like the Lady Hathfertiti, we laugh at shit—but then, we always laugh when a truth is suddenly disclosed and as quickly concealed. The Gods have tickled us with the truth. So we laugh."

"You do not answer the question, my great-grandfather," I burst out suddenly.

"Are you interested?" asked the Pharaoh.

I nodded profoundly. The room rang with laughter, and I wondered of which truth I had just given them a glimpse.

"Yes," said Ptah-nem-hotep when everyone was silent again, "I, too, want an answer."

"I would agree," replied Menenhetet, "that a noble man would reject every foul temptation in his food. So, indeed, his leavings can offer nothing but mean poisons, and that would always be true if it were not that some noble men live with a terrible shame. When offered the opportunity to take a great chance, they do not dare. After all, one cannot welcome every trial presented by life, or the bravest of us would soon be dead. Yet, on the consequence we must recognize that each time a difficult choice is avoided, the best part of a noble man chooses to depart by way of his buttocks."

Ptah-nem-hotep looked again at my great-grandfather. "I still do not understand," He said in a voice that mocked the subject as much as it betrayed His interest, "why the turds of riffraff are not coveted then by My Councillors? How could anything, according to you, be more invigorating for such people than a bath in the worst slops?"

"Your Councillors know better. The poor and wretched have the power to put a curse on their excrement. Otherwise, not even shit would belong to them."

"I am most impressed," said Ptah-nem-hotep, "by this last remark."

"It was so well said, my Lord," said Hathfertiti. Her voice had turned coarse, and I wondered whether it was the conversation, the wine, the beer, the pig, or all of it. She was certainly less respectful to my great-grandfather, and wanton when she looked at the Pharaoh. Several times I tried to enter her head but could see little more than an uproar of naked bodies as bawdy as wrestlers in a pit. Then I recognized the face of Ravah in the swarm, and Ptah-nem-hotep, and my father, and great-grandfather, were also there, my mother among them naked and with her mouth open.

Thirteen

Even by the pale light of the fireflies, I could see that Ptah-nem-hotep was not calm. If at first I thought the cause for His disturbance was equal to mine, and neither of us could forgive my mother for her outrageous inclinations, I soon recognized that my great-grandfather's conversation must have had as much effect on Him. In either case, my Pharaoh's mind was now concerned with buttocks. In His thoughts, they were all about Him. Then they became one great pair that turned into the face of Khem-Usha.

At this moment, my Pharaoh stood up, and, to everyone's surprise, beckoned to my great-grandfather. "Come," He said, "there is a room I would show you." For a moment, I even thought He would invite me as well. His eyes seemed to stare again into mine with great love—or so I believed—but then He stepped out with my great-grandfather, and, much to my mother's vast annoyance at so sudden a departure, was gone.

She stood up as soon as they had passed between the pillars, and walked about like a panther tethered to a stake. I had once seen such an animal in my great-grandfather's gardens, and on the instant he was thrown a piece of meat, the beast would snatch it in the air. So was my mother ready to tear at my father in the moment he said, "I speak not to upbraid you . . ."

"Do not speak," she said.

"I must tell you."

"Is the child asleep?" asked my mother.

I gave a sad whimper, as from a dream, which was not so false, for I always felt sorrow larger than myself when they would fight.

"You do not see," said my father, "how women throw themselves before Him every day. He is bored by such excessive attentions."

"I do not throw myself. I offer myself. And I do it to delight you. For if I succeed, what will give you more pleasure than to know for the rest of your life that every time you come forth into me, He will also be there?" She came to a stop in her pacing. "Doesn't that moisten your little heart? Say you do not want the Pharaoh to know me for a night."

"Please be silent. The air has echoes."

"Everyone knows I am prodigiously faithful to you." My mother gave her coarse laugh.

My father whispered. "I tell you to remember that you are a lady. I do not recognize the woman I see tonight. You laugh so crudely."

"Is that your true speech? I may do what I want, but until I do, please act like a lady."

"I do not think that is what I wish to say."

"Yes, it is. You say it very well. You speak as well as I used to speak when we were first married. You see, old friend Nef, you stole my good manners, and left me yours—which come from your father— that horrible man. If I am too crude for your taste, it is because I, a Princess, made the mistake, when young, of liking you."

After such a speech, my father was silent; indeed, he was always silent after their quarrels. They ended with my mother victorious and carrying herself like a Queen, but then, my father was so sly in his defeat that I often wondered if he did not make himself indispensable to my mother. Could she ever feel so powerful with anyone else?

Still, on this night, my father surprised me. He returned to the quarrel after it was lost. "I think you are stupid," he burst out. "You are doing it all wrong. Admit, at least, that I know Him well. He is a Good and Great God, but He lives with many burdens. So He is not drawn to women who are much pleased with themselves. Such women are overbearing in His eyes."

"You are wrong. He has no Queen, and wants one. He has not even an attractive mistress. In His heart, and I have lived in His heart on this night, He is raw. There is no Goddess to be the sole of His foot, to kiss His thigh and anoint His sword. He is a Pharaoh without a Crook . . ."

"Be silent."

". . . or a Flail. I would be His cunt and His rudder, His precious stone and His slave. I need to hear no more from you about my manners, you son of a shit-collector."

"You are a fool," said my father. "You want Him so much that you will push Him away. Then He will look at me and think, 'I have felt fear before the woman of My Overseer.' He will never forgive me for that."

"I will have Him," said my mother, "before this night is over."

"It will turn out badly," said my father. "If I lose my position, we will be seen as the servants of Menenhetet, and not much more."

She did not reply, but I could feel such a large greed live next to such great fear in her, that I did not wish to be near them any longer. Since I could not discover Ptah-nem-hotep nor my great-grandfather in my thoughts, nor have any idea of where they had gone, so did I slip down the first steps into sleep, but my eyes had barely closed before I met in my wanderings no one other than the High Priest Khem-Usha, and he drew close, and his face was as large and round as the moon. He smelled like the incense that is laid into a winding cloth. Although, by opening my eyes, I could still see my parents, they were not in my dream. Instead, the Pharaoh now came forth and stood beside Khem-Usha.

"Speak to us of spells," said the High Priest to me.

A small force, felt as clearly as a finger pushing on my forehead, brought my eyes up into the large round face of Khem-Usha, and I said, "To set a spell, one must walk around the walls. One must encircle the foe."

"Hear the child," said Ptah-nem-hotep. "You will learn much from him, Khem-Usha."

I do not know why what I had said was worthy of praise, but I spoke the next thought so soon as it came to me. "After you have made a tour of the walls," I said, "you may look for a way to enter them." I did not know what I meant so much as I understood that I was now, and most certainly, in some kind of spell. For by its power, Khem-Usha disappeared and I saw my great-grandfather and Ptah-nem-hotep in a strange room, and listened to their conversation.

Of course, I could not be certain whether my Monarch and Menenhetet had been silent during my parents' quarrel and only began to speak now, or whether all that I would soon hear should have been lost, if not for the power of my spell to bring back their voices.

I do know that I could still see the fireflies in their cages, and my parents lay apart, reclining on separate sofas, the sense of disagreement between them as still as a wall. I continued to lie on my couch but could barely keep before me the pillars of this patio, for I was seeing another room more clearly and it was like the place where painted fish had swum along the floor beneath my feet. Here, however, were paintings of the fields in time of sowing, and the faces of many peasants leading their cattle. I even saw the hooves of these animals spattered with mud, and among them, leopard's tail in His left hand, the golden crook in His right, was Ptah-nem-hotep standing with His golden sandals on a field of mud, but I knew the mud was painted for His feet remained immaculate.

"You spoke," He said to Menenhetet, "with such clarity that I decided to take you here. Since no noble other than yourself has entered this chamber, you will be the first to witness what I have brought forth. Come, I will show you," and He took my great-grandfather by the elbow, a most exceptional courtesy, and led him over to the dais on which was a golden throne. Beside it was a golden trough, and above, a golden shaduf. Now Ptah-nem-hotep lifted the golden seat of the throne to reveal a seat of ebony beneath and it had a hole.

"You were not as alone in your thoughts," He said to Menenhetet, "as you supposed. You could not know it, but each morning it has been My habit to meditate while I sit on the Golden Bowl. For years, I have been contemplating the afflictions of My Two-Lands, yes, our lack of rain and our beneficent flood (on those rare years, at least, when it chooses to be beneficent!). I brood upon our valley so deep in its black soil, so incomparable in its fertility, and so narrow, such a little strip of cultivation between the desert of the East and the desert of the West. Then I sometimes think that our Egypt is not unlike the crack between two great buttocks. Do you know, that curious thought enabled Me to feel a little veneration for the custom of the Golden Bowl. As you know, everyone says of Me that I am lacking in sufficient piety to be a good Pharaoh, but a wise leader does not look to feel false respect. Each morning when the Overseer would take that little golden pot with its contents—My contents—out to My herb garden, I would be cheered by the observation that the Gods know how to take care of many matters through one Pharaoh. So They would employ My leavings as carefully and usefully as My thoughts, My words, the grace of My gestures, or My decrees. As you spoke, it therefore became clear to Me—and most agreeably, most warmly—that My thoughts which had always seemed so curious to Me, so near to unacceptable (even if I am a Pharaoh) were shared by you. I felt stronger in all that I already believed. Each morning, you see, I had told Myself that whatever in Me was failing to serve the interests of the Two-Lands, whatever I might lack in dedication, piety, raw bravery, and martial spirit—for, alas, I am a prudent man— were, nonetheless, all present in My stool. By that path could My gardeners bring forth the most splendid herbs and vegetables and flowers and spices to enrich those priests, officers, and overseers I consider most devoted to the Life-Health-Strength of our Egypt. For years that has been a most reassuring thought. I have made lists of particular men and women who deserve to receive this produce. Even today, I told a scribe to send eight tomatoes to Rut-sekh, that worthy rock-cutter. Contemplate, then, My horror when I discovered in this last year that the Overseer of the Golden Bowl was a thief. On torture, he confessed that he was selling to sorcerers. My garden had been receiving *his* excrement in substitute for *Mine*!

"These are the years when no one in Egypt can be trusted. We do not speak of it, but there are more tomb robberies than ever before— I have studied the records. The grain accounts are calculated by corrupt officials. Theft in high places is frequent. That is bad enough. But the Overseer of the Golden Bowl was stealing from My person. It convinced Me more than any raids on our frontiers that the Two-Lands are weak. I have not gained the respect of the Gods. Not at least as other Pharaohs. They have been able to speak to Them better than I." He was silent, but when Menenhetet said nothing, He went on.

"It was then I decided to entrust Myself to the old artificer, Ptah, My namesake. If no Overseer could be trusted, then so be it, only the waters raised by a shaduf, pumped by Me, could carry away My leavings. I had the pipes laid out in the garden cleverly by different workmen, piece by piece, and the troughs put in here. No one saw it all. Now the waters incline to My garden outside this wall and, do you know, it serves. My plots, furrow by furrow, receive the trickle of this small river. Whenever there is need of more inundation, I pour another bucket down," which He did, and a fly leaped up from the hole in the throne and agitated the air between them. "This all calls for perfume, I promise you, and those blind blacks who clean it all are perplexed by so much sweet air. They know this chamber receives no guests. Yet My herbs and vegetables have never been better. They were served to all of you tonight. You could feel it: those onions and cabbages cast a spell."

"They did," said Menenhetet.

"Tell Me, to your knowledge: Have you ever heard of such a sluiceway as I have brought forth?"

"Not once."

"I knew it was Mine alone. Otherwise, I would not have felt such fear at making the change. I want to ask: Do you approve of what I have done?"

"I do not know."

"Your reply is worthy of Khem-Usha."

"I must say I fear bad luck. It may weaken all that there is." My great-grandfather bowed. "When I was appointed by Ramses the Second to the service of His Great Queen, Nefertiri, She showed me a fine mirror. It was the first true mirror into which I ever looked, and I said, 'This will change all that there is.' I was right. Egypt is weak today. I think Your sluice will stir too many pots."

"No, you do not like what I have brought forth." Ptah-nem-hotep sighed. "Well, you have the courage to tell Me so. But I would prefer that you had liked it. I feel like a prisoner. So much am I bound by the habits of My ancestors. Sometimes I think that the ills of our Two-Lands begin with these customs that bind Me. Then I say to Myself, 'Perhaps I am not fit to be a Pharaoh.'"

Softly, my great-grandfather replied, "Do You wait for me to say that You are?"

"You are right. I am the one who does not think well of this Pharaoh. But then there are nights when I do not believe that the Gods are indeed My ancestors. At such times I do not feel near to Them, nor do I feel that My people love Me. Do you?"

"You call upon me," said my great-grandfather, "after seven years of neglect, and wish me to love You. I do not know if I can. One must serve a Pharaoh to express true devotion. One must be trusted by Him."

"And I trust no one?"

"I cannot say."

Ptah-nem-hotep touched His finger to the side of His nose. "I see," He said, "that My candor must equal yours. I did not think I would, but I will talk to you. I must speak to someone. For I have kept My tongue to Myself all these years, and My heart is like a room that is never opened. I fear that behind the door all is ready to wither."

Fourteen

Now, even as He had promised, the Pharaoh spoke for a long time, or so, within the turns of my spell, did it seem long. My parents did not speak, and only the fireflies danced, but with such close response to the Pharaoh's voice that in truth I saw Him and my great-grandfather most clearly.

"I cannot bear Khem-Usha," said the Pharaoh. "You may ask— why then did I leave My guests to go with him? What could he have said to take Me out of My chair, and away from you and your family? Well, that, I cannot speak of yet. Say it is a matter between Khem-Usha and Myself, a call on a boyhood friendship—except we never liked each other. Now, however, it is worse. I cannot bear priests. They inhabit My thoughts. They are like ants upon the very food of My thought. And he is My High Priest. When I visit Thebes, he up-braids Me for not coming to the Temple of Amon more often, then he dares to scold Me here for not attending the Temple of Ptah. 'Don't you realize,' I said to him, 'that I spent part of My boyhood in the Hat-Ka-Ptah, right here in Memphi. Let Me remind you, Khem-Usha,' I told him, 'that when I was a child, I caught the eye of the King, My Father, and it created such jealousy in the harem that My mother was terrified one of the other little queens would do away with Me. Don't you remember, Khem-Usha?' I said to him, and of course he did. His mother was the little queen of whom My mother was so frightened. There could not have been a harem prince with poorer prospects than My own in those days. There were all those half brothers ahead of Me, and everybody was certain I would become a priest. Nobody knew My kinsmen would die so quickly, did they then?" Now He struck the leopard's tail across His own thigh. "I tell you too much," He said.

"Yes," my great-grandfather replied. "Tomorrow, You will not forgive me for all you have said tonight."

"I will. You would do well to trust Me. I have decided to trust you, My friend."

"You are confident that I am Your friend?" asked Menenhetet.

"At the least, you are the enemy of My enemy." Ptah-nem-hotep gave His short laugh.

My great-grandfather bowed.

"I wish to talk more than you can realize," the Pharaoh said. "I feel a great wrath toward Khem-Usha. I would end his influence upon Me. I do not understand him. Tonight, while we were alone, he spoke for longer than I have ever heard him go on in My presence. I could not believe it! Khem-Usha, the imperturbable. Can there ever have been a High Priest so calm as Khem-Usha? But tonight, he was full of complaints. He is not so indifferent to the Feast of the Pig as he pretends. On all other nights he may act as if his fingers are in the honey of Maat, and he alone knows the sweetness of eternal calm, but tonight I must have roused him more than I thought. He certainly acted as if it were the Night of the Pig." Ptah-nem-hotep smiled. "Once he was alone with Me, a few of his complaints came forth. The true ones. I could welcome that. Kings are lied to by all people, so the truth is air to Me and fresh blood. The Night of the Pig feels like the Night of the Blessed Fields. I come to know the mind of others more quickly. That enables Me to rule with justice, not vanity. And if I rule with justice, then, respect Me or not, the Gods still have to offer Their support. That must be true. So I encouraged Khem-Usha to speak. To My surprise, he complained that his duties were too many. That was a most unusual remark. I have never seen any other man take so many tasks upon himself. Khem-Usha understands piety: Duty brings power. So I did not believe it when he said that he could not continue to act as My Vizier.

"Why, after the last Vizier died, Khem-Usha employed every means to be appointed as acting Vizier. He would, he promised, fulfill the task for Me until I could find a truly suitable man. Of course, he knew there were not many able people in the Court any more. While I did not like him much, I chose him. He did the work. Now he is complaining that the task is too hard. Too hard, he means, unless he is given the full title of Vizier as well. So I decided to tease him. 'That is true,' I told him. 'I think you might give up trying to be both High Priest and Vizier.'

"Do you know, he only nodded when I said this. Then he enumerated his duties as if I were not familiar with them. He just about whined through this speech. I did not appreciate what he was doing. I did not understand how clever he is. On every other day of the year he will never say a word unless he can say it slowly. He has no feelings that are small. His manner looks to move you aside—like a hippopotamus! If I give him a rebuff, he merely adds it to his weight—all the better to bulk him up—one is dealing with a hippopotamus!" Now Ptah-nem-hotep stopped and gave such a curious look to my great-grandfather that I did not know if His mouth was twisted by derision or by anguish, but then I realized He was speaking once more in the exact voice of Khem-Usha, and in his manner as well, that same voice which went on much too steadily for anyone to interrupt. "Each morning," He began, "after prayers are conducted at dawn, I must unseal the heavy doors of the Court so that the office of the Royal Estate may open. Without me, no day of governing can begin. So, there is no morning when I do not read every report that comes from the authorities of the Crown in each nome of the forty-two nomes. Even the most petty official is required to write to me three times a year—on the first day of Sowing, of Harvest, and of Inundation. By this means am I able to see into many lies these same officials have forgotten, for they contradict themselves, or tell the truth today where yesterday they did not. So I am alert to the seed of upheaval in a modest discontent, and can sniff the beginnings of treason in the smallest reluctance to follow orders. In that manner, no nome can stir without my knowledge. As Minister of War, I review each month the disposition of our troops within the Two-Lands, and abroad. As Minister of Ecclesiastical Affairs, I oversee the scribes who tally the gifts given to the temples. As Minister of Economic Affairs, I must know when to proclaim the cutting of timber and the irrigation of the canals. As Minister of Justice, I review the decisions of all judges in all courts, and I not only perform these tasks daily but each season pay a visit to the nomes, and meet Your Officials, so that I may recognize whether they are to be trusted. And these are but a few of my tasks as Your acting Vizier. Yet, as High Priest, I must meet each afternoon with the Treasurer of the Sanctuary, the Scribe of the Sacrifice, the Superintendent of Property of the Temples of Amon, the Scribe of the Corn Accounts, the Superintendent of the Meadows, of the Cattle, of the Storehouses, of the Painters and Goldsmiths, and I do not even speak of my greater duties, yet which of the holiest rituals in the Temple of Amon at Karnak can take place without my person? At dawn, and again at midday, I serve as proxy for Your Person, inasmuch as You so rarely appear in Thebes. Then I must do it again at evening. In the Temple, I am obliged to serve both as High Priest, and as Pharaoh. How much could go wrong unless I am there to instruct the priests in clearness-of-voice, correct gesture, the divine order of the words, and the sequence of the prayers.

"Yet, with the accomplishment of all these duties—and this is my true pain—I find that each day I have failed to instruct You, for on those rare days when You are in Thebes beside me, I can see, as I offer my sermon, that You do not listen. Nor does it matter to You that in Memphi Your day is spent enjoying musicians, or reading from Your favorite love poems, while ignoring the maxims and deeds of great ancestors. Nor that You spend the afternoon speaking to Your cook, plucking flowers in Your garden, or drinking with officers of the King's Guard. Or, to the greater glory of the Two-Lands, You entertain, on rare occasion, a visiting Prince. It does not matter that You are renowned in the gossip of Memphi as a Pharaoh Who cannot wait for night, but visits His harem by day to watch His little queens dance, and—by what I hear—hardly more than that. Yet none of this would matter if You could listen to me and know my words, for then You could stand as Master of the Earth—in Your own Person!—there to fortify Egypt with the Will of Your ancestors. I see a great breastplate on my Pharaoh, and the Crown of the White Land and the Crown of the Red rests upon His head, yet within the robes, no man sits but Yourself, and Your voice is small!"

"He did not say those last words," exclaimed my great-grandfather.

In response to this interruption, the voice of the High Priest left the throat of my Pharaoh, and His own voice came forth. "No, he said it. I was not prepared. His wit was so weak, his feelings were so pompous. I was even sorry for him. To think, he dared to say, 'Your voice is small!'"

"How," asked my great-grandfather, "did You respond?"

"I told him he was an ox and built for burden, and that the fate of Egypt depended more upon the tenderness with which I hold a flower, than upon the reports of a thousand of his scribes. Yet all the while I spoke, I did not believe Myself. My Gods had most certainly deserted Me. I had been chided by Khem-Usha, then insulted, but the walls of his temple most certainly did not crash.

"To My horror, I now began to talk too much. It is due to that unhappy business between us as boys. I said to him, 'I may be no more than the eleventh son of My Father, but My mother had one splendid virtue in His eyes, Khem-Usha, she was loyal through all those terrible times in the harem when His little queens, most certainly including your mother, tried to assassinate Him. That is why I was brought into the line of succession. Of course, that by itself does not bring Me very near to Amon, does it? Yet, this I will say, Khem-Usha, I am the Pharaoh, and your duties exist to no better purpose than to allow Me as many hours as I require each day to meditate upon the needs of the Two-Lands.' Yet all the while I was scolding him, I kept feeling the point of his rebuke. My voice was too small! 'Declare,' I wished to say to him, 'that I am not a good King. Say My third leg is as weak as Horus the boy. Dare even to say that I watch My little queens, but rarely join them. But do not tell Me that My voice is small. For I can speak in all the voices of Egypt, and most certainly your own.' Then I rose in My anger and said aloud to him, 'Let your duties as Vizier be given to another. Serve only as My High Priest.' He was much agitated at what I said, especially when I added, 'Menenhetet may be just the Vizier for Me.' He was aghast, I assure you, and soon left."

"You spoke of me as Your Vizier," said my great-grandfather.

"I did."

"You meant each word?"

"I do not know. At the moment I spoke, it made great sense to Me."

"For if you did not mean it," said my great-grandfather, "we may all be dead." He gave a shrug as if the foundation of pride was to live lightly with such thoughts.

"I believe I know what you mean. Still, I would hear you say it."

"I will not deny," said Menenhetet, "that I have thought of being Your Vizier. If the wisdom acquired in four lives cannot serve a vast purpose, then of what use is it? So I came here with the hope that we could talk of such serious matters. Yet, I cannot say I have been confident. For weeks I have heard that You will depose Khem-Usha as Vizier and replace him with Your Chief Scribe, Nes-Amon."

"Do you believe such rumors?"

"He is a Libyan," said my great-grandfather, "but then, Nes-Amon has been with You for many years. You have raised him to the rank of Prince. He is an able man."

"I have discussed the post with him. The Libyan does not have your knowledge."

"Still," said my great-grandfather, "You can depend on his loyalty. If I were Your Vizier, there would not be a day when someone did not murmur to You that I am no longer to be trusted."

"That is a judgment I reserve for Myself. My judgment of men—if I am given the opportunity to listen—is faultless. Of course, few men dare to speak to a Pharaoh. You do. Indeed, I have just decided to tell

you the truth. Until tonight, I was ready to choose Nes-Amon as My
next Vizier. He is, indeed, an able man. But there is a place in every
servant's heart where he is not to be trusted. I will admit to you that
Khem-Usha, when he whispered to Me, was not speaking of our
boyhood together—far from it! Rather, he said word had come to
him that Nes-Amon was ready to march upon the Palace. The influence of Nes-Amon is large with My charioteers."

"When did Khem-Usha say this would take place?"

"He told Me there was a good chance it would take place tonight.
I laughed. 'You do not have a nose for military matters,' I told him.
'No army likes to move under a full moon, and when it is the Night
of the Pig—all would get lost.' I convinced him. I said: 'If My Palace
were open to you, Khem-Usha, you still would not dare to take it.
Not tonight. Depend on it. Nes-Amon feels no more confident than
you.' I believe Khem-Usha agreed. He certainly became less agitated
about Nes-Amon, and it was then he began to scold Me about the
extent of his duties—I think he was trying to frighten Me by demon-
strating the extent of his influence over the Two-Lands. Yet I do not
know why he dared to speak to Me so at the end. He was taking a
terrible chance. He understands how unhappy I am already with the
situation. Why double the jeopardy of his position by insulting Me?"

"I think Khem-Usha wants You to dismiss him," said my great-
grandfather. "Many are loyal to him now but not so devoted that they
will dare to move against You. You are the Pharaoh. But if You take
away his powers, then those who serve him closely have also lost. So
then they must move with him."

"What would you advise Me to do?"

"I would encourage Nes-Amon to think that he will certainly replace Khem-Usha, and I would convince Khem-Usha that You will
soon make him full Vizier. At the proper moment, appoint a Vizier
over both of them. Leave Thebes and Upper Egypt to Khem-Usha,
and Memphi and Lower Egypt to Nes-Amon. They can each be called
Vizier-to-the-High-Vizier."

"You would be the High Vizier?"

"It would take every skill I possess."

"I should think so." Ptah-nem-hotep gave a cough, rueful as despair itself. "I do not know what to do," He said. "Your enemies will never allow any quality in you more noble than bat shit."

"That is what I fear the least," said Menenhetet. "A man with a dreadful reputation who has just been given terrible powers is treated with great respect. All hope he will not act like a tyrant."

"Then, what is your fear?"

"That You will lose everything tonight. I would raise my guard to man the walls."

"I do not trust My officers. The half who are not close to Nes-Amon may be loyal to Khem-Usha." Now, Ptah-nem-hotep gave a sweet smile to Menenhetet. "My situation is as follows: I detest Khem-Usha, no longer trust Nes-Amon, and do not know you at all. Yet, at this moment, I feel happy. My belief is that the Pharaoh, if He is wise enough to think only of what is before Him, whether it be His Crook, His Flail, or no more than the flower in His hand, is the greatest force in the Two-Lands. No army can move against Him when His thoughts have no fear. Do you believe this?"

"I do not know."

"I will tell you. I do not have the wisdom one needs. But I am drawn to you. If you are wise enough not to deceive Me, and tell Me all that I wish to know, then I cannot fail to increase in strength and wisdom. Of course, it is hard not to suppose that you would deceive Me."

"There are nights," said Menenhetet, "when I would seek to deceive the Lord Osiris Himself."

Ptah-nem-hotep laughed with true merriment. "I want you to tell Me," he said, "of My ancestor, Ramses the Second. He is the one whose strength I will need in the hours and years to come. I want to know what took place at the Battle of Kadesh, and all that followed upon it."

"To tell You might take every moment that is left in this night."

"I am awake until morning." He hesitated. "Will you speak of the Battle of Kadesh?"

"If I think on this matter, I want to be Your Vizier."

"After listening to you, I may have no other choice."

My great-grandfather laughed. "When I tell my story truly, You will learn so much that You will have no further need of me. You will be a Pharaoh greater than others, and Master of the Secrets. Who, but myself, has known the Great Pharaoh, Ramses the Second?"

"You make Me grateful before you begin."

My great-grandfather gave a smile that showed the strength of his face and the youth of the sixty years of his fourth life. "The story of my first life will certainly take us through the night. That is much more certain than that I shall be Vizier. But if this—as I feel with every breath I take—is a night when much comes to an end, and much is ready to change, then let us go back to the patio. I will offer a story far better than any father ever gave a son, but I would like to tell it by the light of the fireflies. You saw them truly. They bring back thoughts of campfires after the roar of the day is done. And I would like my granddaughter to listen as well. And my great-grandson. They are now the nearest to my flesh of all four lives."

IV

The Book of the Charioteer

One

My mother greeted Ptah-nem-hotep with relief enough to suppose He had just escaped the serpents of the sea. She even clapped her hands with pleasure when told that my great-grandfather had agreed to speak of his deeds in the service of Ramses the Second, although I do not believe she would have welcomed this if she knew how long the account might take. But since she did not, she sat up on the couch, and, like a girl, held her chin in her hand.

"I will tell You the story," my great-grandfather began, "as if we did not know each other, and had not spoken of many matters on this night. In that manner, what I say will have the simplicity of my thoughts in my first life, and so we may come to look with the same eyes upon all that happened to me."

"That would be equal," Ptah-nem-hotep replied, "to offering your wisdom itself."

"Wisdom in that life was more like strength," my great-grandfather began. "I was born of the poorest people, and yet became the First Charioteer of Ramses the Second and even lived next to Him in the worst hours of Kadesh." He stopped and looked about him. As if the difficulty of embarking on such a long tale weighed upon him like a stone he was not yet ready to bear, he felt obliged to say: "Indeed, these exploits are inscribed on the temple walls at Abu-Simbel, at the Ramesseum of Thebes, and at Karnak. Also, at Abydos, although not all that is there is correct, and certainly not the spelling of my name. Ramses the Second had a voice to ring in your ear and so His scribes cut my name into the stone as Menni, not Meni."

"Yes," said Ptah-nem-hotep, "I have visited the wall at Abu-Simbel where it is told how the Pharaoh was separated from His troops by the Hittites. It says that you were seized by terror. When I close My eyes, I can still see the inscription. The light is clear on it and the shadows are strong. You said, 'Let us save our lives.' Then, below, it is written that Ramses Mi-Amon replied, 'Take courage, Menni, strengthen your heart. I will go among them like the hawk on his prey. I will lay them in the dust.' It was late in the afternoon when I read those words, so I still see the shadows on the indentations of the letters."

"Those are the words that are written," said Menenhetet.

"Were you really afraid?" asked Ptah-nem-hotep. When my great-grandfather did not reply at once, He also asked, "Did the Second truly reply to you in just so bold a voice?"

"I was afraid," said Menenhetet, "but I would also say there was a moment when Ramses Mi-Amon knew fear. Yet He was the first to be brave. That enabled me to be brave."

"You were braver than is recorded, you say. And He was less brave. Can that be true?"

"I would never say that He was not brave. The Second was the bravest man I ever saw. Yet the story is not as it is told on the temple wall. There was a moment when He knew fear."

"Tell us."

"No, Great Two-House. Not yet. My story must be long like the length of the snake. If I present the head, You will know nothing of the body. Only the smile of the snake. For now, I will say that we both knew some terror. Why, even the lion of the Pharaoh knew fear."

"So the lion is real," said Ptah-nem-hotep. "He truly had this pet beast that is drawn on some of the walls?"

"Yes, the lion fought by the side of Ramses the Second. And pro-digiously." My great-grandfather shrugged. "But if You want to know the truth of all that happened to me, I say again that I must tell the story no more cleverly than I could speak the truth in my first life."

"Why, as slowly as you wish," said the Pharaoh, and inclined His hand most graciously.

So my great-grandfather was ready once more to commence and if we wished to understand what he meant by saying he would tell the story slowly, I came to see that silence was a large part of what he would offer. He did not speak for a while, commencing once, then ceasing, and in the pause, issuing a sigh. "I must," he said at last, "go back to what was there before I begin, even as a journey begins with preparations on the night before. So I would tell you of my childhood in that life I knew first, except I cannot say I had a childhood; I had none, at least none in the way of this beautiful boy, my great-grandson here before us, half asleep. His childhood is full of wonders, but like so many of my people, I had, when I was his age, no more in the way of thoughts than any beast, if not for one thought that left me know-ing I was not like others and would never be. That much I knew be-fore I was born. Because, on the night I was conceived, my mother saw Amon."

"Only the mother of a man who will yet be Pharaoh can see Amon on such a night," said Ptah-nem-hotep. "It seems we are brothers. My mother also saw Amon."

Now, Menenhetet hesitated before saying, "I tell You what my mother told me, no more. My parents were poor people in the poor-est peasant village, and on the night this happened they were lying in their straw, my father by my mother's side. A golden light came to the darkness of their hut and the air smelled sweeter than all the perfumes in the House of the Secluded. Amon whispered to my mother that a great son would be born who would lead the world." Menenhetet sighed. "As You see, I have done less than that."

"You believe her story?" asked Ptah-nem-hotep.

"If You had known my mother, You would believe it. She lived with the earth in her hands. She knew no stories. She told me once and that was enough. When I grew up, we never spoke unless we had something to say. Therefore you never forgot what you were told. Our minds were like a stone and each word was scratched upon it."

"By this one remark," said Ptah-nem-hotep, "I understand My peasants more closely. So, I comprehend your desire to tell the story with deliberation. I would even say that I am prepared to listen with the same repose I might give to watching the river as it drifts by."

"Your Ear," said Menenhetet, "has divined my next words. For I wish to speak of our Nile. It was always in my thoughts and passed through me on every breath. I was born, I may say, at the height of our flood, and the end of my first life was to come on a night when the river had just receded from its highest mark. The last sound I heard was of its waters."

Menenhetet's breath was short, as if this recollection remained arduous. "Now, those who live in the cities have forgotten the extremities of drought and flood. Here in Memphi, we may feel some heat before the river begins to rise, but our discomfort is small. Our noble parks are watered through the year and surround us with their green. We are apart from the desert. But in the land from which I came, midway between Memphi and Thebes, the desert is like . . ." He paused. "No-dwelling-can-contain-it."

I noticed that my great-grandfather's voice, which had most certainly put away its customary edge of mockery, now altered even more, and was outright solemn. But, then, no-dwelling-can-contain-it was an expression used by field workers when they did not dare to speak directly of a ghost which I happened to know because my mother had told me just two days ago, full of her rich laugh at the cautions of country people.

But then, I also noticed that my great-grandfather, having passed through this change of manner, was considerably less like a lord to us now and more like a dignified man of the people, even a village mayor of the sort he would scorn, and I noticed how he only employed words appropriate to a simple man. "Before I tell," he said, "of my military career which began at the age of fifteen when I was plucked

up from my village like a weed from the riverbank, I must inform
You first of how we lived and the knowledge we had of the river,
how it would rise and fall. That was all we knew, and it was all of our
lives. I grew up by its laws. Here, in the cities, we speak of whether
the flood will be a good height for the crops, and we celebrate our
greatest festivals to the rise of our river, we praise it, we think we
know it, but that is not like being born to the sound of it, and fearing
the river when it rises.

"So, let me try to tell You, and I will speak as if You had never seen
it, for in truth to know its anger is like sleeping with Your hand on
the belly of a lion."

I saw my mother give one small look at my father as if to say, "I
hope he knows enough to amuse our Pharaoh."

Ptah-nem-hotep, however, nodded. "Yes, let Me hear of our great
stream in such a way. I find that as you speak of matters familiar to
Me, I come to know them again and they are of different interest."

Menenhetet nodded. "During my boyhood, the air in my country,
when the Nile was low, became as dry as wood-fire. You must think
of how dry was that air. We know nothing like it here, or at Thebes,
but in my country which is between, the fields dried fast after the
harvest. And almost immediately the earth turned old and began to
wrinkle. A thin crack which in the morning was too small for your
big toe was wide enough by the same night to break a cow's ankle. We
lived in our huts and watched our cracks widen, and as they did, these
cracks moved toward us across the fields. Each day, sand filled them
more. The desert was nearer to our scorched meadows. Then there
came a day when the sand surrounded us and the leaves hung like dead
fingers from the trees. The smallest wind blew a fine dust over our
houses and our tables, and we breathed it in our straw when we slept.
Searching over the stubble, our cattle walked with their tongues out.
You could hear them cry, 'I am thirsty, oh, I am suffering from thirst.'
We were thirstier. We had worked in the ditches, even the children,
trying to clean out the bottoms of our narrow canals before the flood,
repairing the dikes, smoothing their top for our carts, restoring the
walls of our basins, every last one of us working while the river was

low. And at night when we rested, too tired to play, you could walk
from one island of reeds to another. Every kind of dead rodent was to
be found in the silt of our canals, and up and down the river came the
sounds of neighboring villages at the same work, all of us filling
sledges with silt that our oxen would haul to the dikes. There we
would pack it with straw and lay such bricks on the embankments. I
tell you, an awful stink was on the land then! Everything dried with
the leathery mean stench of old people. A stinginess is in such corruption, a urine!, and it takes forever. Those hard odors used to go right
up the nose and live under our eyes with the dust and the heat. They
said that to breathe such a smell could cause blindness, and I know my
eyes would pucker. I still remember the bones of one dead fish on the
riverbank by a tongue of sand—each night the crocodile who lived
nearby must have blazed on it with his breath, for there was less of the
fish each day, less of the dried skin near the head and the milky stones
of its eyes, yet the bones had an odor so powerful you would have
sworn the fish had traveled all of the river bottom for its smell to
know so much. I went back day after day to walk around it. The rot
in the bones of that fish knew more evil than any I had ever encountered and I thought the moon must be in it with the river mud. Each
day that skeleton became more of a withered plant until the bones
themselves dried in their joints and the last of the fish blew away.

"That was when we felt the first moisture pass through the air. The
wind came upriver from the Delta, past Memphi, and on to us. The
sluggish green of the Nile, which had been like a soup thickening on
the fire, began to ripple, and we used to say that a crocodile as long as
the river was stirring beneath. You could not see his skin, but the
surface of the water was sliding about. And everything that had died
in the dry heat, lay in a scum on the top. Before our eyes the river
began to fester. Carcasses and dead fish and dry vegetation floated up
on the heavy skin of the new green Nile, and the air turned hot and
wet. Then the new Nile came over the spits and tongues in the middle
of the channel, and the river washed over the islands of reeds. Our
sky was as full of birds as a field with flowers. They flew downstream
with the rise, leaving each island of reeds as it went under, going

down to islands still uncovered by these early waters, then on again, passing over our heads with a rush of wings louder than any current, myriads of birds. Each morning the water was higher than the day before, and the older men in the village began to measure their sticks. Although word always came from up the river that we would be higher this year, or lower, some of the old men claimed they could predict the rise by the color of the stream. As the river came up, so its surface changed into many restless waves, and you could hear the rush in the night as if these new waters were not one throat but an army, and when the color changed from green to the red we see each year in Memphi, we used to say it was heated by the flames of the Duad. And the dates in the palm trees turned red as the red water went by.

"We had no work to do now but protect our ditches, and therefore we could sit on our levees and watch where the water turned beneath in eddies so hollow you could put your arm in the hole and never get wet—so we would tell ourselves but never dared to put out an arm for fear this mouth of the million and one mouths of the river would suck us in.

"Then came the week when the river came right up over the lower banks and flowed into our fields, and on the first day the earth gave a sigh like a good cow gives to the knife in its hour of sacrifice. Even as a boy I could feel the land shiver when the water came over it and closed out the light. Now our one great river became a thousand little ones, and the fields turned to lakes and the meadows to great lagoons. At night, the red water lost the sun, and looked like the Blessed Fields and was silver in the moonlight. Our villages, built so close together along the bank that you could nearly reach one with a stone thrown from the other, were now as separated as dark islands in these fields of silver, and our dikes became the only roads. We would walk along the top and admire the basins below (which we called our rooms—our room-of-the-upper-field, our room-of-the-little-valley) for we had known how to take advantage of any hollow in the ground that was like a bowl, and around it had put our embankments and left openings for the flood, and now closed them when they were full. Rats walked on the dikes with us, even as ducks cavorted in the puddles. Out at the sides of the floodwater, in those fields closest to the desert, scorpions were looking for dry land, and rabbits fled and lynx and wolves—in different years I saw them all—fleeing the spread from the riverbanks. Each year, snakes came into our houses, and there was no hut where the damp did not come up out of the earth of our floors, while our donkeys and cattle could be heard through the night eating the forage we had piled around our walls, thereby dislodging the tarantulas. Sometimes, water rose over the lower dikes, and we could only visit other villages by using rafts of papyrus, and our basins would even wash out our villages while the cranes fed in a frenzy on the banks of the flood because insects would quit their nests as the waters crept higher. Then, there always came one hot morning, more damp, more heavy, and hotter than any that had gone before, when the water in the fields came to rest, breathed up, left a line of silt, breathed up again, and did not pass the line but touched it, did not touch it on the next breath and the ripples lay in a calm, the wind ceased, and the Nile stopped rising. That was the day when you could hear a cry go up from us in the mud on the edge of those fields, and on such hot mornings, the light came back to us from the hills on the horizon. The water was as placid as the sleep of the moon when the sun is high." Menenhetet sighed.

"That was how my childhood passed, and I do not remember any other life than working by the banks of the water, nor do I know how often I thought of what my mother had told me about Amon. I did not see myself as different from other boys except that I was stronger, and that offered much. I remember when a deputation of Officials came one morning to our village to conscript us for the army, I knew no fear. I had been waiting for such service and wanted it. I was bored and ready. The river, I remember, was in the second week of its sub-siding, and the water on our fields had become, in the sun, a lake of gold. I suppose that the Officials saw it as the best of days on which to surprise us, since it was no easy matter, with the fields in flood, for any of us to run away into the hills. I, of course, did not care. In truth, I did think of Amon the moment I saw the Officials. To me, the army was like the right arm of the God.

"I did not know it," said my great-grandfather, "but I was waiting for my career to begin. I laughed at our village mayor when he trembled in his place between two bailiffs, each beside him with a heavy stick. As our names were read, we would lift an arm and call out 'Ho!' to show that we were present, but twice there was no answer. Two boys had run off. The bailiffs at a sign from the Pharaoh's Officer beat the mayor until he was groaning on the ground, and many of us snickered. That mayor had punished us often enough that we did not mind to see him suffer. Then of the eighteen present, the Officials picked us over, looked at our teeth, felt our arms, kneaded our thighs, hefted our genitals and picked the fifteen strongest. While our mothers watched and, I confess, most of them wept, we marched away along the dike and put into their boats and rowed upstream to the South for all of that day until we came to a bend with a great fort and storehouse. There we were locked in together with recruits from other villages, and that night the bakers in the compound gave us round hard black bread." He smiled at the recollection. "I was a poor boy and had eaten hard bakings, but this bread was older than the dead." His mouth worked as if chewing the stuff again.

"To the fort," said Menenhetet, "other recruits came, and we were taught to march, and to wrestle and to use swords. Mine, Good and Great God, was the stroke that was strongest from overhead, and I smashed five shields in such training. They taught us much on the art of the shield for we had large ones then, larger than we use today, and it could cover a man from his eyes to his knees. Yet it was poor protection at best. For unlike Your small shields with their many metal plates, ours, given their big wood frame and their leather, were so heavy that they held only one disc of metal no larger than our face, and it was set in position to protect our arm where it held the shield.

"One by one, we would go up to face the archer and from a distance of fifty long steps he would shoot an arrow at us, and we were obliged, for his aim was good, to catch it on the metal plate so that the arrow would glance away. We were taught to do this with our chest facing to the side so that should the arrow pierce the leather, chances were still good it would miss our body. And of course the leather was strong enough to keep some of the arrows from going through. But it was a sport—to hold that shield and block what you could not dodge. At the end of training, fifty of us faced one hundred archers, and were ordered to advance into their bows. I was busy that morning, I can promise. It was known that I had become skillful with my shield, so many of the archers took pleasure to aim at me."

"Were numbers of men lost in such training?" asked Ptah-nem-hotep.

"There were many scratches, and some wounds, and two men died, but we were skillful dodgers and it helped to make soldiers of us. Besides, we wore quilting thick enough to stop many an arrow although not as much as is worn today. The training was harder then because we were always told to get ready for lands we would soon go to conquer, and were so ignorant we did not know they were lands we had already conquered one hundred years before and they were now in rebellion. Good training, however. We were infantry and our weapons were the dagger and the lance, but they taught us to use the bow as well and the sword. Since I excelled in all contests, in wrestling first, and with dagger, spear, sword, shield, and bow, I was even allowed to enter a special game held to choose one man from our ranks to become a charioteer. In those days, it was only the sons of nobles who could enter such a service."

"And were our chariots at all different then?" asked Ptah-nem-hotep.

"They were beautiful, as now. Unlike our shields, the present chariots do not differ from the ones I knew, not by one bend in the wood, but they were not yet a familiar sight in those days. The oldest man of my village used to talk of how the oldest man he had known when he was a boy could remember the first horse he saw, for that was when they began to bring horses into Egypt from the lands to the East. How it terrified him! But then who would not have been frightened by such strange animals? They heard only the voices of foreign Gods, and spoke in loud snorts, or with a long screaming of wind in their cries. This old man of my village used to say that to approach a chariot with its two horses, was the closest one could get to the Pharaoh. To us, charioteers were soldiers sent from the Pharaoh! They may as well have been dressed in gold. For when they got up behind those four-legged Gods and went off at a gallop, we respected them more than the captain of a great barge going down the Nile. You can see how it was still a rare skill to a common soldier in the years when I was trained, and You may know I dreamed of becoming a chariot-eer. To decide the one common soldier among us who would be se-lected, we were put in a race, and it was the greatest contest we ever knew. Because we were told that the winner would yet ride a chariot like a nobleman. Since we were ignorant and could not command horses, we were made to hold a chariot over our heads and run up one side of a mountain and down the other, carrying the cart with us, wheels and all. The chariots were as light then as they are today, no heavier than a ten-year-old boy, but it was not easy to jog up that great hill with the vehicle on your shoulder and come down the other side unscratched. You did not dare to fall. Be certain if you broke any-thing, they would break your own back with their sticks.

"We set out at a trot. The fools among us tried to go as fast as a horse and soon collapsed on the first slopes, but I set out as if I were the son of Amon and could draw new strength from every breath. I stepped along as if Nut fed my nose, and Geb my feet, while Maat took care of the nausea in my stomach by instructing me not to go faster until I could find a balance between the utmost effort of my body and the demons in my lungs. Still, the earth turned blue, and the sky was as orange as the sun and sometimes became black to me. Then the sand of the desert also turned black and the sky became white. The rocks of the mountain, as I went up, step after step, were no longer rocks to me, but fierce dogs with open teeth and some rocks were beasts large as wild boars—one great stone was a hippopotamus to me—and my heart was before my eyes as I came over the summit, and I thought I would die, but I was over the top, and still ahead of everyone else. On the trip down, another soldier came near to passing me for his legs were long, and he took great bounds and came closer and my perspiration was cold. I shivered in the heat and the chariot weighed on my shoulders like a lion. I swear it had claws that tore into my back. Some of my strength was returning, however, and my breath with it, and I even saw the sky and earth as they were supposed to be, but the spear remained in my chest and the crown of pain around my head. I knew I could not hold off the other fellow unless I tricked him. He was long and thin and built to make this kind of race, but I knew he was vain, so I summoned the last of my legs and leaped with one great bound after another down ten rocks in a row. He was right behind and would soon have passed, for I had nothing left after those ten leaps, but he could not bear the audacity of such long jumps, he must be more daring than me, so he tried to better what I had done, and fell and cracked his chariot. I came down the last slope of the hill by myself.

"That was how I became a charioteer, and went to the Royal School of Charioteers of King Thutmose the Third, and You may be certain I became the best. Although not so soon. First, I had to be taught the care of a horse, how to speak to them and clean them, and horses were mysterious creatures. For the longest time I did not know if they were beasts or Gods, I only knew that they did not like me. They would rear up as I approached. I could not understand their intelligence nor whether they were stupid. By the delicacy of their lower legs, I could see they were animals of some refinement, and the light in their eyes made me believe their minds must travel as fast as an arrow. Given the long curve of their nose I supposed they took their knowledge of what to do next by what they could smell over the next hill. Yet by their teeth they were flat and stubborn. So I did not understand them. But then I was a village boy. Although I did not know it, I was like a horse myself. I did not think, and could barely obey strange commands.

"Learning to guide the reins and turn the horse smoothly became a turn in my own life greater than winning the chariot race," said my great-grandfather, "for the more I attempted to overcome my terrible clumsiness with these horses, the more I became the recipient of much laughter. The noblemen's sons, among whom I now found myself, were born graceful, I used to think, and still do—as witness the beauties of my beloved great-grandson Menenhetet the Second," which he said with a little nod in my direction—"but that only made me more determined to learn. I found myself thinking of a saying we used to have in the fields—it will sound crude to You—but it is a phrase on every farm. 'Know your animal's smell,' we say. It was then, working in the stables, that I understood how much I was in awe of the peculiar odor of horses. Their stables smelled different and better than the fields and coops around our farm. It seemed almost a blessed smell to me, full of the odor of the sun on a field of wheat. Yet part of my fear of horses was that I thought they were more like Gods than other beasts.

"The animal I curried in our stables was a stallion, and particularly fierce to handle. Yet the scent of his hide on my finger proved sweet and friendly, like the odor of the first village girl to whom I made love. She had smelled more of the earth than of the river and most of all she smelled of wheat fields and her own good sweat, strong as a horse, so I had the thought with such a smell on my hands that horses were not Gods but rather might be like men or women who had died, and come back as horses. So far as I knew, no one ever had a thought like that before, and I was sure it was blasphemous. Yet, fortified by the smell of that stallion's soul, as I sniffed it clearly through all the mash of grain and straw, I could feel near to somebody who lived in my horse—whoever it was—that might be a little like the girl to whom I had made love. That morning I began to change the way in which I spoke to the horse. I no longer tried to placate the animal, nor pray to the God in him, and this saved much trouble. For how did one offer prayers to a strange God? On the other hand, I no longer tried to beat this horse like a beast. Not often. No, now, I thought rather of the man who was in the animal, and comprehended that this stallion was envious of me. I spoke and walked upright as he once had done— so I could feel how a punishment had been visited upon a strong soul. In my thoughts, I began to say to him, 'You want to be a man again? Try listening to me. I can be your friend.' Do you know? The animal heard my thoughts. I could tell by the difference in the handling.

"Now, in the beginning of our training, we did not use chariots with two steeds, but small carts suitable for one horse, and they had thick wooden wheels and made a terrible clatter. The sound was atrocious on one's ear, and the jolts of the cart were ferocious to the spine. Only a peasant as strong as myself could have taken such blows as it took me to learn to steer one horse properly. The other students had passed on to chariots long before I could get out of my work-cart. Yet, in the last week, I amazed my drill-major. I had learned how to do tricks with that heavy cart and could even coax my stallion to move it backward. So they promoted me to two horses. Immediately my troubles began again. I had to learn that I was now not like a friend or a brother nor even a man telling another man how to live but more like a father who must teach two creatures to act like brother and sister." He stopped for a moment to clear his throat in the way common people do when their voice is husky. "One cannot build a chair without a saw to cut the wood, one needs one's tool, and I had it now. I lived with these horses and spoke to them with my voice and sometimes with my thoughts, and I taught them how to move together.

"There came a day when I could direct my chariot through turns others found hard to follow, and now I no longer needed to speak to the horses. My thoughts had entered my reins. There even came the hour when I wrapped the reins around my waist and showed the troop you could drive a chariot without hands. To prove the value of such a skill I galloped around the compound with a bow in my hand and let fly arrows into bales of straw. A new practice began. Soon all the sons of noblemen, my fellow charioteers, were trying to drive with the reins around their waist, except they did not learn it so quickly as myself, and the accidents were numerous. They did not live in the mind of the horse as well as I did.

"That was the way I learned my skill, and in the practice of it I soon ceased to think of horses as men or women. By the end, in truth, I thought more about my reins than anything else. Horses could be changed, but the reins were mine and had to be properly treated. In the end I looked only for good blessings to put on the oil. My reins grew so wise, I had no more than to drop them lightly on a horse's back, and the animal was listening to me."

My great-grandfather looked up at us now, and it may have been the glow of light from the cages of fireflies, but his face looked as young as the strength he must have felt in his youth, or at least in that first of his four lives when he was a Royal Charioteer. He smiled then and I thought for the first time that my great-grandfather had a beautiful face. I had only lived for six years but it was the strongest face I had ever seen.

"Shall we proceed," he asked the Pharaoh, "to the Battle of Kadesh?"

"No," said Ptah-nem-hotep in a light and much-pleased voice, "I confess I now want to hear more of your early adventures in the army. Did it all go so well?"

"It went poorly for longer than You would think. I was still ignorant of envy. I could not keep my mouth shut. So I told everyone in my troop how I would yet be First Charioteer to His Majesty. I had not as yet learned how one's advancement into high places owes much to the ability to conceal your ability. That way your superiors find it comfortable to advance you. Having been, as I say, untutored to such wisdom, I can only remark that I am still heedless of it tonight."

"Dear Menenhetet, you will soon be irreplaceable," said the Pharaoh.

My great-grandfather bowed to the remark. I could see that he hardly wished to stop. "In those days," he said, "I used to dream of great conquests in foreign lands, and hoped our success would be due to me. For if a driver could be taught to guide a vehicle with the reins lashed to the waist, then he might also hold a bow, and each of our chariots could ride into battle with two archers. We would be twice as strong as our enemies who rode with one driver and one archer, or, as in the case of the Hittites, given their heavy three-man chariots, a driver, an archer, and a man with a spear. Our two men could be the equal of their three in arms, yet our chariots would be faster, and turn in a smaller circle. I could not sleep for the excitement of this idea. Soon I could not sleep for vexation. So soon as certain noblemen had become curious to test my suggestion, it was declared by the Chariot-Major that, in his opinion, only a few of the best would ever be able to control two horses with the reins around their waist. Finally I was told that my argument was offensive to Amon. Our God had already brought victory to Egypt by way of one archer and one driver.

"I had, however, not learned too much. I still bragged that I would become First Charioteer and lead a troop of two-bowed chariots into battle. For such vanity, I was sent away. An officer who was much my enemy, and by one rank my superior, took care to have me assigned to a wretched oasis in the middle of the Libyan desert out there"—and he pointed with his thumb over his back in the direction of some land far beyond the Pyramids—"a domain of such endless boredom that a mind so brilliant as Yours, my Pharaoh, could not live there for a day. In truth my own mind felt as if it had turned to oil. It smoked in the desert sun. We had virtually no duties, and no wine. There were twenty soldiers in my command, surly mercenaries, village idiots. There was beer that tasted, as we used to say, of horses. But I cannot remember many stories of that unhappy time. I do recall a letter I dictated by way of our scribe, a frail little fellow whose pretty but-tocks were raw from the practices of my soldiers—I may say he was as desperate to escape from the stench of this oasis as myself. So I had him write a letter to my General. 'Make the words look handsome,' I told him, 'or we will never get out of here, and then the hole in your seat will be larger than the one in your mouth.'

"My scribe giggled at that. He was not altogether miserable with such a use of him. But then he saw the look in my eye. It said, 'Get me out of Teben-Shanash.' That was the name of this oasis, and well named, a perfect circle of stench. The odor surrounded our tents. We had, may I say, no huts. There was not any straw to make bricks. The flies were intolerable. I would lie for hours under the date-palms and look down a long sandy road to the horizon. Nothing to see but the sky. I fell in love with the flight of birds. That was all there was to love. The food was atrocious. Bitter dates, and our sacks of corn, so near the moisture of the oasis, were filled with vermin."

"What is the reason to tell all this?" asked Hathfertiti.

"There were dogs. I think there were three hundred dogs, and not one failed to go with me on a walk. Their teeth stank. So did mine. The worm was biting a rotten tooth in my head. There, in the stink of that oasis, where the beaks and muzzles of the scavengers were purple with blood and caked by the sun, there on those dusty roads where these hideous creatures fought over the last maggots on the hot carcass of a donkey, I dreamed of feathers on horses' heads leading the point of a parade. You may conceive of the letter I dictated to my scribe. 'Lead me to Memphi,' I exhorted, 'let me see it in the dawn.' I thought I would die in Circle-of-Stench. I did not know I had a career before me, then another, then a few more. Never in the length of my life, even if it be measured by the length of four lives, did I feel so low."

Menenhetet stopped and ran a finger around his lips as if to recover the memory of an old thirst.

"In composing that letter," said Menenhetet, "I came to witness the power of the God Thoth, and prayed to Him to give my scribe good and proper words, since my own strength was useless for such a test. While the scribe did his utmost to express my desires in a language fit for papyrus, I kept telling myself in terror that the letter had to deliver me. Nothing could be worse than another year in Teben-Shanash. Yet, when I read the letter I was ashamed. I would perish or I would endure, I told myself, but I would not whine to the General, nor beg to see Memphi in the dawn. No, I thought, I will make my request with dignity. So I sent another composed in more calm, and to my surprise I was soon ordered back to the city.

"I have never forgotten that lesson. One must never surrender to desires that damage one's pride. How I sang when the call came for me to return. It seemed my fortunes were in a dance. For not half a year later I encountered the great Ramses the Second in Memphi. He was on a visit from Thebes. My true story of the Battle of Kadesh can begin here."

Two

Even by the light of the fireflies, I could recognize in the eyes of the Pharaoh that look of anticipation which comes at the ascent of a long hill when a view famous for its splendor is waiting; my great-grandfather would tell us at last of the King Who was greater than all others—for so I had heard Him described from the time I learned to speak.

"Yes, I was to come before Him," said Menenhetet, "at the Pillars of Amon in Memphi. It was at that temple He had gone to worship, and out of courtesy was going later that day to visit the Temple of Ptah. I must say that although I had heard of the magnificence of His bearing and the radiance of His face, I was little prepared for what I saw. He was taller than any of us, and His eyes were green like the Very Green of the immense sea beyond our Delta." Menenhetet here debated with himself before he spoke again. "Except to describe Him closer, and You will not believe me, His eyes were not green but blue. I have never seen another man with eyes that were blue."

"Blue?" said my mother. "That cannot be. Gray or green or clear as water, yellow as the sun, but not blue."

"Blue as the sky," said Menenhetet. "And He had a skin dark as ours, yet different and more beautiful, more of a golden-red of early evening was on His shoulders. He looked as if He had lived in the sun like a bird in an oven roasted into red, a lovely and remarkable color. He wore garments of pleated white and the pleats rustled through His long skirt like reeds in the wind. His skirt was white, and yet it had the gleam of silver minnows in the lights of a pond.

"What is most extraordinary is that His hair was more yellow than the sun. A light-gold like flax. Like a Mede, His hair danced in the wind faster than the pleats of His skirt."

"He had golden-yellow hair?" asked Ptah-nem-hotep.

"He did then, at the beginning of His Reign, hair as yellow as the pale sun, but it turned dark in the years He ruled, and His eyes went from blue to green to yellow that had hues of brown. And His eyes were dark by the time He died."

"Even as are the colors in every painting I see of Him," said our Pharaoh.

"Yes, but the artists were forbidden to paint His true colors. He believed, as He imparted to me once, that His hair would mourn and grow dark if truly painted, and indeed He wore a dark wig on all public occasions except when going into battle or visiting the Temple, that is the truth."

"And you saw Him first at the Temple of Amon?"

"I saw Him first with difficulty. I had just come back to Memphi after two weeks of duty in one of our forts, and only as I reached my quarters, did I recognize by the babble of strangers rushing past in the opposite direction, that the young Pharaoh had not only arrived in Memphi on the same morning as myself, but was now at the Temple. By the time I arrived, I could only stand with the mob in the outer court under the full sun and look through the pillars, but the young Pharaoh was lost to view in the Sanctuary. It was like trying to peer across a field into the darkness of a cave.

"When the Pharaoh emerged with the High Priest, however, I knew I was looking at the son of Amon-Ra. Never did a Ramses possess, if not for the exception of Your lineaments, Divine Two-House, a face so close to those noble Gods we see in dreams."

And our Pharaoh at this instant did look splendid in His beauty. I could not cease staring at the chiseled wing of His nostril, or the changing bow of His mouth. He was more exquisite to my eyes than a beautiful lady.

"I am honored at the comparison, but know it is only one more way of proving yourself indispensable," said Ptah-nem-hotep.

Menenhetet bowed with grace, and exclaimed, "My Lord, He was beautiful in the way twenty birds are one bird in the instant they turn. He was as beautiful as the full moon when it lowers its head to go behind the veil of the smallest cloud, and as beautiful as the sun when it rises and is so young we can look into its face and know the God is young. For the first time in my life, I fell in love with a man. It is the only time. I knew I was born to serve as His charioteer.

"From that moment I understood the meaning of a young man's love: It is simpler than other emotions. We love those who can lead us to a place we will never reach without them."

Here, he stopped to nod to the Pharaoh and then to my mother.

"Our Pharaoh had been conducted to the Temple of Amon by charioteers from my own barracks. Seeing them emerge out of the Sanctuary, you may be certain I quit the Temple gate in their company, yet once outside I had to go rushing for my chariot since I had been obliged to leave it with a boy on the other side of the Temple walls. Now, much behind the others, it took a considerable use of my whip on all who wouldn't let me through, plus a few judicious lashes for the horses and one poke of the heel of my hand into the nose of a fool who tried to hold on to my wheel—I still see his face and wonder why he tried to hold me back—then I broke a passage through the crowd and galloped up to the tail of that fast-moving procession of which Ramses the Second was the head.

"What a race began to the Temple of Ptah! In Memphi, rumor had lived among us for a year on the prowess of our new Pharaoh with a chariot. Now I saw that He could race, no question, and He went at such a heat over good roads and bad that the feet of Amon must have guided the hooves of the horses. His animals could have overturned in an instant on many a hole. Beside Him, as calm as if Her ladies were arranging Her hair, was His Queen, Nefertiri, Whose beauty of body was the talk of us all, and is equaled now only by the beauty of my granddaughter, I drink to her here with us tonight," said Menenhetet raising his wine.

"But I know the body of Nefertiri well," said Ptah-nem-hotep, "since there is certainly a statue of this Queen at Karnak where She stands by the right leg of Ramses the Second, not a quarter His size, but famously voluptuous." He now also drank to the health of Hath-fertiti, and my face flushed. In my great-grandfather's house, there was a drawing on one wall of Queen Nefertiri standing nude by the right leg of Her husband, and Her breasts were high and full and con-siderably larger than other Egyptian women; Her belly, if narrow, had a swell; Her thighs were prominent—I had kept thinking for days of this drawing. So now I blushed to think others might look upon my mother's nakedness in the same way.

"Tell us more of this Queen," said my mother.

"Oh, I was not to know anything of Her then," answered Menen-hetet, "although later I would know more, but I felt true respect while looking at Them in the chariot ahead. There are few people who do not show a weakness when seen from behind, even men of great strength or women of grace. Some little clumsiness of the hips or shoulders will be revealed, especially when they know they are being watched. This King and Queen, however, stood on the chariot like two leaves from the same stalk and swayed in the same winds, except it was not wind They met but ruts, and He rode His Chariot so hard it flew from bump to bump. Yet His Queen was there beside Him, standing erect with no more than two fingers curled into His biceps, bending no more than Her knees at each great shock, and all the while They were both smiling at the populace."

"How could you see Their smiles?" asked Ptah-nem-hotep, "if you were traveling to Their rear?"

"As the Good God has just demonstrated to me, I did not see Their faces. Yet I knew They were smiling, for I saw the expression of the crowd, and the people had the happiness of those who have seen the flashing teeth of a great King and His Consort as They go by."

"Of such wisdom as yours, are the best ministers made," Ptah-nem-hotep said.

For the first time I saw how Menenhetet might have looked on a chariot, for the light of an old chase was in his eyes.

"I must tell my Pharaoh," he went on, "that this Ramses the Second, Foundation-of-existence-in-the-Sun, was riding so fast He soon left all other charioteers behind. But then there was no way for the others to keep up at His gallop. Queen Nefertiri was not equal in weight to a sturdy nobleman with shield and spear, nor would our horses be equal. But then neither was our daring. Who could hope to be so brave? Any charioteer who demolished his cart would have to make up the damage. If a horse fell and broke his leg, there were worse punishments. It was folly to try.

"Yet it was also a humiliation to let Him get too far ahead. I was alone in my chariot, and unencumbered by another man's weight. Therefore, I pulled ahead of the Honor Guard, and gained on the Pharaoh at the near loss of my teeth. My lower jaw kept slamming like a catapult into my upper jaw on every unexpected jolt. I gained, however, and soon was riding directly in their dust. Although the young Pharaoh never looked around, nor His Queen, They must have had a glimpse of me around a turn, or could hear my chariot, for as we emerged into the great boulevard that leads to the Temple of Ptah where there was now room for ten to ride in one rank, so did the Pharaoh raise His arm, and with a little movement of three curved fingers, like an adze scraping at the sky, did He wave me forward. As I drew up alongside, He shouted, 'What is your name?'

"When I told Him, I must, in the clamor of the ride, and my great fear of His Presence, have spoken in the peasant tongue of the village where I was born, for He did not hear clearly, and said, 'What does it mean?' and I answered, 'Foundation-of-speech, Great God, is what Menenhetet means,' not knowing enough to recognize I should have said Good God, not Great God, but I was looking for the largest words I could find—Most-overwhelmingly-blessed-by-Ra was what I needed, and I could not remember His other names for trying to keep my horses apart from His. They were furious that other steeds had come near. All the while Queen Nefertiri kept looking at me with distaste. I could feel the dust with which I was covered, and Her annoyance at how it smoked out of my wheels toward Theirs, so I pulled away a few feet, but not before gathering the first knowledge I would always have of that Queen. She adored Her Pharaoh, and wanted to be alone with Him. Here was I, my face sweating through a shield of dust, my white teeth grinning like a crocodile.

" 'If your name is Foundation-of-speech, why do you talk so indistinctly?' asked Ramses the Second, bringing His Chariot near again. Once more, I drew away so as not to cover His Queen with dust, and shouted into the din, 'In the village where I grew up, there were more animals to talk to than people, Great God!'

" 'You have risen through the ranks?' He asked. When I nodded vigorously, He said, 'You must be a splendid driver. Draw ahead and show Me tricks.' I did. I took the chance of wrapping the reins around my waist on that boulevard of long ruts, whereas before I had done it only on parade ground or in fields with few holes, but I took the chance, and leaned forward on my toes so the bit was slack in the horses' mouth, and merely called them. They were off in a new gallop that I proceeded to steer to the left and right of the ruts and then crossed them in a beautiful quick circle to come up again by His side. But Ramses the Second merely said, 'What do you know about the Temple of Ptah?'

"I started to explain in a stammering voice that Ptah was the God of Gods for the people of Memphi as opposed to the people of Thebes who were much in worship of Amon, but the Pharaoh interrupted me and shouted back, 'I know that already.' He did not have," said Menenhetet, turning now to Ptah-nem-hotep, "Your exquisite courtesy when speaking to inferiors."

"He was, after all, a military man," our Pharaoh replied.

"Very military. But unlike most soldiers, religion was also of importance to Him. So, now He asked, 'Is the Temple of Ptah a temple to Osiris as well?' I answered that to the people of Memphi, Osiris was a God of Gods much like Ptah. 'More revered than Amon?' He asked me shortly. 'It is possible, Great God,' I told Him, 'but You may decide for Yourself by comparing the temples.' I knew there would be poor comparison. The Temple of Amon was, in those days, much smaller, and black with the smoke of the sacrifices, whereas only the whitest marble was used for the Temple of Ptah. But again He cut me short. 'It's the opposite in Thebes,' He said. 'There's a temple to Ptah-Seker-Osiris there, filthy little place with old bones and dogs' feet smoldering on the altar. A place where all the whores go.' I was tempted to tell Him it was something of the opposite in Memphi when He leaped onto what was in my head. He was not as learned as Yourself, Twice-a-Great-House, and never as quick in His reply, but like Yourself He could step into the middle of one's mind. So, He gave a great laugh and a cry to His horses and pulled away from me. I did not know if He was inviting a chase, but He quickly slowed up, as if to encourage me to come near again, and said, 'The priests of Amon tried to tell Me that worship of Osiris here in Memphi is only a filthy cult.' Since at this exact moment we came over a rise to see before us the marble walks and white walls and colonnaded porticos of the Great Temple of Ptah, as beautiful in the morning light as the robes of the Pharaoh, He whistled and said, 'Why do they think every young King a fool?' "

" 'You are not only a King, my Lord, but a great rider of the Royal Chariot.' "

" 'And you are better than the rest,' He remarked, 'or can other charioteers also put the reins around their waist?'

" 'A few are learning from me.' I could see the First Charioteer coming up the boulevard fast behind us, obviously determined not to let me talk here too long, so I added before the air felt ready for the remark, 'I think a troop of charioteers could learn to ride in my manner if I were allowed to teach them.' Being a military man, He saw my point. 'We could win on every field,' He said, but added with no pleasure, 'If you can teach those cowards who couldn't keep up with us, you're the son of Amon as much as Me.'

"I would have loved to tell Him my secret, but only said, 'We are all children of Amon.'

" 'Some more than others,' He said, and added, 'You're smart for a good rider. Usually a man has to be dumb as his horse. Like Me,' and He nudged His wife.

"I dared to laugh with Them, but what I did not know until later was that They were laughing at me. He knew the Temple of Ptah well enough to have had His Coronation there. All the same, the face of the First Charioteer, once he had caught up to us, was pale beneath the dust, and for the best of reasons. I was on my way to replacing him. Of course, it was a longer way than I knew that morning."

Three

"He took me back to Thebes, and I was put in charge of a troop. They took to my instruction slowly, however, and years went by. I despaired more than once of my boast that I could show all how to do it, since in the beginning, none could, but for one boy of ten, Prince Amen-khep-shu-ef, the oldest son of Ramses and Nefertiri."

"Now I am a little uncertain," said Ptah-nem-hotep. "How old was the Great Ramses when you first met him?"

"He was married to Princess Nefertiri, His sister, when He was thirteen and She was twelve, and Amen-khep-shu-ef was born within the same year. I would think the Prince was eight in the year His father came to Memphi, and that was when Ramses was twenty-one, and Nefertiri twenty."

"It is not easy to think of this great Pharaoh as young."

"He was young on the morning I met Him," said Menenhetet, "but already the father of a boy of eight, and by the time this boy was ten He had become the first of all the riders in Thebes to learn control of two horses with the reins about one's waist, although with all I taught Him, the Prince never thanked me. A most unusual boy, and stern enough to frighten grown men. Still, if not for His young skill,

I think that Usermare, my great Ramses the Second, would have been most unhappy with the poor progress of the other charioteers, but He was proud of His son, and forgave me much for that, and the others also learned—I think in shame—and finally they grew able. So He became more pleased with me, and on the day I showed Him twenty chariots who could ride at a gallop across a field, their line of attack even, the reins about every waist, all chariots able to turn on a signal, so that now each was riding behind the other, then turn front again, yes, He was so pleased that He made me not only His First Charioteer, but His Equerry which meant that I rode behind Him each morning. There was almost never an occasion when He did not go to the Great Temple of Amon in Thebes—He attended every morning—and that became my next duty.

"What a procession we would make through the streets! It was not like Memphi where we went at a gallop, oh no, we traveled no faster than the speed at which foot soldiers run, and two couriers had to go in front and cry out for the populace to stand back. On we would come, chosen soldiers from every regiment of His guard, each in different colors, the red and blue for the Sherdens, the black and gold for the Nubians, colors I still remember, then the lancers, and macebearers, the archers, all jogging on foot, and to the front of His horses were the standard-bearer and the fan-bearer. He liked them to stay just ahead.

"In Thebes, He would not often ride with Queen Nefertiri. Usually, She would follow in Her own chariot, and I in mine, also alone, and then every nobleman of the palace came behind, followed by charioteers. Hundreds went every day to the Temple of Amon, yet I was the only one allowed to enter the Sanctuary with Him.

"There is one morning of all those mornings," Menenhetet went on, "that I remember clearly, for it was the day war was declared with the Hittites. There are dawns that speak of how hot the afternoon will be, and this was such a morning, and the light and heat come forward in separate steps, as if on the padded feet of a beast.

"On the ride to the Temple, in the midst of the early warmth of that fierce day, one rare cloud came toward us out of the East like a

ship from a far-off place—almost never did we see clouds in the
morning—and it covered the sun. I do not think our horses had taken
two hundred steps before the cloud passed, but my Ramses the Second said, 'At the Temple, there will be unusual events today.' He was
not a Monarch renowned for the quickness of His thoughts, but then
He was as strong as three men and His slow thoughts must have allowed Him to hear the voices of Gods that more clever men do not.
So, this Pharaoh sometimes knew of events to come. On this occasion
He smiled dolefully at His wife and myself, for we had drawn up to
Him when He stopped, and He rubbed His long thin beautiful nose."

Ptah-nem-hotep now murmured: "His nose does not appear thin
in the sculptures I have seen."

"Its shape was to be changed at the Battle of Kadesh. But that was
later. Now, He said, 'This day is the beginning of the end for Me, yet
I will live twice as long as other men,' and He lifted His elbow and
took a long whiff of His armpit as if that was the first oracle to consult."

"As indeed it should be," said my father. We all knew the truth of
this remark. How could the odors that rose from the body of a King
not be close to each change in the fortunes of the Two-Lands? My
great-grandfather took the leisure to sniff at his own armpit in imitation of Ramses the Second, and did it with a strong open mouth as
if swallowing half a jar of beer. "Then," said my great-grandfather,
"my young Pharaoh having come to a stop, the procession stopped,
and that swarm of hundreds of boys who ran ahead of our horses in
order to cry up the alarm on every avenue, courtyard, great building,
alley, and choked-up slum just back of the Grand Avenue of Ramses
the Second (named in honor of His Ascension but a few years before)
became aware, as boys will, how in the tumult of their cries that the
Pharaoh is coming, the Pharaoh is coming, there was now to be heard
an absence of echo. The Pharaoh was not coming. The populace, instead of thronging toward the Grand Avenue, halted instead to watch
the silence of my King.

"But having contemplated the passing of the cloud and the root of
His arm, He had now decided to cross the river instead and make His

sacrifice instead on the West Bank. A most unusual procedure. It would take all of the morning and more. The West Bank, while never as congested as the East, was even then of the same length as it is today from south to north and the New Temple was not near. It would take a while to bring up the Royal Galley and ferry the Nile, not to speak of sending messengers to the High Priest of the First Temple of the East Bank to join us, and wait for that High Priest to order his own transport and pick the order of his First and Second Priests to accompany him—then all the confusion of such esteemed company having to mingle with lesser priests at the New Temple! It could be a most unpopular decision full of acrimony between the Temples. Yet how could He ignore the cloud? I shivered in memory of the chill cast by its shadow. When the Pharaoh looked at me, I knew He was waiting for a word, and so I said, raising my eyes to the sky, 'The cloud has also crossed to the West Bank.' In truth, the cloud was only moving north but our great stream took a bend at this point to the east, and that was enough for Him. We could go where He wanted to go in the first place.

"The horses started up again, the pack of boys ran ahead, the people came out of their shops, their kitchens, their work-houses, the girls in the brothels were up from their beds, children were released from school, and men and women ran in every direction trying to guess the route, for Ramses the Second rarely took the Grand Avenue all the way to the Temple but was even known to draw His retinue through many a dirty square that had no more than a few small shops and an old shaduf with a leaking pail. It was His way of seeing the city. The populace, as a result, was on the move to guess which streets might be chosen. If correct, they would take up their stand as close to the procession as they dared—a chariot wheel was known to cut off a few toes now and again—and the lucky men and women in the front rank had to brace their bodies against the surge of all who could not see from the rear.

"On this morning, now moving very fast to make up for the uneasiness of that moment when He did not immediately know His mind, it happened that the crowds pushed too much. There was an unmistakable cry. I heard the screech that lifts from the groin when the great bone of the thigh is broken, and later I heard of some young fellow who lost his leg to a chariot that day.

"Yet, in our hasty march, we proceeded until we came in sight of the pylons and flags of the First Temple, and could enter on the long avenue that leads past the hundred Sphinxes who line the promenade." My great-grandfather gave these details with a grimace, as though to apologize for the mention of sights the Pharaoh would know well, but I think he described it so in courtesy to me, who had never been to Thebes.

"Then, we entered the gate. Then, as now, many would say that the exterior of the First Temple of Amon of the East Bank of Thebes is equaled by no building in the world. No forest through which I have passed can summon as many Gods as one can hear whispering to one another when the breeze stirs in the Great Hall with its hundred and thirty-six stone pillars, each higher and of more thickness than any giant tree I have seen.

"I would yet go to war in lands where my pride had to grow small before the face of mountain cliffs, the beauty of forest foliage or the magnificence of high waterfalls. I would know that foreign Gods are great because of the extraordinary shape They can give to the land. But, in Egypt, where our country is flat and our mountains, by comparison, are low, the Gods have told us to build the wonders ourselves, and that has cost us much. Instead of feeling an immense pride at what we have done, we are without pride, and terrified of our own works. I know no mountain to inspire me with more awe than the Great Pyramid of Khufu, nor a forest to compare to the Hall of Columns in the Temple of Amon on the East Bank."

"That is all very well," said Ptah-nem-hotep, "but the Hall of Columns of which you speak was only finished by Ramses the Second later in His Reign."

There was a pause before my great-grandfather replied. "To have four lives," he said, "is to live like the passage of the Nile over its cataracts. Four cataracts have I passed over at my four births, and yet it is all one water. That is why I am often in error when I pass each bend.

You are able thus to remind me, You-of-the-Two-Great-Houses, that the Hall of Columns was not finished at the beginning of His Reign, yet it must have seemed completed, at least to me, for the roof was then in place and nearly a hundred columns were already erected; indeed I used to feel as if I wandered, like a child just able to walk, between the thighs of a multitude of Great Gods. There is no sound I have known like the rustling of that Great Hall at night. In my second life, as a High Priest, I used to wander by myself through the aisles and hear the stones communing with each other before dawn."

He paused. "On this morning, as on every morning, there was a multitude waiting in the open courtyard for a sight of our young Pharaoh, and a smaller group was gathered in the Hall of Columns, engaged, if you would believe it, in commerce of the most advanced sort. Land, cattle, poultry, jewelry, vases, and grain were being sold."

"You are certainly not saying there was a bazaar on the floor of the Great Temple?" asked my mother.

"More wondrous than that," my great-grandfather replied. "Business was being transacted between many of the priests and some of the wealthiest merchants and traders of Thebes, yet without an article in sight. Everybody knew one another so well that cheating was not often, I think, attempted. It was impractical. A swindle could be denounced the next day. Then the probity of the trader would be in question for years. Trust was so complete, and the taste for speculation so great, that a piece of land bought one day might be sold the next without the first buyer ever looking at it. If a fraud was thereby passed on, the purchase often had to be traced back through a number of traders before one could find the man who knew the goods were worthless in the first place."

"Does this still go on in the Hall of Columns?" asked Ptah-nem-hotep.

"Divine Two-House, I have not been often to Thebes in my fourth life. But during my third, when I was one of the wealthiest men of Egypt (by my reckoning at least) the practice still ensued, yet by subtler means. The traders would select certain priests and scribes as their agents. It showed more respect for the Temple. Those loud barterings that once howled like wind between the columns were now whispers. But the commerce still existed. This market where objects were for sale, but no buyer could see them, taught me much about wealth. I learned that it was not gold, nor the command of slaves, but rather the power to use another man's thoughts faster than he employed yours that went into amassing it. The absence of anything you could see for sale added to the delights of the game. Only the most astute traders could work in such austere surroundings."

"The priests had no fear of sacrilege?" asked my mother.

"Some did. But it is the severity of the Hall of Columns that makes the value of what one is selling most believable. One hesitates to swindle another in such a place. Besides, the smell from the sacrificial chambers surrounding the Hall of Columns adds to the excitement of this barter. Even as one swears to the authenticity of one's goods, so from the cool of these deep shadows comes the odor of blood and meat and the smell of fifty smokes to remind you that the Gods have Their own market, and it looks down upon ours."

"Did Ramses the Second know of such activities?"

"He used to sweep through the Hall of Columns with never a look at the traders. His mind was on His devotions. We would stop to wash our hands in the Sacred Pool, but then He would rush by chapel after chapel, until He came up to the oldest temple in the compound which in those years was the Sanctuary (until its walls collapsed during the period when I was High Priest) a gloomy room, I must say, built in the reign of Sesostris near to a thousand years ago, large, empty, narrow, of a high ceiling and gray stone walls with an opening in the south wall near the roof, so there was light near the altar from morning to mid-afternoon.

"I would, as I say, be selected to accompany Him into the Sanctuary and on the threshold He would leave the Queen—then, as now, no woman could enter the Holy of Holies, unless, like Queen Hatshep-sut, She had become the Pharaoh Herself. Nefertiri was conducted, therefore, to a large gilt chair and golden footstool in the Hall of Columns, and there She would wait with the King's retinue in ranks about Her, a woman surrounded by a company of nobles, and

yet not a morning would go by that I did not feel Her anger follow
me to the Sanctuary. Through all of the sacrifices that would follow,
through the chants and prayers that came from other chambers, the
pleas for restitution of damage, and contrition for wrongdoing, of all
this multitude of whispered requests and invocations and murmurings, of scoldings, laments and litanies that curled through the smoke
and burning blood of the altars of the chapels around us, I could still
feel the wrath of Queen Nefertiri, more intent than any prayer. I
would wait in silence, my head ringing at the woe that came out of
these supplications, one woman pleading to Amon for life to be given
to her womb, another bemoaning the death of her son"—Hathfertiti,
who by now had moved from her couch to mine, put her arm at this
point around me—"while next to such sorrow could be heard the
pride of a landowner giving over his tithe of cattle and wine and grain
and furniture and one slave per month in honor of the contract made
by him on the promotion of his son to the rank of Third Priest in this
Temple. I would hear all of it, even a beggar's voice full of old sores
long-crusted in his throat while he snuffled forth his request of some
priest passing him by, and to all of this, Ramses the Second was separated by His Sanctuary, and by His pious mind, but so soon as He
entered the Temple and could feel the presence of Amon, my Ramses
the Second was no longer a friend or a fellow-charioteer, but a Monarch, as grand and remote from oneself as the sky. Indeed, as we came
to the great copper doors of the Sanctuary, it was only in a mood of
the most profound solemnity that He broke the clay seal, and we entered.

"Inside, in the middle of the stone floor was a circle of silver soil,
that is, some white sand with many shavings of silver, and Ramses
would kneel upon it, and stare in contemplation on the Sacred Bark
which rested on the silver sand. I, kneeling beside Him, would feel
these filings cutting my knees. The King, however, did not move.
Ramses the Second had little patience in other matters, yet there was
no time of day happier to Him than resting on His knees before the
Bark of Amon. That boat, if I may describe it for my family, was no
more than six paces long, but covered with gold leaf, and ornamented

by a ram's head of silver in the prow, and another in the stern. We
looked at these wonders and rested our knees on the silver sand in this
great stone room old as the centuries, and therefore possessed of the
chill of great age even on a hot day. Besides, the presence of Amon
was enough to bring cold to the air! It was dark, all but entirely dark
in that place if not for the single shaft of light that came down from
the small opening high in the south wall to light up the monumental
bulk of the old altar, but now in the near-darkness it was the ark that
kept our attention more, for its gold sides glowed with fire in the
gloom like the rich light one can sometimes see in one's heart. Kneeling, I could feel the presence of Amon in His cabin on that ark. In His
small cabin, not so high as the space from my knees to my breast, was
the Greatest God, there within! And we could know Him, for His
mood was more powerful than the coming of night to the Nile, indeed we always could say as we knelt before Him whether He was
happy with us or much displeased.

"Soon, the High Priest, Bak-ne-khon-su, would come into the
Sanctuary with two young priests—the one who was Tongue, and
the one called Pure."

Ptah-nem-hotep asked, "Are these the Superintendents of Prayer
and Purity?"

"Their titles have changed," said Menenhetet.

"Ever so much."

"It was different then. Bak-ne-khon-su would wear no more than
a white skirt; his feet were bare. Tongue and Pure would oil their
scalps. Their heads would gleam. I would be impressed by the cleanliness of their dress, for many a priest had linen spattered with the
blood of sacrifice. Some even smelled of burnt meat. But not the
High Priest. He was a man with a simple manner and now he said no
more than, 'The clay is broken and the seal is loosed. The door is
open. All that is evil in me, I throw on the ground.' With that, he
prostrated himself before the Pharaoh and kissed His toe, even as
Tongue and Pure kissed the ground to either side of Bak-ne-khon-su.
All three kept looking up with adoration.

"I can tell you that despite their rank, they were not brothers to know much of matters outside the Temple. Bak-ne-khon-su was most unlike Khem-Usha. If he was a Third Priest by the age of twenty-two, he had to wait until he was near to forty before becoming a Second Priest. During all those years, it was said he remained a vessel of innocence, but little more. No one thought of him with great regard until my Pharaoh made him High Priest. I think his loyalty to Ramses the Second may have been his first virtue. I might also say he conducted all services with exceptional care.

"So, for instance, when Pure opened the door of the cabin, Bak-ne-khon-su not only kissed the ground, but did it with his arms behind him so that he was obliged to incline himself forward until supported by no more than his knees and his nose, yet from this awkward position, he was able to roll his face on the ground in genuine terror at the awesome act of opening the cabin and this was true even if they did it every day.

"My eyes had grown used to the dark of the Sanctuary, so I could see the statue. The gold of Amon's skin was smooth; His hair, and the chin-phallus of His beard, were black; and the black stone of His eyes looked at me carefully. I could swear to that. I felt a new fear this morning, for it may be that I had never dared to look into the face of Amon before, yet He seemed less like a God than a small man, with features not nearly so handsome as Ramses the Second and certainly not so fine as the delicate and somewhat sunken cheeks of Bak-ne-khon-su. Indeed, Amon looked like a wealthy little fellow you might see in the streets. He was certainly being treated with intimacy. The High Priest stood up, bowed in four directions, took a cloth and said, 'Let Thy seat be adorned and Thy robes exalted,' and he reached into the cabin and wiped the old rouge from Amon's cheeks. With another prayer he applied new rouge. Amon now looked more cheerful." I hardly wished to stop listening to my great-grandfather, but it was impossible to ignore my father at this point, who smiled at Ptah-nem-hotep as if he would call attention to the importance of those moments when he, as Chief Overseer of the Cosmetic Box, would apply rouge to the Pharaoh's cheeks.

"Now Bak-ne-khon-su removed yesterday's garment from the

golden limbs and plump golden belly of Amon, and replaced it with
fresh linen and new jewelry. Each piece removed was blessed by
Tongue and kissed by Pure, then laid away in a chest of ebony and
ivory. A perfume of sandalwood was sprinkled upon Amon's brow
and a cup of water was set before Him with a plate containing a few
fine bites of meat and duck and honey. Then the priests lit the incense, and prayed aloud, 'Come, White-Dress,' they said, 'come,
White-Eye of Horus. The Gods dress with Thee, and Thy name is
Dress. The Gods adorn Themselves, and Thy name is Adornment.'

"I was young then and had no idea I would ever die and live again,
and become a High Priest, but even in that early hour, the smell of
incense in the Sanctuary was like no odor I knew, for it was scalding
to the nostrils, yet sweet and mysterious, and with good reason. I
came to learn when I was High Priest that there was much in the incense. I tell it now because You are my Pharaoh, but in my second life
as a priest, I would not have dared to speak of what was in it. Of
course, even as I tell this now, I do not recite the prayers that accompany the mixing, only that this subtle powder held the balm of resin,
and onycha and galbanum and frankincense, and there were lesser
quantities of myrrh, cassia, spikenard and saffron. I can say there were
also carefully chosen amounts of aromatic fruit rind powdered with
cinnamon, then marinated with lye and wine and salt, plus salt of
copper to give a blue flame. Indeed, the lye was best taken from the
root of leeks wherever leeks could be found to grow in high stony
places. This was a secret of the High Priest of those days."

I wished to hear more, but Menenhetet paused. He would wait—
so his manner said—while those who desired could muse over the
salts and powders he had described. These herbs could bring back
memories, after all, of funerals, or perfumed couches, and so his audience was likely to be distracted by many thoughts. But I had no need
to brood on galbanum and frankincense. I waited to hear the story.
My great-grandfather's tale might be full of bends but like our Nile,
it did not matter if the river flowed south for a time since we knew it
would always turn to the north again.

So, I was patient. I knew that the four lives of my great-grandfather

were like the four corners that make the foundation of a box. His
mind could hold what any of us might wish to put within it—there
was no matter on which he had not thought. Even as one can step into
a boat and float down our river, thinking at first only of how far one
has gone, so after hours of travel one begins to see that it is not really
a large distance one has traversed but yet the river is longer by far than
the greatest journey one has taken before—that way, too, did the
long slow current of my great-grandfather's mind give promise to
pass every palace and cave I had encountered in my sleep.

Now when he began to speak again of the presence of Ramses the
Second in the Sanctuary, I could feel the attention of my mother and
father return, then of Ptah-nem-hotep, for He had pondered the
longest over the ingredients of the incense.

"In other places than the Temple," said Menenhetet, "Ramses the
Second was, as I say, impatient. Indeed, He had the impatience of a
great lady just so much as of a great man. His face, as I believe I have
related, would have been as perfect on a woman as on a man. It was
therefore a pure expression of Maat that He had so great an Estate
below. One knew what a man He was when offered a glimpse through
His robes of the stoutest longest friend any man ever carried. The
dissatisfaction of beauty may have been on His face, but the authority
of Egypt dwelt between His thighs."

"I have heard as much," said Ptah-nem-hotep in a voice as dry as
the sands of our desert.

"Yes," said my great-grandfather, "and I have observed that most
of those who are so fortunate as to have been given the great member
of a God often show an uncontrollable lack of patience. Our Usermare, Ramses the Second, on any ordinary occasion, could wait for
delay no more than a lion can be taunted, but in the Temple, He was
as peaceful as the shade of a tree.

"So when Bak-ne-khon-su asked of my Pharaoh which question
the Lord of the Two-Lands might like to present to the Hidden One
this morning after the sacrifice, the Chosen-of-Ra replied only, 'In
the curl of My tongue is the question still sleeping.' In truth, how
could He know His true question after the cloud crossed the sun?

"The door to the Sanctuary was now opened by Tongue and Pure, and a white ram came through the portal, led by two young priests, one at each horn. Two priests followed at the rear holding pointed sticks to prod the ram's flanks. Then, as now, gold cords tied the beast's front feet close to each other. He could walk but not run. I may say, however, that in those days more care was taken with the animal itself. His horns were covered with gold leaf, and his skin was powdered until he was sweet smelling and whiter in appearance than our linen.

"This animal was, however, distraught. Some beasts are at peace with Amon when they enter the Sanctuary, which is in itself a good sign. For then their entrails usually prove firm, and do not excite any dispute concerning the shape. This animal, however, must have seen the same cloud, because on encountering the altar, he gave one mournful sound, as though wounded by the knife already, and defecated. Three large wet deposits were laid on the stone.

"It was three and that is the number of change. We would have preferred four, the base of good foundation. The priests waited, therefore. But when no further tremor showed in the animal's hide, and the ram's mouth relaxed, we could feel Amon stirring in the manner of a guest getting ready to leave. Tongue and Pure came forward then with two handfuls of silver sand from the sacred circle on which the Bark was laid, and they drew smaller circles of silver around each dropping.

"Now the animal was brought to the sacrificial stone. I have not described the altar, but I think it is because I never liked to look at it. The Sanctuary, being the old Sanctuary—it is all rebuilt now—was a thousand years old, old as Sesostris, I say, yet the altar was more ancient. I do not believe it had been washed in that thousand years. Old blood lay upon older blood—you shiver, Hathfertiti, and make a face," said my great-grandfather, "but there is much to be studied, for this ancient blood was darker than the night and harder than stone. The Gods may race through our veins, but They make Their home where blood has dried on the rock.

"Bak-ne-khon-su began to speak to Amon. He had a light voice, and he spoke tenderly as if to the God Himself, using the quiet tones of a man who has spent every day in the service of his ruler, and never uncomfortable in the life he had chosen. While the priests held the ram's head by the altar, its neck above the fount, Bak-ne-khon-su approached with a sacrificial knife and began to utter the words Amon once spoke to the King Thutmose the Third,

'I have made them see Thy Majesty as a circling star
'Who scatters its flame in fire and gives forth its dew.'

"He drew the knife across the neck of the ram, and the animal gave one shake of its horns as if it had just looked into the eye of the sun. Then it stood there shaking to some piteous quivering of its heart. We listened to the sound of blood dripping down upon blood. It is so much more serious than the little cry of water falling on other water.

"Bak-ne-khon-su said:

'I have made them see Thy Majesty as a crocodile,
'The Lord of Fear in the water,
'I give Thee to smite those who live on islands.
'In the midst of the Very Green, they hear Thy roar.'

"And on that," said Menenhetet, "with the skill of a Royal Carpenter splitting a post, so did Bak-ne-khon-su kneel before this ram held by the four priests, and, in the dim light, took a long cut with the knife down the ram's body that not one in a hundred good butchers could have repeated, so quick and certain was the gesture. All of the loose organs, the stomach, the entrails, the liver, and the spleen, fell with a sigh to the stone, and the animal tumbled over. I saw an expression of great beauty come over its worried face and pass from the eyes to the nostrils. I saw its expression change from a twitching terrified beast to a noble one, as if it knew that its life was out there on the stone, and the Gods were offering attention. Like all that lives, the Gods know how to feed on the dead. May the dead not learn to feed upon us."

It was a small remark, yet in the warm night under the soft glow of the fireflies, I knew that fear when we cannot say of what we are afraid. Is it of wild animals, evil friends, or angry Gods? Or are they gathered together in the same air?

"That sacrifice," said Menenhetet, "was of relief to me. I had been close to the dread warriors often feel before a battle, and had hardly been able to breathe as the ram was led forward. Yet the final convulsion of its legs relieved a noose upon my chest, and I took in all the air I could, all the cavernous odors of flesh that had been packed in darkness upon flesh.

"Bak-ne-khon-su knelt then and laid his ten fingers on the entrails and lifted the topmost coils gently to search the turns beneath. Near the center, like a snake that had swallowed a rabbit, was a swelling in one loop, and I felt a congestion in my throat, and will try to explain, for in truth it was an uncouth age compared to ours, that in those days we studied the entrails with much seriousness. The animal might be dead, but in its coils had been left the power to fertilize the land. So these entrails had as much to tell as any piece of gold. The gold we spend may no longer belong to us, but on its travels it inspires great warmth in others."

"If this is what they call philosophy," said my mother, "it has a mighty stench."

"On the contrary," said Ptah-nem-hotep, "I am fascinated by the places through which your heart has passed. You study what others choose to wash away."

Menenhetet nodded at the fine edge of this remark, and went on.

"Standing around the circle of silver sand, our eyes on the navel of the little gold belly of Amon, we waited while the priests cut away pieces of meat from the haunch of the ram, and laid them on the fire of the altar. There, in the thick air of the smoke as new blood charred on the hot stone, we felt the worth of the ram pass into the bellies of the Gods Who were waiting—which is to say I felt close to a great force in the room. Then I heard the voice of Amon stirring His golden belly, even as Bak-ne-khon-su had stirred the entrails of the ram. The High Priest began to speak, but no longer in his own tones, rather in a sound mighty as the echo of a great chamber. Out of the lungs and throat of Bak-ne-khon-su came a huge and unforgettable voice:

" 'To the King Who is My slave. Seven times may You fall at My feet. For You are the footstool of My feet, the groom of My horse, You are My dog.'

" 'I am Your dog,' whispered Ramses. He had trouble speaking, but I could never have uttered a word. My teeth ground upon one another like bone mortared to bone. Never had the voice of Amon been so great in the Sanctuary. Walls could have shattered from the power of that voice. 'Yes, I am Your dog,' repeated Ramses, 'and I live in fear of Your displeasure. This morning, a cloud passed before the face of Amon-Ra.'

"Bak-ne-khon-su was silent, and the voice of Amon was silent, but a babble came from the fire. Through the crackle of the flames, I could hear many voices, and as if this were the sound of many princes and persons inquiring of Him, Ramses the Second now opened His jaws and with as much courage, I am certain, as if I had tried to speak into the mouth of a cave where a beast was waiting, so did He say, 'You Who are Ra and Amon are the God of all good and great soldiers, and I bow before You.' My Pharaoh began to tremble like the ram as He spoke: 'Last night an officer came into My presence with a message from the King of the Hittites, Metella, who declares that he wishes to insult the Two-Lands. He has killed our allies, and taken many cattle and sheep. Now he is in his city of Kadesh with a mighty army and challenges Me to war. He challenges Me! Help Me to avenge this insult.'

"Ramses the Second began to weep—a sight I had never seen before. In a voice that choked, He whispered, 'A cloud covered the sun this morning. I shiver before Him Who dares to insult You. I feel weak in My limbs.'

"The air was heavy with burning meat," said Menenhetet, "an odor so heavy I would not breathe it again until the Battle of Kadesh, but through that thickness of smoke and the lamentations of the Pharaoh, a silence followed. I would swear I saw the corners of the painted mouth of Amon turn downward in displeasure. Yet through

the smoke, and by the white light that still trembled in my heart when
I closed my eyes, how could I know what I saw? I had not eaten since
dawn, and the smell of meat burning on the altar inflamed my stomach. Then, the great clamor of the voice of Amon was heard again in
the throat of Bak-ne-khon-su. In cries of fearful rage, so did Amon
say: 'If You betray Me, Your legs will run like water down a hill, Your
right arm is dead, Your heart will weep forever. But if You are with
Me, they will see You as a Lord of Light. You will shine over their
heads like Myself. You will be like a lion in his rage. You will crush
the barbarian, and crouch over their corpses in the valley. You will be
safe on the sea. The Very Green will be like a string tied to Your wrist.
Yes!' said Amon in a voice so great that Bak-ne-khon-su's lips went
still and the golden statue began to vibrate on the seat of its cabin in
the Bark (until, through my closed eyes, I could see those gold lips
moving beneath their rouge) 'Yes, they will look upon Your Majesty
as My two Princes, Horus and Set. It is Their arms I bring together to
guard Your victory. Bring to My temples the gold and jewels of Asia.'

" 'I am as Your dog,' said my Pharaoh, 'even as the soldiers are My
dogs, and the soldiers of the Hittites are My soldiers' dogs.' He bowed
again and the God was silent. Soon we left the Sanctuary for the banquet room and there ate part of the meat of the ram that Amon had
left for us after His own meal was done. I was much impressed by the
superior taste of this food and thought His saliva might still be flavor-
ing it.

" 'Come,' said Ramses the Second before I was finished with the
meal, and His eyes were still red from weeping, 'come with Me to
cross the river. I want to visit My tomb.' "

Four

"I had much to think about," my great-grandfather told us, "as we were rowed across to the Western Bank of Thebes. I had just heard the most powerful voice ever to enter my head, and my ears rang. In other years, when I became a priest and was instructed in the mysteries of language, I came to learn that the sounds uttered by a God are equal to what He desires. So in ancient days, a God could say: 'chair,' and lo!, there was a chair.

"Of course, in these years, we are not close to the Gods. We can roar like a lion, but we can never call the beast forth.

"I, however, on this morning of which I speak, had just heard a mighty voice issue from a heart of gold. It had captured the lips and throat of Bak-ne-khon-su, and made him serve as the voice of Amon. So we knew that victory would be ours if we were faithful.

"That, all the same, was what dismayed me now. Today, our religious ceremonies had been different from other occasions. Usually, ten or more priests entered with a bull, not a ram, and a Reciter-Priest would stand at my Pharaoh's elbow to whisper which prayer came next, or how many steps to take."

"They have such a fellow today," said Ptah-nem-hotep, "but his manner is not altogether civil."

"It was otherwise, then," said Menenhetet, "and done with great respect. Once, I counted a hundred separate gestures accompanying one prayer and, in my ignorance, missed another hundred I would learn later as a priest. How then could a Monarch like Ramses the Second, with His mind fixed on war, remember the order? Yet if the King could avoid all mistakes during the service, it was our belief—we were simple in those days, I repeat—that Amon would not ignore our request. In truth, I remember how at the beginning of many a service, Bak-ne-khon-su would often place into the golden hand of Amon a roll of papyrus on which the High Priest had written a petition. Then, at the completion of prayers, Bak-ne-khon-su would take it back. Feeling its presence in his palm, he would be able to state whether the Great God wished to say yes or no to the request. Of course, I always believed Bak-ne-khon-su could interpret the word of Amon. There were other High Priests, however, in other years whom I did not trust as well. I thought the answers to their petitions told me more about the servant than about the wisdom of Amon. All the same, when I became a High Priest myself (and I was, I must say, no model of purity like Bak-ne-khon-su, but reached such a position only by my nearness to Ramses the Second in my second life when I was young and He was very old) I learned that I, too, was not ready to pass over the word of the God. No, the feelings of Amon were too fearsome to ignore when the roll of papyrus quivered in one's hand."

"Your lives are as strange as the taste of a new spice," said our Pharaoh and smiled at my mother. At this sign of attention given to her, first in some time, she was quick to smile back, but in her mind (and I, listening to our great-grandfather with all of my attention, had not been near to her mind for a while) now saw her hand move forward in her thoughts to touch her fingertips to a surface as lovely as her own skin, but it was under the skirt of Ptah-nem-hotep that her hand would travel, and His thigh was the one she stroked in her thoughts, upon which the Pharaoh sat up in His chair and felt for His leopard

tail. "You were speaking," He said to Menenhetet, "of the power of
petition of a High Priest."

"Yes," said my great-grandfather. "If my request asked the Pharaoh to enrich the Temple of Thebes, I would know the answer I
desired. A High Priest must increase the wealth of his Temple. Amon's
confidence being gained by gifts, it is gained best by great gifts. So,
my petition might beg Amon to instruct our old Ramses to give over
to the Temple a tenth more of the tribute He had received from Libya
in the last year. My hand, as it touched the petition, expected to hear
no response from Amon but Yes, yet with all my desire for such a result, I could feel the clear displeasure of the Hidden One if on a given
morning He did not desire such added tribute."

"Did you then announce this conclusion?" Ptah-nem-hotep asked.

"I cannot remember, my Lord. My only recollection is that I
would dread such a reply when it came on me. How awful was the
touch of the petition when it said: No! The papyrus could feel as
unpleasant as a snakeskin.

"Now, I, of course, on the day we crossed the river to visit the
tomb of Ramses the Second, knew little of these fine matters. I only
understood that nothing had taken place as on other mornings.

"I was not surprised, therefore, that it became a day where every
event was unexpected. No sooner had we landed at the wharf on the
Western Bank of Thebes than my Pharaoh invited me into His Chariot for the first time, and the horses were as shocked as myself to recognize that Nefertiri was not present. The names of these horses, I
remember, were Strength-of-Thebes and Maat-is-Satisfied, a stallion
and a mare, and the mare, as you would expect, was remarkably like
Nefertiri. She never liked to be separated from her mate. You had
only to command Strength-of-Thebes and it was as if you had spoken
to the eight legs of both beasts. Nor were these horses ever happier
than when the Queen rode with the King.

"But, my Ramses drove off with me, leaving all who had come
with us behind. So I now learned that the people of Western Thebes,
accustomed to see their King only in a procession, did not know to

look up when His Chariot was unaccompanied. They were left with
no more than a glimpse of the War-Crown on His head, thereby to
realize that the Good and Great God had passed, O Double-House of
Egypt," said my great-grandfather, as if apologizing that a Pharaoh
could ride anywhere in Egypt without everyone being aware of His
passage. Menenhetet then struck the table seven times with his hand
as if to ward off any disrespect in what he would next say. "On this,
the Night of the Pig, I could speak of many Pharaohs. I have known
Them as Gods and I have known Them as men. Of Them all—if it
please Your interest—"

"It does."

"—Ramses the Second was least difficult to know as a Pharaoh,
and most difficult to comprehend as a man. Of His piety I have just
given You good measure, yet when He was away from the Temple,
He was indifferent to who might hear His voice. He swore as simply
as a soldier. And when with Nefertiri, He was more like a man in love
than a King. Yet if She was not with us, He hardly spoke of Her with
respect. On this morning, as we started off in His Chariot, He even
said, 'Do you know She had a fit because I told Her to stay on the
Eastern Bank? "Go back," I told Her. "Nurse what You must nurse. I
want to be alone." ' My Pharaoh laughed. 'She does not like to nurse,'
He added, 'She doesn't even like Her wet-nurse,' and He gave a great
whoop to the horses, and a crack of the reins on their back so we were
in a gallop right out of a trot and tearing down the Boulevard of Osiris on the Western Bank like two charioteers with an afternoon to
spend on beer, yes, now I see how He was different from other Kings.
The weight of other Pharaohs can be seen in Their presence on all
occasions, but my good Ramses the Second thought little of that.
Like a boy, He would take off His clothes if it suited Him. He had a
mouth that would look at you as if it did not know whether it wanted
a kiss or a bite out of your best parts."

My mother gave a laugh so full of the depths of her own flesh that
I could all but feel the black hair between her legs and the red face of
a young man with golden hair and lips as red as my mother's smiling
at the sight. I felt Sweet Finger again—except there were a hundred

sweet Fingers up her belly and down mine and I wondered if this man with the golden hair could be Ramses the Second come forward from the dead, and that confused me so thoroughly that I only returned to what my great-grandfather was saying on these words: "I never liked the Western Bank."

"Well, I do not like it today," said Ptah-nem-hotep, and with such vehemence that I saw the picture in His brain, that is, saw the Western Bank as it would look to me now from a boat in the middle of the river. Thereby, I had the sight of a plain with high cliffs to the west and many temples in the valley. There were great broad avenues going in every direction. Yet it did not look like a city so much as a park, and then not at all a royal park for there were swamps between some of the avenues, and long empty diggings of foundations where great buildings must have been planned and never finished. I could see very few people on the boulevards and only one or two wagons. This meant the Western Bank must be altogether different from the East Bank of Thebes which, if it were at all like Memphi, had to be crowded and friendly and full of narrow alleys. Whereas on the Western Bank, there was so much space that you could see a number of new towns built in regular rows between the great boulevards, and climbing into the foothills. But since each stone house in these places had a little pyramid for its roof, I realized they were not houses but tombs in the Great Necropolis of Western Thebes, and indeed looked like a thousand hats planted in the desert, with over there, another thousand hats. Yet the plan of each street was so much the same that my eyes began to water, and I wondered if living people really thought the dead liked to live on streets that did not curve.

My great-grandfather must have heard each of my thoughts (unless I was living in his) for now I heard him say: "The streets of the Necropolis were laid out in right angles on the calculation that the best return is brought back from land sold in small square pieces."

"Menenhetet, you are wicked," the Pharaoh remarked. "I always thought these streets were kept straight to discourage thieves and evil spirits."

"That is also true," said my great-grandfather. "Fewer guards are necessary when one can see from one end of a lane to the other, and spirits are certainly weakened when they cannot dodge and turn. Yet when the decision was first made in the Temple of Amon at Karnak to lay out square plots, none of us knew they would prove so popular. I was High Priest at the time, and can tell You we needed the revenue. I speak of a period fifty years and more after the Battle of Kadesh when Ramses the Second was very old and had no interest in war. So, the Temple could only count on the tribute that still came in from the sons of old conquered Princes. Thereby, we had fewer gifts for Amon. Contemplate the labors of a High Priest like myself when each morning the Great God sneered at me each time I wiped off His old rouge, and Tongue and Pure put on the new.

"I came to the simple conclusion that gifts to make Amon happy did not have to come only from the Pharaoh. Many of the people were wealthy enough to buy plots in the Necropolis.

"Now, I must explain that even on the strange morning of which I speak when Ramses the Second gave me the honor of accompanying Him, there was a Necropolis on the Western Bank. Only it was not like the one today with its thousands of tombs. In that time, there were only a few great avenues. The Necropolis itself was small, and no one but nobles of the best family could be buried in it. I remember the envy I felt at the thought I would never rest on the Western Bank. It seemed to me that a man who has been welcomed into the company of a Pharaoh ought to be entitled to a tomb, and have the history of his life written on the walls. But I knew that was impossible. If you were not a great noble, you could not begin in those years to think of a life in the Land of the Dead. Among the peasants with whom I grew up, we always heard that the pits of Khert-Neter were so terrible, and you encountered such serpents, scorpions and evil Gods, that only a Pharaoh or a few of His royal brothers would dare to make the trip down the Duad. For any ordinary man, the journey was impossible. So, as soon as you died, you expected your family to take you out in the desert, dig a hole, and cover you with sand. If you were a peasant, you did not even brood about it much. But when I became a charioteer, it irked me how many relatives of the Pharaoh had a tomb and could take treasures with them through Khert-Neter, and after this day when I rode in His Chariot, the desire to have a plot in the Royal City of the Dead arose in me.

"So, when I became a High Priest many years later, I knew that rich commoners would want to purchase land in this Necropolis. Because of a special element, however—if I may so speak—in the character of Ramses the Great which developed after the Battle of Kadesh, we did not have to sell to commoners after all. For by His old age, thousands of people in Thebes could claim to be His children, grandchildren, or great-grandchildren. At the least, they were married to His descendants. By then, only the poorest commoner could not claim to be some kind of kin to Usermare-Setpenere, that Sun-who-is-powerful-through-Truth, Ramses the Second.

"That, however, was after the Battle of Kadesh. On this day, riding with pride in His Chariot, who could think of all that was to come? I merely looked at what there was to see while He took us along on a fast gallop down the empty boulevards of Western Thebes. There were not many people there then, as I say, and they all worked for the Necropolis and in the mortuary temples and looked sicklier somehow to my good eyes than people of the East Bank. Even the priests of the mortuary temple seemed thin and drawn compared to those priests who came walking through the Great Hall that is like a forest in the Temple of Karnak. Although these fellows at Karnak also live much in the shade, they grow plump from the sacrifices they consume and the gold they weigh in the vaults, whereas, the ones of the Western Bank, while quite free to enjoy the quiet sun of all their fine gardens and plazas, were bored, I think, by the peace of the ages that you had to breathe in Western Thebes. I think most of these priests wanted to be across the river at Karnak and so their unhappiness came into the air. By late afternoon, I knew it would be mournful. So long as the sun was still high, it was all right, but soon terrible shadows would flow like water from the cliffs to cover the temple gardens with gloom.

"All the while I did not know where my Pharaoh was taking me, but He had decided to visit no place less splendid than the Temple of Hat-shep-sut, and as we drove up, there were, to my surprise, not a dozen priests to turn out. But then there was not even the smell of a sacrifice burning. I think we might have been the first people to visit in days. Of course, it had been built by a woman and looked more like a palace than a temple. My Pharaoh said, 'I used to laugh at this place. Only a woman would build a temple with nothing but cocks,' and clapped me on the back like we were two infantrymen. I was shocked at how He spoke, but then He did say, 'Count the cocks,' and I did, and there were twenty-four columns all holding up a roof, and above was another row of shorter columns, altogether a white and beautiful temple and very large, and the cliffs went straight up to the sky just back of the temple. When my King had chased away the priests who came to greet Him, we mounted onto a patio above the first roof, and there was a garden with hundreds of myrrh trees. I had smelled myrrh in every incense that ever smoked in a temple and knew the power of its odor, but here in the shadow of these cliffs which must have been higher than a hundred men standing on top of each other's shoulders, in the sun of midday with the desert-yellow of the hills all around us, the scent of myrrh from each of these little trees was an odor to fill my head and make me think that the middle of my thoughts could be as clear and empty as the sky. When a priest brought out two gold stools, one for the Pharaoh, and one, to my delight, for myself, to-gether with a golden cup of wine for each of us, I could also taste the myrrh in the wine and it was like a sniff of funeral wrappings with their spices. So, all the while that I felt as alive as the light in the sky, I was still drinking a wine which spoke to me of the middle of the night and strange thoughts.

" 'These myrrh trees,' said Ramses the Second, 'are from Her,' and I thought at first He could only mean His own Queen Nefertiri, but He added, 'Hat-shep-sut,' and was silent. Then He told me they had been carried here for Amon Who had ordered Queen Hat-shep-sut to bring this Land of Punt to His House. Despite the heat, I shivered as I listened, for the scent of myrrh made me cold, and my King told me that a good many expeditions had failed before Hat-shep-sut sent Her fleet. The Queen's five ships came back, however, with myrrh, and ebony and ivory and cinnamon wood and the first baboons and unique

monkeys never seen before as well as new kinds of dogs, the skins of
the southern panther, and natives from Punt with skins so black they
looked more purple than the snails of Tyre. 'Hat-shep-sut was that
pleased She told Her lover Sen-mut to build this temple to Her honor.
Two rows of cocks.' He started to laugh, but then grasped me by the
arm and said, 'One night, I came here with Nefertiri and We were
alone on this terrace. Amon spoke to Me and said: It is dark but You
will see My Light. When Nefertiri and I made love, I saw Our first
child, being made, for We were connected as a rainbow to the earth.
So I do not laugh at this temple all the time, although I hate the odor
of myrrh.' With this He stood up, and we left, and He rode at such a
gallop I could not speak a word. I did not know why, but He was as
furious as if we were in battle already.

"Then, with His eyes, which were quick like the eyes of the hawk,
He saw a movement across a field, and took our chariot off the boulevard, and over rough ground until we passed through a small ravine
where there were many bushes, and two peasant girls walking ahead.
I can tell you that as they stood to the side for us to go by, so was my
Usermare off the chariot, and in the bushes with one girl leaving the
other for me—such was His rush. (He could swing a sword faster than
anyone I knew.) Quick as He spent the vigor of His Double-Crown
to her front and back, He was ready with another set of salutes for my
girl, and offered me His. Of course the new one, like the one before,
smelled of mud, but I fell upon her with more gusto than the first as
if, like my Pharaoh, I was in a charge of chariots. Of course, never in
my life had I been more excited than at the thought of trodding into
a cave where the Pharaoh, so to speak, had just been stepping in His
bare feet."

"You felt no hesitation?" asked my mother. Ptah-nem-hotep nodded. "I am curious," He said, "that you knew no fear. These adventures, after all, took place only in your first life."

"But I could not have felt more awe if I had gone into battle," my
great-grandfather replied.

"Yet," said Ptah-nem-hotep, "if one is afraid, is it not easier to join
a battle than to make love? In battle, you need only raise your arm."

"Yes," said my great-grandfather, "except that I was joined to that girl in battle. I struck her thighs many times with my soft club. In truth, I felt some shame. My member, by comparison with what she had just known, was not what you would call mighty. Besides, the first girl was now screaming with joy at the force with which Usermare-Setpenere was jamming her. Still, I thumped my way into position, and then felt the great call of the chariot. My toes dug a hole in the ground before I was done. For my member was bathing in the creams of the Pharaoh. How good was the smell of the earth. 'I love the stink of peasant women,' the Pharaoh told me as we rode off, 'especially when it lives on My fingers. Then I am near to embracing My great Double-Land itself.'

"I was still feeling a pleasure as brilliant as awakening in the fields with the sun in my face. Even as I had come forth into that peasant girl, her heart came into me. I saw a great white light, as if from her belly, and the waters of the Pharaoh flew across my closed eyes like a thousand white birds. I felt my member had been anointed forever."

"And all," said Ptah-nem-hotep, "from one share in common with a peasant girl."

"Look, the child is sleeping," said my mother.

I was pretending to. I had noticed that as my great-grandfather told more, everyone present took less notice of me, and by now I had only to close my eyes and they would forget I was there. That was agreeable. They did not trouble any longer to cover their thoughts. But then, in truth, I was near to sleep, for I found myself comprehending matters I had never seen, and for which I knew no name.

"We rode off again," said my great-grandfather, "as if nothing had happened, but so soon as we quit the ruts of the field for the greater ruts of one of those unfinished boulevards, He stopped and said, 'In the Sanctuary this morning, in the middle of our prayers, I saw Myself. I was alone, and I was dead. In the middle of the battle I was surrounded, and I was alone, and I was dead.' Before I could reply, He had the horses galloping again. My jaws were slamming against my head.

"I did not know where He would take us, but before long we were out of the town and riding along a narrow road that soon became a trail through a break in the cliffs. Now it grew so steep that we dismounted and sometimes had to stop to lift stones that had fallen on the trail from the heights on either side. Once or twice, I thought He was ready to tie the steeds, but after we climbed through the notch, it widened a little, and I could see it had once been a road.

"When we stopped to rest, we were all alone in the middle of a ravine, and it was then He said, 'I will show you a place that is as secret to Me as My Secret Name, and you will not live if you betray this place.' He looked at me with such warmth that I felt as if I were in the presence of Ra Himself.

" 'But first,' He said to me, 'I must tell you the story of Egypt. Otherwise you would be ignorant of the importance of My secret.' " With this, my great-grandfather came to a complete pause, looked at all of us, and sighed, as though to comment on his ignorance then. "You cannot know, Great Ninth," he said, "how little I understood by my Pharaoh's remark. I had never known that Egypt had a story. I had a story, and there were charioteers I knew with stories, and a whore or two, but the story of Egypt!—I hardly knew what to say. We had a river and it flooded each year. We had Pharaohs, and the oldest man I knew could remember one who was different from all the others because He did not believe in Amon, but I didn't remember His name. Before that, there had been Thutmose the Third for whom our Royal School of Charioteers was named, and Queen Hat-shep-sut, and a Pharaoh, thousands of years ago, named Khufu but He lived in Memphi, not Thebes, and built a mountain higher than anyone had seen in the Two-Lands and two other mountains built by two other Pharaohs were next to it. That was all the story of Egypt I knew.

"He told me of other things, however. We sat side by side on the rocks of the ravine looking out to the Eastern Bank. In the distance, across the river, Thebes was thriving, and we could hear the sounds of its workshops as clearly as the echo of a rock falling in the next canyon. So it is hard to think of myself as dreaming, although I could not separate the stories He told me about Thutmose the Third, and

Amenhotep the Second, and the Third. Yet when He went on to speak of His own Father, Seti, I could see one Pharaoh clearly at last since Seti's picture had been chiseled into the stone of many a temple wall, and this allowed me to understand how the days of Usermare-Setpenere were different from my own when we were boys. I always saw the back of my father. I looked at his elbows while he worked in the fields, but Ramses the Second saw His Father on many temple walls holding a prisoner's head by a hank of hair, there, cut into the stone. I used to feel whenever I looked at such a picture as if the breath of Seti was about to burn the back of my neck, and that I was the prisoner. I used to wonder whether Ramses the Second felt the same when He was a boy but I did not dare to ask Him.

"Then He began to tell me of Thutmose the Third who was supposed to become King but Hat-shep-sut reigned in His place because She had been married to the second Thutmose. So the Third had to live in the Temple as a priest, and was required to tend the incense pots whenever Hat-shep-sut came to pray. He grew such a great anger that when She died and He became Pharaoh, He was not only as mighty in battle as a lion released from its cage, but also ordered His stonemasons to chip away the name of Hat-shep-sut from all the temples. He cut His own name in Her place.

"'Why,' I remember asking of my Pharaoh, 'was the Temple of Hat-shep-sut not destroyed instead of Her name?' and He told me that Thutmose did not wish to enrage those Gods Who loved Hat-shep-sut most—He wished merely to confuse Them. I remember Ramses the Second looked at me and seized my knee with His fingers and gripped it. 'I, too, will be a King to cut His name into stone,' He said, and told me more about the greatness of Thutmose the Third and how many battles He won and the plunder He took. I was told of the ebony statue of the King of Kadesh, for there was such a Monarch in those days, too, and Thutmose defeated him, and took his statue back to Thebes. Then Ramses the Second told me, 'The name of the warrior who stood with Thutmose on His Chariot was Amenenahab. Like all who are named after Amon, he was bold. He understood the desire of Thutmose the Third before the King knew His own longing. You will come to understand as well.' With that, He gave me a kiss. My lips felt as radiant as His Chariot, and I could hardly listen while He told me of other Pharaohs not strong enough to hold the sword of Thutmose the Third such as the Pharaoh Who did not like Amon, the Fourth Amenhotep, a man of odd appearance with a soft round belly, a large nose, and a high head. Yet He must have remembered what Thutmose did to Hat-shep-sut for He did the same to Amon. A thousand stonemasons cut away the name of Amon in the temples, and with their chisels wrote a new name: Re-Aton. That, Ramses the Second told me, is God said backwards, even as Re-Aton is the opposite of *neter*. This Amenhotep the Fourth then changed His own name to Akhenaton, and He built a city in the middle of Egypt that He called the Horizon of Aton. I could not believe all I heard. It seemed strange to me. So soon as it was done, it was undone. For so soon as Akhenaton was dead, Aton's name was struck from the stone, and the name of Amon was put back. 'All this,' said my Pharaoh, 'caused such a weakness in the land, that by now, we paint our sacred marks on wood and do not cut them into the rock. For that reason My Father Seti told His artists to work only in stone. There are many drawings of My Father where He holds the heads of prisoners before He strikes them dead, and they are on stone.' With that, He gave a great laugh, stood up, grasped my hair as if to strike me, laughed again, said, 'Come, I have something to show you,' and we moved up the road.

"Soon we came to a place where we had to tie the horses, leave the chariot, and go up a trail so narrow we were near to climbing the cliffs straight up. For certain, we lifted ourselves from rock to rock and often had to offer our arm to the other. I was glad for the difficulty since His stories of Pharaohs who changed the names on the walls of temples had left me in confusion. If there was one thought as sure to me as the stones of the Temple of Karnak, it was that Amon-Ra was our greatest God. So how could there have been a time when He gave way to another God? And that the Pharaoh of this Aton had been a funny-looking man with a big belly—well, I was short of breath from my thoughts more than the climb.

"When we came to the top of the cliff, I was expecting to find the desert on the other side but saw instead only a descent into a new valley and another rough trail. Standing on the ridge, my King pointed back to the river. 'There is a place named Kurna out there,' He told me, 'where they breed nothing but thieves. It may look like a poor town, but wealth is buried under every hut. Someday, if those thieves make Me angry enough, I will dig up the town of Kurna and cut their hands off. For they are grave robbers. Every family in that town is descended from grave robbers.'

"I soon learned why He said this. If my head was tired from stories of Thutmose the Third, and Hat-shep-sut and all the Amenhoteps, my Ramses now told of the first Thutmose Who had come to visit the mortuary temples of His ancestors here, and saw how many of Their tombs had been entered and robbed of gold furniture and other treasures. Beholding this desecration of dead Pharaohs, the first Thutmose cried aloud to the sky. For when He died, His tomb could also be robbed. Like His ancestors, He might wander homeless in Khert-Neter. 'Then,' said my Ramses, 'He came to this valley.'

"We looked at it together. I wondered if an underground river had shaped the place. For a more uneven ground I had never seen. There were many holes before us that opened into other cavities beneath, and many a large cave. I could feel how water had once come twisting through with a roar, carrying away sand and the softer clay, until only rock was left. Now this rock had holes large as a King's chambers, and halfway up many of the vertical walls in this wilderness of boulders and ledges were what looked to be great caves.

"Now, my Ramses, Usermare-Setpenere, told me how this First Thutmose had found a cliff with a small entrance that you could only reach by climbing straight up, but, once within, was one cave after another behind this entrance and He said, 'Here I will build a secret tomb,' and He had the caves enlarged by the King's Architect until there were twelve rooms.

"The rock from those chambers was carted away to the desert, and the laborers were given no opportunity to speak of their work. My Ramses said no more, but I knew what had happened to the workmen. I heard their silence. 'Nobody ever discovered the hiding place of King Thutmose the First,' Usermare said. 'Not even the Pharaohs know the burial place of other Pharaohs. Behind any of these rocks, high up on the walls, you might find one of Them, but there are a million and infinity of rocks in this place. I do not know if that is why it is called the Place of Truth, but here will be hidden My tomb.'

"Since I lived in the greatest awe of my Pharaoh, I did not want to hear of His secret. So I thought to change the subject. Yet, like black-copper-from-heaven, I was drawn back to talk of it nonetheless. If, I asked, these tombs are difficult to find, then how had the grave robbers of Kurna been able to prosper? Here He took me by the arm, and said, 'Kiss My lips. Vow that you will not speak of these matters. If you do, your tongue is cut from your throat.' We kissed again, and I knew what it was, great Ramses the Ninth, to live in the royal body of a Pharaoh, for again I felt a radiance in my head, and the burden of the secret was on me before it was told, even as His tongue was on mine. I knew the life of my own tongue and how I would never want to lose it.

" 'No Pharaoh thought it wise to let other Pharaohs know His burial place in this valley,' He said. 'Still, someone had to have knowledge. Otherwise, a tomb could be robbed, and the theft not discovered. So each High Priest learned the tomb of His Pharaoh, and before he died, he would give such knowledge to the next High Priest.'

"Now, He told me that a High Priest in the time of Amenhotep the Fourth revealed one tomb to the families of Kurna, and shared the spoils. Then these thieves had a quarrel. The sacrilege was discovered. 'The men of Kurna,' said Usermare, 'brought such fear to the heart of Amenhotep the Fourth that He changed His name to Akhenaton and moved halfway up the river between Thebes and Memphi.'

"I could not believe these thieves of Kurna held so strong a curse that even a Pharaoh would fear them, but as I pondered it, I decided these robbers had been able to invade the tomb because of special prayers said for them by the High Priest, and for the first time I understood how there might be much unholy advantage in being holy. Still, I wondered how these thieves of Kurna had been able to touch the mummy of the Pharaoh. Had any of them died from the fear that bursts your heart?

"Oh, the heat. The trail was open to the last of the sun and my body grew feverish. I was cold in the shade. It was late afternoon, and we were climbing upward in the second valley, in this Place of Truth, which meant—if its name could be right—that the Truth was hot and ugly indeed. Over the next ridge the sun began to quiver. There was a high hill before us with a peak not unlike the little pyramid on top of each tomb in the Necropolis, The Horn, was what Usermare-Setpenere called it—and the sun now passed behind The Horn and was gone.

"It was here, in the deep gloom of this last valley, that Ramses the Second showed me a pinnacle of stone as high as an obelisk. It stood no more than a cubit from the cliff, looking as if it had been split away from the rest of the rock by a blow from lightning. In that cleft, Ramses the Second now put Himself, and by much pushing of His back against the wall, and the clever use of His hands and feet against edges in the pinnacle no wider than my finger, I saw Him climb until He was above my height and then twice and three times above it, a sight such as I had never expected, since His white linen was filthy from the effort, yet He wore His War-Crown all the way, never removing it. Once or twice I thought He could not reach the next grip for need of moving around an overhang that kept threatening to tip His helmet, indeed, it almost fell off when, from one position of great strain, He had to lean back so far that I saw it begin to tilt, but believe me, He held to the pinnacle with one arm and saved the Crown with the other, then reached a ledge on the wall where He could perch, and hooted to me to come up. He was now as removed as the height of one of the columns in the Temple of Karnak, which is like the height of ten men, and I began the ascent with the thought that my King was as high above me as my own life, but then, the climb proved not so difficult as it looked, and was almost like going up a ladder most irregularly built. I grew to love the rock that pressed against my back for I could lean on it when I became tired from the pain in my fingers of a poor grip or a sharp grip, and the rock before me in the pinnacle became as intimate to me as the crevices of a man or a woman. I knew I would dream of it on many a night since I felt closer to Geb holding myself to these wrinkles in His rocky skin than I had known you could come to a God without prayer.

"It took me a while to reach the ledge, long enough to learn that living on the side of a wall is not so different from walking on the ground, no more different than sleep from daylight, and I gave a whoop as I joined Him, and received a quick embrace for the pleasure of our accomplishment. I must say I liked Him then as much as any soldier I had known, and thought of Him as my friend, not my Pharaoh.

" 'Here,' He said, 'this ledge is like any of a thousand ledges, yet there is none like it. For see what is behind the corner of this boulder.'

"It was a stone almost as tall as Himself, of a good thickness, and it nearly divided the ledge in two, but at the rear was a hole large enough for a man to crawl through, and when at His nod I tried it, a lizard went clawing up the walls of a cave inside, and I was in blackness but for the little light that entered.

"In the next instant, Ramses the Second was there beside me, and we sat in the heat, trying to rest despite the scratchings and wails of every creature we had disturbed by our entrance. Bats flew past like whips, and I heard that cry they make so close to the sound of a dying man's breath—that whistle of panic. They spewed us with dung, yet the odor was forever altered by my nearness to the Pharaoh. In the dark, I could feel the nobility of His Presence, and that was as large as the cave, by which I mean His nearness was like a heart beating in the cave, and so the mean smell of bat dung was made sweeter by my Pharaoh's own odor full of royal sweat from the climb. To this day, over all my four lives I cannot despise the odor of the bat altogether since it always recalls to me the warm generous limbs of that young Ramses. Yes.

"We did not sit on the floor of the cave for long, however, before the luminous strength of His body gave vision to my eyes, and I could see better in the gloom, and recognized that this cave was more a tunnel than a chamber, and He laughed at the ingenuity of His scheme, for He would build a tomb of twelve rooms here. Then He added, 'All this is true if I return from the wars to come,' and we were silent within this cave. The lizards still scuttled away from us in a clatter and I knew their Gods were terrified of smelling the sunlight on our limbs.

"'It is the Hittites we will meet,' said Ramses the Second sitting beside me on the floor, 'and they fight with three men in each chariot. They are strong, but slow. They fight with bow and arrow, and with the sword and spear and,'—He took His time to say the next—'sometimes they fight with an axe. They live in a country that has many trees, and they know how to use the axe.'

"In this darkness, I could not be certain of His expression, but I felt a new kind of fear. How wonderful is a new fear! It is like a face one has never seen before. It gives a thrill to new parts of one's flesh. While it was one thing to be killed by a sword, and that was bad enough, there were now lamentations along my back and in my arms and thighs at the thought of being mangled by an axe.

"'The Hittites have long black beards,' said my Ramses, 'and there is old food in such growth, and vermin, and their hair is matted on their shoulders. They are uglier than bears, and cannot live without the blood of battle. If they capture you, they are the worst foe of all. They will put a ring through your lips to jerk your head as you march, and some will flay you alive. So, of the Hittites I capture, I will bring back a hundred, and they will build My tomb.' He smiled, and while He did not speak His thought, I saw those Hittites as they would look when the work was done, and they were without their tongues. 'Yes,' He said, 'it is better than using Egyptians.'

"Now He stopped, and looked at me, and on His face was the same smile He had when He saw the peasant girl. If I could have moved, perhaps He would have done no more than smile, but I did not wish to, I could not, and He stood up then and seized the hair of my head even as His Father Seti held the head of captured slaves, and His member was before me. Then He came forth into my mouth from the excitement of looking into my face. No man had I allowed to do this to me before. Then, still holding my hair, He threw me to my knees, grasped me about the waist, and with not a scruple, thrust up the middle of me tearing I know not what, but I heard a clangor in my head equal to the great door of a temple knocked open by the blow of a log carried forward at a run by ten good men, it was with the force of ten good men that He took me up my bowels, and I lay with my face on the stony soil of the cave, while a bat screamed overhead. I heard Usermare cry out, 'Your ass, little Meni'—even though I was near to His height and could equal His weight—'your ass, little Meni, is Mine, and I give you a million years and infinity, your ass, little Meni, is sweet,' wherefore He came forth with such a force that something in the very sanctuary of myself flew open, and the last of my pride was gone. I was no longer myself but His, and loved Him, and knew I would die for Him, but I also knew I would never forgive Him, not when I ate, not when I drank, and not when I defecated. Like an arrow flew one thought through my mind: It was that I must revenge myself.

" 'We shall never be destroyed in battle,' He said. 'We are now the beast that moves with its own four legs.' And He gave a last kiss and sighed as if He had eaten all of a banquet. But I knew the taste in my mouth of the Very Green and the blood of my bowels kept knocking on my heart.

"We climbed down and walked back in the moonlight, watching the clouds pass over the stars. I could hear their voices. You can hear the voice of a cloud if you are silent enough on a quiet night although that whisper is near to the most quiet sound of them all. In the dawn as we came back with our chariot to the boat on the riverbank, we stopped to watch the flight of a hawk, and I knew that bird of Horus was most intimate to the sun, for it would see the first rising to the east while we still breathed in the dark to the west."

Five

Menenhetet was well aware of how we felt. The smile on his lips was thin when Ptah-nem-hotep looked away. I had seen a thief's face once just before his hand was chopped off in a public square—Eyaseyab having rushed to the sight in the heat of curiosity. The thief gave a smile, that peculiar ridiculous grimace we offer when we have been caught in a trivial act.

The thief lost his smile when the blade came down. I woke up screaming on many a night at the look of bewilderment in his eyes. For the thief looked like he was falling to his death.

Now I saw just such a look on my great-grandfather's face, and I knew he was still living in the dust of the cave of Usermare's tomb. Nonetheless he shrugged. He had the look of a donkey laboring beneath bags of grain he had carried every day of his life.

"I knew," he now said, "that I would never forget. And I did not. But I have never spoken of it until this evening. Now, I will speak of it again. For I have never known more shame than in the days that followed. Yet a great part of this shame was for the joy of remembering. My bowels felt gilded. The light of a God was in my chest. A God had entered me. I was not like other men, although I felt more of a woman."

It was true. As he spoke, the woe lifted from my parents, and from Ramses the Ninth as well. They felt troubled, and I could know their shame—it was not unlike the way I would feel when still too young to control myself in bed, I would soil my linen. Yet I also felt their respect for Menenhetet and it was different now, and not without the finest awe. For he was no longer alone before us. Another presence was with him.

"I remember," he said, "that I did not sleep for two days, and thought the moon had entered my heart. I saw nothing but a pale radiance within. I vowed I would never allow Usermare-Setpenere to enter me again, and that was equal to admitting I was terrified of seeing Him, I, who had never been frightened of any man. Still, if He were to make the attempt, I would have to resist, and that would be my death. So I wondered how to avoid the presence of my Majesty, and kept wondering, until I realized that He, by His turn, was avoiding me. For no sooner had we returned on that dawn to Thebes than my King was occupied with mobilizing His troops for the march into Syria against the Hittites, and messengers were sent to bring up troops from Syene and others went north to Memphi, and Busiris in the Delta, and Buto and Tanis, to inform the garrisons how many men would be called. All the while, we were busy in Thebes collecting our own stores.

"Then, we embarked on boats, some three thousand of us from Thebes, plus a thousand horses, a total of thirty boats, and we took five days going down the river to Memphi. Our bodies sat so close to one another on the deck that when fights commenced from the fretting of one chin on another's back, there was not room to reply in any better way than to bite the other man's nose, and twice I did. They carried the mark on their face until they died. Let me say, and it is obvious, I should think, that I was not on the Falcon-Ship. On most days, that Royal Barge was so far downstream we could not even see the reflection from the gold of His mast, although I could hear the sounds of laughter. That came back over the water. In fact, I did not see my King again for fifteen days until we came to Gaza where the army was at last assembled, but even there I was never near Him alone for we camped on a vast plain full of dust from the drilling of new detachments, and the clouds left by our chariots. It was, all the same, preferable to the boat. There, two hundred of us had been packed in, the support for your back no more than the knees of the soldier behind you, and no way to feel sorry for yourself, because on either side of our rank of six men was a poor oarsman pumping on the oars even as he pumped his life out. They say it is easier to row downstream, and it is, but not much when you are rowing steadily, and besides, the pace is faster. Pressed together in the open hold with the red mainsail spread over us as an awning, we were not able to see the sky—just as well in that heat. We had nothing but the gasp of those fellows pulling on their lungs to the creak of the oars, and I never saw more than the bodies in front of me, or the naked sweat of the oarsmen to either side, their raised benches blocking all view of the horizon. Nor did I even feel the thousand limbs of the river passing beneath, nor hear the rustle of the water, no, in the hold of that boat with two hundred other soldiers, we heard nothing but grunts, and were fed nothing but grain and water until we farted like cattle. With so much fermentation in the gas, you could get drunk from breathing it. There was a monkey that belonged to the captain and I believe the monkey did get drunk, or maybe it was his excitement at being handled by so many of us, whatever, he was the only entertainment we had. He would make me laugh until the veins in my head came near to breaking, for when the captain would stand in the bridge near the bow, his fat buttocks squeezed together, his hand shielding his eyes against the glare of the river, so would the monkey do the same, and we would roar. Yet all the while I was laughing, I was also sitting on my sore seat, not knowing if I had a wound in which to take pride or shame, and so feeling like the lowest servant of the Gods. Like the monkey among us.

"In Gaza, I never saw the city. They said it was now an Egyptian city, but we camped out in the desert and drank goats' milk, which did not reduce our gas. To travel is to break wind—as our saying goes—and in the tents we talked of nothing but fresh food. Once our legs were back, for I could hardly walk after two weeks on the boat, we charioteers went out foraging and even ate some goose. We roasted it near a grove of dead trees and the wood of the fire was silver and blazed with a heat like the sun from the fat that dripped on it. There was a happiness in that fire as if the wood, drier than bone, had slaked its thirst at last.

"Then the King called a great council of all of us together in His leather tent which was as large as twenty tents, and more than a hundred of us sat in a council of war in a large circle about Him. Our Ramses the Second never looked more magnificent, and had made a new friend since last I saw Him. A lion, on a short leash, stood by His right side.

"This lion, Hera-Ra, was a remarkable beast. How it had been tamed, I do not know—it came in tribute from Nubia—but the Pharaoh received it only the week before we left, and it was said that neither the King nor the animal could now bear to be without the other. That gave me the first jealousy I ever felt. I did not know whether I had been treated lately like the lowest of charioteers because Usermare-Setpenere had lost respect for me, or just found the lion more attractive. I even wondered if the King dared to treat the buttocks of the lion in the way He had mine. It was not an absurd thought if you knew Ramses the Second. Left to yourself, your will might feel strong as rock, but when He looked in your eyes, or seized you, like His Father, by the hank of your hair, then your will flowed away into the thousand limbs of water. Certainly, there was an understanding between Him and this Hera-Ra. Face-of-Ra indeed, the lion had a head more like a God than a man, and looked at everyone with a large and intelligent calm that had much friendliness in it, something like the way a two-year-old noble will think of all who come near as bearers of great pleasure for himself. The noble, of course, is spoiled, and flies into a rage so soon as the first wrong sound offends his ear—like this, was the lion. Like this, for that matter, was Usermare-Setpenere. They both looked at you with the same friendly interest.

"But it is true. I was jealous of Face-of-Ra and felt a weak smile on my lips at the way the lion listened to all that was said, then turned to his friend and Monarch. Once, when two officers spoke at the same time, each trying to gain the King's ear, Hera-Ra was on his feet, his great blunt nose pointing in turn toward each of them, as though to fix their smell forever in his nostrils, these disputants. He was no doubt thinking that he would bite their heads off. All the while, I was telling myself that if it came to it, I would bite his nose off before he came near mine. Yes, I hated that lion.

"I had never been in a council of war before, and so I would not have known if it were always as calm as on this meeting, although the presence of Hera-Ra gave caution to all that was said. Even the quiver of his hind leg offered a suggestion of impatience, and once when he yawned at a long tale told by a scout who had discovered nothing of the enemy in his searches, it was obvious the fellow had spoken long enough.

"As each said his piece, I came to learn that many of these strange officers were Governors or Generals who ruled over many places in this region from which our Two-Lands received tribute. So my Monarch had summoned them to Gaza to report on the armies of the Hittites. Those legions seemed to have disappeared, however. There was no word of them. In Megiddo and Phoenicia the country was quiet. On the banks of the Orontes, no movement. Palestine and Syria were sleeping. Lebanon was calm.

"The Prince, Amen-khep-shu-ef, now spoke, and as He did, Hera-Ra laid his paw on the knee of the Pharaoh Who in turn covered that paw with His own hand. 'My Father,' said Amen-khep-shu-ef in a clear voice, 'if I may speak My opinion.'

" 'No opinion could be more valuable,' His Father said.

"The Prince, now thirteen, was already like a man. He looked more a brother than a son, and since Nefertiri, as I believe I have said, was Usermare's sister, you could say the father was the uncle as well. It is certain Amen-khep-shu-ef spoke to the Pharaoh as to an elder brother of whom He was envious. 'Having listened,' He remarked, 'to all that has been said, I am ready to think the King of the Hittites is a coward. He dare not come to us in battle but will hide behind the walls of his city. We will not see his face. So our armies must prepare to lay siege. It will be years until the last of the Hittites has fallen.'

"He not only spoke like a man, but an adviser. He had a deep voice, and if you did not look at His young face, you might have thought He was as old as His father. Certainly all who heard Him were impressed. Some of the Generals could not have followed His words more closely if they had been listening to a command of the Pharaoh, and they nodded when He was done. A few were even so brave as to ask permission of Usermare to speak, and then offered their agreement to the words of the Prince. Since they rushed forward without knowing the opinion of the Pharaoh, I thought them so stupid I would not have liked to serve in their command. Then I realized they were all of the same party, and must have spoken to each other before this council, everybody from Amen-khep-shu-ef in His white pleated skirt and jeweled sword to the roughest of our provincial Generals with chest-hair as thick as the hide of a bear, and a broken face looking as mangled by old battles as the rocks and gullies of the Place of Truth. But I soon ceased to wonder what they would gain. It was simple. If Usermare-Setpenere agreed with His son, He would not wish to lead the campaign. Given the breadth of His impatience, how could He bear a mean struggle in which His armies would be reduced by illness faster than by battle? Indeed the prospect might prove so boring that He would soon depart, leaving Amen-khep-shu-ef to conduct the siege. That could be agreeable for the Prince. In His Father's absence, He would live as a King.

"It was obvious my Pharaoh was not happy with this discussion. I was hardly prepared to say anything at this point, but on the next instant, Ramses the Second, not having had a glance for me during all these weeks on the river, nor at Gaza, now passed over His other advisers and, as if I were the veteran of ten campaigns, inquired what I thought. I must say I had a tongue that had rested through these weeks and was in secret as lively as a horse in need of exercise. In fact I had to take care not to speak too quickly. To make the Pharaoh strain to follow your argument was a discourtesy. So I reined in my voice. Yet I still had much to say. (I had, after all, heard much gossip on the boat.) 'Foundation-of-Eternity-in-Ra,' I began, 'the King of the Hittites has called forth his allies and it is said that the Mysians, the Lysians, and the Dardanians are with him, as well as the soldiers of Ilion, Pedasos, Carchemish, Arvad, Ekereth, and Aleppo. These peoples are barbaric. While they may be fierce in battle, they are also impatient.'

"Now I saw the King close His eyes, as if a thought unpleasant to Himself had passed through His mind, and Hera-Ra yawned in my face. Already, I had spoken too much. I can say that the crease between my buttocks began to itch, and the loins of this lion were so unruly that I could swear they began to swell. A red tip appeared, and all for the word *impatient*. All the same, the seriousness of our discussion obliged Ramses the Second to separate His temper from His irritations. He gave a thwack to the back of the lion, as if to say 'Do not frighten this soldier until he has finished speaking,' and gave a nod. He would forgive me for reminding Him that there could be similarities between a barbarian and Himself. I went on, therefore: 'These enemy soldiers want our bodies to roast by the fire. They want plunder. If that does not happen soon, they will talk of going back to their own countries. If I were the Hittite King, I would not wish to keep such troops for a siege. I would want to bring them into battle.'

" 'Then where are they?' asked my King.

"I bowed, I struck my head to the ground seven times for I did not wish to insult Ramses the Second a second time by disclosing my reply too quickly. Instead, I addressed Him by so many of His great names that the tongue of Hera-Ra lolled in pleasure, and then I said, 'The King of the Hittites knows every hill and valley of Lebanon. I fear, Good and Great God, that the Hittites will try to come down on our flank as we march.'

"I knew the Prince Amen-khep-shu-ef was furious. I had made an enemy. But I also saw that our King was as the center of a wheel on a chariot. We, who were advisers, were His spokes. We could never be friends with one another. 'The peasant who knows so much about horses that he has become Your First Charioteer,' said Amen-khep-

shu-ef, 'speaks of impatient barbarians as if that is the truth on which
we may depend. But where is the King of the Hittites? No enemy
walks in our sight. No spy speaks to us. I say they hide in their forts
and will stay there. Barbarians do not possess that royal strength some
see as impatience. Rather they are stupid like cattle and can wait forever.' The Prince now looked at me with all the force of the oldest
son of Usermare-Setpenere. Although He resembled His mother
and had dark hair, His Father's confidence was in His manner. Any
thought that came to Him was an offering from the Gods and so could
not be false—so said His manner.

"Yet, I believe He had now offended His Father. For if the Gods
spoke more quickly to Amen-khep-shu-ef than to the Pharaoh, there
was cause for rage.

" 'You talk,' said Usermare-Setpenere, 'with a voice worthy of a
King-yet-to-come-forth. But You are a young bird. You must break
out of Your egg before You fly. When You are older, You will have
learned more about the battles of Thutmose the Third. You will follow the campaigns of Harmhab. Maybe You will know by then that
it is not wise to speak with certainty about a battle that has not begun.'

"A heavy sound came out of all of us, a grunt, indeed, of the satisfaction uttered when a truth is deep. 'Hear the Pharaoh, He has said
it,' we all said. And Hera-Ra roared for the first time in this council.

"I saw a flush on the face of the Prince, but He bowed. 'May-Your-
Two-Houses-be-great, would You give us Your desires?'

"Usermare said that He had decided to break camp and march
from Gaza to Megiddo. From there, He would go down the valley to
Kadesh, but He would not advance more rapidly on any road than
His detachments on the ridges flanking the march. He would also
send scouts by other routes to Kadesh. One squad of charioteers
would cross the Jordan. Another would take the road to Damascus.
I—and I looked up as He spoke my name—I would be sent on the
road to Tyre. I could take a squad, He told me. But when I looked
into His blue eyes, I knew that until I had been alone long enough to
follow each of my thoughts down to the bottom, I would have weakness in my belly, not strength. Indeed, I wondered if I could lead men

well with the scorn of the Pharaoh still smarting on my buttocks. So I bowed and asked if I could travel by myself. It would be quick, I said, and He had need of His troops.

"A hoarse murmur came forth from more than a few of the Captains and Generals around me. A man by himself on strange roads would have to face new beasts without a friend. He could meet new Gods. My Pharaoh nodded, however, as if I had said the right thing, and I wondered if He wished to respect me again."

Six

"On the journey, I learned, however, what it is to be lonely. I had never been so much by myself before. Now that I am coming to the end of my fourth existence, I am left with memories of people who lived near to me once and now are dead. But in my first life, I had always found myself among many people, and that permits but one kind of thinking. Others talk; we reply. It is usually without thought. On important occasions, it is true, a voice might come into my head and speak for me and sometimes it was so powerful a voice, I knew it belonged to a God or His messenger. But now, going to Tyre, there came an hour when I could no longer listen to my two horses, nor to the complaints that came from the frame and wheels of the chariot, and I became alone in such a way that whole processions of thought passed through me, as if I were no longer a man but a city through which soldiers were marching.

"Of course, these were not my feelings on the first day, nor the second or third. In the beginning, there is such terror to find oneself alone that no thought has the liberty to speak—it is rather as if you walk beneath the walls of a fortress waiting for the first stone to drop. My eyes, I remember, were like birds, and flew from sight to sight, never resting. Nor were the horses comfortable. I was not traveling in my own battle chariot which was agile and weighed little. For the rigors of this trip I had chosen a training cart used to much abuse and newly repaired. I had also selected two strong but stupid horses who would be able to work all day even if they were much confused by commands they had heard in a hundred voices. I was sure I could train them to my purposes, and did, but my first request was that the horses not wear out, and these were born with stamina.

"One was called Mu, an old word for water, and it would have been an odd name for a horse except that Mu never failed to urinate at every halt. The other was Ta. He was close to the land and always fertilizing it.

"I set out by riding across the long flat valley that leads from Gaza to Joppa, and it was near to familiar country for me. The soil was as black as our own after the Nile recedes, and the heat was no different, nor the look of the villages and huts. Except I did not see a face on all of the road, not for all of the morning and afternoon of the first day. Of course who would be about to approach me? I rode with the reins around my waist, my spear in one quiver, my bow and arrow in another, my shield hooked to the prow of the chariot, and my short sword in its scabbard. I had a scowl on my face, a helmet on my head, and a coat of mail on my chest and back. I must say that in those days we did not know how to make a coat of mail from metal. Mine was of thick quilted stuffs with strips of leather, a coat so heavy you paid for its protection as your strength wilted in the heat. Still, I wore it like a house around my heart. Although I may have looked fierce, my tongue was as dry as an old piece of meat salted in natron and I could hardly breathe. The horses and I passed through nothing but these empty villages, their silence also breathing in my ear. Since we had already pillaged everything, you could find nothing. No food, no flocks, no people. Nothing in these empty huts but the spirit of each abode. I rode on, looking to the hills on either side of the valley, and in the night, when I made camp, I could see fires in fortified towns high on the ridges, and knew that the villagers who had fled were up there standing watch on the walls. In the valley beneath, I stopped just off the road and tried to sleep and heard my heart beating beneath me all night. Then in the morning I set out to the same silence. Even the blue of the sky was like a wall above, so much did I feel alone.

"Still, it was familiar ground, and that was better than what came next. The black soil gave way to a reddish-brown country full of sand and clay, colors common enough, but then some trees began to show themselves on the low hills, and soon there were more of them, then considerably more. They were nothing like our high palms, but short trees with thick, stunted trunks and twisted limbs, the most unhappy looking creatures, as if the wind had been a torture every day of their lives. I did not feel comfortable with these woods, nor did the horses, and soon we were in our first bad place. Brush had begun to grow, and you could not see anything but the road. A thicket more dense than any of our Egyptian swamps settled in next to the trees. Sometimes we crossed little streams and hardly knew it for the road was so muddy that water was always flowing in the ditches. Now I dismounted from the chariot as often as I went up on it, and kept pushing the wheels through the mud until in one swamp of this low forest, I saw a crocodile go sliding away. That put me back on the chariot again. In the marshes I was devoured by insects.

"I felt I was not only in a strange place, but at war. There was a most unfriendly spirit in these low trees, and I wondered at the animals I might find, the bears and the boars, and remembered talk of a hideous hyena native to these parts. The forest made me feel as if I voyaged through the maw of a beast. I perspired from the gloom and heat and felt the absence of Ra, and wondered what foreign Gods were here in such dark marshy land. Every time a small branch snapped across my face, the horses gave a lurch. My fears went through them like arrows. On we went, bumping from rut to rut and back to the mud again. Often I had to get out and dare the crocodiles.

"Then this narrow road mounted above the wetlands and the thicket diminished, the trees grew taller. Now it was easier to ride, except for great roots that grew across the road and near upended my vehicle whenever I put the horses in a trot. The height of the trees grew awesome, and I could no longer see the sun very well but merely felt Him above. My head was full of the oppression of all these bowers of leaves, and then I passed a terrible place where a great tree had fallen over. I could see that the roots were nearly as long as the branches, and the cavity left in the ground was as large as a cave and ugly like the mouth of a serpent. I knew the entrance to the Land of the Dead must look like this hole. Even the worms that crawled at the base were odious to me, and I began to shiver with fright at the thought of the battle to come. The naked roots of this tree made me know how my shoulder would look if my arm were chopped off by an axe.

"What fear I knew of such weapons. The Overseer of Carpenters in our squadron of charioteers was a wizard at working with wood and now I remembered him telling me that black people in the jungles would never cut down a tree unless they sacrificed a chicken first, and its blood was dripped on the roots. Then, after the first blow of the blade, you had to put your mouth to the cut and suck the sap until you were in brotherhood with the tree. But I knew I would never dare to put my tongue on the sap of these strange trees. They were too fierce. My horses trembled when we stopped, and Mu could no longer urinate, or did not dare.

"Still, I began to think of the goose we roasted on those dry silver boughs in the desert. Ra had held each branch in His hand and given heat to it. If I died in the sand, I might become as dry as my bones, but I would not burn for much. Yet each one of these trees would blaze with flames as high as themselves. It was then I had a vision of all the fire that lived in the forest, and felt again like a city through which soldiers were marching.

"By evening, I was completely out of the marshes and crossed my first ridge which gave me a sight I had never known before. Ahead were nothing but mountains covered with trees. These lands ahead must be as much unlike Egypt as a Syrian with his thick beard is different from our clean cheeks, and that made me sigh at the weight of this view. I could not believe how alone I was. For two days, no caravans had passed me in either direction—no merchants, it was evident, dared to be on the road—and every village through which I went was empty. What fear they kept of our army!

"On the next day, I learned much for I came to a place in the mountains where three roads could be taken to Megiddo, and it brought back the voice of my Pharaoh telling me of Thutmose the Third. For He was the Monarch who had come to this same fork with His armies only to learn that He could approach Megiddo by the long route to the north through Zefti, or by the open southern road through Taanash. There was also the Pass of Megiddo between, but that went over the Ridge of Carmel to the gates of the city itself, a dangerous trail, and narrow. 'Horse will have to pass behind horse,' said His officers, 'and man behind man. Our advance guard will have to fight their armies on the other side while our rearguard is still here.' I, having brooded so long on the nature of these strange trees and forests, must have come to live in the echo of the voices of these long-dead officers of Thutmose the Third, for I knew I would choose the route taken by Thutmose. 'I shall go forth at the head of My army,' Thutmose had said, 'and I will show the way by My footsteps,' and He brought most of His army through the pass before the Kings of Kadesh and Megiddo were ready to meet Him since they had thought He would go by the long southern road to Taanash.

"Now I had to take my own way through the pass. If I had not known that an army had gone through already, I might have given up. The hills were steep and the trees grew as high as the columns of the Temple of Karnak. So, it was cool in this forest, and strange. The road kept climbing upward and the hill on one side of the trail was high above, but to the other it fell away so steeply I could see the tops of trees beneath me, and that was different from what I expected, and soft to the eye like pillows. I felt faint and wished to fall upon them so powerful was the spirit of those trees calling me down to them (and I did not even know the names of the spirits!). I had only been in this kind of forest for a morning, yet I felt as if I had lived here half so long as the years of my life in Egypt, and my heart never stopped beating in fear, not for a moment, as I rode through. There was no place where you could feel close to the sun. Instead of the pale gold of the desert, everything was green, and even the sky, where I could see it, looked more white to me than the blue of our sky above the Nile. How twisted were the spirits of this forest. The horses kept crying to one another.

"Then we came to a place where the hill fell away on one side; on the other it rose straight up. I could see the sun at last. We had climbed above the trees. The trail was now so narrow I did not know if I could take the chariot through. To the one side was a wall of rock, by the other a precipice, and the horses would not move. I had to free Mu, who was nearest to the fall, from her harness, and then tied the tail of Ta to her bridle so that Mu could walk behind. The chariot I pushed myself. In that way we proceeded, step by step, the outside wheel of the chariot hanging—it happened—over the abyss. I, at the rear, leaned all my weight to the side of the chariot that was near to the wall. You may be sure I cursed in terror whenever a rock made us stop, and I had to lift the chariot over. Before we were through, I knew why Thutmose the Third was a great King.

"Yes, it was difficult. Never once, may I say, did I think of that other wall in the Place of Truth where we climbed up to the tomb of Usermare, nor did I want such memories, although I believe the fear in which I lived on this trip, a fear so great as to make me think of myself as another person, and a weak one—came from my abject silence when He took me by the hair. No matter, I was one sweating charioteer by the time the horses and I came through and reached a rise from which I could see ahead. Below, the pass widened, and there on a hill in the distance up the other side of the valley across green forests and plowed fields was the town of Megiddo. I saw it through the battlement of the mountains.

"Thutmose the Third had descended this pass, and gone into battle, and captured chariots of gold and silver and left the champions of the enemy 'stretched out like fish'—such was the word of Ramses. Thutmose took thousands of cattle and two thousand horses and much gold and silver. Hearing of such plunder I had supposed the city would be a rich sight with white marble palaces like our own

Memphi, or temples of gold, or, at the least, wooden mansions painted in the richest of colors. Yet, on the next day, as I came near, it was only a poor town, and dirty in appearance. Maybe it had been poor ever since Thutmose had conquered it. All the same, it was a fort, the first Syrian fort I had seen, and it was not built square like ours with our straight brick walls. These palisades were made of rough stone, and went up and down with the land, the walls following the hills. Every few hundred steps was a high tower so that you could not charge the doors of Megiddo without a hundred arrows shooting down. A mean place. You would look to starve it out. I began to see the argument of Amen-khep-shu-ef.

"On this day, however, the gates were open and the market was busy. I did not enter. There was no need. The King of Kadesh would not be hiding an army inside the walls of Megiddo when you could walk into the city and look about. So I knew that Monarch was not here with his men. Besides, Usermare would reach Megiddo in a few days, although by an easier road, and He would ask the questions that receive good answers. Whereas one dirty soldier with a battered chariot and two unseemly horses was more likely to be tortured himself than coax any truth out of strange tongues. So I drove around the walls of the town which took a long time, for the lanes were muddy, and it was a big town, but then I found a road on the other side that some had spoken of in Gaza. This road was easy to recognize, for it had paving stones and oak trees planted on each side, a royal road straight out of Megiddo to the north, yet I was the only vehicle on it.

"I soon knew why. The paving stones ended on the other side of the first hill and now I was on a wagon trail that had to be renowned for its ruts. Soon the fields disappeared and the forest grew in on me, and the horses and myself were afraid again. We were on the direct road to Tyre, but it was not direct. It curved like a snake and even coiled back and forth on itself to climb the higher hills. In the dark of late afternoon, I thought again of all I had heard of this road and its bandits. Even before I left Gaza, I listened to stories of how they raided caravans, and any merchant who did not know them well enough to pay tribute, was sold as a slave. Usually a merchant could write, and thereby serve as a scribe—a valuable slave! Then the bandits kept the horses and sold the goods. There were so many thieves that it gave occupation to the men of Megiddo. They could always hire out as an armed guard on a caravan.

"All the same, I was more afraid of the forest than the thieves. It would take four or five such robbers to bring me down. Afterward, one would be without an arm, another a foot, and maybe a third would never see again. I would die with my thumbs in somebody's eyes. They would gain nothing but a body, two mediocre horses, and a chariot they probably could not sell. The cart was close to coming apart. Unless I was carrying a sum of gold—which I was, but hardly looked so prosperous—I was not worth attacking. They would see me as a soldier who was lost, or a deserter ready to join any pack of thieves, or even as the scout I was indeed. And if they saw me as the last, why, they could do worse than offer a favor to an Egyptian scout in the army of Ramses the Second. Among our allies in Gaza had been a few Asiatics from nearby tribes, and by what they said, I knew there was a large fear of the new Pharaoh. Syrians might be used to Egyptian garrisons living among them, but in a quiet year no more than a few envoys would arrive from Thebes to collect tribute and talk to the Prince of the territory. They did not try to change the laws, nor interfere with the foreign temples. We Egyptians had a saying, 'Amon is interested in your gold, not your God.' A sensible arrangement. Usually there was no trouble.

"When a new Pharaoh ascended the Throne, however, it was different. The young Princes of Asia were more defiant. So, in all these lands of Lebanon and Syria had come the word: Ramses the Second was arriving with the largest army ever to march out of Egypt. If I were a thief, in that case, hiding in these dark hollows, with many a merchant offering a bounty for me, I would look to make an Egyptian my friend. Therefore, I did not hesitate. I took the most dangerous road to Tyre. Maybe I would fall in with a few brigands who could give me information. My fear of travel might be great, but even larger was my fear of rejoining Usermare-Setpenere with no information to offer.

"So I kept moving. Here, the trail was wide enough for both my horses. Yet by evening the forest and hills were still around me. I bedded down in a grove, fed my horses some grain, ate of it myself with care not to crack my teeth on any pebble, and then prepared to sleep, using my charioteer's cloak for a ground-cloth. It proved, however, too cold, and I soon preferred to sit with my back against a tree. That was better. The trunk felt like a friend behind me. It was as if we sat on watch, back against back, and searched the darkness. To my surprise there was more to see than I would have thought. No farther away than four or five long throws of a stone, a spark flew up in the darkness, and watching, I soon saw a small campfire.

"The spirits in this wood were silent. They encouraged silence. I could feel those spirits going deep into the earth, yet I could also feel them returning to the tree, and they were light as the feather of Maat. I heard the leaves speak to them on every little wind. So, too, was I able to hear the quiet of these woods, and by their hush did I pass through the wall of my own ears and into the movements of every small animal. The keenness of my hearing was so fine that I wondered if I had been blessed by the spirits of my tree since I felt no fear, and was strong for the first time in weeks.

"I kept looking at the campfire. I could see little more than its light, yet by the sound, there could not be more than three men around it, probably two, and they spoke in a language whose tones were strange.

"In the wild of this forest, I found it peaceful to hear these thieves' voices. I knew it was the peace that comes when you can choose what to do with another man. You can kill, or let him go. There is no peace so calm as that. Indeed, my Pharaoh always seemed to live in just such a way.

"Now I felt the same power. My arm was ready to slay the first thief before the second would know I was there.

"I stood up then. The horses were asleep and I sent them a thought as sure as the flick of my reins. 'Sleep in peace,' I told them, 'and blow no wind through any hole.' I meant it. Then I took off the coat of mail so that my skin could feel the nearness of any low bush, and in the darkness I began to walk toward the fire. Almost at once I lost my strength. My hearing disappeared. The fear came back. The forest was no longer my friend, and I had to sit down once more against a tree.

"Now I could hear the voices of the men again. Courage returned to my loins and my back. I was eager to move, but so soon as I was on my feet, these powers departed. Only the touch of the tree, it seemed, could give me strength. Was I not like a blind priest in the Temple of Karnak feeling his way from column to column?

"Unable, therefore, to move, I told myself I could hardly approach the campfire if I did not have my strength.

"One thought, however, did come. If I was in a strange land, why did the Gods who lived in these trees offer Their confidence to me? Why did They not give it to the thieves by the campfire? It was their country. Maybe it was because those two good fellows—I could hear now that there were no more than two—were drunk, and so their minds were like a swamp and seeped out in all directions. Such is the power of wine. It is, after all, the juice that comes from a dying grape—to get drunk is to know how it is to begin to die. So they were far away from nearby Gods. But I was close, as close as the touch of the leaves overhead. It was then I understood that the Gods of these trees were offended by the rudeness of those who dared to get drunk among Them. So I might not need to touch a tree if I thought less of the task ahead and stayed close instead to the spirits of the nearest branch. At this moment I felt blessed by the forest. I could even smell those trees who were happy, and know those who were not well—what a difference! One complained of its roots which were growing between many rocks, another was fresh and young but shadowed by a taller tree. Still one other had been split by lightning and grew to a great size after being struck. It stood there like a crippled giant and inspired silence. I bowed my head as if truly passing a giant of a fellow who now stared only at the sky. Now I could understand that these trees would give me their good force if I showed respect, and I paid attention to each step before me. Feeling, thereby, a fine peace, I passed through what these trees had to offer me (and their thoughts were so pure they came to my senses like perfume) and at last I reached the edge of a very small clearing where the fire burned. I saw two drunk thieves. They were wrestling with each other in a kind of dance, and laughing, and wet from the heat of the fire, each with his member sticking out through the old animal skins they wore.

"They gave a shriek when they saw my sword, then flew apart, a wise move. Now I could not attack one without showing my back to the other. Yet it gave the choice of who to attack first. Both were tall, but one was slender and sly as a quick animal while the other was rich in his muscles, a body I could recognize as near to my own, and on the calm instinct, the wisdom, if I may speak of it so, that the trees had offered, I nodded to both, smiled, and with a speed of arm faster than any I had shown before, put my sword through the slim man's chest and felt his heart go right up my arm. I blazed within as if touched by Usermare-Setpenere. Until then, never, not even with my King had I known such a moment, equal to lightning, I would say, if lightning were bliss, and then the slim thief's face began to change. The tricks he had played on others came over his expression one by one— thievery, betrayal, and ambush were his hidden faces—but by the end, I saw a good man, not without bravery, and he died with a peaceful look.

"The other thief could have run away in the time I took to look at what I had done, but he seized a rock instead, and threw it at my head. I ducked, and by then he had two more rocks, and I laughed in the happiness that we would have a contest, and advanced on him. He threw one rock. Again I ducked. Then he hurled another at my chest, which I caught with my free hand. As he reached to the ground to pick up another, I knocked him flat with the stone I held, a good blow to the neck that finished his fight. As he lay on his knees, groggy as a cow given a blow in preparation for the knife, I took my sword and with the flat beat him on the back until he was soft like a steak that is pounded, very much alive, I promise you, for he yowled like a wounded beast, but soft. He had no will to send to his muscles.

"It was then I discovered the gift Usermare-Setpenere had left in my bowels. Gift it was. I had known from the time He seized me by the hair and took me by the place no other man had ever reached, that something new had been left in me and I did not know how to use it, but then I had never had such an hour before. Now, I could feel the gift. It was nothing to take a boy from the rear, or a man, for that matter, if he were weak enough. I had done as much ever since I was a boy myself—weaker boys, animals, girls when I could find them. You had to find a girl whose father and brothers were more afraid of you than you of them, but, in any case, it had all been nothing, I was a soldier, not a lover, not even a soldier but a river. A flood rose, and I rose with it."

Here, Menenhetet paused before he said: "I would make it clear again, Good God, that I speak out of the innocence of mind I knew in my first life. In those years I never had a thought for the body I entered. Rather I did it to find the peace that comes from the Gods. An animal knows as much. I may say that I have seen such light in an animal's body. So there was nothing new about this thief except that he had a back and ribs that would have looked like my own if not so thoroughly marinated by the flat of my sword. Yet I never enjoyed a buggery so much. My hand flew into the thick hair at the back of his head, and I felt my member swell to the size of a King. I was large with the gift of Ramses the Second. No door could have withstood my horn. The thief shrieked like a beast disemboweled. The first slash of the butcher has gone wrong and the poor animal runs around the shop with its tripe falling out while the customers scream and the butcher curses. Those were the sounds this fellow made beneath me and I even felt the last of his strength—that power which is attached to each man's Secret Name, if so I may put it—for it came right into my belly, as if my loins were drinking it from him, oh, how I loved his ass. It belonged to me. I could hardly take air through my nostrils so thick were my feelings. I had used holes before, but only to give me peace, as I have said. This time I was ready to steal the seven souls and spirits of this wretch, and when I came forth it was with all that had been put into me by Ramses the Great, the very message He inscribed on the walls of my insides. Even as the very center of me had been stolen by my Pharaoh, so did I steal it from another, and knew it could never stop. I had an appetite as strong as the color of my blood and knew I would keep trying to steal the seven souls of all I met, indeed when I was done, I kissed this fellow on the lips, and wiped my prick on his buttocks as a courtesy for the pleasure he had given me, then slapped it into his mouth in order to grow hard again.

"But you need no more in the way of such description. I took him through the night as if I possessed the Royal Member of Ramses the Great—may I speak with the truth that is found in the balance of Maat—I came to know the strength and the bravery and the cheap treacherous shit of this cutthroat whose name I never asked (I spoke none of his language and he knew fifty words of Egyptian) but before I was done, I had acquired all of his character that I would care to use and a few of his bad habits as well, or so I would have to think when I would find my fingers looking into the possessions of others, yes, I took him so thoroughly that there was a thief in me for the next ten years, yet by the time I left him sobbing on the ground, grateful for the tenth time that he was not dead, he was also mourning all those qualities in himself he would never know again, and I had learned one matter of interest about the King of Kadesh—it was that he had a woman on the Street of the Jewelers in the city of Tyre, of New Tyre, not the Old, and she was his secret whore. Of the armies of the King of Kadesh, this thief knew nothing except that there were armies.

"I speak of this knowledge as if the thief and I both owned the same language and had met in a beer-house for a drink, but getting him to tell me took half the night, and a few tortures of the hair on his head. I ripped away half his scalp before all desire for him was out of me, and even then he stammered forth whatever words he had. Maybe he would have answered sooner if not for his lack of Egyptian words. They have narrow ears, these Syrians, so it took long. I would ask a question, but then I would enjoy the power of my body over his body so much that he could not even try to give the answer. I felt as if I had grown a tree out of my crotch and it was on fire and this tree was being rammed into those secret turns of the bowel where the Secret Name is held." He paused for breath and I felt my own Sweet Finger stirring.

"I always knew that men took a great deal of pleasure in each other," said my mother, "but I never understood the price."

"It is not always like that," said Menenhetet. "Indeed, the night was unusual."

Ptah-nem-hotep said: "Perhaps our good Menenhetet also takes pleasure from the recollection."

"One must," said Menenhetet. He shrugged. "In the morning, I kissed that poor thief again and sent him limping back to Megiddo, and worked the horses toward Tyre. I was over the worst of the mountains and it was a quick trip down—too quick—coming out of one of the ravines, we were going fast around a turn, hit a rock, and spilled. I went leaping off the road but landed on my feet with no more than a bruise for the bone of my heel. The horses were screaming in their traces and the shaft that goes from their harness to the cart had split at the fastening. In my pouch I had two hardwood spikes and leather thongs, but still lost half the day. Let me say I was no carpenter.

"By the time Mu and Ta were harnessed again, the sun was overhead. What a ride was ahead of me! The road became no smoother and the chariot groaned through every one of its fastenings. I did not know if I could get it all the way to Tyre and hardly knew why I wanted to. At this point, it would be faster to travel on one horse with my weapons on the other, but then no charioteer wants to lose his cart. Mine, of course, had little to distinguish it—just a wood wagon. Still, it had the lines of a chariot, so my sense of what was proper did not suffer. While only a few specks of paint still stuck to the wood, and it certainly looked—with those thongs around the shaft—as though it was waiting to fall apart again, I liked it enough to laugh, for my own post was sore at its root. 'Better you than me, old soldier,' I said to the chariot, and we went on.

"The road dipped, it climbed, it turned, but the forest began to open into fields, and around a knoll I could look down through the ravines to the sea. There was air in my lungs of a sort I had never breathed before, not even on the Delta, a smell—it had to be—of the Very Green itself, and wholly composed of fish, with an odor refreshing to my nose, not like the fish that rotted on the mud flats of the Nile. No, this good smell that came up into the hills from the loveliness of the Very Green was amazing to me, as clean as if I were breathing the very scent of Nut when She holds up the sky, so dainty, so different from the meat that gets into the sweat of men and some women. I began to cry because I had never known a lady like that. I do not mean that I wept like a child nor in weakness, but with a healthy longing now that my pride (because of what I had done to the thief) felt much restored. Besides, the water went out to a great distance, extending beyond the strength of my eyes until I could not find the place where the sky overhead came down to meet the sea and that was part of why I wept, as if a sight of the greatest beauty was being withheld from me. Then there were the ships. I was used to our own sailboats on the river, and the royal barks with their huge red and purple sailcloth, and their gold and silver hulls that gave more show of our great wealth than watching a royal procession, but these boats here on the Very Green—so far away I could not even see the color of their hulls—had white sails, and that was also a sight I had never known before. They rode through long curves of water that almost buried them, and their sails spread out like the wings of white butterflies. I could not believe how many I saw, and some by their direction were rowing away from Tyre and some were sailing to it, although, as I descended, I could not see Tyre itself, only the stones by the shore.

"Now, riding by the rocky coast, the road would sometimes climb over a spur of mountain that moved right into the sea like an arm in front of your nose, and sometimes our wheels would wobble along a trail that almost came down to the rocks of the sea, and these low roads were wet. I had never before seen such streams of water to come at you. The sea was like a serpent rolling down a hill, if a serpent were to do such, then smashing on the rocks. I was covered with spray from the Very Green and what a taste it had—of minerals and fish and the soft little devils that live in shells and something mysterious as well—

maybe it was the smell of everything I did not know. All I can say is that the feel of the Very Green as it sprayed on me still had much to do with a lady for it was also light and contemptuous and playful, but could leave you chilled.

"Then it grew dark and I realized there were many Gods and Goddesses in this sea, and Their feelings could shift. Certainly the serpents that rose from the water now smashed with more force on the shore, and left a noise like thunder. The spray began to sting my eyes. I was happy to climb a hill that lifted me above such spite, but realized even as I got out of the chariot to lift the wheels from one smooth bump to the next that here the hill was of solid rock, and workmen—back so long ago as Thutmose the Third, or was it nearer to the beginning with Khufu?—must have labored for years to cut these steps on the road to Tyre. It was truly a stairway and would have impressed me more if not for our Egyptian works that are so much greater. Still, I learned another truth about the sea. For in the dark, the water struck the wall below the road, and this shock was like standing on the parapet of a fort while a siege army pounds on your gates with a battering ram. The spray flew up here to the height even of fifty or a hundred cubits above the sea, and when I looked down in the near dark, the Very Green had a million and infinity of mouths with white spit on all of them, and it growled and sucked at the ledge like a lion tearing at its prey. Even while I watched, came one massive blow of the largest serpent of water I had yet seen, a snake as large as the Nile, and it smashed the cliff so well that a full slab of rock gave a groaning sound, wrenched forth from its socket and fell into the sea. I was trembling so much at this encroachment on my road, and at the endless anger I could feel in the true Gods of the Very Green, that I wondered how I would even dare tomorrow to embark on a ship and ride over such serpents to the Island of New Tyre. I can only say that so soon as we were past the hill, the road, to my relief, moved inland, and I made camp, ate some wet grain with the horses, then slept shivering in my damp clothes.

"In the morning, I had another fine view. The mountains now moved away from the sea, and I could look across a long valley that had fields tended like gardens, and orchards of olive trees. In the distance, a city stretched out along the sand. Across from it, far away in the water, were the towers of another city seeming to grow out of the Very Green itself. I knew the place on the beach was Tyre, and the one in the water was New Tyre, and there I would learn much about the King of Kadesh, or so I hoped. My chariot had a comfortable sound despite the groaning of the shaft against the leather on our way back to the shore."

Seven

"Good and glorious Ptah-nem-hotep," said my great-grandfather, "when You spoke of the purple snails, I was silent and did not tell of my experiences in Tyre and Old Tyre. In truth, I had almost forgotten these purple snails and their stench. How that is so, I can hardly understand, for the old city stank of their corruption as one came near, and the alleys made you hold your nose. Yet the purple of the paving stones on every street with a dyer's shop was so bright, it hurt the eye. One could even see the sky reflected in that wet purple. Still, the odor of those poor snails was so squalid that my first thought on riding through the gates was to suppose I had come in by the beggars' quarters. The breath in my nose was like nothing so much as a whiff of the curse which comes with rotting teeth. You would think that is a scent to wilt the feather of Maat, but such is the purity of its odium that the horses began to frisk with each other for the first time in days. Since this put a strain on my crippled shaft, I had to dismount and hold Mu and Ta, all to the amusement of everybody watching. Witness my second surprise. I had never seen so many well-dressed people on such a mean-odored street. That was the cost of wealth here—you were obliged to breathe the air.

"I confess, however, that the sudden playfulness of my horses was a common sight in Old Tyre. I do not know why foul-smelling places have such peculiar appeal—although Nut, we must remember, was able to fall in love with no one but Geb—yet in this first life with my quick eyes, I never failed to find lovers busy with each other in caves and ditches, under bushes, in the cellars of vaults, and here in Old Tyre, down every dank alley. Never was I in a city where people fornicated so frequently in public. Maybe it was the sun on the hot beach in the daytime, and the glistening purple of the walls under moonlight, or something intimate in the nature of the snail turning in upon itself, but I remember my proud shaft was full of blood from the hour I entered.

"Tired of the battered virtues of my homely chariot, and the stupidity of my horses, I left them in the keeping of the stable boy in the courtyard of the House of the Royal Messenger of Ramses the Second, at least so soon as I could find his street. Indeed there were few people I approached in Tyre who did not understand what I said and they spoke back to me in a hoarse and somewhat guttural use of our language that rubbed agreeably on the lining of my ear and stirred some cockles of good feeling in my chest, although with it all, I still felt like striking them for how they disturbed the ceremony of our well-spoken tongue.

"The Royal Messenger, I soon learned, was not in Old Tyre. He came to the House once a year to pick up tribute from the Phoenicians, and then went on to collect in other places; I could see, however, that his arrival in this place would be like a visit by one of the sons of the Pharaoh. The Royal Messenger certainly had the largest place on the beach. Even compared to the villas of the wealthy of Tyre, it was near to a palace, and the servants of the Royal Messenger, many of whom were Egyptian, kept the House ready for his return. Never before had I seen such scruples in servants when the master is away, but then I came to understand that just about every Egyptian trader who passed through Old Tyre paid a call here to pick up the gossip of other merchants. In one room, I even saw a wall with cubbyholes in regular rows, containing many a roll of papyrus with a gold string and a seal of wax—letters left by the last Egyptian or Phoenician ship to come from the Delta. Certainly, the servants kept the place up and I was content to rest there.

"A day went by, then another day before I was ready to take a boat from Old Tyre to Tyre, indeed, that much time I needed to recover from my trip. I was not tired so much as confused. There was gossip to pick up in the home of the Royal Messenger, but after I heard it, I did not know whether the King of Kadesh was weak or powerful, cautious or aggressive. The only matter of which I could be certain was that everyone had information to offer, spoke in a voice that was full of authority, and contradicted what the last fellow had said.

"Of course, I was also curious to see this Old Tyre. I had never visited such a town. While the poor quarters were old and, with the stink, more miserable than anything you could find in Thebes, yet much was interesting, and the new streets made you think of a mouth with missing teeth. On every new street there were so many empty plots. Even the town wall had breaches, and there were breaks in many a fence. The best streets often had ruins. Yet the town was prosperous. A trader explained it to me. The new Tyre out in the bay, having been built upon three islands, was impregnable. No army that marched in by land could take it, since such armies would be without boats when they arrived. Nor, for that matter, was there a navy who could defeat the fleet of Tyre. So that city on its three islands was equal to a fortress with a moat, and if it came to siege, they could never starve. Food would be brought in by sea—as was done already. So the people decided never to defend Old Tyre on the shore inasmuch as New Tyre could make more in trade than it would cost to rebuild Old Tyre after an army came through. That was why I saw so many empty plots and so much new building. Old Tyre had been taken by the Hittites two years ago. Yet, the old city, I heard a lot of people say, looked newer than the new city.

"All the same, New Tyre paid tribute to Egypt. I concluded that this was not from fear, but for profit. Every utnu they gave us brought back a hundred in trade with the Delta. Yes, they were certainly the first people I met who did not think themselves inferior to us.

"On the third day, I took the ferry to New Tyre, and watched the oarsmen take us up the back of each rolling serpent, then slide down the other side. There were tears in my eyes from the wind, and I felt much consternation in my legs at the pitching of the boat. These were no thousand limbs of water, but more like twenty bodies in a beerhouse shoving you about, and the spray slapped my face. For that matter, it washed so far up my nose I could smell the end of the snail all over again. Yet when we got to New Tyre, it was like nothing on shore.

"This city on three small islands had no horses, for one matter, and everybody walked or was carried. In most places only three could go abreast. The walls of a house on one side of the street were never so far away from the other that you could not touch both walls with your hands, and then I had never seen buildings that went so high. One family lived on top of another, five families high, and the walls drew nearer to each other as they went up. It was nothing to leap from roof to roof, you almost stepped across. The door on the patio of each roof, as a result, was more securely barred against robbers than the door to the street.

"I remember that as our ferry approached a landing, I could not think of a more crowded town to visit. There was no beach to the island, nothing but heavy sea and much wind, and jetties built out by the placement of one rock on top of another. Hundreds of people stood on every dock and quay. Behind them, the city had the look of cliffs facing other cliffs and there were the most extraordinary towers on some of these roofs. You could also see every color of the palette on the painted walls. So it was the prettiest and most fearsome looking place. A thicket. These three islands were so close together that you could cross from one to the other by bridges built of wood above the water, but once in the city, you could never see the sky, no more of the sky at least than the little space between the buildings. There were no gardens, and no town squares. In the market, you could not move because the alleys were that narrow, but then, the place not only stank of snails, but the alleys curved like snails. You were always lost until you reached the outermost point of whatever little island you were on. Then you could look at the sea from the end of the alley before plunging back down another alley. I would get thirsty on these walks, but there were no shadufs nor fresh water. You had to drink what you could of rainwater from the cisterns and they were filled with the salt of the stones in that place. Everything was covered with spray that kept coming in on fogs and ended in the cisterns. I even wondered what the Phoenicians did for fresh water, until I learned the wealthy had their boats—you were not wealthy in that place unless you owned a boat and crew, which cannot be said of all wealthy Egyptians—and the lady of the house would send to the mainland for spring water. I purchased some in the market and drank it all before I could stop.

"Never had I been in a place where land was so valuable. Even the most expensive shops were small, and the workshops were more cramped than the houses. The traders offered wares made of gold or silver or purple glassware and vases. They even sold imitations of our Egyptian amulets and I heard they could trade with them in every port of the Very Green because of the esteemed reputation of our curses and our charms. The poor fools who bought these copies in faraway ports would never know. But then you must imagine what was made in these workshops for foreign lands. Egyptian swords and daggers that never saw our Nile looked nonetheless like they belonged to us, and rings with scarabs had our cobra, or our lotus, engraved on the metal. I heard it said that you could go through Rhodes and Lycia, Cyprus and some other islands of the barbarian Greeks, and everywhere natives would be wearing Phoenicia's jewelry, their bracelets, their collars, their damascened swords, chased swords, and every kind of material you could dye purple."

"But what," asked my mother, "did such barbarians give back in trade?"

"Some had gold to offer. Probably they robbed it from other traders, or they paid in jewels, or bars of silver. Often, they sold their young men, their young women and their children. In some lands, that is also a crop."

"I have noticed," said Ptah-nem-hotep, "that even though the

Greek slave is as hirsute and rank-smelling as any Syrian when he arrives, he does seem to learn from us. And quickly."

Menenhetet nodded. "I can tell You that the secret whore of the King of Kadesh was a Greek, and there were few who could still teach her. But then, the prostitutes of Tyre were regarded with respect, at least the more famous ones, and while I did not enter the Temple of Astarte and can give You no account of the priests, I heard it said that, under certain conditions, prostitutes were like priestesses there and much respected. This was, however, told to me while I was still in a state of confusion from all I was seeing. Never were so many people from so many lands gathered in a single place. Going the length of one alley that ran from the quay where I landed to the Temple of Melkarth, I saw Phoenicians and Amorreans, mountaineers from Lebanon, Turks and Sagalosians, Achaeans and Danaeans, tattooed blacks, men from Elam, Assyria, Chaldea, Urati, and every archipelago, sailors from Sidon, crewmen from Mycenae, and more costumes than I could distinguish, high boots, low boots, barefoot, colored shirts, white shirts, red and blue wool capes, animal skins, our white linen, and the hair of Your head in a hundred styles. Most of the Phoenicians were, themselves, nude to the waist and wore short cotton skirts of many colors. You could recognize the rich because they had their hair done in ringlets down their back, and four rows of curls on top like four serpents of the sea, back to back. With it all, everything stank worse in New Tyre than Old. All day long, people were combing snails off the rocks of these three islands, and children would dive for them. I had never known that people could swim, yet here I saw ten-year-olds go beneath the water like fish.

"My room on this island was in an inn, and my sheets were of red silk, the walls of purple fabric. The sarcophagus of an Egyptian merchant of no great wealth is larger in size than that room. You could not stand up in my abode and the hall was so narrow people were not able to pass each other. Later, I heard the sound of a couple thumping away over my close ceiling, and realized that mine was only one of two little bedrooms, one above the other. All up and down my floor, two bedrooms to one true ceiling! Of course, each sarcophagus had a window, I will say that, and through it you could pour your leavings. I had learned of that local habit already. My boots could have told you more. A true sign of poverty in Tyre was to walk barefoot."

"I cannot believe everything you are telling us," said my mother.

"On the contrary," said my father, "I have spoken to a few who trade in Tyre and it is still the same."

My great-grandfather nodded. "What can we know of such a life? Here, on our desert, we have room for all. Sometimes I feel my thoughts extending out so comfortably, that all of me, that is, my thoughts and myself, could fill a tent. In Tyre, however, there is only space on the sea. Never had I felt the presence of others so powerfully, and I discovered that in the midst of such congestion, it is impossible to think. My thoughts felt bruised. Yet my heart was warm. In all the stink of those decomposing snails, human bodies were sweet. Even old sweat smelled like perfume next to such putrescence, and of course no one bathed, not when water could be measured in gold."

"That place is a pestilence and a nightmare," my mother said.

"No," Menenhetet told her, "I came to like it. You could walk along the canals they cut into each island. They would put boats up in dry dock by the side of these canals, and the people of Tyre respected their boats as if they were Gods, and built them of the best timber from Lebanon—from the forests, indeed, through which I would soon pass—and from the oaks of Ananes. What boats they were! What crews! It was told to me that of all the ships in the Very Green, only the Phoenicians did not hug the shore and worry about making port each evening, but traveled instead through the darkness, daring every monster that came to the surface during the long night. These people could even steer by the stars, and if the one they followed was covered over by clouds, they would guide their trip by calling upon another star. Where there were none, have no fear, they would steer into the waves and wait for the sun. 'We can sail to the land of the worst dreams,' was one of their sayings. How can I tell you? These sailors were as proud as charioteers, and the poorest of them acted like a rich man in every beer-house. I saw fights in those dens that were good preparation for war.

"Then there were wine-parlors with long benches where you sipped your drink, and the elbow of your neighbor was on your neck. That was all right since your own elbow was on the next neck. One could not call one's skin one's own, and the wine was sour as vinegar, yet we lived in a happy delirium, for on a raised platform just large enough for one girl, there was a whore who took off her skirt and—since the boy is asleep I will tell you—showed the center of herself with such readiness that your eye might have been looking through a keyhole at another eye. She was some kind of Asiatic with the darkest hair, and a body the color of leather but the lips between her thighs were like an orchid whose petals are black at the tip and pink in the center and I do not know if till then I ever desired a woman so much. Perhaps it was the look on her face. She wanted all of us. As proof, she arched her back, put her belly up, and displayed herself in turn to each man. I remember I put my desire into my eyes, and her petals quivered before my look even as a lotus plant will wave slowly when you look on it hard enough. Then more desire rose in me out of what came back from her. In the circle around that whore, men were putting gifts on the platform, and when the music finished she went off with the highest bidder. I did not show my gold. It was the Pharaoh's and to be used only for the purchase of information. So I was desperate. How had that woman put so much into my loins?

"Then I learned she was not only a prostitute of this quarter who went from wine-parlor to wine-parlor along the alley but was also on this night a priestess. Before the dawn, she would fornicate on the altar of Astarte in the dark temple near the dry docks. It was the belief of these Phoenicians that in the filthiest could be found the finest, and in the most debased, the colors of the rainbow, which is why they were so happy with their stinks of snail and the royal purple glistening on every wet stone. My head felt like thunder trying to comprehend their religion. For in showing herself to all of us, she had also been serving her Goddess Astarte (whom some called Ishtar), yes, the whore was working for Astarte, collecting the lust of all of us in her black (and pink) orchid just as a flower receives the blessings of Ra, except here in the new city of Tyre, they never saw the sun in their

alleys, and so it had to be the heat in our belly that was served up to
the Goddess, why that whore would collect enough of you to make a
sacrifice splendid and glowing right out of the heart-meat of her
thighs, yes, send it up to the roof of the Temple of Astarte.

"I was ready to burst. It was a common sight in these alleys to see
people urinate, or expose their buttocks for the other relief, but my
member was feeling horrendous now, and I felt so foolish and wild
that I rushed back to my room to smother my fever. The truth is I was
looking for a man as much as a woman. The thief had given me a taste
for that. How I longed to be at Kadesh and with the battle begun.

"Yet as soon as I lay down in my bed, I felt an impulse to get up,
that is not to stand for you couldn't, but to squat under the beams and
look out my window. There, another orchid was to be seen! It belonged, as I soon found out, to the secret whore of the King of
Kadesh.

"In our own Egypt, we know what it is to live in the thoughts of
another. We are famous for our power to lay the most effective curses,
and this is due, of course, to the comfort with which we can leave our
own mind and rest in the next. One has to know one's enemy before
one can curse him, and such power, I should think, comes naturally
from our desert and our river. In great spaces, the mind can travel as
well as the body. On this unspeakable island of congestion, however,
this damp Tyre, given the closeness of all our bodies, no thought
from one mind could ever penetrate another. In Memphi or Thebes,
I would not have been surprised if the secret whore of the King of
Kadesh had taken abode in a house across from me—assuming she
was the person I had come to find. Our minds race ahead of us and
summon strangers. But in this beehive, this ant-heap, no! Later, when
I pondered it, I was amazed that I came upon the secret whore so easily. I did not yet understand that in Tyre, in the absence of every
message that one mind can give silently to another, the tongue substi-
tutes for the brain. Gossip is even more common than money in Tyre.
So it was known that I was a strange charioteer, and, given the cleverness of these Phoenicians, was either a deserter, or an officer on a

mission for Usermare-Setpenere and must certainly be the second since I did not have that unhappy look no deserter can avoid."

"I agree," said Ptah-nem-hotep, "that this woman must have heard you were in town, but how could she know you wanted to see her?"

"That is the point, Good and Great God. She was the one who decided to meet me. Retaliation was what she wanted upon the King of Kadesh. Of course, I did not know that then. I saw only a woman who wore nothing, lying on a bed across the street from me, her window no more than an arm's length from my window. She was beautiful in a way I had not known before. Later, over the years of my first life, and through the experience of lives I was yet to know, I would come to learn that women are as different from each other as our desert from the Very Green, but I knew nothing in those days except that there were beauties so lovely they lived in the Pharaoh's gardens and were called little queens, and then there were the whores you found in beer-houses. Nor could I speak about ladies of good birth. I knew such noble ladies were not like other women, just as you could not speak the same word for courtesans and common prostitutes, but then, for all I knew to say to either, ladies and courtesans were more alike to me than not, by which I do not mean I was familiar with any of them, but only that ladies took pleasure in the way they spoke, and courtesans knew how to sing, and either way I was always completely uncomfortable with their splendid manners, whereas any woman who was lower than me felt comfortable, speak of the ugly farmgirls I knew when I was a boy and peasant, and the good-looking farmgirls and beer-house girls and servants when I was a soldier, I took what I could and thrust myself into all of them as if to shoot an arrow— there was hardly any difference between a man and a woman, except with a woman, you were more likely to see the face and that could be preferable. All the same, as I have said before, I made love like a soldier, simple as that.

"With this secret whore of the King of Kadesh, however, I was in the presence of a magician. Just as we all know when we are kneeling before a person of great power, so did I know, looking through my window, that this woman was no whore to make you eat out your eyes in a wine-parlor or carry your lust to the altar, no, she might be without clothes, and her gates open, she might lie on her back, knees out, yet never was a woman less unclothed. She was, if you take the fear in my heart, a temple. I felt no haste to go over to her. Just as one must make no error when offering a sacrifice to Amon, and try to go through each step in a ceremony with no faltering, so did I lift myself from my bed, remove my own white skirt and boots, and in the most grave and comfortable motion, as if I were a cat walking the rail of a balcony, leaned out of my window, four stories in the air, and leaped across to hers. Then, with a smile that had no triumph, only my courtesy, I approached the bed on which she lay—it was all of purple silk—and knelt at her feet and was ready to touch her ankle, but as I drew near, it became more difficult to move, no, not more difficult, more circuitous, as if I could not approach directly but must respect the air, and halt. I was not two steps away from the bed, yet I could as well have been climbing a long stairway for all the time it took, and through it, her eyes and mine looked into one another for so long that I came to understand how an eye does not have a surface like a shield but is deep and something of a passage, or so you may believe on the first time you look into eyes that are the equal of your own. Hers were more beautiful than any I had known until that day. Her hair was darker than the hair of any hawk, but she had eyes of violet-blue, and by the light of a candle, they were near black when she turned her head to the shadows, yet against the purple sheets, blue again, even a brilliant purple, except it was not their color I saw but the transparency of her eyes. I felt as if I were looking into a palace, and each of its gates would open, one by one, until I could look into another palace. Yet each eye was different, and each palace was wondrous in size and had the color of every gem. The longer I stared, the more I could swear I saw red rooms and golden pools and my eyes traveled toward her heart. Since I did not dare to kiss her (I did not know how to kiss a woman, having never done so) I put my hand on the bed near her thigh.

"Once, during those days I traveled alone, the mood of the forest had become so powerful I stopped. The air was too heavy to breathe. I raised my sword then from its scabbard and drew it down slowly as if to cut through invisibility itself. Such had been the stillness that I swear I heard one fine note as pure as the plucking of a string, at least so clearly had I cut the air of the mood, and in a resonance of all my senses that was now as deep, I laid my touch on her flesh, and she returned a sound from her throat as pure and musical as a rose if the flower could speak. I knew then that I would make no mistake. Every sound that came from her mouth was a guide where next I could lay my touch, and to my surprise, since I had never heard of such an act, nor even thought it possible, my head, like a ship rounding the point to harbor, came down past her knees and I put my nose into that place out of which all children are born and smelled the true heart of this woman. She was rich and cruel and lived with a terrible loneliness in the center of this congested old city of New Tyre, although with it all, there was such loveliness in the quiver of those lower lips, and such subtlety of experience that I began to kiss her there with all my face and heart, with all the happiness of an animal learning to speak. Never had I known that my lips could offer such delicacy of movement, it was as if splendid words I had never uttered were now at the tip of my tongue, and soon I was wet with her from eyelashes to chin, wet as a snail, and indeed she smelled like the sweetest snail and more, she was the only garden on the island. I felt as if I lived in a light close to violet itself. All the while she never stopped humming her song of encouragement, as unrestrained as the purring of a cat in pure heat. Again, I knew I could make no error, and before long was introduced to the pleasures of that two-backed beast which lives with one head at either end, and her tongue felt like three Goddesses bringing peace to all the clangor of sword on shield that had been the harsh sum of my testicles, my asshole, and my cock, may the Pharaoh forgive me for so speaking in His presence, but this is the Night of the Pig."

"I am content that the child is asleep," said my mother, but her voice was sweet and carried the nicest rough edge to stir through my chest as I lay by her knee. Having listened to my great-grandfather speak of wondrous palaces in an eye, I now felt a kingdom stirring in the forest of her thighs while his voice went on to tell us more.

"In that manner, with a sense of respect as wide as the tide of the sea when it washes against the beach, and so gently as if I were hold-ing a small bird in my hand, I lay with the brow of my member on the edge of those lips I had kissed with such devotion and promises that were new to me pushed so powerfully within my belly that I was tempted to have it all now and live with the fire left behind. But I could feel an invitation to know her further, and so I entered this temple that was like a palace, and descended step by step in the puls-ing of my muscles, and felt the brush of her hair against mine as we went down into a splendor of many lights, rose and violet and lemon-green were their hue, and then a great serpent of the sea washed over me and I was gasping in the rush of my seven souls and spirits for they leaped out of my body and into her, even as her seven parts were com-ing to me. Some battle took place while each of us made great swings of a sword that cut no heads, and we were in a garden again, her gar-den, and it was very sweet. Her loins kept pulling on me. It had not been bliss—not as I was to know it later—indeed, in the middle, my loins knotted, but I also knew for the first time what it was to make love and be given the full value of a woman's heart, her greed, her beauty, her rage, and all equal to my own. May I say it was my first great fuck.

"There are men who measure their life by success in battle, or by the victories of their will over other men. There may even be a few like myself who can measure each life by other lives. In this, however, my first life, I had just learned that it can also be a journey from one extraordinary woman to another. The secret whore of the King of Kadesh was my first."

"How did you know who she was?" asked my mother.

"How, I cannot say—maybe it was the sight of those palaces in her eyes. By the time we were done, however, I did not doubt that I knew the King I soon might meet in battle. I knew him. If I met this King of Kadesh on the battlefield, I would know how to fight him. His heart was in my possession. By the way she gave herself to me she held her King in contempt. Do not inquire how I, who knew so little about women, could now know so much—it was the gift she had to offer. Women's gifts are never so profound as when they take revenge on a lover.

"Yet I did not even say her name, and would not see her again. A night so beautiful as this could not be repeated unless one was ready to live with the woman forever. I speak now out of the extravagance of four lives and twenty such women, twenty such lost empires, but the secret whore of the King of Kadesh was the first, and we held each other until the dawn, and laughed, and told each other little things like the common name in Egyptian for the common act. She was much amused that it is written with the sign for water above the sign of a cup. 'Nak,' she kept saying, and repeated after me, 'Nak-nak,' giggling as if it were a wonderful sound and had a true echo, all the while pretending she had never heard it before.

"I wanted to know about her, I, who had never had curiosity for a woman's story, but all I learned was that she had been kidnapped by Phoenicians when a child. A boat came to her island in Greece, and the captain sent two sailors to shore. Would the chief and his daughters come out to the ship? She had gone with her sister and her father. As soon as they were on board, the boat pulled up anchor. So she had been brought to Tyre. Now, she was the High Priestess of all the whores in the Temple of Astarte, yet remained true (except on festival nights) to the King of Kadesh. She even had three children by him.

"How much of this was so, I cannot say. She told it like a tale she had told often. Besides her use of our language was limited. Still, I was certain she hated the King. Finally, she told me where she thought he was hiding. With her finger she made a small circle on the purple sheets to show me Kadesh, and drew another finger down from the circle to show me a river. Then she made small hills with her cupped hands. 'He is in the forest,' she said to me, 'but not for long. He has boasted too much of how his army can destroy the Egyptians. Still I never know when he will visit. Maybe your Pharaoh will not know either.' She sighed. 'I think you need your eyes.' She kissed me then on each one of them, and prepared to leave. It was close to dawn, and I had to wonder if she would join the other whores in the Temple of Astarte.

"After she was gone, I stepped across to my room and lay on my red sheets and tried to sleep but I could only think of the war to come and all the ways a soldier could die, and I hoped I was not afraid of the King of Kadesh but that he would know fear of me. Before the sun was up, I took the ferry back to Old Tyre, returned to the House of the Royal Messenger, and inquired about roads into the mountains toward the East.

"I soon had a decision to make. The shaft of my chariot had been repaired by the carpenter to the Royal Messenger, but since he did not have a piece of seasoned napeca wood and the other chariots had shafts too small to borrow, he had merely made new splints and attached fresh thongs. I did not think it would hold me to Kadesh, nor did I want to ride by the main road. There could be Hittites on the route to capture me. So I decided to leave my chariot and go by horse. That was certainly a change in my feelings from the way I arrived in Tyre, but I had no information then, and did not wish to meet Ramses the Second with neither a report nor a vehicle. Now my message would take care of the loss. So I packed my equipment on Mu, saddled Ta—traded the chariot for the two new harnesses—and went up into the mountains by a trail that must have belonged to a wild ram, or maybe a wild rabbit, it was that narrow. The horses' bellies were soon raw both sides from the scratch of branches. Yet I enjoyed it. I knew I could make no great error. The sun was up and I could take direction from that. Besides, I needed only to climb up an ascending floor, then cross a great ridge, travel across another valley, climb another great ridge and beyond would be the valley of the Orontes. I knew I would find the armies of my Pharaoh near that river. It was the only route He could follow. The great cart that held His great tent had six wheels to a side, and eight horses drew it. You would not have to wonder which road He was on, only that it be wide enough.

"On my route, however, I was not halfway up to the first ridge before the thicket grew dense and the briers so agitated the horses that

I was in a lather of perspiration myself what with pulling thorns from their hide without getting kicked as they thrashed, and the cedars were now so tall I could not see the sky. To the rear, the sun was only a dull glow and cast no shadow. I might never have left Tyre if I had known the gloom of these steep woods.

"So I made camp and slept. Next morning I was up to travel through all of the day and then another, and thought I would never come to the end of the forest. In great gloom, I had to sit each night with no fire. I did not dare. There could be Hittite scouts in these hills. Shivering, I was on the move with the dawn, leading my horses through the early mists while thinking for the first time in many a year of Osiris and how His Ka must have traveled through mists like these in the time of His great loneliness when His body was still in fourteen scattered parts, yes, these were sights appropriate to the Lord of the Land of the Dead, the pillars of these forests coming forward like sentries one by one as we walked in file through the fog, and I only kept my direction by the knowledge that I had not turned astray for the moss still grew on the same side of the rocks. I kept the moss to the right of us. Through a long day that made me feel as old as some of these trees, we climbed to the second ridge and by evening made it through a gorge where the boulders were so huge I had fear of serpents lurking in the caves of these great rocks. Then, after we had gotten through, it grew dark. I tried to sleep with my back against a tree, but I was no longer in Lebanon, I calculated, rather in Syria, and these great cedars belonged to another God. No strength came to me. I felt weaker than at any time since I left Megiddo and knew then that the secret whore of the King of Kadesh had taken more of my strength than she had given me of hers, although, of course, I had to suppose such strength had come in the first place from the thief whose back I had beaten with my sword, which was a thought to suggest that those who make love for a night had better be as adept as thieves. At last, I fell asleep between the horses, all three of us together for warmth, and let no one say a horse is not the equal of a plump woman except no woman ever passed so much wind.

"Then, in the morning, the dawn was up before I awoke, and

through the thinning of the trees, I could see the fields of Syria in a long plain. Far in the distance, half a day's march, must be Kadesh, and I thought I saw the glint of sun on chariots, hundreds, or was it thousands of chariots, somewhere behind the town to the north.

"Beneath me, not an hour's ride straight down the last of these slopes, I could see the van of my own armies. The Honor Guard of Usermare-Setpenere was camped there by a ford of the river. Looking on them, I knew—for I can still feel this sensation to a certainty—that other eyes were watching as well. Back of me in the forest, like a rock falling with my thought, came the sound of hooves as a horse began to ride away with news to be brought to the King of Kadesh, yes, the echo of fast-moving hooves."

Eight

"The fields were empty, and I must have been visible from a long distance as I cantered in on the last long slope to the river. The outpost of my Pharaoh's armies nearest to me had Libyans for soldiers, and they promptly tied me up in the Egyptian fashion. May I say how well it works. To sit on the ground with your wrists lashed behind your neck is cruel. I thought my sword arm would come out of my shoulder. However, a charioteer recognized me as I came down the ridge, and he galloped over and soon had me released.

"It was a sure sign, however, that the outposts were fearful. On our ride into camp, I found out from my charioteer that the bivouac here at the ford of Shabtuna would not be broken this morning. So the troops could have an afternoon to take care of equipment and rest their feet. The officers, however, were not at ease. Usermare-Setpenere was in a great state of anger, I was told. His scouts had still picked up no knowledge of our enemy, and everything was taking too long. The vanguard might be here at Shabtuna, but only the Division of Amon was close behind. The Division of Ra was half a morning back and stuck in the passes of the Orontes. The trail being too narrow for any quick passage of wagons, the Divisions of Ptah and Set were just at the beginning of this march, a full day to the rear. I had a picture then of how they must be stuck in the middle of the gorge, and I could even hear the cursing of the wagoners and the fearful voices of the horses.

"Worse than that, explained my friend, nobody knew what we would find at Kadesh. Last night Usermare-Setpenere had said to His officers, 'The Monarch of the Hittites does not deserve to be a King.' Our Ramses was in a rage. It was maddening that He must advance to Kadesh without knowing whether it would be battle or siege.

"I was trying to decide the worth of my news. Would He be ready to hear? I was not, however, to see our Pharaoh so quickly. There were ten officers waiting to speak to Him, and I, full of the most unusual uneasiness, went walking around the camp with a void in my torso as if my stomach had died.

"In those days, we still made camp in the same manner as in the age of Thutmose the Great. So, on this morning, the pavilion of the King was erected in the middle of the officers' tents, and the royal chariots were on all four sides. This square was surrounded by our cattle and provenance, and infantrymen were placed to the outside, their tall shields planted vertically on the ridge of an earthwork dug the night before. In that way, we were like a fortress of four walls of shields, and you even entered through gates, except they were not real gates, just the road and a platoon of infantrymen either side of that opening. Inside, you could stroll about, and visit your friends. If not for my message, it might have been good to feel like a soldier again. On ordinary days little made me happier than to be inside a camp, even if many did nothing but snore, or sharpen the blade of a dagger for one hour and then another.

"On this day, in the expectation that we might still be marching into battle—what life had an army without rumors?—many a Nubian put on his helmet, and would not take it off. These blacks, some in leopard skins, some wearing long white skirts with an orange sash slung from the right shoulder, made quite a sight. The blacks liked to be seen, and I watched five of them arguing in one place, and ten sitting so quietly in another that their silence was stronger than clamor, curious soldiers about whom we charioteers disagreed, some saying the Nubians would prove brave in combat, others said no. I knew they were strong, but I thought of them as horses, brave until frightened, and much in love with their plumage. Like horses, the Nubians would put at least one yellow feather at the top of their leather helmets. What a contrast they made to the Syrians who often had bald heads, no helmets, and big black beards.

"About the time I realized it would be afternoon before my King might see me, all discomfort went away, and I relaxed in the sun with other charioteers and told of my adventures, keeping the best to myself, and walked back and forth through the inner and outer square, the goodness of Ra warming my flesh, so that at last I was down to no more than my sandals and a loincloth, lolling about like half the soldiers on that ground, and the day grew lazy. I stopped for a while at the shop of the Royal Carpenter to tell him of the loss of my cart, but he was too busy to care, for he was putting together a chariot from two broken buggies, and promised to do better for me than that, since his workmen could return you six chariots ready for battle out of seven half-dismembered carcasses, and I listened to him while he stood in the middle of his shop with chariot wheels in one stack, the spokes for wheels in another pile, and heaps of broken parts on the ground. I did not know how he would ever be able to move.

"Then I watched other infantrymen carrying paniers of water up from the ford to a large leather bag hung from three sticks in the center of camp, and horses being walked to the blacksmith shop. I watched soldiers drinking wine, and a few were wrestling, and two others led a couple of cows to the field kitchen. I smelled the sweat of the day and the odor of roasting meat. Two of the soldiers drinking wine began to skirmish with daggers. They had been doing it for a long time and knew how to lunge at each other, then stop short. A Sherden, sweating like a fountain in his red and blue woolen cape, was beating a donkey who had gotten his nose into a bag of provisions. The food so excited the beast that he promptly got an erection. The Sherden kept beating on him and the donkey kept scampering away but never lost his excitement, nor took his head out of the bag, not while I watched. Next to him, another donkey, excited by all this, was rolling in the dust.

"Most of the men were sleeping. The afternoon grew lazier still, and I could feel the fatigue of all the days of the march that had brought these troops this far, and then felt my own fatigue, and went back to a tent I was sharing with other charioteers and fell asleep on a ground-cloth, only to be awakened by word the King would see me now. In bewilderment, still dreaming of forests and thieves, I stood up, threw water on my face from a bowl, and went over to the King's Pavilion. I had been dreaming of the Hittites and saw a road where they planted sharpened stakes, and Egyptian soldiers were dying on them. Slowly in my dreams, bodies slid down the stakes. My bowels were cold. I took a slug of wine from a skin, and that made me sweat. Looking like a man whose insides must belong to others, I entered the great tent of Ramses the Second.

"It was as much a fine house as a tent. He had not only His sanctuary for prayer, and His bedroom, but a dining room as well, and then a great room for anyone to whom He would give audience. On this day many officers and Generals and the Prince, Amen-khep-shu-ef, were with Him, yet when I entered He was so impatient that He began to speak before I had finished touching my head to the ground. 'Would you,' He asked, 'give up the richest province of your lands without striking a blow?'

"'My Lord, I would try to fight like the Son-of-Ra.'

"'Yet, some here tell Me that the King of Kadesh is two days' march on the other side, and dares not come nearer. He is a fool. I will let all know his shame. The stone I put up to celebrate my victory will show that the name of the King of Kadesh is equal to what you see between a whore's thighs!'

"It was hot in the tent from the sun coming down on the other side of the leather, and hot again from forty officers' bodies, but the greatest heat came from my Pharaoh. He was like a fire on a hot day in the desert.

"'Who says he will not defend Kadesh?' I asked.

"My Pharaoh pointed to two shepherds sitting quietly in a corner. By the dust of their long robes, they looked as if they had been traveling with their animals for a hundred days. Now, with smiles that showed their teeth—the teeth that were left—they bowed seven times. Then the older spoke, but in his own language. The Overseer-of-Both-Languages, one of our Generals, exchanged the Bedouin's words for ours, but only after each breath the shepherd took, and he took many breaths.

"'O Beloved Ramses, Adored-by-Truth,' I heard, 'does not the Good and Great God know happiness when He cuts off the head of His enemy? Does that not give Him more delight than a day of pleasure?'

"I saw my Pharaoh smile.

"The shepherd spoke in a long slow grave voice as deep and full of echo as any prophet, 'O You-who-are-the-Majesty-of-Horus-and-Amon-Ra, You-Who-are-firm-on-His-horse-and-beautiful-in-His-chariot, know that we have come to Your throne of gold'—and indeed my Usermare-Setpenere was sitting on a small chair of solid gold—'to speak for our families. They are among the greatest of the great families who are sworn to Metella, King of Kadesh and chief of the Hittites. Yet our families say that Metella is our chief no longer, because his blood has become the color of water. His force is to Yours as the eye of the rabbit to the eye of the bull. Metella sits in the land of Aleppo and cannot find the courage to march to Kadesh. So our families have sent us to You, as a pledge of their desire to become Your subjects.'

"'I am honored,' said Usermare-Setpenere, 'because I know you tell the truth. He who does not tell the truth before Me is a man who will soon lose the limb that makes children. Behold, he must look upon his lost parts with both eyes before his eyes are sent to join the lost parts.'

"Never had I heard my Pharaoh speak that way, but then I had never felt such heat come off His body. 'I believe these men are telling the truth,' He said, 'how dare they lie?' But in the same anger, He turned to me and said, 'Do you believe them?' When I was silent, He laughed. 'You don't? You believe they are so brazen as to deceive your Pharaoh?'

" 'I believe them,' I said. 'I think they tell the truth that is the truth of their family. Yet it is several days since they have left. While they have been making their journey to us, so may the armies of the King of Kadesh have also been traveling. O You-of-the-Two-Great-Houses,' I said, so frightened that I also struck my head seven times to the ground, 'in the dawn, this morning, as I descended from the hills, I saw to the north, near Kadesh, an army.'

" 'You say an army?'

" 'I saw the light of an army. I saw the light that is made by lances, and swords, and the polished metal on shields.'

" 'But you did not see the swords?' asked the Prince Amen-khep-shu-ef. 'Only the light?'

" 'Only the light,' I admitted.

" 'The light is from the river that flows around the walls of Kadesh,' said the Prince. A good many of the Generals laughed. When our Pharaoh did not, however, they were silent. Now I knew why the heat that came from my Pharaoh was so strange. Hera-Ra was not by His side. I remembered then how much of the heat used to come from the beast. Yes, the Generals were now silent before Usermare-Setpenere the way once they had been silent before Hera-Ra.

" 'On your travels, what did you hear about the King of Kadesh?' I now was asked.

" 'That Metella hides in the forest near the city,' I said quickly. 'That he has a large army. That he will come on us suddenly.'

" 'It is untrue,' roared the Pharaoh. Under the black and green of His cosmetic, I saw how the whites of His eyes were red. 'It is untrue,' He repeated, 'yet I believe it is true.' He glared at me as if I had taunted Him.

"A discussion began whether to break camp in the dawn and march to Kadesh with the first two divisions, or, whether—and here I could not keep silent and was soon in the debate—it would be wise to wait one more day. Let the last two divisions come through the gorge.

'Then,' I said, 'we can march onto the great plain with a horn to the left and a horn to the right.' I said 'horn' because I remembered that on the day we traveled to His tomb, Usermare had told me how Thutmose the Great never said 'wing' or 'flank.' He spoke of His armies as if He had a head and two horns, a Mighty Bull.

"My Pharaoh nodded. He looked into Himself and saw His Chariot at the center of a great army on a great field with two horns, and I thought He would give the order to wait. But Prince Amen-khep-shu-ef also knew His Father, and said, 'On that great field we may wait for another week, while the King of Kadesh does not come. Our men will fight with each other. They will desert. We will look foolish, and our horn will crumble.'

"The Pharaoh nodded to that as well. Now, the council was concluded. He gave the order. We would break camp in the dawn. That evening, Usermare-Setpenere stood on the cage that held His lion. One night in the forests of Lebanon, Hera-Ra had eaten one of our soldiers. So a cage had been built for him next morning. Now our Pharaoh spoke to all of us from the top of that cage, while Hera-Ra roared beneath.

"'The battle of Megiddo was won by the Great Pharaoh, Thutmose the Third. The King, Himself, led the way of His troops. He was mighty at their head like a flame. So will I be mighty at your head.' The soldiers cheered. I knew again that I was part of an army, for the evening was red once with its own light, and red again with our cheers. 'Thutmose went forth to slay barbarians,' said our King, 'and none was like Him. He brought back all the enemy Princes even though their chariots were wrought with gold.' We cheered again. Each time our Pharaoh spoke of gold, we cheered. 'All fled before Thutmose,' said our King. 'In such fear did they run that their clothing was left behind.' A great snickering laugh huge as a river of mud came out of us. 'Yes, they abandoned their chariots of gold and silver'—we gave a sigh like the whisper of moonlight on water—'and the people of Megiddo pulled their soldiers over the wall by what was left of their skin. In this hour, the armies of Thutmose could have captured the city.' Here, our King paused. 'But they did not,' He said.

'Our soldiers gave all their attention to the plunder left on the field. So they lost the treasures that were in the city. The men of Megiddo were stretched on the field like fish, but the army of Thutmose picked at their bones like gulls.' A groan came up from us. 'Do not act,' said Ramses, 'like gulls. The city that was not taken on that day had to be besieged for a year. The army of Thutmose had to work like slaves to cut down forests so that they could build walls to approach the walls of Megiddo. And the work was not done until all of the wall of Megiddo was surrounded by the wall of Thutmose. It was a year's work. The city starved, but in that time, they also hid their gold. It was lost to us. No good slaves were taken. Only the dead and the plague-ridden greeted the armies of Thutmose. So I say to you that we will fight a great battle, but none of you will take plunder until I give My word! It is Asiatic hands I want to see on the pile, not Egyptian.'

"We cheered. We cheered with fear in our throats and disappointment in our loins at the thought of less plunder, but we cheered, and the lion roared. Next morning at dawn after a night when few of us could sleep, we broke camp and crossed the ford at Shabtuna. Although the water in the deep places came to our chest, not a man nor a horse was drowned. Disturbed, however, in their nests at the riverbank, beetles gathered like clouds and came between us and the sun. The swarm of their flight was so thick that it left us in shadow. No one saw a good sign in the rising of these beetles.

"Once we were across, we formed our ranks and set out on the great hard plain in the valley of the Orontes that leads to Kadesh. Its soil is as baked as a parade ground. May I say that our horses and our chariot wheels rode over the bodies of all the beetles that had tired of flight. We left the mark of our route as much behind us as if we had trampled through a field of berries. Beetles were in our hair and clothing like a pestilence.

"Again I could feel the impatience of my Ramses. He was in the vanguard of the march. His charioteers, taken together with His Household Guard of the strongest Sherdens and Nubians, giants all, had, counting everyone, not five hundred men. We were certainly in the van. There was a clear distance behind us and the first troops of the Division of Amon. Worse. Looking back from a rise, I could see how far we had marched this morning across the plain. But the troops of Ra were just crossing the ford. It would be half a day before the Division of Ptah could follow. As for Set, those men were still jammed in the gorge. They would be no use to any of us until night.

"All the same, I was happy to be in the van. The dust was less. Clouds rose from the hard-baked clay of this plain that were thick enough to drive away the beetles, and such clouds drifted back on Amon and its five thousand marching men. It would have been like passing through smoke to ride with that division.

"How we must have been visible from Kadesh! Through the dust, we could see it in the distance where the sky met the hills. The city was not an hour's ride away on a fast horse, but would take us until afternoon, I knew, because now we were winding through lightly forested rises, and could see ahead no more and so could not go forward without pause, but had to send out scouts, then wait for their return.

"I was carrying a weight in my chest like the heart of a dead man. Yet, I felt neither weak nor spineless, but even in the midst of my oppression, alert, as if throngs were waiting inside me for the battle to begin. I tried to think of what I would do if I were Metella, the King of Kadesh, and where in these woods would I choose to attack the Household Guard of the Pharaoh so that I could capture my great Ramses? Then it seemed to me I would prefer to wait until half the Division of Amon was past, or even half the Division of Ra, so that I could strike at a large force when it was stretched out on the trail of the forest as long and vulnerable as a worm you could cut in half. Still, the effort of trying to think as if I were someone other than myself, especially a foreign King, made me know vertigo, and I supposed I was living with a fearful gift from the secret whore of the King of Kadesh. Maybe I was not trying to think like this Metella so much as I was indeed living in the thoughts that came from his heart. If that were so then our vanguard would go forward untouched and the Division of Amon as well. It would be on Ra that the thunder would fall.

"My fear was replaced by woe. At this instant, we were in no danger, yet in a greater danger. I could never tell this to Usermare-Setpenere. He was riding with His son Amen-khep-shu-ef in my place. That left me as a driver for no one better than the Overseer-of-Both-Languages. This fellow was a General called Utit-Khent, but, of course, this name, 'Mistress of Expeditions,' was only an army joke. He was said to have a rectum like the mouth of a bucket. So I knew again my Pharaoh's anger. He would have me share a chariot with such a man. Of course, He was now listening to the advice of His son. So soon as He discovered the power of my thoughts to reach into the thoughts of our enemy, so might I be His driver again. In the meantime, Utit-Khent babbled along about the dust, but in so clever a way I began to laugh for, lo, he pointed out there were Gods for every fish and cat, and the God of beetles was a Great God, but no God ever bothered to inhabit the dust. You could not name such a God. He was harmless, this General, a clown for other Generals, he commanded no men, and had been a flunky for Prince Amen-khep-shu-ef, but I had to wonder if this poor Utit-Khent had once been a strong soldier but had grown weak serving the father of Usermare. Maybe, that Pharaoh Seti had held him by the hair.

"We were not on a bad trail, indeed it was more like a road wide enough for one chariot to pass another. That was comfortable and it was cool in the forest under the heat of midday, but none of us were comfortable—Kadesh was too near. Besides, you had to wonder where a squadron of chariots could strike at us. While the forest reached to the road in most places, still we also crossed fields, and an army could hide at their edge. Five thousand men could charge down on five hundred, yet now my good King, impatient at delay, did not bother anymore to send out scouts. He must have believed the gates to Kadesh were open.

"Into the early afternoon we traveled, and passed another wood, and many a cultivated field, even saw a farmer or two who ran off at the sight of us, but we kept moving with the Orontes at our right, and the river was shallow here and slow-moving, and had several fords wide enough for an army, if this was where Metella wished to attack from the other bank. Still, nothing happened, and we came around a turn in our road and saw before us, there in full view to the north, the walls and towers of Kadesh, and no Hittite army was drawn up in front of it. There was nothing before us but the river which wound around its walls to the left. We had been marching so long to reach this town, so many days on the Nile and in the desert and the mountains, that I think my good King could not stop, not yet, but must keep going while He passed the city on our right hand. Soon, the walls would be behind us, and here, as if confused by the absence of any soldiers, or even any face in the windows of the towers of Kadesh, in this silence of the hills where the largest sound was the groaning of our chariot wheels, not a large sound, for we hardly strained on the level ground, Ramses the Second finally gave the order, and in a thin wood with many small fields and scattered trees, we halted beside the river in a place too steep to cross. The three open sides to our square that looked out on the land were quickly faced off with our shields, and an earthworks to support the shields was begun by the Nubians right about the Pharaoh's pavilion. Here we waited in silence, no sound but the digging. The Division of Amon soon followed, and built a larger square around our square, which enabled the King's Guard to move back from the Orontes. Now, the Division of Amon had the river for a fourth side. There was still not a sound from the town.

"Around us you could hear the echo of the five thousand men of Amon digging away, although with no great effort. In another hour we might be moving again. So they carried on with the ease of men unharnessing their horses, feeding their beasts and their own mouths, and in all this unyoking of the provision trains, there was a feeling of safety at the size of our numbers. Only I felt oppressed in my breath. Even though I did not want to fight beside Utit-Khent, still I worked on the chariot I might yet have to ride with him, grinding the bronze rim of the wheels with a rare hard stone I carried in my leather bag

until the edge was sharp as a knife. That would not last for long, but,
oh, what cruelty a wheel, freshly honed, could commit on the body
of a fallen man. All the while, I continued to feel heavy in my lungs.
When we came to this camping ground, I had seen no sign of another
army, no litter whatsoever, and the red pine needles of the forest floor
were smooth. Yet they did not look smooth so much as swept back
into order. I had the feeling an army had been here before us, even this
morning, and wondered how easily pine needles could conceal their
traces. Besides, I could smell the God of the pine trees and He was
almost as strange as the God who came with the myrrh from Punt.

"Men kept coming to the Pharaoh's Pavilion with little pieces of
equipment. Here was a wagon-spoke unfamiliar to us, or a broken
leather cinch with a strange-smelling oil. More and more did a sentiment become powerful to me that the forest was stale. Then I thought
if I were Metella, yes, I would stay on this north side of Kadesh well
hidden by the forest, even as Usermare-Setpenere moved forward
from the south. Only when He came up to the walls, would I cross
the river to the east and hide on the other side to keep the city between us. Then, if He came even farther north to this place, so would
I move altogether to the south and still be hidden by the walls of
Kadesh. That way I could cross the river in the place where there were
many fords and strike into the middle of the Division of Ra, there in
that open field south of the city.

"Even as I was considering such maneuvers, an outcry began in our
camp. Two Asiatics had just been brought in by scouts, their faces
covered with blood. Soldiers in the middle of cooking a meal stared
as the captors led these prisoners to the Pavilion of the Pharaoh. Then
came many screams and the sound of the flail. By the time I entered
the King's tent, the backs of the prisoners were as bloody as their features, and I was glad I could not see their expression.

"Each bite of the flail whipped loose a piece of skin large as your
palm. Usermare-Setpenere now pulled off a strip from the prisoner's
shoulder like a ribbon of papyrus, and threw it to the ground. Then
He said: 'Speak the truth.' That Hittite could not have known a word
of our language, but he knew the voice, he knew the eyes that looked

at him. The light from those eyes was as full of flame as the sun. So to Usermare-Setpenere, by way of Utit-Khent, he said, 'O Son of Ra, spare my back.'

" 'Where is your miserable King of the Hittites?'

" 'Behold,' cried the Asiatic in his language, and 'behold' said our Overseer-of-Both-Languages in our language, 'Metella the King of Kadesh has gathered many nations in great numbers. His soldiers cover the mountains and valleys.'

"He continued to speak even as Amen-khep-shu-ef was twisting this man's arm behind his neck. I thought his shoulder would dislocate, for even the bleeding stopped, so white did his back become from the pressure. Yet the scout said it all, every word, waiting each few words for Utit-Khent to express what he had said, all the while swallowing his groans. Now, Usermare-Setpenere raised His sword. 'Where is Metella now?'

"He could hold out no longer: 'O my Lord, Metella is waiting on the other bank of the river.'

"I thought the sword would fall. It hovered. Instead, our King let go of the Hittite, and turned to us. 'See what you have told Me,' He cried out, 'see how you have spoken of the King of Kadesh as a coward who flees.' Now I thought He would take the sword to His son. The Prince struck His head to the ground seven times, and must have had many thoughts, for when He looked up, He said, 'My Lord, let Me ride back to tell the Division of Ptah. We will need them.' When our King gave a slow nod, as if forced to agree despite His wrath, the Prince was out of the tent, and at once, I suppose, on His way, although none of us were able to know what another did, for in the next moment, chaos fell upon us. I heard a far-off din, a nearer uproar, and then the voice of a hundred horses, a most fearful clamor, a pandemonium, the shock and crash of chariots. We did not know that the shattered legions of the Division of Ra, horses without chariots and charioteers without horses, were now running our way, infantrymen chasing wagon trains pulled at a gallop by horses without drivers, and all of this disorder came down on us. Only later would I learn that the Division of Ra had been cut in half even as I had foreseen it, there in the road where they were long indeed like a worm. Now the rear of Ra was running back to the Division of Ptah, and the front half was on us in their rout, some already falling under the first chariots of the first Hittites, while the survivors were staggering up to the shields and earthworks of the outer square of Amon. The armies of Metella, like a serpent of the Very Green, had washed right up to the shore on which we stood. In this clamor, we saw the sky become as dark as the metal in an infantryman's dagger."

Nine

"I could tell you," said Menenhetet to our Pharaoh, and to my mother and father, "of how we spoke of this battle later, when each man could tell it to his own advantage. Then, it was only by comparing the lies that you could begin to look for the truth. But that was later. At this moment, there was nothing but noise, and much confusion. Yet I do not find it hard to remember how I felt through all of that long afternoon to follow when so many of us were nearer to the dead than the living, because I never felt so alive. I can still see the spear that passes to the left of my shoulder, and the sword that misses my head. Once more—it is as near to me as falling from my bed in a dream—I am thrown out from the Pharaoh's Chariot by the shock of a lance against my shield. It was the greatest battle of all wars, and in my four lives I never heard of anything like it. Of course, my mind did not speak to me on that day as on others, and it is true that the most unusual moments and the most unimportant passed equally like separate strangers, but I remember that in the instant when the clamor first beat about our camp, Usermare-Setpenere turned to me, and said, 'Take your shield and ride in My Chariot,' and I who had dreamed of this moment down the Nile, in the dust of

Gaza, and through the mysteries of Tyre, could only nod my head and think that the work I had spent in sharpening the wheels of the chariot of Utit-Khent was work worse than lost, for Utit-Khent would probably cut his own leg off falling out of the chariot, and such is the shock of battle where events become as shattered as broken rocks whose pieces fly in all directions, so I was seeing fragments of what was yet to happen, and Utit-Khent certainly did fall out of his chariot, and his leg was mangled by the wheel I sharpened even as his horses in panic ran over him.

"As I say, all I could feel at the instant was that I must now find my leather bag and my stone and begin to sharpen the wheels of His Chariot. But even to have such a thought was stupid. A squad of soldiers—the Royal Guard of the Chariot-of-the-Mighty-Bull— were forever polishing the gold and silver filigree, and working many royal stones on the treads—you could lose your finger running it along His wheels. So I climbed up instead on the cage of the lion to get a better view of all that was happening about us. Immediately, Hera-Ra started roaring beneath like a drunken beggar, hooking at his cage so furiously I almost fell off. Standing on those slats, the beast thumped my feet with his tail and shoulders and head, while I looked in all four directions, my organs in an uproar to match a confusion of sights multitudinous as the foam of the Very Green. I could certainly see the King's square surrounded on all four sides, for the larger square built in such haste by the soldiers of Amon was now lost. Beyond our square was a chaos and a carnage. The Division of Amon were fleeing their meals, their games, their tents, their wagon trains and their animals. While our inside square stood fast for the Pharaoh, outside I could see no more than a few of ours to face hordes of Hittites overrunning us so quickly they were caught already in their own rush. These Asiatics were not riding in one careful rank behind another of charioteers in perfect order the way we Egyptians like to advance, no, just a mob of hundreds of chariots, three men in each, wearing odd yellow hats, nor did they fight with bow and sword but tried to run everything down with their axes. In this din, our chariots, at least those still fighting, kept weaving in and out, our charioteers, some even at this hour with the reins around their waist, were pulling bows, quick as sparrows fighting boars. The enemy was so big and clumsy that I even saw two Hittite chariots crash into each other, three men in one catapulted out even as the other three were hurled to the ground. Yet over every hill, through these thin woods, came more ranks of Hittite chariots, some at a run, some at a walk, and then I saw the nearest thirty or forty, maybe a squadron, riding at a gallop toward the King's square itself. They charged our breastworks, up and over, and nearly all spilled. Those who did not, landed among the strongest of the Pharaoh's Sherdens who seized these Asiatic horses by the bridle, and held their footing long enough to turn the horses' necks and halt the chariot, at which moment, other Sherdens ripped the horses' bellies with their daggers. Then they pulled off the Hittites. Of the thirty who charged into our square, not one was left, and I, like a boy quick with excitement on the cage of Hera-Ra, had only an instant to see that the Pharaoh, His head down, His eyes closed, was still praying. Out of His mouth I heard these words: 'In the Year Five of My Reign, third month of the third season, on this Day Nine of Epiphi, under the majesty of Horus, I, Ramses Meri-Amon, the Mighty Bull, Beloved of Maat, King of Upper and Lower Egypt, Son of Ra Who am given life forever'—so I heard Him call on all His names, and even as a shaduf lifts its pail of water up the hill, so was my Pharaoh pumping up His blood as though the very water of the Land of the Dead must be lifted into His heart until He feared no death, and the dead as well as the living would listen: 'I, Who am mighty in valor, strong as a bull, Whose might is in My Limbs like fire'—so He kept speaking while on the battleground of woods and fields outside our square I saw a horse go over backward with an arrow in its neck, down on its own chariot with its own three Hittites, and one of our charioteers with a short spear in his chest fell forward onto the shaft between his two horses. On their backs, everywhere, were dead men staring at the sky. The nearest was farther away than I could throw a stone, yet, brilliant as a bird's eye was his eye. I could see it. Near him lay another dead man clutching his genitals. Then I saw a man whose arm was caught in the hub of a chariot wheel, and a Hittite came along and hacked at his head with an axe. All the while, most of our army was running into the woods. I could not believe in what panic were the men of Amon.

"Now my Pharaoh had finished praying and He unhooked the door to the cage of Hera-Ra who came out. Then, to my surprise, Usermare-Setpenere leaped into His Chariot on the driver's side. I, thereby, to the other, and He rode in a circle through our square, nearly striking some of our own men as He called, 'We are going to attack. We are going to attack.'

"Six chariots, seven, now eight, followed in our circle. Others saluted but did not move until the next time around. Now others joined, but not enough.

"'Follow Me,' said Usermare-Setpenere, and with a force of twenty chariots, He rode at full speed to the southern side of our square, choosing the lowest place in the earth wall, and we drove over it and down the other side, banging against one another badly; but then we were on the field, Hittite chariots before us in every direction, and, when I dared to look behind, half of our force was still with us. The other half had not dared to make it over the wall. We were surrounded already, if you could speak in such a way when our Pharaoh, having pumped the courage of the dead into every one of His limbs, not to speak of the force of Strength-of-Thebes and Maat-is-Satisfied, fastest horses of any land, and Hera-Ra bounding at our side, his roars louder than an avalanche of rock down a cliff, were, all of us, galloping through every bewilderment of battle so fast that none, not even our own men, could keep up with us, although some tried. The Hittites parted before our passage, as well as any poor Egyptians from Amon or Ra whom we passed, and for the length of a field, through a wood, and down another field, not one arrow was shot at us, not one did we shoot, and no Hittite came near, not man nor chariot—perhaps they were all afraid of the brilliance of the chariot of Usermare-Setpenere and the face of Hera-Ra, bounding beside us.

"Behind, like a tail that becomes so stretched the end must pull off, were our charioteers. I knew what it cost to keep up with the Pharaoh over rough ground, and only a few stayed with us now. When I dared to look, for I felt as if my good life depended on keeping eyes to the front, I could see how some of our men were surrounded by Hittites, and some had turned back, or were fighting their way back, and still my Ramses the Second galloped south, no one more happy, nobody so brave, nobody so handsome—He looked as if the sun shone out of His eyes. 'We'll break through,' He shouted, 'and find the troops of Ptah. We'll kill these fools when we come back,' and with that, we met a hundred Hittite chariots waiting in the next field.

"Now I saw more battle than a man could fight. Never will I be certain how many of our chariots were still with us, if any. For when our Ramses drove with His golden vehicle full-force into the center of these heavy Hittite carts with their three men, there was nothing for the next few minutes I saw whole. So I saw the spear that came at my shield and the axe that just missed my head. I saw Hera-Ra leap across three men of one chariot onto the horses of another. I saw him hanging upside-down with his muzzle on a horse's neck. Hidden from the arrows of the Hittite charioteers, he clung to the horse, his jaw on the blood of the stallion's throat, the claws of his hind legs opening the belly, until the horse stood up in such extremity of pain that his mate stood up too, both screaming, and they fell backward on their drivers, even as Hera-Ra leaped from the horse to a man and bit off an arm, or most of an arm, I could not believe what I saw, all from the side of my eye, between the movements of my shield, a hundred arrows seeming to come at once, all at the Pharaoh, as if no one could think of the horses nor of me in view of His golden presence. Those arrows were wild, but not the ones I blocked. They came at us hard as birds flying full tilt into a wall, and their points came through the leather of my shield, evil as the nose of your enemy.

"All the while, Ramses the Second would draw His bow and loose an arrow at full gallop, swerve by one Hittite chariot, then another, and was so adept we could stop, wheel, then charge away to stop short again as chariots converged on ours. 'Your sword,' He shouted, and there, not moving, two of us against three on either side, we fought back to back with our swords against their six axes, only it was not so unequal as that, for Hera-Ra charged one chariot, then another, and with such bloody fury that others did not come near, and we were free again, we had broken through, we were on our way to the south once more, we could reach the Division of Ptah, so we thought, so we shouted to each other, only to find another hundred Hittites facing us in still another phalanx.

"Sometimes a few of our own chariots caught up so we were not always alone, but five times we fought like this, five times we drove into a mass of men and horses so thick the only forest you saw was swords, armor, axes, horses, limbs, and chariots turning over. Vehicles raced by empty of riders, and ran into one another. The trees quivered. Ramses' great bow, which nobody but He could draw, had a force to drive its arrow through a man so hard it could knock him from the chariot to the ground, yet these sights I saw in fragments like the eye of a face on the shard of a pot. So, for instance, did I see a Hittite hold up a man who was expiring in the flood of a wound, while two others galloped away in a chariot without reins. The third Hittite had fallen off already. Many a soldier was trampled by horses or run over by wheels—I saw so many of those Hittite wheels with their eight spokes that I dreamed of them for years, foul dreams, the little wheels puckered as a strange anus, and there were sights full of folly: I even saw a Hittite attacking his own horse in harness; such was the fever that the fellow killed the beast with his axe. Maybe it had tried to run him down. I did not know, I never saw more, I was ducking a blow, sticking a lance, or reeling from the impact of the Pharaoh's body against me when He slammed our horses through a sharp turn, once I even fell off, landed on my feet and jumped up again. My lungs knew the fire of the Gods. I saw Hera-Ra leap at three men who stood motionless in their chariot, transfixed by the loss of their horses. They were still looking at their useless reins as he clawed down on them.

"Loose horses were everywhere. I saw one on broken front legs, trying to rear, and a charioteer lay on the ground, holding the tail of this horse until the animal flopped around to bite him. Another man was all alone in his wagon, his horses walking in stupor with loose reins. Then the man fainted, and I saw him slide to the ground. To the other flank was a riderless horse trying to crawl into a fallen chariot. It was a madness. One pair of horses, stripped of all three men, tried to dash over a collision of other chariots, but stumbled, and the empty chariot catapulted overhead while the horses stampeded into the ground. I never heard such a scream come from animals before. The worst was a howl from a steed Usermare-Setpenere struck in the chest with an arrow when it tried to leap between our stallion and mare. Everywhere, beasts in panic were defecating as they ran. On it went. We would think we had broken through the Hittites only to see another phalanx to the south, and we would attack again, even break through, but on the sixth attempt, we saw a thousand Hittites coming toward us in orderly formation.

" 'It can't be done,' I said to Him, 'we can't get out!' He glared at me then as if I were the worst coward ever seen, and said, 'Strengthen your heart. I will lay them in the dust!' I looked at those thousand soldiers and at my King's face, and in it was the expression I have seen in the eyes of mad beggars when they believe they are sons of the Pharaoh, yes, my Ramses the Second could swear to destroy all who called themselves Hittites, and I could feel His certainty so powerfully that I believed in it myself, although in a different way, and I said, 'Let us return, my King, to Your Pavilion, and we will gather Your troops and fight and destroy these Hittites from there,' and on that word, He wheeled our horses and we went charging back to the north, back to the remnants of the King's square that was two hills, three fields, and I do not know how many small woods away.

"There were enemy everywhere, and none of our chariots to be seen, yet no Hittites came to intercept us. They were all too busy plundering the deserted camp of the Division of Amon. So we swept back into the King's square and heard the cheers of all the men who were left. Officers came running forward as we halted, telling in great excitement how they had defended our square by the north side, the south side, the west and even by the river until the Hittites had retreated—with all their thousands, they had failed to take the square—but Ramses listened with wrath. To hear of their exploits, you would have thought we had none of our own, yet the arrows were still sticking in the quilting of our horses and the face of Hera-Ra was more red with the blood of the Hittites than the chest of a man laid open with a sword. I could not believe how red was the brightness of blood when you saw a great deal of it."

Menenhetet paused. "In what I have told you, there is not the heart of what I truly felt. Those sentiments were magnificent. During all that time we tried to break through to the south, I had been like a God, I felt twice my size—even as They are twice our height—and I was four times my strength, even as Gods know the power of four arms for each of Their shoulders. Never had I been so tireless in so heavy a work, and never was my breath so close to Them. I could have fought through the afternoon and night with the love I knew for Ramses and the horses and all that came forth from how we moved together. Often as not, I had no more than to think of a quick turn to the left for my King to perform the move, and, as if given vision in the back of my head, knew to swing my shield when a flight of arrows came down on us, never did I know as in those moments that we live for Them to see us, see us well, and thereby let us feel like Gods ourselves. I could no more have fled from the field than cut off my feet, at least so long as the Gods were with me, yet I lost them in the instant I saw the chariots of the thousand Hittites, except I do not know if I really did, for I was not full of fear when I saw that frightening sight, merely cool and calm and tired, my arm was suddenly heavy, and the voice that spoke to me was the same God's voice I heard in the flame of the hottest combat, still the same voice now said in my ear, 'Do not let this fool attack, or you are both dead,' and I say to You that the voice was amused—it is the word—It was amused, yet so fine and quiet a voice I could swear I did not hear from Amon with His mighty tongue but the soft tone of Osiris Himself. Who else would dare to speak of my Pharaoh as a fool? Only the Lord Osiris Who gave me the advice to return quickly to the King's Pavilion. And so I said to myself, 'Even if I am the son of Amon, it is Osiris who saved me today.'

"Now we were back in the middle of the Household Guard, and in the joy of our return, so did I feel the strength of the Gods once more.

My height doubled again, at least to myself, and I desired combat so much I felt the swelling of my member, and did not know whether to laugh or cry out in exultation. I saw Hera-Ra bounding about, licking our soldiers' faces with his bloody face, and mighty for a cat was his member, also fully extended, he was one in good spirits with me. I do not know if it was the blood on the field, or the jubilation of these troops that they had held their square, maybe it was the early fermentation of the dead bodies around us before their seven souls and spirits had begun to depart, but I can only say that the air in our nostrils was like a rose at evening when the light of the sun is also the color of rose, just so fine smelled the air with our desire for new combat. I thought again of my mother's story at how she awoke at my father's side and a God brilliant in the gold of His breastplate was above her, and the hut was filled with a perfume lovelier than any she had ever smelled.

"Now I knew what she had known, and it was equal to the tender odor of this air, and whether we owed it to Amon or Osiris, I could hardly say, but I was moved to climb onto the cage of Hera-Ra, and this so pleased him that he, in turn, walked with humorous thumps of his paws into the space beneath where he began to purr. Only then did I look out to all four sides, and the Hittites with their thousand chariots and a thousand more behind were walking their horses toward us in two great semicircles coming in from the west and the south. To our north was devastation. All of Amon and Ra were long departed, and I saw nothing but corpses, abandoned chariots, shattered tents, and provision wagons being plundered now by the Hittites on the field. The wisdom of Osiris must still have been with me, for I whispered to my King, 'At the east by the river, the line of Asiatics is thin.' It was true—fewer Hittites were there than on any of the other sides of our square, indeed the river was not two hundred paces away, and so He, adding the force of Amon to the mind of Osiris, shouted to the brave Household troops on all our four fronts, 'Come with Me. To the river!' Leaving our flanks and rear unprotected, Ramses mounted His Chariot and we took off at a gallop, followed by our remaining chariots, and foot soldiers from all four sides.

"There were not fifty steps from our line of shields on the east side to their line, and we crossed before you could blink three times. That was just as well since I never saw so many arrows coming our way. They surprised me. A moment before, these Hittites by the river had been somnolent, as desultory in shooting at us, as we at them. So long as arrows went back and forth from one entrenchment to another, you collected what fell, and soon the arrows you returned to the Hittites were sent back again. All the same, I was amazed at the number that now came at us as we galloped across. I heard foot soldiers cry out as they were struck, and then in the full shock of combat, for so it is, full shock, we slammed into the shields before us, and our good horses, Maat and Thebes, took us up over the earthworks of the Hittites, and we came down on their chariots with all our own chariots behind us.

"I do not know what it is like to fall into a river and be dashed over rocks. Since I cannot swim, I will never know, except I do, for the golden chariot of my King, stronger than any beast and beautiful as a God, was met by three Hittite chariots at once. With nine men, six horses, and three heavy carts did we collide, and all four of the vehicles went over I think, it is certain we did. I remember striking the ground and the King with me, and our chariot coming over on us, its wheel, much blunted now, still scoring my back, then we were bouncing up and the horses were trumpeting, and even as I was coming off the ground, so His Chariot was up again as well, I do not know how unless it kept tumbling with the horses, it was His, after all, and we jumped on once more, and rode in a circle, firing arrows into the Hittites. With it all, these collisions, bumps, falls, and recoveries had been happening as slowly as you would slide down a mountain in a dream. Never had I had as much time to arrange my body for each new shock, nor been this quick with my feet.

"Neither can I tell You how well we fought. It was nothing like the maneuvers we had practiced for years, no orderly sweep of rank on rank, no herding of infantry into a corner, no, we were in a rush to drive them to the river and fast, very fast, before other Hittites overran the King's square we had just left. Maybe it was the desperation of where we were, no front, no rear, no flanks, and probably no King's Pavilion to return to, but we fought like Hera-Ra, and so great was our lust to win a victory on this dreadful day that we were forever jumping in and out of our chariots, Ramses and I often fighting back to back, and many a soldier we wounded, and more than a few we killed, and back to our chariot against new Hittites. Everywhere I could see our vehicles circling their heavy carts with our skillful turns. On the ground, the Nubians were impaling Hittites with their short spears. I saw a man bite the nose off another man, and more than one Nubian had his yellow sash turn red. Three Hittites galloped by, and one of them had an axe in his hand and an arrow in his buttocks. He kept looking backward as if to see who had bitten him.

"We drove them all into the river. Foot soldiers, chariots, charioteers, even their Princes. It was fierce, but our swords were strong, our desperation was the virtue of war itself, and snorting, sobbing, growling at each other, charioteers on foot and infantrymen so crazed they leaped up on loose horses, we fought them to the edge of the embankment of the river, and then one Hittite chariot went over, down the bank and into the stream, a scream, a splash, they were washing away. Speak of rock and a rapid river, the river was narrow here and deep, and downstream a rapids began with many rocks. The first chariot to go shattered on those rocks, and I heard water swallow up the middle of a man's cry.

"Now, river at their back, the desperation of these Hittites matched our own, but we were close to a triumph here and our soldiers were berserk. Since we had overrun their campfires, some of us seized burning branches and hurled them, and I even saw a Sherden swinging a leg of half-cooked beef, and Hittites fought back with torches, and with daggers, and sword against sword, and axe against sword. We pushed them all in, every last man who had not fallen on the field, and the few who clung to the slope of the wet and precipitous bank were struck in the face with arrows, although one of our Nubians was so emblazoned by now with the heat of battle that he slid down the bank to push a Hittite in, and failed. Both men drowned instead, biting at each other, arms around each other's throats.

"What a sight! We stood at the riverbank and cheered, breathless and sobbing we cheered. It sounded like the demented wails you hear in a funeral procession, and over the water we looked, and there were sights no one would ever see again. A horse was swimming downstream with a Hittite trying to climb its back, and falling off, and trying again until he slipped off and drowned, but the horse reached the other bank, and other Hittites pulled the animal out of the water. There was a Prince washed up next, that I knew by his purple raiment, and the Hittites held him upside-down until I could not believe the liquid that poured out of the man's throat, and later I heard he was the Prince of Aleppo, no less. So I saw royalty held by its heels, and then my eye flew to another Hittite who was sinking. Clearly I saw him wave farewell to the land as he went under the water, and another man swept by right beneath me, his arms around his horse's neck as if he would kiss the creature, and he was speaking to his animal, I heard him weep with love before the rocks struck him and the horse. Behind him went a man who had already drowned, but so fat he floated with an arrow in his belly. I even saw one soldier make it with his animal to the other bank, and crawl ashore and lie there dying from a wound. As he expired, his horse licked his hand.

"Then we saw the Hittites come out on the other bank of the river. Out of the woods they emerged, too far for any of our arrows to reach, and I, practiced at making a quick count of a hundred men in a field, or a thousand, here saw something like eight thousand. I was happy they were on the other side of the river at this place where there was no ford, though I must say so soon as our Ramses saw them, that was equal to destroying His pleasure at what we had gained, whatever it was.

" 'Attack again,' He cried. 'To the west.'

"I never knew if my King was wise in battle, but then wisdom is a word by which one judges a man not a God, and He never looked to see if His command was followed. Instead He charged back over the old camping ground that lay within the entrenchment of our four sides, and everywhere were plundering Hittites, their backs to us and their faces to the ground. Like maggots on meat, they were as blind.

The fools were so hungry for spoil they had stopped short of bearing down on us from the rear while we were at the river. Instead, they attacked our riches. Two hundred of them were ransacking the King's Pavilion when we came back. We set fire to them there. In that way I could never understand my Pharaoh. No one loved His treasures more than Himself, yet so great was His heat in battle that He was the first to pick up a burning log and throw it on His tents, and a hundred of us added to the blaze, indeed our chariots ran a relay from the campfire to the fine stuff of His tent itself. Its walls were now collapsing upon the Hittites plundering within, and as they ran out, their beards on fire, their woolen capes on fire, even their groins on fire, our Nubians met them with short clubs, and cracked the heads of these fools on fire, twice fools for they died with the plunder in their arms. The stink of the leather of the King's burning tents was even worse than the odor of burning flesh. Yet the smell was like a marrow to give us blood for the battle. I felt vigor in my sword, as if even the metal could know exhaustion and look for new spirit.

"We destroyed the Hittites in the King's Pavilion and came down like a scourge on the petty plunder of the wagon trains. We took back our four sides and were a square again. Again, we gave a cheer. The two semicircles of Asiatic chariots who had been advancing upon us at a walk now stopped some hundreds of paces from our lines. They, too, were busy at plundering, but it was their own infantrymen they stripped. For those soldiers were still picking up the spoil left behind by the troops of Amon until the Hittite chariots scourged them like big animals eating little animals.

"Now the King's Pavilion was down. Its leather was consumed. White ashes lay on the ground, and some still glowed. My Ramses said, 'Who will bring Me our God?' and the Captain of the Nubians pointed his finger at one of his blacks, a giant of a man with a huge belly, something in build like Amon Himself, and the black stepped into the hot ash and ran to the middle of the fallen tents, picked up the blackened statue—may I say it took all his strength—and staggered out. Given its weight, the Nubian had to hold it against his body, and his breast was burned, and his belly, his hands, his forearms and his feet, yet once he had set the God down by my King's feet, so did Usermare-Setpenere kiss him, kiss this black—what honor could be so great as for a black to be kissed by the Pharaoh?—and then my Ramses knelt beside Amon, and in the tenderest voice began to speak to Him, talking only of His great love equal to the rapture of the sky at evening, and He took one end of His skirt and wiped all that was black from the God's face, kissing the God on the lips even though His own mouth blossomed at once into two great blisters which He wore in combat. A frightening sight it made, for now He could only speak out of the swollen rope of His upper and lower lips.

"I would have wondered at the power of the black to bear such pain, and even the love for Amon that would lead my Pharaoh to seek such pain, but at that moment a broken feather flew loose from the headdress of Maat-is-Satisfied and drifted to my feet. When I picked it up, the feather was heavy with the blood and grime of battle and moved in my hand like a knife, it had weight. I knew enough to kiss it. So soon as I did, a terrible heat went out of my Pharaoh's lips into mine, and, lo, I, too, was now to fight with white and swollen blisters upon my lips.

"Can I tell You of the rest of the day? Our battle, You remember, had begun under a dull and heavy sky. In that gloom, so strange to our Egyptian eyes, the sweat was cold on our bodies whenever we paused for breath, and our thirst was dry and cold and as desperate in our throats as our situation itself. Now it was easier, and as the Hittites came back into formation from plundering each other, and began to attack us, so were we also stronger. The Army of Amon that had deserted us was coming back from where they had fled, and many a skirmish was fought between these returning soldiers and the Hittites. Seeing the desire of such lost troops to make their way back to our square, my King, to help them, rode forth many times with our charioteers of the Household Guard on either side. Five times we rode out and felt the shock of battle but it was less each time for now we knew that the first of our advantages were the bows. Our arrows flew farther and so we did not have to crash against their heavier vehicles, but would stop short and send off as many arrows as we could afford, and pick up those that came back. The Hittites were hurt in this combat. Many of their horses, struck by us, would drive their other chariots amok with confusion, and often they were forced to retreat. On these scenes, the skies parted, and the Sun was revealed. We were warm in the late afternoon and grew stronger. It was then my Pharaoh lost all sense of how much we were outnumbered. Without a word to any but myself, out of the very warmth He felt from the Sun, and the burn on His mouth, with the reins hardly flogging our good horses, and Maat and Thebes no longer horses to me, but giants, may I say, in the bodies of horses this day, so did He gallop toward the largest circle of Hittites and at such a speed that we came to where they had put up the tent of the Hittite leaders, and in that place, before their phalanxes, alone with me again, my King approached their flags and standards. We were all but surrounded by a circle of the Asiatics' chariots. Hera-Ra roared at them with such fury that I think each enemy was afraid to draw his bow for fear the lion might attack his face alone. I do not know why they did not charge, but there was peace for this moment on the battleground as if no one could move, and even Hera-Ra was silent at last.

" 'I am with Amon in the great battle,' said Ramses the Second, 'and when all is lost, so will He cause them to see Me as the two mighty arms of Amon who are Horus and Set. I am the Lord of Light,' and He raised His sword until the sun glittered upon it, and then jumped down from His chariot, and walked ten steps toward the Hittite leaders.

" 'Tie the lion,' He commanded me, and He waited, sword in hand, until I tethered Hera-Ra to our chariot. Then He held up the fore-finger of His hand as a way of saying He wanted to fight their best soldier.

"From the Hittite leaders came forth a Prince with a terrible face. His beard was lean, and one eye was as flat as a stone, the other was bright. He, too, was dismounted, and in the moment Usermare saw him, I think my King was not at ease.

"They began to fight. The Hittite was fast and his movements were quicker than my Good and Great God. If this Prince had been as strong with his blade as my King, it would have ended soon, but Usermare attacked with such force that the other went back in a circle away from His great arm. Still, the Hittite's parries blocked the sword of the Sun from above and below, and now, given the chance, he struck back. Behold, there was blood on my King's leg. He limped now, and moved more slowly, and the look in His eye was not good. He breathed like a horse. I could not believe it—the sword of the Hittite grew bolder. Soon he began to attack, and my Lord retreat. The weight of all these hours of fighting was on His mouth, and, then, fending an overhead blow from the Prince, my Ramses' nose was broken by His own shield. I thought He was lost, and it may be that He was, but the end of the fight was interrupted. For the lion had become so agitated that I had to cut him loose from the tether or he would have turned on the horses.

"The Hittite, seeing the beast bound toward him, lost no time running back to his own people, and, Usermare, much fatigued, leaned on His sword. The lion licked His face. A sound like the bellowing of hippopotami came forth from the Hittites, and I was certain they would charge us where we stood. If so, we were done. Usermare might not have the strength to lift His sword, and then the lion and I would be alone. Yet at that moment, a Hittite trumpet blew. I heard a call for their retreat. Now, to my astonishment, they moved out quickly, leaving their royal tent behind.

"I was certain of a trap. I could not believe they would leave such spoils for us. Not when they were so strong. Yet in the next moment, I saw their reason. The Division of Ptah had come on to the field at last. The phalanxes of its chariots were moving up fast from the south. So the Hittites were now in a rush to reach the gates of Kadesh before Ptah crossed the line of their retreat. We had been left alone on the field.

"I think my King had a vision then. It was other sights He saw. I can only tell you that He staggered across to the abandoned tent and emerged with a bull in His arms made of gold. It was the God of these Asiatics, and had great furled wings, and the face, not of a bull, but of a beautiful man with a long Syrian beard. It also had the pointed ears of a monster, and a castle in the shape of a tower was its hat. I had never seen a God like this. He was screaming now, in some harsh language of the Asiatics, a hideous host of lamentations, and must have been naming all the larger catastrophes, locusts and boils for being deserted by His troops. In truth, it was the most horrible voice I ever heard. It spoke through the blistered lips of my Pharaoh, the oaths resounding in Usermare's throat until He threw the God to the ground. Whereupon fumes came from the mouth, yes, from the golden mouth of this bull-beast came smoke, I swear it. I did not know how my Pharaoh could be called the Mighty Bull of Amon, yet here before us was another bull, also a God, with wings, and a beard. It was then I saw the face of the secret whore of Kadesh. It was her features I saw on the winged bull, a beautiful woman's face with a beard. So I knew that the cries of this voice came from Metella's God. We were hearing His agony that the battle was lost. Maybe it is in war that you come to the place where the rainbow touches the earth, and much that has been hidden is simple."

Ten

"With the departure of the Hittites, the fields were empty. We were alone, as I say, and Hera-Ra raised his head and gave a lonely cry. It was a sound of much confusion as if the animal did not know whether we were victorious or desolate. In the distance I could see the legions of Ptah give up their attempt to reach the gates of Kadesh before the Hittites. They wheeled instead toward the King's square. Yet my Pharaoh disdained to raise an arm to greet them. We returned over these bloody anguished fields to the sound of many an injured cry and more than a few of the dying to give us a cheer. One fellow even managed to make a sound with his head half off. You saw nothing but the hole in his neck out of which he seemed to speak. My Pharaoh, however, ignored the pandemonium with which our soldiers cheered and as we came through the opening of our square, He drove to the ruins of His Pavilion in silence. He did not dismount.

"Even as His officers came toward us, bowing, then crawling forward on their knees, so did He speak only to the horses. 'You,' He said, 'are My great horses. It is you who rode with Me to repulse the nations, and you were under My hand when I was alone with the enemy.' If there had been sparks when He struck the sword of others in combat, now there was flame in His eye as He looked at His officers. They did not even dare to beat their heads to the ground. 'Here,' He said, pointing to the horses, 'are My champions in the hour of danger. Let them know a place of honor in My stables, and let their food be given to them when I am fed.' Now, He stepped down from His Chariot and caressed each of their noses. They gave an answer in voices full of pleasure. Their feathers were in shreds and their hides were red, their legs shivered in fatigue, but they called forth a thanks to Him. Then my Ramses heard the voice of His officers.

"'O Great Warrior,' they cried out. It was a babble, however, of one hundred names of praise in six or seven languages, and all in a rush. 'O Twice-a-Great-House,' they cried, 'You have saved Your Army. There is no King that fights like You.'

"'You,' He said to them in return, 'did not join Me. I do not remember the names of those who are not beside Me when I am in the midst of the enemy. But here is Meni who is My shield,' and He put His arm about me, and patted my buttock as if I were a horse. 'Look,' He said to all those officers. 'With My sword I have struck down thousands, and multitudes have fallen before Me. Millions have been repulsed.'

"They all cheered," said my great-grandfather. "Some had fought, and some had even fought a lot. Many were bloody with their wounds. Yet they listened in shame and lowered their heads and when the Generals of the Division of Ptah came forward to greet our Monarch at this reunion, He did not thank them for saving the day, nor reward His son Amen-khep-shu-ef for the rigors of that ride to join the legions of Ptah, but only remarked, 'What will Amon say when He hears that Ptah left Me alone on this great day? I slaughtered the enemy beneath My wheels but other chariots were not there, and neither was My infantry. I, and I alone, was the tempest against their chiefs.'

"We could only bow. A desolation worse than the swords of the Hittites was being felt. His officers touched the ground, they struck their heads, they lamented. I, in the most peculiar of positions, also bowed, but out of caution, and tried to keep from smiling. I thought that perhaps I was in error and should, unlike the others, remain standing so that my King should never mistake me for them, and I wondered if His mind had not taken a wrench from the screams of that Asiatic God who roared out of His throat. I did not know, but my King was soon silent and sat by Himself, alone by the blackened statue of Amon, and with the linen of His own skirt cleaned the soot from the belly and limbs of Amon, and pressed His forehead to the golden brow in a long embrace.

"We surrounded Him in silence. We waited. As the gold of the late afternoon lowered with the sun, and evening was near, He said, 'Tell the men they may begin the counting of the dead.' By these words the officers knew they might speak to Him again.

"Yet, I know He lifted His head from the brow of Amon with the greatest regret. So long as He sat with His forehead touching the golden forehead of the Great God, so did He see a sunset behind His closed eyes and feel the peace of our Egyptian wisdom enter His mind and pass into the scourged flesh of His throat and mouth. I could not believe it but when He looked up, the blisters were gone from His lips. (They still remained on mine.) So I could see that in all the splendor of the pure gold out of which Amon was made, there was also balm as cool as dew. What merits in this metal of the Sun!

"Soon, the counting of the hands was begun. We used to lay the hands of thieves in a heap outside the gate of the palace, even as we do now, but, in that time of Ramses the Great, the counting of hands was also done after battle. Usermare-Setpenere stood in His Chariot and soldiers came forward in a line from the Household troops to be followed by the soldiers of Amon. Many hundreds, then thousands of these soldiers passed one by one before the Pharaoh on this night even though we did not know yet if all of the battle had taken place or it was only the first day. Metella still had his infantry and his chariots, and both were inside the gates of Kadesh. They might come out tomorrow. So we could not say whether we had won or must get ready for the dawn. But the field where we fought this afternoon was ours for tonight, and that is like having another man's woman. She may go back to him tomorrow, but no one can tell you tonight that you have lost. So the longer this evening went on, the more it became a night of pleasure. As if in contempt for that enemy who had gone behind his walls, we lit so many campfires that the field was scarlet and gold and its light prevailed through the darkness like a glow of sunset on one of those miraculous evenings when night itself still hovers, or so it seems, on the last, and then the very last, and then beyond the last light of evening and nobody loses their shadow. So was our field luminous on this night, and the light came from that part of the sun which entered the trees in their youth, and now came forth again while the wood was ablaze.

"All through the night, our fires burned, and through the same night, Usermare-Setpenere stood in His Chariot under a full moon and received the severed hands of the slain Hittites one by one. Since He spoke to no one but the soldier who came before Him on His right hand, and then to the scribe who sat at His left hand entering the name of the fellow bringing in the trophy, so was I able to move away often and come back. Yet on all that long evening, for so long indeed as the line lasted, so did Usermare-Setpenere stand in the same place on His Chariot and never move His feet. I realized once again how to be near Him was to gain all knowledge of how a God might act when He is in the form of a man. He looks so much like a man and yet reveals divinity by even the smallest of His moves. In this case, it was that He did not move His feet. To receive a thousand men, and another thousand, then another, to take into one's right hand the severed hand of a man dead since this afternoon, or dead in the last hour—we were still killing our prisoners—to inquire the name of the soldier who has given over to you this cold hand, or this warm hand, then tell it to the scribe, then throw the hand on the pile without ever moving one's feet, was an exhibition of such poise that one saw the mark of a God. He never moved His feet. Each time He cast another hand onto the pile, and may I say the pile grew until it was the size of a tent, He threw it with the same grace by which He steered Maat and Thebes when the reins were about His waist, that is, He did the task perfectly. One could not think of another way to have done it. He was showing us the nature of respect. The right hand of a dead warrior, the same right hand that might have seized His own in a treaty, having been given to Him, so did He cast it onto the pile with care, and to the place where by His eye it belonged. The pile grew like a pyramid whose corners are rounded, and never did He allow the base to become too broad nor the top too blunted. Yet He was also careful to avoid the vanity of building too fine a peak, for then one misplaced throw could destroy the shape. No, these hands were added to the pile in a harmony between the height and the base that was equal to the harmony with which our Ramses received His soldiers." Here Menenhetet closed his eyes as if to recollect whether it was all so perfect as in his description.

When he began to speak again, he said, "You may be certain that the calm of this ceremony was not matched by the scenes on our campground so recently a battlefield, and now a campground again. It is one matter to kill a man in battle, another to find time at that instant to cut off his hand. Oh, there were sights even in the worst of it when your chariot was overturned, yet through the spokes you'd still see one of ours on his knees sawing away at the wrist of some Hittite he'd just dropped. You'd even see some fellows so blind and red-faced for their trophies that they did not see the Hittite who came up behind, killed them, and started to cut off their lips, the lips! Can you imagine if we had lost the battle to the Asiatics this day?

"You can see then that no good soldier would stop to claim a hand during the tides in and out of such a battle. Figure then the disputes that arose among us that evening when men who had been the bravest on the field were without a prize at night. Those hands were worth much to a soldier. You were able to say your name to the Pharaoh, and have it put on a list. Benefits, even a promotion, could follow. Besides, it was humiliation to go through battle and not have a hand to show. What, after all, were you doing? I can promise that fights broke out. When one squadron of chariots who had fought with the King's Household discovered that a company of infantrymen from Amon, the first to run, were now approaching the Pharaoh's line with a larger collection of hands than the charioteers themselves, a second war nearly began among our own. Soon the officers were in a council to make peace on this matter.

"They knew there would be terrible argument unless they agreed on some allotment. A fracas could spew forth in front of the Pharaoh. So, forcibly, we had to declare how many Hittites were slain by each company. That way we could determine the numbers of hands to be passed out, platoon by platoon. If it came to five for every eight soldiers in one company, you may be certain the five strongest men then seized their hands regardless of how they had fought that afternoon. Let me tell you—more than one ear got bitten off in the little fights that continued. Given the outrage of real warriors who had been passed over, not to speak of the bravado of many a big fellow who had been a coward earlier but was not remembering it that way now, we embarked on a night I will not soon forget. Another fifty of our own must have perished before the darkness was done.

"It was worse with the captured Hittites. Wherever one was not guarded by brave and responsible officers, he soon lost his right hand. More than a few bled to death. More than a few had the stump bound with a leather thong and went on to live and be brought back to Egypt. Naturally, they could expect the prosperous future of a slave with one hand. All the while, those of our men who had not been allotted a trophy went searching the bloody ground with their torches, and some even dared to cut the hands off our own slain, although to be caught in such an act was equal to losing your arm. After all, everyone's trophy would be tainted tomorrow if some of the hands proved to be Egyptian, so, count on it, every dead soldier of ours who was found mutilated at the wrists was stripped of his few clothes and his face soon made unrecognizable—I will spare you more. Even so, the corpse still looked like one of ours in the morning. With or without a face, a dead and naked Egyptian does not look like a naked Asiatic. We have less hair on our bodies.

"Speak of hair, these poor Hittites had beards like thickets and probably hoped to protect their necks from a sword. They also had hair on their head as tough as the hide of a helmet and that may have been to shield their skulls from our clubs. Small use now. Even a helmet cannot protect you from all blows. As the night went on, we used these captives, we gorged on them, we devoured them, of that I will speak. Everywhere was the comic if piteous sight of ten or twenty Hittites all tied with their hands behind their necks, the same cord binding them to the throat of the next fellow, until when told to walk, twenty would hobble along in a lockstep, their eyeballs squeezed out of the heads by terror, their necks at an angle, yes, so hunched up and bound together you could mistake them for a clump of figs on a string, except that these figs groaned frequently from the pain of their bonds. May I say their captors guarded them poorly. Any gang of soldiers who came blundering along could cut off the first or last on the line—it was too much work to untie a captive in the middle. Then you would see some sights in the blaze of the campfires. Many a poor Asiatic's beard was treated like the groin of a woman, and his buttocks as well; why, you would see five men working on one fellow who had already been turned into a woman, and one poor captive was even put into harness like a horse while our soldiers played with him as they would never dare play with a horse. This Hittite could not even get his mouth open to scream—it was filled near to choking. Picture the fury of the man who straddled his head.

"You would have thought with all the blood we had seen this day that some would want no more. But blood is like gold and feeds the appetite. You could not smell it enough and some could not even taste it to their full content. All of us, despite the discomfort of being covered by it, sticky with it, crusted over, came, sooner or later, to want more. It was like fresh cosmetic over old. Blood was now as fascinating as fire and nearer to us. You could never travel to the center of a fire, but the blood was here in everybody's breath. We were like the birds who collected in a million and infinity on this battlefield and would feed through the night on all they could tear from the flesh of the slain. They would fling themselves into the air with a heavy tilting of the earth as we came near and give a clap of sound like thunder, but it was only the uproar of their wings breaking away from us and the blood. Then there were the flies. They enraged us with their bites as if they now carried the fury of those we had killed. In the pestilence of those insects, I brooded much on the nature of wounds, and thought of how a man's power goes out of his flesh when he is injured, and travels into the arm of the man who gave the wound. On the other hand, so soon as you laid a cut into a man, you could treat his pain. If you were sorry for what you had done, you could spit on your hand and that might reduce the suffering of your victim. The Nubians had told me so. But if you wished to irritate his wound, you did well to drink hot and burning juices, or wine heated over a fire. Then would his wound be inflamed. So I was thinking of the Hittites who had given me the cuts and slashes I knew on my chest, my arms, and my legs, and I looked about until I could find a Hittite sword. All through the night, I oiled this blade and took care to bury it in cool leaves so that it would ease the festering of my body tomorrow. I also drank hot wine to irritate the wounds I had left on my enemies.

"I remember some of us even took the heads of Hittites and put them on long pointed sticks. While others held torches, we waved them aloft. We stood on one side of the river, across from the walls and gates of Kadesh, and we mocked them in the night while the banks began to stink from the early corruption of the bodies and would be a monstrosity in hot days to come.

"As we stood at the river, arrows came our way from the walls, not many, so few as to make me wonder at the thousands of Hittite soldiers who had not fought today—why were they silent with their arrows?—it hardly mattered now. We were so drunk that when one of us, a charioteer next to me, was struck with a spent arrow in his chest, the point going just deep enough to stick in his flesh, and thereby oblige him to remove it, he threw the head and shaft away, rubbed the wound with his hand, and with a laugh, licked the blood from his fingers. When his chest still bled, he painted his skin with it. When still it bled, he cut some locks from the beard of the dead Hittite on his pole and stuffed that into the hole in his chest."

"There is," said my mother in a sudden intrusion on this story, "nothing to compare to the monstrousness of men." As she spoke, I was close to her feelings, twice close because of pretending to be asleep, and I lived in her emotions once more. Never had I felt such rage at my great-grandfather, yet I could also feel her courage to scold him sink into itself as she looked at his face, for she was also much excited. Her belly had an ache of expectation that settled in my head like the pain of a tooth. It was enough to make me cry out.

Menenhetet merely shook his head. "On the other side of the river," he said, "at the top of a tower, was a woman who looked out at us and saw the Hittite whose beard had been shorn of a lock. She began to scream. Maybe it was the face of her lover that she recognized, or her husband, or a father or a son, but I tell you her shrieks tore the sky. Her moans were bottomless. I have heard women cry in that way ever since. We know those who make such sounds at any funeral. Hypocrisy is the possession of such women. For their grief speaks of the terrible end of all things in their heart, yet a year later that same woman will be with a new man."

My mother answered in a deep voice. "Women search," she said, "for the bottom of their grief. If they can find it, they are ready for another man. Why, if I were ever to weep for a lover and learn that my sorrow was bottomless, I would know he was the man I must follow into the Land of the Dead. But I cannot be certain of such feelings until I wail." She gave my great-grandfather a triumphant look, as if to say: Have you ever believed you could be that man?

Ptah-nem-hotep gave a small smile. "Your account, dear Menenhetet, has been so exceptional that I have had ten questions on every turn of the battle, yet I did not wish to divert your thoughts. Now, however, since Hathfertiti, out of the depth of her feelings, has spoken to you, let me ask: What are the sentiments of My ancestor, Usermare-Setpenere, during all of this, this dreadful night? Does He really see none of it? Do His feet, in truth, not move?"

"They never moved. I had been, as I said, standing near Him, and I would also, as I said, go away. When I came back the pile would be higher, but nothing else had changed, unless it was the mood of the Pharaoh. That grew more profound. No matter how well one came to know Him, even if you were to see Usermare-Setpenere every day, be certain you would not approach with ease. If you found Him jovial, then even from some paces away, you would feel the same as you did on entering a room full of sunlight. When He was angry, you were aware of that before coming through the door. On the battlefield, His fury was so great it served as our shield. The Hittites could not see into the dazzling light that came from His sword. The horses of our enemy were afraid to charge. One does not ride up to the sun!

"As this night went on, however, I saw He was not only the Beloved-of-Amon, Blessed-by-the-Sun, but also a King to live with the Lord Osiris in darkness and be familiar with the Land of the Dead. It is certain that the longer He conducted this ceremony of asking each soldier his name, repeating it to the scribe, and making a throw of the hand onto the pile, so did the weight of His presence grow heavier on me until I would have known with my eyes closed that I was somewhere in the presence of Ramses, just as a blind man can tell that he has stepped into a cave, even a large cave. On this night, my King filled the darkness, and the air near Him, unlike the fires of the campground, the red lick of the flames, or the breath of us drunks, was an air cool with the chill of the cave. He was observing the spirits of the dead, or at least that much of them as could be known by their hands. Even as we appreciate something of a stranger by taking his fingers in greeting, so could my Ramses know a little about each of the enemy soldiers as He held their last manifest for an instant. So He understood a bit of the character of the fellow and his death. Never had I seen my Monarch brood in such a way, and His mood continued to deepen until it was much like the sound that holds your ears in the roar of the Very Green.

"Indeed, as I stood near Him, which is to say as I entered the cave He inhabited this night, I could not know if each thought I comprehended was mine or my Pharaoh's. I only knew that the longer I looked at this pile of hands turning to silver in the moonlight, the more I thought of how the power of the Hittites was now in our possession, and we owned the field. They could not put the curse of their dead on us so long as our Pharaoh touched each evil thought in the hand of each lost soldier, and drew strength from it for future battles. So did my Pharaoh hold the fortunes of our Two-Lands together.

"I stayed so near to Him for so long that whenever I left to go wandering around the campground, I think I shared a part of His thoughts. Or maybe it was no more than the keenness of His nose for what was next. I know I was hardly surprised to come over a hillock and there between two rocks find Hera-Ra half-asleep under the full moon. I do not know if the lion had never been put back in his cage or whether some of our soldiers had set him loose, but he was quiet and only half-awake. Still, such were the fires of this night on this field just a hill away from the solemnities of our Pharaoh, that Hera-Ra now gave a great broad grin at the sight of me, rolled over on his back, spread his legs, showed me the depth of his anus and the embrace of his front paws and invited me to roll on his belly. I never knew the day I would have been that brave. Not in four lives. I patted his mane, kissed him on the cheek. With a grunt and a growl, he rolled over again, got up, and burped in my face to give a sour whiff of all the blood he had drunk; but then, my breath with its wine could have pleased him no better. At any rate, we were now friends enough to go for a walk. I do not know if I ever felt any more life, health and strength than making the tour of that flame-filled bloody field with ten thousand of our madmen spread over all of these meadows and a thousand fires you could look into for a carouse, yet I was the only one with a lion! It was a wealth of sights—more buttocks than faces!

"Let me say that there were also women among us. A company of camp followers had marched along with the Division of Set, for these were the soldiers last to arrive and they came in on the full moon. They were famous as a lot of fornicators and buggerers, this Division of Set. The tortures that had been tried up to now on the captured Hittites were nothing compared to the practices of the fresh troops who had just joined us.

"They had done little that day but march, and toward the end, as they got word of our victory out of the mouth of some messengers from the Division of Ptah, they had broken into their provisions and were drunk when they arrived. Now lines of men were waiting before each whore brought in by these soldiers from Set (who incidentally were collecting Hittite spoil in recompense). I saw more ways of making love that night than I would see again in three full lives. Since there were more men than women, it behooved you, if you had concern for your own buttocks, to see who was behind. I swear, it was a disgrace. Those Nubians are big, and it is the practice of their males to use one another until they are rich enough to afford a wife. On this night, woe to the poor Egyptian soldier if he waited in front of a Nubian, for he was soon on his knees, Egyptian or not. We are a smaller people. That night, a good deal of our strength was given over to the Nubians and the Libyans, and for what good return? To be able to shoot the few arrows you had left into the loose cave of a mongrel whore? The rush was so great in the fires of this night that many a man could not wait for his place at the front, and so took the girl between her cheeks, while she was busy up forward, and thereby made a three-backed beast, a copulation of serpents. Now, a new man was at her mouth, and another in the third man's bottom. They looked worse than those captives who had been tied like figs. Others, waiting, kept yelling 'Hurry up, hurry up.' Over it all was the smell of sweat. I could smell the buttocks of half an army. A fit husband was that odor to blood and smoke. I would speak of these acts as abominations but it was less than what was yet to come. Besides, I will offer no judgment. After all, is not our word for a night-camp the same as one of our expressions for fornication? I can only say I was part of it, and much stimulated. I swear, if it were not the Night of the Pig, you would not know so much of this. Enough that Hera-Ra and I moved through campfires and snoring drunks, through lovers and plunderers and scavengers, even past the groans of our wounded—for in the middle of it all, men were still dying, our men mostly (theirs already gone)—our amputees and our belly-gutted fevered, dying first of thirst, then of wine given them to drink. Sometimes you could not tell the oaths of pleasure from the wails of the doomed. Through such cries did Hera-Ra and I walk among the flames. Occasionally the lion

would trample over a group of copulators, squeezing their grapes, so
to speak, and many a soldier, catching the breath of the lion in his
nose, or the wild look in his eye (and Hera-Ra, even when feeling like
a kitten, had the wildest pale-green eye anyone had ever seen) would,
staring face to face with such a beast, lose his erection for this night
and more. Such frights, like a sword, cut you off. The whores, be it
said, loved Hera-Ra. I have never seen women so insatiable, so brutal,
so superior in pure joy—it is their art, not a man's. Even in this riot,
where one came forth so much more than one wanted that the joys
were like the throes of one's death, it was still extraordinary with
these women. They were only camp whores with putrid breath, but I
saw the gates of the Heavenly Fields open in my loins—these women
took the sweetest shoots right into the center of themselves. It must
have been all the blood and burning flesh. Maybe Maat approaches
with love when all are choking with smoke. You have to wonder how
many Generals are conceived on campgrounds such as this.

"But I spoke of burning flesh. You cannot know the hunger that
comes to your stomach on a battlefield. It mocks the hunger of your
private parts. I was ravenous, and Hera-Ra was ravenous. All of our
army was hungry, and after we ate all we had plundered from the
Hittites, we broke into our own provision trains. I saw salted quarters
of beef thrown into the fire, then pulled out, and sawed up for steaks,
one side black, the other red. Then the cow was thrown back again.
Soon they were cutting into the dead horses as well.

"It was, however, a peculiar hunger. I do not know for how many
I can speak, but each taste of meat gave me the desire to taste another
kind. I could not satisfy myself on beef, nor even on horse, although
there was something already in the flavor of the cooked blood in a
stallion's meat that spoke of strange truths and new strengths. I just
kept eating to fill a hole in my intestines. Maybe it was the presence of
the lion. He kept poking his snout into the wounds of the dead, and
before it was over, many of these men had become as ravenous in their
taste—how can I confess it to you? Walking next to that lion, he became my best friend on the field. So I could see into his thoughts as
clearly as into my Pharaoh's, and the lion, to my surprise, had a mind.

Now he did not think with words, but with smells and tastes, and every sensation put sights into his eyes. As he ate the raw liver of a dead man—I think he was dead, though he twitched—Hera-Ra was seeing our Pharaoh. I knew, by the gusto with which he chewed, that the valor of our Pharaoh had made him happy, just as happy as the liver of the brave warrior he was eating. Then it turned out that the dead fellow was not so brave after all. A taste of bile came into Hera-Ra's throat. Like a dirty vein through the liver was the secret cowardice of this warrior.

"I watched Hera-Ra nibble on dead men's ears until he found those that pleased him most. It was then I could see that as he ate, he had before him a heaven with stars more brilliant than our own smoke-filled sky so obscured by mist and scud. Indeed, my own mind felt blessed as he ate, for I was learning that our ears are the seat of all intelligence and the very door to the Blessed Fields. Now Hera-Ra began to lick the skin of many a forehead. With deliberation and much choice in his taste, he passed from head to head comparing the taste of their salts. Soon enough, I knew why he enjoyed such licking. For the picture he gained from the forehead that pleased him most was of a soldier running uphill, forcing his face up the hill into a stiff wind; truth, the fellow he finally chose had been a monument of perseverance. Then Hera-Ra ate him by the testicles as well and chewed into the groin. The soft growls of Hera-Ra were enough for me. I realized he had selected this fellow as the very seat of manly strength.

"I must tell you more. Before the night was over, I, too, indulged the meat of a limb, burned it in the fire, took a taste, and knew that the pleasures of a cannibal were going to be mine this night. Suffice it that the first step in what is considered the filth of my habits was taken. It has led me through many a wonder and many a wisdom. But then you do not really wish to hear more of the Battle of Kadesh. Let me say only that human fat, gorged in considerable quantity, has an intoxicating effect. I became as drunk as Hera-Ra."

With these words, Menenhetet shut his mouth and did not speak again.

Eleven

We were left with much curiosity. The silence broke, but only into another silence, and our Pharaoh gave a wise look at the fireflies and said, "I hope you will continue. I would like to know of the next day."

Menenhetet sighed. It was the first sound of fatigue he had uttered on many a breath, and the insects quivered behind their fine linen. Did I see what was not to be perceived, or did the glow of these mites fade in salute to the dawn that came outside the walls of Kadesh when the fires were burning down and exhausted soldiers began to sleep? It is certain that their light was less. But then I could remember Eyas-eyab telling me that the finest food for these fireflies was themselves, and they ate each other.

"I do not know how much there is yet to tell," said my great-grandfather. "Metella must truly have been cursed by his secret whore; he did not come out in the morning with his eight thousand infantrymen, nor with what were left of his chariots. Even when we took a captured officer, tied his arms to his chariot, and drove him into the river so that he drowned under their noses, Metella did not come out. I thought he was a fool as well as a coward. He should have attacked. We were so festered and unruly that morning, so entangled in a million and infinity of evil spirits that Metella could have overrun us—unless his troops had also had a night like ours.

"We held a council. Some of our officers spoke of siege, and tried to tell how Thutmose the Great had cut the fruit trees in the groves surrounding these hills in order to build the siege-walls that He brought forward against the walls of Kadesh. In the months ahead, if we did the same, the city could be taken. My Ramses listened, and looked affronted, and said at last, 'I am not a slayer of trees.' By that afternoon, camp was broken.

"It proved no easy departure. First, our dead had to be buried, and our wounded gotten ready for the trip. It took a lot of digging before the bodies were covered over, and the pits were never deep enough. These dead men were pressed down so tightly that a hip, an elbow, or even a head would push up and the birds must have had their pick. Of course, the insects devoured the other half. Seeing those myriads swarm over the pits before they were even covered, I knew the answer to one question forever. I learned why the beetle Khepera is the creature closest to Ra. In the middle of any hot night, beneath the silence, give a moment's attention: You will hear the mightiest sound of them all. It is the drone of insects. What multitudes! They possess the silence.

"Needless to say, a few of our dead were saved from the birds and the maggots. Each division had a platoon of embalmers who carried a sacred table with their wagon, and they soon wrapped the Princes and Generals who had fallen. Even if you were no more than an officer (but also happened to be the dead son of a rich merchant) there was a good chance someone would speak up for your remains. No embalmer could be unaware of the award he would receive in Memphi or Thebes if he delivered a well-wrapped son back to the family. Before it was all over, a hundred officers were stacked with care on the different work carts, and though the task was done in the field, only a few of these wrapped bodies began to stink.

"The wounded were worse. Some lived. Some died. They all stank. The Divisions of Amon, Ra, Ptah, and Set traveled behind

each other in so long a line that it took a day to move from the van to
the rear. Now we were truly like a worm cut in four pieces. Yet the
smell connected us. We moved slowly, a thick river, full of rot, and
the screams of the wounded were terrible when their wagons shuddered over the rocks of the gorges.

"Of course, we were all in pain. Who did not have foul cuts and
scrapes? I soon grew a dozen boils to meet my other afflictions, and
you could feel the poison of these wounds growing in new places
even as they were being worked out of the old. Some of us were demented by fevers after the third day, and in the heat of our march,
what had seemed a victory quivered before us like a defeat. By the
fourth day, we were being attacked. A few of Metella's best troops
began to follow, not enough to matter, but in sufficient numbers to
raid our rear. They would kill a few, wound a few, and ride away. We
would lose time in chasing them, more time in burying our dead.
Since the carts for the wounded were filled, foot soldiers were now
used as litter-bearers and some dropped from the heat and were left
behind and had to catch up again. Others were lost altogether.

"One of the Hittite raids even tried to steal a few of the donkeys
transporting the hands. We used more than ten for this purpose alone
and each carried two large bags, one for either side of their back. The
smell was not atrocious unless you came close—there is finally so little flesh on a hand that the skin dries quickly and by itself—although
the odor from one of those baskets (if you were fool enough to put
your head in) was as clear to the nostrils as rotten teeth. A true curse.
Leave it alone and it would hardly stir. Go too near, and the stench
lived in the lining of your nose. Hera-Ra could not keep away. Un-
tethered, he would bother these donkeys in the worst way. Trying to
bolt, they tangled in their harness, nearly strangling—donkeys in
doubt always climb over one another—and in the confusion, a bag
broke. Hera-Ra made a meal of what fell to the ground. I came running up to pull him away since I was the only one he obeyed besides
our Pharaoh, but I was late. He had gorged on a dozen of those hands,
and then more. Pictures of the Pyramids danced in his brain, then
sights of great cities. I had never seen buildings like the ones Hera-Ra

now envisioned in his head. They showed thousands of windows and great towers and went to vast heights. It was as if a part of great buildings yet to come was in the knowledge of those hands he ate. Yet what a dreadful meal! Hera-Ra had teeth strong enough to break your bones, although not quite—his mouth was happier in soft flesh which he liked to tear to strings. Now he broke one of his own teeth, and whimpered like a baby at the pain, yet kept on eating—all that unspeakable swallow of leathery skin, cursed smell, dried flesh, together with those little bones of the hand that crunched so hard. All the same, something in their odor drove Hera-Ra to more. He growled in real rage at me when I tried to pull him back. He wanted to take this curse. Some curses we dare—we wish to penetrate them. A dull anger went up from these mutilated hands at this second destruction. But then, that was why Hera-Ra took on such a fury. It gave him visions of the future. Again, I saw buildings high as mountains.

"The lion turned ill from his meal. By the next day he could not walk. His belly swelled, and his hind legs, which had suffered any number of slashes from Hittite swords, began to fester. On his shoulder, an open hole from the point of a spear turned black. He could not keep the flies away. His tail was too weak to brush them off. We built a large litter and six men carried him, but Hera-Ra's eyes took on the dull shine of a dying fish. I knew the hands in his belly were gripping his vitals, the little bones flaying his intestines like knives.

"My Pharaoh was with us ten times a day. The Royal Wagon's golden walls and golden roof were deserted by Him, and He walked along the litter beside Hera-Ra and held the beast's paw, and wept. I cried as well, not just for love of Hera-Ra, but in the terrible fear of knowing that the animal would not have gotten ill if I had kept him away from the donkeys' bags.

"Once, His tears washing thin lines through the black and green cosmetic about His eyes, Usermare-Setpenere said to me, 'Ah, if I had vanquished that Prince of the Hittites who met Me alone, all would be well with Hera-Ra!' and I did not know whether to nod or deny His words. Who could decide whether it was better to encourage His

wrath against Himself or take it on my back—I should have known
the answer. My good Pharaoh Ramses the Second was not made to
bear His own anger.

"Then the lion died. I wept, and more than I would have believed,
and for a little while my sorrow was all for Hera-Ra. I even wept because no man had been my friend so much as that beast.

"Few of the embalmed Princes had also been granted the honor of
having their organs properly wrapped. The provision wagon of the
embalmers could carry a few sets of Canopic jars, but how many can
you treat when it is four jars to each fellow? Even Generals were having their organs thrown to the woods. For Hera-Ra, however, the
embalmers used the next to last set of jars, and his wrapping was su-
pervised by Usermare-Setpenere Himself. Indeed, I heard the rage in
His voice when He examined the intestines and found bits of broken
bone protruding from the coils like arrowheads of white stone. By
the look my Pharaoh cast at me, it was clear that I was out of favor
again.

"My punishment, however, was not so simple this time. He had
me travel with Him often in the Royal Wagon. We sat on chairs of
gold and looked through open windows at the chasms of the gorge,
while we rocked perilously within. Certain bumps so tipped the
wagon (which was high enough inside for us to stand) that we all but
went over.

"Sometimes, He would not say a word. Just wept silently. The
eye-paint streaked. The Overseer of the Cosmetic Box would repair
Him, a nimble fellow, nimble as Nef"—this with a nod to my
father—"and we would sit in silence. Sometimes when we were alone
(for on occasion the King would wipe all cosmetics from His face and
dismiss the Overseer) He would speak briefly and in gloom about the
campaign. 'I did not win, I did not lose, and so I have lost,' He said to
me once. Since His eyes did not leave my own, I nodded. It was the
truth. But not even the Gods love the truth when it scores each breath.
Before the day was out, He said to me in the gloom of the carriage,
'You should have given your arm to Hera-Ra before you let him eat

those hands.' I bowed. I struck the floor seven times with my head even though the floor of the carriage was bumping like a rock in a fall. It hardly mattered. A sigh, long as the sound of the death that had come out of the lion, now came from the throat of Ramses our Second, a terrible sound as though the eyes of the lion were losing their light once more. What can I tell you? I thought often of the meaning of that sigh, and realized that the death of the lion was the end of Usermare's happiness at the sight of me. In the heart of His rebuke was the thought that if I did not know how much my good fortune depended on the health of His beast, then good fortune and I were best separated.

"We were. By the time the troops returned to Gaza, I was transferred from the Household Guards of Usermare-Setpenere to the charioteers of the Division of Amon, and I may say that no division of the four was in worse repute after Kadesh. Still, we were given a good reception by the natives of Gaza, and I was not surprised. In the last days of our return, people cheered us on the road. A runner traveled in front to tell them that the Armies of Ramses the Second had scourged the Hittites from the field.

"I think my Pharaoh must have listened to His messenger. He had healed from His wounds and looked magnificent. On the last day I would see Him for what would yet be fifteen years, He was on the parade ground at Gaza. There He displayed the winged bull of the Hittites and gave it to the city as a gift. This captured God, He told the multitudes, would protect our eastern frontier. By the next day, we began our march to the Delta, and, once there, sailed up the river to Thebes. I sat in the same crowded galley with my back pressing against the knees of the man sitting behind me, and since the winds were not steady, our trip upriver was even longer than the descent. Soon after our arrival, I was sent on duty into the depths of Nubia. That is to say, my King was banishing me to a distant place called Eshuranib. In command of a small detachment, I went up the Nile as far as a boat could go, and then had twenty-four days of march across a desert whose heat I will not soon forget." Even as he spoke these words, I could see such a desert before me. "In that time," he said, "I gave my farewell to every great and exalted moment I had known. The desert was hotter than the steam that rises from the Land of the Dead, and I was an officer without a true command." He ceased, he nodded, and said, "I think I can end my recollections here."

Twelve

There was a sigh.

"It is true," said Ptah-nem-hotep, "that I asked you to tell us of the battle and you have done this well. Yet I cannot say that My desire is to hear no more."

"Praise from the Pharaoh is a blessing," replied Menenhetet, but his voice remained dry. "Good and Great God," he said, "a life of monotony and foul work were now my reward. Do You truly wish an account of my years in the desert?"

My mother, who had been listening to my great-grandfather with more patience than she usually possessed, said, "I agree that we may not wish to hear this." She laughed at the boldness of her remark, and looked into the Pharaoh's eyes, indeed, lay her long black eyes on Him much as she might have ensconced her breasts upon His chest. "I wonder," she murmured, "that I do not flee in panic for daring to decide what might be of interest to You."

He gave a tender smile, but spoke to Menenhetet.

"How long," He asked, "were you at Eshuranib?"

"For fourteen years. They were long years."

"And the gold mines were already there?"

"They were."

Our Pharaoh told Menenhetet: "I would hear what you will say. For how could you live in any place and not see what others fail to observe? Besides, gold is never without interest."

Menenhetet gave a curious bow, and by the light of the fireflies I was aware suddenly of all that shone of gold, of the flat collar around my father's chest and the snake of gold on my mother's head, the gold bracelets of Menenhetet, or, for that matter, the gold in the houses of all nobles we would visit. It was then I thought I heard, like a faint cry, some echo of the labor that had delivered this wondrous metal, and I saw the Pharaoh nod wisely as though He had also heard such groans and they were part of the curious value of gold.

Much like moistening the memory of old dust, did my great-grandfather move his tongue. "Your desires," he said reluctantly, "are the source of my wisdom."

"Spoken like a Vizier," said Ptah-nem-hotep.

Now, Menenhetet took a swallow of his beer. "I will say," he told us, "that there was never a time in my four lives when my throat suffered so. If there was an affliction worse than others in the mountainous deserts of Nubia, it was the dust on one's tongue. I remember that my sufferings began on that twenty-four-day march through the desert. My detachment was sent off without any better company than our platoon of prisoners, my few fellow-soldiers, and two guides who seemed to live on a handful of grain a day, drank little water, and took pains to defecate once a week. They prayed at dawn and at dusk. That was their nearest approach to a vice. What soldiers they would have made. I needed those guides, for in the heat of the march, which was greater by far than any that I had known in Egypt or at war, the desert was full of dangers, and I saw many Gods and demons in the air, and knew Osiris was accompanying me since I heard His voice tell me that when I died I would not have to take the long trek to the Land of the Dead inasmuch as I had already crossed the desert. I believe I even saw Him. (Although who could know what was seen in these valleys when great mountains of rock quivered before your view as if ravished like wood in a fire?)

"We arrived in Eshuranib at last. I saw a cliff with stone huts at its foot, but the quarry had neither a stream nor an oasis. Before us were no more than two great bowls of soft stone, cisterns to hold our water. We were free to drink every drop of rain that fell from the eyes of Nut when She wept for Geb, but even this water, so vital to our throats, had to be used first for the ore. So our thirst continued and lived with us like an illness through all our work. We used to dig our shafts into the quartz of the cliffs before us, setting a fire at the head of the passage—as if Eshuranib were not fire enough—and then the children of our miners would crawl forward into the fissures to pick out the ore that had cracked loose from the rock and was now brought forth to be ground on a wheel of granite. When the rocks were too large and would not crumble, they would be raised by means of a leather rope as thick as my arm, then shattered on a great flat stone. The leather rope, I remember, was always breaking. So the curses and the beatings never stopped. Nor did the sound of running water ever end. It flowed from our cisterns to inclined beds of stone where the ore was washed. Afterward, when the sediment had settled, we would drink a little, then carry what was left back to the cistern. When I think of Eshuranib I can still taste that water." Since my great-grandfather now paused again, Ptah-nem-hotep said, "Yes, I am most interested."

"We had," said Menenhetet, "hundreds of workers, mostly Egyptians. Some were criminals from Memphi and Thebes who had been sent to this place for crimes they could no longer remember. They were soon stupefied by the heat, and blinded in the sharp dust of the mine shafts. Yet children were born in this place, and I saw a few who had grown to manhood here although they only spoke in some mixture of language I cannot describe, but that is because the soldiers who guarded these criminals were wild Syrians with great beards, Ethiopians with painted scars, and pale-colored blacks from Punt with curved Egyptian noses. Their languages mixed together until I knew the meaning of no sound, yet I was the commanding officer of this paltry legion."

"Why," asked our Pharaoh, "did Eshuranib have need of a charioteer?"

"In the reign of King Amenhotep the Second when they began to dig, it is said that three were assigned. I know what purpose those charioteers served in their day no more than I know why I was needed there. Soon, the other two charioteers and myself grew so bored we took to driving a cart filled with quartz from the mines out to the stone tables where the ore was washed. Then I grew so bored I even tried to improve our methods for crushing the larger pieces of quartz. The leather rope, as I said, was always breaking, so I worked at tying knots until I found one that would hold better and not snap the rope like a knife. Some hard years began, and for the longest time I learned nothing but the secret of boredom which tells you that no Gods, good or ill, are near.

"But, even as I was brooding, the rock would drop on the stone, and our river of gold would be dug out of the earth, pebble by pebble. It was a fever." Menenhetet sighed. "All the same," he told us, "the search kept some kind of fire alive in the heart, even if it was never our own gold. Still, it was cruel. There may be no torture like the years when one learns little after years when one has learned much."

"And you learned nothing?" Ptah-nem-hotep asked.

My great-grandfather was silent.

Now I saw how fine was the mind of our Pharaoh. He said, "Can this be true? I feel as if you are keeping knowledge to yourself."

"What I could tell You," my great-grandfather said in reply, "is not large."

"Yet I would suppose there is as much to learn from this small matter as in all you have told us tonight."

My great-grandfather's voice showed admiration. I do not know that I had heard such a tone come from him before. "You hear what I have kept beneath my thoughts," he said into the eyes of our Pharaoh. "Yes, You have searched it forth. I was not about to tell, but Your knowledge of me is as powerful as a command. I may as well confess that there was indeed a small matter from which I learned much. For I found a prisoner in those gold mines who passed on to me one secret that is more valuable than any other I have acquired." Here, he paused as if he had already said too much, and yet, reluctant to say more, must therefore say it quickly. "This prisoner was nothing but a poor Hebrew sent here for a crime his friends had committed. All the same, he interested me from the moment I saw him inasmuch as he looked like the Hittite who fought alone with Usermare at the Battle of Kadesh. Like that warrior, he had two different eyes. It was as if one looked on yesterday, and the other would see tomorrow. His name was Nefesh-Besher, which are the words of his people for Spirit of Flesh. I called him, therefore, by the good Egyptian name: Ukhu-As. After all, he had been born in our Eastern Desert near Tumilat, and therefore the truth of his name could come just as well with *our* Spirit of Flesh as with the Hebrews'. I may say he came to hear it often for I gave him as much attention as if he were the Hittite. People who look alike are alike. They are formed by the same agreement among the Gods." Now, Menenhetet nodded again. "Yes, I owe much to that man.

"He was very sick when I met him, yet his wife—who was the nearest to what you might call a good-looking woman in this place— still thought enough of her mate to share his captivity and march across the desert by his side. How she nursed him. Ordinarily, a fellow like this would have been buried in a few weeks. However, I was curious enough to keep him alive, and, as a result of the good share of food I sent their way, Ukhu-As became confiding. He was going to perish, he said, yet he would live. So he said. At first I thought he must be in fever, but he was so quiet, and so sure of what he said, that I began to listen. He had been given the secret by a Hebrew magician named Moses whom he had come to know in the city called Pithom, which the Hebrews had been building for Usermare ever since He became Pharaoh. Moses had been sent out to the Eastern Desert to serve as leader of these people. For that matter, I thought I remembered a tall Hebrew by the same name—Moses—in Thebes. If that

was the man, he used to ride among the hundreds of nobles who followed Usermare on visits to the Temple of Karnak. Since he was Hebrew, this Moses had to wait outside, but some thought he might be
a son of one of the little queens in the House of the Secluded from the
time when Seti the First was Pharaoh. We never knew. I did not see
him often. Now Ukhu-As told me that in the same season when
Usermare marched to Kadesh, Moses arrived in Pithom dressed as an
Egyptian officer and told the Hebrews he would take them to a land
in the East they could conquer. Ukhu-As said he got that tribe to
march into the desert early one morning without one of them being
caught. Yet this feat was simple. During the night, Moses had taken a
few of the strongest young Hebrews on a raid and they killed the
Egyptian guards of Pithom in their sleep. So, no pursuit was possible.

"Ukhu-As told me that he, however, did not flee with the others.
His wife was away that night visiting her parents in the next oasis, and
he loved her so much that he did not want to leave her. Since he surrendered himself to the authorities, he was not sentenced to death,
only to Eshuranib.

"When I asked him if he hated Moses, he shook his head. Not at
all. Moses had passed on a great secret. It was how, on your last breath,
you could put yourself into the belly of your wife.

"Here he was. This Nefesh-Besher, this Ukhu-As—dying—yet he
spoke of living. And not at all in the way some speak of continuing
one's name through the respect of one's descendants. No, he told me,
the child you make in your last moments of life can become a new
body for yourself. To hear this said with confidence out of the mouth
of a sick man was unforgettable. While he could not give me the Hebrew words for the last prayer to be said within your woman's body,
there, at the last moment, still, I had been his benefactor, so he would
pass it on to me through his flesh. And he instructed me to do something most disagreeable, but I did it on the night after he died. It is not
easy to tell. I have explained how Hera-Ra taught me the ferocious
virtues to be obtained from eating the flesh of others, but that was in
the thick of the night which followed the day at Kadesh. When you
grabbed a bite from a roasted limb, you did not ask from where it

came—blood mixed as easily with blood as meat with meat. Here, however, the fellow had been sickly, now he was gone. And he had told me to wait no longer than one day after he expired. In that way, he could serve as my guide without a prayer."

"How disgusting and unforgettable is this thought," said Hathfer-titi, but her voice was without strength. Menenhetet merely looked solemn. "I could not," he said, "have done what he asked except there was nothing to greet me at Eshuranib but the old boredom. Still, I approached this little meal with such revulsion that it took many at-tempts to swallow one morsel. Yet I held it down. I felt no new knowledge within me, yet I did—I could not say.

"A few weeks after Ukhu-As died, his wife told me she was preg-nant. Nefesh-Besher had been well named. His spirit was certainly in her flesh. It was just that he did not survive as well in her loyalty. She had taken such good care of him that she had used up her affection. When I saw the look in her eye, I began to do little favors for the widow. Soon enough, she became my mistress.

"I was weary of the smell that rose from the cheeks of men weaker than myself. So I kept this woman. Her name was Renpu-Rept, and that was a good name. When she gave herself up to the joys of making love, she was to me—in these harsh ovens of Eshuranib—like a young plant and a Goddess of the Nile. How I enjoyed speaking to the little Ukhu-As who was now within her. Soon I came to realize that one's member can say much to an unborn child. Do you know, I felt the ambition and the great rage of the new Ukhu-As, still unborn. Of course I had no fear of him, and I laughed. His former wife was such a pleasure. Why, Renpu-Rept taught me as much of his wisdom as he had known himself. He used to make love without letting his seed come forth, she told me, and I was quick to acquire his practice. To believe that the longer one waits, the greater will be your reward, was the only belief to keep you alive at Eshuranib. So I became acquainted with living at length in the cave of a woman, and many were the lita-nies she taught me to say to myself until I was the master of my own river and could send it curling back to my groin. That offered me one more road to the Land of the Dead. There were times, lying with her through those hours, when I felt as if I floated on the brink of my own extinction so long and so well did I hold my breath, and my heart within it, indeed, so high did I rise on the very roar of the sounds within myself that I could have been above a cataract that would wash me out of myself forever into her. So I knew the way. I could run those waters. So I speak of it, but I was not curious to try. For steeped in the sentiments that rose from her flesh, I was happier to meditate through the night, and such hours were sweet for me. I felt as fortunate as a Pharaoh in the House of the Secluded and had splendid thoughts, and lived in the reverberation of all things.

"Sometimes, during our long embrace, Hera-Ra would come to visit, and whether it was his true ghost I cannot say, but he was near and I was like an animal myself, and thereby close to the sound of all languages. In the arms of Renpu-Rept, the cries of the wild creatures outside, and the babble that rose at night from the huts of the village, began to speak to me of the mystery of many languages, and I came to see how certain sounds may say the same thing in all tongues. I would ponder over each word for mother among the different people of Eshuranib, for they all had the sound of 'm' within, and would ask myself why a barbarian had only to speak in rage to remind you of the roar that is heard in the letter 'r.' Homage to Hera-Ra! Deep in the going-forth and the back and forth of nak-nak, I would ask myself if 'k' was the sound of all knocking, even as 'pa' might be there for the sound of men, like the sound I made in her cave with my club— pa! pa!

"Through the long days at Eshuranib, I had made efforts to learn how to read, and it had been simple so long as there was a sacred mark for each of our sounds, but now I began to ponder some of the more curious tones for which there were no hieroglyphs. 'Eh' is without one, and 'oh' came out of my throat like the long note of the wind, and needed no mark. Nor was there a writing you could make for the scream you hear when someone feels a pain that cannot be endured— 'eee' is that sound of pain, even as 'oh' is the reverberation of the belly, and again there is no sign for that. I had heard such cries all my life, but I began to listen to them more closely in the gold mines of

Eshuranib where our barbarian guards were always beating the prisoners. And now, at night, there were also other sounds, softer cries,
oo and ah—those moans that come from the lowest part of the stomach where one feels the pleasure common to all. At evening, you
might expect such murmurs in every street and house of Memphi,
but it was different to hear it rising in the dark out of the shacks of the
workers of Eshuranib, their pleasures coming to my ear like the trip
across water from one island to another. After all, we live in a sea of
sound.

"Afloat on such thoughts, deep inside her, close to that heaven
where Nut meets Geb, there, through those hours of bathing in her
waters, while the rage of the unborn child moved against me, I
brooded on these matters of language and longed for a sight of our
Nile, and the baby grew larger in her belly.

"Then, there came a day when I knew great excitement, for I saw
Ukhu-As again. He was right. He possessed the power he claimed.

"I saw him on the day he was reborn. Two separate eyes looked out
at me from the face of the infant just delivered, and those eyes hated
me. For yesterday and tomorrow! What pleasure I had enjoyed with
Renpu-Rept! Yet this tiny creature was too powerless to offer a curse,
and could only wave his fists. Never had I felt such excitement looking at an infant just born. You know, I would have been ready to raise
that child. What could prove more interesting at Eshuranib?

"It never happened. The dust of the mines came into the baby's eyes
and Ukhu-As-of-his-second-life was blind at the age of three months,
and soon died. That taught me more about these arts of being born out
of yourself. It is not enough, I learned, to conceive your next life in the
last minute of this one—that may be a bold art, but you need enough
sense to pick the right woman for your mother.

"Yet how I liked my tender young shoot, my Goddess of the Nile.
I stayed in that hut at Eshuranib with Renpu-Rept for many a year,
and was not too desperate, for in time she became nearly so beautiful
in these practices as the secret whore of Kadesh, and in all of my first
life I can say that I never knew such peace as with her—but at a mean
price, for each day, out in the sun, the stone was raised, the stone was

dropped, the quartz was crushed, and the waters ran over the sloping tables to wash out the dirt from the gold. More gold! The beatings went on, the cries resounded in the night. There were times in my despair when I came near to gambling most dangerously with the gifts given by Nefesh-Besher and I thought to die and be born again. But what folly to be born in that place! Yet one time I all but expired before I brought myself back, and a child was conceived. When, nine months later, I saw her face, I loved her, and when she died, I mourned her loss like my own limb, but I also knew I could not live forever in Eshuranib.

"Then it became a question of whether I would take Renpu-Rept with me. I came face to face with the cold features of my own heart. How much would I value this woman if I were back in Thebes? She was not a wife for a Master of the Horse, or, better, a General—which I was determined to become—more than ever after the loss of these years. Then—I do not know if it was misery at the death of our daughter, or horror at the cold she sensed in my heart—but my only true wife, Renpu-Rept, also died of a terrible fever. I could not believe how I mourned her. 'No one,' she said to me at the last, 'will ever be so near to you again.'

"How long I might have survived alone I cannot say, but I was released from my captivity one hot afternoon fourteen years after arrival, and this sum resounded in my mind for the rest of my first life. It was equal to the pieces of Osiris' body. Therefore, in the hour of my release, I wondered who my true God could be—Amon or Osiris—and the question never left my first life. But more intoxicating than my wonder at these fourteen years was the sight before me of a detachment of new soldiers. A charioteer was with them. My replacement. He handed over a papyrus to tell of my orders to return."

"So the King had forgiven you?"

Menenhetet nodded.

"I would expect of My ancestor, Ramses the Great," said our Pharaoh, "that He would never forget, and He would never forgive."

"He never forgot, but there came a year when He needed my help."

"Can you tell Me truly that this was the year?"

"No," my great-grandfather confessed, "it was not."

My mother found a weakness in the composure of my great-grandfather. By way of her mind, I entered his mind, and my great-grandfather's thoughts were full of shame. He could speak of eating from the ham of a dead man, but he could not bear to confess cheap practice. He sat becalmed in his seat.

"You bought your way out of Eshuranib," said my mother. "You are no better than Fekh-futi."

Thirteen

There was an exclamation from my father at this mention of his father, but a glint came into Menenhetet's eye like the light I had once seen on a merchant's face in the sharpest moment of the bargaining.

"Yes," he said, "I bought my way out of Eshuranib. But I cannot boast that it was clever, merely that I was able after fourteen years to put aside enough gold to make arrangements for a large payment to a General in Thebes. In return, my name was put on the list of charioteers assigned to the Royal Household."

Ptah-nem-hotep asked, "How many of the officers who drill in My outer courtyard have been promoted by comparable payments?"

Menenhetet did not look away. "What matters is that they ride well. There is no cure for injustice other than committing another injustice to correct the first—let the river wash away the bad blood."

My father nodded profoundly as if this last remark were the thighbone of all wisdom.

"Not the least," said Ptah-nem-hotep, "of your qualities as a Vizier will be your ability to take our petty vices and return them to us as virtue."

"That is the way it may now seem," agreed my great-grandfather, "but I can tell You, Divine Two-House, it was not easy then. I had to wait a year after I made the payment. All the while, since I did not tell Renpu-Rept, I began to wonder if I could desert her, and after she died, I thought of those Hittite hands we collected at Kadesh and was terrified that my own would soon be added to such a pile. Remembering those exceptional cities Hera-Ra saw while eating his last meal, I decided the most terrible punishment must be to lose your hands, for it would prove the same as loneliness. Without our hands, we cannot know the thoughts of others. We are left only to our own thoughts. Do not ask me why this is so, but I know it. To reassure myself, I looked again and again at the papyrus I had been sent from Thebes. It told of my 'zeal to guard the gold of the Pharaoh from all who would steal it.' Well, I did my best to believe this."

"I must leave you to the Lord Osiris," laughed Ptah-nem-hotep.

Menenhetet touched his head lightly to the floor. "Good and Great God," he said, "I brooded much on the nature of proper behavior in those days. Since this papyrus bought with stolen gold testified to my honesty, I came to realize that a man who lies can be as comfortable as anyone who tells the truth, provided he keeps lying. For then no one can catch him. Such a man has a life as true as an honest life. Consider it. An honest man is miserable once he begins to lie. For then he must remember the truth, and what he said that was not the truth. So is the liar miserable so soon as he speaks in an honest voice.

"I say this because Ramses the Second—as I soon learned on my return to Thebes—had become a liar. Forgive me, but it is the Night of the Pig. I discovered I was known to all, and for the worst of reasons. My name was on every new temple wall, and I can promise that in the years I was gone, many temples had been built. Usermare was always erecting some monument to Himself, large or small. You could not fail to see His statue at any bend of the river, and commemorative pillars in every grove. Be certain that in each new temple was an account of the Battle of Kadesh and there was I with my name on the wall, forever crying out, 'O my Lord, we are lost, we must flee!' and I would shake my head on seeing it as if that could erase the sacred marks. 'Go, Menni,' He would answer, 'I will fight alone.' Even my name was wrong. I, who had learned to recognize MN on a papyrus now found it cut into the stone as MNN. I was still ignorant. I did not see how there could be any error on a temple wall. I did not know then, as I would learn in my second life, that scribes know less than priests but are all too ready to inscribe a stone. I did not realize I was looking at a crude error. I stepped backward, as if the temple wall could fall on me. I thought of all the prayers I had offered to great and little Gods, ten hundred such Gods, but I had addressed Them with the wrong sacred marks in my heart. 'MN beseeches You,' I had been saying when I should have said MNN.

"Now, if the misspelling of my name bothered me so greatly, think of my confusion about what was written in stone. That could not be false. I must have said things in the battle that I had no memory of saying. Yet in the same temple, on another wall, as if the truth was no better than the wall at which you looked, I would read, word by word: 'Lo, His Majesty hastened to His horses and stormed forward— He alone.' I would awake in fever that night with the wall pressing on my chest. Had the Pharaoh been alone in His Chariot through all of the Battle of Kadesh? It took me years to comprehend that, to Himself, He was by Himself. He was a God. I had been no more than the wood of His Chariot.

"All the while, as if to mock me, I became renowned. My name was cut in stone. My deeds might count no larger than the works of a worm, but I was a sacred worm. In the barracks, among the charioteers, a subtle derision greeted me. One or another would always cry out on my arrival, 'Here is our hero of Kadesh.'

" 'What do you mean by that?' I would ask. I did not like the word he used for hero. It could also mean 'bird' or 'coward.'

" 'I mean that you are a hero. We know that.' There would be much laughter. I could do nothing about it. These charioteers from the best families of Memphi and Thebes were not about to fight. It was well known there was no officer I could not defeat. So they mocked me in their noble manner, which was to play with words until the meaning was as hard to catch as a minnow with one's hands. I took a vow they would serve under me before I was done.

"Then an event took place which did, indeed, teach me new ways. Word came to Thebes that Metella had died.

"Now, while I had been in Eshuranib, many small wars had been fought with the Hittites, but so soon as Metella was gone, his brother, Khetasar, proposed peace, and was accepted. It may be that our Ramses was tired of war. Each year for fifteen years, He had found Himself in the field. So, at Tanis, in a splendid temple just completed, He received the new King of the Hittites. Khetasar brought with him a silver tablet on which were more than a hundred lines of writing clearly engraved into the metals, and I still recall what it said, for all of us in the Household Guard who were at Tanis looked at it closely: 'This is the treaty which the great chief of the Hittites, Khetasar, the valiant, son of Merasar, the valiant, and grandson of Seplel, the valiant, has made on a silver tablet for Usermare-Setpenere, great ruler of Egypt, son of Seti I, the valiant; grandson of Ramses I, the valiant: This good treaty of peace and brotherhood sets peace between these nations forever.'

"I read all of it, taking in the words one by one, and was much impressed that it had been composed by the Hittite King, for our Pharaoh would not have spoken in such a way. I may say that this tablet of silver had the light that comes from the moon, and that gave me a new fear of these Hittites. With their dirty beards and clumsy chariots, they had seemed crude, yet how wise was this tablet. The phrases were in such fine balance that you could feel peace was near: 'Between the great Prince of the Hittites, and Ramses the Second, the great Monarch of Egypt, let there be a beautiful peace and a beautiful alliance, and let the children's children of the great Prince of the Hittites remain in a beautiful peace and a beautiful alliance with the children's children of Ramses the Second, great Monarch of Egypt. Let no hostilities arise between them.'

"Why, this Khetasar even said: 'If a man flee from the country of Egypt to the Hittites, then shall the great Prince of the Hittites take him into custody and cause him to be brought back to Ramses the Second, the great Monarch of Egypt. But when he is brought back, let not his crime be brought against him, nor shall his house be burned, nor his wives and children killed, nor his mother slain, and he shall not be beaten in his eyes, or in his mouth, or on his feet.' And it would be the same for any Hittites," said Menenhetet, "who fled from their country to ours. I was much impressed with the good sense of this. It takes no great effort to make people go back to the land from which they have fled, if they are not afraid of terrible punishment. I was even more impressed when our Ramses allowed the name of the Prince of the Hittites to come before His own. That had to be due to His respect for all these fine words written on silver. Besides, the treaty concluded with the names of the most powerful strange Gods. It was said, 'A thousand of the male and female Gods of the country of the Hittites, together with a thousand of the male and female Gods of the country of Egypt, will be with us as witnesses to these words: "The God of Zeyetheklirer, the Gods of Kerzot, the God of Kherpenteres, the Goddess of the city of Kerephen, the Goddess of Khewek, the Goddess of Zen, the God of Zen, the God of Serep, the God of Khenbet, the Queen of the Heavens, and the Gods and all the Lords of Swearing, the Goddess and the Mistress of the Soil, the Mistress of the Mountains and the rivers of the land of the Hittites, of the heavens, the soil, the great sea, the wind and the storms."

"That was how it ended," said Menenhetet, "'the wind and the storms,' and there was a hush when all was read and we were finished. Ramses pressed the cartouche of His ring on the soft silver of the tablet, and the mark was made. He embraced the messengers. Lo, the war was done."

When Menenhetet was silent, our Pharaoh yawned. He did not seem pleased to hear the names of so many strange Gods, and remarked, "Hathfertiti may be wise in her wish that you return to more amusing matters. Yes," He said, "You hide yourself too much in this account. You are too modest." He shook His flail as if to clear the air of all echoes of this treaty. "Do you know," He said, "that when I first ascended the throne, your name was always on the lips of My little queens?"

"My name?" asked my great-grandfather.

"None other."

"But I have not been in the House of the Secluded since the year I served there for Usermare."

"For that, you were mentioned all the more. I grew to detest their fascination. Even when they were silent, I was obliged to hear the little queens think of you."

On this pause I lived in the mind of my mother, and knew her discomfort. It was as simple as the beating of my own heart: Our Pharaoh spoke so easily of hearing the thoughts of others. Now, He must be enjoying her thoughts far better than she could hope to dwell in His! On that instant, like a cloth thrown on a spill of soup, the inside of her head became as clean as a floor that is wiped.

Ptah-nem-hotep gave a smile. I wondered if He was amusing Himself with how empty and polished were the thoughts presented to Him; then He laughed. "Yes," He said, "no man in Egypt attracted more attention than you, Menenhetet, among My beauties. They live in a sea of gossip, and you were the storm that hides in the wind of the sea. Even now, they suffer a perfect fury that not one of them was invited to be with us. I can hear them" —He pointed an indolent finger in their direction. "So be it. They will talk of you tonight, and tell again all the stories I have already heard about your second life, and your third, and your fourth. Of course, your first life is their favorite. They will never quit speaking of how you were General-of-all-the-Armies, and yet, so great, they say, was the prestige of the House of the Secluded in the years of Usermare, that you were made Governor of the Secluded."

"Is that how they speak of it?" asked Menenhetet.

"By half," said Ptah-nem-hotep. "Some of the little queens keep a high opinion of their importance. Others wonder how a General-of-all-the-Armies could bear to become a keeper of concubines. They have quarrels over this, I assure you. Still, I expect you fascinate them for a better reason. No story absorbed My harem beauties (nor My-self) so much as the one that is always whispered—for they believe it is a sacrilege. Indeed I can hardly believe it either. Especially since your account of your first meeting with Ramses the Second and His Queen is most innocent. But they say—you see, I whisper it Myself—they say you became the lover of Queen Nefertiri. I even heard that you departed from your first life and entered your second by way of a knife left in your back. That you died as your seed went forth into the Queen."

Ptah-nem-hotep smiled, a true sweetness on His lips. Had He been waiting through this night to encourage Menenhetet to tell us about the love of Queen Nefertiri? He was certainly amused by the shock He had given to all.

My mother had every thought at once, including every one of my father's. His thoughts leaped into her. He saw Menenhetet lying on Nefertiri's belly. Indeed, my father was so overcome by the sight of family flesh upon royal flesh that his groin was plucked, and he came forth right there and was wet beneath his linen. My mother was in-stantly offended by the waste. The fresh seed of my father was the finest lotion she had ever found for her face.

Menenhetet began to cough. A desert wind could have been whis-tling down the caverns of his body. Yet so soon as it was gone, he was quick to speak.

"I do not wish," he said, "to contradict Your amusement, but there is much I cannot recollect. To be born more than once, as I have been born these four times, is not the same as remembering each life clearly."

"All the same," our Pharaoh replied, "My request is that you tell us of your friendship with Queen Nefertiri."

"I served first as Governor to the little queens," said Menenhetet. "Only later did I become Companion of the Right Hand to the King's Consort, Queen Nefertiri."

"Then I would hear of these matters in order. As you tell us, so may you remember much that you believe is forgotten."

Menenhetet bowed, and touched his head to his fingers seven

times. "I will," he said, "say again that these matters are more difficult to relate than the story of one great battle."

"Yes," said our Pharaoh, "but I feel no haste. It is My preference to be entertained on this night through all the hours of darkness."

"And to be amused by Your guests," said my mother.

"Yes, by My guests," said Ptah-nem-hotep, and as if her attention— if it became too sulky—would spoil His own, He gave her a dazzling smile, then turned back to Menenhetet. "Find your memory, old friend," He said.

"May I speak," asked Menenhetet, "of the years after Eshuranib when I rose in the army? I think that may warm my thoughts. For I confess, it is not comfortable for me to move so quickly into the Gardens of the Secluded."

"I say again," said our Pharaoh, "tell it in your manner."

Menenhetet nodded. "I would go back to my careful study of the treaty with the Hittites written on silver. For I would never have become General-of-all-the-Armies if not for the influence of those words on me. I had never read language so fine. It suggested to me that I must learn the arts of subtle men. This Khetasar had known how to address Usermare. All I had gained until then had come from the gifts of my body, but, now, if I would thrive in the world, I must learn the arts of speech."

"Did you discover many principles for such use?" asked my Pharaoh.

"One principle above all: Avoid all subjects of which your superiors are afraid. All men are afraid, I learned, and do everything in their power to conceal what they fear the most. Those, for example, who are cowardly will tell you of their acts of courage so long as you were not there to witness them.

"I, who used to believe all that was told me, began to look for the lies. I soon could recognize ambitious men by the traps they set to discover if you told the truth as little as themselves. I came to enjoy such games and the people you could play them with. Be certain I studied flattery. That was still the fastest way to become valuable to one's superior. Of course, by the balance of Maat, I also had to learn that it was not wise to become too indispensable, or you would never be given a promotion. Look at the best of house-servants. They always die in the same job. The trick, therefore, is not only to please one's superior but inspire a little uneasiness—the fear, at least, that you know his fear. That will make him wish to promote you. He can still receive your compliments but at a safer distance. I even had to learn how to keep my inferiors from advancing more quickly than myself, which was a skill I had always scorned before. What need had I of flanks in my early days? Like Ramses, Beloved-of-Amon, I believed in nothing but attack. Yet I had learned, by way of Hera-Ra, that the unforeseen could destroy you. So I was careful to slow the ambition of officers beneath me, yet quietly, so they did not know, and to my superiors I tried never to be unsettling. I had come to understand that no one hates the unforeseen so much as men of powerful family and mediocre ability. Amuse them, titillate them, confirm them in their habits, speak softly to their fears, but do not alter their day. They are terrified of all that is larger than themselves."

"Never have I heard you speak more eloquently," said our Ptah-nem-hotep. "It is the voice of the highest servant." He reached across the table and tapped Menenhetet with His flail. "But why," said Ptah-nem-hotep, "do you tell these truths? Why not hold more closely to your principles and offer a few lies?"

Now, my great-grandfather showed a smile. "The art of the liar is to speak so well that You will never know when he is ready to betray You for the first time."

"You set My heart to beating," said Ptah-nem-hotep. "Now, you must tell Me what is next." I could see, however, that He was greatly amused for He had succeeded in making my great-grandfather eloquent once more.

Fourteen

"I may," said Menenhetet, "have spoken too much of these low arts. It would give the impression I was not a true soldier. That is misleading. While the Hittites never rose again, our armies were always in some small war, and I fought at Askelon, at Tabor in Galilee, in Arvad and the lower regions of Retenu, a hundred battles, although none like Kadesh. We were always strong, and never were we surprised again in our camps.

"All the same, we fought for years. Each year we would gain much territory and take several towns. Then we would go back to Thebes and the territories would be in revolt again. Our Majesty took so much in taxes and spoil.

"My career, however, prospered. I was the only Egyptian officer who could make war in the field, yet had studied the skill of flattery in Thebes. Our High Priest, Bak-ne-khon-su, was so old by now that on many a day, he sent one of his Second Priests for the daily audience with the King. So I learned the art of flattering Second Priests. That is the most demanding practice. May I say it helped if you brought something to eat—at least to those priests who were fat. The thin

ones proved more difficult. Sometimes, they could only be charmed
by one's knowledge of special prayers. But then the fat fellows were
always happy to tell you which verses appealed to the thin priests."
He smiled. "I must say there were some very thin servants of Amon
who were satisfied only if you gave them gifts of the rarest papyri, or
stones of fine color brought back from the wars. Misers are the same
in all occupations. Be certain I cultivated each priest, fat or thin, who
could speak to Ramses the Second, and I watered them like my own
tree. Of course, my Pharaoh did not like me a great deal better than
on the day He had sent me away to the Nubian desert, but how could
He name a Libyan or a Syrian to command His Armies when an
Egyptian as suitable as myself was near? I also knew how to speak of
the infinite love of Amon for my Pharaoh's face. He did not really
want me for General-of-all-the-Armies, but when the choice came
down at last to Amen-khep-shu-ef, or myself, I think He found that
He did not trust His son. How can any terror be greater than the fear
of being betrayed by one's own blood? I was at last promoted, and
given my gold carriage.

"I think I would have been His General for many years, if not for
a trait in Usermare-Setpenere that caused great imbalance in the stability of those days. While our Two-Lands were never more powerful, nor a Pharaoh more esteemed and more beloved, yet His desire
for women was insatiable. How he thrived among the rivalries, jealousies, intrigues, and detestations He stimulated among them in the
near to thirty years since the Battle of Kadesh. Only a God could have
lived so far beyond the balance of Maat. In this manner, He was also
Ramses the Great.

"He was, of course, much changed from the young King Who
rode with Nefertiri. I would even say it was the great and horrible day
at Kadesh that affected Him forever, and in all ways. Certainly, His
love for Nefertiri did not remain the same. Until that campaign, my
King might spend an afternoon with one of His little queens from the
House of the Secluded, or knock the cup of a farmgirl, or two farmgirls, as He did with me on that ride into the valley of His tomb, but
that was no more than a sport. Nefertiri was His sister, the love of His

childhood, His first bride, His only Queen. On the day They were married She was twelve, and He thirteen, and they say Her beauty was so full of light you could not look at Her. Even in the first years I knew Him, I do not believe He had many thoughts which were not of battle, prayer, Nefertiri, or His other true taste—the buttocks of brave men.

"After the Battle of Kadesh, however, He was like an oasis that finds new water beneath its palms and divides to a hundred trees where before there were three. Our good Pharaoh came back from Kadesh with more hunger for the sweet meat of women than any man I knew in all of my four lives. He must have gained the seed of the Hittites He killed, for His loins were like the rising of the Nile, and He could not look at a pretty woman without having her. But then, He could like ugly women as well. Once, after He spent a night with a little queen from the House of the Secluded who was so ugly I could not bear to gaze on her (she looked like a frog) He told me, 'By the balance of Maat, I hoped to find beauty within for the bad view without, and it was true. This woman's mouth has captured the secrets of honey.'

"After Kadesh, if you had a wife, your wife was His wife. To belong to the Court of Usermare-Setpenere was to have His child in your home, yes, often a baby as handsome as the Pharaoh. Of course, on many a hunting trip, He would still hop on a passing girl. Along every road of Egypt, it was known that Usermare could come forth twice in the interval other men took to show themselves once. He wished to know as many women in a day as there were intervals between His duties—it was as if the great plow of Egypt was here to till the field. These were the years when He began our horde of Ramessides, that tribe now so large that by my third life, the Necropolis was closed to all but the blood of Usermare-Setpenere. His seed is in the seed of all of us. No man ever created so many after him, but that is why the beauty of our Egyptian nobles is known by every land. He was beautiful, I tell you. At night when the Royal Barge slipped down the Nile, the wave it left behind made a sound so fine against the shore that women would turn over on their bed at the washing of its passage, and that was true. I was sleeping once when His Majesty went by, and my woman shifted her belly and gave me her back."

"How splendid!" said Ptah-nem-hotep.

"May I say, Divine Two-House, He was beloved, but not wholly beloved."

"Who but Queen Nefertiri, yourself, and a scattering of jealous women would not love Him?" asked my mother.

"One's harem is never to be ignored," said Ptah-nem-hotep.

Menenhetet bowed his head seven times, but so gently as to stir no glow from a firefly. "Yours is the divine wisdom," he said.

"Not at all," replied our Pharaoh. "As you know, there was a plot to assassinate My Father by a few ladies in the House of the Secluded."

"That I remember clearly," said Menenhetet. "The trial of these women was held in secret, but it became the talk of Memphi and Thebes. It was said of Your Father that He did not know His Notables, nor how to hold the roots of their loyalty. But I can tell you that Usermare did. In His Reign, the Gardens were filled with women from noble families. I do not think my Pharaoh ever thought of any man or woman for long, but He understood the pride of such families. He knew how much disruption He caused whenever He chose one of their daughters for the Secluded. So, He also knew that one must hold such a family close. Loyalty is never more dependable than when it rests in shame and must call such shame, honor.

"Your Father did not know that so well. Too often, He ignored the families. Many of the Secluded would appeal to their fathers or brothers after an injury to their pride. I think that is how the plots to kill Your Father began, the plot that failed, and the one that may have succeeded. For His death was curious."

"Yes," said Ptah-nem-hotep, "I have thought as much Myself."

"That was twenty-five years ago," Menenhetet said, "but already we have had Ramses the Fourth, the Fifth, the Sixth, Seventh and Eighth—merely think of it, great Ptah-nem-hotep, in the seven years You have reigned, You have held the throne longer than any of Your brothers and cousins."

"Yes I have also had that thought—" He smiled. "I remember that

My half brother, Ramses the Fourth, was most fearful. He wanted no girls from good families among His Secluded—He would take on no enemies. He closed the harem in His first year, and when He opened the Gardens again, behold, the girls were stout and strong and common, and their fathers had no noble titles. Just merchants and traders.

"It was not attractive. Nor did any of My relatives improve matters. So soon as I was on My throne I paid a visit, and I was startled. So many fat women wearing so much jewelry! All with garlic on their breath! Now, the House is sweet again, although not so sweet, I know, as that time one hundred and how many years ago that you were transferred from General-of-all-the-Armies to Governor of the Secluded?"

My great-grandfather did not reply at once, and I pretended to be asleep. A sadness passed over me. I was looking at the fireflies. Through the night, they flew in a cage from which they would never escape. I thought of the swamps near the Palace. Some hundreds of slaves with quick hands must have stood in that low water this evening catching them one by one. My sadness spread out from me until I felt as large as a man.

It was then I realized that my own sympathy had been much increased by the sorrow behind my great-grandfather's smile, a considerable sorrow, composed of many matters, the first of which must have been his recognition that he would continue to offer the Pharaoh more. My Pharaoh, by His own fine art, was cruel, no matter how He smiled, and my great-grandfather, for all his calm, still wished to be Vizier and so would please the Pharaoh's questions.

"Yes, it is one hundred and thirty years ago," he replied, "that I became Governor in the House of the Secluded."

"And were you pleased at this great change in your career?"

"I was appalled. I remember I had just celebrated my fiftieth birthday. I do not know for what I had saved myself but my body was powerful to behold and more beautiful to me than a home. I was General-of-all-the-Armies, yet felt as if my life had hardly begun. I still lived in barracks, but now thought I was ready to make a splendid marriage—I need only choose the lady. All was before me.

"Yet, like the cloud that crossed the sun, so did the shadow of Usermare's life come between me and any easeful wealth. For my Pharaoh had a fear in His heart that was like the gloom that came to me from the myrrh trees of the Temple of Hat-shep-sut. Except, it was not the Hittites of whom I thought today, but His own wife, Nefertiri, and there was reason for such gloom. He had taken a Hittite Princess for His new Queen. Now, while it was true that even before Kadesh, He had married another Queen, she was not to be compared to Nefertiri. Although a daughter of the last High Priest of Amon before Bak-ne-khon-su, and of a sublime family, so that the marriage wed the Temple of Amon to the Son of Ra, still this second Queen, Esonefret, was ugly, and Usermare soon ceased to give Her any place beside Nefertiri. He chose instead to build a palace for Her down the river at a small town named Sba-Khut Esonefret, the Concealed Doors of Esonefret, and it was a good name. He bothered to visit just long enough to make a child from time to time. Nefertiri sat as the only Queen in Thebes. It was said for many years that Usermare would dare the displeasure of the Temple of Amon in preference to the rage of His First Consort.

"Yet, when Usermare dared at last to marry a third Queen, the choice was as bold as the manner in which He drove His Chariot. For the new wife was the daughter of Khetasar, and young and beautiful. Her mother, the Queen Pudekhipa, was an Aryan from Mede, and it was said by all who saw her daughter that the pale blonde hair of the Hittite Princess was more luminous than the moon."

"Here, I must interrupt," said Ptah-nem-hotep. "How long had you been General-of-all-the-Armies when this third marriage took place?"

"For five years. The Princess Mernafrure arrived in the Thirty-Third Year of the Reign of Usermare, twenty-eight years after Kadesh and thirteen after the treaty. I know these dates well, for I became General-of-all-the-Armies eight years after the signing of the treaty."

"One matter," said Ptah-nem-hotep, "still confuses Me. You speak of the furies of Nefertiri. Yet, at the time of the treaty, thirteen years before, it was already arranged that this Hittite Princess would become His wife."

"Your knowledge of such matters is close indeed," said my great-grandfather.

"Not close enough. I do not understand why Nefertiri agreed to this third marriage," said our Pharaoh.

"The Hittite Princess was only seven years old then, and not all matters in a treaty are equally honored. In those years, moreover, Nefertiri could not count as yet on the power of Her oldest son. But by the time that Usermare married the Hittite, the Prince Amen-khep-shu-ef had become a great General, and could prove a hazard to the throne. Besides, there was nothing now to be gained from marrying this Princess, indeed there was not even wealth enough at Kadesh to pay back loans Khetasar had taken on signing the treaty. Khetasar sent Mernafrure as tribute, no more. Usermare did not even receive Her. She arrived after a difficult journey, and as a gesture of contempt, was put into His harem at Fayum. There He met Her. No one in Thebes ceased speaking of it. For so soon as Usermare encountered this lady, He was overcome by Her beauty—so I heard—and removed Her from His harem, married Her, brought Her to Thebes. Worse. Her name being Mernafrure, all called Her Nefrure, which, being too close to Nefertiri, our Pharaoh changed Her name to Rama-Nefru so that it be near His own. Those who knew Nefertiri said no insult could be worse."

Menenhetet brought his hands together, and lay his face into the cup they formed as if to drink from the past.

"This then was our situation: a Queen on either side of Usermare. Many changes were upon us. I did not expect, however, that the first would fall on me. Usermare had come to the decision to send Amen-khep-shu-ef far from the Palace. His First Queen and oldest son must be separated. Yet He did not dare to send Him off to new wars in Libya without promoting Him. Since my rank was higher than the Prince's, Usermare decided to give it to Him."

"Without a word to you?"

"I should have taken the measure of His distress. He was making great plans for His Third Festival of Festivals which was nearly a year away, but would be the greatest of such festivals in His Reign. So He lived in terror that He would die in this year for He knew great uneasiness at His own deeds. He was building a grand chamber for the festival—The Hall of King Unas—but to His wrath, He discovered it would take two years to quarry the stone upriver and bring it in. So He made the decision to pull down our Temple of Thutmose in Thebes, and worse, the Temple of Seti at Abydos. He would use His Father's stones! These, and the stones of Thutmose, were the only marble suitable. I cannot tell You how many priests had to be present at these works of demolition each day the stones were removed, and their curses—by way of the priests' prayers—dispelled. Sometimes, the old inscriptions were chipped away. More prayers! Sometimes, the writings on these stones were turned to the wall, and so were hidden from sight. How many great names were thereby buried in the Festival Hall of King Unas.

"To the fear He knew of Nefertiri, therefore, was added the terror of shifting these great blocks. I remember that on the day He brought me with Him out to the stone works, He took me later into the room where He slept in the Little Palace, a great honor, for no one but His First Queen and His Second were usually invited there. Yet before He came to the purpose of our conversation, He talked for a long time of plots and intrigues.

"Now, my Pharaoh had a heart that was not like others. If our hearts were made of rope, none would have knots so great as His. His anger, and His fear, His breath, and His pleasure, were all wrapped around one another so closely He never knew the reason for what He did, yet He did all things with great force. The strength of all that passed through His heart had force enough to bruise the air itself. I do not think He even felt a whisper of His true fear of Nefertiri or Amen-khep-shu-ef, yet He felt, nonetheless, a terrible fear. It was so great, He even spoke to me. 'There will come a day,' He said, 'of fearful bad luck in all three parts of the day. In those hours, someone will try to kill Me.' It was His belief that some of the women in His House of the Secluded might know the assassin.

"I felt His terror. It did not attack His chest like the sharp point of a sword, but more like a poison in His thoughts. Over and over on this day, He talked of plots, and while I did not understand it then, I can speak now of His fear. It is because so many come before a Pharaoh that His memory can never be good. To remember, one must be able to look backward. Yet the Pharaoh is pushed forward by those who think of Him at every moment. Their thoughts are always shining into the darkness ahead for they wish to give Him the power to see truly into what is still to come. Only a Pharaoh can be our guide. Yet Usermare lived in so much fear that He was like a man who looks at a field glistening in the sun and thinks it is a river. Indeed, it is a river, but of light, not water. So did Usermare have an ear for treacherous voices and a nose to sniff out any plot against His glory, but He obtained His whiff of burning meat before the fire was lit. So did Usermare see so far ahead that He even glimpsed the plot that was going to arise more than a hundred years later against Your Father. To a God, one hundred years is like the interval between two breaths. So He saw the blow falling on Himself.

"Therefore, He distrusted the House of the Secluded. After many a pause, He told me that He had decided to place me there. I was the only man in the Two-Lands who was wise enough to discover whether there was a true plot or none. 'Yes,' He said, 'at Kadesh, who else but you could know the mind of Metella?' He took my arm. 'No task,' He said, 'is more important than caring for Me. That is noble work for any General,' and He began to tell of great Generals of the past who had become Pharaohs. Powerful was His breath!

"Yet, He was sending me into a place where there would be none but women. When I did not dare to refuse, I knew that the warrior in Him—even if it was His own order—must despise me.

"So, I had to wonder if my new title—Governor of the Gardens of the Secluded—was also His way of telling me that thirty years might have passed, but He had not forgotten how I bled like a woman on the day He separated my buttocks. I might be a General to others, but from His exalted view, I was a little queen. Grand Nanny of the harem. Could this be His humor? I nearly choked on the rage in my throat.

"So soon as I was away from Him, I began to pray. 'Let there be a plot against Him,' I begged, 'and I will lead it myself!'"

V

The Book of Queens

One

"In the Gardens of the Secluded, I learned what I could not have been taught in other places, and was introduced to beguilements as different from war as the rose from the axe. While I cannot speak of how it may look today, a hundred women lived there then and it was the loveliest part of the Palace. Behind its walls were many fine houses, and from each kitchen you could hear much gaiety for many of the little queens loved to eat and were merry when there was food before them. And of course they loved to drink. Each day, after all, was like the one before. The little queens arose long after sounds from the Palace beyond their walls had awakened everyone but themselves, and through the morning they would dress each other and hold long conversations over what they would borrow, and told odd tales of what they had lost to one another. For if the Pharaoh happened to visit a little queen while she was wearing a borrowed necklace, it became her own necklace. Since the King had seen it on her, there was no question of giving it back. Of course, His gifts were never loaned so lightly. Any adornment that came from Usermare was not to be touched by anyone else. Once, a little queen broke this rule, but she was obliged to pay a fearful penalty. Her small toe was

severed from her left foot. As quickly destroy the first column of a
temple built by Ramses the Great as lend one of His gifts. Afterward,
this little queen did not dance, in fact, she hardly moved, and she ate
tidbits like the candied wings of birds to restore the ache left by the
stump of her little toe, and became so fat that everyone called her
Honey-Ball. I was told of her when first I entered the harem.

"In those days—was I more weary of my old command than I
knew?—I would kneel to study the flowers at the edge of each royal
pond. There was one bloom, an orchid I would suppose, but of an
orange hue, and I spoke to it many times, which is to say I would utter
my thoughts aloud and the flower knew to reply, although I could
not tell for certain what it said. With no breeze passing over us, it
would still stir when I came near and sometimes it swayed on its stem
as undulantly as one of the little queens in a dance, indeed its petals
trembled in my presence like a girl who cannot conceal her love. Yet
this would happen when none of the other flowers were moving at all
in the still air. It was as if the stem of this orchid had roots as deep as
the thoughts of my heart, and I could breathe with the same God we
knew tonight when He brought together those two pieces of black-
copper-from-heaven. What spirit was in the flower I do not know,
but the filaments would curl beneath my eyes, and its tiny anthers
would grow larger under the power of my gaze until I could see the
pollen gather.

"Like those anthers were the eyes of the little queens when they
chose to adore the sight of you. I do not suppose there was one who
was not ready to look at me in such a way before the year was out. But
then, any man who was not a eunuch would have found it unnatural
to serve in the Gardens of the Secluded and know the nearness of so
many female bodies. Since they belonged to Usermare, one would no
more breathe their perfume too closely than drink from His golden
cup. Death to be caught in the act with any one of these hundred
women. While I had looked at death two hundred times already, and
often with a shout of happiness, I had been at war. Death, in the moment you know your glory, can seem like an embrace by the arms of
the sun, but now I was weak with the knowledge that I wished to

live, and so had no desire to be dispatched with the Pharaoh's curse on my back.

"I spoke to the little queens, therefore, as if they were flowers by the edge of the pond, and did my best to show a General who cultivated a face of stone. Each of the scars on my cheeks might have been shaped by a chisel.

"Of course, such fear did not please me. Each morning I awoke in the House of the Secluded with more desire to learn the ways of these beautiful women. I saw that my peasant beginnings, no matter how they had been dignified by the achievements of a soldier, would be of no use for comprehending the airs and silly disputes of this harem where I was now the Overseer, especially when I did not know if their arts of cosmetic and story-telling, of music and dance and kingly seduction, were as common here as an ass and a plow to a peasant, or partook of magic itself. Nor could I decide if the passing quarrels I witnessed each day were as important to the Gods as any battle between two men. Indeed they seemed to be fought as fiercely in some God's service! I was such a stranger to the House of the Secluded that in the beginning I did not even know how the little queens were chosen nor how many were daughters of the noblest families in each of the forty-two nomes. But then the woman who could have told me much about them, the ancient matron who was their supervisor, had just died."

"I do not like the way you tell us of the harem," said Hathfertiti. "Since I have never been in the House of the Secluded, I cannot picture for myself how it looks. Indeed," said my mother, with every sign of annoyance, "there are no faces in your thoughts, nor anything for us to look upon."

My great-grandfather shrugged.

"Surely, you are not tired," said Ptah-nem-hotep, "now that we are near to these stories of love so much more curious to relate than the encounters of war?"

"No, I would not say to You-of-the-Two-Great-Houses that my thoughts are weary, but still I hesitate. It is not easy to describe. I think it was the most curious year of my life. Do you know, I had

never had a home before? I had one now—in the Gardens—and servants to keep it for me. I was free to leave whenever I wished. I could,
if I desired, have gone to visit any one of several women I knew on
the outside, and yet I was like a creature in the grip of black-copper-
from-heaven. I did not dare to move from the Gardens. It was as if all
I was now trying to learn would disappear the moment I stepped
out through the gates and struck the clatter of the streets of Thebes.
Besides, I was not so free. There was the unspoken command of
Usermare-Setpenere. He would not wish His Governor to be away
from the Secluded on any undeclared hour when He might arrive.

"Moreover, I had all the years of my life until this hour to contemplate." My great-grandfather looked sad. "Ah," he said with a sigh,
"the tiny birds need stirring," and he waved his hand at the nearest
cage. The fireflies remained somnolent. Behind the fine and transparent linen that confined them, I could hardly see them stir.

My great-grandfather did not speak anymore, and we sat in silence.
This night, I had listened to his voice so many times that I did not
need to hear it any longer. I could imagine virtually all about which
he spoke. Indeed, what he had to say became clearer than his voice,
which is to confess that I began to have many pictures of the gardens
in the House of the Secluded and saw the women as their likeness
appeared in his thoughts. I could have stood upon a small bridge over
one of the ponds in these gardens, and heard the little queens speak to
one another. And I could see my great-grandfather's face as it must
have been then (which was certainly as stern and as marked with the
cuts of swords as he had told us) but now I needed to keep my eyes
open no longer, for so powerful became his thoughts that I could not
only hear the voices of the little queens but his voice as well, and it
vibrated inside me like the heaviest string on a lute.

As I lay there on my cushions, asleep for all, my body feeling as
agreeable as sleep itself, my eyes closed but for the veil of my eyelashes, I could see as I never had before. Even as I had wondered at the
paintings of Gods on the walls of many a temple and tomb my mother
had taken me to, because such people never appeared on the street,
nobody, for instance, with a long bird beak like Thoth, nor Sebek, the

God with jaws like a crocodile, so could I understand that there were
hours like this when you could see more than one face on a single
person's head, and my great-grandfather became one by one, as I
looked at him, the people of whom he thought, and I began to witness his story as if these people were in the room, and would even
have been ready to walk among them if I had not been enjoying more
the composure of my limbs. These thoughts no longer seemed to belong to my childhood so much as to what must be the wisdom, I
supposed, of a man of twenty, but such enrichment was due, I believe, to my great-grandfather's reveries as they passed through others
before drifting on to me. The patio of the Pharaoh soon became,
thereby, many rooms, and no part of it was of any certain size. Where
before I could have been looking at a couch, now I saw a road, and the
arch between two columns became like the great doors Menenhetet
saw at the entrance to the House of the Secluded. I even saw the two
stone lions on either side of the Gates of Morning and Evening, and
knew (my understanding of these Gardens of the Secluded as rich as
Menenhetet's in his first days there) that these lions were a gift to the
Pharaoh from a place called the City of the Lions down the river, and
I was taken past these marble beasts and went into the Gardens. I
could even see the splendid bodies of the four black eunuchs who
stood guard at the gate, and they wore helmets of gold. Their teeth
were as white as the linen of the Pharaoh.

Then we were in the harem, and the trees were so many, and the
grounds that full with flowers I could recognize and others I had
never glimpsed before I thought there must be more blooms here than
grew in all of Egypt, such reds and oranges and lemons and golds and
golden greens and flowers of many colors with violet and rose and
cream and scarlet and petals so soft as they came into Menenhetet's
thoughts that the sweet lips of the little queens might have been whispering on my cheek, never had I seen such color before, nor these
black-and-yellow bridges with silver balustrades and golden posts
crossing the ponds which wandered through. A green moss covered
the banks, as brilliant in the soft light as any emerald. It was the most
beautiful place through which I ever wandered, and a perfume came

from the flowers and the fruit trees until even the blue lotus had a sweetness of odor. Since it usually had none, I did not know why I could sniff it until I saw black eunuchs on their knees painting the blue lotus with scented oils, perfuming the carob trees, and the syca-mores, even the roots of the date-palms whose fronds, above, deep-ened the shade of the garden. One could not even see the sky for the branches and leaves of the low fruit trees and the lattice of the grape arbors, and this shade gave back the lavender light of evening as one sits within a cave.

Everywhere, birds flew from tree to tree and glided above the royal palms. There were ducks of every color in the ponds, bronze-hued ducks with wings of saffron and garnet, and a black swan with a bright red beak who was called Kadima, the same as the name of one tall black Princess, Kadima-from-Nubia, one of the little queens.

Never had I seen so many birds. Flying above our deserts and our river, they must have glimpsed the green eye of these gardens from a heaven away, and they came in such a splendor and confusion and outright gabble of voices that I could not have heard Menenhetet if he had still been speaking, for all of them, the geese and the cranes, the flamingos and the pelicans, the sparrows, the doves, the swallows, the nightingales and the birds of Arabia (faster than arrows but no larger than butterflies) covered the lawns and the swamps and the branches. One breathed in the hum and flutter and drumbeat of birds' wings until their power to speak tore out of my chest like a breath I could hold no longer, and flocks of them flew up in a cloud of wings while others settled to the ground. Overhead, above the palms, other birds were fighting, and the cry of these battles also came down to us. Kingfishers soared, falcons soared, ravens went through their turns, while below were all the flights of smaller birds, full of messages for one another, as if all that would yet happen in our harem and our city was being told by one bird to another. There were hours when the Gardens were as noisy as a marketplace.

Then as if the flowers knew how to calm the air, a peace intent with the sound of many a small sweet bird would come to us, and one could feel the cool of the day, and the murmuring of water. Now we could listen to the flowing of a brook whose stream was lifted from the Lake of the Gazelle. Beneath the songs and disputes of the birds came a steady pumping from one shaduf above another, lifting water from the pool to a stream bed that led down to another pool, a splendid sound as it reached my ear on this late night, as comforting to me, on all these borders of sleep, as the unhurried beating of my own heart, for no sound was more virtuous than water being lifted by the strength of slaves.

The streams were beautiful. The waters flowed over glazed clay bricks and over precious stones set within the bricks. The streams reflected the colors of the stones. I saw waters red as ruby, and violet streams, and a golden waterfall where the stream tumbled over plates of gold. I saw brooks with a bed that was mother-of-pearl, and one grotto was rosy as the setting sun, although here the shade was deep. By this bank, beneath the scent of an orange tree, one could see, since no lights were on the water, how the fish would pass. None was larger than my finger, and they would all turn at once if I inclined my wrist, these silver minnows looking like moonlight in the water. I could have sworn they cooled the garden with their silver light.

By one pond were no trees, but a lawn, green as the moss, and watered through the day by the black eunuchs. Too hot at noon, it was cool by twilight, and the little queens would sit on small golden chairs their servants had brought, and watch the passage of Kadima. The swan chose to pass at twilight as if she too wished to watch how the sky would draw in the night, and the birds came to settle. Then the eunuchs slaving at their shaduf could cease to turn the pumps and the water-pails moved no more. The little queens would lift the leaves from bowls of fruit. The smell of a pear ready to be tasted would join the scent of the flowers, and the feathers of the swan lifted and left ripples in the darkening air. So I knew we were in the hour when the little queens would begin to stir, some to go down to the lake to bathe, others to return to their houses, their servants and their children. Before long, the sound of lutes could be heard in every corner of the night and the laughter of their games. Some little queens were commencing their nightly beer-house. Menenhetet would walk through the gardens, following the stream from one pool to another, and the water, now that no eunuchs were turning the pails of the shaduf, made no murmur, and all the surface was dark but for the one brook whose bed was lined with gold. There, in the moonlight, shallows were bright as burnished copper, and Menenhetet, passing by the stream, would look at the silver minnows, the music all about him in the darkness, and the merriment of the beer-house. Standing by the gold bed of the stream that flowed from the Pool of Beloved Wisdom to the Pool of the Blue Lotus, he shivered at the babble of sound that came from the little queens. There was a disloyalty in their voices he could not name, an affection for each other that held no sound of awe for Usermare, as if there were happiness at His absence! Disloyalty stirred then in Menenhetet, and his breath became hushed as the water. He was ill with desire for the little queens. It was vivid as shame to be alone among so many women with not even a boy about older than ten, but then by that age, the children born here were off to the priests for schooling. All he heard were the voices of women who had no husband nor friend nor any lover but the Good and Great God Usermare. Worse. About him were all the plump eunuchs with their black muscles enriched by the air of their easy life. Thereby they were appealing to all—the hundred women and Menenhetet—attractions powerful to his senses. His loins ached, his throat was gorged, and his mouth was so hungry he would not look through their windows at the beer-house these little queens were making. In the dark, like the horse that hears a murderous beast in the rustle of a leaf, he started at each breeze. At this hour, there were eunuchs everywhere in the gardens, fondling one another with their fingers and their mouths, giggling like children, and the flesh of Menenhetet was inflamed. A desire for satisfaction came to him like the urge for carnage that follows battle. Yet he could never go near a eunuch. They gossiped like children. Every officer would hear of it. To be near a hundred queens and lie down with a eunuch. Menenhetet walked the gardens as if he were the ghost of a sentry who cannot give up old soldierly duty.

In the morning, it was easier. The little queens sang as they brushed each other's hair. They searched through one another's chests for clothes to exchange. They played with their children, gave orders to their servants. Since they could not leave themselves, their cooks were sent to the market for food, and scolded on their return for any flaws in the onions and meat. At the height of the day, the little queens ate at each other's houses and exchanged gifts of fruit and oil, then decorated each other with flowers, or sang new songs. They trained their pet greyhounds, their cats and their birds. They told each other stories of their families, and taught their children of the Gods of their family's nome, and the names of the Gods of the planets, and of the five senses and the four winds, and the Gods of the hours of the day and of the night. And in the late afternoon, after the little queens had slept through the heat of the day, they would meditate on their books of magic or mix their perfume. They would offer prayers and some would visit other little queens.

At twilight, they might go to the pavilion to wait for Usermare. On nights when the moon would be full, He was likely to arrive at just that hour when the light would rise upon His Chariot, and Menenhetet would watch from the tower gate as the Royal Runners raced ahead of Usermare through the street, then fell to the side and kissed the stone lions as the doors flew open. Then He rode in, leaving behind the two platoons of the Royal Guard, the fan-bearer and the standard-bearer, the mace-bearers and the lancers, and they, in turn, bowed to an escort of Princes and dignitaries who wheeled in their chariots and returned to their homes through the streets of Thebes, standing beside the grooms of the chariots in the near-dark, their bodies jolting to the clatter.

He was now inside. There were times when everyone knew He was coming; other nights He surprised all but the wisest of the little queens. Yet once within, nobody could say His mood. He delighted in presenting Himself as stern when He was pleased, or might be charming to a little queen and then leave her to weep in her chamber through many a night. "Leave now," He might tell her, "your breath is impure."

Sometimes, when early, He would sit by the pavilion and feed Kadima as she went by, and on that lawn He would often remain, talking first to one little queen and then another, well into the night. Sometimes, it was only after the rise of the moon that he would select a woman and go to her house for the rest of the night. Of course, He might select so many as seven women and there had been festival nights when He celebrated with twice seven, but on a night much like others, it was not common for Usermare to appear too late. So the little queens who waited eagerly for Him when He did not come, having been given signs by their Gods that the occasion was favorable, were obliged now to assume that other Gods had intervened, or had prayers been spoken in an unclear voice? They would raise a hand for their servant to carry away their golden chair and, furious with the perfume they had chosen, which could also have betrayed them, would walk down to the lake and wash in the moonlight, bathing away the scent of its failure.

There were little queens who might dress every night with attention, yet never be spoken to once by the King. Then, as Menenhetet came to understand, they were at last like defeated soldiers and did not try to charm the King again for many months but would stay in their homes and teach their children and wait until another season had come. If they failed on Flood, they might even wait through all of Sowing and Harvest until the fields were bare again. Some never tried a second time. There were little queens who had lived for ten years in the Gardens of the Secluded and never saw His Splendor—it was enough if they could serve as friend to a little queen who was, for a while, a Favorite. Of course, Favorites changed.

In the dry season, after Menenhetet had been Governor of the House of the Secluded for many months, Usermare arrived one night so late at the gardens that the disappointed women were already bathing in the lake. He was drunk. Never before had Menenhetet seen him so. "I have been drunk for three nights on kolobi," said Usermare, "and it is the strongest brandy in all of Egypt." Here I opened my eyes long enough to see Ptah-nem-hotep nod as if the drink came into His mind with all its fiery virtue at the moment it came into mine. "Yes, drink kolobi with Me," said Usermare as He came through the Gates, and Menenhetet bowed and said, "No honor is greater," and gulped it out of the golden goblet passed to him. Usermare asked, "Is the kolobi hard to swallow?" When Menenhetet did not reply, He said, "Does what I say have an evil smell? Drink!"

On this night, Usermare went down to the lake. It was a place He had never visited for so long as Menenhetet had been there, and thereby He surprised the few little queens who were bathing in the moonlight. Indeed they were frolicking before the eunuchs who waited on the shore, holding their robes. Now, they gave a squeak and a cry and the splashing sound of bathers trying to hide themselves. Usermare laughed until one could smell His brandy in the air.

"Come out of the water and amuse Me," He said. "You've played long enough."

So they emerged, some more beautiful under the moon than they could ever be in the light of the sun. Some were shivering. A few of the most timid little queens had not been near to Usermare for the longest time. One woman, Heqat, named after the Goddess of Frogs, had been, on occasion, His companion, and another, the fat one, Honey-Ball, had even been a Favorite until her toe was cut off. Now, she bowed before Him but with a flash of her eyes so intense that even in the night, the white of her eyes was whiter than linen. Although Honey-Ball was very fat, she carried herself as if she were the greatest little queen of them all, and did not look fat at this moment but powerful. Her hips were like the hips of a horse.

Then they were all out of the water, and their eunuchs put forward golden chairs so that they might sit about Him in a semicircle, but Usermare asked, "Who will drink the kolobi with Me?" and of them all, only Honey-Ball reached forward her hand. He gave it to her and she drank and handed back the cup and Menenhetet poured more kolobi for the Pharaoh.

"Tell Me stories," said Usermare. "I have been drinking this brandy of Egypt for three days, and I would have done better to swallow the blood of a dead man. I have awakened each morning with a blow in My head from the ghost, but I do not know which ghost, although I could swear he is a Hittite, is that not so, Meni? Hittites carry axes," and He cleared His throat, and said, "Once in the mountains of Lebanon, I came to a valley that crossed another valley and in the center was a hill. From that hill four streams flowed. There, I have told you a story. Now tell Me one."

The smell of His brandy lay on the night air, full of the wounds of the grape. Usermare had lungs to breathe the flames of fire itself, but the little queens sat with throats full of unseen smoke. Heavy was their fear of the invisible fire of the brandy.

A little queen named Mersegert, small in size and loud in voice, was the first to answer. Named after the Goddess of Silence, she was the noisiest in every group. Where others might be silent, she would, when in panic, rush to speak, and now she tried to tell a tale of a poor King who wandered with his horse in the dark because the stars were covered. "O He-Who-brings-great-pleasure-to-the-altar-that-is-between-the-thighs-of-all-beautiful-women, listen to my tale," said Mersegert in her funny voice that came from the nose like a reed pipe. "This King was unhappy and poor."

"Of which country was he Monarch?" asked Usermare.

"Of a country that is far to the East," said Mersegert.

"Get on with the story, but tell it loudly. Your voice is best when you do not lose it."

"In the darkness, this King could not see," she said. "He knew no direction. Yet the sky was visible beneath the hooves of his horse. It could not be seen above, but below, the stars were shining. The King dismounted from his horse, and lo, he was standing on the sky. The stars were beneath his feet. So he knelt and picked up one star, and saw it was a precious stone and had a God in its light. That told him to look for many more stones, and by their light, he was able to return to his kingdom, and was rich again."

Usermare broke the air with a loud hiccup. Everyone laughed at Mersegert.

"I want a better story. It's dark down here. We could use a few precious stones." He squinted at each of the women. "Who have we? I see Harmony and White Linen and Hippo—" He gave a nod to Honey-Ball and a few of the little queens giggled at the name He had

just given her—"and Nubty and Amentit, and Heqat and Creamy.
And Rabbit. Rabbit, do you have a story?"

Rabbit was the tallest of the little queens and among the youngest,
and shy. She merely shook her head. "Oasis, what have you to tell
Me?" He asked. That was Bastet, named after Bast, the Goddess of all
cats, but her eyes were beautiful and looked like two wells, so everyone called her Oasis.

She sighed. She had a beautiful voice, and used it well, and spoke
of the nine full moons before a child could be born, and the nine gates
through which it must pass in the belly of its mother. Usermare-
Setpenere was, however, so bored that He interrupted Oasis to say, "I
do not want to hear any more," and took another drink of the kolobi.
A silence came forth.

"Heqat," He said, "it is your turn to amuse Me." He burped again.
The queens giggled. The sound might lap at the edge of His fire and
soothe it. Tonight, however, He had had so much of the kolobi that
they laughed in great doubt, not knowing if their mirth was soothing
His temper, or inflaming it.

"Great and Noble Two-House," said Heqat, "I would wish to tell
a story that does not displease You."

"Tell no stories of frogs, then. You are too much like a frog yourself."

Usermare always spoke to Heqat in just this manner. It was appar-
ent He could not bear her appearance. She was the ugliest of the little
queens, and for that matter would be the ugliest in many a group of
women. The skin of her face was splotched, her neck was thick, and
she was imperfectly formed. Her skin exuded a moisture. Menenhetet had not a friend among these little queens who would tell him the
truth, but several of the eunuchs offered up their tales, and if they
could be believed, for they giggled even more than the women, it was
true that once a year, on the height of the flood, the frogs would pass
through the Gardens and swarm over the floor of every house. Then,
on one of those nights, once a year, Usermare would go to her apartment and spend hours with Heqat in the darkness. Afterwards her

place reeked from the labors of love. The eunuchs knew, for they would clean it, and on such a night two years ago, there had been a hailstorm, and half-formed frogs were found on her patio dead and dying and looked like men and women wrongly formed, a host of them come forth from the slime. On hearing this story, Menenhetet had thrust his arm through the air as though to wield a sword against the words of the eunuchs, for he wished to sever the image of User-mare and Heqat in such repulsive acts.

Now, in the darkness, by the bank of the lake, Heqat said, "In Syria, to the east of Tyre, the brides of many men are bought at auction. The most beautiful bring a good price to their family, but for ugly women in whom there is no interest, the father of the bride must pay the groom. So there comes an hour in the auction, when the passage of money changes its course, even as the tides of the Very Green wash out and then wash back. Much money is paid by the father of the ugliest bride."

The story had succeeded in capturing Him. There were murmurs from the little queens. "It happened," said Heqat, "that one woman was so ugly her new husband grew ill when he looked at her. Yet soon after her marriage, she was befriended in a dream by the Goddess Astarte. Good and Great God, our Astarte is the most beautiful of all Goddesses in the temples of my land, and we even say that She is to us as Isis to the Egyptians. Now, Astarte said, 'I am bored by beauty. I find it common. So I take notice of you, poor ugly girl, and offer these words-of-magic. They will protect your husband and sons from every disease but the one chosen to kill them.' Then Astarte disappeared. The husband of this ugly woman, however, grew so rich in vigor that he made love to his ugly wife every night and they had many children who were also healthy. When at last the husband died of the one disease chosen to kill him, the woman asked to be auctioned again. By this time her power to enrich those who lived closest to her was so well known that she commanded the highest price at the auction. More was paid for her than for the loveliest bride. Thereby, every principle of beauty was turned about on that day. Now, in my land, they cannot tell the good-looking women from the ugly, and they honor long crooked noses."

She bowed. Her tale was done. A few of the little queens began to giggle, but Honey-Ball commenced to laugh. Her mirth came from a powerful throat, yet the sound was so rich at its foundation and spoke so well of the recollection of old pleasure, that Menenhetet thought it beautiful.

"Have more kolobi," said Usermare. "Take a good swallow. Your tale is next."

Honey-Ball bowed. Her waist was as thick as the waist of any two women beside her, but she bowed well enough to touch her knee.

"I have heard of a Goddess," she said, "who has rose-colored hair. None know Her name."

"I would like to see such a Goddess," said Usermare. His voice was as powerful as her voice.

"Great Ozymandias," she said, and there was mockery as delicate as the lift of a wing in the manner she spoke the name for it was the one by which nations to the East would call Him, "if You were to see this rose-colored Goddess, You would hold Her, and then She would be a Goddess no more, but a woman like any of us."

The little queens giggled with great happiness. The insult was safely contained in the compliment, and Usermare could only reply, "Tell your tale, Hippo, before I give a squeeze to your belly, and the banks of this lake are covered with oil."

"A million and infinity of apologies," said Honey-Ball, "for delaying Your amusement. Oh, Great Ozymandias, the skin of this Goddess with rose-colored hair was white, and so She loved to lie in a marsh by the green of the wet marsh grass. There came one day a shepherd who was also beautiful, and stronger than other men. He wanted Her as soon as he saw Her, but She said, 'First you must wrestle in My pool.' He said, thinking to tease Her, 'What if I lose?' Oh, She told him, he must give Her a sheep if he lost. The shepherd seized Her hair, and pulled Her to him. Her head smelled as sweet as the rose, but his hands were trapped by the thorns in Her hair. So She seized him by the thighs and threw him, and sat on his head. Then he discovered thorns in the hair of the other forest. Oh, his mouth was bleeding before She let him go. He had to give Her a sheep. Next day, he came to fight again, and lost, and gave up another animal. He fought every day until his flock was gone, and his lips were a sorry mouth."

Now, Honey-Ball began to laugh and could not stop. The power of her voice, like the first rising of our flood, had a strength to pull in all that was on the banks. One by one, other little queens began to laugh, and then the eunuchs, until all were sharing the spirits of this story.

Maybe it was the kolobi, or it could have been the whim of the King, but when the merriment of the little queens did not cease, He, too, began to laugh and drank half a goblet, and passed what was left to Honey-Ball. "Ma-Khrut," He said, "you are True-of-Voice indeed," and by the way I heard it through Menenhetet's ear, resonant as a bell, I knew that Ma-Khrut had been her name in the days when she was slender and beautiful, and that caused my mother, my father, and my own Pharaoh to utter a small cry of astonishment in their thoughts, for as I now learned, Ma-Khrut is a title given only to the greatest and wisest of priests, only those who are most True-of-Voice, those who utter the sounds of the most profound prayers in the clearest and firmest tones (since in that manner they are able to send back in recoil, like an army in flight, all Gods who might interfere with the prayer). Only High Priests are granted such a title of respect. Yet here was Honey-Ball given the name of Ma-Khrut. It could only mean She-who-is-True-of-Voice.

"Usermare-Setpenere," said Honey-Ball, "if I speak with clarity, it is because of the awe I know at the sounds of Your name."

The little queens murmured their assent. Their piety was added to the mist on the lake. To pronounce the many names of Usermare in the most immaculate tones was said to be a power great enough to rock the earth.

"That is good," said Usermare. "I hope you always say My name with care. I would hate to cut off the toe of your other foot."

One of the little queens gasped so unexpectedly she could be heard. The others ceased to laugh. Honey-Ball turned her head as if slapped. Still, she murmured, "Oh, Sesusi, I will become twice as fat."

"No bed in the House of the Secluded will then be strong enough to bear you," He told her.

"Then there will be no bed," she answered, and her eyes flashed again. Menenhetet was much affected. Her presence on this night was so different from other occasions when she was merely fat and limped about on feet sore from her weight. Tonight, ensconced on a gold bench, for the golden chairs were much too narrow, she seemed massive, yet majestic as a Queen, at least in this hour.

"Tell another story," said Usermare, "and tell it well."

"Why, if I do not, Great Ozymandias," she said, "I will of my own choice give up a finger." A few of the little queens could not help themselves, and laughed aloud at her audacity, most of all Nubty, the little goddess of gold, who had been given such a name because lately she had taken to wearing blond wigs, which is to say, hair from a lynx dusted in gold, and all said it was to encourage the Pharaoh to see her as like to Rama-Nefru when He was among the Secluded.

"Make this story long," said Usermare. "I like long stories better."

"There is one that tells of two magicians," said Honey-Ball. Her speech was like a wind that holds birds motionless in flight, just so full was it with the sound of her voice. "The first to know is Horus of the North. Before he was even born, he was allowed to sleep at the feet of Osiris.

"The other magician was called Horus of the South. He was black. He had been given his name by Nubian priests who stole many rolls of papyrus from the Temple of Amon at the First Cataract. Back to the jungle they took this knowledge and practiced for a thousand years until they were very wise. Then they became the teachers of the black magician, Horus of the South, until he left for Thebes to frighten the Pharaoh."

"Which Pharaoh?" asked Usermare.

"Great Beloved of the Sun, I cannot say, or I will bring misfortune upon Egypt."

He looked furious but did not dare to insist. "Tell your story, Ma-Khrut. I will see if I am happy when you are done."

In the darkness, one white butterfly came over the heads of the women on a wandering flight, and the silence was so profound upon the lake that I thought I could hear the flutter of its wings.

"On his way to the Court, across all of the distance from the jungle of Nubia to Thebes, this Horus of the South took care each night to take a papyrus from his book of magic and dissolve it in wine. Then he would drink, and the magic words written on the papyrus would travel to the interior of his thoughts. Thereby, Horus of the South grew impregnable with wisdom. By the day he appeared at the Palace it could be said of Horus of the South that the lights in his eye had the Secret Name of Ra. Yet when he knocked on the door to the Twin-Gates, a charioteer was there to arrest him. For many witnesses had run forward in advance to say that the strange Nubian who approached had the odor of sorcery. That was true. One cannot swallow too many words-of-magic without reeking of roots and rocks."

"I like this story," said Usermare.

"Horus of the South said to the guard, 'No bonds will hold me.' He raised a finger, and the cord that lashed his wrists broke into many pieces that scurried away like worms."

"Did you see it?" asked Usermare.

"Great Lord, in my sleep, there I saw it."

Usermare drank more kolobi and expelled His breath. "Look," He said, "at My magic. Even the white butterfly is singed by the fire of My mouth." The butterfly, passing, most certainly wavered. The little queens giggled.

Honey-Ball waited until her silence became more powerful than the sound of Usermare drinking His kolobi. Then, she said, "Since no cord could hold him, Horus of the South walked across the parade ground and said to the Pharaoh, 'I am Horus of the South. I have come like a plague upon Egypt. No magician has strength against me. I will take You back to the Kingdom of Nubia and my people will laugh at You.'"

"Aiiiiiigh," shrieked one of the little queens, but Honey-Ball did not pause.

"Before the Pharaoh could even reply, Horus of the North came out of the House of the Secluded, and said, 'My magic is as powerful as this plague!' The Pharaoh shook His Flail seven times to declare that He would like a contest between these magicians but His nobles begged Him to wait. They knew Horus of the North as the son of one of the little queens, no more. They had not seen him sleeping at the feet of Osiris in the Land of the Dead. But the Pharaoh knew," said Honey-Ball, and all the little queens clapped their hands at His wisdom.

"Horus of the South did not seem frightened, however. He held forth his empty hand, and, lo! a stick was in it. '*Medu*' he said, 'is the word for *stick*. It is also the word for *word*. Therefore I draw a magic *word* with this stick.' He said all this in a great mumble: 'Medu is the medu for medu, as is medu, medu. Whereby medu may beget medu.' But with the point of his stick he drew a triangle. A flame rushed out and burned in the air with such a great noise that all of the Court drew back." Now, Honey-Ball ceased speaking and looked most solemnly at Usermare before she continued.

"Horus of the North, however, stood up and drew a circle about his Pharaoh. The flames drew back. Now, in the other hand of the magician of the North appeared a golden cup which held a little water. Horus of the North hurled those few drops into the air, and they came down as a mighty rain that put out the flames. Horus of the South was left as wet as the river that brought him here, but Horus of the North and his Pharaoh were dry. Yet, when all the nobles began to laugh, Horus of the South laughed back and most heartily, and without hesitation drew the rude figure of an anus in the air. That is a circle with spokes like the wheels of the chariots You have captured, great Usermare. It was dreadful! Into this circle came a mighty wind out of the terrible jungles from which this Nubian had come, and in it was the smell of all the foul wind expelled by the Nubian lords to show their contempt for the Court of the Pharaoh." Despite themselves, a few of the little queens giggled, but Honey-Ball pretended not to have heard and went on.

"In reply, Horus of the North waved the tip of his stick in upon itself like a spiral, and all the winds loosed by the Nubian were spun into a tight skein around the shaft. Poof! Horus of the North withdrew his stick from these braided winds, and the skein burst into flame.

"Now Horus of the South showed his teeth, and his head became as ugly as a serpent. He said to the Pharaoh, 'Hear me: Your Court will be Your tomb!' and, with that, cast his stick into the air. At the height of the throw, the stick refused to come down, but floated overhead and spread out until it was like a great flat stone above. Now, Horus of the South said: 'This roof will collapse and You will perish beneath unless You agree to come with me to the Land of Nubia.'

" 'What will happen in Nubia?' asked the Pharaoh.

" 'My people will see You on Your knees.'

" 'Then I will never go,' said the Pharaoh.

" 'Perish.'

"In great fear, all waited for Horus of the North. He was pale, but the color of his eyes turned to silver, and he smiled under the shadow of the great stone roof that hid the sun. With a cry, he, too, threw his stick into the air. As they watched, it turned into a barge which rose upward until it came to rest beneath the great roof of stone, and then it heaved and groaned until it was able to raise the stone roof back into the sky.

"Horus of the South now said three strange words. On the instant, he was invisible. It proved of no protection. At once, Horus of the North repeated the three words backwards, and Horus of the South was obliged to come forth again. Now, he was a black cock, his wings clipped. In such a situation, he could only utter the most terrible howls of lamentation."

"How did they bury him?" asked Usermare.

"Oh, not yet, great Sesusi. Horus of the North called forth a soldier to cut off the part that lives between a cock's legs. At this, Horus of the South made much commotion. He begged the Pharaoh to save the life between his legs.

"'I will save you,' said the Pharaoh, 'if by the balance of Maat, you agree to let me make eunuchs out of all Nubians I capture. Do you assign such rights to Me, and to the sons of My sons for a thousand years?'

"Horus of the South wept. 'I am lost,' he cried out, 'so all of Nubia is lost. Do what You will. I promise not to come back to Egypt for a thousand years.' When the Pharaoh nodded, Horus of the North gave a sign. The cock grew feathers and flew away. But the leg between the legs of all captured Nubians was lost, and they learned to serve in the House of the Secluded for all Pharaohs to come."

"That is the truth," said the eunuchs of the little queens, "that must be the true tale of how we are here," and a sigh came up from them.

"Is this the last of your story?" asked Usermare.

"All but the last." As if to show that many Gods were with her this night, whatever light could be found in the waning of the moon lay on her face, and the eyes and nose and mouth of Honey-Ball were beautiful, or at least would have been, if not surrounded by the full circle of her face, round as the moon. Within that face, however, her eyes were large and dark, her nose was most delicate, and her mouth was curved and very soft for so strong a woman.

"What is the end?" asked Usermare.

"Oh, great Sesusi," said Honey-Ball, "since the time of which I speak, more than a thousand years have passed. Horus of the South may now be ready to return."

"If that is so, how can I find Horus of the North?" asked Usermare. He spoke lightly, but His voice was heavy with the kolobi.

She shrugged. In the dark, the force of her gesture was felt in the air. "Let me offer a prayer to the Ka of Horus of the North. The great magician may wish to find his successor."

Now, it was no longer Honey-Ball's voice I heard in my ear but Menenhetet's. I sat up straight as if tugged by the hair. So deeply had

I been listening to his thoughts, that his voice was now as startling as the cry of an animal next to your tent. "So soon as she spoke of a successor," my great-grandfather most certainly said, "I began to shiver. In the warmth of the night, I was trembling. One little queen pointed to me, and cried out, 'Why do you fear the story?' I told her that I was not afraid, only cold. But I was afraid. Honey-Ball had looked at me more than once, and I had dared to look back into her eyes. A thought had come then from her to me. It said: 'I will teach you a little of these arts of magic.'"

Two

Now that his voice had, however, risen again to the surface of his thoughts, my great-grandfather looked much refreshed, and began to muse aloud on several subtle matters.

"In this hour of His drunkenness," said my great-grandfather, "I think Usermare was much disturbed by that tale of two magicians. For, as You know, it was His belief He was going to be killed in the Gardens of the Secluded. Now to speak of how He was right about such a suspicion when it was not true, must prove confusing. He was never assassinated. Yet, by another measure I would say He was all-but-killed in this year, and I was the one to do it, even though, as we all know, He lived until He was very old, old-as-Ra-is-Ramses-the-Second, we used to say, and I was even a High Priest in the late years of His Reign. Indeed He died only a few years before my second life was lost. I still remember children saying at His funeral: 'God is dead,' and they wondered how the sun could shine. He was a Pharaoh for sixty-seven years. Yet after this night, even though He would reign for another thirty-four, I still do not think there was a season when Usermare did not fear the return of Horus of the South.

"Of course, I did not know it that night. He showed no fear. To the contrary. If the story told by Honey-Ball had immediate power over my Monarch, it was to arouse His desire. One could almost feel the glow of His belly. It rose in my great Pharaoh like a fire beneath the fumes of kolobi. The eunuchs began to chant. Their hands struck their thighs with many little taps in a rhythm so quick I could hear the chirping of the crickets and the hooves of horses. One of these eunuchs even had a way of running his fingertips over his knees with a slipping sound to give you the patter of a brook or the slap of the smallest waves. To this accompaniment came forth many moths and butterflies from the dark and they flew in and out of our ears as if we were water-grass and they as numerous as little fish. Honey-Ball began to hum, and her voice was so resonant that once again I could not recognize the woman I saw. Other times, she had seemed without shape in her clothes, yet from the moment she came out of the water tonight, her body looked firm, and she was not without beauty. Like some who are fat, her flesh was slack in dejection, but could fill with blood when she was happy.

"Tonight, she sang a ballad of the love of a farmgirl for a shepherd, a sweet and innocent song, and Usermare drank kolobi to the sound of it, and wiped His eyes. Like many powerful men, he liked to weep a little on hearing tender sentiments. But not for too long. Soon Honey-Ball sang the next verse. The melody was the same but now the shepherd had no interest in the girl, and looked instead at the buttocks of his sheep, a wicked ballad. Honey-Ball began to cry out in the pleasurable cries of the beast as it was taken. 'Oh,' she groaned, in a voice to wake us all, 'Oh,' and the air throbbed.

"Usermare was now ready. 'Come,' He said to her. 'You, Heqat, Nubty, Oasis!' With a voice that did not bother to conceal the heat of His slow fires on this night, He added, 'Let it be in the house of Nubty.' Then as if a thought had come to His hand, even as Hera-Ra used to stand by His side and lick His fingers, Usermare said, 'Meni, you are to come with Me,' and He took my hand, and that way, we walked together.

"It is curious, but in His eyes, I had become Hera-Ra. It was to the lion, not myself, that He offered friendship. To myself, therefore, I now became absurd. Beneath all my vows that I would know revenge, I had been so starved through these years for one sign of His affection, that I was ready, doubtless, to roar like a lion if it would only keep His hand in mine a little longer.

"Yet, now, as we walked, strange events occurred. If I was like Hera-Ra to Him, I can only say that beside me, I could feel the hoof-beat, quick, of a wild pig. What a companion! If my first thought was that this pig had to be a gift from Honey-Ball, I do not know that I was wrong, and I can say that after the night which was to follow in the house of Nubty, the wild pig was often at my side until it was killed, about which I will also tell You, but that is later. Certainly on the next day when I walked along the lawn where the black swan sailed by at twilight, so was the wild pig with me, and when I would stop at the house of a little queen to watch one dress the hair of an-other, then, too, was the pig at my side. I came to know his face and know it well, but no one else could see the creature. Everywhere he walked with me, yet I could not summon him. While to think of his face was enough to make the pig appear, sometimes he would not, and on those nights when I was alone, I could not bear the sounds of the beer-house. The noises made by the little queens proved offensive to me. Indeed, once accustomed to the companionship of this silent creature, I became most censorious without him.

"I already knew that these hundred little queens did not always wait for an offering of pleasure from our divine Ramses, but some-times ended by making love to each other. This discovery was objec-tionable to me, even if it should have been familiar. I grew up in a crowd of boys who were always on each other. Our expression for a powerful friend was 'he-who-is-on-my-back.' So as a boy, there was nothing I did not know of being on the others' bodies, although my pride, since I was strong, had been that nobody was on mine. Still I could not bear to think of these women with one another, nor the way by which the most powerful of the little queens often treated the gentler ones as if they were slaves. On those nights when His Chariot did not enter the gates, and you would not hear the thunder of His fornication, there would rise up instead the sweeter cries and harsher screeches, the moans and music of many a woman in many a room. It was common whenever women were at such play that one would pluck a harp to accompany the others. And I, hearing such sounds, could not, in my mind, forswear the sights. To see a little queen at the sweet-meat of another was to gorge my blood. But then I did not have the royal disregard of my Monarch. We all knew that He liked to watch His little queens romp with one another. 'Oh, yes,' He would say, 'they are the strings of My lute and must learn to quiver together.'

"I, however, especially when I was without the pig, used to think of this as part of the filth that rose on the flood, a pestilence out of these women, and I sometimes dared to wonder if they loved Him as much as they came to love each other. Sometimes two little queens would virtually live in one house like husband and wife, or brother and sister, and their children would speak equally of either little queen as their parent. It seemed to me that for a woman to love another woman more than her Pharaoh was equal to praying for the plague. So marched the legions of all those thoughts in me that were loyal to Usermare, but when I walked through the gardens with the pig, I became another man and was tolerant to their games and coveted the little queens for myself. Indeed, I even liked to observe their eating and their dancing, the songs they sang as they brushed each other's hair, or searched through each other's chests for finery to wear. Indeed, there was a time when I, like Nef-khep-aukhem, could name every cosmetic they used."

"Are there any I do not know?" asked Hathfertiti.

"There is no oil of a flower you have not decanted," he replied.

"But what of the herbs?" she insisted.

"Only the finest and sweetest perfumes were chosen. They had no need of the bitterness of galbanum or cassis."

"Yes," said my mother, "but what of the ointment of spikenard?"

"That they used, and saffron and cinnamon and the sweet wine that leaves the very odor of love when it is rubbed into the thighs with oil and a little of the gravy of roast meat."

Now, Ptah-nem-hotep stirred with annoyance. "To tell too little,"

He said, "is becoming your sin. I wish to know: What was done in the house of Nubty?"

"I have no way to inform You," said Menenhetet, "without presenting myself as a fool."

"That is hardly possible," said Ptah-nem-hotep. "If I listen to you for so long, it is because you are not. But I can hardly expect that you were the master each night of your four lives. Even a Pharaoh may play the fool. There, I have made the most intolerable remark."

"If I tell it, well then, it will be done quickly," said my great-grandfather, and he leaned forward, as if, even to begin this unwilling engagement, he must go in at a gallop.

"The little queen, Nubty, had a statue of Amon whose belly was no larger than my hand. Yet the staff that rose between His golden legs was not hidden, no, to the contrary, it was half as long as the God Himself was high, and Usermare knelt before this little God, and raised His own hands as if to say that all of Him, Himself and each Ka of His Fourteen, were in service to Amon. Then, He put His mouth around the gold member, the very staff of the God Amon.

"'No man has ever penetrated My mouth,' said Usermare, 'but I am happy to kiss the sword of Amon, and know the taste of gold and rubies.' Indeed, on the tip of this gold member, on the knob itself, was a large ruby.

"Then, He rose, and Heqat and Oasis removed His chestplate and His skirt of linen. 'Here, Meni,' He said to me, 'pray to Me as if I am the sword of the Hidden One,' and His phallus was in my face, and I swallowed it, and felt the flood of the Nile rise in Him. My head was bobbing like a boat and the little queens giggled as the heat of His kolobi rushed into my throat and down the inside of my chest. Through it all, down to my navel, I knew now why the pig was with me. None of the little queens would have dared to touch one of their painted nails to my skin, but the pig had his thick nose between my cheeks and would have liked to swallow the semen of my King if it could have passed through me so fast. So I was not scorched by the heat of Usermare's loins, only the contempt. There, I have told you the worst," my great-grandfather said, "the first of the humiliations I was to know on this night before my Pharaoh, and that after I swore He would never shame me again. It is this which has delayed me, this which is difficult to tell. Yet now I feel as if a stone is lifted. So I will tell you the rest. For much was done.

"They anointed Usermare. On this night, as on others when I had not been there, He would sit like the God Amon, while the little queens would serve Him in the manner of Tongue and Pure, by which I mean that they would wipe His face most carefully and apply new cosmetic to His eyes. They would take off His garments, and dress Him in fresh linen, then speak verses over the jewelry they laid on Him. Each piece removed was kissed by one of the little queens, as well as each garment they laid on Him. Since in those days I did not fully understand the difference between kissing and eating—which peasant could?—I thought they were making these small sounds with their lips to show that the taste of the linen of the Pharaoh was good.

"Now, on this night as on others, they sprinkled perfumes on His brow, and into their mouths, each one of these queens, one by one took His sword while the others murmured, 'The Gods adorn Themselves and Thy name is Adornment.'

"To my astonishment He gave Himself up to the little queens as if He were a woman. He lay on His back with His powerful thighs in the air, His knees farther apart than the width of His great shoulders, and my hand was held in His with such force I could hardly have freed myself. Yet that was only at the commencement. I was still full of fear and expected the house of Nubty to roar up around us in flames, yet the walls only staggered, as from shock, and still were standing; indeed, it could have been my own body that was quivering. I still lived then as I say in fear of catastrophe, but when it did not happen, my terror grew less, and so, too, did His grip relax.

"Toward the end, He held my hand softly and I could feel His pleasures as they swelled into Him out of the cunning mouths of the little queens, indeed, even now, I can tell You, great Ptah-nem-hotep, of all that was in Usermare as He grew ready to come forth. I was able to know Him in those moments as none who is not a Pharaoh can ever know so Good and Great a God. In that pleasure when the four little queens knelt before the great and beautiful body of Usermare, I came to know Him. Heqat had taken His feet in her mouth and licked between His toes like a silver snake that winds through golden roots, and Oasis, with the skill of long practice, had given light licks and long kisses to the sword of Usermare even as Nubty knew His ears and His nose and the lids of His eyes with the tip of her tongue, yes, all of these caresses from Heqat, Oasis and Nubty had passed through His fingers into me and I felt more beautiful than all the flowers in the Gardens of the Secluded and lived in the air of a rainbow while there He lay, legs apart, His knees bent. It was then that Honey-Ball brought her lips to that mouth of Usermare which lived between His buttocks and she kissed Him there, her tongue coming forth into His gates, and she knew the entrance to His passage. He lay there, and with my hand, I was with Him. So I knew what it was to be in the Boat of Ra going up the river of the Duad in the Land of the Dead, and that was a wondrous place from such a boat with serpents and scorpions at every turn, flames in the mouths of beasts more terrible than I had ever seen, and Blessed Fields whose grass was sweet even in the night. Usermare floated through the Land of the Dead, and I with Him, the pig at my vitals. He saw the Sun and the Moon as His cousins. Then the river began to rise into the ruby of His sword there in the sweet lips of Oasis, and I heard Him shout, 'I am, I am all that will be,' and even as the women cried out, He came forth and the ghost of the kolobi was like a fire with red and emerald light in me.

"So did I come forth at His side, all the powers of His own rising having surged through His fingers into mine, but then my coming forth was blasted back by the snout of that pig and thereby I felt owned from mouth to anus, great Monarch and curious pig owned the two ends of the river that ran through me, even as Osiris commands the entrance and exit to the Land of the Dead.

"I found no cause for celebration. Usermare had no sooner recovered from coming forth as a woman than He was ready to stand as a man and now was interested in none of the mouths that lived between the thighs of His four little queens, but took my poor cheeks, rooted in all night by the snout of the pig, and before the women, made a woman again of me. 'Aiiigh, Kazama,' they cried with many giggles, and it was then I learned that Kazama was their name for me. Slave-Driver was the thought they held when they spoke the name to each other, but now the slave-driver had become the slave. 'Aiiigh, Kazama,' they cried in their laughter. But I did not. Holding His hand, I had lived in the waters of paradise. Not so with His sword. That gave me pain. I saw no vision. I swore that if this was the second time He had penetrated my bowels, there would not be a third even if He cut off all I had and left me in the compound of the eunuchs."

At this, Menenhetet's voice fell silent, and I, who had been listening with all my attention, eyes shut, now opened them to see my mother across the room, and on her knees before Ptah-nem-hotep, and I thought His sword was in her mouth. Yet, whatever passed between them ceased so soon as I sat up. My mother, however, still purred like a cat. My father slept. At least, he did not move, and his eyes were closed. He snored openly and in misery. The fireflies glowed so brightly that I thought I could witness the expression on my great-grandfather's face, and he was far from us. That was certainly true. In the next instant, he began to speak in the voice of Honey-Ball.

Three

I knew they were her tones. All the while I had lived in my great-grandfather's thoughts, I had heard her speaking. Now, his eyes rolled up like the eyes of the dead, and out of his throat came the voice of Honey-Ball.

"Kazama, I did not see you leave," she said. "But I laughed with the others for He made a woman of you. You jerked like a worm on the hook of His strength. Yet, now, I do not think of Sesusi, but of the injury to your proud heart. You feel soft like the earth when the river flows over. Tell me it is not so."

"It is so," said my great-grandfather speaking in his own voice out of the very heart of this spell, and yet, by the diminishing light of the fireflies, I knew he was calm once more, his voice older than any I had heard and looked one hundred years old, more than a hundred. The patio smelled like old stone. I was trying to remember some opening of my own jaws in a vault so dank I could not breathe. The voice of Honey-Ball spoke again, however, and I was back in every murmur of the night. Through the mouth of Menenhetet, I heard her say, "How I felt the pain of your thoughts. They suffered the convulsions of a belly when a child is born. Is it so, Kazama?"

"It is so," said Menenhetet.

"In that hour, you could not say if you were a man or a woman. You could only wonder why men pass over into women, and women into men."

When the last echo of her voice was gone, Menenhetet's head came forward, and he looked at all of us as if he had slept for a hundred years. His face came back from the old age that had lain upon it, and I never saw him look so young, a man of sixty who could have stood among us for forty and stronger than a charioteer. My father ceased his snoring to come awake, and my mother had a look of satisfaction on her lips, as if she had tasted nothing so much as the center of a secret.

"Yes," said Ptah-nem-hotep, "tell us more of this Honey-Ball for she sounds nearly so curious as My great ancestor, may I be welcomed by Him in the Blessed Fields," and He made a loud smacking sound with His mouth to remind us that it was still the Night of the Pig, and piety might offer less protection than sacrilege. "Yes," He said, "tell us before the dawn burns our eyes. Soon Hathfertiti and I may wish to find our sleep." With a laugh of great gaiety—in the first true sound of real happiness I had heard from Him, our Pharaoh came to His feet and kissed my father on the brow.

"It is so," said my father.

"Speak again in the voice of Honey-Ball," cried Ptah-nem-hotep to my great-grandfather, as if He, too, had been drinking kolobi.

"Divine Two-House, I slept for a moment and feel well-rested. Did You hear her voice?"

Ptah-nem-hotep laughed.

"It must be true," said Menenhetet. "I think of her now."

"Yes, go on," said our Pharaoh. "I would enjoy it."

"If I remember," said my great-grandfather, "the night was without a moon when I left the house of Nubty, and, to my unhappy eyes, as dark as the most awful of my thoughts. I found the pond where the black swan liked to stay at night and tried to speak to her, yet I could think of nothing but my shame. It was then I took a second vow. Shame, like any other poison, needs its own outrageous cure. I decided to seek the courage of madness itself. I would dare what no one else was ready to dare, and put myself in the bed of one of the little queens.

"It was bravery itself to breathe twice on one thought such as this. For it is on the second breath that others hear what you think. Yet I knew I must speak the vow clearly. So I told myself, but I was shaking so much the swan began to shudder as well. Her wings clapped, and little waves went out from her body to set the water of the pond to frothing loudly. I was certain every house in the Gardens of the Secluded would awaken. Then the pond was still again. I began to think of Honey-Ball. Out of the breasts of that round woman rose a tenderness for me that was like the rise of the river when the earth is dry, and the pig's snout came up behind me then and nuzzled my thigh.

"Let me not speak of the days it took until I made my first visit, nor of each fear I managed to conquer only to lose my footing on the next fear. All such tales are the same. I do not know that I could have entered her house if in my dreams, I was not always walking toward it. How I wished to lie on my back like Usermare and know her mouth at the lower gates.

"Say that I was drawn as one bar of black-copper-from-heaven is seduced toward another, for on a night when Usermare did not visit the Gardens of the Secluded, I presented myself at her door. Although on that visit I did not even try to sit beside her, I asked on leaving if I could come tomorrow, and she agreed but said, 'No one must see you here again at night,' and she led me out to a tree by her own garden wall over whose branches I might climb. That way I could enter without awakening her maidservants or eunuchs. Touching the branch, I remembered a night when I sat with my back against another tree on the way to Kadesh, and I nodded, and she put her hand to my neck and rubbed it slowly. A strength came to me from her plump fingers like the force I once received from the Lebanese wood.

"After I left, I could not sleep again. In the night the power of her attraction was upon me. I had never liked women so heavy as herself, and yet the thought of such plumpness stirred like a sweet wind in my belly. I confess I felt all but equal to one of those eggs in the middle of a ball of dung that our scarab beetle pushes up the riverbank, for in the midst of trying to sleep, I was as rich as Khepera Himself, and warm, and full of earth, and knew again the smells of our Egyptian dung so replete with all that rots and dies and still reeks of the old greed, and wondered if this were the odor of Honey-Ball's flesh when her perfume was gone. Yet I also felt full of gold, and saw a golden sky beneath my closed eyes and heard its thunder as though the light of Ra, not content with offering light to corn, to the reeds, to the glint of the river, and to that richest ore of earth, gold itself, had also to warm all filth and penetrate to the very center of this oven of dung that was my pleasure. With that, I sat up, hating the foul attraction I might find in her arms, yet determined to know her, for I was worse than dead. My shame, carried for so many years, was now inflamed.

"So I got up and walked through the gardens, and climbed the tree outside her walls, crossed the branch and dropped within her garden. She was waiting for me in her room, but I fell into her arms with such fear that my sword was like a mouse. She felt larger than the earth. I thought I embraced a mountain. On that night, I did not have the strength to enter a lamb. The trickle drawn forth from me had none of the serpent's flame or the radiance of Ra, I flew on the wings of no bird, but was dragged out of myself, and indeed, she pulled me forth, her hand plucking me up and down until the waters were lifted to the end of my belly and beyond. I knew what it was to come forth in fear. I did not even feel shame when we were done, but much relief. Soon I could be gone.

"She was not in the same haste, however, to see me leave. By my side, she gave a heavy sigh, heavy as the shadow of a large bird when it crosses your shadow, and said, 'I will lead you out to the tree.' But even as I was putting on my sandals, she took me in another direction, and we passed through a door into a room that had many odors from the powders of beasts and animals long dead, and in a corner by a niche was a small bowl of alabaster with oil in it, and a burning wick. By its light, she took three fingers of powder from a jar, stirred that in wine, drank half and gave me the other half. I knew a taste older than a coffin.

"She laughed at my face. It was a laugh loud enough to wake others, but she put a heavy hand on my shoulders, as if to tell me that her servants would not be surprised by any noise she might make in the night, and I knew, since she was speaking to me with barely a word, that the drink we had taken together was a bridge from her throat to mine. Over it would pass my thoughts. So I knew also that this room next to the chamber where she slept was her abode on any night when she could not close her eyes, and then, indeed, my nose told me as quickly of little sacrifices performed in here. I could see the altar, a table of granite, and sniff the old blood of many a small animal who had given up its last fears to her. Then I knew that even as I had lain in my bed and felt the beetle of Khepera stirring my bowels, so was the powder in this wine come from a beetle she had captured and dried (after its head had been removed). She must have pounded it, sifted it, then spoken the words of power. Now, together, we had drunk that wine, and that caused me to think again of our dung beetle. We are so in awe of its strength that we do not study its subtler habits. But I, as a boy, had spent many afternoons on the riverbank with no more for amusement than the beetle to watch, and I had seen them push the ball up the bank to the hole where they would bury it. That dung would serve as food for the eggs laid within. Yet if you confused two beetles and changed their balls, they still strained to the task and did it for the other's eggs. I tell you this because I understood, standing next to Honey-Ball, that she had been putting our purposes together and mixing our thoughts until Usermare would never envision us side by side. Before I left on this night, as if she would own more of me than He did, she cut off the ends of my fingernails with a sharp little knife, collected these parings and minced them small with her knife. Then she ate them in front of me. I did not know if I was with a woman, a Goddess, or a beast. 'If you are here for love of me,' she said, 'your hands will learn caresses. But if you were sent by Usermare, your fingers will share the pain of the leper before they fall off.' Again, she smiled at the expression on my face. 'Come,' she said, 'I trust you—a little bit,' and she kissed my lips. I say 'kiss' because that was the first night I could truly try it. I had known the secret whore of Kadesh and my woman in Eshuranib and many a peasant girl and I had known the sharing of our breath which is agreeable. Peasants tell each other, 'Nobles eat from plates of gold so they also know how to touch each other's mouth.' Here, she lay her lips on mine, and kept them there. I felt swathed like a mummy, only it was in wrapping of a cloth finer than I had ever felt. Her tongue was sweeter than any finger, and yet like a small sword when it pressed into my mouth. No, say it was like a little serpent that undulated in honey.

"'Come to me tomorrow night if He is not here,' she said, and led me to the tree. I had no sooner departed than my desire was back. Yet when I returned on the following night, I was weak again. Her hand, like the shaduf, was there to lift me above myself. Once more, I knew only the walls of her body, and could not enter her gates. But she was gentle on this second night and said, 'Come to me when you can, and on one good night, you will be as brave as Usermare Himself.' As if to speak of how many nights it might take to acquire such knowledge, she introduced me to her scorpions. She had seven: Tefen, Befen, Mestet and Mestetef, also Petet, Thetet and Metet—I could not believe that she knew them each by name, for in the box that was their nest they moved about like beggars who owe one another nothing. Yet she would lift them out with her fingers, and lay them on her eyes and lips and never fear any sting. 'Their names are the same as the seven scorpions of Isis,' she told me, 'and they are the true descendants.' By the light of her oil lamp I could see that these scorpions covered the seven gates of her head: her eyes, her ears, her nostrils and her mouth. But then she plucked them off, and put them back in their box and kissed me. She said that the ancestors of these seven scorpions had created our seven souls and spirits. Then she sent me home. My instruction had begun.

"Now, I was, as I say, the only man living in the Gardens who was not a eunuch. So I did not wish to think of the amusement that would be stirring in every house as these little queens, one by one, heard of my night with Usermare. I stayed behind the walls of my own garden and no longer went visiting through the day from one home to an-

other. Such visits had been most agreeable for the gossip they offered,
but then by way of the eunuchs, and the Chief Scribe of the Gardens,
also a eunuch—of whom I will tell you later—there was no story
about any Prince, Governor, High Priest, Royal Judge, Third Overseer to the Vizier, or even"—with a nod to my father—"Assistant to
the First Overseer of the Cosmetic Box, that did not come back to us
in the Gardens. I say to us, but the eunuchs knew the gossip first, the
little queens received it next, and I was lucky to hear it last. Even so,
I knew more of the good and bad fortune of everyone in Thebes than
in the old days when I was a charioteer galloping through the city. So,
it had been agreeable to visit the little queens, and eat their cakes,
smell their different perfumes, admire their faience, or their golden
bracelets, their necklaces, their furniture, their gowns, their children,
until all compliments given, we would come to our greater interest
which was gossip and I would hear much about many a Notable although by the end, they always spoke of Queen Nefertiri and Rama-
Nefru. The little queens had their preferences, of course, like schools
of priests who worship in different temples, so you could hear that
Rama-Nefru would only be the favorite for this season, or as easily
that She would be His beloved for many years. I soon saw that these
were only a reflection of stories the little queens told about each
other. For you could count on it. To listen to the tale of one was to
believe that another little queen had just lost favor.

"Thereby, I came to know quite a few of their secrets, and even
before I began to visit Honey-Ball at night, had an understanding of
her that came in part from her friends, as well as from little queens
who were not. Hearing two sides of the same story was like eating
two foods at once—together were they digested in the belly. Long
before I climbed over her tree, or heard Honey-Ball sing by the lake,
I knew of her loss. Indeed I could all but hear the echo. I had seen
men killed by the thousand and their bodies eaten, but that might
weigh less in the balance of Maat than the woe felt by these little
queens for the amputation of one toe. In the Gardens of the Secluded,
Honey-Ball had been His Favorite—on that, her friends and those
who did not like her were nearly ready to agree. She had not been fat

then, and even the eunuchs did not dare to look at her when she bathed, so voluptuous was her beauty. Ma-Khrut was her name for all occasions. But she was vain, vain even for a little queen, indeed after all I heard of good and bad about her, it became my conclusion. She was vain. So she traded to Heqat—the ugliest of the little queens!—a necklace that once belonged to Usermare's mother. Then she dared to tease our Pharaoh. She told Him she had exchanged the necklace for a bowl of alabaster, and could Sesusi find her another bowl to match? They were alone in her bed when she said this. He stood up, seized His knife, and holding her foot by the ankle, severed the toe. Merse-gert, that Goddess of Silence who never shut her mouth, told me that the screams of Ma-Khrut can still be heard over many a pond on a still night, and her enemies spoke of how she rushed to have the little toe wrapped, and then embalmed. Some said that after this night she was constant in her study of magic. She grew fat, and her garden sprouted rare herbs and rank ones, her rooms were filled with stuffs she col-lected. Where once she had had the finest alabaster of any little queen, now the bowls were chipped. There was much handling of the roots and skins and powders that moldered in them. Foul smokes were al-ways rising from the fire-pots in the chamber where she performed her ceremonies and you could sniff the dung of birds and lizards or snakes in cages of all sorts. Needless to say, she not only had names for these beasts, but also for various stones and branches she kept, not to speak of her wrappings of spiderweb, her spice, her herbs, her snake-skins, whole and minced, her jars of salt, her dried flowers, her per-fumes, her colored thread, her consecrated papyrus, and many jars of oil, native and foreign, some from plants and trees strange to me, some to be used beneath the light of the moon and others at the height of the sun. She knew the name of many a rare root of the fields that I had never seen before, and hair of all description, a curl from the brow of many a little queen, and more than a few of the eunuchs.

"Each morning she drew a new talisman for herself on papyrus purchased the day before by her most trusted eunuch, Kiki, which was the name for an oil made from the castor bean. It was a girl's name as well, although it did not matter—you could call a eunuch anything. Castor-Oil was just as good as the name of her second favorite, Sebek of Sais, so described for his mournful resemblance to the crocodile. The way those two eunuchs looked at each other while serving at her morning ceremony, you would have thought the crocodile had fear of being cooked in the castor-oil. Just so awesome was Honey-Ball. All the same, that woman could charm the snakes she kept, and by no more than the movements of her heavy arms—so much like large snakes themselves—or by her magic words. It was this last she employed to call spirits forth, since, as she would yet explain to me, no presence can resist its Secret Name—it hears it so seldom."

"I have heard many descriptions of these spirits about us," said Ptah-nem-hotep, "but you make them sound like strange birds or beasts."

"Ma-Khrut would often say that our thoughts, once they are mixed with the breath of the Gods, become creatures. They are invisible but they are still creatures. Some spirits even dwell together like birds of the same plumage or congregate to become as powerful as armies. They can gather in a mass like mountains, or great cities on the river."

"It is true," said Hathfertiti. "I have known emotions so powerful that they will live long after I am gone," and she looked at the Pharaoh with all the depth of her capacity to show such emotion.

"Yes," said Menenhetet, "it is not uncommon for those with strong feelings to create a few spirits. But once they are made, not many of us can call them back. That is because we do not know the Secret Name. Ma-Khrut, however, had a power to move spirits near and far and knew which substances to employ. She could choose, so to speak, between the blood of a bull and the blood of a frog. While it is royal, even divine, to hear someone else's thought on the moment it awakes in the other, Honey-Ball knew how to travel alone down those invisible rivers which are formed by the thoughts of us all. When I was a priest in my second life, I learned how to draw near to the vast force that rises to the heavens as soon as the servants of Amon, and the worshippers who attend the ceremony, contemplate the Hidden One together. As we travel along the waters of a common prayer, our thoughts are as alike as the little waves of the river. Priests, thereby, can serve as helmsmen to the vessel of their large congregation.

"Honey-Ball had no such congregation to draw upon. But she knew how to call separate spirits forth, and could coax them to draw up others. I say she worked harder than any priest."

"Tell us, then, of the wonders she performed," said Ptah-nem-hotep.

Menenhetet touched his head seven times to his hand. "I do not speak of the true wonders of an age that could know battles between Horus of the North and Horus of the South. No, I would tell You instead of the Gardens of the Secluded, and of her house and garden within. Not a large house by the measure of the Secluded, and outside the walls was the Palace and all the temples of Usermare.

"So, to take proper account of her work, one must measure it against the vast number of prayers the priests sent up. What a multitudinous river of spirits was kept flowing between Usermare and the glorious sun of Amon-Ra.

"Whereas Honey-Ball had only her own ceremonies. Yet these she would perform for all of a day and sometimes into the night. Sometimes when I visited at night she would be in the room where she kept her altar. Much time might go by in obedience to the purity of her ceremony before I could speak. All the while, she made no move that was not perfect, and if you ask me what I mean, I could not tell you, except that the triangle she would draw in the air with the tip of her wand proved to be no ordinary triangle, but before my eyes looked ready to blaze into flames. Her voice as she uttered her invocations had the tones of the opening and closing of doors, the fall of great stones upon the flat bed of other stones, the slithering of lizards and the flapping of wings when many birds spring up into the sky at once. The sigh of the wind came into her chest when she took a deep breath, and the roar of a lion was back of her throat as she spoke, yet all of this was but a natural part of her work, and she had many other tasks. There were the pots, for instance, on her altar fires and many ingredients to be fortified by words of power before being put into those pots. Sometimes, in preparation for a ceremony, she spent the day in reading from the rolls of papyrus that Castor-Oil or Crocodile brought back to her from the libraries of the temples, and she would copy passages onto her own papyrus. Of all the little queens, she was the only one who could write as well as a Chief Scribe, and sometimes I would pick up some of these old temple rolls and open them to their tiny painted birds and the papyrus would tell me much I could not name, so powerful were the thoughts contained.

"Watching her write, I would think of all the little scribes I had known who engaged in such tasks, and I would brood on the power of this act, and ask myself why such puny men were able to appeal so greatly to the Gods even though, when they spoke, they were never true-of-voice but frail as reeds, scratchy voices most of them. Yet the words they painted onto the papyrus were able to bring forth the power that rests in silence. So they could call on forces the true-of-voice would never reach. After all, to speak is to offend the power of silence.

"She respected that power. Once I saw two small lacerations on the inside of her upper arm, little cuts that ran in the same direction, side by side, but then she had sliced each cut in punishment upon herself for saying a word when she had vowed to be silent. On other days, she would speak, but never mention herself. If she wished to dine, she would tell the servants, 'Eating is begun.' She wished, when necessary, to live outside herself as if not in the room, move from her body to her Ka so that her Ka could walk out from her and look at her.

"That enabled her to work to many a purpose. Some were large, and some as petty as a ceremony to repay a small injury. She knew, as would everyone here, how to keep mosquitoes away, and was so adept at such practices that she never had to draw any circle about her head or recite appropriate prayers. Instead, at the first whine of such little beasts, she would raise her closed hand and open it. Away they would fly. You could hear the cry of their retreat."

"I have unguents so powerful in their odor that mosquitoes will never come near," said Hathfertiti, "and I use them when I cannot remember the prayer for the circle, or my fingers feel weak. I do not see where your Honey-Ball is more advanced than myself."

"Since she lost the favor of the King, and you may have gained it, there is much in what you say," replied my great-grandfather.

Ptah-nem-hotep was delighted. "Your family," He said to Hathfertiti, "is never without a reply. Nonetheless, I would be careful not to speak too poorly of this Ma-Khrut."

"The wisdom of the Ninth is great," replied Menenhetet. "For it is true. A little queen who had too cruel a word for Honey-Ball might as well have been stung by her scorpions. Since the Ka of Honey-Ball knew how to wander away from her body, she would on occasion even welcome an attack by many mosquitoes. How many times did I not see her sleeping helplessly on her bed, or so you would have declared, for that heavy body was covered with mosquitoes enough to kill another. Yet she was outside of herself. Afterward, on her return, she had the use of their venom in her veins. One little queen who had spoken ill of Honey-Ball was so bitten by the largest mosquitoes after such a night that she could not leave her house for days. That swollen were her features.

"It is a small story to tell of her powers. I would offer a better one. Each night that Usermare remained away from the Gardens, I would awake in the dark, and with the pig nuzzling at my desire, I would be drawn to the branch that carried me over her wall. With a good look to be certain no eunuchs were near, I would leap up from the land where I was Governor and drop over into that garden within the Gardens where so much grew that was strange, and I had no power. Each night I would hold her in my arms, but my sword was like a snake with a broken neck, and when she kissed me, I did not know how to live in the pulsing of her lips. The full weight of her mouth had the heaviness of honey poured upon itself.

"In such moments I could not taste the pleasure. Too full was my recollection of her face at the gates of Usermare. Warmth rose at the memory of her mouth on Him, and I was like a woman again, so rich was my pleasure, but nothing like a man—so little was I able to stir myself. And all this pleasure only turned around in me like oil that is never poured from a jar. I began to hate how clearly I could see her mouth on Him and even began to dislike her, that dull weight of her body, the odor beneath her arms as it came through the perfume. Like many another fat woman, it seeped out to the damp eaves.

"But on one night, after seven nights of failure, she said, 'You live in His wrath. I will make a boat to rise above Him.' Upon my closed eyelids, shut in weariness, and close to despair, she drew with her fingernail, lightly but firmly, the hull of a ship. In the darkness these lines were as clear to my closed eyes as fire. And as I saw each part of the ship, so did she say its customary name in her own voice, but reply with a whisper for the Secret Name. The sound of this second voice seemed to come out of the straining of the wood, the pull of the ropes, or the smack of the sail when the wind took it. I heard the groans of the oars in their locks, and did not dare open my eyes for fear I might lose the image of this vessel.

" 'I am the Keel,' she said, and in the other voice, replied: 'My Secret Name is Thigh of Isis.' Then the first voice said, 'I am the Rudder,' and the answer came: 'In my Name is Leg of the Nile.'

"The more closely I listened, the shorter became her speeches until she had to say no more than 'Oars' and the reply would come from the creaking of the boat itself: 'Fingers of Horus.'

"Soon, she was speaking only to one ear, and I was hearing the Secret in the other. 'Bow,' said she, and 'Chief of the Provinces' was the response. 'Sail,' she said. I heard the whisper: 'Sky.'

" 'Tying Post,' said Honey-Ball, which brought forth: 'Dweller in the Shrine.'

" 'Pump,' declared Honey-Ball, and then her own deep voice spoke out: 'The-Hand-of-Isis-wipes-away-the-blood-of-Horus.' With that, her hand took my poor dead snake and pumped it. Like a wind that touches the water as lightly as Your fingertips, so did the breath from her nose blow over the top of all she held in her hand, until at last she said, 'Mast,' and without moving, muttered, 'Bring-back-the-lady-before-she-leaves.' On those words, she put her mouth on the blunt head of my poor snake, but it was dead no longer and more like a wounded sword. Then as the boat moved forward in the water, so did her mouth ride up and down the waves, and I do not know if it was Ra I saw in my body, or the royal pleasure of Usermare, but she lay back, and pulled me over. It was so quick, I plunged. I even screamed. Fire and rocks threw me about, then cast me out of her as I came forth, but my boat flew over the edge of the sky. She was kissing my mouth. So I knew. My flesh had dared to enter where only a Pharaoh could dwell. I was still alive. So soon as Usermare read my thoughts, I would certainly be dead. Yet I had never taken a breath with such exaltation.

"But she drew the circle of Isis about my head—a double circle— and the gates to my mind were closed. 'Go,' she said, 'and come back tomorrow.'"

Four

"No risk in the Battle of Kadesh was ever the equal of this," said my great-grandfather, "for when the battle was over, it was done, but now I would be on guard every day of my life. No matter. I could not wait for the next night. Through all that morning, as I discharged the little duties that came my way, I was also possessed of a vigor which had me near to laying hands on several little queens. I felt as if I were still on the boat—or what was left of my boat!—and sailed with the sun.

"At evening, He arrived, so I could not see her. Usermare spent His time with other queens, but still I could hardly take the chance to visit Honey-Ball. His presence kept the eunuchs awake and stirring in every bush. Besides, the little queens were also listening to each sound. The night was like a dark ear. I could still have made the attempt, yet with Usermare only a house or two away, I might find myself as inert beside her as the heat of this darkness itself, and that shame I would not risk again. So, through the night, I had to hear His loud laugh, and the grunts that came from His throat. Like Ra, He was close to the beasts, and the Gardens were filled with the lion, the bull, the jackal, and the bark of the crocodile, even the high cry of a few birds and the cooing of a dove came from His throat. When I could not sleep, my pig came back again, and breathed on my groin.

"Next night, Usermare stayed away, and I was with Honey-Ball, and ready. So soon as we lay down, I was in her, so soon as she moved, I could not stop, and before her body was in a gallop, I had ridden through. This time it was I who heard the whimper, the cry, the small moan of rage, and the fall reverberating through her.

"Still, there was a difference most agreeable for me. Until this night, I had no more than to come forth and I was ready to flee her arms. Tonight, however, I wanted to do it again and, before long, did, and it was better. At last I could feel master of my feelings. The knowledge that her mouth was a slave to Usermare gave me sufficient disdain of her (and of myself) to remain within my bounds, and most nicely, able to rock back and forth as if lolling on a boat, even to take her hips through the pounding waves, indeed, took her on a voyage of both our bodies through the river of the night until the small stirrings of every caged animal in her garden became like the sounds on the riverbanks, and even the mice in fascination ceased running through the cracks in the walls. I tried this art of kissing at which she was adept, and although she was but a few days removed from the taste of Usermare's parts (which gave me a great revulsion insofar as He was a man) still He was also a God and nothing may issue from a God that is not fit for a feast, indeed it used to be said that our flesh is formed from Amon's leavings, and perfume is the sweet smell of His corruption. So I was able then to keep turning between admiration and disdain, bringing myself back each time I was ready to go forth, and we galloped at the end in equal bounds, throwing each other about, and afterward felt true repose in the circle of our arms around each other, the little pig at me again, but most tenderly.

"From that night on, I could speak of a sweeter warmth. For I thought she was beautiful. Even the great weight of her hips spoke of the power of large beasts, and her waist had the vigor of a tree. I adored her back. It was strong and full of the wonderful muscle I used to feel in the haunches of Hera-Ra, and her arms were like the thighs of young girls and led me to her mouth which was honeyed. Honey-

Ball's thighs when I took them in each of my arms were as full of satisfaction as the waists of two young girls I might hold at once.

"Each time, then, I knew her better, and thereby underwent more misery on those evenings when Usermare came to visit. One night when He chose Honey-Ball in company with several little queens, the sounds of their pleasure so disturbed me that I came near to bursting in. Such an end would have been peaceful compared to the cruel state of listening. For I was crawling with ants in the hot baked desert of my heart.

"On the next evening, He was there again, but I could recognize the little queens' voices and He had not chosen her. Uncertain whether to be pleased, or to despise her lack of charms to capture Him a second time, I overcame all caution, climbed her wall, entered her bed, and knew jealousy when she spoke. She told me she had been witness to all He did last night, yet entered none of it. When He asked why she stood before Him in such chastity, she said that she had been communing with demons in preparation for a holy ceremony, and wished to avoid the risk of attaching these unseen ogres—who might be near—to His divine flesh. When He asked the purpose of her ceremony, she replied that it was for the Life-Health-Strength of the Two-Lands. At which He grunted and said, 'You could have chosen a better day,' but asked no more.

"That was the story she told. I did not believe it. The night before, in my suffering, I had heard her laugh many times. Besides, Usermare had small patience toward anyone who could not please Him. When I was ready to tell her so, she put her fingers to my lips (though I promise you, we were speaking in tones next to silence itself) and whispered, 'I said that if I did not touch His flesh on this night, I would be twice full of Him as a result.' Honey-Ball giggled in the darkness. Although she had made the double circle of Isis about us many a time so that not one fleeting thought could depart into any-one else's thought, still she did it again to protect us for laughing at Him. 'What did He say?' I asked.

" 'Oh,' said she, 'He told me He would pay double attention when next He looked at me,' and with a bawdy grin, she spoke in the language of the streets, her mouth in my ear. 'He said that since He was Lord of the Two-Lands and twice King of Egypt, He would have me by my cunt and my asshole.'

" 'And what did you say?' I whispered.

" 'Great Two-House, it will take all of us to kiss You clean.' He started laughing so hard He never stopped. It almost ruined His pleasure. That is the only way to speak to Him.'

" 'Will you do that?' I asked.

" 'I will do my best to avoid it,' she said, but with the same bawdy mirth on her mouth. I was tempted to strike her, but instead, I seized her foot.

"Now, no matter how else we held each other, she had never let me near them. They were tiny for so big a woman, that much I could see, tiny like the feet of her mother, reputed to be the most elegant among the rich and noble ladies of Sais, and delicate in her size. Honey-Ball told me that was the mark of a noble family, small feet, and when I asked why such delicacy was of importance, she looked at me with scorn. 'If our hair is able to feel the whisper of the wind, we can have thoughts as delicate as birds.' 'Yes,' I replied, 'but by the balance of Maat, our feet should be sturdy like the earth.' She laughed. 'Spoken like a peasant!' she said, and laughed again and opened the circle of her thumb and forefinger so that I could enter her thoughts. I now saw myself jiggling like a doll at the tip of Usermare's sword. That made me angry enough to strike her, but I did not. She would never let me enter into her mind again. 'Sweet Kazama,' she said, 'the deepest thoughts are held by the earth. Through our toes—if they are fine enough—enter the cries from the Land of the Dead.'

"Simple enough. A good reason for delicate feet. So I would never have touched them, if she had not mocked me again with her laughter. But that puppet who moaned and whimpered and jiggled on Usermare's hook—I saw Him in the mirth of her mouth, and seized her foot.

"By the way she fought back, I knew at once I had committed some terrible act. But I was too busy wrestling to understand in all this silent fury (for we did not make enough commotion to wake one

servant) that the foot I had grasped was the one with the missing toe.
Then, since I held it with both hands, and she was kicking at my wrist
and head with the other leg, it was all I could do to explore the poor
missing place where the little toe had been, now as shiny to the tips of
my fingers as the amputated nub on the wrist of a thief, yet so soon as
I truly held it, I knew this rape was the only true seduction I would
ever have of her, and feeling by now strong as a tree myself, I merely
offered my skull to each of her kicks, while deliberately kissing this
shiny little place. But my head was ringing so much from these blows
of her leg that I saw her family pass before me in a noble boat, a golden
panoply on the broad waters of the Delta, and then her fight was
gone, and Honey-Ball burst into tears. Her sobbing became the loudest sound of the night in all these gardens, and it was as soothing to
the heavy silence as the washing past of waters, for where was the
house with a little queen who had not wept? Usermare would never
be concerned with such a sound. Honey-Ball's body became soft
again, and I lay holding my captive foot and imbibed all the sorrow
that came up from it, even the odor of the little caverns between her
toes was sad, and so I knew with what misery she lived, and rose up at
last and kissed her on the mouth to taste the same sorrow, ah, there
was a feeling of tenderness in my chest such as I had never known
before.

"From that hour I began to see her as a sister. We had a saying in
my village. 'You can sleep in a woman's bed for a hundred years, but
you will never know her heart until you care for her as a sister.' I
never liked that belief, I find no pleasure in sentiments that take care
of matters forever, but now I believed I understood why Honey-Ball
had grown so fat. One had only to touch the stump of her little toe,
as I alone had done, to feel the loss within her—the nub of that toe
was like a rock in a silent sea, and I could feel her thoughts beat upon
it. So I came to learn how her feelings toward Usermare might have
only a little love to mix with a hatred larger than mine. Holding her
as she wept, her heart spoke to me, and we were of the same family—
you could not find another man and woman in all of the Gardens or
the Court as consumed as ourselves with the heat of revenge. It took

two of us even to confess the one thought, and we did it with our breath, no other sound. Even from far away, His ears were as alive as the net to the bird, and you never knew when His nose might point toward an enemy so unwise as to say a curse aloud. Now, with the wisdom of my four lives, I can wonder at our audacity to share such dreams of revenge—why, if not for the circle of protection she put about our hearts, I think even the birds would have feared to stir."

"Yet, to me, her unhappiness seems excessive," Hathfertiti now said in a voice of much authority. "Surely she was a spoiled woman to have carried on so."

"In all deference to your understanding, my granddaughter, I would say that I have not yet told you all of her reasons. This punishment, petty to you, was nonetheless so painful to Honey-Ball that it changed her life and doubled her weight. When Usermare took out His short knife, grasped her foot—which is why, I expect, she fought so furiously when I seized it myself—and promptly took away the toe with one stroke of His blade, He then handed that bloody little half-worm back. They say she screamed and fled, all true as she told me, but she also embalmed the toe in natron for seventy days and kept it in a small gold case somewhat in the shape of a sarcophagus. That is the act of a woman who puts immense value on herself, but you must understand that to her family she was not a little queen, but a Queen. Her mother used to say: 'After Nefertiri, comes Ma-Khrut.' It was never true, of course, yet to the eyes of her family, it was. So the insult to her foot disturbed the heavens. So she saw it, and so she ate of many rare and prodigious fats, of swans, of large snakes, and of domestic boars to draw faraway spirits to her."

"I still say: For the loss of a toe, she gave up her figure?" my mother persisted.

"She used to say," said my great-grandfather, "that it was in obedience to Maat. Having gained many powers by the care she gave to this lost toe, she was now obliged to carry them. A larger house for a larger treasure. So she would explain herself to me, but I would say she felt most vulnerable. It is no small matter to descend the royal steps from First Favorite of the little queens to a woman whose name

He speaks twice a year. Like a mummy I think she had to cover herself with three coffins.

"Besides, she had brought great dishonor upon her family. In Sais, she told me, the good families gossiped so much about her loss, that one of her sisters, engaged to a young noble, received word most suddenly that the suitor would now marry into another family. Honey-Ball sighed as she said, 'They might as well have buried me in a sheepskin.'

"Now, in these days, she began to speak of what could prove to be another humiliation. She did not know if she would be invited to the Grand Councils. I did not see why this evening should have so royal a name, but, still, it was Usermare's habit to give one small entertainment a year for a few of the little queens in His Palace, at least, in the part we used to call the Little Palace. He would even invite some of the nobles of Thebes. As evenings went—I knew, since I used to attend when I was a General, that the occasion would prove no great affair—a small feast, and singers and dancers. Yet for the little queens chosen, it was a rare opportunity to come out of the Gardens.

"Since there had not been a Grand Council in the last two years, gaiety stirred. Many little queens had hopes. So, too, did Honey-Ball. She even cast a few small spells, although the smoke had been too thick, she told me, and her thoughts too scattered. Her most powerful spirits were not appearing to her summons. She would never be invited, she said. 'I do not know if I wish to be,' she added bitterly. Of course, I did not believe her. It meant much to her. The last time, three years ago, still slender, still possessed of all her toes, she had been the first of ten little queens to be presented to Nefertiri, and the Queen asked her to sit nearby. Nefertiri even had a word for Ma-Khrut's voice. 'They say your throat is so sweet it encourages others to sing,' the Queen had remarked. I wondered at these words, but Honey-Ball saw it as a grand evening.

"Now, when we learned who would be invited this year, I knew the blow to her heart. 'It is a small matter,' Honey-Ball said, 'and yet the pain is not small.' I felt her true woe. In this year with the Festival of Festivals approaching to celebrate the Thirty-Fifth Year of His

Reign (and who among us did not know it was going to be the largest festival in anyone's memory?) some little queens, of whom Honey-Ball was most certainly one, had needed an invitation to the Grand Councils to make certain that one would not be passed over at the Festival of Festivals.

"I must say her fear of missing this far greater occasion was not without basis. Most of the little queens would be able to leave the Gardens each day to mingle with many nobles in the newly built Hall of King Unas, or in the Great Court—a rare occasion for a little queen to invite her parents to Thebes. It all depended, however, on being one of the mothers of His children. His sons and daughters would be present to see their Father in His Godly Triumph. On the consequence, there being a great many such children, any little queen who had not borne His child could not with any confidence expect to be invited. Hence the Grand Councils might open the way. Honey-Ball's dejection was deep.

"I think it was the failure of her magic that hurt her so. With our growing familiarity, she had become more modest and did not always seek to display her powers, indeed, there were nights when she was my sister, and spoke of small pains and miserable little sorrows. So I began to hear from her lips the old saying one heard often in Thebes about people in the Delta: 'Those who inhabit the swamps, know not.' The meaning had always been so obvious that I never questioned its truth—to live in the swamps was to be wet, pestered with insects, and weak with heat. Everything grew too easily. The balance of Maat was missing. One lived in stupor and knew not.

"'It is true,' said Honey-Ball. 'It is true except for those about whom it is not true.' And she went on to tell me how her family, of twenty generations in the city of Sais, had had the pride to overcome the apathy of their swamp country. 'Our desire,' she said, 'is to stand in balance to our neighbors who know not.' Then I would be obliged to listen as she pondered the depth of the Nile and the height of the stars, the Gods of the deep water in the river channels, and the Gods of the shallows near the banks, the warnings of the stars whose eyes never closed, and the stars who blinked. How it annoyed her that I

did not even know the month of my birth. She would unroll a papyrus to show me charts that could measure the date of one's death by
the hour one was born. 'How long will you live?' I asked her, and she
replied, 'For many years. My life is long.' Then she sighed and said,
'But I will lose more than my little toe, and soon enough. So say the
stars.' Her sigh was heavy.

"Even after the Grand Councils were past, and I could assure her
that it was not a grand affair, and neither Queen Nefertiri nor Queen
Rama-Nefru had even been present, Honey-Ball's spirits did not improve. For Oasis and Mersegert spoke of it as full of light and wonder,
and said they received many attentions. Honey-Ball said, 'Sesusi does
not value me because I am from Sais.' The pit of this drear mood was
that in the last few days, to avenge herself against Usermare's indifference, she had given much to her rites, and received little. Each night,
she had performed a ritual to turn-the-head-of-Usermare, and had
cried forth the names of Gods Who had much weight, her voice quivering with exaltation. But next day, the sum of all she had exhausted
in herself, was most visible on her face.

"I began to ask myself how any magician could turn His neck?
Usermare was able to call on a thousand Gods and Goddesses: He had
a myriad above, and now, after His marriage to Rama-Nefru, a Hittite myriad of Gods below.

"Yet, each night, as I lay beside her, much as if her magic was able
to turn my neck far better than our Pharaoh's, I was not bored with
her unhappy moods, and loved her. We could each drink in the other's sorrow. I would lie beside her, my face between her breasts, and
steep myself in the solemnity and deep resolve of her heart until I did
not think she was silly for suffering over the Grand Councils, but
understood that she saw it as one more injury to her family. It would
be a true misery if she could not invite them to the Festival of Festivals. I was coming to understand that this family was raised higher in
her heart than Usermare. In her two great breasts lived all that she
would cherish, her father, her mother, her sisters, and myself. Feeling
myself in her flesh, I thought that if she was slow to stir, and I might
never again enjoy the liveliness and wickedness and love of the dance

that women with pert breasts might bring to bed, that could not weigh against our sweet deep silence, its warning in one's flesh that the love I would find in this massive bosom would not be small nor soon pass. Listening to the secret intentions of her heart as its beat came to me out of the depth of her flesh, I knew she had decided against all caution to trust me—which could only mean that she must work her spells from out of my heart as well as her own, bind us so closely that an error in the magic I learned could cause a great rent in hers. So I also knew that if I did not stand up straight away in the dark and leave her room, never to be alone with her again, I would lose the power to command what was left of my will. Yet so strong was the power of her heart that I felt no panic to move, and indeed, was a slave already, and close to her.

"That night she initiated me, and I took my first step toward Horus of the North. Of course, these matters are full of treachery and peril. Now, looking upon the result, I do not know if I was set properly on my way to the power and wisdom of a magician."

Five

"In that square chamber which held her altar, there were no windows. The ceiling was as high as the floor was long. In the center, she had had inlaid on the stone, a broad circle in a narrow band of lapis-lazuli, while against all four walls, low tables of ebony held her boxes, and high chests her costumes. Other than the door, the only opening was a wind-catcher on the roof into which smoke from the altar could rise.

"On the night she initiated me, I remember every act, but I will not relate it now in the exact order for fear it could be abused. I know that You, Good and Great God, may not be pleased if I fail to tell You all that is true, and in its proper place, yet there is no truth in a magical ceremony but for the performing of it. Even as I have trusted You, and confessed to matters that no one in my fourth life has known before, so must You now trust me and know that in all I say, my first desire is to safeguard Your Throne and the Two-Lands upon which it sits."

Ptah-nem-hotep inclined His head. "Your words are polite but have a rude edge, for they assume that we are equal and must trust each other, whereas you know better. It is for you to trust Me. However, I will listen to the way you tell it and may ask for no more. The magic I seek is of a higher nature than the one you now relate. To the measure that you bring the secrets of the past forward into My thoughts (so that the past lives in My limbs like My own blood) you will have performed an honorable work of the highest magic. I do not object at this moment, therefore, if you conceal the exact order of your ceremony of initiation."

Menenhetet touched his forehead seven times. "I thank the great wisdom of Your mind," he said. "This much is safe to tell: Honey-Ball had purified her circle of lapis-lazuli with many preparatory rites, and invoked friendly Gods to be our witness (although some had names I never heard before). Then, before we began, she asked, 'Are you ready to join my Temple?' When I said yes, I could feel a swelling in my chest larger than the clamor of battle, so she asked again, and once more, and after listening carefully, as if the beating of my heart could tell her more than my voice, she said at last to her Gods, 'He was asked three questions, and three times he knew the same answer.'

"Now we stood within the circle of lapis-lazuli and she blessed my naked body in an order that was most precise. This I also tell: She passed incense by my navel and my forehead, by my feet and my throat, by my knees and my chest, and gave a last pass to the hair of my groin. Then she anointed the same seven places with drops of water, with pinches of salt, by the flame of a candle that she brought near enough to warm me, and last with drops of oil. I was now blessed and prepared.

"From the altar she took a knife with a fine white marble handle and a point so sharp your eye would bleed if you continued to look at it. Now she removed her gown of white and stood before me naked as myself. With this knife, she pricked me on the belly just below my navel, and mixed my blood with hers, for she did the same thing to herself, and in the same place. From there, she repeated each step of the blessing, taking a drop of blood from my forehead and hers, from my big toe and hers, out of my right breast and hers, and a drop of blood from each of us just above the hairs of the groin. And each drop of blood clung like a tear to the point of the knife until it was brought to the same spot on her body so that when we were done, our blood was mixed in these seven abodes and we stood together by the altar, grave, naked, and equally marked.

"Now, I was ready for the consecration to her Temple. Within the circle, with only a burning wick in a saucer of oil for illumination, she had me lie down on the stone, raised high a scourge, and struck me twice, four times, then fourteen times.

"I had been whipped often as a boy. I had been left to crawl away and look for mud to staunch the bleeding. In my first life, no matter how high my rank, nobody could ever have mistaken me for a noble—I had too many welts on my back. A whipping had no strange taste for me. Yet to be scourged by Honey-Ball was unlike other lashings. She laid on the strokes with a lightness of touch that carried far. If you were to toss a pebble into a pond and succeed on your next attempt to drop a second pebble into the center of the first circle, and at just the right instant (so that you would create no confusion on the going-out of the wave but would deepen the ripple) then you would be close to Honey-Ball's art. Pain permeated me in the way that scented oil will reach into every corner of the cloth. On other nights, she had taught me much about how to kiss, and I lived in the wealth of such embraces, and knew why kissing was a sport for nobles: Now, I came to pass through the vales of the scourge. A vertigo close to intoxication came into my thoughts, which is to say I passed into an adoration of my own pain, for I felt as if it purified me of all disgrace. While I could nearly not endure it, and might have leaped into the sky out of the very torture of the touch of the flail, a tenderness nonetheless came from her. How can I explain such a clash of sentiments? Let me say she laid on the scourge with perfect strokes, once to the cheek of each bare buttock, then twice to each buttock, then once to all the fourteen aching parts of the body of Osiris that for all I knew was now my own as much as it belonged to the God. She scourged me once upon my face with my eyes closed, and once with my eyes open, once to each of the soles of my feet, upon each of my arms, and each of my fists, on my back, and on my belly, on my chest

and my neck. At the last it was once upon my testicles and once like a
snake did the scourge whip around my limp worm. High in clouds of
fire I even listened while Ma-Khrut recited in the clearest voice after
each slash, 'I consecrate you with oil,' and oil she laid on every one of
those flames from the fourteen strokes of the scourge until the fires
cooled and were more like the warmth of my own body. Then she
said, 'I consecrate you with wine,' and brought the astringent of wine
to the fourteen flames, and my skin shrieked again. To which she
bathed me lightly in cool water until the steam rose out of my heart
from the quieting of the blaze, and said, 'I consecrate you with fire,'
but she merely passed the smoke of the incense bowl by each sore
place. Then she said at last, 'I consecrate you with my lips,' and kissed
me on the brow with my eyes open and again with my eyes closed,
kissed me on each of the soles of my feet and on the large muscle in
the crook of each arm, kissed the knuckles of my fists, and my back,
and my belly, my chest, my neck, and then finished by licking me
long around the circle of my testicles, and most gently on the head of
my sword which rose out of the soft swamp of my loins until it was as
mighty as a crocodile. Then she said, 'I make you First Priest of the
Temple of Ma-Khrut Who Dwells in Osiris. Vow that you will be
loyal, vow that you will serve,' and when I cried out that I would (for
this was the last of fourteen vows she had demanded through each of
my fourteen parts) why then she lowered herself upon me like a wondrous temple of sweet shuddering flesh, and whispered my Secret
Name, and with a welling-up of every one of the fourteen oases
where I had swallowed the sweats of pain, my river came forth in
flood.

"That was the end of the rite but only the beginning of the pleasures of that night. Now, it was I who scourged her buttocks, and
they were as large as the moon and as red as the sun by the time I
finished, and I say it, I learned the art of the stroke, for it was not my
arm that held the scourge, but her heart drawing it in upon herself,
so that I felt as if I were beating upon the swell of her heart itself, and
then to my astonishment and to my horror, since I had never done
this for anyone before (not even for Usermare) I grasped those great

mounds of her much-whipped buttocks, and put my face into the fold of her true seat, and with a mighty voracity kissed her in the place where all that is soon to die is most redolent. And what with all these exertions, she smelled stronger than any horse. She did the same to me, and we rolled about with our faces buried in the ends of each other, and were married by this ceremony, and would never be the same. Then she gave so many kisses to the gates of my buttocks that by way of her caresses, I came to feel like a Pharaoh lying on His back, and did not know whether to claim I was the husband or wife of all Egypt. Carried on such lovely currents, I could feel again how there were purposes of which she did not speak, and I was becoming the servant of her vast intentions.

"I use the word *vast,* and it is proper. In nights to follow I could lie beside her as happy as a man asleep on a boat, yet dreams would stir in those great breasts that left our boat on a ledge of the highest cliffs, and we would come awake, clinging to the rock. For I knew the intent of our magic—it was our magic now—could be no less than to take away the strength of Usermare, and often when I looked at her face I would see the fine intelligence that lives in the eyes of that most austere God, Osiris, and that would make me feel much like Horus of the North. Indeed, staring into one another's eyes (and like Queen Hat-shep-sut, she would often wear a long and narrow chin-beard) Ma-Khrut had all the bearing of the Lord Osiris."

"What," asked Ptah-nem-hotep, "was your Secret Name?"

"I did not expect my great-grandfather to be quick to give this answer, yet to my surprise he did. "Why," he said, "it was 'He-who-will-help-to-turn-the-neck-of-Usermare,' and the name soon rebounded on me. I had to give it up."

"And you will tell us of that?"

"I will. But later if I may. Indeed I knew it was a dangerous name. However, she was most frank about that. If I was to be the great servant of her magic, I must be ready to die. That she told me often, and always added, 'But no longer like a peasant.' No, now I must learn to die in the full regalia of embalming. Like the art of learning to kiss, death belonged to nobles. I used to laugh at her. I need this strengthening of the will?—I, who had looked at a thousand axes—but she knew better. She understood, as I would soon, that to die peacefully can be the most perilous way of all, since one must then be ready for the journey through Khert-Neter.

"Over and over, she wished to assure me that no servant of her body and heart, certainly not I, would lose Ma-Khrut's protection. Neither in this world nor in the next. I told her that in my boyhood, in my village, we knew it was only nobles and the very wealthy who could travel in the Land of the Dead with any hope of reaching the Blessed Fields. For a poor peasant, the serpents encountered were so large, the fires so hot, and the cataracts so precipitous that it was simple prudence not to try, indeed never to think of it. Easier to rest in a sandy grave. Of course, as I also began to remember, many of our village dead did not accept such a rest, and came back as ghosts. They would pass through the village at night and talk to us in our dreams until the burial practice in my region became so harsh as to cut off the head of a dead person and sever the feet. That way a ghost could not follow us. Sometimes, we would even bury the head between the knees and put a man's feet by his ears to confuse him altogether. She gave a silvery laugh when I told her this. The light of the moon was in the tenderness of her thoughts, whatever they were.

"It was then she rose from our bed, and picked up a sarcophagus no longer than my finger, yet Ma-Khrut's face and figure were painted upon the lid. Within was a mummy the size of a short caterpillar, so carefully wrapped in fine linen that it needed no resin, indeed, its touch was as agreeable as the petal of a rose. I was holding the carefully embalmed mummy of her little toe. Yet before I could so much as decide whether it was of great value, or disagreeable to behold, she began to speak of the travels of her little toe through the gates and fiery courses of Khert-Neter, and when I babbled that I did not know how any part of the body, much less a toe, could travel by itself, she gave her silvery laugh once more. 'By way of a ceremony known only in my nome,' she said. 'Sometimes those who are from Sais do not know so little,' and she laughed again. 'My family had the Ka of this toe betrothed to the Ka of a fat and wealthy merchant from Sais. Yes, they even provided him with the appropriate rolls of papyrus.' I knew her well enough to understand she was serious, and at last she told me the tale. On receipt of a letter from her mother, Honey-Ball learned that this merchant died on the same night she lost her toe. So, even as her toe was lying in its small bowl of natron, so was the merchant lying in his bath, and both of them to be steeped for seventy days. Messages were exchanged to make certain they were wrapped on the same afternoon, and installed in their separate sarcophagi, the large and the small, and both on the same evening, the toe in Thebes, the fat merchant in Sais ten days' travel away on the river, yet such is the natural indifference of the Ka to any measure of distance that her toe was ready to take the voyage to Khert-Neter with him.

"Then she spoke of how her mother had had to assist the fat man's family during the preparations. The widow was instructed in which kind of shabti dolls to order, and who were the best craftsmen on the Delta. 'A shabti doll may weigh no more than your hand, but it has to stand properly on its wooden boat. This poor woman didn't even know where to place the dolls once he was in the tomb. It is terrible when a family makes its wealth so quickly that no knowledge adheres to the gold. They couldn't name which rolls of papyrus to buy. Nor did the widow understand that, no matter how much it cost, she was obliged to buy the Chapter-of the-Negative-Confession.'

"'The Chapter-of-the-Negative-Confession,' I repeated wisely, but Honey-Ball knew I was as ignorant as the fat man's family.

"'Yes,' she said, 'the widow complained about the cost. She was stingy! Finally my mother had to pay for it herself. She was not about to let the Ka of my little toe go wandering through Khert-Neter unless he had the Negative Confession. The night before the funeral, my mother had to hire two priests, and it took them until dawn to inscribe it properly on thrice-blessed papyrus. But now at least the merchant could show the Gods, the demons, and the beasts that he was a good man. This papyrus testified that he had never committed a sin. He had not killed any man or woman, nor stolen anything from any temple. He had violated none of the property of Amon. He had never uttered lies or curses, and no woman could declare he had committed

adultery with her, any more than a man could say he had made love
to other men. He had not lived with a heart full of rage, and he never
eavesdropped on neighbors. Neither had he stolen desirable land, nor
slandered anyone, and he did not make love to himself. He had never
refused to listen to the truth, and could swear that no water destined
to flow onto the property of others had been dammed up by him. He
never blasphemed. He had not even raised his voice. He had committed not a single one of the forty-two sins, not one. Most certainly he
had never worked any witchcraft against the King.'

"Now Honey-Ball laughed with as much pleasure in her voice as I
ever heard. 'Aiiigh, Kazama, what a foul man we helped! There was
no sin he did not commit. His reputation was so putrid that everybody in Sais called him Fekh-futi, although not to his face.'"

Both Hathfertiti and Nef-khep-aukhem stirred here at the sound
of this name, but neither said a word, and with hardly a pause, Menenhetet continued. "'Do you understand,' Honey-Ball said to me,
'the powers of this Negative Confession are so great that the Ka of my
toe is safe.' She nodded. 'In my dreams, that is what I am always told.
Fekh-futi thrives in the Land of the Dead, and my little toe beside
him.'

"'Thrives?' I said to her. I was much confused. The night before,
seeking to impress me with how much wisdom she had acquired from
these travels of her toe, she said that no priest could instruct me as
well in what to say to the fiery beasts and the keepers of the gates. She
not only knew the names of the serpents, but was familiar with the
apes and crocodiles on the banks of the Duad, and her Ka had spoken
to lions with teeth of flame, as well as to lynxes with claws like swords.
She could use the words of power to take you past lakes of burning oil
and had learned the herbs to eat when traveling through the quick-
sand in the darkness beyond each gate.

"Moreover, she could consecrate any amulet I might need in
Khert-Neter. The amulet of the heart, for example (which, properly
blessed, would offer new strength to my Ka) or the two gold fingers
(that would enable me to climb the ladder that ascends to heaven) she
even knew how to purify the amulet of the nine steps (that led to the

Throne of Osiris). Moreover, she was ready to paint onto papyrus the words of many a Chapter I would need, and began to tell me their separate titles: Of-Coming-Forth-by-Day and Of-Living-after-Death, the Chapter-of-Passing-over-the-Back-of-the-Serpent-Aapep, the Hymn of Praise for the West, the Chapter-of-Causing-a-Man-to-Remember-His-Name-in-the-Underworld, the Chapter-of-Repulsing-the-Crocodile, and the Chapter-of-Not-Allowing-the-Heart-of-a-Man-to-be-Carried-Away. I did not know if I could follow it all, there were so many: the Chapter-of-Living-upon-Air, and the Chapter-of-Not-Dying-a-Second-Time, the Chapter-of-Not-Eating-Filth, or, Holding-a-Sail (so that the vessel of one's Ka might be blown forward through the worst of the stink). There was the Chapter-of-Changing-into-a-Prince-among-the-Powers, Into-a-Lily, Into-a-Heron, Into-a-Ram. Nor was that all. There was the Chapter-of-Driving-Evil-Recollections-from-a-Man, or Of-Not-Allowing-the-Soul-to-be-Shut-In. Also the Chapter-of-Adoring-Osiris, and then there was a Recitation for the Waxing of the Moon. Each time I thought she had come to the end, she would remember another—the Chapter-of-Coming-Forth-from-the-Net, and the Book of Establishing the Back-Bone of Osiris. She spoke softly, but these names began to sound as loud in my mind as the cries of a vendor.

" 'You're equal to the Royal Library of Usermare,' I said.

" 'I would do all of this for you,' she told me. I could hear how much love was in her voice. She would, indeed, take true care of me in the Land of the Dead. She wished me to have no fear of that place. That way, I would have less terror in her ceremonies.

"I was now altogether confused. She had spoken of the need for me to have all these amulets and Chapters, yet with it all, Fekh-futi had still been given one little piece of papyrus full of lies, blessed by who knew which drunken priests fondling one another through the night.

" 'Oh,' she said, 'the thrice-blessed Negative Confession was not written for Fekh-futi alone. It is also for the Ka of my little toe.'

" 'Can you say that you have committed none of those forty-two sins?'

" 'The virtue of the papyrus is not to be found in its truth but in the power of the family who purchases it,' she admitted at last.

"Her words sat heavily on me. Ma-Khrut might claim to be able to do much for me, but the more likely truth was that we were both in peril.

"I told her this. I hardly had to. She knew my thoughts.

" 'We could be killed together.' She said this calmly, even as we lay side by side in her bed.

" 'Then why do you tell me the names of all these Chapters? You would not be left behind to write them for me.'

" 'That,' she said, 'is why you must commit the words to memory.'

" 'All of them?'

" 'It can be done.'

" 'You have done it,' I agreed.

"Ma-Khrut might know how to memorize the prayers she would need, but her memory was mightier than my muscles. I did not even feel the desire to try such feats. She might be as wise as the Royal Library, but she was also so stupid as not to know there was going to be no bath of natron for me. Usermare would cut me into forty-two pieces, and strew the parts."

It was at this point that my mother (whose thoughts had strayed into her own childhood) now asked, "Who is this Fekh-futi?"

Menenhetet, annoyed at the interruption, did not look back at her. "Not the same man," he said, "but another Fekh-futi in an earlier life, even as I am not who I was yesterday." With no more than that, he went on, "It was in this hour, I tell you, that I recollected the wisdom of the Hebrew, Nefesh-Besher. Maybe I, too, in my last breath, ought to leap out of myself into the belly of my woman and be born with a new body and a new life. But so soon as I had this thought, I wanted to return to my own bed. There I could draw a circle around my head forty-two times in order to keep such thoughts from traveling. Indeed, so soon as I left her side and was back in my own house, I began to drink from a jar of kolobi and soon swallowed all of it. The sad truth was that I did not know if I wished to end as a child in her belly.

Did I want to be the son of a woman who had tasted the leavings of another man?

"It was then I knew how much I was married to Honey-Ball, and how much I was oppressed by her. Even in my own room, I did not dare to have any thoughts. Saying this to myself, the near-empty jar of kolobi in my hands, feeling as drunk as the Good and Great God Usermare, I made the circle forty-two times about my head and fell away from vertigo. The trials and ambushes of the Land of the Dead had become as twisted in my mind as coils of entrails.

"When I awoke next morning in the stupors of kolobi, I turned over on my bed and said to myself, 'The evil spirits of the night are abroad.' For behind the protection of my forty-two circles, I still hated Honey-Ball, and was most happy with the few thoughts she could not reach.

"All this while, the cries of children playing outside my house were in my ears. How many there were! Retching over the ghost of the kolobi, I could hear (as I had never before) the sound of their games, larger even than the cries of the birds. These children's shouts flew in all directions. Now I heard them as they bathed in the pools and chased the geese, or climbed high in the trees to talk to the birds. Over my head came a gabble of nurses scolding, mothers scolding, long whimpers and every kind of laughter, all these children, every one, sons and daughters of Usermare. Watching these children, there were tears in my eyes. As strange and sweet as a fall of rain in a desert, I was remembering my daughter, born of Renpu-Rept, dead for so many years. I still supposed she would look like a child. Then I was moved by the thought that Honey-Ball was one of the few little queens who had not borne any of Usermare's children. Could it be that she was so rare as not to love His loins, and might in truth prefer mine? I felt close to my heart at this instant and could hate her no longer. She had been ready, after all, to die with me.

"So, if I had awakened with every oppression, now I could breathe again. My heart stirred at her generosity. It was as if I understood, and for the first time, how no one would provide for my future travels so well as this woman. It brought me to understand the true power of a family. As Ra had His godly boat for travel through the dark river of the Duad, so were a wife and children one's own golden vessel on such a trip. Honey-Ball and I had been wed by the secret ceremony of marriage—knowing each other's buttocks, we shared the property of our flesh. Now, I would have children with her. Yes, I told myself, we must escape from these Gardens. I, like Moses, would flee with her into the Eastern Desert. From there, we might travel to New Tyre. How, with her great knowledge, could we fail to prosper in such a curious city?"

On these words, Menenhetet looked up at my mother and at Ptah-nem-hotep to see whether they would agree with his rich belief in the virtue of marriage, but to his surprise, and to mine, for I had been listening only to my great-grandfather's voice, I could now witness that they were most certainly gone. During his talk, they had fled. My poor father was still asleep.

Six

Not only could I still feel my mother's presence, but she was not far away, and I knew our Pharaoh was with her. Since my great-grandfather, however, had no one now but myself to listen, he no longer offered his voice. Instead, his thoughts were given to the silence of the night, out to the Gods and spirits in the darkness beyond the light of the fireflies. I knew that in whatever room, or on whichever path of the garden my mother might be, the story of my great-grandfather and Honey-Ball was visiting her by every silent path of the night, by the scent of flowers and in the breeze through the palms. I even knew that as much as my mother had desired to leave, my great-grandfather was not that much displeased for he could still feel our Pharaoh's attention, quick with thirst to hear the story. Indeed, the night had never been more alert.

Once again I began to lose all sense of my own age, even as the echo of a sound may wonder whether it is the sound itself. So I sat in all the power of his silence, and heard the murmur of long-gone voices, even the whisper of little queens as they passed through the royal palms on their way to the lake, yet I felt so close to my great-grandfather while he sat staring silently at me, that his meditations

rose like water from a spring and I was wiser in knowledge than when
he spoke aloud, and saw him on the night he crossed the gardens to
ask Honey-Ball if she would flee with him to New Tyre. It was then
he remembered the story Heqat told of the ugly woman who kept her
husband free of every disease, and he laughed aloud. Honey-Ball's
face was beautiful as he held her, and her body was as great as the
wealth of Usermare, yet he knew she must be the ugly woman of
whom Heqat had spoken. He would never suffer any ill while he lived
with her, nor would their children. She would protect them all. So he
loved her for these riches, and when, late at night, he slipped back to
his own house, he could not sleep for the clarity of the sentiments he
felt. He could smell the keen air of every morning they would know
in the mountains on the long road from Megiddo to Tyre, and even
the perils appealed to him as pleasures. He could show Ma-Khrut the
resources of his courage once they were in the forests. More than ever
before, he felt bold as a God.

On the next night, therefore, in the sweet silence that followed
love, full of honor, and most content that they had embraced without
a ceremony of magic on this night nor the night before, but had come
forth in all the quiet yearning of a brother and sister, he held her face
between his hands, much aware of the great sky above her house
where the Gods might be listening, and whispered of how they would
yet be wed and live with many children. And as he spoke, he knew the
perils of the journey, for he perceived how much they would need
her magic to reach any other land.

She answered, "It is better here."

He had a clear view through her eyes of all she would give up: the
jars and boxes that held her amulets, her powders, and her animal
skins. She saw them as equal to a city, even as the fortress of her powers, but so soon as he was ready to tell her that she would have all of
that again in another place, she asked, "How dear will children be to
you?"

"We must have many."

"Then you do not want to run away with me," she said. Her eye
had no tears, and her voice no sorrow as she told the story, yet when

she finished, she began to weep. The child of Usermare had been in her belly, she said. And she had lost that child, her first child, on the night Usermare cut off her toe.

"I do not believe that," he said.

"It is true. I lost the child, and I lost what was in me to make other children." Her voice was as firm as the roots of the largest tree in the Gardens of the Secluded. "That," she said, "is the true reason I grew fat."

In the pain of listening to her, his thoughts ran past like riderless horses.

She got up from the bed and lit a pot of incense. With every smoke he took into his throat, he had the certainty that his life was shorter by each one of these scents, and the hour of his most unlucky hour was coming in, even as his breath was going out. On the inside of her belly would his last seed expire.

Unable to bear the misery of their silence, he began to make love to her again, but he felt thick with stupor. He might as well have been asleep in a swamp and lay beside her, wondering whether the power of the circle drawn forty-two times around his head might keep her from knowing how foul were the pits of his mood.

She did not speak, but upon them, sour as the odor of old blood, was the weight of her purposes. No love would ever be so near as the triumph of her craft. Lying silently by her side, he spent the night waiting for that hour before the dawn when he must leave. He did not wish to stay, but the depth of her thoughts (which he could not enter) lay upon him like the carcass of a beast, and indeed they passed the night like two much-wounded animals.

Yet, in the last interval before he left, she allowed him to come close once more to her thoughts. As a traveler on a barge can listen to the murmurings of the Nile and know the spirit of the water, so did he perceive that she was searching through her wisdom for a ritual that could strike Usermare with force.

Nor was he surprised in the morning when he returned to her house and saw, by the nature of her preparations, that she would make an Address to Isis.

Honey-Ball had spoken of how dangerous this ceremony could be. Her choice was as bold as his own plan to escape, and a breath of love returned. His daring might have inspired hers. So, Menenhetet refused all food offered to him this day, touching neither melon nor beans nor goose, and went early to the house of Honey-Ball. It was common for Menenhetet to take his dinner with one or another little queen, even a good omen. The appearance of the Governor might induce a visit by Sesusi Himself. On this evening, however, neither he nor Honey-Ball took more than a dish of cooked wheat on a plate made of papyrus. Then, in full view of her eunuchs, and of any little queens strolling by the house, he left. He even lingered in the lane outside her walls and spoke to other little queens and waited for the darkness. There would be no moon tonight, and a visit by Sesusi was unlikely. So soon as the eunuchs of Honey-Ball were dismissed, he came back over the wall.

Honey-Ball was wearing white sandals and a gown of transparent linen. Her perfume spoke of white roses and her breath was sweeter than her perfume. He wondered if it was the presence of Isis rising from the wheat they had eaten. Honey-Ball had a breath that could come forth like a blossom, or reek of foul curses, and on many a night, he knew the stench of the Duad. On this evening, however, her breath was calm, and the red amulet of Isis about her waist gave composure.

Now, she entered upon the invocation. Honey-Ball would call upon Isis in the voice of Seti the First. Ma-Khrut might be esteemed by many powers and spirits, but only a Pharaoh would be admitted to those elevations where Isis dwelled. Indeed, Honey-Ball had found a spell in the Royal Library of Usermare that would call forth the full powers of Isis if spoken by a dead Pharaoh. So she must summon such a Ka. Enveloped in His presence, she could speak like a King.

She stepped outside the circle, therefore, to remove her gown, and took out a white skirt, golden sandals, and a golden chestplate large enough to cover her breasts. Then, to the astonishment of Menenhetet, she opened another chest and withdrew a Double-Crown of fine stiff linen made, he realized, by her own hands, and it was more than a cubit in height. She placed this upon her head, with a chin-beard to her mouth, and by the time she stepped into the circle and laid the red amulet on the altar, her full mouth was now altered into the stern lips of Seti—at least as Menenhetet knew him by many a temple drawing.

Then in a voice of much authority she began the invocation that would bring the Ka of that Pharaoh forth.

While Menenhetet lay on his back, his head against the altar, and her foot upon his chest (so that he looked up at a body and face as fierce and massive as the great Pharaoh who had been the Father of Usermare) Honey-Ball began to recite a poem:

> "Four elements
> "In their scattered parts,
> "Will bring their hearts
> "To these events.
> "May the Ka of Seti come to birth,
> "May the Ka of Seti know our earth.
>
> "Air, water, earth, fire,
> "Seed, root, tree, fruit,
> "Breathe, drown, bury, birth,
> "Air, water, fire, earth,
> "O Seti, come to me."

She said it, and Menenhetet, lying beneath her, repeated it, their voices in unison, and the lines were said many times. As she spoke, she lay pinches of incense on the burning pots beside his body until the room was heavy with smoke, and the heat of her heart rose higher. Her voice moved through air so thick her breath shifted the smoke like clouds.

"O You," she said, "Who were the greatest of Pharaohs and the Father of the Great Usermare, and are twice the greatness of this Pharaoh, Your Son, Who is called Ramses the Great, know, then, the sound of my voice that calls to You for I am Ma-Khrut, the daughter of my father, Ahmose of Sais, who was born in Your Reign.

"Great Seti, Greatest of all Pharaohs, let Yourself be known by Your Power, by Your Rage, and by the Glories of Your Reign. For Your Son, Usermare-Setpenere, has torn down Your Temple in Thebes. He has turned to the wall all the great words that are spoken of His Father Seti. In these Temples, praise for His Father is silent. The stones have been choked. If You hear me, may Your First Ka descend upon me like a tent." She was silent. Then she said: "O Seti, come to me."

She spoke in the clear and perfect tongue of a Pharaoh, her left hand pointing out before her North to the altar, North to the lands of Sais on the Delta, and Menenhetet felt the Ka of the dead Monarch descend upon her like a tent of the lightest linen, and she-in-the-Ka-of-Seti stood with her foot upon him. He saw the green circle on the floor, and it burned with the red of the amulet on the altar. The cries of birds came across the silence of the sky from the time of Seti, and Menenhetet sat up so that the hand of the Father of Usermare could grasp his hair, and indeed his hair was seized, and he felt the great force of the Father of Usermare in the hand that was on his hair, and it lay like the weight of a bronze statue upon him.

Then Menenhetet heard the voice of the Ka of Seti speaking to Isis: "O Great Goddess," said this voice, "You are the mother of our grain, and the Lady of our bread. You are the Goddess of all that is Green. You govern all clouds, swamps, fields of wheat and every meadow of flowers. So, You are stronger than all the Temples of Amon." Now a mist arose from the altar, and a smell of the sweetness of the fields was in the air.

"Great Goddess, hear the shame of Seti the First. For His Son moves the stones of His Temple. The blocks of marble are turned. The glories of Seti are turned to the wall. What has been to the front is now to the back."

"It is true," said Menenhetet.

"Old odors stir from these stones. They speak from the earth that has buried them. Let these stones fall upon Ramses. Let His Heart be crushed by the stones of Seti."

Waves went out from the Ka of Seti and passed through Menenhetet. Waves went out through the wind and through the water,
waves of flame, and great contortions of the flesh, and all of it was in
the hand above his head.

"Your mouth commands Ra. The Moon is Your Temple. All
mountains come down to You."

On the altar, the amulet was glowing with a molten light white as
the fires of metal. Now, Menenhetet could not breathe. The altar
trembled and tottered and crashed like the stones of the temple of
Seti. The cry of a captured bird shrieked in his ears. Now, Menenhetet was shaken by a great fury and the Ka of Seti passed from her to
him, even as the altar had fallen, and although he had been told by
every one of her instructions that he must remain motionless at the
end to aid her in thanking Isis (and thereby assisting Her departure)
and then must stand up to thank the Ka of Seti, Menenhetet made a
sound instead like a beast, and the Ka of Seti that was in him became
as fierce as a wild boar. There, beside the shattered altar, he mounted
Honey-Ball and made love as he never had before, and she was sweet
beneath him even as Menenhetet came forth in a voice loud enough
to wake Horus of the South (so that in the morning, more than one
little queen would say the serpent of all evil must have traversed the
Gardens last night) and Menenhetet knew that the hands of the thousand and one Gods Who surrounded Usermare were no longer joined.
For in the sound of his own great roar was the voice of Seti thundering in wrath at the overturning of the stones in His Temple, and again
Menenhetet made love in a fury to Ma-Khrut, and turned her about
so as to know her by each mouth, the Mouth of her Flower, the
Mouth of her Fish, the Mouth of the Pit, and gave both of his two
mouths to her so that she knew him well. Beyond the walls of the
Secluded, in the great plazas and gardens of the High Palace and the
Little Palace, out to the city of Thebes itself, and down to the river,
he could feel the wrath of Seti enter the mutilated stones of the new
temples, and Menenhetet knew that Usermare was disturbed in His
calm, like the water of the sea before a storm.

Yet when all was done, Honey-Ball said, "I do not know what happened. The Ka of Seti the First was not supposed to pass from me to you."

Through the night, she was much agitated by the unforeseen turn of the ceremony and greatly depressed through all of the following morning.

Seven

By the next evening, however, there was no one in the Gardens who had not heard what had come upon the Pharaoh. Visiting the Palace of Nefertiri in the middle of the day, He had been eating with His Queen when a butler spilled on Him a bowl of steaming soup. The servant fled to the kitchen pursued by the King's Guard who, hearing the Pharaoh's roars of pain, proceeded to beat the poor steward so brutally that he died before the sun went down. Among the Secluded, there was no end of talking on this matter, and Honey-Ball laughed with the sweetest gaiety Menenhetet had heard in her voice for many weeks. "The powers of Isis work directly," she said.

Not two days after the accident, Usermare commissioned the writing of a great number of papyri with magic words until not even the Royal Scribes could make a count on how many amulets were being prepared.

Menenhetet, at the prompting of Honey-Ball, took one of his rare trips out of the Gardens and went to visit the great chamber where the Scribes of the Court were at work. Five hundred sat with their palettes and paint-boxes writing letters to brother-scribes of the Temples, of the House of Gold, the House of Grain, of the Troops, scribes of the Law Courts, scribes, when you came to count them, of every royal purpose in every province of the kingdom, the great chamber like a temple itself, for there were no walls, only a roof, and many pillars, and the scribes not only worked, but went back and forth to gossip with each other until Menenhetet began to see much in their activity that was like the flurry of birds carrying messages to the Gods and beasts as they flew between air and earth. How few in comparison were the thoughts of Ma-Khrut. Yet how powerful they had been!

On this day, gossiping with a few of the Chief Scribes, Menenhetet learned that the production of His Amulets was no longer sufficient to satisfy the Pharaoh. Much disruption had come upon the Scribes' Chamber. Many of them, accustomed to composing letters to officials in far-off nomes, were most uncomfortable with this new craft.

When Menenhetet told her, Honey-Ball laughed again. "The powers of Isis also work slowly," she said, and added that much in the mind of Usermare must be distraught. For the thought of unpracticed scribes making amulets was absurd. Exactitude of procedure was crucial to any papyrus being so prepared. No amulets were better than those they made in Sais where she had learned the art, and in that city they used to say one error in an amulet could taint twenty others. The scribes who had just been put into service were good only to keep inventory of cattle or tell you the number of geese sacrificed for a festival—they were *scribes*. She gave her giggle of derision—they were like monkeys to her, or eunuchs. If they could never speak the word that was silent, how could they make amulets?

Then Menenhetet told her of the exceptional story he had heard that afternoon. It came from Stet-Spet, known as Pepti, who, being the Scribe of the House of the Secluded, was also, of necessity, a eunuch, indeed the only scribe who was, and that made him an incomparable gossip. Having no children of their own to protect, eunuchs were always ready to talk about all forbidden things, but then, the same, he said to Honey-Ball, was true for scribes. Spending much of their lives in one room, scribes felt natural envy for those whose duties took them to lively places, and so talked about their betters prodigiously. What then, Honey-Ball agreed, could be said of a man who was both a eunuch and a scribe? They laughed together at this. Actually, they would not mock him to his face. Stet-Spet was no one to have for an enemy. Only a few years ago, he had been one of the lowest of the Royal Scribes of the Superintendent of Agriculture, yet his wish to rise out of the ranks had been so ardent that he asked for the operation that would make him a eunuch, and survived the purulence which followed upon wounds in such swamplike parts of the body. Menenhetet respected that. It was not easy for an Egyptian. They were less hardy than Nubians and not always able to endure the atrocious infection of castration. However, the opportunities to be a Chief Scribe had been so few, Stet-Spet once told him, that he rushed to request the operation so soon as he learned that the former Scribe of the Secluded, an aged and exceptional Nubian, had begun to show the final signs of going blind.

Now, Stet-Spet worked in the Gardens, which is to say he had the best task of all scribes. He ate at the homes of all the little queens and could have lolled in the harem more than he worked, but no detail of his office became too small for him. So he heard about every love of each little queen for another little queen, and even knew the pet names they gave each other. The women, in turn, had put on him a new name, Pepti, inasmuch as the old one, Stet-Spet, meant Trembling-Pole. If they even thought of his operation, they would titter too much when speaking to him. Of course, being a eunuch, yet feasting at so many homes, Pepti grew fat until he was as heavy as Honey-Ball. It was said that no two people equaled either of them in wisdom, but that of the two, Honey-Ball was wiser. Pepti's knowledge came to him by the nature of his task. Since no lady in these Gardens would ever fail to inform the Scribe of the Secluded that she had received the seed of Usermare on the night before (the date to be scrupulously set down in his records so that no question could arise of the time of conception) Pepti had a list of every little queen chosen by Usermare in the three years he had been Scribe to these Gardens. No little queen could rise or fall, therefore, in the esteem of the Pharaoh without Pepti's knowledge.

He also had heard what happened to Menenhetet in the House of Nubty. Pepti had it all by morning—aiiigh, Kazama! He had been told by Heqat and Honey-Ball before they even went to sleep, inasmuch as they were at his house to record the coming-forth in them of Usermare's seed. Of course, Pepti did not keep the story to himself, and a laughter cruel as the coils of a silver snake twisted through the Gardens. The eunuchs put a hand to their lips as they passed their Governor. Menenhetet would think of the Scribe of the Secluded telling this story, and see the fat belly shaking with mirth, yet he could not hate him with the burning light that is the foundation of revenge. Menenhetet knew the story would have been told no matter how. Besides, such stories quickly became old in the Gardens and rotted like fallen figs. Moreover, he did not dare to make an enemy of Pepti for then the Scribe might tell the eunuchs to spy on him. So, he kept his manner pleasant. For that matter, being the only high officials in the Gardens, they were obliged often to converse over the records. All purchases made in the market by eunuchs had to be marked by the Scribe and examined by the Governor.

Afterward, Pepti would gossip with Menenhetet. Pepti gossiped with all. A story not told was equal to food not eaten. So on this morning when Menenhetet passed through the Chamber of the Scribes and met the eunuch talking to old friends, he offered a ride in his chariot. Pepti, speaking just below the din of their clatter over the stones of the paved squares and the ruts of the dirt roads, was able to insinuate his voice between the cries of every merchant and worker in the market of Thebes, and so Menenhetet heard more about the bowl of soup. The meal, it seemed, had been spoiled from the onset, for Amen-khep-shu-ef had returned to Thebes that morning after a surprisingly quick and successful campaign in Libya. He had even been present with Nefertiri when Usermare entered, and then the Prince had sat close to His Father without proper invitation, and so disrupted the air that no one was wholly surprised when the bowl was overturned. Usermare even cursed His son for the burning sensation upon His chest and left, His skin beginning to blister beneath His gold and enameled chestplate. Without pause, He had crossed to the Palace of

Rama-Nefru. The Hittite was now certainly His favorite—so the Scribe assured Menenhetet. Several little queens had told Pepti that the name of Rama-Nefru was heard more often on His lips in the coming-forth than the name of His First Queen. Moreover, He had not spoken to Nefertiri since that night, nor the Queen to Him. Nefertiri had chosen to go into mourning for the servant who had been beaten to death. It seemed he had been with Her many years. Of course, it was a frightful rebuke to Usermare. And Amen-khep-shu-ef was most menacing with His presence these days.

Now, when told of this, Honey-Ball was much impressed that Usermare had been so deranged, and she spoke of summoning the Ka of Nefertiri's butler. When Menenhetet asked how the Ka of any servant could be of use in dealing with Usermare, Honey-Ball told him that sudden death, when unjust, gave much vigor to the Ka, no matter how common the person. So she would call on the servant.

But even as she was contemplating this, Menenhetet choked on a bone, and it lodged so deep in his throat that his eyes grew as large as eggs. Honey-Ball called at once for her servants, and Castor-Oil and Crocodile carried him into the middle of her circle of lapis-lazuli.

With no further preparation, Honey-Ball cried aloud, "O bone of the ox, rise out of his belly! Rise out of his heart! Rise out of his throat! Out of his throat, come to my hand. For my head reaches the sky, and my feet rest in the abyss. Bone of God, bone of man, bone of beast, come to my hand." The bone disgorged from his throat with his vomit, and he could breathe again, but Honey-Ball began to vomit as well. Gods Whose name she did not know had attacked the servant of her heart, Menenhetet.

Later that night, he felt strong enough to return to his home but when alone was miserable and decided to go back, yet, on the path, felt so weak that he could hardly climb the tree to her gardens, and once inside, found her morose and puffed up as if she had been weeping since his departure.

"My purposes have been twisted," she said. "I knew it on the night when the Ka of Seti passed over to you."

When Menenhetet spoke of his remorse at disobeying her instructions, she replied, "No, it is not your fault but mine. I forgot about the creature."

He had never spoken of the pig, although he always supposed it came from her. "Did you send it," he asked, "so that I would come to you?"

She nodded. She sighed. "He does not belong entirely to me. He was also fashioned from the evil thoughts of Sesusi. Now the creature may upset every one of our ceremonies."

Having spoken this aloud, he knew she must perform the service quickly.

Taking a small square of clean linen from one of her ebony boxes, she carefully wrapped the piece of bone that had lodged in his throat, and laid it in the hollow belly of a carved ebony statue no larger than her hand, but it had the face of Ptah, the crown of Seker, and the body of Osiris. Quickly, she placed this on her broken altar, and built a fire of dried khesau grass. Then she took from the bodice of her gown a small mound of wax, and made of it a figure of Aapep.

She said: "Fire be upon you, Serpent. A flame from the Eye of Horus eats into the heart of Aapep." The blaze on the altar leaped to the mouth of the ceiling, and the heat in the room was great. Menenhetet sat cross-legged in the pool of water that flowed from his skin, while Ma-Khrut uncovered her bodice to show her great breasts. By this light, they looked as red as the fire. "Taste of your death, Aapep," she said. "Back to the flames. An end to you. Back, fiend, and never rise again." Now she lay the wax figure of Aapep in the fold of a papyrus on which she had just drawn a serpent daubed with the excrement of her cats. Then she laid the offering into the fire of the altar, and spat upon it and said, "The great fire will try You, Aapep, the flame will devour You. You shall have no Ka. For Your soul is shriveled. Your name is buried. Silence is upon You."

Menenhetet's own throat was still swollen from the bone, his eyes ached, his lungs were choked. In his head, he knew the wrath of many Gods, but he did not complain. He did not dare. Legions of Gods collided on fields he could not see. He could even smell some of the dead and wounded in the smoke of the cat dung on the khesau grass.

The battle was joined, and he was an ignorant soldier, but he would never desert Honey-Ball in such an hour. "O Eye of Horus," she cried, "Son of Isis, make the name of Aapep to stink." And Menenhetet smelled the dead and wounded Gods in the foul breath of the smoke. When Honey-Ball embraced him her lips were slippery like snakes, and her breath was as foul as the smoke. His sore and injured throat began again to retch.

She stepped forward to the altar, and said, "Arise, Pig of the Forbidden Meat. Enter the Circle. Reek of the Seven Winds." Then she sang in seven voices, each voice uttering one sound, each voice lower than the one before, as if she descended a ladder into a pit where the Pig was kept. "I," she sang, until her lyre, hanging from a cord on the wall, began to quiver, and "ee" she sang until he could hear her bowls of alabaster rattle, "ay" and his teeth ached, "oh," and his belly moved, "oo," went into his groin, and on "you" the ground stirred beneath his feet. In the lowest voice of all, in a sound of much contentment, lower than the throats of the beasts who lived in the swamps, she sang "uhhh," and at the end he heard one clear grunt, and felt the stiff hairs of the Pig's snout nuzzle him between the cheeks in the way it did those nights when Menenhetet walked alone through the Gardens.

Now, standing before the altar, she raised her knife, point on high, and said, "I invoke You, God of destruction. I invoke You Whose name is Set. I call You by all the names that others do not know." She said names stranger than any he had ever heard. "You Whose name is Set I call by Iopakerbeth and Iobolkhoreth, by Iopathanax and Aktiophi, by Ereskhigal and Neboposoaleth, by Lerthexanax and Ethrelnoth. You will come to me as I kill all that is evil in the Pig," and she turned in a circle, knife out, and Menenhetet felt the Pig's tongue grow rigid like the end of a cut branch, then push upward for an instant between his cheeks and fall away. Menenhetet could feel blood beneath his feet, but when he looked down, the floor was dry. He saw the face of the Pig, however.

It was dying, but the light did not leave its eyes as in a common death when water seems to sink slowly into sand. The light from the eyes of the Pig went away in a flash of lights and sudden shadows, like a stream falling over rocks, and Menenhetet saw many expressions pass. He saw fear in the face of Usermare from the day at Kadesh when the Hittite broke His nose, and a great pride, wild as a glint in the eyes of a boar, reflected back from the moist nostrils of the beast. Then the animal died and its face was like the round features of Honey-Ball when her eyes were asleep in the circle of her face. He could see the Pig no longer.

This ceremony had been different from others. For now he felt no desire for Honey-Ball. That was done. The Pig was dead, and with it had gone the fury of his member and the pleasure of his heart. Menenhetet was sad.

"I did not mean to kill the Pig," said Honey-Ball, "only the part I did not make myself."

"Who can know what will come?" he said slowly.

She smiled, but did not answer, and Menenhetet was moved by her next thought. "It is over with us," she told herself, and gave him the measure of her love by the sorrow that overflowed in her. It was then he knew that his Secret Name was lost as well. He-who-will-help-to-turn-the-neck-of-Usermare belonged to Menenhetet no more, and now he had nothing with which to resist his Pharaoh.

Eight

Now, on the next night, Menenhetet was obliged to hold the hand of Usermare in the House of Heqat, the Pharaoh of the Two-Lands lying on His back, flat as the valley before the rising of the river, while the little queens made love to Him. Heruit and Hatibi were at His toes and Amait and Tait at His chest. The river was beginning to rise and so His nipples must be caressed until they swelled like Hapi, the God of the Nile Who had the breasts of a woman. An-Her, the spirit of harmony, gave long slow windings of her tongue to the folds of His belly, and Menenhetet, holding Him by the hand, could feel His navel trembling like an ear, and Heqat gave licks of her tongue to His sword, her lips like the tents of the Blessed Fields that are made from the petals of roses, inasmuch as the beauty of her mouth was equal to the ugliness of her face. By His head, Djeseret, the Sublime One, and Tantanuit would kiss Him as He inclined His face to one, then the other, all of these eight little queens as devoted to His body as if they prayed by His side in the temple, and their tongues were comfortable with one another. By the light of the burning wick in the saucer of oil, their eyes were as full of gold as the eyes of a lion, and their limbs gleamed.

Yet Menenhetet also felt His woe. Black as the mud at the bottom of the Nile was the gloom that lay beneath, and it shifted in the depths of His body like monsters in the unseen fields of the river mud. Old trapped odors of the most terrible fear drifted into Menenhetet's nostrils from the stones that had been moved to face the wall. Mixed with His lust, rich as the beating of a stallion's heart, Usermare was most uneasy in His belly from the shift of these stones, and a thought came to His mind across many years. Clear as a voice that Menenhetet could hear, Usermare said to Himself: "In the old days when I made love to Nefertiri, I could feel My Kingdom turn within."

From Menenhetet's fingers, along the length of Usermare's arm, and through His body to His sword, Menenhetet felt Usermare enter Nefertiri as in the days when she was as young as Rama-Nefru, and Usermare knew Nefertiri in that way now by the mouth of Heqat on His sword. So, Menenhetet could live in the belly of young Nefertiri and that was as tender and royal a sensation as evening in the last roselight of the sun. Menenhetet could not help himself, and his loins spurted, and he was wet in all the weakness of a field slave caught pilfering by his Overseer.

Usermare threw off the kisses of His little queens, and inquired, "What splendor brought you forth?"

"I do not know, my Lord."

Like a woman giving birth, the stones of the ancestors of Usermare were grinding in His bowels, but Menenhetet had come forth, and so he could no longer feel his Monarch's pains. Instead he was left in all the loneliness of his own poor wet thighs. Yet, even as he closed his eyes, he saw the great stone doors of the Temple of Seti knocked down that week, he heard the clinking in his ears of inscriptions being chipped away.

Through such a route did the Governor of the Secluded return to the dark thoughts of the Pharaoh, and Menenhetet felt once more by way of Heqat how Queen Nefertiri was near, yet within Her was Amon, and the sword of the Hidden One was like a rainbow of light in the small forest between Her thighs. The gloom that lay like mud on the heart of Usermare was the name of Amen-khep-shu-ef, for that Prince was the child of Amon. It was Amon who had taken the place of Usermare between the thighs of Nefertiri.

Usermare's blood raced with the anguish of the hare when caught in the jaws of the lion. The member of Usermare grew soft in the mouth of Heqat, for the rainbow who was Amon whispered to the young Nefertiri, "You will give birth to a Prince Who will slay His Father." Nefertiri groaned in great pain and much delight, while Amon came forth in great size and radiance, even as Usermare came forth with none into the mouth of Heqat. A woe from the blackest caves of Seker lay on the heart of Usermare. He saw a son who wished to kill Him.

"I will cut off the nose of anyone who conspires against Me," Usermare now said to the eight little queens and glared at them so fiercely that no hope of joy was left for the evening. Once again, He lay on His back, deep in gloom, holding the hand of Menenhetet while the little queens attended Him, and Heqat now stood to the side, trying to summon the Gods He desired to be near.

"O Great Pharaoh," said Heqat, "King of the Reed and the Bee, Lord of the Two-Lands, Host of Thoth, Most-Favored of Ptah, Son of Ra, we anoint Your body." Heqat laid an oil blessed by the High Temple of Amon between His toes, and other little queens anointed His orifices and laid oil on the muscles of His chest which were like the waves of the Very Green. Yet the despair of Sesusi was profound.

"O Golden Falcon," said Heqat, "You, Who are Horus, Son of Osiris, You unite heaven and earth with Your wings. You speak to Ra in the sky and to Geb in the fields. You are Horus Who Lives in the Body of Great Usermare." Heqat lay her face upon the groin of Sesusi, but He did not stir. He lay as if in His tomb.

"O King of Upper and Lower Egypt," said Heqat, "Lord of the Two Lords, Horus and Set, Your speech is like fire . . ."

"I know no fire," said Usermare. "I am cold. Amon has hidden Himself."

"Amon has hidden from the treachery of men. But none can destroy Him," said Heqat. "For He has made heaven and earth and He scattered the darkness on the waters. Amon made the day with light, and has no fear. Amon made the breezes of life for Your nostrils."

"For My nostrils," said Usermare.

"Amon," said Heqat, "made the fruit and herbs and the fowl and fish for Your subjects. He will slay His enemies, as He has destroyed all who dare to revile Him. Yet, when His children weep, He hears them. O You Whose speech is like fire, You are the Son of Amon." Heqat took into her mouth all that was in the groin of Usermare and the King gave a great groan, but nothing stirred.

Then, Menenhetet, holding the fingers of Usermare, felt a new fear. For his Pharaoh heard the seven sounds as clearly as if He had been present last night at the Execution-of-the-Pig, and the seven sounds crashed together, while the soup fell again upon the chest of Usermare. His heart burned with wrath, and a mist rose in His bowels from such heat. "I must gather My powers," He said aloud, "so that I may calm the flood." Why did He lie on His back if not to guide His thoughts toward all thoughts in His Kingdom that would soothe the flood? The high waters of this year must not rise too high. Yet He could not calm His thoughts. He was in a rage, and weary. He sighed heavily. No caress could relieve the dread upon His chest. "Never poison a Pharaoh, but at the time of the flood," He murmured, and fear of Amen-khep-shu-ef returned like a foul smoke. Usermare sat up to stare at each of the little queens before Him. He looked at Heruit and Hatibi, Amait and Tait, An-Her and Heqat, Djeseret and Tantanuit, and he thought of other little queens not there, of Mersegert and Merit of the North, of Ahuri who performed the swallowing of the sword so well, and of Ma-Khrut—equal to Heqat at such services. His fingers gripped the hand of Menenhetet fiercely so soon as His mind saw the face of Honey-Ball. But His thoughts moved on to think of Oasis and Tbuibui and Puanet, of Squirrel and Rabbit and Creamy and many others. Like flowers waving before Him at the edge of the pond where Kadima swam at twilight, so did Usermare think of each little queen and wonder which one had sent out evil words.

He stopped before the ugly face of Heqat, and said, "You are from Syria. So you know the prayer of my young Queen Rama-Nefru. Say this Hittite prayer against the demons who are as numerous as the dust."

"Do You speak of the incantation against the worms, Good and Great God?"

"That is the one," said Usermare. "Say it before the enemies who are in the air can escape."

"These worms," said Heqat, "cannot be seen. But their howling is heard in the Palace when the night is still."

"I hear them," said Usermare.

"They can be found in the rafters of every house. No gate can keep them out. They pass beneath the door. They separate the wife from her husband."

"Call forth the Gods who will chase them. Call upon *your* Gods," said Usermare.

"I call upon Nergal," said Heqat, "who sits at the top of the wall. I call upon Naroudi who waits beneath this bed. He will bless us if we give him food and drink."

Now, Usermare stood up. Once the little queens had begun to offer their gifts, He usually did not rise from the bed until He came forth many times, but on this night, as if disturbed by the Nile, whose murmur could be heard across the distance of all these gardens and parks, agitated again by the sore irritations of His thoughts, He stood up and told Heqat to bring food and drink to set beneath the bed for the Syrian God Naroudi. Then Usermare grasped Menenhetet in the full sight of the four little queens, and said aloud, "It is Isis I desire."

Menenhetet did not know whether it was his own terror, but a giddiness began in his feet. He could not speak for the fright. Usermare, despite forty-two circles of silence, was near to his thoughts.

"Do any of you," asked Usermare, "know the Ceremony to Invoke Isis?"

The little queens were silent.

"You, Heqat, who are ugly as a frog. You are a Syrian and know words of magic in two tongues. Invoke the Nearness of Isis."

"Great Sesusi," she said, "the ceremony is reserved for a Pharaoh or a High Priest."

"It needs a High Priest?" asked Usermare. "You, then, Menenhetet, will serve. For this hour. No more. More would offend Amon."

"Lord of the Two-Lands," whispered Menenhetet, "I do not know the words."

"Heqat will say the words. You will hear them." Menenhetet's hair was rudely grasped by His hand. Then Usermare lay back upon the bed, and brought Menenhetet's nose near the divide of His buttocks.

"Pray," said Usermare, and Menenhetet heard the scream of Isis as the body of Osiris was cut into fourteen parts.

Yet, the first fruit of such prayer was the clear voice of my great-grandfather himself. Menenhetet began to speak aloud once more as if his voice could not only reach our ears, but was ready to travel through the night and be heard by Hathfertiti and Ptah-nem-hotep, no matter where they might be.

"Yes," said my great-grandfather, with a look of much sympathy toward my father, as if to state that he, Nef-khep-aukhem, asleep or not, would understand, better than any, those sentiments that came from licking the Royal Buttocks, "you are one to know of these matters," yes, none could know better than he how my great-grandfather felt.

"Through the gilded nails of Ramses the Second," said my great-grandfather, "by way of His royal sweet-breathing palm, I had already entered some of the great and powerful halls of His thoughts. But that was as nothing before the entrance to His Kingdom provided by the Mouth of the Pit. I knew no more defiance than a slave. I even girded myself to breathe the putrefaction of the swamp, but it was otherwise. For I saw the light of Ra at the end of a great and golden chamber. This was no foul exchange like swilling in the traps of Honey-Ball even as she, in homage to the balance of Maat, would bury her mouth in me, good pig to pig, no, I was drawn forward by the tip of my tongue. Like the paw of a dog scratching the earth for new mysteries, so did it quiver to kiss the buttocks of Usermare. Even to suffer my nose as a plow, or my tongue as a spade (for His hand was

rude!) did not make me feel as if I were being buried in Egyptian
mud, no, it was more like entering a temple, I swear, He had been so
much anointed and by so many little queens, that He smelled of perfume, and I, entering, learned of royal passions that grabbed at me as
quickly as the hook that enters your nose for the old dead stuffs of the
brain. So His rage came to me, and His royal desires. He lay there,
attended by the others, washed by their tongues from His ears to His
belly, and by Heqat on His sword whose base rubbed like a pillar on
my head when she sucked at it, and buffeted me like a lion's tail whenever she forsook it long enough to intone, 'O Goddess of the Green,
Great Isis Sister of Osiris, Nephthys, and Set, child of Earth and
Sky, Lady of the Swamps,' on the words went until she must suck
again, but I, rooting in the pit like a beast, was the only one to know
the thoughts of Usermare, and I can tell you that He was dreaming of
how He would devour all the Gods in the Land of the Dead, at least
all Who were His enemies. He traveled on a ship that was like the
Boat of Ra and it went past fiery furnaces on the banks of the Duad.
I could see the damned squirming in ditches while Goddesses vomited forth a great fire from burning rocks to consume these souls and
shadows who were enemies of Usermare. I even thought I beheld the
body of Amen-khep-shu-ef in flames. Certainly I saw devils of mist
and rain, and the fiends of cloud and darkness.

"In this boat with Usermare was a great Pharaoh, and He was as
strong and beautiful and as great in height as Usermare. I knew it was
His ancient ancestor, the Pharaoh Unas for whom the Festival Hall
was being built. Now, in the company of Unas, Usermare moored the
boat and went onto the shores of the Land of the Dead in order to
hunt other Gods. I saw the chase. Many of these Great Lords were
soon caught, and servants to Unas and Usermare cut Them up and
cooked Them in great pots. I saw Usermare eat the parts of these
Gods, even as His ancestor Unas also devoured the best and finest,
while older Gods Whose flesh was dry were merely broken like wood,
and Their brittle bones used for fuel. But the spirits and souls of the
best Gods were taken into Usermare, and He grew Their features.
Now, I saw His mouth, His nose, and His eyes as they came to Him

from the Gods. He was Horus, the son of Osiris, yet He was Osiris Himself, and Usermare sat with the Lord of the Dead, side by side, there with Osiris on the Great Throne that is made of a material clearer than water and brighter than light. Usermare sat in the place of Isis.

"All this was in the mind of my Pharaoh, Great Ramses the Second, Usermare-Setpenere, lying among us with His scented body, our own God, Sesusi, in the warmth of His flesh, and I, suffused with the blood of the fires He saw and the meals He consumed, radiant with the glow of the luminous fields where the flowers of the stalks of grain shone like golden stars, was close to believing that I would never breathe again, just so cruel was the pinch of His buttocks on my nose, yet I was relieved that He had suspicions of me no longer, and merely enjoyed Himself eating those Gods. His gloom was gone. The base of His sword trembled against my forehead even as He came forth into the mouth of Heqat. Then He lay in repose against a golden field of grain. Yet He would not release me.

"So I continued to kiss and to lick, seeking to give pleasure to Him Whose appetite was best satisfied by the body of a God, and in the peace that came upon all of us now that He was no longer in His most woeful mood, so did I go back to the village of my boyhood, a boy again, if indeed not a child just born, and was returned to calm memories of my past, as firm and certain as the stone and clay that are baked by the sun. I lived not only in my Pharaoh's heart but in my own, and that was like being in the Two-Lands. One is the knowledge of all that is behind us, and the other must be our vision of what is yet to come. In that manner was my mind equal to two minds, and my hands held the separate buttocks of my Great King whose cheeks were as firm as the haunches of a horse. Out of His heart, into the wisdom of my hands did I begin to live in the despair and joy He knew of His two Queens, of Nefertiri and Rama-Nefru.

"Although I had been near to Queen Nefertiri but once, and never to Rama-Nefru, now they were like the Two-Lands of His two buttocks, and by His right mound was I led to drift on His sweetest memories of Nefertiri, for He had gone back to the year of His ascension to the throne. In that season when the young King meditated on the works of His dead Father, Seti, He searched for feats to excel His Father, and by that path came to think of the dry wells on the roads that led to the gold fields of Ekayta. No water was to be found on the route, and half of the laborers perished on every trip. No gold had come out of Ekayta to celebrate the Reign of Seti.

"Yet in the first weeks of Usermare's ascension, there was a night when He plunged so deep into His young bride that the beer in the jugs by Their bed began to froth. Later, when They lay beside each other, Nefertiri said, 'Water will come out of the mountain on the road to Ekayta.' Hearing the confidence in Her voice, Usermare ordered a well to be dug, and there, water was found, and its flow enabled the laborers to bring back much gold in the early years of the Reign of Ramses the Second. So, He took a vow upon Nefertiri's body that He would know love for no other woman.

"Yet, now, forsaking His right buttock for the touch of His left, so could I see Rama-Nefru as clearly as Nefertiri, and Rama-Nefru was no older now than the other had been then, and thinking of Rama-Nefru, He was as tender as a young lover.

"Rama-Nefru might have been the daughter of a Hittite, and in Her childhood only known men with beards and been raised by women with noses more curved than a sword, but She, Herself, was like the loveliness of a clear morning on our river. So I knew why She was beloved by Usermare. In Her arms, He heard the birds at dawn, and saw the clear light of the Palace courtyard when the sun is high. By night She offered a tenderness like the smallest flowers of His garden. That much did I learn by the touch of my fingers to His left buttock. For into my heart passed the cup of His happiness. The harsh appetites of my King did not occupy all His heart. To Him, the luster of Rama-Nefru's hair was like the light falling on the transparent Throne of Heaven. Yet, the purity of His feelings were such that He could not be with Rama-Nefru when His heart was black with fear, or She would suffer from bearing His heat.

"Later that night, after Usermare had mounted the bodies of each of the eight little queens and took each of them with a fire to bury the fires of Khert-Neter, coming forth each time like a God, He became at last as calm as the waters of a pond and dressed with me, and we walked together in the Gardens hand in hand. He had not been so calm in a long time. His breath smelled powerfully of kolobi and I understood how near we had been to the body of Isis through the night. For all which was in the grain belonged to Her, and everything in the grape. And all that came down to us on the rise of the river.

"This time, it was not like that occasion when He hesitated to tell me that I would no longer be General-of-all-the-Armies but Governor of the Secluded. He said, 'I have lived in indecision for many months, but it has come to an end. Tomorrow, you will begin to serve as Companion of the Right Hand of Nefertiri.'

"When I asked, 'Who will be Governor?' He replied, 'I am giving the Gardens to Pepti. He will do well there. But you belong in My First Queen's Palace. You have the wisdom to serve Her well, and serve Me even better.' He nodded, as if the greatest wisdom were His own. 'You will stay close to Nefertiri. You will not leave Her. If word should come that I am dead, you have only one instruction: Slay Her where She stands.'

"Now He kissed me. 'Kill Her,' He said, 'even if others will slay you in the next instant.'

"I bowed. The dawn was as lovely to me as the thought of my own life. 'That is the best death for you,' He said. 'You will be able to accompany Me in the Golden Boat.'

"He was my King. So I did not dare to say that I might wander in Khert-Neter and not be welcomed by Him on any boat. I merely bowed again."

Nine

Once, sitting with my mother in her bedroom, I saw her pick up a round plate of silver with a handle of gold, and hold it beneath my face. I nearly cried out. There, floating on the polished surface, was my Ka looking back at me. I had seen this face in the water of a pond on a calm day, and learned I could not touch such a Ka for it rolled away in many small waves so soon as I reached out. Now, my mother said, "This is the veil-of-the-Ka-who-stands," and it was true. When I brought my finger to the surface of the plate, another finger came forward to meet me, but the face did not move— it stood there as solemn and respectful as my own. At that moment, I felt as far apart from a six-year-old, at least in age and wisdom, as my great-grandfather himself. I knew there was no rare thought I could not understand if I looked long enough into the silver light of the veil-of-the-Ka-who-stands. For with my face before me, I shared the wisdom of the Gods—if only in that instant.

Now, something of the knowledge I had then must have come into my breath, for when I opened my eyes on this patio, expecting—I do not know why—to see my own face, I was staring instead into the eyes of my great-grandfather, and we looked at one another unti I lost all sense of where the horizon might be on this dark night. Now I could not be certain I belonged here any more than on my knees in some chamber of stone in the center of a mountain of stone, and my mouth was open, and my great-grandfather's eyes remained motionless on me. All was still.

I began to know the emptiness of this late great hour of the night. I could feel the darkness upon us until I did not believe I would see the sun again. The fireflies hardly stirred and so dim was their light that one could barely see the cloth of their cage. Now my father moved in his sleep, and a groan came from his lips. For the first time, I felt near to him, and then—I do not know if he was wide awake or spoke right out of his sleep—but his hand reached out for mine, and the current of all his feelings ran from his fingers into mine, although with no similarity to the heart of the Great Sesusi. My father was in all the pure simple pain of a throat as sore as Menenhetet's after he swallowed the bone, and I knew we had entered the hour when Ptah-nem-hotep and my mother lay deep in each other's embrace, while the touch of their flesh, naked to each other, lay directly on my father's feelings, as cruel and copious as an onrush of blood. So I knew then how powerful was my father's adoration for the beauty of my mother. Nor was the depth of his anguish lessened by the excruciating pleasure of knowing that she gave herself (and all the wealth of herself) to the man (and the God of all the Gods) to whom my father was nearest. So it was as if my father, out of love for my mother, and love for Ptah-nem-hotep, now met the scorching onslaught of one adoration fallen upon another, and thereby suffered like a lion devouring its own entrails. Yet—how much like a lion!—his heart also knew glory.

It was then, as I say, that I entered his thoughts. I had grasped a few before this night, but only in the way a throwing-stick may strike a bird as it rises overhead. So many impressions are in the air that you bring one down merely by making the effort even as the stick cannot fly through a cloud of birds without breaking a wing. Tonight, however, I learned that if one could be true-of-voice like Ma-Khrut, so could one also be true-of-thought and be borne on the stream of another's meditation. In that manner I was carried on my father's dreams and realized that he saw the same throwing-stick (curved like a serpent, and of splendid ebony) just hurled into the sky by my thoughts. Yet so fine are these tricks of the mind when it is not one's own eye that sees what is before you, but another's thought, that the same black throwing-stick became on its trip down the marvel of my mother's pleasure. She exclaimed at the skill of Ptah-nem-hotep, and would have jumped for delight if she had not been standing next to Him on the most fragile little skiff of papyrus, its sheaves delicately lashed together.

Yet it was only after I saw the stick come down and go up again that I also knew my mother was younger than I had ever seen her, and alive with the sauciness that gleams in the eyes of a young Princess when she enjoys much pleasure, yet has earned it at no cost. Even then, it was not until I saw her sandals, made of palm leaves and papyrus as fine as the skiff, and put together to endure no longer, that I realized (and only by way of my father's hand in mine) that I was seeing the sunshine of an afternoon seven years ago and Ptah-nemhotep, to match her sauciness, was still a young Prince crowned as Pharaoh in the same year, and with the same regal fastidiousness of a very young King, so that as He flirted with her, and they spoke with their heads close together, so did He still stand, even on the skiff, with His back straight and His eyes smiling more than His mouth. For to His chin was attached the long thin beard that only the Pharaoh may wear.

"Oh, look," she cried, "at the monkeys." As they rested for an instant, the skiff drifting through the reeds (while the birds they roused settled into other grass) the sunlight dazzled along the length of the tall stalks at the border of one of His gardens. Up in the trees, monkeys were picking figs for the eunuchs and busily throwing them down. One could not tell who was laughing more, the gardeners or the monkeys. Both saluted Him as He poled by, and that encouraged Hathfertiti to laugh in her turn. Down in the marsh, the sun was lighting on the water-pads, and on the flowers at the head of the papyrus stalks. Silence came again. They were near to another flock of

birds, and standing erectly, side by side, their balance as keen as the
tilting of the skiff, He ran into the reeds, the air quivered, the ducks
flew upward with an ongathering cry like a herd of horses trumpeting
up the hill, and His stick flew with them. A bird fell down.

So the afternoon passed. As quickly as a cloud passing beneath the
sun. The sounds of my mother's laughter scraped twice on my father's
heart. He had made love to her almost every night of his fifteenth,
sixteenth, and seventeenth years and had always known he would
marry her and yet as she stood in the skiff, the slim upright grace of
her body matched to the balance of the poised body of Ptah-nem-
hotep, her happiness offered a delicacy Nef-khep-aukhem had never
glimpsed for himself. All the while he watched from the branches of
a tree at the edge of the swamp, his cheeks became more swollen from
the bites of mosquitoes. She would laugh again when she saw him in
the evening. For these ludicrous lumps on his face spoke of an afternoon so absurd that he had been trapped in a tree by mosquitoes. Besides, she was savage. There had been the illimitable disappointment
that Ptah-nem-hotep, having brought back the skiff, did not pursue
her very far although her thighs quivered for Him with a beating
more rapid than the wings of the birds. Then, after the lingering of
their farewell, she had been seized in the twilight by her grandfather,
who, having made love to her since she was twelve, now made love to
her again on this day with all the passion of four Pharaohs, and Menenhetet would have died even as he was about to come forth if he
had not realized how much she desired the still silent smile of Ptah-
nem-hotep. Twice denied, once for too little, once for too much,
Hathfertiti had laughed at last in full cruelty at the face of her brother,
while he took her with an anger and appetite as great as her grandfather or any Pharaoh, and they traveled over much of the floor of that
room with their bodies. It may be that I was made in that hour. Or it
may be that I was made in the hour before by my great-grandfather.
Or was I also conceived on my mother's side by the love of the young
Pharaoh's eye? All I knew at this moment was the pain in my father's
heart. He still gazed back into the sunlight of the swamp and wept
within, for he saw my mother and Ptah-nem-hotep together in their

embrace, and was overcome that his Pharaoh, uplifted by the vigor of His ancestor, was tonight, if not the equal of Usermare, at least His descendant. The exquisite happiness of my mother's cries scratched like a dagger on my father's ear.

By now, of course, I was so immersed in my mother's heart as to be able to do without the intercession of my father. So I saw my father as my mother did, knew the meat and pleasure of their matrimony, and understood that my mother enjoyed my father more than she wished, indeed, they were glued to one another. Therefore, my father—and this was part of his pain—had to be aware that my mother might enjoy all the riches of Egypt when he was in her, yet with so low a longing that the slap of their bodies resounded in her ear like the smacking of riverbank mud. So there was never a time when she did not look to betray my father with my great-grandfather. In Menenhetet's arms she knew more of the Gods on one night than she saw with my father in a year. The odor of Menenhetet might be strange to her, as perfumed and dry as the remote dust that lies upon the loneliest sunbaked rocks, but he could be many men. Afterward, she would tell Nef-khep-aukhem (for my father always understood that it was part of her pleasure—with all the spite of an older sister—to tell him, yes, to tell him) that she not only made love to Menenhetet but that her grandfather was like a Pharaoh, and so she could be the Queen of a Pharaoh, whereas with her husband, ah, dear man, it was just his low appeal. With him, she felt as comfortable as a field in the afternoon sun, but then she could see nothing better than peasants trodding the seed. Saying this, she would poke her full breast into his hungry mouth, considerably parched by the truth of listening to her confessions, and my father would suck hungrily on her tit, like a baby, like a younger brother, like a wounded husband, and grasp her buttocks with the desperation of a lover who can find no mastery in the force of his grip. Hathfertiti would meow in imitation of her favorite cat, and grasp his wretched half-erect little limb, weak in this hour, and draw it in and out of her mouth with all the languor and sweet teasing wit of a tongue that could and would tell him how she had done as much for Menenhetet and more, and the cream of my father's coming-forth would be tasted by her, and thoughtfully, indolently, wiped on her face and breasts, while still smelling the spit of his mouth and her mouth and all the other mouths in a bond that sealed them to each other still, and reminded both of all the joys they had known when she was fifteen and he was thirteen and they did it in every hidden place. In those days, she used to believe that she betrayed her grandfather with her brother. Now, were both men betrayed, and even I lived like them in my mother's flesh while the Pharaoh was inside her, full of the feast of our Pig, our good Pharaoh, Ramses the Ninth, in no ordinary joy after listening to the stories of Menenhetet. Like Usermare, Ptah-nem-hotep was feeling an army of Gods in His body. Uplifted by the times without number my father had been joined to the body of Hathfertiti, yet had given his kisses, my poor father, to the feet and buttocks of his Pharaoh over these seven years, yes, the fields and heavens of all His subjects and His ancestors were joined as my Pharaoh grasped the full near-to-bursting flesh of Hathfertiti, and came forth from the source of the Nile, came up, Ptah-nem-hotep, behind the cataracts and felt Himself roaring down in flood into the mouth of the Delta there to be buried in the Very Green with Hathfertiti moaning beneath Him like a lioness. Then He was done, and she was still thrashing about with abandon enough to flow over the banks of any river, sealing His mouth with a kiss.

In the chill that always came upon Ptah-nem-hotep after the coming-forth, He was repelled by this cheap woman, the wife of His Overseer of the Cosmetic Box, the spouse of a servant (with the flesh of that servant all over her) and her mouth stuck to His Mouth like the jelly that came from the boiling of a bone, all repellent, a sealing fully as complete as any real marriage with its contracts written on papyrus. Like such a sealing were their mouths glued together, a slavery, an entombment, a joining of His Double-Throne with her insatiable greed.

So did His colder sentiments also come into me, but no longer by way of my mother, no, the heart of the Pharaoh spoke to me, and was heard by the night and in the night, through the pain of my father that was like an open ear. By way of my father I learned of His feelings, and my father's pain was doubled for knowing himself despised.

Yet Hathfertiti felt none of these drear stirrings in her Pharaoh, only the burden of His power. She took in His royal fatigue. She had never felt more tender toward a man. These emotions I received as directly as if she had spoken, and understood, if I had ever doubted, that being possessed of two separate eyes and two ears, two arms, two legs, two lips for taste (one for the good taste, one for the bad), two nostrils by which to breathe (the male Gods to one side, Goddesses to the other), and that even as Egypt was the nation of the Two-Lands, and the Pharaoh had a Double-Crown, and a Twice-Royal Seat, the Nile had two banks, and there was day and night, so could my mind receive the thoughts of two people at once. To my mother, Ptah-nem-hotep was the sweetest sensation of love she had ever known, even sweeter than her love for me, whereas the feelings of the Pharaoh were now in a fever of fury at all the insistent pleasure of this woman's charms, that sealing of her lips, her firm body soft in every corner it could be plundered, even the crisp brush of the stiff hair that grew like foliage over the wet meat between her thighs, was irritating to Him. He began to make love again with all the skill He had acquired from His small harem of ten little queens, all of whom He knew better by far, He could say, than Usermare knew any of His hundred, and indeed there was no caress He had not felt, only the absence of any Goddess He might revere, and Hathfertiti was no Goddess at all, yet she was inspiring in Him the most appetite He had known in the seven floodings of the Nile since He had ascended the Double-Throne. And all the while He caressed Her flesh, Ptah-nem-hotep had more thoughts for Menenhetet than for her.

In the chill that followed His coming-forth, He had seen again how the mighty phallus of Usermare entered the gates to His Governor's buttocks, and that gave vigor to Ptah-nem-hotep. By the breath He took through one nostril it gave Him vigor, but it also left Him in no way superior to Menenhetet by the other, inasmuch as Usermare was also entering Him, if by no more than the tongue of Hathfertiti

commencing her music again. Now, feeling her wet breast by one
hand, and the crevice of her hips by the other, recollecting the view
of her open thighs as He saw them in the light of a flame in a censer
of oil, the Gods gleaming in the wet flesh of her hair, He knew a second pleasure, and His life stirred inside her belly and began to grow
long as the Nile and dark as the Duad. The great force of the phallus
of His ancestor, Usermare, covered His own phallus like the cloak of
a God. At that instant His Secret Name must have opened the door
for He had an instant when the Gods went in and out of Him a second
time and the Boat of Ra flew past as He came forth. The Two-Lands
shivered beneath. He had dared to speak to the Gods on the body of
the wife of a servant, and as this terrible thought passed through, so
did my mother see again the great stone obelisk we had encountered
this morning on the river and felt in her belly the strength of those
men rowing upstream against the great weight, for the sword of Ptah-
nem-hotep was like that obelisk and possessed of a golden tip. By its
light she climbed the ladder of heaven.

Indeed Hathfertiti was uplifted so high into the radiance of her
feelings that, try as I desired, I could not remain in her exaltation but
floated down to the thoughts of my great-grandfather who continued
to stare at me. He was searching for the mind of Ptah-nem-hotep, and
I wondered if our Pharaoh had fallen asleep, or was passing through
His own darkest thoughts, since I could no longer feel His presence,
only the stirring of my great-grandfather's recollections of Queen
Nefertiri, yet I knew such memories must be as turbulent as the rough
water around the islands of New Tyre. Nonetheless, he must have
found those thoughts of the Pharaoh for which he searched, since my
great-grandfather was so calm and firm that I did not realize at first no
sound was coming to our ears, only the thoughts, and if a servant had
entered they might have thought we were sitting in silence. Indeed
we were, but for the clarity of each and every unspoken word I heard.

Ten

I confess to You, Great Ninth of the Ramses, my great-grandfather commenced, that Queen Nefertiri as she lives in my thoughts is not close to the expression one sees on Her last statues. There the sculptor, for want of better knowledge, made Her look much like Usermare Himself. I see the same long nose with the majestic curved nostrils, and the exquisitely shaped lips, and that was a fair estimate for the sculptor, since She was Usermare's sister. But I knew Her very well and it was not like that, not altogether. Yet—and this is the most curious difficulty of living with a memory that has passed through four lives—I cannot be certain now if the face I see before me when I think of Nefertiri is indeed the one I used to love when I knew what it was to desire a woman so completely that there was longing for Her even in the ends of my toes, as if like a tree I could draw strength from the earth. I knew Her face, yes, and yet as I remember Her now, She is not unlike Honey-Ball. She was not fat, of course, yet, all the same, she was a voluptuous woman, at least in the season I knew Her, and the face of Nefertiri, like the face of Honey-Ball, had the fine short nose, the same wondrous curved lips whose warmth was like a fruit and tender in expression or merry or cruel as the whim would take Her. Of course, Nefertiri's hair was dark and lustrous like no other woman's, and Her eyes belonged to a Goddess. They were deep in color but not brown nor black, more like darkest violet, or is it indigo? They were as purple as the royal dye that comes from the shores of Tyre and they spoke of the wealth of royalty itself, as if one were forever staring into the late evening sky. That is how I remember Her, and yet I cannot be certain it is Her fine face I see, or only what I recollect.

My great-grandfather held out his hands, a most peculiar gesture for him, since he rarely made a move that was not exact, and yet this uncertain lift and fall of his arms spoke of the sadness that comes from recognizing that one will never know all that it is essential to know, and new error, therefore, must forever be conceived out of the old.

I remember, however, he went on, that on the morning when I first entered the Throne Room of Nefertiri in Her Chambers of the Royal Wife (which was itself a palace among the many palaces of the Horizon of Ra) and there was introduced to Her Court as Companion of the Right Hand, that the sunlight was entering from the open pillars behind Her, and dazzled my eyes as it glittered over every carved lion and cobra of the carvings of Her golden throne.

Let me say that I had been passed quickly by Her sentries into Her presence itself. My new rank, of obvious and considerable worth in Her Court, opened gate for me after gate, and I went through a great pair of double doors into the gold and splendor of Her great room. I was prepared to be blinded by the light from the throne—the little queens who could inform you of everything they never saw, had told me much about the splendor of the light in the morning when She sat by the eastern bank of columns, but I was not prepared to grow faint. I had spent so many hours with Usermare that I thought my feet would be steady before Her Presence. It was not so. I threw myself on my belly and kissed the ground, which was the accepted ceremony then, as now, for that first occasion when you are presented in Court to the Great Two-House or His Consort (thereafter, one need only bow profoundly) but on that first meeting, no noble, no matter how proud, would fail to taste the dirt, in this case, the polished marble floor of Egypt, against his teeth. My teeth rattled, however, against the stone. I was in the presence of a being near to the Hidden One. Amon, not Usermare, was in the room with Her, and I can only say that as I threw myself down, a cloud came over, my sight failed, the river of my sweat came forth, and my heart—then I understood what they meant by the expression—was no longer in my bosom, no, it flew out like the Ba.

"Rise up, noble Menenhetet," were the first gracious words of the Queen Nefertiri to me, but my limbs were like water when there is no force of a wave, only the weight, and yet, as if like Amen-khep-shu-ef I must learn to climb the steepest cliffs, so did I raise my head and our looks met in the silence.

That gave me much strength. I had heard from the little queens of the remarkable color of Her eyes and was prepared, except that the beauty of the color gave me strength even as a dying man knows happiness when offered the petals of a rose. So our eyes met, and I lived with Her in all that perturbation of the Nile when it is divided by an island, just so great a change did Her eyes of indigo make in me, but then we did not merely greet one another, and step back into ourselves, but met like two clouds of different hue traveling on different winds and there was much dancing in the air between. Her face and body were in this first instant like a mosaic of sparkling stones— I could not even see Her whole—but knew I loved Her, and would serve Her, and be Her true Companion of the Right Hand. A happiness came into Her eyes, and She laughed with a sweet peal of rollicking laughter, as if, behold, it would be a better day than all the signs had foretold.

We did not speak much more on that occasion. I made my presentations in a low voice full of respect, and, in such a situation, with what is better than respect, offered by my voice a not all-controlled quiver of admiration for Her beauty, so spoke my tones. Then, I stood up and gave what was, for a charioteer who had risen from the ranks, a noble bow so full of the grace and manner of—I was to learn it just then—of a particular nome, that the Queen asked, "Are you, dear new friend Menenhetet, from Sais?"

"No, Great Consort of the King, but I have lived among the people of Sais."

"And it is said that some of the little queens are from Sais."

I bowed. I had no answer. I was too confused. Indeed, I cannot tell you how many courtiers were in the room, whether five or fifteen, I saw only Her and myself.

Later that day when the House of a Royal Companion was assigned to me, and I saw the gold of my chairs and tables and wardrobe chests, my new clothes of linen, and gold bracelets, and the faience of my new chestplate, each piece of the thousand and one pieces of blue stone limned with an edge of gold, and when I smelled the choice perfumes delivered to me by the bounty of the King—or was it from Nefertiri Herself?—when I surveyed my new servants—all five— and passed through the gracious rooms of my new house, seven rooms in full (to hold a scorpion, each one!) my kitchen, my dining room, my receiving room for guests, my own room for meditation and ablutions (as explained by the new keeper of my keys, a scribe with a face like Pepti, and a name, Slender-Sticks, to make you laugh—he was so fat!) my bedroom, and the two small rooms at the end to hold my five servants who were my cook, my keeper of the keys (and accounts and correspondence) my groom for the golden chariot, a gardener, and last, my Major-domo who was all in one a butler and houseboy, I knew I was now blessed with more rank than General or Governor, and no longer lived in a small house, but a large one.

So I was happy in this new place, if for a day, but by the conclusion of my first few days, I was as vexed as a sail when the wind blows by both sides, for if the Palace of Nefertiri lived in all the brilliance of sunlight upon gold, I could not say the same for Her people. Her Officers were inferior men, Generals you would not trust with a command, Governors who governed no longer (like myself!) and a former Vizier who now reeked of kolobi and told long stories of his provident decisions in the early reign of Usermare. Her priests were full of vices of which the first was greed, and Her maids, once beautiful, were no younger than Herself. Their minds, as I came to know them, were narrow and connected only to the fortune of their Queen, their

own families, and their entertainments. Yet they knew less of arts and
refinements than the little queens—it is obvious to me even as I speak
that I lose the passage of the days for one does not learn that much
about a Court so quickly, yet I believe my years in the army were of
use. When I was General it took no more than an hour's visit to a new
command before I could form one indispensable opinion: the troops
were ready, or too weak for my purpose. I saw much luxury in my
first hours in Her Court, and the subtle manners of many aristocrats
were displayed, but I also knew that Usermare need not fear Her people—ambition was twisted here upon itself, and honor was sour.
These courtiers would worry more about what they might lose than
ever they would dream of the rewards that boldness might gain. No
plot could come forth here.

Years later, and in another life when I was a High Priest, and knew
all the royal and wealthy worlds of Egypt like the lines of my hand, I
would understand at a glance what took me much time then. By my
second life I would have walked into the Court of Nefertiri and said,
"They do nothing but gossip here," and I would have been right. I
heard again every story I had heard before among the little queens,
but in Her Court, these stories were told with those little details that
can be more dear than ornaments themselves, and are presented to
one another like gifts. So in the Palace of Nefertiri, I heard more of
Rama-Nefru than of the First Queen, and if I learned on the first visit
to my house by the former Vizier who drank kolobi, that Nefertiri
made much mockery of Rama-Nefru because She wore nothing but
blond wigs, Nefertiri had been forced to discover by the boasts of
Usermare Himself—and on the night the soup was spilled!—that
Rama-Nefru's own hair was also blond between Her thighs. No man
had ever seen a sight like that. On hearing this truth, Nefertiri had
burned every blond wig in Her wardrobe. Here the Vizier did not
continue, but only closed one wise, sad, much-dimmed eye on me
and opened it with a wink. "The head of Rama-Nefru will yet be as
bald as mine," he murmured.

That was the first visit paid to me, and others followed. Where the
decorum in the Gardens of the Secluded was so great that I never

touched a little queen's hand, but for the one I did, here I could have had five men's wives in as many days, and they had arts for seduction. It is the only sport left to those who grow no more beautiful. Needless to say, they were adept at finding the poisonous point of their gossip. So, Nefertiri was always hearing of the youth and beauty of Rama-Nefru, or how He Who used to speak of Nefertiri as "She-Who-sees-Horus-and-Set," was using the same words now for Rama-Nefru. The lady who told me this gave a low wail at the horror of living with Nefertiri afterward.

Now, my duties as Companion of the Right Hand were to be near the Queen. It was understood that I must accompany Her whenever She left the Palace, which was not every day, although often enough, for She delighted to search out rare sanctuaries throughout Thebes. Unlike Usermare, She was not only dedicated to Amon, but to Gods revered in other cities, as Ptah in Memphi, or Thoth in Khnum, not to speak of the great worship of Osiris in Abydos, but these Gods also had Their little temples here with Their loyal priests, plus many another God my Queen would find in many another temple, and often in the meanest places—at the back of a muddy lane in a slum of Thebes with the children so dirty and ignorant they did not bow their heads at the sight of Her nor express any sign of awe, but merely goggled their eyes. Still (the lane too narrow for Her palanquin) She promenaded on Her fine feet and golden sandals to the very bottom of the alley, there to have her toes washed by the priests of this shabby little temple of—be it—Hathor or Bestet or Khonsu, or in finer quarters down broad avenues, past the gates of mansions with their own pillars, sentries, and privately commissioned small stone Sphinx, we might pass through the slender marble columns of a "divine little temple," as She expressed it, to pay homage to the Goddess Mut, Who was Consort to Amon, or to the Temple of Sais-in-Thebes which revered the strange Goddess Neit. I found it hard to follow, all these temples of Ombos-in-Thebes, and Edfu-in-Thebes, Dedu-of-the-Delta-in-Thebes, or the temple of Ptah-in-Apis which worshipped the God as He appeared in the body of the bull Apis; I had much to keep me busy with these new temples, and more than a few pilgrims to shoulder aside. The priests were often rendered so stupid at Her sudden appearance that they were slack to clear the way to the shrine themselves.

Afterward, She would shop. We would travel in our small procession of chariots with Her guard behind us, and myself with Her in the golden Carriage-of-the-Consort, and stop to visit a jeweler or a dressmaker, but these visits in these fine quarters of the market interested Her less than the dirty little shrines. I think She wished to seduce the allegiance of many a God. How I suffered on these trips. As Her Companion, I was Her protector, and if in the true privacy of my orders, I was Her nearest enemy, well, I could hardly think of Her death when on these little expeditions, I saw a fellow or two who might be trouble to Her life.

Besides, another difficulty was there. When He was not out in the field, it had been Amen-khep-shu-ef who accompanied Her to the markets and temples. Now, I was replacing the Prince. He might be the General who had replaced me, but that did not count for Him. He let me know by His first look of greeting how welcome I was. Each morning I expected Him to meet me at the double door to Her bedroom and say, "I will accompany the Queen today. You need not go." Would I know how to reply? At Kadesh, He had still been a boy, although fierce enough already to die before He would lose a battle, but I had known for years that He was beyond my own strength. Indeed, He was still so tall and straight that His name among soldiers was Ha!—just so quick was the sound of His spear through the air! You only had to look at Amen-Ha, and the Gods in yourself rocked backward. So I would not dare to oppose Him directly—yet I could never watch my Queen ride off with Her son. For on just such a day could an assassination of the King be plotted. There, right in the hour that the Good God might be expiring in His own blood on the marble floor of His own Palace, She could be safe with Amen-khep-shu-ef in any one of a hundred noble mansions, or away in some secret little hovel in the maze of Thebes. I was by Her side to protect Her, but I also had to be ready to reach Her side, and in the next instant, Her heart. Like my Monarch, I inhabited two lands at once. Of course, on

any day that Amen-khep-shu-ef ordered me to stay behind, and I
dared to refuse, the Prince could slay me before the echo would be
heard. Then He could tell whatever tale He wished. So it was not
comfort I found in my new house.

Yet, how I enjoyed each day with Nefertiri. In all the hours I had
spent with Honey-Ball, I still did not know how to treat her. She had
been as much a priest, a beast, and a fellow soldier as my own woman,
and besides we were always working at one ceremony or another. Or
so I remembered our life together after fifteen days away. Still, I tossed
at night until I could have been in a storm at sea. I did not know if it
was I who longed for her, or she for me, but, Execution-of-the-Pig or
not, there was some longing left and I understood again how much
she suffered from the loss of her little toe, since the suddenness of our
separation now had many strange effects upon me. One morning I
even woke up with her little toe throbbing in mine. So I knew how
agitated was Honey-Ball, and how far from separated we were still,
indeed when with Nefertiri, I could feel Honey-Ball sending me favors or withdrawing them. I might pour a wine with a decorum as
perfect as a Goddess coming to drink from Her own pool, and know
it was Honey-Ball's hand that guided the calm measure of mine, or,
equally, I could leave a ring of moisture on the table from the base of
the golden pitcher, and be certain my former mistress had led me to
dribble a few drops off the lip.

Yet, give me an hour alone with Nefertiri, and I knew happiness.
She spoke so well. It was magic. With Honey-Ball, I sometimes felt,
when most dejected, that magic had the weight of a ritual practiced
much too much in the caverns of the night. Sitting beside Nefertiri,
however, I learned of the other magic that rises from the song of birds
or the undulation of the flowers. It is certain She seduced the air with
the sweetness of Her voice.

It hardly mattered of what She spoke. She had been obliged to be
together so much with the people of Her Court that She delighted in
the smallest conversation with me, and wanted to know about the
hours of my life which I would tell to no one else. Soon I realized that
in all the years of Her marriage to Usermare, She had never spoken at

length to anyone who lived in the Gardens of the Secluded, and so She always wished to hear of the little queens. There was not one whose name She did not know, for She had learned much about them from their families who were always eager to tell about the early lives of their little Princesses, lost to them. She corresponded prodigiously, and on many a day I sat on Her patio with Herself and Her scribe, a dwarf called Nightingale, whose back was hunched but whose small hand was exquisite, and watched them write letters. Often, he would read to Her and She would reply Herself, Her own hand at the palette, Her own calligraphy a gift to those who would read the papyrus. Sometimes, She would show me Her work, and I was so seduced as to feel I had received a dear caress. The purity of Her divine little sticks and snares and pots and curves, the colors of Her letters, and the precious life of the birds She painted made the papyrus tremble in my hand as if the wings of the birds furled by Her fine brush upon the page were now unfettered and could glide through my fingers in their flight. Golden were the hours I sat beside Her while She composed these letters.

One night, She had Amen-khep-shu-ef brought together with myself for dinner, and it was clear Her purpose was to encourage friendliness between us, or, failing that, bring us to some recognition of how we were each servants of Her "great need" as She came at last to put it, and it was then I came to understand something about the grandest ladies. One could not be a Queen without a *great need*. Whether Hers might be to injure Rama-Nefru, lay revenge on Usermare, or establish the Prince of Her flesh, Amen-khep-shu-ef, in succession to His Father—who could know? I remembered soldiers with terrible wounds in their stomachs. If they could bear the pain, their dignity became their highest honor. Those Gods one could respect the most seemed to gather about them. I thought of one charioteer who spoke to me in the calmest tones while the moon was rising, then he died. No sign of his pain did he show, yet I felt all of it.

Now, Nefertiri spoke to us of the lightest matters, of the amatory exploits of Her greyhound, Silver-Heart, who, sitting beside Her, kept looking at each of us as She spoke, and my Queen mused on how

Silver-Heart mourned for his family left behind in the incense countries to the east of the Red Sea. Hearing that, Silver-Heart mourned,
indeed howled as if to oblige his mistress, and She gave another sweet
peal of laughter in which was all of Her unhappiness, all of what I call
Her great need that I, in the soft light of Her dinner table, was so
ready to serve.

Yet I suspected that Amen-khep-shu-ef was not likely to be my
friend. Like Nefesh-Besher, He had a cast in one eye and never looked
at you so much as His sight flew over your head like a bat. He, too,
made me think of the Hittite who had come across the field of battle
to fight, sword against sword, with Usermare. While Amen-khep-
shu-ef had the long bridge of His father's nose, the curve of His nostril was crueler than the arc of a scimitar—no, He would never love
me. He loved His Mother too much, and with the wrong mouth as
we used to say in the charioteers. Indeed, She even called Amen-
khep-shu-ef by His little name as if the thought of His spear was always in Her thoughts. "Amen-Ha," She would say, "why do You
frown so?" and I, seated in the middle of the long table, felt smaller
than myself, and not at all in the conversation. He spoke to Her only
of matters about which I knew nothing, of His brothers and their
wives, of hunts in the desert when She had accompanied Him, of a
day most recently when She had stood beside Him in a boat of papyrus while He struck down eight birds on five casts of His throwing-
stick and the last bird had fallen into Her lap: there was a purity of
understanding between Them I could not enter.

She made efforts to bring the conversation to me. When I compli-
mented Her on the beauty of her writing, I was treated to a little explanation on the rarity of the school to which She had been sent as a
child. It was one of the very few of the Houses of Instruction in
Egypt where girls might go, but many were the difficulties for the
teachers. The students happened all to be Princesses, or, at the least,
the daughters of Nomarchs (as was Honey-Ball, daughter of the
Nomarch of Sais, and a classmate of Nefertiri, I would yet discover)
and so could hardly be whipped by their teachers. "Yet," She said, "as
every scribe must tell you: 'The ears of a boy are in his seat, and he

learns best when he is flogged.' Yet where were they to strike a Princess? No, they could not. Still we suffered. The ears of a girl are in her heart, and we wept when we made errors, and I could never learn to count. Each time I drew the sign for seven, I could think of nothing but the little cord that held My robe together. After all, the writing is the same."

"Sefekh," said Amen-khep-shu-ef. "I never thought of that."

"Sefekh," She said. "It is the same. I always mixed one with the other, and then the seams came apart in My head. All untied!" "Sefkhu," mother and son said then both at once, and Their mirth could frolic over this fine word, so near to the other, but it meant taking off one's clothes. I tried to smile, yet They knew words I did not, and laughter lived between Them like a wind I did not share. Of course, it was not the first time I had come to think that our language was too subtle, for I was well aware, having been tricked more than once, that the best Egyptians from the finest families know how the same sound can have many meanings and be written several ways. I thought, "I am as low as dung before Them, yet They use this same sound 'dung' to mean 'bleached linen.' Who is to know what They mean? They conceal much from those who were born beneath Them and then will turn a word into the opposite of itself."

But then, going back so far as my first days in the charioteers, I had noticed that what characterized a noble most, even more than their fine accent, was much private wit. As a simple charioteer, I had often not known at all what they were saying. How could I when each one of our words in Egyptian has so many meanings? They might use the sound for "breasts" which is the word *menti* but they would be speaking of eyes. Yet another word for eyes is *utchat,* eye-of-a-God, also the word with but a little difference in tone, for "outcast." One had to be clever to serve these nobles when they could play with many a meaning for each sound. All the same, no one had ever done this so well as Nefertiri. By a lilt in Her throat when She said *"hem-t,"* She could change a "hyena" into "precious stones." That, too, was magic—Her wonderful use of the inflections of words until light sparkled on every sound. How She would move from one meaning to the next!

"*Khat,*" She could say in disgust, but you had to know, by Her expression, whether She was talking of a "swamp," a "quarry," or the "Land of the Dead."

Still, such games did not go on too long this evening. In His royal manner, Amen-khep-shu-ef was more a soldier than a noble, and not able to play at this so well as His Mother, indeed, left to Himself, He had a solemn dogged mind. Despite His effort to talk of matters where I did not belong, He was obliged at last, with the help of Her sympathy for me, to come back to a subject where I could offer a few remarks myself, and yet I cannot say I was happier that She turned the conversation to war since His exploits had usually been more celebrated than mine. "Foolhardy," was how He was always described by the Generals closest to me, but even then, being handed the worst end of each story about Him, I knew how brave He was, and in the Gardens of the Secluded, although they never saw Him, the Prince was much admired by the little queens.

I was obliged to admit, despite all my desire to think less of Him, that no commander had ever had so great a reputation for conducting successful sieges. We took care when I was General-of-all-the-Armies to have the Division of Amen-khep-shu-ef away on the frontiers of Syria, but I never ceased to hear of the towns He took by siege, and some were strong cities never before fallen. He built forts to roll forward on wooden wheels, and one was even three stories high to equal the wall he would face. No labors were too endless for Him. He dug moats around towns so that none of the women and children could slip out—the wails of the starving gave strength to His troops, He would say. Yet the little queens spoke less of such cruel and stubborn skills than of His daring. So if I heard once in the army, I would hear again in the Gardens of how He not only climbed the face of high cliffs to accustom Himself to problems He would encounter on the battlements of cities, but had taught one squadron of His charioteers to climb nearly as well as Himself. On His last siege in Libya, to which His Father had dispatched Him in the hope He would stay away, Amen-khep-shu-ef and His men had been able to scale the walls without ladders on the first night of a siege before a single trench had been dug! His armies had only reached the place that afternoon. All talked of it. A siege that did not last a night! It was clear that Amen-khep-shu-ef wished to let everyone in Egypt know that He would be greater than Usermare.

Of course, there had been constant gossip in the Gardens over His prospects. Would Amen-khep-shu-ef ascend the Throne? Or might the Pharaoh choose another Prince? Rama-Nefru had given birth already to twins, and though one had died in His first week, the other thrived. Rare was the day, however, and rare the gossip, that did not carry a hint of some threat against little Peht-a-Ra who, having been given this mighty name of Lion-of-Ra, was also called by His Father, Hera-Ra. Of course, to spend a season in the Gardens of the Secluded was to learn, if you listened to the little queens, that no Prince ever followed His Father to the Throne before ten of His half brothers by other women had been brought to a sudden death. I heard so many stories of death in beer-houses, on the field of battle, in bed with treacherous women, or suffocated in the cradle, that I believed none, not until I saw the size of the guard around the Palace of Rama-Nefru, and found myself thinking of the obstacles awaiting Peht-a-Ra before He, half a Hittite, would be King of Egypt.

I must still have been brooding on such matters, for at the end of dinner, Amen-khep-shu-ef took me by surprise. After making clear mention to His Mother of the beauties of the noble lady who waited for Him in Thebes tonight—I could see He wished to leave Her jealous—He spoke directly to me at last. The point was clear, and He made it in contempt. "You are a friend to My Father's ear," He said.

"No man like myself can make that claim."

He smiled. He would remind me that He might yet be my King. And a meaner one. He said, "Speak well to My Father Who rewards you."

Not only was He much pleased at the cleverness of these last remarks, but His Mother clapped Her hands, and kissed Him full on the mouth before He left.

"What do you tell His Father?" She asked of me.

"Not a great deal," I said. "The Good God does not listen." I sighed. "It is sad to be the wretch whose limb is crushed between two great stones." Happily, I managed to put a smile on my face, sly and wicked I knew, and She smiled back. "You are as helpless as oil," She said, "and have nothing to fear from two great stones."

This joke is a fine example of what I mean by Her use of our language. "Helpless" and "oil" had the same sound and so were typical of Her magic, light as the wings of a starling. Indeed, it obliged me to ponder why the same sound could make you think both of oil and of helplessness, even as the word for "think" can mean as easily that you are thirsty, or you are a vase, or are dancing, or are ready to stop. Our word for "meditate" was next to "blasphemy," even as our little sound for "ponder"—*mau*—could also mean "the light-of-a-God." Or it could speak of your "anus." There was no end to the nets that held our thought. Could it be that Nefertiri, because She wrote these words so often, knew how the drawing of a little God or some curlicue at the end of a word could take one's meaning away from the light of the sun to the darkest coffin on the inside of your belly? Often, She would amaze me with the delicacy of Her offering. I, who was used to the urgent strength of Ma-Khrut, now came to appreciate how light was the touch of those who are near to the Gods. I knew, despite Her adoration of Her tall son, that She was also glad to be alone with me, but then it was in the nature of a great Queen and Consort of the God to live as if, truly, like Usermare Himself, She, too, had not one Ka but Fourteen, and so there were many women in Her, and each could find its pleasure in a different man.

May I say She knew me very well, for Her first act now that we were alone, was to go to a golden coffer that stood upon a large chest, and from it remove a disc of ebony as wide as one's brow, and with a handle of electrum. Carrying it carefully, so that I could only see the back of this ebony disc, She sat beside me and placed it by its base on the table. Then She said, or so I thought, "Have you ever looked into a fine *revealing*?"

Once again, I was bewildered. I did not believe She could be speaking of the night when Amon came to Her and gave Amen-khep-shu-ef to Her belly, but, in truth, I was much embarrassed by the

directness of such a question, for I supposed She could not mean anything like "conception" which was certainly one of the meanings of
"revealing," but, no, not by the light smile on Her face—no nearness
to Amon there! So I took another meaning for the word, and wondered if She meant, "Have you ever looked into a foulness?" but
again, by Her expression, I knew that could hardly be so. At last, and
with what relief, I concluded that She had said, "Have you ever
looked into a fine river?" for indeed I had, who has not seen the quiet
Nile when the water is calm and clear, and your own face ripples on
the surface of the small waves, so I nodded and said, "Yes, I know
nearly all of the Nile," much relieved, whereupon She reached up,
pinched my cheek, brought a candlestick near to us, and turned the
ebony disc around. I drew back in fright. By the glow of the flame, I
saw the face of a man who had something like my own face, but more
intimate than the surface of all those rippling waters where I had half-
seen it before. Now, I truly saw my own features on this perfect plate
of polished silver, and how much I looked like you, Nef-khep-
aukhem, husband of my granddaughter, Hathfertiti, yes, I had the
expression of one who serves the Good and Great Gods, and was startled by how much caution now dwelt in a man who had once been a
charioteer. How smooth and worried were my cheeks. All those rub-
bings from the cheeks of Honey-Ball! A tomb of corruption must be
my heart! That was the first thought at seeing my face, and it came
from the side of myself that is noblest in spirit, nearest to the brave
Gods, and most demanding of myself, but the next voice I tell you
was from the sweetmeats of myself, and they were delighted with this
look at me. I thought myself handsome, and knowledgeable in the
desires of women, indeed, I was so handsome that I stirred unmistakably and almost came forth like a hound in a frolic, that intoxicating
was the sight of myself. Then I was full of fear because I realized it
was not my own face I saw, but my Ka, which lived on the surface of
this silver, this polished lake of silver. Nefertiri stroked my cheek
with the most mocking touch of Her fingertips, and said, "Ah, the
dear man does not know a mirror."

"Never a mirror like this," I managed to say back to Her, but I

could hardly speak. "Why this," I wanted to say, "will change all that
there is." For I knew that if every soldier and peasant could see his Ka,
why then all would want to act like Gods. Oh, I had looked into common mirrors, scratched and dull, their surface so impure that one's
eyes and nose twisted as one moved it about, but this was a mirror like
no other, it must be the finest in all of Egypt, a true *revealing*—ah,
there was the word She had used—and my Ka was before me, and we
looked at each other.

Then I understood once again how cruel it must be to wander in
Khert-Neter with no tomb for a home, nothing but the banks, the
monsters, and the flames of the serpents. For I saw that my Ka was
virtually me and there before me and so alive. He was the one who
would be destroyed in the smoke and the stink. I wished to cry out
against such monstrosity. So vivid was all I saw of this face, that even
the light of the candle seemed like the flames of Khert-Neter, and I
knew that I loved my Ka and it did not matter how much corruption
was in those features when my life was also in them. Then I gasped.
For by a turn of Her wrist on the handle of this "revealing," so did I
see Her Ka, not mine, and Her indigo eyes, blue as evening in the
flame of the torch, looked back at me from the polished disc, and I
could dare to lay my eyes full into the eyes of Her Ka, this One, at
least, of Her Fourteen, and by my expression must have told Her how
much love I knew for Her since She blinked as if She also saw the
shadow of unseen wings. I think it was then She knew that I must kill
Her if Usermare was dead. By way of the mirror we looked at one
another until the tears came forth in both our eyes.

Yet by the strength of our gaze into each other, so did I enter Her
thoughts for the first time, and before we were done, I took Her
hand—I dared and took Her hand—and was able by way of Her fingers (just so well as with Usermare) to enter Her heart. The thoughts
were not small. She was thinking of the night Amon had come to Her
bed, and She conceived Amen-khep-shu-ef. Yes, the jealousy of Usermare was well-founded. My own had begun at the touch of Her palm
in mine. For I saw Her in the lap of the God and nobody was more
powerful than the Hidden One. The rush of Her thoughts came over

me in this gallop like a thumping of horse's hooves, a true set of blows
to pay for daring to touch Her fingers, but then She was calm again,
and wicked, and leaned forward to whisper in my ear, "Is it true that
Ma-Khrut cannot keep her hands off you?"

Now I do not know if it was my thoughts She could hear, or the
lonely desires of Honey-Ball, or, whether, given the free passage of
eunuchs, so much like birds, from the kitchens of one palace to the
gates of another, Nefertiri had heard it all as gossip. Still, what a clam-
oring in my heart if I was now part of the common gossip.

I did not answer. I thought that if I pretended the question was not
understood, why the dignity of a Queen might keep Her from asking
again. I did not yet understand, so exquisite were Her manners, that
Nefertiri's desires were as close to the roar of the lion as Usermare
Himself. "Come," She said, "is it true? Ma-Khrut has said it." Now,
I had to wonder if Ma-Khrut was so intimate with the Queen that
they spoke to one another through trusted friends.

I could have smiled like a fool, or merely looked wise, but some
strength out of the heart that once spoke in me as a brave man drew
my eyes back to the mirror, and I reached forward with my fingers
and turned the handle so that we could speak again from the eyes of
my Ka into Hers, and I said, "If it were not for the loveliness that
surrounds Your Majesty, I would think often of Ma-Khrut." In such
an instant I understood that the true desire for revenge is like a serpent. If its tail rested in the pits of my dream its head spoke in the eyes
of my Queen. We both felt the breath of Ma-Khrut, as if she did not
give us her blessing so much as the power to use her curse. Nefertiri
and I still looked at one another through the mirror, but now it might
as well have been the high bank of a river past which flood waters
wash in the great force of a bend. We saw each other with all the surprise one might know when looking at a stranger in the marketplace—yes, by Her size and by the poise of Her hips, so equal to mine,
does that woman draw me forward, and by Her age as well—She is
my age, and has my wisdom, She is a stranger who could be my mate.
So I saw Her, and knew She saw me, She as a woman, not a Goddess,
and I as a man, not a servant. It was wondrous to me how we met in

all that is equal, and were so well met. We smiled tenderly at one another. Alas. That Ka was only one of Her Fourteen.

Still, we were as tender as new-found friends, and She took my hand again and began to explain to me, now that we were near, a matter I had never understood before. Yet much which had been incomprehensible to me in the Gardens of the Secluded was now restored to its place, and it gave me much new knowledge of my Pharaoh. I saw why He came back from Kadesh as another man. For She told me how on the day of the great battle when the Hittites broke through, and Usermare prayed in His tent, He had asked Amon to give Him the strength to meet His foe, and the Hidden One had told Him that His wish would be granted. "You do not ask Me for a long life," were the words of Amon, "and so You will gain much strength."

"He has lived," said Nefertiri, "for twenty-nine years since that day, but He still waits for the hour when Amon will come to take Him.

"That is why He is now with a woman of the Hittites," said Nefertiri. "He hopes Amon will not dare to go to war with Hittite Gods." I saw the anger in Her eyes. "He knows great fear when He sleeps with the Hittite Princess and tries to be close to Her Gods. For He still wants Me." Her voice was as deep as the night, and as grave as the weight of the stone that She would lay upon His tomb. "I despise Sesusi," She said, "for His fear."

Eleven

Sometimes, sleeping alone in the House of the Companion of the Right Hand, I would awake in the middle of the night and feel Honey-Ball near to me. There was not a bat who passed through my window, nor a bird scattering the hush of the night who could not have been a visitor from her garden, and I felt the Gods rising like the inundation. Just as villages would soon become islands, so would my fortunes ride on a floodwater. I knew I must seize whatever was offered.

I say this because the next offering was foul, and I was sick of such practices. Yet nothing that came my way offered more service to Nefertiri. Once, Honey-Ball, while mixing the dung of her cat with the ashes of a plant and the blood from her arm, said, as if to herself, "It is the leavings of Sesusi that I need the most," and I felt a revulsion so large that the food in my stomach nearly came forth into the stew of her magic. Yet I never forgot her words. For I understood they were true. I brooded much on the nature of such stuff when I lived in the Gardens of the Secluded—how could I not? Sometimes it was as near to me as the earth to my feet. I even supposed that dung must be the center of all things, and that was its reason for departing from us

by the center of the body—a true compact between Set and Geb!
Certainly I came to the sad conclusion that excrement was as much a
part of magic as blood or fire, an elixir of dying Gods and rotting
spirits desperate to regain the life they were about to lose. Yet when I
thought of all the transformation that dung contains (since it is not
only good crops which sprout from it, but one has to take account of
the dogs who eat it, and the flies who swarm over it) I began to think
of all those Gods, small and mean as pestilence itself, Who dwell next
to such great changes. "How dangerous is this excrement," I said to
myself, and knew one terrible thought, even if I could not explain it.
To hold the leavings of another must be equal to owning great gold
and wealth.

Was it for such a reason that all who visited the Court would wear
as much gold as they possessed? I still remember how in the Great
Square between the Wide Palace and the Little Palace, the gold would
glisten on their bodies like sunlight on the surface of the Lake of
Maat. By its bank was a patio of white marble under a gold roof, and
in that cool place all used to congregate, every nobleman and rich
merchant in Thebes, and every man of consequence who had traveled
up the river from the Delta or down from the nomes of Upper Egypt.
Like cattle who come down to the river to drink, they were all there,
and that would yet contribute to my offering.

To enter the Wide Palace was not permitted without a papyrus
from the Office of the Gates, and the Little Palace was forbidden to all
but intimate servants of Usermare. So, on this patio between, by the
Lake of Maat, the wealthy of Egypt would wait for Usermare to pass
in His route from one Palace to another. He was always carried, and
eight visitors would bear Him—eight chosen from the hundred and
more who waited for word to issue from the doors of either Palace
that the Good and Great God was coming forth. These visitors would
then become a mob, jostling with one another like the first froth of
the rising waters for the right to carry Usermare on the Golden Belly
(which was what we called His palanquin) but then this was the only
time when such fellows could serve Him. The other moves He might
make from Court to Temple or to the streets of Thebes or down to

the Royal Boat-House were carried out by officers assigned to His Guard who served at a particular position, indeed, there used to be a name for each of them—Third Bearer of the Right Limb of the Golden Belly was the kind of title. The Guard were, however, not used on the many trips He took between the Wide Palace and the Little Palace. For that, any merchant esteemed enough to enter through the Double-Gate by the river, could, if fortunate, obtain the privilege of carrying Him those few hundreds of steps around the Lake of Truth (that is, the Lake of Maat) into the doors of the other Palace. It was not a long trip, but one heard of men who waited through a hot afternoon by the doors of either Palace, there in all the most terrible hours of the heat, crushed against one another, stinking in the oven of the sun if they did not carry their perfumes—woe to the body who stank in the nostrils of Usermare!—but in that terrible press, some would prevail, some would seize the honor (and talk about it for the rest of their lives). No matter how exhausted from the hours of waiting, they were delighted to cheer in unison carrying Him and His Golden Belly with His Seat upon it. They would cheer even as they ran, and never seem to fear that any would drop dead from the pace at which they went, while another crowd of prominent men from far-off nomes would wait at the next doors in the hope He would soon come out again.

That was when I knew how high was my own station. I looked with contempt upon men who would make such fools of themselves. If, when General-of-all-the-Armies, I did not yet have entrance to the House of Adoration (which was our other name for the Little Palace) still I rode in my chariot behind His Chariot through the streets and out to the courses where we had our races in the deserts to the East, and when His route was not so long, and He chose to be borne on His Golden Belly, I had a place to His right, second on the bearing-pole behind His Vizier of Lower Egypt, a weak fellow whose load I used to help support. Then, in the Gardens, as Governor of the House of the Secluded, I had held His five fingers. Now, as Companion of the Right Hand, I had entrance to the Little Palace at any hour and by any door. How could it be otherwise if my King lived in fear of His Son and His Wife? He had told me to tell Him all I heard. Often He would summon me and ask many questions. Rarely, however, would I please Him since He did not hear what He was waiting for—a tale of Nefertiri's disloyalty, or an intrigue by Her son. Instead, I used what skill I had to suggest that little could be learned until She came to trust me more. I made much, however, of small sighs from Her lips, and the cruel expression on the mouth of Amen-khep-shu-ef. By exaggerating such trifles, I succeeded on the one hand in convincing my King that I was loyal to Him—no easy matter—yet allowed Him to conclude that there was no sure evil to be found in His Wife or His Son. That also pleased Him. But then a Monarch with a Double-Crown must have Two-Lands to His mind: if Upper Egypt desired true tales of treachery, Lower Egypt was delighted with Her fidelity. All the same, after Nefertiri told me of His great and secret fear of Amon, I decided to let Him know what She had said, even if I hardly knew how I dared to confess so much. He had received me in His bed in the great room where He slept, and in His arms, Her golden hair covering His chest, was Rama-Nefru, yet I told it all, and with no pain that I was betraying Nefertiri. Indeed, I believe She knew I would tell it to Him, and wanted it so. Certainly, She grew greater in all our eyes as I repeated Her words, "I despise Him for His fear."

Usermare shouted in a voice to bring the walls of His temples down on my ears, and Rama-Nefru looked at me for the first time. Although I had been in His bedchamber twice before when She was there, I had seen no more of the Hittite than the back of Her head. Neither time had They moved while I spoke, and when I had no more to say, I left, so, now, it was in pride, I think, at the boldness of my Queen's words that I repeated them, and could have sworn I acted properly.

Certainly, Rama-Nefru sat up in bed, and showed the wickedness of Her little breasts (which were wide apart) and cried aloud, "She is evil, Her eye is evil," words I could barely understand, so strong was Her emotion, and strange words to come from a young face as open as a flower, but I knew by the pain of Her voice that She was wiser than Her own anger. She knew Usermare would not think of Her for the rest of the morning. By the fury of His desire to lay hands upon this insolence (but could not—They were not speaking!) so would He be living with Nefertiri this day rather than with His young bride.

It was then He ordered me to take the Golden Bowl by His bed and empty it in His garden, and the command was uttered with such contempt that Rama-Nefru smiled at me as if to draw half of the insult back upon Herself, a kindness I would not have expected from a Queen. I bowed to Her, and to my King, picked up the Bowl, and stepped backward from the room to be met immediately by a priest who waited in the vestibule. He was the Overseer of the Golden Bowl, and offered this title before I could even turn around. My duties were concluded, he told me.

I did not argue. The tips of my fingers still burned in shame from the manner in which I had been dismissed. Though no tears were in my eyes, I knew the terrible rage, so full of its own weakness, that children suffer, for I hated my Pharaoh, but such hatred was worthless since I wished to be able to love Him. Indeed, I knew I did love Him, and it was hopeless. He would only love me less. How I wished to destroy Him.

I had such thoughts. Walking beside the priest while he carried the Golden Bowl, I wondered that the earth did not tremble from all that was awesome in my head, but the light of morning remained as golden as the surface of the Bowl even if my hands still shook from the intimate warmth of the metal where I had touched it. My palm burned like the sun.

"There is," said the priest, seeing I still accompanied him, "no lack of respect for your own high office, but it is His command to perform these duties in solitude."

"That is true for all other days," I said, "but this morning, I was told to stay with you. Ask the One."

I knew he would not dare. Beneath his shaven head, was a weak and selfish face. He nodded as if his first pride was that few matters could surprise him. Still, I could see he was worried. Were his duties to be reduced?

We went by a path through a garden. I may say that he walked with his arms thrust out like one who carries an offering to the altar. Wherever we passed a soldier or a maid or a gardener, so did they bow low before this Golden Bowl, and I noticed that the priest inclined his head like the Pharaoh Himself, just so stately was the gesture.

Before a green wooden door on which I could see the outline of a wild pig painted in black, we stopped, and the priest drew forth a wooden key from his skirts, opened the door, and looked at me once more. He was still in doubt that the One had truly told me to come so far. But I inquired with confidence, "What is the name of this wild pig?"

"Sha-ah," said the priest, and proceeded to become most learned. "That is the name of Set when He fought with Horus and became a wild boar."

"Yes," I said, "this is the same name of the door that the One told me to enter." I did not know why I wished to go in, yet I did, and with all the certainty one knows when close to the orders of the Gods. Which is to say, close to those Gods Who are awake within you. Who can be so fortunate as to know Their names?

We entered a modest garden in which many herbs were growing, and this priest knelt by one small furrow, set down the Bowl, removed the lid, and began to knead little pellets which he tamped into place around the base of each plant until the Bowl was empty. I also knelt beside him, and must have looked as if I would touch one of the leaves, for he said, "These are herbs of wisdom, and may be plucked only by me as His Overseer." I nodded. This would agree, my manner said, with all I had been told, and I stood up. Of course, he had been looking so suspiciously at the hand close to the leaves that he had not watched the one near the roots. In my fingers I now held a pellet, and it was as warm as the blood of Usermare, but then it came from the seat of the Two-Lands. I bowed, and the priest knelt by a small altar and prayed. Then he washed his hands in holy water, and withdrew from this small garden, myself a pace in front of him, only to quit the fellow on the walks outside and proceed at my own quick gait from the grounds of the Little Palace, around the Lake of Maat to the Wide Palace, and from there I walked even faster through other gardens and by many a shrine and temple until I stood before the gates of the Chambers of the Royal Wife, and was welcomed into the Throne Room of Nefertiri, and from there, so soon as Her morning audience with Her Officials was complete, went into the bedchamber where we had sat last night by Her mirror, and all the while my hand throbbed as if I held the heart of Usermare in His leavings.

When I showed it to my Queen, She was grave and quick, and more deft than Ma-Khrut. She did not wait for darkness, nor proceed through any invocation, but merely took the pellet in Her palm, closed Her eyes, spoke some words to Herself, and handed it back. "Go," She said, "to the Lake of Maat and drop His gift in there."

I did as She said. Later that afternoon while the eight bearers of the Golden Belly were carrying the One from the Wide Palace to His Little Palace, so, by the right bearing-pole, even as they passed the Lake, not one man, but two, collapsed at the same instant, and the Golden Belly tipped over. Usermare fell out of His Seat from a height higher than the saddle of a horse, and His head struck the marble. He did not move, and some thought He was dead. All knew He was near to dead. Nothing stirred but the wind in His throat.

He was carried to the House of Adoration by the Guard of the Adored who were nearer than the Guard of the Wide Palace. Once brought to His bed in the Chamber of the Blessed Fields, He was attended by four royal doctors, priests from the School of Sekhmet. Fomentations of dried herbs from the Garden of Sha-ah were put to boil, and their steam entered His nostrils. The half-chewed meat of Nubian lions was pulled from their jaws to be mixed with fourteen vegetables for His Ka, all Fourteen, and His head was anointed where He struck the ground. The priests sang prayers, and Rama-Nefru entered and began to wail in Her own language of the Hittites, after which, Nefertiri, so soon as the other was gone, paid a visit with Amen-khep-shu-ef and They sat in silence by His bed, myself behind Them in the second rank next to the doctors from the Goddess Sekhmet. Usermare never stirred.

It was then, looking at His silent body, that I realized the Good and Great God might die, and I prayed as well. For if He did not live,

I would have to kill Nefertiri, or meet His wrath in years to come when I went to Khert-Neter.

Now, whenever I looked at Her, I would see myself with a dagger in my hand. She was there on Her golden seat, sitting in silence on the third morning. Outside, across all the patios and gardens, the King lay unmoving in the Little Palace, and the vigil of the doctors did not cease. No man moved across all of that paving of marble around the Lake of Maat, and beyond our walls, the city of Thebes was near to silent. So in the silence that lay upon Nefertiri, did I sit and stare at Her and wonder if I could obey the secret command of my King.

While I thought of no orders but my own, I knew that throughout the Horizon-of-Ra, great nobles and Viziers were plotting with priests as to who should become the "well-beloved friend" of the next King. Amen-khep-shu-ef was with His Mother often, but rarely without His guard, and they, as I expected, were in the state of all good soldiers when a battle is near, and death, wounds, or treasure are close. They had the happiness of the best warriors and suffered that they had to walk about with unhappy faces. They were feeling, I knew, as cheerful as great beasts and wanted to smash each other's heads on the marble floor for all the impatience of waiting.

In these days, I never saw Amen-khep-shu-ef when He did not show the wild eye of a falcon. He glared at me often, until at last I chose not to look away but let our glances meet. We stared at one another until all decorum was lost. My eyes could not have been more oppressed if His fingers had been squeezing them. But I was weary of humiliation. Besides, I had fought beside His Father in the greatest battle ever fought, and this Amen-khep-shu-ef had been in the wrong place that day. Yes, I stared back with all the power of the Gods Who passed through me at Kadesh, and dwelt in the invocations of Ma-Khrut, and so, when our eyes locked, mine may have been as fierce as His. The contest remained equal. I think we would have gone blind staring at one another if Nefertiri had not come between, and said quietly, "If Your Father dies, I will need both of you."

Amen-khep-shu-ef left the room. He could not bear to be cheated of a victory. Since He never believed He could lose, the interruption from His Mother had stolen a prize. So He saw it. But I do not know. If I had blinked my eyes before His, I think I would have drawn my short sword on the next breath, and if I killed Him, She would have been the next, then everybody who came at me until I was done. At that moment, I knew again all the happiness of the brave, and felt equal to Nefertiri. It was Her life She had protected by placing Her hands between us. It was then I believed again as I used to when I was young that I, too, was a true Son of Amon, and the Hidden One had come to my mother. How else had my eye proved equal to the eye of Amen-khep-shu-ef? There could be no other explanation. And I laughed that in His rage He had been such a fool as to leave me alone with Her.

She smiled softly, but said, "Why did Sesusi choose you to be My servant?"

"Do You ask because I am Your friend?"

She did not reply at first, but came nearer to me. "I know the doubts of Amen-khep-shu-ef," She said.

I bowed. I touched the ground seven times with my forehead. I did not know what I would reply until my words came forth. "I am to be here when Usermare dies," I said. "That is His order to me."

She nodded. She knew what I did not say. The nearness of Her death came about Her like a garment held by a servant.

"Why do you tell Me?" She asked. "Is it because you will not obey Him?"

I was about to say, "I will never obey Him. Your heart is of more worth to me than His heart," but I did not. The wisdom of the most cunning Gods touched my tongue and I said, "I do not think that I will, yet I cannot swear."

She looked at me in another manner then. I saw an expression in Her eyes that offered more than tenderness, indeed, there was respect in it. She felt admiration that I would dare to kill Her. Such courage must belong to the Gods. But, then, how could a Queen be drawn to any man like myself unless the God spoke through him?

"Yes," She said, "it must be true. Ma-Khrut cannot keep her hands off you," and She gave a delightful smile which said clearly that I need only be brave enough, and all could happen.

Of course, She was a Queen. A Monarch's heart is like the labyrinth of the entrails. Snakes coil at every turn. So did I also know that next to the little love She might feel for me, was the fire of Her marriage. How could She not believe that Usermare still wanted Her if He had ordered Her sent to join Him so soon as He died?

Twelve

Usermare did not die. By the fourth day, He opened His eyes; by the fifth, He spoke; on the sixth, He raised His head; and on the next, He was standing. Soon He was back in His Chariot, and paid a visit to the Secluded. I still spoke to Pepti and even met him at the gate to the Gardens on many a morning. We would tell each other much, he on his side, I on mine, and so I learned that on His return to the Secluded, Usermare had spent the night with Ma-Khrut, and the sounds of their pleasure had been louder than the lion and the hippopotamus. Next day, she acted like a Consort, and moved in much radiance.

I smiled through every word offered by the damnable Pepti (whose face had that smugness peculiar to eunuchs as if they are the seed itself of the Blessed Fields) but I knew the cold woe of a merchant who is left naked in the moonlight after his caravan is robbed.

Yet, on reflection, I did not know whether I had gained or lost. A few of His best curses might now belong to her. I do know that on my return, Honey-Ball's eunuch, Castor-Oil, was waiting outside my house, and he handed me a long red feather, then left silently. That was a message on which we had agreed before I left the Gardens. It was word from Honey-Ball to see her as soon as I could, and by any means.

Now, through these days of His recovery, the Palace had been in disarray. Much of the disturbance came from those who had the most ambitious plans on how to act after His death. Such hopes had been lost on His return. And who could begin to measure the disorder among the Gods? So many had been invoked by priests and nobles praying for a particular successor. I know that in the days of His convalescence, much went wrong. Ceremonies in the Temple were improperly conducted, and errors of addition began to be found in many a sum laid before His Officials. There was abominable crowding in the halls outside the Great Chamber. Stewards and scribes, even Governors of nomes had reports to offer that no one had read while He was ill.

I ignored most of that. I would pass by the Great Chamber and not enter. I stayed at the side of Nefertiri even more than before, and She wanted me near. Since we did not know what I would have done if Usermare had died, we certainly did not know what we would do now that He was alive. A day did not pass but She would bring forth the mirror, and we would look at one another, and study the Ka of the other's face, and many of Her Fourteen I came to know, at least by a little. A cloud could not touch the edge of the sun, nor a breeze enter the pillars of the patio, before Her Ka would leave and another of the Fourteen enter the mirror. Sometimes, She would speak to me in this manner only, our eyes connected by the mirror, particularly on those mornings when it was known through every mansion of the Palace that He had gone to visit Rama-Nefru. Nefertiri would even say, "He will not come to Me until I beg His pardon for the soup spilled on His chest, but I won't. He had My servant flogged until the poor man died." She nodded with all the weight of a numb heart. "The daughter of this dead butler," said Nefertiri, "is blind, and used to have the finest voice in my Chorus of the Blind. Since her father was killed she has not been able to imitate the sound of one bird." Nefertiri looked at me. "It is the fault of the woman with the dyed hair."

That was how She spoke of Rama-Nefru. So great was Her detestation of Rama-Nefru that She used the word for bleach, *sesher,* that is also our word for dung. She wove *sesher* in and out of what She said until the beautiful hair of Rama-Nefru came to sound like intestines left white, emptied out, bleached out—I did not like the cruelty of this Ka in Nefertiri's face, for, once begun, it never wished to leave the mirror. "The Hittite hates Usermare," said my Queen. "He suffers miseries He cannot know—He is too strong to know His own misery. Why, He would not have fallen so heavily from the Golden Belly if His senses were not stupefied. That is what comes from making stupid love to that Hittite with the bleached hair."

Finally, She said to me, "I wish Her hair would fall out. There is no gift I would not offer then."

How much power those few words gave to me! I revered Her, I fear, like a Goddess. I did not believe, try as I would, that I would remain firm should She ever choose me. I might be the Son of Amon, but there were greater Sons. She repeated, however, "There is no gift I would not offer," and Her eyes spoke so clearly to the seeds and snakes of my groin that for the first time I wanted Her with the spirit of the swamp. The God Set came awake in me. I desired Her between Her thighs there in the Ka-of-Isis.

Nefertiri now said, "You must pay a visit to Honey-Ball."

I did not tell Her how difficult that would be. I bowed instead and left Her chamber, and then bowed again, for Amen-khep-shu-ef was approaching. Now, we did not look into each other's eyes. We would never look into them again unless our swords pointed at one another. But He was here to say goodbye to His Mother, so I learned, for we actually spoke (each of us looking at the other's mouth as if it were a fort to take by siege) that He would go with His barges down the river today, off to fight one of His little wars in Libya, another town to besiege—such were Usermare's orders. I wished Him well with the best of my manners, and thought it was a good omen He would be gone.

After His departure, I wandered by the Gates of Morning and Evening at the Gardens of the Secluded, and told one of the two eunuchs standing guard to send for Pepti. Soon we spoke through a narrow opening in the wall by the side of the gates.

"There is peace with me," I told him. "I hope there is peace with you."

"There is peace with me."

He could not go on. He began to laugh, which for him was much the same as to cry. Many eunuchs, I had noticed, did not seem to know the difference between laughing and crying—their lives were so different from ours. "In truth," he said, "there is a disturbance in the House of the Secluded," and went on to tell me of quarrels between the little queens, and rudeness among the eunuchs. Certain houses looked slovenly. The night that Usermare had spent with Honey-Ball left confusion in many. He sighed. "I think it is the rising of the river."

"I have come to tell you of a greater disturbance. Households are going to be moved, and Great Queens will sleep in new beds."

He cried at the magnitude of such change, that is, tears were in his eyes, but I did not know if he was laughing. "There won't be such a disturbance soon," he said. I looked into his eyes which were large and swollen forth as if someone were squeezing his throat. "The One," he said, "loves the pale gold of the sun. When He is with Her, He holds the sun in His hand."

"That is how it used to be. But since His fall, He has been weary of the Hittite."

Pepti shrugged. "He told Ma-Khrut to give Him magic to make the Hittite love Him more."

"Ma-Khrut tells you more than she would tell me."

"I am a eunuch."

I nodded. "You are also wise. I have said to Queen Nefertiri that you are the wisest man I know. She said, 'We need such a man as our Vizier!'"

He was pleased, but did not believe me. He was too wise for that. "You were not there to hear the warmth of the Queen's voice when She spoke of you," I said. "Do you know how She hates the man who now is Vizier?"

"I have heard." He might indeed be wise, but also he wanted to believe me. "Does the One," he asked, "ever listen to Nefertiri?"

"Soon He will."

Pepti looked at me as though I were a fool.

"No," I said, "you are mistaken. Others come and leave. Sooner or later, He always goes back to Her. And when He does, She never forgets those who were loyal. Be loyal to Her now, and She will get you the highest rewards."

He looked glum. "Even if it is all as you say, the One would never accept a eunuch for His Vizier."

"No," I told him, "you are wrong. The only men trusted by Sesusi are eunuchs." I said it bitterly as if, but for that, I could be a Vizier myself. "Sesusi does not trust men," I said, "only eunuchs."

Now Pepti did believe me. It was the cruelty of my remark. Cruelty he could always trust.

"You," he said, and he was crying now, "would like me to become a Vizier. Then you could command the Court through me."

"That would not be true," I said. "I would never make such an attempt."

He smiled as if my lies were absurd. Yet, he believed me more. I knew his calculation. If he were Vizier, I would discover that there was more to his will than the sword he no longer kept between his legs. "My friend," I said, "let the day come when you are a Vizier. Then we shall see if I speak through you, or you through me."

"I do not feel close to the Queen Nefertiri."

"Still, if you help Her now, She will never forget."

"How would She hear that I was the one who helped Her?"

"She has asked me to speak to Honey-Ball. She knows that cannot be done unless you are Her friend."

"If I am discovered, they will cut off my hands."

No, the task was easy, I told him. He could send one of the two eunuchs here at the gate off to the market. The other could be given work in the house of a little queen, and Pepti could occupy his place. Then, Honey-Ball might come through the Gardens and stop by this small opening in the wall. Round as she was, no one could see her there, not for all the foliage of the bushes.

He was cautious. Even in the present disorder of the Gardens—"and there was a beer-house last night noisier than any I remember," said Pepti—he still did not believe that Honey-Ball could walk the length of the path from her house to this wall and attract no attention. Honey-Ball did not walk for too little. All the same, he would have a conversation with her. If I returned this evening, he would be at our little opening in the wall.

No Vizier could have dismissed me with more dispatch. That night, when we met again, he told me that Honey-Ball was ready to be of service to Queen Nefertiri, but wished in turn that her own dignity be honored by a special invitation from the Queen to her and her family for the Festival of Festivals.

Nefertiri was displeased. Of course, She could do it, but She paced back and forth. The calm of Her bearing was gone. I saw another Ka of Her Fourteen.

"I am ready to reward Honey-Ball," She said. "It is understood she will be rewarded. But I cannot bear her family. I was entertained by them on my last visit to Sais, and they are common. Very wealthy and common. They have a papyrus factory, and make contracts with every Temple of Amon in their nome. Most respectable in their airs. But the great-grandmother of Ma-Khrut was a prostitute. So it is said. So I believe. You can see it in the way they eat. That family wipes their fingers too carefully. They are quick to speak of their ancestry while the wine is passed. They go back twenty generations. They assure you of that. They have the audacity—oh, they are truly common—to present the names of their forebears as if one were speaking of people of substance. They went on in that manner to Me! I came near to telling them that as a matter of family, I could mention Hatshep-sut and Thutmose. But no, we did not talk of anyone but their forebears. Twenty generations of harlots and thieves! These are people of the swamp. No," She said, "I really do not want them seated in My circle. Nor do I know, for that matter, whether I care to have Honey-Ball near Me. She has an excellent education, and knows as much about perfume as I do—I would not say that for any other woman—but I detest her for growing so fat. It is an absolute abuse of Maat. I like Honey-Ball, we knew each other as children, I adore her voice. If she were blind, I would treat her like a Goddess for the joy of listening to her sing, but I also tell you this: I consider her a hippopotamus and a slut. She has noble blood, but of the lowest sort. Her family does business with shit-collectors."

I felt so bold as to answer, "It was only to protect her toe."

"The one Usermare cut off?" When I said yes, Nefertiri laughed with much agitation. "Sesusi never told Me all of *that*. He does not tell a story well." She sighed. "You believe that I should invite her?"

"It is better to have Ma-Khrut for a friend than an enemy."

"It is even better to have Me for a friend." She sat down at last. "Come here. Look into the mirror." Her eyes were merry. "I like Ma-Khrut. When Sesusi and I were younger, Ma-Khrut was the only little queen of whom I was jealous. Tell me, Kazama, was I right to be jealous?"

"I would not know, Good and Great Goddess. It is forbidden to go near a little queen."

"Everybody knows of you and Ma-Khrut. Even her sister knows. That is how I found out. Her sister writes to Me. You see, I am really very friendly with her family. It is just that they are common."

"Does the Good and Great God know?"

"I would think He does."

"He is not angry?"

"Why should He be? He has had you by the asshole, has He not?" Now I saw Her fury. I had dared to bring this request from Honey-Ball. But no, I concluded, Usermare could not have heard of my affair in the Gardens. Nefertiri was merely punishing me. I was beginning to understand how profound was Her displeasure that I did not produce the magic of Ma-Khrut without a payment in return. She looked at me in the mirror. I saw no love whatever. "Tell Honey-Ball that I will keep a seat for her, two for her parents, and one for her sister. No more." Her eyes turned away from the mirror and looked at me directly. I could have been a servant. "Sleep well," She said. I did not.

Thirteen

I saw Pepti next morning in the Wide Palace. He was on the other side of the throne in a file of Officials waiting to address the King. So I could do no more than meet the question in his eye with a nod of my head, and had to wait until evening to meet him at the Khebit Kheper which was the grand title given by little queens to the hole in the wall where Pepti and I spoke to each other. How ironic was this Hole of the Beetle, this Hole of Becoming. For nothing became of it. At best, a few whispers between a charioteer and a little queen.

By the aid of a stick, Pepti pushed out to me a packet from Honey-Ball wrapped in linen and smelling of incense. It was longer and narrower than her well-wrapped toe, but its emanations spoke to me of nothing I knew.

On my return the Guard of the Vizier was waiting outside Her Throne Room, and within was the Vizier speaking to Nefertiri. The visit had put Her in a most gracious manner. It was his first appearance at Her Palace in many a month, so She mocked him slightly on presenting me, saying, "Kazama is *My* Vizier," of which he took full notice. He was a man to observe the changing fortunes of others like a river pilot stays keen to the wind, and he bowed to me with a look that spoke of future conversations between us. Then he left, whereupon She said, "That man does not make many mistakes. I hope the same may be said of you." She took my little wrapping. Within, was a piece of papyrus and a tress of blond hair. She held this last with a look of no pleasure on Her face. "It is as coarse as the tail of a bull," She said, and began to read from the papyrus. "Well," She said, "it *is* hair from the tail of a bull," and looked a little further. "Black hair," She read from the papyrus, "blessed by words-of-power, then dyed. As black hair turns blond, so does blond hair fall away." Now, She gave a cry of much displeasure. "Look," She said, pointing to a dark, congested little stream on the papyrus, "this is not wax but a dead worm! She tells Me to mix this with my own pomade and to sleep with it. Sleep with this worm in My hair, and the tail of the bull under My bed. No," She said as She continued to read, "under My headrest itself. I am ill."

She did not look well. I did my best to soothe Her. I explained that any sorcery powerful enough to pull out the roots of an enemy had to create a considerable disturbance. One could not send such illness to another without suffering a part of it oneself. I did not ask Her why, if she could use the leavings of Usermare so adroitly as to crash His head to the marble, She need suffer feelings of fastidiousness here. I understood, however. A woman knows more fear at attacking another woman with her magic than a man. Nor did I even dare to speak of Pepti's last instruction to me. Each night, for seven nights, of which this was the first, I must go to the Khebit Kheper for another wrapping. Each night Nefertiri would receive a new message.

Indeed, on the second night, it was worse. She was told to take the blond fibers that She had kept beneath Her headrest for the first night and now hold them in Her hand while She slept; on the third night She had to put them in a sack around Her belly; by the fourth, around Her neck. Be certain that by the seventh night, She slept with it between Her thighs and was no longer so outraged. The magic was having a most powerful effect.

By then, there was no one in the Court who had not heard of the

suffering of Rama-Nefru and the dreadful purge of Her stomach. I
saw Her myself on the fifth morning. The King held Her in His arms,
and Her body contracted like a snake and sprung forth, contracted
and sprung forth, while the Royal Doctor held a golden saucer to Her
mouth. I was asked to leave the room. I knew the Golden Bowl was
also in use. From the roots of Her stomach and the roots of Her entrails was She discharging. Later that day, I heard Her hair had begun
to fall out. So did the word pass through Court like the rise of the
river.

Usermare called on Heqat. The little queen was summoned from
the Gardens, a Syrian to treat a near-Syrian, and Heqat asked for the
shell of a tortoise from the shores of the Very Green. Doctors and
messengers went through every market of Thebes before such a curious object was found, and Heqat boiled it to a jelly, then mixed in the
fat of a hippopotamus just killed. They used this pomade every day,
but it was said Rama-Nefru had already lost Her hair.

Nefertiri never ceased speaking of Heqat. "To be ill is misfortune
enough," She said, "but to be nursed by a woman with a face like a
frog is a catastrophe. Tell Me, did Sesusi ever make love to Heqat?"
When I nodded, She shook Her head in admiration. "He is a God,"
She said. "Only a God could enjoy Honey-Ball and Heqat." She
looked at me again. "And on the same night?" I nodded. "He is sprung
from the loins of Set," She said. But Her expression could not have
been more merry. "You must tell Me all about you and Honey-Ball."

"I do not dare," I said.

"Oh, you will tell Me." Her good spirits could hardly be measured. I wondered why Nefertiri was bothered so little by Usermare's
continuing loyalty to Rama-Nefru. This dreadful illness did not seem
to drive Him away. Indeed He had not made even one visit to the
Gardens in all the days Rama-Nefru was sick. Yet the splendid mood
of Nefertiri diminished so little that I began to wonder if it were a
folly caused by the magic—a subtle working of the balance of Maat.
Indeed, Nefertiri began to limp a little in these days from a twinge in
Her bone where the thigh entered the hip, and this limp, so long as I
knew Her, never went away. Yet, speak of folly, it had no effect that

I could see on Her fine mood—She ignored it. She was a Queen and there were more intimate matters of concern. Once, She even said, "Sesusi will always tell you of His loyalty"—She pealed with laughter—"but He is very easily bored. He will remain true to Her until the day He cannot endure Rama-Nefru for one more instant. Then He will send Her, bald head and all, back to the Hittites with a wig, a *blue* wig, and they will declare a great war on us for the insult. Amen-khep-shu-ef will find glory instead of growing old with little sieges, and Usermare will grow very old with Me. I will yet know the power of Hat-shep-sut!" She held my hand as She spoke, and I could feel the fever in it.

Others must have begun to reason in Her way, however. The visits of high Officials to Her Court were now more frequent. Before, there had been days when you could see no one in Her Chambers but the Keepers of Her Apartment, the Keepers of Her Wardrobe, the Keepers of Her Kitchen, the Keepers of Her Carriage, plus a number of old, petty, and garrulous friends. Now the Governor of the Treasury of Upper Egypt came one morning with his scribes, eight of them— to show the extent of his courtesy—and Privy Councillors visited, Princes, judges, even the Governor of the Palace, a Lord Chamberlain—old men, many of them, and to my eye not the most powerful nor the closest of Usermare's Councillors, rather, old friends, it seemed to me, of the days when Nefertiri stood alone as Queen. I would have been more certain of a turn in Her fortunes if nobles closer to Rama-Nefru were among the visitors.

All the while, Nefertiri would complain to me in the happiest tones. "I enjoyed My days more," She said, "when you and I could spend the hours of the evening looking into the mirror," and She would touch me lightly under the ear, or draw Her fingertips along my arm. Never had I felt sensations that traveled so far in me from so delicate a touch, unless it was in my memory of the secret whore of the King of Kadesh. Her eyes spoke to me now without a mirror, Her fingers teased my neck, and when we were alone, Her gowns became more transparent. I had known there were marvels one could weave of linen, and many ladies on great occasions would wear the gauzes of

Cos, so that you could see their bodies beneath their gowns as clearly as their husbands would see them later, but I was to learn that even in these thin veilings of woven-air, even finer than the woven-air worn by my granddaughter tonight, were some of a lightness to make you swear that spiders had spun the thread. Nefertiri kept them in the subtlest colors so that you could not swear whether her gown was tinted like the yellow rose or if it were the light of the candle, but the gold of Her body was visible to me, and when the beauty of Her breasts touched Her linen, the golden-pink of the nipple of Nefertiri deepened in the shadows to a rose-bronze.

I would stir, I would growl mightily in the silence, but only to myself. I was a lion without legs. Never was I more aware of the poverty of my beginnings than when I measured the emptiness of my strength before Her Ka-of-Isis, and knew that even if Nefertiri were to minister to me with the crudest arts of Honey-Ball (which doubtless She would not) I might still be numb and equal to the dead. When it comes to making love to a Queen, a peasant carries a boulder on his back.

So I stared at Her in the mirror, putting all the hunger of my limp loins into the ferocity of my eyes. With my eyes I desired Her, and with such adoration, enriched the air with honey. She seemed to enjoy these evenings when the others were gone and we were alone. Her desire for me looked ready to rise with the river beyond the Palace walls, but my loins felt like a land where it rained and the mist was cold. I thought of Her low opinion of the family of Ma-Khrut with their twenty generations, and wondered why She desired me at all. I concluded (was it the wisdom of Ma-Khrut in my ear?) that no insult could be more profound to Usermare than the touch of peasant flesh on Hers.

So, She sat beside me, evening after evening, in a gown of woven-air, while I, transfixed by every view She gave of the grove beneath Her belly, began to feel like a priest ready to kneel before the altar more than like a warrior able to enter Her gates. Yet, at last, this must have begun to please Her profoundly for there came a night when She chose to tell how Amon made love to Her, and I wondered how I,

who could never have the loins of a Pharaoh, was supposed to rise out
of the ashes left by Her tale.

"In the year I was a young bride," She began, "Usermare was the
most beautiful of all the Gods but I saw the Hidden One. His spear
grew out of My husband's sword like the fork of three branches that
springs from the loins of Osiris, and I saw lightning flash and wild
boars fought with hippopotami. The darkest of His three spears entered the cavern of Set, yet My Ka-of-Isis could swallow the Secret
Name of Ra (which is the second branch) and His third sword (that
was like the arrow of Osiris) lifted in a rainbow above Our bodies and
We drove in His chariot over the sun. That night I became the Queen
of Upper and Lower Egypt."

I did not recognize my Queen as She told this story. I must have
glimpsed the First or the Last Ka of Her Fourteen. Never was She
more beautiful. The lights in Her eyes were like phosphorescence on
the midnight sea. I knelt and placed my face upon Her feet. They
trembled at the touch.

My Queen's ankles had the scent of perfume on a stone floor and
felt as cold as my loins, but then, Her toes were equal to my loins, and
I took those cold feet and thrust them beneath my short skirt, and lay
my face on Her knees. Her toes turned to the hair of my groin, and
nestled there like frightened mice. I felt how She was alone and like a
fire in an empty cave. All the while those toes nibbled at my bush until
they lost the chill of the flower that perishes on the stone, and were
like mice, furtive and sly.

An unaccustomed wind came through the pillars of the patio, not
steadily, but enough to touch my thoughts, and on one of these
winds, I felt pain stir in the hair of Rama-Nefru, still and dry like
drying leaves, vulnerable to every breeze, and Nefertiri must have
known my thoughts for as I looked up, and withdrew my head from
Her knees, so did She seem to know that it was better to speak, and
She told me how She came to recognize that the bleached hair in the
tail of the bull which came from Ma-Khrut was of no commonplace
animal but from an Apis bull of Festival, the kind that is tended by
priests and washed in hot baths. Its body, She explained, is always

perfumed with sweet unguents and odors of sandalwood, and for such bulls, the priests even lay out rich linen each night for the creature to lie upon. On the day it is to be slain, they lead the bull to the altar, and wine that has been tasted by the priests is sprinkled on the ground like drops of rain. Then the head of this bull is cut off and the marble of the altar-floor runs red. She raised Her arms and said, "I learned, however, that My tail had been stolen after the bull's death, and by one of the priests. To pay his gambling debts, the priest sold it to a rich family."

She shrugged—not at all the gesture of a Queen. "I might as well tell you," She said, "that the young priest who sold the tail is My youngest son, Kham-Uese, and He is a poor excuse for a Prince, and a dishonest priest. You have met Him."

When I looked at Her in surprise, She said, "He passed with you through the Door of the Black Pig. He is Overseer of the Golden Bowl."

"Is that an office fit for a Prince?" I could not stop myself from asking.

"Not even for the son of a little queen. But His theft was discovered. The Temple made ready to embalm the bull and lo! there was no tail. So, He confessed. A priest from a poor family would lose his hands for such a violation, but not a Prince. Instead, He was made the Overseer of the Golden Bowl. His father rarely speaks to Him."

Before I could begin to think of this curious Prince Who had been so weak in the performance of His duties, at least with me, She said, "A single theft brings much disorder to magic, but then the tail was stolen again, and sold to Ma-Khrut for a high price. I must say you could feel its powers. I did not have to hold it for long before I could discern that this was a true beast of Apis, and so I was happier. I inquired of Kham-Uese and He told Me that, even as a calf, it had been splendid, black with a white square on his forehead, and on his tongue the marking of a black beetle. Not one in a million-and-infinity of bulls is so perfect in these signs."

Nefertiri placed Her hand on my knees, and I felt the warmth of Her body. "When I was young," She said, "in the year before Amon came to Me, an Apis bull was chosen for a Festival to honor Seti, the Father of Usermare. They searched through all the nomes for an animal with proper markings until such a creature was found near the Delta, and the priests sent him up the river to Memphis. There, the bull, to great acclamation, was led through the city and fed cakes of wheat mixed with honey, and roasted goose, and a crowd of boys was brought forth to sing hymns to him. Then the bull was put to pasture in the Sacred Grove of the Temple of Ptah and cows were set aside for him. How beautiful he was. I know because I was visiting relatives in Memphis before My marriage to Sesusi. My aunt, a woman with an everlasting appetite for men, took Me with her to the Sacred Grove of Ptah. There I saw how none but women were allowed to look at this bull of Apis, for when he was near, some would place themselves full in his view, and lift their skirts, and expose all that they had, and all that they were, to the eyes of the animal. I saw My aunt do this. She was a lady of exalted birth and almost a Goddess. Still she put her thighs apart and grunted like a beast, and the bull pawed the ground.

"I felt too young to expose Myself, but the pleasure of My aunt entered My navel, and after My marriage to Sesusi, on the night Amon came to Me, His eyes had the light that was in the eyes of Apis, and I spread My legs like this." So did She now raise Her skirt of woven-air, open Her thighs, and take my face into her Ka-of-Isis. The smell was noble as the sea, and the spirits of many silver fish lived between Her lips. I kissed Her and lay with my mouth on all that was open to me, and She began to quiver in many a part. I felt the hooves of the bull of Apis ride into Her belly and through the grove of Her bush. The Ka-of-Isis was wet on my mouth, and I believe She was carried on the Boat of Ra.

I, however, gained no more than I had learned by way of my mouth. When She was calm again, and had put back Her skirt, I was near to Her, and happy that a part of me would know Her forever, but the rest of me was no warmer than before.

Yet, as if She knew the ways of my becoming better than myself, She told another story and thereby I learned of the great love of Queen Hat-shep-sut for the architect Senmut who was a man of the people and not of noble birth. But Hat-shep-sut adored him, and he built Her many palaces and temples, and even brought Her two obelisks from a quarry, and covered their summits with twelve bushels of electrum.

"She was a mighty Queen, and great as the greatest Pharaohs," Nefertiri said, "She attached the chin-beard to Her face that all Pharaohs wear. And even as the God Hapi has breasts, so is it said that Hat-shep-sut had the divine member of Osiris, strong, and with three branches. With it, She could make love to Her architect." Here, Nefertiri began to laugh, and with much pleasure.

Hat-shep-sut was a Queen of strength, Nefertiri told me, because She was descended from Hathor. No Monarch who has such a Goddess for an ancestor can ever be weak. Terrible punishments would come down upon cities when Hathor would attack, and She was so fierce in Her massacres that blood would even flow uphill so much was it pushed by the blood behind. In the face of such fury, Ra saw that no one in Egypt would be left alive. So He sent many Gods to the barley fields, and They fermented grain in this blood and brought seven thousand jugs of this beer to Hathor. Her lion's mouth crusted with gore, She was still slaying the troops of all mankind. "Pour out the beer," said Ra, and the Gods inundated the meadows until Hathor, looking upon the new lake, began to drink and was ferocious no longer, but drunk, and wandered about, ignoring mankind until it could begin to recover.

As Nefertiri told me this tale, so did I remember the Battle of Kadesh, and smell again the field where we roasted meats in the night, and the Division of Set arrived with camp followers. I thought of all the men and women I had known by two mouths or three that night. No sword had been so strong as mine but the sword of Usermare, and He was in the other field counting hands. I could see again the tent of hands, and blood on earth, red once from the wounds and again by the light of the campfires, and I was returned to the joy of seizing lovers I did not know and entering them. So, the smoke of those fires returned to my chest, and my Queen Nefertiri had thereby warmed me further. In the mirror, Her eyes had the light of campfires. Beneath the woven-air, Her breast rose and fell. Even my awe before Her was no longer like the chill of a temple but more like the cold blue fire of the altar when salt is in the flame.

Now, She set aside the mirror, and gave Her attention to my short linen skirt, only She did not look upon it with desire, but calculation, in the way I might approach a new horse before considering whether I wished to mount. Then She gave a sigh. Whether it was at the monumental rage of Usermare if He knew Her thought, or my own not so subtle tortures, I cannot say. However, She most certainly drew a circle around Her head before proceeding to tell me another tale.

That was of still another architect. Back in the era when people were crude, and there were no monuments, there had been a sad reign of a Pharaoh Horus Tepnefer-Intef, a weak King Who stored His plunder in a vault built by the architect Sen-Amon.

Horus Tepnefer-Intef feared for these riches and so the walls of the vault were of great thickness, the stones even chosen by Sen-Amon himself, for he was a mason as well as an architect. At night, however, after his laborers had left, he polished one stone, and set it on so perfect an incline that he could draw it forth from the wall. So Sen-Amon slept with the knowledge that the riches of Pharaoh Tepnefer-Intef were, if he desired, his own. But he was old and stole nothing. He merely visited the vault with his oldest son, and counted the King's fortune.

When Sen-Amon died, his son, however, went in with his younger brother, and they took as much gold as they could carry. Since the Pharaoh also liked to count His hoard, He soon discovered the theft. Full of consternation, He set a trap.

When the thieves returned for more, the lid of a sarcophagus fell on the younger brother, and he cried out: "I cannot escape. Cut off my head so no one will recognize me." His older brother obeyed.

When Tepnefer discovered the headless man, He was frantic with terror. He hung the body by the wall of the main gate and told the guards to arrest whoever would weep beneath. "This was," said Nefertiri, "a terrible act for a Pharaoh to decree. We honor the bodies of the dead. Tepnefer-Intef must have been a Syrian."

"The mother of the poor dead thief did not weep in public, but she told her oldest son to rescue the body of his brother, or she would claim it herself. When he went by the wall at evening, therefore, he fed the guards wine. Soon, they were drunk and asleep, and he cut down his brother and escaped."

"Is that all of Your story?" I asked. I was disappointed. The stone that slid in its socket moved in me as well. As the brothers stole the gold, I had felt a first stirring in myself. Yet now, the thought of a headless body lay on me like the weight of a coffin's cover.

"There is more," said Nefertiri. And She told me that this peculiar King, Tepnefer-Intef, infuriated by the cleverness of the thief, was unable to sleep. Tepnefer-Intef even commanded His daughter, Suba-Sebaq, famous for Her wide-open thighs—"they can only be Syrians," said Nefertiri—to open Her house and receive all men, noble or common, who came to visit. Any of these men would be free to take his pleasure by way of any of Her three mouths if he could entertain Her with a true account of the most wicked deed of his life. So She learned of the escapades of the worst men in the reign of Tepnefer-Intef. Many of these stories exciting Her, the men learned much of the smell of the meat in the three mouths of Suba-Sebaq, "that slut"—now did Nefertiri's clear voice deepen in my ear. Such was Her excitement, that Her thighs came apart and I could see in Her parted hair, the eye of Horus gleaming. Then Her voice, rapt as the oncoming of the river, went on to tell of the ingenuity of this oldest son of Sen-Amon. To prepare himself, he cut off the arm of a neighbor who had just died, and concealed it beneath his robes. Then, he went to the Princess. In Her Chambers, he told how he had rescued his brother's body. But when the Princess tried to seize him, he gave Her no more to grasp than the arm of the dead man. It came right out of his robe, and Suba-Sebaq fell backward in a swoon. Then, while She lay beneath him, the thief made love to Her by all three mouths.

"After he left, Tepnefer-Intef so admired his boldness that He sent out word He would pardon the fellow. Thereby, the son of Sen-Amon disclosed himself and married Suba-Sebaq and became a Prince whose wife was known by half the men of Egypt."

Now, Nefertiri kneeled before me, raised my skirt, seized my swollen but still sleeping snake, gave a small tug with Her slim and playful fingers, said, "Ah, this arm does not come off," and proceeded to give Her beautiful face to my limb. As the royal mouth came down upon my honor, my desire, my terror, my shame, my glory, I began to feel the seven gates of my body with all their monsters and snares, and a great heat, like the burning of the sun, blazed in me. Then I was alone again, and the fires were subsiding. She was no longer on me with Her mouth. "You smell like a stallion," She said. "I have never smelled an unperfumed body before."

I knelt and kissed Her foot, ready like a hound to slaver atrociously upon Her sandal. I wished to abase myself. The sensation of Her lips upon the head of my phallus remained, and that was like a halo. My cock felt as if it were made of gold. A glow rose in me. I could die now. I need feel no shame. The woman of Usermare had given me Her mouth, and so my buttocks were my own again, yes, I could have kissed Her feet and chewed upon Her toes.

"Truly, Kazama, you smell dreadful," She said in Her fondest voice and wiped Her mouth as if She would never have any more of me. But then, She knelt, and despite Herself, gave one queenly teasing lick of Her tongue, light as a feather, along the length of my shaft, down into the tense bag of my balls, and around, a fleeting lick.

"You stink! You smell of the end of the road," She said, which, in the Court of Usermare where people spoke so well, was the worst reference you could make to the anus, and I wondered if something out of the marrow of Ma-Khrut's fats, some thirst of the lost Pig, or slime of the hippopotamus, must be oozing forth from me, an abomination, or so I would have said until I saw Nefertiri's face, and another Ka was on it. Her delicate features had their own thirst. She was full of folly.

Fourteen

"Oh, I adore how dreadful you are," She said. "Did you visit the Royal Stables? Did you rub the foam of a stallion's mouth all over your little beauty?" She took another lick.

I nodded. I had indeed gone to the Stables before coming here. I had rubbed myself, and with one of Usermare's horses, no less, back from a ride with his groom and not yet rubbed down, I had managed to get my hand full of the slather of the beast, nor had I known why.

"You are a peasant. Common as Lower Egypt," She said, and teased what I had anointed by way of Her fingertips, clever as starlings' wings, but with Her tongue and lips as well, a flutter into the ferment of my seed.

I knew what a mighty revenge She was taking upon Usermare. She never left the crown of my shaft, indeed She called it that, "the crown," and in a crooning voice, almost so pure as one of Her blind singers, said, "Oh, little crown of Upper Egypt," and laid on the butterfly wings of Her light tongue, "Oh," She said, "doesn't the Upper Crown like to be kissed by Lower Egypt," whereupon Her tongue curled like the cobra that comes forward from the Red Crown, and She laughed at the mating of the two, as if She would laugh again when the White Crown and the Red of Usermare were together on His head, and He was solemn with His ceremony. "Oh, don't you spit at Me," She said, "don't you dare, don't let that wickedness of yours begin to shine, don't let it leap, don't let it dance," all with the sweetest little kisses and tickles of Her tongue, trailing the fingertips of one hand like five little sins into my sack and over my shaft, and all the while She played with words in the way I had so often noticed among the most exalted, but all such games were nothing to what She said to me now. It was as if Her heart had tasted no pleasure in so long that She must croon over my coarse peasant cock (and She called it that) and called it by many other names, for after each tickle of Her tongue, I was "groaner," and "moaner," "knife," and "stud," "inscriber," and "anointer," and then, as if that were not enough, She spoke of my "guide" and my "dirty Hittite," my "smelly thickness," and lo, they were all much like the sound you hear in *mtha,* although a little different each, and then using a word so common as *met,* which I heard every day, now came such sweet caressing sounds as "Do you like the way I tickle your *vein,* My *governor,*" and She gave me a nip with Her teeth, "or is it *death*?" Yet, if it were not for the cleverness of my ears after the Gardens of the Secluded, I might have thought She said, "Do you like the way I tickle your governor, My death, or is it the vein?" some such nonsense, but we were laughing so much, and enjoying ourselves so freely that She began to flip my proud (and now shining) crown against Her lips, and She cooed at it and called it "Nefer" but with a different meaning each time so that it was sweet. "Oh My most beautiful young horse," She said, "My *nefer,* My phallus, My slow fire, My lucky name, My *sma,* My little cock, My little cemetery, My *smat,*" and She swallowed as much of my cock as Her royal throat could take, and bit at the root until I screamed, or near to it, but then She kissed the tip. "Did I hurt My little *hen,* My provider, My *hemsi,* My dwelling place? Oh, is he coming forth?" and indeed I would have been all over Her face and spewing on the woven-air across Her breast, and there to watch Her rub it into Her skin slowly and solemnly as if painting the insult to Usermare upon Her flesh—such was all I saw in Her mind—but the coming-forth turned upon itself with all rude force, clear up my fundament, into my cave, seizing my heart, and drew all the joy in the head of my cock right back into my sack, and I knew we had made no small commotion. Yet I had small fear of that. Her Palace was not like the Secluded where every house had its walls yet every sound belonged to all. Here were no walls around Her rooms. Her bedroom opened to a patio that gave on a garden which ended in an arbor beyond which was a pool. So royal was the air, however, and so sweet and heavy the music of birds, and the cawing and barking of Her falcons and greyhounds, that She had no concern for gossip. Who would care to carry such a tale? Her body servants were not only eunuchs, plump as geese from rich food, but silent as fish. For they were also without their tongues—a considerable cruelty, to be certain, but done, I learned later, not to silence their speech, although it did, but by order of Usermare so they could not lick Her. Indeed, if it would not have made them too hideous in appearance, He would have cut off their lips as well. Of course, He did not protect Himself altogether. Once, later, She whispered to me, "They have marvelous fingers, these Nubians."

I speak of such matters, but by now the desire aroused in me was like a fire that could melt a stone. As I stood before Her, trembling, all but flinging myself and my seed in all directions at once, a fire in my stick, and honey in my bowels, my mind was aflame with the stories She had told, and I had to seize myself at the brink before the cream of my loins was shining on Her queenly face. But I had another desire now, large as Usermare Himself. It was to fuck Her, fuck Her good, good and evil. She was murmuring, "Benben, benbenben," but with such little twists and stops of Her mouth, such a beat of Her breath that as I heard it, benben said all too many words, "Oh, *come forth* with Me, you little *God of evil*, you *fucker*, give Me your *obelisk*"—for that was also a *benben*—and then Her gown of woven-air was gone, and Her field was open before me, Her thighs like slim pillars, and Her altar wet with the passions of my tongue. *"Hath, hath, hath,"* She panted like a cat in heat, "Let us *fuck*, let us *fly*. Come into My *flame*, My *fire*, My *hath*, My *cunt*, come into My *snare*, enter My *sepulchre*, Oh, come deep into My *cemetery*, My *sma*, My little *cemetery*, unite with Me, *copulate* with Me, come to your *concubine, O heaven and earth, hath, hath, hath!*"

We kept looking at one another, She on Her back, I on my knees, and I drew into myself all I could remember of the most reverent moments I had known—anything to hold me from shooting every white arrow at once—I saw the solemnity of Bak-ne-khon-su when he sacrificed the ram, and the grandeur of Usermare as He received the hands of the Hittites, and all such thoughts I took in upon my fires like smoke, my lust steaming on the hot stones of my will. I knew all the madness of the lion. "Would You like," I said to Her, my lips as thick as if they had been beaten, nay, scourged, "would You like my obelisk in You, Queen Hat-shep-sut?"

"In my *cunt,* yes, in My *weeping fish,* oh, speak to My *weeping fish,* enter My *mummy,* come into My *spell, work your oars,* work your *spell, slaughter* Me, *shet, shet, shet,* oh, come into My *plot,* come into My ground, come to My *pool,* yes, fuck your *Ka-t,* fuck your *cunt.*"

Yet when I entered, Her breasts looking at me like the two eyes of the Two-Lands, all the reverence I had drawn into myself made me ache with a radiance equal to a rainbow in a storm. Having banked the fires of my balls, I entered Her with the solemnity of a priest who reads a service, and lay upon Her lips, but the lips of Her enclosure were so hot that my fires almost flamed over the river. Then all was calm again, and She was lying on Her back. My obelisk was floating on Her river. She made the sounds of a woman in birth, *aq* and *aqaq,* and yet with all the clarity of a greeting to enter, "*Aq,* please *enter,* come to My *sunrise,* come to My *sunset,* Oh, *aqaq, raid Me,* spy into My *entrance,* look on My *uba,* rest in My *Court, read the prayer,* rest in My *gate. Uba, uba* live in My *cave,* move in My *den, ri, ri, ri, mover of stone,* you are a *mover of stone, haa,* you *travel by sea, be My embarcation, haa,* My *entrance.* Oh," she said, going suddenly still, "do not *burst into flame,* do not *burn up, haa,* paddle away, *khenn* and *khennu,* oh, slip into My *snare, hem, hem, hem,* crush My *majesty, hu, hu, hu,* let it *rain*"— I heard it all. She sang of the beauties of my testicles (which She held with fingers that had learned the tongueless art of the Nubian) She governed me with words of power, with *heq* and *heha* and *hem,* and as

She sang to me, I entered the Land of the Dead that was in all the life of Her, and felt like a noble. She kissed me on the side of my mouth with those lips that had brought royalty to the head of my cock, and our mouths were on one another and our tongues met like woven-air and I felt Her voice on my ear, "*Netchem* and *netchemu* and *netchemut*," She crooned, "Oh, what a merry fuck you are, *ri, ra, rirara*," and on Nefertiri's face was such tenderness that *rirara* rose in me and I could not enter enough into my *nefer* of my most beautiful Queen, my *nefer-her*, beautiful like rain in the fourth hour after rising, She was a Goddess, She was Her majesty, and She was shameless. *Tcham*, I fucked Her by *Her youth, Tcham, Tcham, Tcham*, by Her *Sceptre* and Her *youth*, and our hips moving together, She cried out, "*Shep, shep, shepit, shepit*, and all such words like *shepu* and *shepa* and *shepat*, Oh, *light*, oh, *radiance*, oh, *brightness*, oh, *blindness*, oh, *wealth* and *shame, vomit* and *shipwreck, shef, shef, shef, ram* into Me, *swell* into Me, give Me your *weapon*, give me your *power, shefesh, shefesh*, I have your *sword*, I have your *gift*, give Me your *evil*, give Me your *wealth. Khut, khut, khut, tehet, tehet, tehet*. Oh, by the *sacred backbone of Osiris*, give me *tcham, tcham, tcham, qef, qef, qef*, show Me to My Ka, *dead white, dead black*, I am a *fortress, ai, ai*, what *light*, what *splendor*, go deeper, you obelisk, fuck Me into glory, take Me to flame, I am *rich*, oh, stop, I am *fire* and *light*, I am your *filth*, your *offal*, your *devils*, your *friends*, your *guide*, oh, good, good, good, give Me your *benben*, evil fucker, *nek, nek, nekk, nekk*, fuck me, slash me, murder me, *aar, aar, aar*, I am your *lion*, your *bird*, your *lock of hair*, your *sin*, I come, oh, I come, I come forth, I am the Pharaoh."

And even as I was rising into a celestial city by a field of golden reeds, there to know a change as great as death itself, I heard the deep sounds of the bowels and the high sounds from the wind in my throat, the cries of my heart roaring in the water rising in me, and I flung myself out to fly to the heavens, or crash on the rocks, and saw the legions of the Land of the Dead and a myriad of faces, all the damned and perfected souls that Nefertiri could command, and rammed into the last gate of Her womb with the moan and groan of a peasant cock, the radiance of Amon blazing in me like the Hidden Sun of my mother's belly, and She rebounded beneath like a beast, Her limbs storming over mine with the strength of Usermare as I was borne aloft, but not by Her so much as by the wrath of my Pharaoh Who lifted me high like a feather over the flame, and slammed me down like a rock, then gave me another blow and another blow of Her queenly cavern, my tomb. I gave out within Her while the storm still blew, and She washed over me. She came out of every great space that Usermare had left in Her. "She was much more powerful than myself."

Saying these last words aloud, my great-grandfather Menenhetet fell from his chair to the ground, and there his body began to shake. His head rapped on the marble of the floor. Out of this seizure, he continued to speak, but now it was in the voice of Ptah-nem-hotep.

And as I heard the tones of my good King, Ramses the Ninth, so did the limbs of my great-grandfather quiet, and his body turn still. But the voice continued to speak out of his face, cultured and noble, weary and bemused as Ptah-nem-hotep Himself.

VI

The Book of the Pharaoh

One

"I cannot bear the limbs of this woman. She entwines herself too much about Me. I feel wrapped in the arts of the embalmer. Her flesh suffocates. Yet, I cling to her. My fingers search her depths. My mouth is sealed with hers."

It was His voice. I heard it in my ear, the voice of Ptah-nem-hotep, as it came from the throat of Menenhetet, but I had dwelt for so long within the thoughts of my great-grandfather that these strange sounds came over my head in a babble.

A sweet smell rose from the patio, a perfume sweet to me as the scent of Nefertiri, and across the hours of the night I now remembered the scent of rose on Ptah-nem-hotep's ankles when I kissed His feet. So I knew these thoughts were His. How else could such an aroma have risen? Yes, I was being carried in the sentiments of my Pharaoh, lifted on the odor of His perfume even as water will carry the colors of a dye, and now I heard the voice of my mother as well, for she and Ptah-nem-hotep were speaking, which is to say, laughing. I could hear them fondling one another, and the small slap of His hands on her hips, the proud little smack of her mouth on His ear as if He were not only the treasure of all treasures, but dear as a child like me. The same sound of possession was there. I even knew the moment when the harsh reserve of His voice was gone, and He no longer thought of the weight of her limbs, but of bliss, and it was then I knew that my mother had succeeded in carrying off His woes, His fatigues, even His distaste, had taken it into her heart out of the force of her adoration of Him, had softened His body with her caresses until He was like a field trodden for the seed, had lain with Him while His flesh, after every panic, had begun to breathe the calm of her pores—how well I knew this power of my mother!—and now it was the voice of Hathfertiti that came from my great-grandfather although I had no need to wonder what she might say. I heard her in my thoughts, and she was speaking at this moment of the day, seven years ago, when she and the Pharaoh made love.

She lied. I knew it by the honesty and simplicity of her voice. My mother could lie with such art that her lips trembled with truth, and Ptah-nem-hotep came near to believing what she said no matter how He remembered that they had not made love. Indeed, He could still recall the touch of His hand in hers. That was all His timidity had been able to muster on a day when His distrust of Hathfertiti had not been small. Even as a priest in the Temple of Ptah, He had heard of her license with her brother and grandfather. It was the gossip of Memphi. Of all the women who presented themselves to the Apis bull, she, the youngest, had been the most impudent. Now, His hands deep in her several treasures, He said to Himself that if gold were as malleable as flesh, her flesh was gold. For He was beginning to feel as if the best she might offer was yet before Him, just beyond His fingertips. So He did not deny her when she spoke of their act of love seven years ago on the banks of the pond after they had left the skiff of papyrus, nor did He even shake His head as she breathed into His ear, "My son was conceived in that hour."

But then He turned her over, and His hands upon her breasts, His mouth on her lips, He began to laugh and said, "You are in error. I became Pharaoh without ever knowing a woman, and so I remained for all of My first year." He began to laugh. "There," He said, giving a good slap to her hips, "no one has known before you."

"I knew it on that day," she said. "You were so fine. I had never seen a young man who could stir me so. You know, I did not think of You as a King, but a priest."

"Then how do you say we made love?"

"I must whisper it to You."

I lived on the whisper. I did not wish to listen to the curious sounds that came like broken words from my great-grandfather's dreams, although my mother's voice was in them, but I was near enough to her—no matter how many courtyards might separate us—to know she told Him now that they did not make love on that day as they did tonight. The true love—for which one must be ready to die, she said, as she was now ready to die for Him—had no, not been made, He had not entered her, that was the truth. Yet, out of the sweet touch of the water sliding beneath the skiff through all of that golden afternoon, they had felt so near to one another when they returned to the shore, and she had stood beside Him with such joy, that He left His seed within her hand. She then anointed herself. His seed in her palm had been worth more than the seed of all others.

"And did you anoint yourself in My view?"

"I do not know. I did not hide what I was doing, but You may not have looked. We stared into each other's eyes until we could have wept, just so much did I love You on that day. Your eyes aroused me more than the strength of other men."

In those days, He was thinking, He had left His seed in the hands of many women. It was said, He knew, that the palms of women were closer to Him than their mouths. Such gossip must have been common. So, now, she could be lying. Yet He did not know. It could be the truth. Of course, she had the will to keep a truth (that did not exist) in her head. When He looked for what was in her thoughts, He could see nothing but my face. Then she whispered, "He is Your Son. He has Your beauty, and His mind inhabits Your mind."

My Pharaoh thought of those years when He left Himself in the palms of women. What He next said to Himself, I heard clearly from the mouth of Menenhetet: "He is My Son, you say?"

"He was conceived in my heart," she said, and she rubbed His palm against her breast.

Now, Nef-khep-aukhem started out of his misery. The fierce snoring that came from his throat was broken. Lying there between my great-grandfather and myself, he cried out in his sleep, "You have all. I have nothing. You have taken my treasure."

An oppression came over me. I knew the weight of a coffin lid. Such weight was upon me so heavily I could not move, or I would have touched Nef-khep-aukhem and looked to soothe him. His pain was not to be ignored. I felt this with all the wisdom I possessed much more than from any gathering of love for the man who had been my father in the first six years of my life, and now might be no more than my uncle, my mother's brother! I knew a kindness for him, but it came as much from fear as from any sweet measure of my heart. Let me say, I was afraid of the Gods to Whom he might appeal. It was my new Father I wished to protect more than the old.

Yet, even as I lay there, unable to move, I felt again the full force of my Pharaoh's thoughts. They were of me. I was His son. He would accept me as His son. I felt a strength in His breast, and it was different from the gloom of His former thoughts. If He had chosen to become my Father, I was in no doubt of the reason. He was now, by way of my mother, nearer indeed now to all that Menenhetet might know, nearer, therefore, to what He desired the most—which was to dwell in the heart of Usermare. To live in the voice of the great Pharaoh was to gain the power to become more like the great Pharaoh from Whom His own flesh descended. When He spoke, therefore, out of Menenhetet's throat, it was in the tone of a Court Crier announcing the entrance of a Pharaoh. It was, however, not only a large and sonorous voice but startling in its declaration. He said:

"By way of the descendant, Hathfertiti, of the Goddess Nefertiri, I, Ramses Ninth, choose to enter the thoughts of the God, Her husband, Usermare-Setpenere, on the first day of His Great Festival. It was that Third Festival, His Godly Triumph, which renewed the power of His coronation in the Year Thirty-Five of His Reign, which, after all the years of His Reign, would be the greatest Festival He ever held.

"By way of Hathfertiti, the descendant of Menenhetet who becomes in this hour like My left arm, and by the blood of My right arm that flows directly from Usermare-Setpenere to Me, I seek to enter the breast of the Good and Great God Ramses the Second in the dawn of the first morning of His Festival of Festivals."

So I listened to my *Father's* voice. If my blood was His (and now, not even I could be certain my mother had told a lie) then my blood came from a God. I came from the Pharaoh, Ramses the Ninth, Who was, with all else, a God. So He was not only my father but of greater eminence, my *Father,* the Good and Great God, a man and a God. Now I heard all that was divine in His voice, and knew He was seeking to raise Himself to an eminence where He could enter the domain of His ancestor, and live in the power to rule of the great Usermare. Out of the throat of my great-grandfather came the voice of my Father, and Ptah-nem-hotep said: "His Majesty Horus enters. The Strong Bull, Beloved of Maat, His Majesty Horus, Lord of the Diadem, now enters. Egypt is protected and the barbarians are subdued. O Golden Horus, great in victories, King of Upper Egypt, King of Lower Egypt, enter!" Even as He spoke, I felt a coursing of the blood in my own limbs, and a greater strength came into me, as if I were truly the Prince of my new Father, and I was with Him as He felt Himself entering the knowledge of His ancestor Usermare, dead for sixty or more years before my Father was even born. Yes, the wisdom of my great-grandfather together with the wealth of my mother's flesh—and ancestry!—had brought the wings of Horus to our own Pharaoh. Now, He could partake of the five days of this Festival of Festivals one hundred and thirty years ago when Usermare-Setpenere would look again for the Strength-to-Rule.

It was for this great power that my new Father, my own Ptah-nem-hotep, Ramses the Ninth, now sent all of His new-found knowledge, gained breath by breath from my great-grandfather in the course of this night (and much aided in this last hour by my mother) out into the most vertiginous effort of His unhappy Reign. For He wished to leave the burdens of His own throne, and ascend into the exaltation of His ancestor. Toward the fulfillment of this desire had He led Menenhetet on this night. And that purpose, I could now comprehend, for I learned it in the moment He became my Father.

If there were three ways to increase His knowledge, the first being the lessons of His life, and the second deriving from the favor of the Gods (and the proper use of Their Ceremonies) the third was the greatest. Indeed, the first and second were no more than a preparation for the third—since that was the godly power to rule Egypt. Not even the secrets of the dead were equal to such godly power which could come only from the heart of a great King. So I traveled with my new-found Father into the divine and exalted breast of the Mighty-Justice-of-Ra, the Chosen-of-Ra, User-Maat-Ra, Setep-en-Ra, His own Usermare, and I was with my Father in the hour He entered into Ramses the Second as the great King awoke on the first morning of His Festival of Festivals, and stirred in His bed before walking across the marble of His courtyard to bathe in the dawn by His sacred pool near that place where He had fallen head first from the palanquin to the stone, the curse of Nefertiri on His back.

TWO

On this first morning, Usermare awakened in the dark and entered the caves of Himself that lived within. There, embraced
in the heavy arms of His fear, He felt near the force of all-that-did-
not-move. He lay in a stillness upon His limbs, in a darkness which
abhorred the light, in the place where cold chilled all that was warm,
and knew awe before the great force of Atum. The First God, Atum,
had been able to rise against all that was dark and inert when He ordered the powers of lifelessness to descend into the Land of the Dead.
So the living could begin to breathe. Now, too, did Usermare order
away from Himself all powers of lifelessness.

Thereby, awake, and able to feel the vigor of His body, Usermare
stood in the Sacred Pool whose waters were as calm as the balance of
Maat (even as the pool was named the Eye of Maat) and prepared to
adore the sun at its rising, the pool spreading out before Him to the
East. There, Usermare waited for the golden face of the sun to rise
out of the water, aflame from the fires of the Duad.

For each morning of the five days of preparation before the five
days of this Festival would commence, He had arisen out of the same
darkness to bathe in the dawn, and had waited for the shoulders and

limbs of the God to come up behind the crown of fire, even as the head of Ra lifted above the horizon.

Each of these five mornings, He had bathed in the dawn, and when He was done, had stood in the silver light, the last of the Kings who had come before Him, and the first of the Kings to follow, and knew the sun could not rise in the East on this first day of the Festival without His consent. So, His breathing was troubled as He stared at the Eastern sky. For when the fires of the Duad showed on the dark horizon, then He could feel Himself pass through the ages of the Pharaohs, and all the dead Kings stirred, and He saw the first day of creation and knew how the First Hill rose from the waters when there had been no land, even as that First Hill could now be seen forever in the Great Pyramid of Khufu.

Usermare contemplated the millions of men and the infinity of stones which had been moved, and lo! all had the same thought as the Pharaoh Khufu: A pyramid as large as the First Hill must be built. Now, all the temples of Egypt were blessed by a handful of earth from the ground near the Great Pyramid, laid in their foundations with the blood of a ram, and Usermare held His breath as the blood-red head of Ra was crowned upon the horizon, and light gave the first of its warmth to the silver water and all the birds speaking to the Gods. Usermare saw the sun rise as on the first day of creation, and Atum was the name given to Ra for that first light of the sun before men had been born to see it. Then, Usermare closed His eyes as the sun rose in its revealing and showed so red on the horizon that He knew His own warmth, and the Pharaoh passed from the Good God Who had awakened, to the Great God Who stood in the waters of the Sacred Pool, and He spoke His own name to the rising sun and said, "I am life to the Horus, and King to the Two Ladies. I am the Adored of She Who is the Cobra of Lower Egypt, and the Beloved of the One Who is the Vulture of Upper Egypt. I am the Horus of Gold. I am He who belongs to the Sedge and the Bee. I am the Son of Ra!" And He knew the blood of the first Pharaohs in all His limbs, and what belonged to Menes was in His arms, and the power of Namer was in His legs, while Khufu the Great lived in His throat, even as Unas, Who could devour many Gods in the Land of the Dead, took up a place in His heart. He said a verse to Unas.

> *"O, Horus takes dead King Unas to His side.*
> *"He cleanses Unas in the Lake of the Fox,*
> *"He purifies Unas in the Lake of the Dawn,*
> *"He soothes the flesh of the Ka of Unas."*

Standing in the pool, the warmth of the sun upon His breast like the fires of Kadesh upon His heart, He said to Himself the names of each of the Gods Who came from Atum, beginning with Shu and Tefnut Who were the children of Atum, and the parents of Ra, and that was so because Ra was the grandson of Atum even though Ra was Atum. It was true. The God begets the God Who will be His father. For the Gods live in the time that has passed, and the time that is to come.

So did Usermare stand in the great gold of the sun that lifted free of the horizon, and He contemplated the reflection of its fires which hovered like an isle of flames in the Eye of Maat. And Usermare-Setpenere thought of the small pyramid of gold on top of the great obelisk of Hat-shep-sut in the Temple at Karnak and that gleamed like a drop of the golden seed of Atum which gave birth to the First Hill.

It was then that a bird flew between Him and the sun, and Usermare-Setpenere remembered the hour when the palanquin fell. The whisper of a breeze came to Him across the stillness of the Eye of Maat. The fire in the isle of flames quivered. So, then, did He also think of the stillness of the river in the year, thirty-five years ago, when He first ascended the throne. The water in that year had been low.

Now in the Thirty-Fifth Year of His Reign, the Nile was full and the abatement of the waters had begun. Today, the first day of the Godly Triumph, was the first day of the first month of the Season of Coming Forth, and all of the flood was risen and the land sat in the communions of the high water. The birds were quiet. The flood was in. The pure waters were long in, all the young waters that came from the sweat of the hands of Osiris and the tears of Isis, and all the liquids that had run from His dead body to carry away the putrefactions of the land. Usermare stood in the sweet heat of the early rising of the sun and a warmth was within His head and within His chest, and His arms extended to the golden heat in the red heart of the sun, and He meditated on its radiance.

"I came," said Usermare-Setpenere across the water of the Eye of Maat, His words lifting into the breath of the birds, "I came to My throne as Horus, and on My death I join Osiris. I will become Osiris. Each Ka of My Fourteen will go to each of the fourteen parts of the body of Osiris, and I will live in Him," and the breath of Usermare-Setpenere came with less weight and He knew less fear of death, and stepped out of the water.

The Washer of the Pharaoh and the Superintendent of the Clothes of the King came forward and dried Him with linens, and He left the pool and passed through His gardens. By the sycamores and date-palms, the mulberries, the persias, the fig trees, by the tamarisks and pomegranates, He walked in the dawn. And the smell of smoke was everywhere from the fires of the night before. Through all of the five holy days of preparation to make ready for the Godly Triumph that would commence today for five days to come, so had the Lighting of the Flame taken place, and through every village and city of the Two-Lands, at every crossing of every avenue in Thebes, and before many a shop and home, had torches been lit for the five days of the year that would be like no other festival from the Thirty-Five Years of His Reign.

Now, Usermare walked through the Court of the Great Ones, and the sun came high enough to shine on the courtyard, and all silver left the face of the marble and it was white, and Usermare approached the steps of the Hall of King Unas that He had built in this last year with stones from the mortuary of Seti and Thutmose the Great, and each of these new walls caused a terrible stirring of His bowels as if the Ka of the stones had been disturbed.

He stood on the steps before the Great Door of the Hall of King

Unas and it opened and a priest came forward from the depth of an interior which was as dark as the night, and the priest spoke.

"His Majesty Horus enters, His Majesty Horus, Strong Bull, Beloved of Maat." Now the priest kissed the left foot of Ramses the Second for Amon, and the right foot for Ra, then he bowed seven times for Geb and Nut and Isis and Osiris and Set and Nephthys and for Horus the brother, and the priest said: "He is Ra, Strong in Truth and Chosen of Ra. He is the Son of Ra. He is Ra-meses the Beloved of Amon. He is Horus. He is the throne of the Two-Countries. He sits in His Double-Throne among men while Ra, His Father, sits in the heavens."

The sun was lifting up the steps even as Usermare listened to this greeting. From the depths, from the dark interior of the Hall of King Unas came a column of light as the sun rose high enough to shine through the square hole in the center of the roof. Through the open door, the light could be seen and Usermare was blinded by the radiance of Ra and bowed His head before the Great Mouth of Gold.

"He is," said the priest, "the beautiful Silver Hawk of the Two-Lands, and with His wings gives shade to mankind. Horus and Set live in the balance of His wings. Amon said, 'I made Him. I seeded the truth in its place.' O Great Pharaoh, at the sound of Your name, gold comes out of the mountains. Your name is famous in all countries. All know of the victories Your arms have won. King of Upper and Lower Egypt, Great Pharaoh Who is strong in truth and has come from the loins of Ra, Lord of Crowns, You are our Horus Who is Ramses the Beloved of Amon."

He passed through the door, and His strength quivered through the room, and He knew all who saw Him would tremble. The Monarch Who could support the Double-Crown of Egypt entered the Throne Room, and it was a great room, fifty long steps by thirty. Before He could even see, the odor of incense also greeted Him, and He breathed it deep.

Three

In the Throne Room, light came through the opening in the roof, and lay upon a golden table. Now, as the sun lifted, so did the light also move and the priests shifted the golden table in order that the light continue to shine upon the Crown of Lower Egypt and the Crown of Upper Egypt set next to one another, side by side, and the Double-Crown offered such a force as He came near that He was again a youth approaching His Father, the Pharaoh Seti, and the long high White Crown of Upper Egypt and the Red Crown of Lower Egypt were alive to Him and like two creatures. Now, as He placed the White Crown of Upper Egypt within the Red Crown, so did He feel how the Two-Lands had been apart through the night and full of chaos in the dark. Now they were brought together, and a calm came over Egypt as He lifted His White Crown and His Red Crown, thereby making Them His Double-Crown of the Two Ladies: of the Vulture who was Nekhbet, and the Cobra who was Wadjet; and He prepared to place Them upon His head. And He said:

"Let there be terror of Me like the terror of Thee,
"Let there be fear of Me like the fear of Thee,

"Let there be awe of Me like the awe of Thee,
"Let there be love of Me like the love of Thee,
"Let Me be powerful and a leader of spirits."

The High Priest put the Double-Crown upon His head and the courtiers and priests who stood beside Him embraced the ground. The power He had known while bathing in the dawn came to Him again and was much increased. For, even as He had absorbed the light of Ra in its rising, so had the Double-Crown been steeped in the power of the Cobra and the Vulture through the night, and They stirred in Their power and were alive upon His head.

He walked to the Robing Room at the rear of the Hall of King Unas, and it was a great and crowded chamber with many smaller rooms and cubicles. Courtiers came forward and surrounded Him, and He greeted them by the special and ancient titles He had bestowed for these five days: the Superintendent of the Clothes of the King was one, and another was the Special Custodian of the Sandals—here to recite hymns to Geb for all that touched Usermare's foot. There was the Washer of the Pharaoh (who had accompanied Him to the Eye of Maat) and all the Overseers of the Wigs, and the Underdress, the Short Skirt, the Overdress, were also in the Robing Room, and the Custodians of the Headdresses—all the sons of Nomarchs. And the son of the Vizier was there to be Keeper of the Diadem of the Gods, and he laid on and took off the great Headdress of the Horns of Khnum with its two cobras, and two great feathers and disc, and other Lords: the Chief Bleacher who must oversee the cleanliness of all that was worn and remove every stain from the linen, the Chief Artist of the Royal Jewels and others, a crowd of men in the Robing Room, and next to each noble with his special title was a skilled servant to perform the task. On each day of these five days that were yet to come, Usermare would pass into the Robing Room and out again for each of the separate ceremonies in which He would participate at different shrines of the Court of the Great Ones outside the Hall of King Unas. On the shelves and tables, therefore, and within the cubicles were war helmets and ointment boxes, wine cups and incense

burners, crooks, whips, crowns, ceremonial helmets and flails, lions
of gold in many sizes, amulets, necklaces, breastplates, bracelets, sandals, dresses, overdresses, short skirts, underdresses, loincloths, wigs,
jars, vases, standards and great and little feathers, and all the Overseers
and their servants for the bowls of alabaster, diorite and serpentine,
the bowls of porphyry, black and white and purple porphyry, even an
Overseer of all the bowls of rock crystal.

In clamor did these changes of costume take place, and with piety
and blasphemy. Usermare was as often praying with a priest as swearing at His nobles for the poor appearance of a wig, the mangled pleat
of a skirt, or the lack of high polish on the golden fingernails placed
over His fingers. This uproar would increase so soon as He strode out
of the room, for many of the nobles surrounding Him must in their
turn change costume for the oncoming visit to the shrine of another
God, and many were these Gods, and much confusion, since by the
first day of the Festival, not all the Gods had yet come in from up or
down the river, some being transported great distances from Their
local shrine to the landing place by the Royal Quay of Thebes.

Now, dressed for His first ceremony, walking in skirts of pleated
linen so fine and so stiffly pressed that the cry they made against His
thighs was like the clatter of sheets of papyrus, Usermare, holding His
flail, came out of the Robing Room and prepared to depart. Yet, He
was unready. The turmoil of changing His costume was still upon
Him, and so He stopped by the Double-Throne in the center of the
Hall of King Unas and mounted the dais, stood upon the thick carpet.
Two thrones sat beneath two canopies side by side, and Usermare sat
first in the Throne of the King of Lower Egypt. The Crook was
placed in His hand, and its power passed into His arms. He smelled
the odors of the swamp as they came to Him from the North of
Egypt, and He closed His eyes and saw the dark marsh where Horus
fought Set, and Usermare lived again in the hour when Horus was
wounded. His closed eyes throbbed with pain and He knew a pang
within the sockets of His head as Horus plucked forth His own sight
to punish Himself for the crime of beheading His mother.

Usermare-Setpenere entered into the God Horus. Beyond His

shoulders, He could feel the wings of the God Horus, and they were large. The walls of the Hall of King Unas were not great enough to contain them. He thought of the clouds He had seen on the horizon in the dawn, and the vast feathered breast of the hawk who was the God Horus was in those clouds, and He saw the spread of the God's wings from horizon to horizon.

Usermare opened His eyes and descended from the dais. He took four measured steps to the South and mounted to the Second Throne of the Two-Lands. In His nose, many scents changed. He knew no longer the smell of the swamp but now inhaled the dusty odor of a peach tree by a road at the foot of a dusty hill. And He thought of His own coronation thirty-five years ago in Memphi at the Temple of Ptah where the First Hill had risen from the water, there within sight of the Pyramid of Khufu.

In that day of His coronation, the High Priest had set Him a meditation to contemplate through every festival for the years of His Reign until the Festival of Festivals, and He had done so. He had done as He was doing now, and He set His thoughts upon the center of His meditation.

The priest had said that even as the name of Osiris could be heard in the ear as Ausar which is equal to the Seat-Maker, and the name of Isis is Ast, which is the Seat, so was it natural for the Seat-Maker to know His Seat. "Now, for all the days of Your life that You are Horus," said the priest, "so will You, too, sit upon the Seat of Isis, Your mother."

The golden Seat of Isis was hard and cold in the early morning (even as it would be warm by midday) but there, in Her lap, He was the Pharaoh. "I have come forth from Thee," He murmured, "and You have come forth from Me." That was what the High Priest had told Him to say.

In the hour of His coronation, all those thirty and more years ago, the Double-Crown had been placed on His head, and He had become the Pharaoh. The God Horus had come to live in Him. And He lived in Horus. They would be together until the day of His death. Then, He would leave to join Osiris. In that hour, His Double-Crown would be placed on the brow of the Pharaoh Who followed. That Pharaoh would become Horus. "I have come forth from Thee," He said to the Double-Crown, "and You will come forth from Me."

Around Him, the courtiers were silent. He sat upon the Throne of Upper Egypt and lived in His meditation.

Then He stood up. He was ready. They brought Him the Sceptre of the Lotus, and on its staff were many lotus blossoms. Now, His thoughts would be open to all the desires in the land of Egypt for the lotus was the ear of the earth. So He stepped out from the Hall of Kind Unas, His Sceptre of the Lotus in His hand, and waiting for Him were many little queens and their children and lines of nobles in linen whiter than the bones of the Gods, hundreds long, to accompany Him on His trip to the river this morning to greet the Gods arriving on Their boats.

Yet even as I witnessed this, and kept running in and out of the crowd of courtiers to catch a better sight of the approach of the Pharaoh Usermare-Setpenere, now did I also see Him before me here on my own patio, and He was with His Queen, and one of her breasts was bare. The rose of her cosmetic had been rubbed away from her nipple, and Her face did not show Nefertiri's features nor Rama-Nefru's, but the powerful beauty of my own mother! The head of King Usermare no longer belonged to the Second, but to the Ninth—my Father's face, His long thin nose, His beautiful mouth—yet I recognized neither Father nor mother on the first instant. They were so alive and so much like the others who walked as Queen and Pharaoh in the years of Usermare-Setpenere that I did not know in which time I lived, nor in which city, Memphi or Thebes, until the sight of my mother's saffron gown brought me at last out of the webs and caves of my sleep, if sleep was what it was, and I smiled at them. They smiled at me.

At this moment, Nef-khep-aukhem awoke. He stretched, he yawned, he took in the sight, and then he jumped to his feet. He was about to bow to Ptah-nem-hotep, but did not. Instead, without a word, nor any sign of respect, he stood up and walked away so fast that if I had closed my eyes for the length of a thought, I would have lost the sight of his back.

His departure, however, had a most unhappy effect. My misery, in the first instant, weighed no more than the fall of a feather, except it was not truth I felt, but uneasiness. I did not wish that to weigh on the joy I knew in looking at my Father and at Hathfertiti. They were as sweet to my heart as the violet light of this patio. For Ptah-nem-hotep looked at me with eyes of love. All the love that had come into my heart as I heard His thoughts had been true. That was why the voice of Usermare had sounded just so clearly in my ears as a ring tapped on a table. It was then I was twice certain Ptah-nem-hotep must be my Father since I could live in His thoughts so comfortably, it could almost be said, as in my mother's, and even see—and this was more of a gift—what they saw when the Gods of Egypt, like golden birds, were wheeling above their heads.

So I knew that the difference between being loved by one's mother alone, or by one's mother and one's father, might prove as different as the White Crown alone upon a ruler's head compared to the greatness of all Egypt that a Pharaoh could know when Red and White were both on His brow, and all of these feelings would have been as lovely to me as the most splendid garden if not for the departure of Nef-khep-aukhem. My first father had lived in our house like he-who-is-without-a-dwelling, and like a ghost he had left. There had been the sound of no door to close behind him. Only a curse. I had just learned that it is the smallest men who leave the largest curses.

As if my mother had an intimation of how this weight might increase on my heart, she beckoned, and I sat down between her and Ptah-nem-hotep Who put His arm around me. The hand of my Father was as tender and wise as the silver light on the Eye of Maat, and, oh, what a warmth came forth from my mother! I nestled between them in the nicest confusion since each was full of the odors of the other, and I felt like a small animal in all the redolence of its nest while they lay back and pleased themselves with sharing my heart, now so full of sweetness. I gave a little sigh of contentment.

That may have been the sound to bring my great-grandfather forward from his sleep. He opened his eyes, took in who had come, and
left, and began, without any greater sense of disturbance, to speak.
His voice was his own again, with no sound of the accents of my Father. Yet so deep were the caverns in which he had lain, that my great-
grandfather must still have been in a spell. Though his eyes passed
from one of us to another, and all he said was clear, still he did not
seem to notice how our Ramses held Hathfertiti as closely as a wife.
He spoke only of matters that concerned himself, and as if nothing
had intervened, as if, indeed, the Festival of Festivals had not commenced, but was still a month away. So, listening to him might have
been full of a sense of much dislocation if not for my Father's arm.
Otherwise I might as well have been lifted from one boat to another
in a mist, indeed, each boat so quickly out of the other's sight that you
could not tell if they were going in the same direction.

My parents did not seem to suffer this vertigo, however, and calmed
by them, I began to appreciate that what Menenhetet had to say was
so clear I did not need to hear his voice, nor feel obliged to know
whether he spoke aloud. My Father, I soon discovered, happened to
be listening in the same manner. For He was convinced that the finest
secrets of His great ancestor were soon to be acquired. So I could feel
His attention lift from His weary limbs to the appetite for understanding that was in His heart. Even more than His pleasure in my
mother, or His joy in me, must have been the taste of this desire.
Lying so near to Him, it kept me awake. I did not even mind that we
were no longer with Usermare on the first day of the Festival, but
back with my great-grandfather in the Palace of Nefertiri. If a story
was like a flower, and once interrupted, was plucked, roots and all,
well, I told myself, a story might also be like the garment of a God,
and a God could change His clothes.

Four

I do not remember how I said goodnight to my Queen Nefertiri, Menenhetet began. I only remember the next morning, because I awakened late in my own bed to a happiness I had never felt before. I could not wait to see the great Queen Who had become my lady. This happiness was perfect. I was so rich in the recollections over which I had just slept and these memories were so balanced by the pleasures I hoped to feel soon again, I knew such worth in my opinion of myself and such peace in my achievements, that my heart was like a sacred pool.

May I say it was a happiness I was not to know again. Majordomo came in with a message to report to the Vizier at once, and this command was so exceptional that I was soon on my way. In the chambers of the Vizier I was told that Usermare, on awakening this morning, had given orders to transfer me from the service of Nefertiri to the Palace of Rama-Nefru. The move was to be made this morning. All that I owned could be carried by my servants to this office of the Vizier where other servants, now to be my new gardener, new butler, new cook, new keeper-of-the-keys, and new groom, all in the livery of Rama-Nefru, would transport them the rest of the way. I was now Companion of the Right Hand to Rama-Nefru.

The happiness with which I awoke was, as I say, never to be known again, not in any of my four lives, and for good cause. There was no sentiment as dangerous to one's security, I had now discovered, as happiness itself. I cannot believe that I would otherwise have so separated my attention from the heart of my King. Not for so long as a night's sleep! In sleep I might travel through those markets and palaces where my dreams could take me, but now I knew I must never wander too far from my Monarch's heart. Happiness had left me without a sentry. So I had neither warning of the shift, nor a sure suspicion from whom it had come. I did not know if the Hittite Queen had cajoled Usermare into making such a change so that She might spite Nefertiri, or whether He had awakened to the sure knowledge that I had sported on His flesh, tasted it, left my taste. Yet, if that were so, why would He now put me where He did?

When I went to see Nefertiri, my confusion became chaos. She was pleasant, but distant, as if I were the one who had plotted for such a move. She did not refer to the loss of me as a triumph for Rama-Nefru, not once, and so I could not know if She were troubled, or too proud to show a hurt. In the few moments I had to be alone with Her (and I could not delude myself that She wished to see me for long but could not—no, She chose to keep the meeting short) it was clear: She was not altogether disturbed. Indeed, She had the look of relief I had seen on other women when escaping from an imprudence. She held my hand, and spoke of patience, and said at last, "Perhaps you will observe Rama-Nefru for Me," and when I bowed at this invitation to be Her spy, and made the formal gesture of kissing Her toe, I nonetheless whispered up Her skirts, "When will I see you again?" My heart and loins were in such an uproar they could have been grappling with one another. She did not tremble from my breath upon Her legs, but kissed me on the forehead, and most solemnly. Whether this was to be taken as Her vow, or more as a caress to calm a nervous horse, was more than I could know. "It is wisest if you do not come back," She said, "until there is much to tell Me of Rama-Nefru."

At last, however, She let me look into Her wondrous eyes, deep as the royal-blue of evening, and all that I wanted to see was in them—love, loss, and the tenderness of flesh that has shared a few secrets with your flesh. I was sick, I say, with confusion.

By afternoon, the move was done; by evening I had my first audience with Rama-Nefru, and it was short as well. She greeted me in a sweet voice charmingly laden with the accent of the Hittites, and told me that Her need for my services was great (although She did not mention a single matter upon which I might begin). Then She added that I must talk to Heqat, who could instruct me about Her people. "We are simple next to the Egyptians," my new Queen said, "but then no nation has desires that are easy to learn."

She was gentle in manner, and certainly most courteous. I was much moved for the way She had suffered. I did not know if all Her hair was gone, but She wore a golden wig, much more brilliant, though of a less refined color, than Her own pale-gold, and the hue of this wig showed how ill She must have been. Her skin was green in its shadow and sad in its lack of luster, and a considerable sadness was in everything She said. I began to wonder, since She had such small idea what to do with me, whether Usermare had not made this change to divert Her. Was I a new interest for His sick Princess? This question now coming upon all the others, sent me away from Her chamber with an ache in my head that was worse than the feelings of a God buried alive.

So I cannot say I was of much use to myself or to anyone the first day. While the Palace of Rama-Nefru had been given so lovely a name as the Columns of the White Goddess, and was a lively place to visit whenever Usermare was there (what with the officers of His Guard congregating in every courtyard) I found it somber when He left. The baby, Her Prince Peht-a-Ra, lived in a wing enclosed by a new wooden fence of tall posts with spikes at the top. Around that barrier was stationed most of the Queen's Guard. Rama-Nefru's soldiers, loaned to Her by Usermare, not only walked around the fence but down the corridors within, and there were even soldiers on duty with the nurse in the Prince's own chamber. I would come to know

Rama-Nefru, but I hardly saw the baby—He was guarded too closely. Nor did it improve my first impression of these Columns of the White Goddess to recollect that the Goddess in question was Nekhbet, the Vulture. While Rama-Nefru did not look like any bird of prey, the Palace, all the same, had a taint in the air. A whiff of carrion rose from the garden where Her plants had animal meat ground into the compost, and thereby gave the odor of a wild bird's nest high on a cliff with the shreds of a few victims scattered about.

Of course, it was a Hittite palace. If it were white on the outside, and had as many columns as its name, and so could not have looked more Egyptian—but for that hideous fence!—it was Hittite within, or what I thought Hittite must be. Rama-Nefru had covered the walls of many rooms with pale purple tile that came from Tyre. No finer color existed for the pale gold that Her hair used to be, but then the more I looked, the more I understood that Rama-Nefru looked to decorate Her palace with fine materials from the lands between Thebes and Kadesh, as if these would prove the most beneficial substances for Her marriage. So Her furniture was made of copper from Sinai and timber from Lebanon, of malachite, turquoise and alabaster from the lands between. How dark were Her rooms, but how strong! As I wandered through, and many of Her chambers were empty for hours at a time, I longed for the Palace of Nefertiri where one could also pass from room to empty room, yet all were open to patios and of white marble, and alive with light. Now I had the sadness of knowing that I must lose my hours in this stronghold while understanding so little of the Hittites. When I would look at the personal servants walking about within, heavy and bearded men who, no matter how hot the day, still wore their wool garments, I would think of what a gloomy people they must be. I knew nothing of their Gods nor of their sentiments, but on my first sunset in the Columns, and on each sunset thereafter, I noticed that these Hittite servants had a long droning song to offer the evening, and their voices wailed with much misery. Heqat, who soon became my first friend here, was able to tell me what the words meant in Egyptian, and their meaning was cheerless if not downright terrible.

"What seems good to us, is woeful to Them,
"What feels bad for us, They *say is good,*
"Who can know Their *thoughts?*
"They are as concealed as the waters."

"Who are 'they'?" I asked of Heqat. "Do the Hittites speak of Egyptians?"

"Oh, no," she told me. " 'They' are the Hittites' Gods."

Of course, Heqat was not a Hittite herself, but a Syrian. Nonetheless, the two countries were much nearer to each other than to Egypt, and she had much to tell about Rama-Nefru, and did. She spoke to me with the intimacy of those who had served the body of Usermare-Setpenere together, so I had not been talking to Heqat long before I learned a good deal.

In my loneliness, I was ready to see more of her than ever I did in my days in the Gardens, and soon discovered that this ugly little queen was also lonely here. She had no home to keep, nor advice to give, nor gossip to hear, and no beer-house with the other little queens, only her attendance on Rama-Nefru. So we spoke often and she taught me about the Hittites. They were much different from the Assyrians, I was soon told (I had always thought they were nearly the same) but, no, the Hittites came down to Kadesh from the North, and had only been living in that country for the last four or five Kings. All the same, they had learned a lot from the Assyrians and dressed like them, even as the Libyans and the Nubians knew how to imitate the Egyptians. Only these Hittites, said Heqat, were more a vagabond people. They had also learned from the Mittani and the Babylonians, the Medes, all the others, although—with all said—they were most like the Assyrians.

I could not believe how odd they were. Whenever they had to live through many years of trouble they would decide to cleanse their cities of ill fortune. At such times, mothers could not scold their children, nor masters castigate their servants, and all lawsuits were forbidden. They burned cedar in huge bonfires at the crossroads, and psalms were sung at night. They would also repair all the damage and wear on the old temples. I learned that this was very important, since they thought the weakening of the timbers in an old building also showed a weakening of the bonds between the Gods and the people. Then Heqat tried to tell me about a code of laws that the Hittites copied from a king named Hammurabi, but I could not believe such statutes. Hammurabi ordered death as the penalty when a proprietor of a wine-shop dared to shelter an outlaw, and he had other laws that said you could burn a priestess if she went into a wine-shop. A wife who stole something from her husband might be executed. Yet if she stole something from a neighbor's house, they could only cut off her nose! After a while, I began to follow the reasoning. If a woman was in a fight with a man, and crushed one of his testicles, they cut off one of her fingers, but if both testicles were damaged, they tore out her eyes.

Now, despite herself, Heqat showed her teeth. I knew it was at the thought of a wife who could smash her husband's testicles. I gave her wine and began to laugh with her, but I kept up my questions. I wanted to know more about the Gods of these Hittites, for when it came to serving one, I thought I had better know Her lords, and what She might call on.

Ugly women, however, are very clever at knowing what it is you really want from them, so when I asked too much, Heqat continued to laugh. She told me I would never remember Their names. Too difficult.

"The Assyrians have a God named Enlil," I told her. "I don't see why I can't remember that."

"His name in Hittite is Kumarpish. He is also called Lukishanush." Now she began to tease me. The Hittites, she said, had a Goddess Ashkashepash, and near Kadesh, in the land of Rama-Nefru, they had local Gods with names like Kattish-Khapish, and Valizalish and Shull-inkatish. "It is not a religion to try to understand," she said. "You could never sit long enough to listen. You see, there is also the God Maznulash, and Zentukhish, Nennitash and Vashdulashshish." Now she laughed boldly in my face like a little queen. I must have shown my displeasure, for she thought to soothe me by saying that there were so many prayers and exorcisms the study was hardly worth the work. Besides, she whispered, she didn't know that their Gods did as well for them as our Egyptian Gods for us. The Hittites had many epidemics and where was the happy family? It was a wet country much of the time with evil demons under every roof. They were simply not as cheerful as the Egyptians. In truth, they were so gloomy that they grew long noses. In winter these noses even had a drop of water on the tip. Of course, they had a lot to cry about. After all, they believed the Gods wanted people to slave for Them. And disaster waited everywhere. In fact, their Supreme Deity, this Enlil, who was as great as Amon, was called the Lord of the Storm.

If I was frowning, it was not because I thought they had no right to give their Gods such peculiar names as Vashdulashshish—although they didn't!—but for the simple reason that the more I heard of the Hittites, the less I could understand of Rama-Nefru who was so fine and pale in Her beauty, and so delicate a lady, at least so far as I knew. So I asked Heqat if our Princess—I was not yet ready to say *our* Queen—was of a spirit to share such gloom, and Heqat only said, "These Hittites have two natures. You may think She is a silly young girl with lovely hair," Heqat went on, "but She is thoughtful, and frightened of many matters you would never notice."

"Tell me of one."

Heqat had her own charm. She liked to give you the feeling that if you liked her, she would not keep to herself all that was true on a matter. "When She looks at the Great Door of a temple, She does not see it as you do. That door is like a God to Her. When it is open, She sees a God's mouth."

I thought of how the air within a temple held other spirits than the air without. Perhaps I could come to know Rama-Nefru.

"Of course, She is not much like other Hittites," Heqat added. "Sometimes Her spirit is as light as woven-air. I think Her parents must have conceived Her in the dew. Do you know, Her moonblood lasts no longer than the dew?"

I decided that Heqat knew little of Rama-Nefru. How could an ugly woman understand the beauty of a young Queen? Once again, I was obliged to wonder, as did everyone in the Garden of the Secluded, why Usermare made love to Heqat once a year, and the gossip of the eunuchs came back to me. A plague of snakes and toads always passed over the Gardens afterward. In the morning, there would be slime on the ground, and everyone would think of the eight ugly Gods of the first slime, of Nun and Nunaunet, Kuk and Kauket, of Huh and Huahet, and of Amon and Amaunet, all there at the Beginning which was so full of wind, darkness, boundlessness and chaos, long before there was Nut and Geb and Osiris and Isis. Then the world was nothing but blind frogs and snakes and wet mud and the great seas. This Heqat must have Gods who came from there, otherwise, why was she so ugly?

All the same, I liked her better now than when I knew her before, and while her face might be no better to look at than a sick toad, speak of doors, her eyes were two, and you could look into them and see many gardens. Her eyes were luminous, and all of the loyalty she would give, if you valued her first, was in them. Be certain that I gave her many an idea that I valued her. My confusion at being brought to this Hittite palace in the midst of Thebes was so profound that I searched for a little understanding the way a man in the desert will be good for nothing but to look for water.

We had conversations so rich that Heqat told me at last of one secret I could even bring back to my first Queen. It was that Rama-Nefru most certainly believed Her illness had come from Nefertiri. The first morning that She was ill, there had been two small punctures on Her neck. When I suggested it might have come from Her necklace, Heqat shrugged. "Or a cobra," she said. Then she leaned forward and gripped my knee. "My friend," she went on, "Ma-Khrut may speak to the Gods, but there are Hittites who summon dead people."

"Is Rama-Nefru one of them?"

She would not say. She seemed not to have heard.

"If Honey-Ball is wise," she said, "she will call forth no more spells."

It was then I had an idea why I was in the Palace of the Columns of the White Goddess. Could it be at the suggestion of Heqat? I know I did not tell her how little I could speak to Honey-Ball these days. Let all who were in this place continue to believe in our nearness to one another.

Five

Late that night, after my last talk with Heqat, I went to see Nefertiri. Given my knowledge of the ways of Her Guard, I succeeded in reaching the room where She slept, and even had the notion of slipping into Her bed. However, there was no question of that. She was still awake and Her disposition was not friendly. "You reek of the Hittites," She said.

I was pleased at Her cruelty all the same, and hoped it was a sign of the loss She felt at not having me near.

I did not stay long. I did not wish to be near Her when interest was not present. My desire had been so great, and would again perhaps prove so large that I must never attempt even one caress with this Queen if my blood was not full of the thought of Her. Therefore, I did no more than speak of what Heqat had said, at which She frowned.

"I do not care about Rama-Nefru anymore," She said. "She is an empty woman. You could observe Her for years and have nothing to bring back to Me." Then She pinched my cheek as if I were an old and trusted servant, no more.

There must have been some force in my expression of which I was not aware, for She relented. "You are very dear to Me," She said, "but I cannot concern Myself now. The celebration of the Godly Triumph is too near. For such a Festival, one does not think of husbands nor of lovers, but of what one will wear." She smiled. "Tell Heqat that her friend will not have to worry about Honey-Ball, but about Me."

I left with much numbness of feeling, but had time to reflect, once back on the other side of the Eye of Maat, that nothing could be more painful for Nefertiri in these days of preparing to celebrate His Godly Triumph than Her own position, and with the sigh of a most unhappy lover, found my rest. There is no slumber without truth, even some unhappy truth, and mine was that Nefertiri would think only of Usermare in these days. I must acquire the patience to wait. Yet how much I also felt a brute hardening of my feelings because Nefertiri felt so little for me as to be this capable of restraining Herself.

By morning, however, some of my confusion had lifted. Having, at last, recognized that I would be at these Columns for weeks, if not years to come, a stampede of restlessness came to rest in me. I was not only resigned to living without Nefertiri, but strengthened (by the vow I took on awakening) that I would have Her again, whether it be days or months, and so I could breathe at last and look about me, and even enjoy my conversations with Heqat. As a consequence, I began to feel the presence of Rama-Nefru in many a corner of Her Palace, and took the first comprehension of Her practices. If I was still not to see Her for a day, and another, and several more again, She seemed nonetheless much nearer to me, and I was intrigued by Her methods. Any servant in the Columns of the White Goddess who was able to read could be certain of receiving from Her at least one message a day written in Her language for Hittite servants, or in our Egyptian signs for all others. These messages usually said no more than, "For protection against colic, feed Peht-a-Ra from the yellow herb that is in the southeastern corner of My shade garden," "Examine all the maids for lice," or "Be certain to sing outside My window—I love your voice." (This last was sent to my gardener—much to his terror!) There was even, "I will soon have need of you!" which came to me every day.

That She had been able to learn our sacred letters left me much impressed, and it was agreeable that She would choose only the finest papyrus, and then roll it, and seal it with wax.

Her seals, I soon came to see, were a special aspect of these Hittites. Rama-Nefru had many such seals in Her collection, Heqat told me, and they were all of stone, little cylinders, no longer nor thicker than one's finger, but I could see by the picture made upon the wax that they were remarkably carved. I did not know how the artist could cut such fine little scenes of Gods and Kings out of lapis-lazuli and serpentine, or from jasper and agate or chalcedony. I began to think of that blond Princess alone in Her room writing on papyrus, then choosing the proper seal. Each time I broke open the wax on one of Her messages, I felt as if tiny Hittite Gods collected immediately about me like clouds of gnats.

Then, one day Her message said, "Visit Me this morning." I did, and we talked for an hour in Her garden and more on the next day. I discovered that for one who looked as delicate as Herself, She was a most practical woman and loved to gossip. Where, at first, I had thought She coveted me because I had been so close a servant to the other Queen, now I began to wonder if She was not more interested in my days as Governor in the House of the Secluded. She never spoke of Nefertiri, but wanted to know all I could tell Her of the Gardens, especially of Usermare's children in that place, and which of the little queens were His favorites. She had heard it all from Heqat, but wished to be told again by me, and once, laughing, I complained, "You know it already." She answered fiercely, or so it seemed from the funny uses of her accent, "We have a Hittite saying: Learn with one eye, learn with the other. Then, see with both eyes."

I could not be certain, but I soon began to suspect that Her love of gossip had its purposes. She wished to learn which, if any, of the children in the Gardens might have a chance to ascend to the Throne. Soon, we grew more intimate for part of the pleasure of Her company was that you never had to speak to Her as a Queen, but as a Princess, to be certain, even a spoiled Princess, but enough in need of intimacy to put on no airs. Truly it was not unlike Heqat and myself speaking to each other. It was then I teased Her by saying, "You care for nothing but that Peht-a-Ra become the Pharaoh." Her eyes gleamed.

"You cannot enter the thoughts of a foreigner," She said. "You will never know when I am telling the truth."

"No, I cannot enter," I said. It was true. From Her pretty face with its small features, no thoughts escaped.

"I am weary of My wig," She said. "Do you mind if I take it off?"

When I bowed, She did. Her poor head was bald but for the few blond hairs that grew like the fuzz of an infant upon Her scalp. Yet I knew why She had removed it. She was more beautiful without, and most strange. A fragile Goddess. Did She wish me to carry word back to Nefertiri that Usermare might find Her more delightful now than before? Yes, like all who gossip, She had no reticence about Herself.

"In Egypt, if you are the Queen," She said to me once, "then you are also a Goddess. Is that not so?"

"The Pharaoh is a God," I said, "and His Consort is a Goddess."

"I do not know why. My father, Khetasar, is not a God. He is only a King, I can promise you. Enlil does not speak to him as a God. Enlil tells him what to do. And then he does it. I am not a Goddess but a woman. What do you think of that?"

Oh, I didn't know, I told Her. She must speak to Usermare.

"He does not want to talk of that. He wants to make love." She giggled. "I think I am the only woman in the world who can tell Him, 'No, I don't want to.' Isn't that amusing?" She spoke with Her head to the side as if She had a tame crocodile for a husband, and did not know what to do with it.

I was thinking that whether She was a woman or a Goddess, She had certainly performed a few wonders in Her life. I recollected that when She first arrived in Egypt as the gift of King Khetasar, Usermare had been so rude as to put Her in the harem He kept at Fayum, which was where He kept the little queens who aspired to be invited to the Gardens of the Secluded. Yet Rama-Nefru had been brought back to Thebes as Usermare's Third Great Wife. I, and everyone else, assumed She had performed wonders upon His body that no other woman could discover.

Yet She certainly did not carry Herself that way. When alone with Her, I never thought of myself as a man, nor of Her as a woman. We were friends. We lived to gossip with each other. Once, after I made a reference to Fayum, She said to me, "I never had anything to do with Him there. I said, 'I won't let You hold My hand. My father sent Me to You as a Queen. I will not allow You to come near in this filthy place.'"

"What did He say?"

"He said He would throw Me in a fire. I said, 'Please do. You have no respect for My father and none for Me. I'm better off dead.'" She giggled. "Actually, I was hoping He would send Me back to Kadesh. Instead, He took Me here. Who would have expected that?"

"No," I said, "it is not true. Heqat tells me You adore Him."

"That's for you to find out," She said.

"I cannot," I said. "I cannot enter Your thoughts."

"Not until the day you do," She said.

When Usermare would visit, which was usually in the late afternoon, She would receive Him in Her bedroom, whose silks were all of a purple-lavender to match the purple of Her walls, and indeed, I thought often of the silk sheets of the bed on which I had once made love to the secret whore of the King of Kadesh. I did not know as yet which pleasures Usermare looked to find with Her nor how often She would go over to His House of Adoration (where I had seen Her on the morning He passed the Golden Bowl to me) although I was beginning to wonder whether She spent as many nights with Him as once I thought. When He visited Her, it was usually in the late afternoon, and frequently He would invite Heqat and myself to sit with Them, although He would talk to Her as if alone.

I knew the vanity of my Good and Great God—I had seen Him by so many of His Fourteen Ka that I could walk about Him as if He were a statue. Yet now I saw another face. He was much delighted in Rama-Nefru's cleverness (and His own) and I think He did not wish

Their words to be given only to His fellow Gods but also desired Heqat and myself present as witnesses. He took a great delight in how artless She pretended to be. Even the way She would scold gave Him pleasure. What novelty to be upbraided before us. He was like a giant stallion who neighs with delight at a sly use of the reins by a most skillful new rider.

"You could improve the Royal Library," She said to Him one day, and when He grunted, and finally replied, "There is not a library anywhere its equal," She said, "All the more reason to improve it!" whereupon He guffawed and said, "Well, You poor bald little thing,"—She did not wear Her wig when alone with Him, no need, His eyes were delighted with Her face—"You bird with no feathers, how would You improve My library?"

"In My country," She said, "My father knows the customs of traveling merchants, and many of them like to carry a papyrus, or a book of tablets. They wish something to study on their long travels. The pious keep prayers to look upon each night. In Kadesh, My father requires all such itinerant merchants to leave their writings at our own Royal Library long enough to be copied."

"I would not like such a practice," said Usermare. "It would put many disturbances into the air. All that strange writing being copied at once. I prefer a story I have heard already," He said. "Is that not true, Heqat?"

"It is true, Divine Two-House," said Heqat.

"Like the story you tell of the ugly woman whose husband never gets sick. Meni, do you remember that story?"

"I do."

"Do you think Heqat could be as good for you?"

"Good and Great God, I have not asked myself the question." But I did now. Could this be revenge? I did not understand my Usermare any longer. He might no longer kill you for too little. Rather, He would enjoy your suffering. How fine His laughter if I were married to Heqat. Yet, again, I did not know His thoughts, and longed for the wisdom I used to have when near to Honey-Ball.

But He was bored. So He said to Rama-Nefru, "Speak to Me in

Sumerian." He was very proud of Her command of such a tongue, which, as Heqat had explained to me, was studied only by Hittite girls of the best families (who would try to emulate the Babylonians and Assyrians). No one spoke it anymore, but it was considered very cultivated among the Hittites to be familiar with so old a language of religion and learning. "Do you know," He said, "She can tell you many things in Sumerian."

"Oh, I do not want to, today," She said.

"Tell us about the eunuchs," He insisted.

She was playing with Her cat, a beautiful silver-gray animal with a tail as high and arching as a palm leaf, and now She stroked this tail between Her thumb and forefinger. "Mer-mer," She asked the cat, "do you wish to hear of the Sumerian eunuchs?" and when Mer-mer stretched her back, Rama-Nefru smiled. "She says yes, so I will tell You, but if Mer-mer said no, You would not hear a word." Now, Rama-Nefru stretched like a cat. "When I was still in school at My own palace, My girl friends and I used to suffer from Sumerian. It was so difficult. We would cry. But in our Library, we found a book with all the forbidden words. How My girl friends and I used to laugh at these expressions. Do you know that in Sumerian there are three words for eunuch? Yes," She said, "there is *kurgurru*, there is *girbadera*, and there is *sagursag*. The first is for the eunuch who has lost his sack, and the second is for the one who has lost the finger between his legs but keeps his sack. So he is still a man. The third is the word for the true eunuch. He has nothing at all. Oh, we used to giggle over these words. Because the first kind, the *kurgurru*, are gossips, and sour as vinegar; the second kind, since they still have their sack, make fearless warriors, and the last, who own nothing, are honest eunuchs and peaceful as cattle."

"I like that story," He said. "Tell Me another."

"No, You are insatiable," She said. "You are not the Pharaoh Ramses but King Sargon."

"Tell Me about Sargon," He said.

She consulted the tail of Mer-mer before She decided to speak. "Sargon," said Rama-Nefru, "was a great King of the Sumerians and reigned for fifty-six years. He conquered all lands. You are My Sargon."

"Do you hear?" said Usermare. "Fifty-six years."

"You are My Sargon and My Hammurabi," She said.

"Why am I *Your* Hammurabi?"

"Because You are so cruel and so just."

He had a keen look of pleasure on His face. He loved the sound of Hammurabi. It was vigorous on His ear.

At a sign from Heqat, I stood up, and we left Their room, but I might as well have been on a long tether for we had gone no farther than the next chamber before I could feel the strength of His will ordering us to wait. We might not witness what They did, but we were certainly obliged to listen.

"Hammurabi," She said, when They were by this manner alone, "why do Your Egyptian women have so many husbands?"

He laughed. "You have it wrong," He said. "They have one husband and many lovers."

"Then I am not very Egyptian," She said. "I have one husband and no lovers."

"You," He said, and He laughed with more happiness than I had ever heard Him, "are not very Egyptian."

"It is true," She said. "I was told in Kadesh that of all the nations, Egyptian wives are the first to practice adultery."

"For once," He said, "they know what they are talking about in Kadesh."

"They also say," She said, "that You are the one who made all those wives so adulterous."

He roared with laughter. I had never heard Him laugh so loud. "Are You jealous?" He asked.

"No, I am pleased that You like Me. Come here, Mer-mer." I heard Her petting the cat. "Aren't You," She asked, "ever afraid that You will injure all of Egypt by teaching such frightful desires to the women?"

"Oh, no," He said. "Egyptian women have always been like this." Now He told Her a tale of a blind Pharaoh who asked the Gods to restore His sight. It was simple, They said. So soon as He found one faithful wife among His subjects, He would see again. "Well," said Usermare, "this Pharaoh couldn't find a wife to cure Him." Now I heard His sigh. "Will You always remain faithful to Me?" He asked.

"Always," She said. "But not because I love You so much. It is only because I do not think I am a Goddess. Egyptian women believe they are. So, of course, they cannot stay with one man. But I know better."

Sitting in the next room with Heqat by my side (and the true uneasiness for me was the ease with which she moved near) I waited in the darkness of these purple tiles, and listened to the cries of the cat in Rama-Nefru's chamber. She was a noble little animal with fur so smooth one could have been feeling the fondest part of oneself, and she was most composed. Now, however, Mer-mer uttered outraged cries, as if the body of her mistress were being disturbed, yet all I could hear was Rama-Nefru's giggle and the rustle of much tickling and touching.

So far as I could determine, and They made many small sounds, there could not be much to see. I had an impression of Usermare much engaged in the act of holding Her hand, and when my curiosity became as sharp as teeth nipping at my vitals (for in my mind I saw Them so clearly!) I stood up at last, and peered into Their room. They were exactly as I had placed Them—side by side, Her royal fingers in His. But I was not prepared for the look of passion upon Her face, quick and tortured. I heard Him murmur, "I am the Strong Bull, Beloved of Maat, I am His Majesty Horus, Strong of Truth and Chosen of Ra."

A sweet but most peculiar sound came forth from Her, not a groan nor a squeak, but some protest of Her flesh at its own pleasure, like the turn of a hinge, and She said, "Yes," and gripped His hand, and said, "Keep speaking to Me," and He said in a low voice, as pure as the trembling of earth, "I am the Throne of the Two-Countries. My strength is famous in all lands. At the sound of My name, gold comes out of the mountains."

If I had not seen the shaking of Her body, I would have known from Her quick little screams that She was coming forth, there, fully dressed and beside Him, no more than Their fingers entwined. In turn, pressed back by the intimate force of these sentiments, I felt obliged to sit next to Heqat again, and that lady, much aroused, was ready to welcome me with all she could offer.

Honey-Ball having instructed my body in the uses of the swamp (by which I learned that the most intoxicating caresses are fermented like spirits out of the worst rot) I had come to understand the half of love, the lower half, be it certain, but Honey-Ball could also offer the bountiful splendor of flesh, whereas Heqat, by this measure of the swamp, was not even a beast, but (for the blessing of her eyes) a lizard or a snake. Now, I knew why Usermare saw her once a year. For I felt within myself the eight fathers and mothers of the slime, and was stirred by all that moves in the dark earth beneath the blackest water. I shuddered beside Heqat, resisting the temptation to enjoy every demon she could command as if I would thereby be sealed into marriage on the spot (and not even by my own lack of will, but rather by all she must now command of Usermare's powers). So I stood up then, and knew—do not ask me how—that if I did not remove myself from Heqat, Nefertiri would be lost forever. The gesture cost me dear. My loins had known such a turning of the springs that I now felt disemboweled—such an abrupt quenching of these sudden heats— no, say I was nothing but smoke in my lower regions.

It was at this moment that I heard Usermare making extraordinary sounds, not like the convulsions of choking, yet a voice of the greatest urgency was certainly coming out of His throat. The shriek of a bull with a rope around his neck would not be far from these strangled moans! I dared again to look through the door, and there He was, my King, with His head between Her legs. Never had I seen Usermare's mouth on a woman, not in any sport, no matter how abandoned, with any number of little queens, no, the sight struck me as vividly as a gleam of light entering my eyes. He gorged like a wild boar on an exquisite root of the damp forest, here no more than Her blond little nest, and growled as He came forth and shouted something about the heart of the Hittites, and sunlight on the sea—a gabble! I hardly knew what He said for noticing that She remained unmoved. So soon as He was done, indeed, She reached for His hand again and spoke of His royal fingers, and Her hope that they were not weary.

I moved back from the door and sat down, a tingle of miseries, while Heqat, on the other side of the room, was left in the bubbling of her heats. All the while I was obliged to listen to Rama-Nefru's clear voice telling Him that She worshipped His fingers on Hers, She *said* it, She even said, "I love Your hand!" and indeed, I thought, "This is how Egypt enters Her!" but mocked Her less in my heart when I remembered the wondrous feel of Usermare's grasp on mine, and how much it told of His joys.

Yet one could know nothing of Rama-Nefru if one would forget what a most practical lady She was. They had hardly done with Their compliments, Their sighs, and Their temporary contentment before She was offering Him questions of a sort to stir every uneasiness in me. No one in the Two-Lands that I knew would ever ask the Pharaoh about such matters, but She was as direct in Her manner as She was silvery in appearance—there, I had it! I knew of what She reminded me: It was no less than the silver tablets on which Khetasar had inscribed his most sensible treaty of peace.

Now, She wanted to know how He, Her husband, Her mighty husband, had become Pharaoh. Was it by way of being the oldest son, She asked? She did not think that was the custom here, She said, and none She knew could tell Her. No, He could tell Her, He said, it was not by that, but by way of marrying His half sister, for Nefertiri, by Her mother's side, was in the highest royal line.

"You have a daughter with Her?"

"No, but I have a daughter, Bint-Anath, from Esonefret who is also of acceptable line. Of course, She is plain, She is foolish, and She is always with priests. Bint-Anath will never make much of a Queen."

"Yet a son of Nefertiri could become the Pharaoh if He married Bint-Anath?"

"I suppose so. It is far away. Do not continue to talk about it."

"But I want Peht-a-Ra protected. I want You to protect Him."

"You wish to betroth Him to Bint-Anath? She is as old as You."

"It does not matter. I want You to protect Our son. The Gods formed Our son in My womb."

"Which Gods?" asked Usermare.

"Which Gods?" She repeated.

"You cannot name Them," He said, "You do not know the Egyptian Gods."

"My Gods are Yours," She said stubbornly.

"Tell Me about Them."

"I do not wish to know Their secrets."

"You do not even know the secrets of Your own Gods."

I could feel His thoughts. They lay heavily on my brow. The fear of great and terrible things had begun again in Usermare. His fear was like the weight of gold and full of majesty. I do not know if it was because of Heqat, but I heard the next of His thoughts, and so clearly that I would have sworn He said it aloud, yet He did not. "The longer I stay with Rama-Nefru," He said to Himself, "the farther I will be from My Kingdom."

She must have heard the echo of this. For She said, "You do not need Me to be near Your Gods. If You would sleep in the Temple, Your dreams would keep Them near. That is what My father does."

Usermare snorted. His fear rose up from Him like the undulation in a swamp as a boat goes by. Nor was I surprised by the place to which His brooding had taken Him. He had begun to think of the dilapidation of the tombs of Pharaohs long gone by. Through His eyes, I saw the broken walls of the temple of Hat-shep-sut at Ittawi. He sighed. "Osiris is the only ancient God," He said. "Who is worshipped everywhere. No priest allows His temples to molder. That is because He had a wise wife who knew the Gods. Isis was the Seat to the Seat-Maker and She made a wise wife."

I felt Him mourn for the lack of love that had come between Him and Nefertiri. I was close to His misery as He rose from the bed of Rama-Nefru. She was so ignorant of all He needed. I heard Him say to Himself, "She is not a Goddess, She tells Me, and that is true. She does not act like one." He left without saying more.

If I thought He had tired of Rama-Nefru, however, I was quick to learn my error. Even as He passed through the outer chamber, I saw by His elbow that I was to follow, and we walked together around the Eye of Maat. He now desired that His old charioteer should begin to instruct His Hittite beauty in the nature of the Egyptian Gods.

Each time I tried to say I would not understand what to teach, He would hear no more. "You know the Gods as I know Them," He said. "That is good enough for Me. It is, therefore, good for Her. I don't want a priest who will tell Her so much She thinks She knows more than Me." He sighed. "You will do this," He said, "and one day I will surprise you with a gift you do not expect."

Six

It was not long before I was in the worst difficulties. Twice around the Eye of Maat, and Usermare returned to Rama-Nefru's room to tell Her that instruction should begin at once since the Godly Triumph was but a few days away. Then He left. She asked about papyri with which to commence Her study, and I could only reply that the best rolls were to be found in the Temple of Amon.

"Get them now," She said, but I took the moment to tell Her it would be better to start in the morning. Indeed we could visit the Temple then. We would go in disguise. Like a child, She clapped Her hands in delight.

Next day, dressed as merchants from the Eastern desert, Her face in shadow beneath a woolen cowl, we left by the servants' gate of the Columns of the White Goddess, crossed many a palace ground and pool and park and garden, passed through the gates of the last wall, promenaded down a great avenue, skirted the walls of the Temple grounds, passed through a Temple village of alleys and huts where many a workman for the priests lived with his tools and his family, and came at last to the Street of Scribes that ended before a courtyard and a chapel, next to which were Temple workshops and many buildings of the school. Everywhere was the industry of these priests. You could see young ones who were student painters practicing the art of temple drawings on a white wall, and on the next wall, other students were painting over yesterday's work so they could begin new tasks tomorrow. We passed a Chief Scribe while he was scolding a student sculptor who had just cut a name in a cartouche, but had made a terrible mistake that even I could see. His Eye of Horus was with a spiral that turned in the wrong direction. Then there were musicians in the next alley practicing Temple music for the chants, and one school of scribes stood before other inscriptions on a Temple wall and copied as fast as they could, yes, it was a contest, and groans came out of the losers when the first fellow finished. We went by other courtyards and larger temples where you could see nothing through the great open doors but the white robes of priests listening to a discourse.

I took Her at last to the top of the Western Tower where there was a good view overlooking the boats moored to our quays, four or five lashed to one another out from the wharves, and more than I had ever seen before, were coming up and down the river.

The four corners of our tower were honored by four wooden masts, sheathed in gold, their flags languorous in the light winds of this bright morning, and before our view, many avenues went out like rays of light, and each avenue was lined with statues of rams or sphinxes. In the distance, we could see the canals of Thebes leading up to the docks, while the roof of the Great Temple of Amon spread out beneath us like a terrace. Everywhere was the sight of laborers scrubbing the tiles and flagstones of the monuments and patios of Thebes, and from markets came the sound of music. What a preparation for the Festival of Festivals.

"It is beautiful," She said, "and rare for Me. I never see the city of Thebes." Through Her eyes, I witnessed another beauty, for the gold on the pyramidion of many an obelisk in these Temple grounds, had picked up the glow of the sun and shone like leaves of gold on a green and dusty tree. The sky above seemed larger than all the Gods to fill it. "Let us go," She said, "to see the teachings in the Temple of Amon."

"That will take long," I told Her. "Even the First Priest has to wash his hands seven times before he can touch a holy papyrus," but when She insisted, I was obliged to explain that the priests would never let us, dressed as strange merchants, enter such holy rooms, whereas to tell them who She was, would create the most injurious gossip in their schools. Besides, we would lose this incomparable view and the nearness of the Gods to all that we would say.

She was annoyed to be thwarted, yet after a silence, said, "May I ask any question?"

I was fearful, but I looked back into Her eyes and nodded calmly.

"You will not think it is a silly question?"

"Never."

"Very well then," She said. "Who is this Horus?"

"Oh, He is a Great God," I told Her.

"Is He the Only One? Is He the First First?"

"I would say He is the Son of Ra and the Beloved of Ra."

"So He is the same as the Pharaoh?"

"Yes," I said, "the Pharaoh is the Son of Ra and the Beloved of Ra. So the Pharaoh is Horus."

"He is the God Horus?" She asked.

"Yes."

"Then the Pharaoh is the Falcon of the Heavens?" She asked.

"Yes."

"And He has two eyes that are like the sun and the moon?"

"Yes. The right eye of Horus is the sun, and the left eye is the moon."

"But if Horus is the child of the sun," She asked, "how can the sun be one of His eyes?"

My legs were crawling with ants. So they felt. I did not like to talk of these things. I knew my arm, but I was not an artist and could not draw my arm. She needed a priest to tell Her. "It must be so," I said. "The Eye of Horus is also known as the Pharaoh's daughter, Wadjet, who is the Cobra. The Cobra can breathe fire, and kill all of the Pharaoh's enemies." I was tempted to tell Her that while I had not seen the fire of the Cobra at the Battle of Kadesh, I had certainly felt it.

"I do not know what you are talking about," She answered. "It is like a rope that is twisted."

"Well," I said, "that is because They are Gods. The Pharaoh comes out of the Gods, but the Gods also come out of the Pharaoh." When I saw the dying look of any hope that She could follow me, I said quickly, "I do not know how that can be, but it is so. That is how it is with the Gods. Amon-Ra is He-Who-begets-His-Father."

"But who is Osiris? Is He Amon? There!" She said. "I have not dared to ask that question in all the time they have kept Me in Egypt."

"Osiris is not Amon," I said, and was pleased I had something clear to tell Her. "Osiris is the Father of Horus, and He is also the King of the Land of the Dead. His Son, Horus, because He is also the Pharaoh, is the Lord of the Living." I should have been silent, but to the understanding I now saw in Her eyes, I added, "And to Osiris belongs all the trees, all the barley, and the bread and the waters, also the beer because the fermentation of the grain is halfway between the living and the dead."

"I thought all the grain belonged to Isis."

"That is also true," I said quickly. "It belongs to Isis as well. But then Isis and Osiris are married."

"Yes," She said, "but what belongs to Horus if He is the Pharaoh?"

"I cannot tell You of all the things, but they are many. I know the Eye of Horus is oil, but it can also be wine, and sometimes it is eye-paint."

"You say He is the Son of Osiris?" She asked unhappily.

I nodded.

"But if Horus is the Son of Ra then He is the Brother of Osiris, not the Son," Rama-Nefru said.

"Well, He is also the brother," I agreed. I could no longer see the avenue below us. A haze was over my eyes. Whether it was from the return of my former confusion, or from the many waves and currents I felt between my ears at the thought of all the Gods I must yet name, I do not know, but I felt faint, so faint that no matter how rude it might seem to leave Her standing alone, I squatted suddenly and rested my buttocks on my heels. Whereupon, She also squatted and continued to look at me eye to eye.

"We must go back to the beginning," I said. "Before Ra, there is Atum, His grandfather. Atum had two children, Shu and Nu, but we also call Nu, Tefnut."

"Shu and Tefnut," She repeated.

"They gave us air and moisture." I could see that She repeated this to Herself as well. "From Shu and Tefnut were born Ra and Geb and Nut. The last two are the earth and the sky. Geb and Nut made love to each other." I started to cough. "Some say," I muttered, "that it is Ra Who made love to Nut." Now, I continued to cough. I did not wish to interrupt myself but was obliged to. "They do not know the father," I said, "but Nut's children are Isis and Osiris, and Set and Nephthys, and also the God Horus. He is the brother of Osiris, except that He is also all the other Gods as well—Shu, Tefnut, Ra, Geb, Nut, Isis, Osiris, Set and Nephthys."

"Then how is Horus the Son of Osiris?"

"Because Horus died. He fell from a horse. So He had to become the Son of Isis and Osiris in order to be born again. That was after Osiris was killed by Set. Yet Isis was still able to make love to Him."

"My legs are weak," She said. "I will never learn all of this."

"You will," I said.

"I won't. You talk of many Gods. But we are standing on the tower of the Temple of Amon and still you do not speak of Amon. Nor of Ptah. Sesusi is always telling Me of His Coronation at Memphi in the Temple of Ptah. I thought this Ptah was a Great God."

"Oh, He is," I said. "He comes out of the earth. In Memphi, they do not believe it was Atum in the sky at the beginning but Ptah. They think everything that there is rose up out of the waters with the First Hill, and this First Hill belonged to Ptah. Out of the First Hill, the sun was born. In that way, Ra comes from Ptah, and Osiris does also, and Horus."

She sighed. "There are so many. Sometimes I hear of Mut and Thoth."

"They, too, can come from Ptah."

"They can?"

"Well," I said, truly perspiring—the faintness would not go away—"They really come from the moon."

"Who?"

"Mut and Thoth. And Khonsu."

"Oh."

"The moon is the other Eye of Horus."

"Yes."

"The first eye, as I said, is the sun. You can see it in the kernel of corn. The kernel of corn is shaped like an eye."

"Yes."

I did not tell Her that the Eye of Horus was also the vagina. I did, however, explain how the two ladies of Upper and Lower Egypt, Wadjet the Cobra and Nekhbet the Vulture (who was also the White Goddess) were in the Double-Crown that sat on the Pharaoh's head. Even as the Pharaoh Himself was Horus, but also Horus and Set.

"How can He be Horus and Set?" She asked. "They fight each other all the time."

"They do not fight each other when They are in Him," I explained. "The Pharaoh is so powerful that He makes Them live in peace."

She sighed again. "I cannot understand any of these matters," She said. "I grew up in a land that has four seasons. We speak of spring and summer and fall and winter. But you have only three seasons in Egypt, and it never rains. You have a flood instead. You do not have our beautiful spring when we see the new leaves."

"No, it is simple," I told Her. "Here, all the Gods are like the other Gods. That is because They can join with each other. Sekhmet is a lioness, and Bastet is a cat. A cat as beautiful as Mer-mer. But Hathor can be either. Yet, when She wishes, Hathor is Isis. And all our Gods can be entered by Ra. Even Sebek, the crocodile from Fayum."

"Is it the same with Amon, when He is Amon-Ra?"

"No, that is different," I said. "Amon-Ra is the King of Gods." But I did not like to talk about Amon while standing on His Temple.

"Let us go back," She said.

So we returned along the Great Avenue of the Temple of Amon which led to the palace grounds, and She was silent. She did not speak again until we were back in Her chamber in the Columns of the White Goddess. Then, Her gloom was deeper. I do not know if the curse of Heqat was upon me, but the rooms of Rama-Nefru were still heavy with the last unhappiness of Usermare, and I felt the ugliness of Heqat in the restlessness of every joint and folding of my body. It came upon me with much woe that with all I had told Rama-Nefru of the greatest Gods, I had never spoken the name of Kheper and He might be among the greatest of all. Yet when I thought of how He was born in the darkness of dung and inhabited the blackest holes of the earth, I did not think I could explain to Her that the beetle also had wings and could fly, and so knew all worlds.

"Tell Me about the moon," said Rama-Nefru. "Who is that God?" Her skin in the lavender shadows of these rooms was as pale as the moon. "I suppose," She said with a pout, "it is your Eye of Horus."

"No," I said, "the Eye of Horus *is* the moon." I was feeling hungry by now, and not at all sweet-tempered myself. "Osiris is the God of the moon," I said, "and so is Khonsu."

"Khonsu? Did you say His name before?"

"He is the son of Amon and Mut." I despaired. I had yet to tell Her of Amon and Mut. "Of course, Thoth," I said hurriedly, "is also the God of the moon, but some say it is the vulture Nekhbet. For Whom Your palace is named," I said again. "When it is Their desire, any of these Gods can serve as the God of the moon."

"Do They all go there at once?"

"I do not know," I said. "No one ever asked such a question of me before."

She called to a servant who brought us roast goose in a sauce of peppers that must have come from Kadesh for it had a fire in its taste that was not from our swamps or deserts. Then we drank it down with beer.

"It is not so complicated," I said.

"Please don't say that anymore," She told me.

"In the forests of Syria," I said, "you can have five kinds of trees.

Each one comes from a different God, yet on one hill you can find all five. And there must also be a God of the hill. So the five Gods of the five trees may also be part of the God of the hill."

"That is true," She said and yawned sweetly. "Do you like our peppers?"

I nodded. I did not wish to cease teaching. I felt as if I were beginning to understand it myself. "At Yeb," I said, "up by the First Cataract, there is the God Khnum. He has ram's horns. He guards the Nile. Yet He also lives down at Abydos near the Temple of Osiris where He is the husband of Heqat—not Your Heqat, but the first one, the great Goddess Who is the first frog. Khnum can also live in Ra. And in Geb. Each one of these Gods will let Khnum think with Their thoughts. Of course, that helps Them to think with the thoughts of Khnum. There are times when They need to, because Khnum is the potter who makes our flesh out of clay."

"You have told Me so much," She said. "You are a wonderful teacher."

I thanked Her, and said I was not. She put on Her blond wig. This morning, at the Temple, to conceal herself, She had worn a black wig which She had removed so soon as we were back in Her chamber. While we ate, She wore no hair. But now She put on Her blond wig.

"You have told Me of so many Gods," She said, "yet you do not really speak of Amon."

"Oh, Amon," I said. I swallowed more beer. "Amon is the Hidden," I said. "He is behind all the Gods."

"Is He always there?" She asked.

"Always." Indeed, I decided not to tell Her that if you said the wrong thing, you could feel Him hearing it in the air.

"Always?" She repeated.

"He was there at the beginning with the wind. He was the first of the eight blind Gods who were the frogs and snakes in the slime, but even in that darkness, He was the air." I never liked to speak about the air, or even say the wrong thing. The air that was in your ear was Amon. I was glad at this moment not to be like Usermare and know the hand of Amon on my heart.

"I have heard," She said, "that Amon used to be only a little God here in Thebes. He was just the little God of the city of Thebes. But when the greater Gods could not agree on who was most great, They chose Him. Now, He is the Great God."

"That is also true," I said. "Both are true. That is why Egypt is the Two-Lands."

"You are more a priest than a soldier," She said.

I bowed.

"Amon is the God of the air?" She asked.

I bowed again.

"Then He is like our Enlil." She smiled. "Our Enlil enters into all trees, and then the branches wave at us when He passes." She finished Her beer and pondered the empty mug.

"Do you think your Gods are different from ours because you have so few trees?" She asked. "In My land, we have so many." She spoke of Her own land as though the perfume of the cedars of Lebanon were in Her throat. So I did not trust Her voice when She began to speak now in praise of Egypt. Nor did I treat Her like a Queen. For when I saw Her looking at my beer, I wiped the lip of the mug, and poured what was mine into Her empty vessel (which I would never dare to do with Nefertiri, not even if there came a morning when I would know Her by all three mouths). Rama-Nefru, however, drank with pleasure, and Her eyes were saucy. "Do you know," She said, "there is much that is splendid in your country. My father says that there is no land so elegant as Egypt, and I agree. He says you all make traps to snare the Gods. That, he says, is how you Egyptians do it. When you make one of your little pieces of jewelry, or any of your little wonders, it is so beautiful that the Gods are delighted and come down from the sky to touch it."

I did not know of what She was speaking, but She picked up Mer-mer who had passed in front of Her nose, tail up. As I looked at this cat I could understand how Rama-Nefru was thinking not only of our pools and gardens, our jewelry and our woven-air, our plates of alabaster and our golden chairs, but of this cat as well, raised from one generation to another until one knew that the Goddess Bast could

never leave this animal inasmuch as Mer-mer might be the most beautiful creature in the Two-Lands. Rama-Nefru made love to her now,
tickled her, laid Her cheek upon her haunch, grasped her tail, tapped
her paws, fluffed her fur, and then lay back upon the couch and allowed this creature to walk upon Her. The voice of that sensual contentment which is deeper in cats than in any man or woman came
from Mer-mer, and she hummed with her nose in Rama-Nefru's
throat.

But then, as she explored the chin of her queen, Mer-mer's lips
were met by the mouth of Rama-Nefru who kissed her. I do not
know if it was the odor of the beer, but on that instant, Mer-mer
scratched Her across the cheek, and quick as the first act, the second
was done. Rama-Nefru flung her against the wall. At first I thought
the beast was dead. Then she scuttled away.

"You can go now," said Rama-Nefru to me. "You do not know
how to teach."

I passed through the adjoining chamber. It was still heavy with the
wisdom that lies on the breath of the swamps, and in that purple light,
I wondered whether Rama-Nefru might yet chastise a few more of
our Egyptian Gods.

Seven

The thud of the cat against the wall was heard so clearly that I realized I had been present with my great-grandfather as he recalled these events, and I knew that Ptah-nem-hotep heard the same sound for a shudder went through His body. My mother was the most agitated. Her disturbance passed through me as if she had been slapped, and she begun to speak most quickly and eloquently.

"I do not know," said my mother, "what can be more untrustworthy than this thin desire of Rama-Nefru toward Usermare. It is like a blade of grass ready to be torn in half. But then I distrust even more the much misplaced passion that Nefertiri has shown for Menenhetet. A Queen must never betray the Pharaoh. Why, the treachery of Generals has cost Egypt less." My mother nodded at the force of this. "An offering of such value," she told us, "should have been given only to Usermare."

"Your loyalty to My dead ancestor delights Me," said Ptah-nem-hotep, "but, surely, that is not the true cause of your concern."

"No," she confessed. "It is that I did not expect there would be another woman in Egypt who knew as much as me," and with these words, both laughed with much delight in each other, while Menenhetet looked at them. I had to wonder at his thoughts. For none came forth to me.

"Tell us," said Ptah-nem-hotep, "are you in accord with what you hear?"

Menenhetet touched his forehead to his fingertips, as if giving the short bow of a Vizier intimate with the Pharaoh's works. "I have spoken so much on this night," he said, "that now may be the hour for me to listen."

"It is a night for celebration," said my mother. What she added next was so wise, however, that my great-grandfather's thought leaped out of his mind, and I knew he had just said to himself: "She will yet make a good wife."

Holding my Father's arm across her body, my mother said to Him, "I would be pleased if You would tell us more about the Festival of Festivals." I could perceive her wisdom. No suggestion was closer to the liking of the Ninth than to return in this hour (rich in the light of His union with my mother) to the Godly Triumph of His ancestor, Ramses the Second. Indeed, I could not believe how powerful, sensual, and comfortable was the face of my Father in the late moonlight upon this patio. His voice was now as composed as His face, a rich full voice, to be certain, and He could even speak of His ancestor with a tone of equality, or so seemed the response of the air about us. For in everything He said was the hope that one day many years from now, twenty-three years from now, He would have His own great jubilee to celebrate the first thirty years of His Reign, and it would be like this. Since my Father spoke with as many gifts in His voice as a painter has colors in his box, so did the feathers of every bird and beast come to my eyes, and I saw the jewelry of the nobles and the passage of the crowds through the markets of Thebes on the royal route Usermare took after leaving the Throne Room.

Of course, my Father had not been a student in the Temple at Memphi for too little, nor lived in the spirit of Ptah, the Great Craftsman, without acquiring the power of well-chosen phrases to invoke the shape of all that is before us no longer. Nor had He failed to learn how the powers of men greater than ourselves can be acquired not

only by emulating their feats, but also by living to the full in the hours
of their ceremonies. So my Father confounded us with His knowledge of Usermare on the days of His Godly Triumph. What study He
had given to this! He told it to us now, hesitating only at the superior
knowledge of my great-grandfather before some occasional small
matter.

I saw it all, therefore, and was witness to the first hour of the first
day of the five days of the Festival (after the five days of preparation)
when Usermare in the early air of morning strode down the steps
between a file of Nubians wearing red sashes across their chests and a
file of Syrians in long blue wool caftans with embroidered white
flowers. A eunuch came forward with a headdress of two feathers,
each almost as long as his own torso, and the body of the eunuch was
painted in blue. He wore only a necklace and a short skirt of red and
yellow. Behind him came another slave who, dressed the same, might
have looked the same if his body had not been washed in white, and
these two painted eunuchs led the Pharaoh down the file of Nubian
and Syrian soldiers to a gathering of little queens who waited with
their children at the end of this promenade. Now, the little queens
knelt and threw flowers at Usermare, and you could hear the giggling
of their children. A long cheer now began in the markets of the city
in response to the hubbub of acclamation that first greeted His appearance when He came out of the doors of the Hall of King Unas,
and the echoes began to pass back and forth from the Palace to the
city, and from the alleys, avenues and embankments of the river back
to the royal grounds, a penetrating of cheers into one another that
was like the meeting of clouds in a storm, and soon became a din.

Having passed through the file of Nubians and Syrians, Usermare
inclined His Double-Crown toward the little queens, gave His blessing to the children, and walking alone, passed through an arbor of
trees leading to the Court of the Great Ones. There, in that prodigious place, a thousand long steps in length by a thousand in width,
were the hundreds of His retinue waiting. And across the Court,
gathered on the far side before the shrine of Isis, were thousands of
barren women who had come here in the dawn of each of the five

days of preparation, and would come again for the five days of the
Festival, all of them on their knees, or on hands and knees, praying.
And between them and the retinue, across the great walks and flowered avenues and marble fountains of this plaza, in every corner and
bower, were the shrines of Gods carried to the Court of the Great
Ones in these last few days after being rowed down or having sailed
up the river in Their Sacred Barges. Everywhere were such chapels,
put together quickly of reeds and as quickly washed with white clay
in imitation of the ancient chapels and shrines of the first Gods in the
reign of Menes and Khufu there back at the creation of the earth and
the water, the heavens and the fires. For the first shrines were no more
than reed huts, so said the priests.

Now, high courtiers with the special rank for these five days of
Friend-of-His-Feet—a title bestowed for this Festival—rushed forward from the ranks of the retinue to wash His legs before He would
put on His sandals again, enter His palanquin, and embark on His first
procession through the city on the first day of the Godly Triumph.
When the Friends-of-His-Feet were done, other courtiers came forward in a great rank of the mighty ones of Upper and Lower Egypt,
forty-two Nomarchs from the forty-two nomes, and they kissed the
ground before Him.

Then His sons came forward in the bright sunlight, three of the
four sons of Nefertiri (only Amen-khep-shu-ef was not present) and,
carried by His nurse, was Peht-a-Ra, a child with black ringlets, curly
as a Hittite, and surrounded by a guard of twenty, together with the
seven sons and daughters of the plain third wife, Esonefret, and they
were all followed by the hundred sons and daughters of the little
queens from the Gardens of the Secluded and from His other Gardens
at Tanis, Fayum, Hatnum and Yeb, and, of these, the youngest who
had never left their homes before were much bewildered, while the
older children, now full-grown, carried themselves with importance
on this day. Being sons of the Pharaoh, they were, no matter how
removed from Their Father, in command of such offices as Superintendent, or Treasurer of a nome, or were High Priests or Prophets,
Chief Judges, Reciter Priests, Scribes of the Divine Book, Governors,

even Generals, and yet these sons of little queens, and their wives, and the daughters of little queens with their husbands were only a small part of the retinue that now formed after much jostling into a procession and began to move out across the Court of the Great Ones, through the grounds of the other Palaces, across all of the Horizon of Ra until they passed through the gates and into the city. It was a file thousands of paces long, and twelve of the Royal Charioteers were runners to carry the Great Golden Belly, built for the occasion of this jubilee, and sweated themselves to the task with its high honor and heavy difficulty inasmuch as the soldiers were obliged to run with the palanquin as fast as the horses pulling the chariots and carriages. Behind were other squads to replace them at every halt, while on either flank were His Guard, those files of Nubians and Syrians through which He had passed on leaving the Throne Room, now also running beside Him. Then came the long line of the retinue for this first day, a host of golden carriages and chariots bearing His officers, and His Princes and Princesses with the palanquins of the Court Ladies and the little queens and Lords of the Bedchamber and all the standard-bearers and fan-bearers, the mace-bearers and lancers of each Nomarch of the forty-two now standing in chariots driven by their grooms. How many plumes the horses carried! Their harnesses had been worked upon for months, the leather embossed with a filigree of gold and silver leaf.

On this first morning there were fires at every crossroad still burning from the night and by every gate to the quarters of the city. Before some of these fires, the Pharaoh would halt, stand in His open palanquin on the shoulders of His charioteers, and, towering above all, would wave His left arm to one side and His right to the other before bringing the fingertips of both hands together so that His arms might encircle His own Double-Crown. The crowd, watching, cried out with pleasure at the sight of the procession, and the gleam of the sun looked back at them from the broad golden collars that everyone near the Pharaoh was wearing. The fan-bearers arched their immense fans of great reeds and feathers about Usermare's head, people waved bouquets of flowers as He passed, and the town children rushed ahead in order to wave again, while His runners strewed the street with oil of flower-water so that the Good and Great God would smell nothing that was not sweet. And now in front of Him, and to the sides, pressing to keep the crowd back, Nubians and Syrians were swinging clubs and crying out, "Make way for the God. Back up, back up. The One is coming." Often they had to shout to be heard, while the crowd laughed at their accents, and gave way only after much pushing. "Listen to my word," the Syrians shouted, "do not make me use my stick." Sooner or later, they did, and blood would be on the route from a bleeding scalp, and wretches with bloodied noses would wave in happiness at the procession since in years to come they could speak with pride of the day they came so near to the Pharaoh that they were whipped until they saw their own blood.

Now, as they passed, priests came out from each temple and burned incense. Drummers and harpers played for the Pharaoh as He went by, then joined the rear, and townspeople followed in greater numbers until the procession went through the markets. There, everybody came out of the shops. It would take half the morning for the last of the retinue to pass through some of these narrow streets.

Usermare went by the carpenters, the joiners, the cabinet-makers, and the veneer-maker, down the Street of the Metalworkers, past the copper forges and the lead forges, the tin shops and the bronze shops of the armorers, down the Street of Fine Metalworkers where He waved to all who knew the Crafts of Gold and Silver and Electrum and to their families. He nodded to the shops of the boot-makers, the weavers and the potters, and greeted their hundreds of apprentices. He was cheered by the weavers of woolens and linens, by the shops that made thread and the shops that made lampwicks, and through the Quarter of the Jewelers where they worked in red and yellow jasper, and carnelian, and malachite, and alabaster, carved the scarabs of lapis-lazuli and the little lions and cats. He passed the wagonmakers and the wheelwrights, the furniture makers and the ivory workers. They went down the Street of the Sculptors where the bas-reliefs were prepared for the palaces and the tombs, and the inscriptions were struck, down the long dank street of the sandal-makers and tanners, full of the stench of hides being cured, a low occupation. Even on these festival days when the tanners did not work, no amount of perfume cast by the runners could keep off the smell, and it was the same with the heavy aromatics of the sawdust of the fine woods in the Street of the Coffin-makers, worse in the stench of the gutters of the papyrus-makers. Then the promenade went by the butcher, the brewer and baker all selling their food to people in the street and many cheered with a full mouth before they crossed the alleys of the basketmakers, and painters, and came at last to the canals along the Square of the Boatbuilders with their long sheds and wharves. The river was near. They had arrived at the place where they would meet the Sacred Barge of Ptah sailing up the river from Memphi these last ten days.

Here my Father ceased to tell us any more, as if He would reflect on the sights that had moved before us, and my mother sighed and said in a voice of admiration that she was amazed how much Ptah-nem-hotep could know of these-years-that-were-behind-us. What He had told was like a wonder seen clearly by a blind man.

I could feel His pleasure at the praise but He only said: "I have studied every papyrus that speaks of the Great Festival of Ramses the Second, and the Third Festival that I now relate to you, which took place in the Thirty-Fifth Year of His Reign is the greatest, and I believe what I told is near to all that passed, at least by every exactitude of the records. I must, however, apologize that I cannot give the titles of all the courtiers and servants who attended this Festival since User-mare employed the charming custom (also taken up by My Father for His Godly Triumph after His first thirty years) of bestowing titles whose sounds have not been heard for the last twenty Kings, and sometimes, if one could measure, for more than a thousand years, back to Khufu and Menes. That is the difficulty. Not all of the titles have been recorded, and some of the papyrus in the Royal Library may have been moved too roughly from the old vaults in Thebes to the new in Memphi, for it is frayed. Some of the titles have also been misspelled. They are unfamiliar. But there! I am as fussy in these matters as a Chief Scribe. I do not know if it is My old allegiance to Ptah, but I have a great respect for Him, the best of all craftsmen, and so I try to know the old quarters of Thebes as they were then, even as I know the shops of Memphi now."

When my great-grandfather nodded, and said, "All You have described is justly placed," there was a respectful judgment within his voice, or so I felt, taking it in through the exquisite ears of my Father whose pleasure in His own description was thereby not lessened. He quickly said, "You, of course, were there."

Menenhetet nodded.

"In the retinue of Rama-Nefru?"

"In Her Household Guard," said my great-grandfather. "No one of the Three Great Consorts was there the first day, not Nefertiri, nor Esonefret, nor Rama-Nefru, but I was at the head of the men of Her Hittite ranks, and there was much discomfort when I walked by the few officers of the Royal Guard of Amen-khep-shu-ef who were in the city. Even if the Prince had not yet arrived in Thebes, they were here, and it was clear they knew His opinion of me. That was so ugly I told myself not to enter any bar where they might be drinking during these five nights of celebration, unless I wanted to be beaten half to death."

"Yet it is these matters," said Ptah-nem-hotep with new delight, "that I wish to hear, for they concern subjects a scribe is not trained to express."

"I will respect Your desire," said my great-grandfather. His eyes did not move from the sight of us on our couch.

"Was what I told of this procession without error?"

"It is better than my memory," said Menenhetet. "On that day I saw only what was near me, but You see it all."

"Still, you must think, I am certain, of matters I failed to tell, or did not know to tell."

"Only the smallest incident," said Menenhetet. "It is amusing now. For I can say that the procession through the streets of these shops is true as You have told it, but the last street before the Square of the Boatbuilders passed by a corner of the Whores' Quarters—which were larger by far in those days than now. A great jeering burst forth from those women. They were sitting in their windows when the little queens went by, and might never have recognized them (since each little queen was dressed like a Princess and rode in a gold carriage) if not that all the little queens were together with their children and no men were near. Besides, I confess it, the little queens looked as merry as whores. They had passed before the vast admiration of half the men of Thebes and were so unaccustomed to such warm looks that their cheeks were flushed redder than paint."

"Was there a scandal at the outburst?" asked Ptah-nem-hotep.

"No, the jeers from the Whores' Quarter were soon overcome by the most frantic sizzling of the sistrums and the loudest pounding of the drums in our procession, and we quickly went on, just as You say, down to the Royal Quay to meet the Sacred Barge of Ptah."

"You must inform Me of anything that took place about which I do not know. For it is My wish to enter these five days and breathe with the heart of Usermare."

"I understand all that You say," said my great-grandfather. He looked again with cold eyes, powerful in their certainty, at each of the three of us, and said, "I will serve."

"Spoken like a Vizier," said Ptah-nem-hotep.

My great-grandfather touched his forehead to his fingertips. "I will serve," he repeated.

Now, my Father began to speak of the acts of Usermare on the first day of the Godly Triumph. As the Pharaoh and the front of His procession reached the riverbank, the cheers were larger than any sound heard in Thebes for many years. Half the city must have been waiting for the other half to arrive and this ovation was even greater than the great cheer that had gone up two months ago when the obelisk had arrived after its long trip down river from the quarries near the First Cataract. Now, in the five days before the first day of the Godly Triumph that commenced on this dawn, the High Priest, the Vizier, and even Usermare had gone out in smaller processions to meet the greatest of the multitude of Gods arriving, and had once more received much acclamation. Indeed, for all of these five days of preparation, large crowds had been gathering again and again on the banks to

watch the Gods being removed from Their cabins, carried to shore
and brought up the avenues to the Court of the Great Ones on the
shoulders of Their priests who staggered from the weight of palanquins that had to carry not only the God but the burden of His traveling shrine, often built in the shape of a small boat. According to the
wealth of the temple, these boats were made of gold or of silver or
merely of bronze inlaid with gold, and were heavy. Depending on
the customs of each God, some were exposed to the throngs in the
Court of the Great Ones, and some were never seen, the doors to
Their shrine remaining sealed, but whether the God was well known
in Thebes, or from a faraway nome with none but poor, sweaty, be-
draggled priests to bear Him on their much-used shoulders, a horde
of children and beggars would always follow such minor Gods
through the city. One crowd had never ceased to be great over the last
two months. That was the mob about the obelisk. Its progress on
rollers up the large slopes from the Quay to the Court was, to be certain, not quick, but there had been fascination for everyone watching
because of its length and the silent wisdom of its black granite, imper-
vious to all sights and smells.

Now, however, the Sacred Barge of Ptah was arriving, and no God
who had come to Thebes in all of these days was so mighty as Ptah of
Memphi. His boat, even as seen in the river, was as long as the great
barge User-Hat of Amon, the Strong Heart of Amon, and it would
have taken a man seventy long steps down the quay to equal its length.

Actually, it had sailed the last few bends to Thebes during the
night, and tied up in the early morning to wait for the arrival of the
Pharaoh. Runners between the boat and the procession had been
going back and forth since dawn, but now, even as Usermare came
forward to the Quay, so did the Barge of Ptah come around the last
turn and gleam upon the water as if the God were standing in its
masts. All of its cabin and its spars, its rudder, and even its oars were
made of gold or covered with gold leaf, and there was much music on
the riverbank and many cries of joy. Those who could see told others
of the beauty of its cedar wood and the gold on its cabin inlaid with
precious stones, but then Usermare had chosen His route this morn-

ing through the congestion of the craftsmen's shops rather than proceeding down the great avenues to the river because He had wished to
give homage to the multitude of Ptah's works and skills in the city of
Thebes.

Usermare stood by the stone hawser on the Royal Quay as the Sacred Barge came near, and He caught the mooring rope. Even those
who were too far away to see still cheered, and the ladies and nobles
in the golden carriages stood to applaud. The High Priest standing by
the palanquin that carried the silver shrine of Ptah sang a hymn, then
broke the seal, threw back the bolts, opened the doors, and before the
eyes of the crowd, brought forth the God, holding Him in his arms.

He was no larger than a doll, but Ptah had limbs that moved, and
His black lips and golden chin could open and close upon His golden
face. Courtiers from the ranks of Usermare came forward and laid
fine wines and fruits and roast-meats and goose in a semicircle of
plates about the High Priest of Ptah and the God he held on the Quay,
while Usermare knelt, and said, "We, of the Temple of Amon, offer
food and drink to the Great God Ptah." The God stared back at Usermare and looked upon the food, and His golden eyelids blinked to
give assent. Like all divine beings, He needed sustenance. He had now
obtained it. For even as a God may create what He wishes by calling
forth its name, so could He eat by gazing upon His food.

Then Ptah spoke to the people on the riverbank in a great voice
that came from the heart and lungs of the High Priest who held Him,
but it was truly the tongue of the God. The High Priest was in a
trance and could move neither his eyes nor his limbs, yet the eyes of
Ptah were open and His golden arms moved as He spoke.

"When I receive You," Ptah said to Usermare, "My heart rejoices,
and I hold You in an embrace of gold. I enfold You with permanence,
stability, and satisfaction. I endow You with wealth and joy of heart.
I immerse You in gladness of heart and delight forever."

Now the High Priest of the Temple of Amon came forward to
stand beside Usermare, and in his arms he held a large vase in the
shape of the *sma,* and at the sight of the long neck of this vase entering into the heart-shaped body, people began to weep. The vase had

the shape of a divine phallus and a godly vagina, and thereby spoke to the people of Thebes of the wonders of love they had known in the past. A cry of pleasure came up from the townspeople as water was poured from the vase onto the feet of the High Priest of Ptah. "Ahhhhhhh," they shouted for the union of the Two-Lands.

The Good and Great God responded to the sight of the vase. To the benedictions of the God Ptah which were now repeated, "I immerse You in joy, I immerse You in rejoicing, forever," Usermare now brought forth from beneath His skirt an erection of prodigious length. Already, it had pushed His garment forward like the prow of a ship, and, now, since He could not conceal it, He parted the folds of His skirt and showed it forth to the populace. No cheer heard in all the day was like that one. The best and most powerful sign of good luck for all of the Two-Lands was in this confluence between the Gods Ptah and Amon. Cheers that the Horus had been able to feel such strength and sweet emotion. Indeed, all who were holding sticks with a lotus attached, now turned the cup of their flower toward His erection, and all cried out His name with much love for this feat as He stood before them, their proud King revealed.

Eight

Ptah-nem-hotep now paused and looked with expectation at Menenhetet, who in his turn nodded profoundly. "It is as You have told it," He said. "You have seen every sight. I witnessed only a few."

"It is all true?" asked my Father.

"There is no error."

"The last was as described?"

"That is certainly true. I never saw Him with a greater sword." Menenhetet, however, now hesitated. "No, I did again, perhaps, in days to come."

"There was no such description in the papyrus I studied. My knowledge comes from the understanding of Usermare that you have imparted, as well as by the rumor of the legends, I confess." Now my Father ceased to speak and hugged me with pleasure. "I have told you of the First Day," He said to my great-grandfather, "but you can instruct us in what I have not seen."

"You saw every sight," my great-grandfather repeated. "I remember those five days as a chaos. For in all we have said, I have not told enough of the fear that was also present at the Godly Triumph. While the Pharaoh is never more our King than on these five days, yet in that period, He is also uncrowned. He can wear the Double-Crown but it is not His, not for five days."

"I know that," said Ptah-nem-hotep.

"Yes. But in our years, we believed it as no one does today. I can tell you that in all of Thebes there was a fear of which no one wished to speak—which is why there was such elation at the size of our Pharaoh when He stood before Ptah. Yet, despite such a good sign of His confidence, I can say that on that night, and for each night to come, there were few in the populace who did not fear their house might burn, or their wife leave. For that matter, with all the torches on the avenues and the bonfires at the crossroads, more houses burned than on other nights, and it is astonishing how many good wives were unfaithful. Fornication was everywhere. So I would repeat: the erection of Usermare may have been a gift to the city, but it was a curious one, since afterward, even old men walked about with their pride in front of them, at least by dark. Decorum was only to be seen in the processions of the day.

"All the while, beneath all other feelings was terror. I cannot say it enough. There had been fear until the last few days that the flood would come too high, but now, in the abatement of the waters, that fear was gone. Good enough! Who could enjoy a festival if the river was still rising? But no matter. Fright still came flooding out of us with every merriment. People would laugh and cry and laugh again while trying to finish one song, and drunkenness, even in the daytime, was everywhere. Besides, there were curious sights to behold. Great numbers of boys and young workers from the poorest quarters of the city had decided to shave their heads. You never saw such a riffraff of what might have been young priests, but were not. Even vain fellows, proud of their hair, had taken it down to the skull, then anointed their scalps with oil. They ran in packs, yet were most pious beasts and never attacked anyone. Often they marched in procession from shrine to shrine, or from temple to temple, or even made pilgrimages to the Court of the Great Ones, thereby adding to the legions of priests and nobles and merchants and soldiers and clerks and workers and general rabble who came in crowds on those hours of the day and night when they were let in to mill about the shrines and bowers and reed huts. Sometimes all of Thebes seemed to be in that gathering. Nonetheless, these platoons of bald heads were prominent everywhere, and often followed by a gang of unshaved friends who jeered at the oil on the others' scalps, yet followed them like the wake of a boat, all the while reminding these shaved heads what they did last night with their sweethearts, or their boy friends. 'Oh, how good we are today!' the unshaved ones kept shouting. This was part of the unrest. Needless to say, the beer-houses were busy.

"Indeed, after the first procession, Usermare could not often leave His Throne Room in these five days, just so numerous were the ceremonies He granted to Nomarchs and deputations from foreign nations.

"Even the simple courtesy to greet the arrival of small processions from noble families kept Him most occupied. Only twice did He go back to the river to greet a God, once for Amon, and once for Osiris. The others were brought to Their bower in the Court of the Great Ones, and Usermare might leave the Throne Room to pay homage, but so many Gods arrived that some He never did visit. Besides, many hours of His day were engaged in changes He must make of costume.

"I do not know if it was inspired by the variety of ancient skirts and cloaks and skins and mantles that He wore, but I never remember a time in Thebes when you could see as many priests in ostrich feathers, or bearing the head of the hawk or ibis, or walking about with the horns of the ram. The more exceptional the costume, the wilder were the cheers in the city. Through all these five days, the air of a great entertainment was always with us, and a small pandemonium followed a deputation from a town called Nekhen in Upper Egypt who debarked from their boat with a Herdsman at the head wearing the hides of many wild animals, even part of a lion and part of the skin of a crocodile. On each side of this Herdsman was a servant wearing on his own skull the furry head and jaws of a wolf, while to his buttocks was attached the tail. These two servants when asked who they were, would point to the leader who always replied, 'I am the Herdsman of Nekhen.' Then all three would dance about each other, and wave high sceptres.

"For some reason that no one could explain, these three people caught the fancy of the crowd. I do not know if it was the lion and crocodile skins the Herdsman wore (as if the beasts of the hills and the swamps were now approaching the Palace) but even when it was realized that all three must be priests of some sort, still they were cheered, and eventually, all three marched up the Grand Avenue to the gates before the Court of the Great Ones, entered, and were even presented to the King."

"These Wolves of Nekhen were much honored," Ptah-nem-hotep murmured, "as spirits serving Horus. I can tell you that he who was dressed as the Herdsman on this occasion was First Scribe to the Vizier and not from upriver at all, but lived among us in Thebes."

"Yet his face was wild on that day," said Menenhetet. "It was a wild face for a scribe."

"I have read what was done," said Ptah-nem-hotep, "but you saw what was not described." He repeated, "I would like to know all you can tell Me of such matters."

So my great-grandfather kept speaking, but now his thoughts began once more to enter me as quickly as his voice, and, being seated in such fine comfort between my mother and Father, I found this manner of listening more agreeable than any other.

I can tell you (came to me by way of my great-grandfather) that each day, the drunkenness of everyone increased, and with it the confusion of ceremonies. Thereby, it became less necessary to appear at one's formal station in the retinue. For that matter, Usermare had gone back and forth to so many shrines in the Court of the Great Ones that even the most scrupulous of officers found it difficult to be always in the proper place, especially when our Pharaoh grew more impatient each day at delays in the formation of His processional marches. Moreover, much fever simmered in us at the heat of encountering so many Gods. It did not seem to matter, therefore, if you were not always in the proper carriage, nor running in perfect position behind Him. Besides, I was in tumult, and hardly able to think.

On the second night, therefore, I deserted the Court of the Great Ones and wandered through the city, stepping over the bodies of drunks, and listening with sadness I had never felt before not only to the sounds of psalms rising from the temples but was also tender to the moans of tethered animals as if their pain or plain beast-misery at being hungry were my own. So, too, was I moved to concern by the cries of children, and even made happy by their shouts in the late evening as they played (with all the excitement children know as the Gods of evening move in from the horizon) and at last, as it grew late, I listened to the slow oncoming sound of men and women making love to one another. (For that also came to me from every alley in every quarter and warren of Thebes.) I could no longer hold back all that was most painful in me, and I thought of Nefertiri. But then there had been no moment I had not thought of Her since the afternoon of the First Day when the waters from the vase shaped like a *sma* had been poured to the ground, and Usermare stood forth in majesty. I was shaken twice then, and by two convulsions: For even as the multitude of the crowd uttered up the sweet moans and harsh cries of their own most triumphant hours of love, so was I captured by my despised allegiance to that godly phallus—yes! I wanted to be used by Usermare again. What a destruction of self-esteem to say it to myself! Yet, having said it, I was near again to Nefertiri, and knew how much I had held in myself through these miserable days of serving a Hittite Princess I could not comprehend. My loins ached for Nefertiri. I had an erection of my own. I could hear Her saying, even as the water poured from the vase, "You are My slow fire, My lucky name, My union, My sweetness, My *sma*," and heard myself groan with all the others and could not take my eyes from the Pharaoh's full erection. So I shivered twice. Since then, I had wandered through the ceremonies and through the city, and by this second night was ready to look again for an entrance into Her bedroom, but now guards were everywhere about Her Palace, and besides, much as I wanted Her, I felt no hope. My senses were too thick. I was drunk three times over each day and never sober before I began again. I was near to stumbling and my voice was hoarse, and only Her voice in my ear was keen, stirring my limbs and warming my body more powerfully than the wine. I fell asleep that night in my own bed alone with my hands on my loins to hold the pain, and that is a poor posture for a man over fifty who is still called a General.

In the morning I slept late and then went to the Robing Chamber where Usermare came out dressed in no more than a short white kilt with a bull's tail attached, a golden necklace for His chest, the White Crown of Upper Egypt for His head, and His staff with its several lotus blossoms. When I saw that He was holding in His other hand a square of fine stiff papyrus with gold leaf piping on the four borders, I knew that He was about to dedicate to Amon a field that belonged to Nefertiri, a fine plot near the river. Since the gift was from Her, I can tell you that no matter how I had gorged on meat, and drunk too much wine, even my toes came alive at the thought that She must finally make Her appearance. Indeed, She must. The field had been given to Nefertiri by Usermare on the day of Their marriage. Now, it was being given back. On the day She saw the Vizier, She had even told me that their conversation had concerned this ground. "It is the perfect gift for His Godly Triumph," She said then, and I knew it was Her protection against being ignored entirely for all the five days and nights. Her intentions were successful. I had also heard Rama-Nefru asking Usermare why He was obliged to be alone with Nefertiri while dedicating the land to the Temple. "It is Her field," He said at last, "and I cannot, in courtesy, ask You to be there in that hour," at which Rama-Nefru walked out of the room.

It is an indication of how bloated I had become with pity for myself, and all its pollutions of misery, that I did not think enough of this occasion in advance, nor see how it might offer an opportunity to have a word with Nefertiri. When the hour came, therefore, I found myself at the wrong end of the procession. On this day, Nefertiri's sons were among those honored by carrying His Golden Belly, and I, in the colors of Rama-Nefru, was many carriages back. As we came near the field, a lovely grove with the rarest shade trees on the bank of the river, indeed, an idyllic place for the Temple to Amon that would soon be built, I was obliged to dismount at some distance from Usermare, and only then saw Nefertiri approaching from another direction in a large covered sedan chair mounted on a carriage and drawn by six splendid horses. She stood up while the priests and royalty invited to this most exclusive service applauded Her passage, but, by an instruction to Her coachman, She came to a halt on the side farthest away from us, enough away indeed so that I could not catch Her eye.

Now, Usermare held up His papyrus and began the ceremony that would deed the land to the Temple.

"Do you know the name," asked Ptah-nem-hotep, "of this papyrus?"

"I do not."

"It is the Secret of the Two Partners. They are Horus and Set." I could feel the pleasure of my Father at this knowledge. "No gift from the Pharaoh," He said, "could be consecrated in those days without receiving the Will of Geb. That Will is embodied in any papyrus with golden edges."

"I had forgotten," said Menenhetet.

How much was stirring in my Father's limbs! I could feel His desire to speak again in His ancestor's voice. He stood up and began to stride around the four sides of the patio, even as Usermare must have been walking the four borders of this field returned to Him by Nefertiri. "I run," I heard Ptah-nem-hotep say in the voice of Usermare, and it was such a great voice to hear, and came out of such caverns in my Pharaoh's chest, that only a Great God would not tremble before it. "I run," said my Father, "with the Secret of the Two Partners. For this is the Will given Me by Geb. I have seen His eyes. I know the fire in the cave. I touch the four sides of the land."

Closing my eyes, I lay against my mother. I could hear a chorus from the riverbank, and I do not know across how many years such sounds came to me, but I heard that chorus sing:

"The Pharaoh passes the four quarters of the field.
"He touches the four sides of heaven.
"The field passes over to its new master."

And in my Father's voice, equal in my ears now to Usermare's voice, the reply came: "I am Horus, Son of Osiris. Amon is My breath. Ra is My light. Amon-Ra is My Divine Light and Breath." Now, Usermare was walking in the sunlight, and each breath He took was in the woven-air of the Gods. The field passed over from the Palace to the Temple, and the crowd gave a long sigh like a mother who is freed of the birth, and this sound I knew for I had heard it often in the servants' quarters when a child was born.

Now, Usermare held up His staff of the lotus blossom and He could hear the voices of Egypt speaking to Him. The blessing of the Two-Lands descended. His erection came forth again and was immense. Now He walked to the far side of the field where Nefertiri was waiting in Her sedan chair, and He entered this carriage and closed the door so that none could see Him. But I heard His voice. It came to me through my Father's voice.

"The Eye of Horus is between Her legs. It knows the caverns of the Earth." I heard the sound of Usermare's breathing. "The Backbone of Osiris beats upon the Eye of Horus. The Gods are joined." Then I saw the image of the sun in the reflecting pool, and it burst between Her thighs.

In the next instant, I heard my Father mutter in the voice of Usermare, "I did not speak to Her. It was the Gods Who spoke." My Father, exhausted by how closely He had lived in His ancestor, moved away from all of us and sat by Himself on another couch.

Menenhetet spoke aloud. In a small dry tone, he said, "Everyone who was on the border of that field saw Usermare close the door of the sedan chair. Nor was there uncertainty at what passed. All heard Nefertiri give a loud cry of joy. Her sobs of pleasure were rich, Her groans were deep. The Gods had most certainly been joined. By night, there would be no official, noble, or servant who would not have heard of this event, and as Usermare walked from the field, He knew the woe of every beggar in Thebes before the uncertainty of the night. All that was uneasy in the city about what was yet to come began to rise in the alleys."

And I, sitting beside my mother, was much aware once more of the absence of Nef-khep-aukhem. That was like the wrath of a ghost.

Nine

When Ptah-nem-hotep continued to sit by Himself, and would not reply, my great-grandfather said to Him: "I do not know by what union of Your wisdom and my description You have come to such understanding of Your ancestor, but all is true. The words of Usermare-Setpenere were as You have described."

My Father gave no indication He had heard. An exhaustion was on Him. I think that by the bold act of taking into His own throat the mighty voice of His dead ancestor, He had been like a timid rider who lets himself be carried in a gallop on a wild horse. Like all who have dared too much, he is speechless afterward. But my great-grandfather, as if tempting a convalescent with fine dishes, now began to speak. He said that as he stood on the field, knowing Usermare was with Nefertiri, the heart of his pain was most intimate. He had never been closer to Usermare's thoughts. That, he said, was because he had talked earlier, if only for a little while, with Honey-Ball herself.

The gleam of the late moon on this night could be glimpsed again in my Father's eyes. They showed interest, and He moved a little, and was aware once more of my mother—which I could recognize by the quickening of her flesh. My great-grandfather, encouraged, continued to speak, and I, in my turn, slipped back once more into that half-sleep so comfortable for me where I did not have to listen to every word, but knew, nonetheless, all that was told:

Yes, he declared, I saw Honey-Ball just before the Dedication of the Field, indeed I came upon her as I was walking by a line of many dignitaries from the nomes of the Delta. There, in the midst, appeared Honey-Ball with her parents and her sister. I was now presented to her parents, the father a man of obvious great wealth, patted and pampered by slaves. He had that smoothness of skin so much like plump buttocks which only the faces of the very wealthy obtain, and he was dark from the sun, and fat. Honey-Ball's mother, however, was tiny, a jewel of beauty. There, between them, was Honey-Ball and her sister, neither as fat nor as beautiful as my own Ma-Khrut.

I bowed and kissed her hand. I knew by the absence of any stir in her father at the sight of me, that he knew little of us, or did not hear my name, but now to my longing for Nefertiri was added the disruption of seeing my old companion in this place so at odds with the roots of our memories. I did, as I say, no more than kiss her hand, and yet I knew then that in some fashion I would dwell with Honey-Ball forever. I might never see her again, or never intimately, my body would not enter her again, and yet I would dwell with her forever. It was not the happiest house in which I might choose to live, but it was the one that would be my home in time to come. That much I knew by the force of the wave of all that came washing back upon me, so that I almost swooned—or was it drowned?—in the suffusion of her influence on mine, and I felt the force of her power to protect all that she loved, and the great dull weight of her spirit as well. Her father, in the little we spoke to each other, had managed to inform me that no one in Sais ever raised a stone larger than the ones he could lift above his head when he was young. Such strength was in her. I remember as I walked away, that I knew a prodigious nearness to Usermare, as if He were by my side, no, better, I could have been back in the days when I walked in the Gardens with the pig's snout between my cheeks. So I felt, and with more certainty on each step away from her, that Honey-Ball had been chosen often by Usermare since I left the Gardens.

That was another great commotion for me, but nothing to what I was to suffer out on the field when by way of the new powers Honey-Ball must have offered to me, I felt Nefertiri's joy as She gave the eye of Her love to Usermare. Her womb come forth with the frenzy of many Gods, and I was knocked about in my heart.

Afterward, in the sorrow of early evening, as I wandered back to the Columns of the White Goddess, I could begin to feel the woe of Rama-Nefru. No sooner did I enter the walls of Her Palace, than Her thoughts also came to me, and they were more palpable than a scent. The end of Her love for Usermare was in all She thought. It fell upon me like a cold rain in Lebanon. The rooms about Her chamber were as mournful as if Her son were ill, but even before I saw Rama-Nefru's face, I knew that the touch of my lips upon the hand of Honey-Ball had opened my mind to Rama-Nefru as well. If I did not know Her language, still I could be near what She thought. So I knew that She had gone back to living with Her own Gods. They came before Her—heavily bearded were Her Gods—and I recognized Marduk for He looked as I had seen Him on one of Her Hittite seals. There, in Her thoughts, She was visiting a grave in a place no one dared to go. Much wailing came out of the ground. I do not know if this was Marduk's grave, but I saw the chariot of a God go by and the vehicle was empty. The chariot raced down a deserted road beneath a dark sky, and careened from side to side.

When Rama-Nefru summoned me, Heqat and I were obliged to wait at Her side while She performed a Hittite service. Into a bowl of water, oil was poured from a little jar and She studied the shape of this oil as it spread. Such shapes would be no different in Her own land, She said to us. "If I had never gone to Egypt, and knew none of you, but did the ceremony on this day at this hour, so would the oil have the same shape in the water. For it would say the same thing." I did not tell Her how much I doubted this. The Gods in the air of each land were different, I knew. But She looked up from the bowl to tell us, "One of the little queens has given birth to a monster. The seed of My husband harbors monsters." With that, She stared into my eyes. She would have done better to look at Heqat who gave a cry of fright since it was no one other than Heqat who had had the birth a few months ago.

Now, whether Rama-Nefru spoke without the knowledge of this monster and truly learned of it from the shape of the oil, or whether She wished, for whatever reason, to chastise Heqat, I did not know— Her mind had now become as empty as the Eye of Maat before the dawn—but She went on to say, "In My land, the birth of such a monster must hurt the fortunes of a King," and soon enough, Heqat left, complaining of congestion in her throat. I wondered if the purpose of Rama-Nefru's magic was to be alone with me, for She nodded, and summoned a servant who brought in a covered silver bowl. The lid, when removed, disclosed a sheep's liver. So soon as he was gone, She took it out and laid it on a silver plate, whereupon She touched it in many places with Her forefinger, and looked for a long time at the lobes of this liver, all the while—as a sign of hospitality—concealing no thoughts from me.

So I knew She was remembering the animal as it had been when alive. Indeed, She had chosen this ram for its twisted horns. Before the sacrifice, She had even whispered a few words of Egyptian into the beast's ear—it was, after all, one of our animals. "Will My baby become the Pharaoh?" She had asked. Now, the shape of the liver said to Her, "He will, if other Princes do not kill His Father," or that was how I interpreted the message. For She saw Amen-khep-shu-ef plunge His knife seven times into the back of His Father while User-mare lay on a woman, yes, the woman was Nefertiri. But I do not know if these were thoughts Rama-Nefru obtained from the liver, or whether She chose to offer such sights so that I might speak of them to the Pharaoh.

We sat in silence.

She said, "Did you know that the old dead Pharaoh, Ramses the First, the grandfather of My husband, was a common man?"

"I did not know," I told Her.

"He died in the second year of His Reign. I think a common man dies of fright when he has to be King." She nodded. "That has happened."

"I have no knowledge of these matters," I said.

"Yes, Ramses the First, the grandfather, was only a soldier. I learned about this from a papyrus in the Royal Library. He was a Superintendent of Horses. Later, He was promoted to Superintendent of the River Mouths, and then He was made a Commander of the Armies under Pharaoh Harmhab Who, I must tell you, was also no more than a soldier."

"I knew that," I said, "yet I did not."

I could have told Her that nobody ever spoke of this Ramses the First Who came before Seti. One could tell stories of old Pharaohs like Thutmose and Hat-shep-sut, but They were dead long before any of us had seen the sun.

"Your Seti the First," She said, "was a respectable King and He reigned for near to twenty years. Still, He is the son of an upstart. Such a son remains an upstart. So does the grandson. When I came to Egypt I did not know that Sesusi was the grandson of an upstart. I think My father would not have sent Me if he had known." She sighed and pushed away the sheep's liver. "I find My husband difficult to comprehend, don't you?" Before I could begin to answer such a remark, She said, "I have never known a King who spends as much time with priests. I think that is because He is an upstart."

I was thinking of Queen Nefertiri lying in the dark of a closed sedan chair. Her legs had been parted by a Pharaoh whose grandfather had been a soldier like me. Yet, Her blood was descended from Hat-shep-sut.

Why had Nefertiri never spoken of Ramses the First? Was my Queen ashamed? Now, in this moment, when I thought of Usermare, I did not dare to say it, but if the majesty of a Pharaoh was a virtue granted Him because He was crowned, then the Gods of Egypt, if They chose, could make any man a God. I told myself that I had been General-of-all-the-Armies, and therefore, could become a Pharaoh! Even as had Harmhab and Ramses the First before me.

Rama-Nefru said, "Here, take My hand. When I am lonely, I need a friend."

Since I knew how the touch of one hand upon another could produce astonishing results in Her, I was uneasy. Yet such were the thoughts I had just had, that I also felt ready. I took Her hand. The surprise, I may say, was delightful. She had the softest palm I ever held. Then She gave a radiant smile, as if no bleak thought could live beneath the radiance of Her golden wig, and handed me a flower. It was a fresh pink rose. She said, "Its bloom has opened this morning."

I held it to my nose, my other hand touching Her hand, and felt a sorrow lift from Her and come over to me through the petals of the flower. I did not know if I liked Her, yet out of that music in Her heart, so different from mine, one note must have been the same. For we felt the same sorrow.

We sat there holding hands, and memories of the Battle of Kadesh came back to me. She had been born after that day, but lived in the shadow of the battle. So, I knew, as I say, Her misery. I even heard Her silent lamentations as Usermare and Nefertiri came forth in one another.

Now, Her chamber may have had no window with a long view, but I was still so close to the thoughts of Usermare that I soon became aware He was on His way, and indeed was approaching across the Palace walks. In truth, I was ready for His visit so nicely and with such calm that I did not withdraw my hand from Rama-Nefru until I could hear His step in the next chamber. Then our fingers came apart with the lingering touch of two lovers separating from a kiss.

I waited in the anteroom. Now, Usermare was with Her and holding Her hand. I listened. I had never felt as gentle, nor as unlike a man before, not even when I had been treated like a little queen by Usermare. At such times, all of me had been in a terrible contraction. The more He had made me feel like a woman, the more I knew the anguish of a man. But now, as if the cries of pleasure uttered by Nefertiri left a wound in me whose bleeding would not be staunched, I felt as peaceful as the Nile in the abatement of its flood, and never more immersed in sorrow. The river might as well have contained the water of all who ever wept. That sorrow increased as Usermare began to hold Her palm. For with all Their sighs and heavy silences, I could feel the infidelity of Rama-Nefru's hand as it lay in His.

The Hittites, I told myself, had four seasons, not three. So Her hand was like a fourth mouth, and Her heart more subtle than ours. Like the turns of the lobes of the liver She studied for so long, Her cruelty might be as subtle as Her heart. I do know that on this night She chose to speak of the Battle of Kadesh, and never uttered a word about Nefertiri. Yet I was certain that before She was done, He would suffer injury.

Here, Ptah-nem-hotep interrupted my great-grandfather, the sound of His voice bringing me back from the sweet indolence of my absorption. For my Father's voice was harsh, as if He had recovered His strength but was in a rush to exercise it before losing such force again.

He began: "You have not said what was in My ancestor's mind."

"I have not," agreed Menenhetet.

"Did you know His mind in this hour?"

My great-grandfather nodded. "Under the spell of Ma-Khrut, I can say that I knew His thoughts."

My Father was pleased but agitated. "I, too, would claim," He told my mother, speaking to her as much as to my great-grandfather, "that I am under your family spell. For I also know His thoughts. I, too, can see Him returning to the Columns of the White Goddess, and such a sight is rare, but . . ." Ptah-nem-hotep hesitated, as if daring much, ". . . He is, on this occasion, alone on the path."

"That is the same," said my great-grandfather, "as the way I see it."

"Tell Me then if what I possess of His thoughts is exact. I believe He is trying, even as I, to recollect the noble exploits of great Pharaohs before Him. He is telling Himself that Amenhotep the Second killed more than a hundred lions. He also thinks of Thutmose the Third and the ships of Hat-shep-sut. Now, He is so unfortunate as to pass by the place in the reflecting pool where His head crashed to the marble. On this recollection, He feels a terrible pain in His groin. Is this exact?"

"It is true measure," said my great-grandfather.

"His stomach," my Father said with more confidence, "is full of pain. He knows a fear of Thutmose the Great. The stones of Thutmose grind in His bowel. Then Usermare stumbles and nearly falls from the force of the kolobi He has been drinking since the hour with Nefertiri. Many Gods pitch about in His thoughts. All the same, He begins to sing:

> "An Egyptian Princess has deep and bottomless eyes,
> "I will spend the night with Her under the stars.
> "How sweet is the taste of honey in Her mouth."

Menenhetet rose to his feet.

"Did He sing that song?" asked my Father.

Again, my great-grandfather nodded.

"But the song," said Ptah-nem-hotep, "does not take away His fear. As soon as He enters the halls of the White Goddess to see Rama-Nefru, His chest thumps like the heart of a stallion. All the while He repeats to Himself the name of Kadesh. The battle reverberates in His heart until He can feel Himself a Pharaoh like none before. Indeed He loves the names of the Hittite Gods because they remind Him of Kadesh. He says them to Himself: Kattish-Khapish. Valizalish. Is that true?"

"It is exact. You have heard it with exactitude of measurement," said Menenhetet, and to show how moved he was, he crossed the patio, knelt, and kissed the ground before the Pharaoh's feet. My Father, with a smile of happiness on His face, knelt in turn, and with His hand grasped the big toe of Menenhetet.

I had learned the word to describe all that was most exquisite to these two, great lords. It was *exactitude*.

Ten

This time, my Father's strength was not consumed by entering the thoughts of Usermare, and He came to sit with my mother and me. Indeed, if not for His heavy breathing, I believe He was left most content with the achievement. The wind in His chest ceased to sound like a storm, and with a small gesture of His hand, He requested that Menenhetet resume what He had been telling. I, at the moment, happy my Father had returned, if only from across the patio, was soon listening again (in the manner I enjoyed so much) at the very entrance to sleep, and every voice soon became a murmur.

I can tell you, my great-grandfather related, that Ramses may have entered Her room with Kadesh on His tongue, but when Rama-Nefru did not upbraid Him, and gave instead the gift of Her hand, He was relieved to sit in silence and restore His calm. Then, to His surprise, Rama-Nefru began to speak of the battle, and told Him what She had heard of it in Her childhood. Listening in the next room, I soon decided that no story could be better chosen to suit the air of Thebes on this night when fires were burning at every crossroad. Indeed, one's breath was nearer to the smoke of Kadesh than on any evening I had known by the Nile.

"In the year before You came with Your mighty armies against us," She said, "our Hittites went to war with the Medes, and we won a great victory. As a child, I often heard of the splendor of that celebration. From the town wall, our people hung draperies of the most brilliant colors, purple, red, and blues richer than the sky of the day, and all these cloths were much embroidered until the walls looked like the interior of a palace.

"Then My uncle Metella and his officers had a great party where they drank from gold and silver cups he had taken out of the temples of conquered nations, and My uncle found much pleasure in using these sacred vessels of the vanquished. Having asked for a trellis to be built in his garden, he hung the head of the King of the Medes there. While he drank, he liked to look at this head hanging from a branch, and it gave him strength. Although My uncle did not need such strength. He was near to a giant in size."

"I did not know that," said Usermare. He waited in much doubt, but finally asked, "Was he taller than Me?"

"I have never seen a taller man than You," She said.

"Yet You were still a child when Metella died. So You cannot know."

"I cannot know," She agreed, "but where is the King who can lift his head nearer to the sky than You?"

He grunted. "Do You feel well?" He asked. I could feel His desire to offer His tongue to Her blond hairs.

"I feel weak at this hour," She replied, "but ready to tell You more."

"I wish to hear it."

The people behind the walls of Kadesh knew, She told Him, that the Egyptians were coming. They had had word of the departure from Gaza. Spies with fast horses had come to the city each day bringing news of the advance of the Egyptians. Great was the uneasiness. Even as the Armies of Usermare marched forward, so did the full moon draw near. But the morning after a full moon was called the Day of Sappattu and on that day, strenuous activity was forbidden. The Hittites could not fight on such a day. It was the hope of Kadesh that the Egyptians would arrive on the morning before the Day of Sappattu so that the city would not be lost. To induce the Egyptians to march into battle a day early, they even conducted a ceremony. Within the walls, many fires were lit, and priests spoke prayers into the flame. Metella, however, did not attend. It was reckless to expose the King. The person of the King was never to be attached to the flame. "Magic," said Rama-Nefru, "when it does not burn one's foe, can eat oneself."

"Well, where was he while the fires were going?"

"In his Palace preparing to sleep. He was looking for a sleep of truthful dreams."

"How would he do this?"

"I have told You how. Many times. By fasting all day. The question to which one desires an answer will also be hungry."

Metella did not know whether the Egyptians would advance on Kadesh by the left or the right bank of the river. He hoped to be able to address the question to Marduk Himself, although the God was not easy to reach. It was equal in difficulty to walking across a chasm on one of the giant hairs that grew out of the God's head. So it was necessary to have the purest sleep in order to know the best balance.

"What if Marduk had told him of disasters to come?"

"Then," said Rama-Nefru, "one could prepare for one's doom. That is better than to wait blindly."

"I never want to hear bad omens," said Usermare.

"We believe it is better," She said, "to know, than to hope."

He snorted. "What happened while he slept?"

"In the middle of the night, he awoke with a headache."

That was no good sign. If the Gods did not speak, then a vow would have to be taken. The priests shaved Metella of his beard and the hairs of his body. The heavy black curls, when collected, overflowed a bowl.

The High Priest stuffed this hair into a vase, and sealed it, and the vow was taken to carry this vase all the way to Gaza and bury it there. While the battle would certainly take place before any messenger could reach such a distant place, the vow would be secure if he was on his way before the armies met. So, in the middle of the night, they sent off a man.

Yet once the messenger was gone, the King's headache remained. All who were near Metella thought an earthquake was close. The stones beneath their feet felt as slippery as the back of a snake. This must be a sign that the enemy would overthrow the walls. In an earthquake, the land loses its reason and many trees fall.

The High Priest of Kadesh engaged the King, therefore, in a rare ceremony. He asked Metella to put down his sceptre, take off his ring, remove his crown, and unbuckle sword and scabbard. Then, beside a statue of Marduk, the Monarch bowed before the High Priest. Since Metella was without any of the kingly appointments, his person was not inviolate, and he could be treated as a man. The High Priest thereupon struck him in the face many times, and did not stop until tears came to Metella's eyes. His headache, however, was lessened. Now the people of Kadesh could have hope that the trees would not be uprooted. Still, the omens were poor. Outside the Palace, people were wailing in the middle of the night. It had become known that the King, trying to find a true dream, had wakened with much oppression.

When Metella's headache still did not pass, the priests declared that more daring spells must be cast before the battle. This, however, would leave the King wholly unprotected. Metella had, therefore, to be removed from the battle. A substitute would be sent out in his place.

The King's wrath, Rama-Nefru said, was great. Yet, having accepted the ceremony, he was bound to the word of the High Priest. All wept at the pain of Metella that he would have to remain behind, and he battered his head against the walls of his Palace.

Next day, no one knew who had been chosen as the King's substitute. Indeed, he did not declare himself until the hour when Usermare asked for a Hittite to meet Him on the field. Then the fellow stepped forward. He was the First Charioteer and a great swordsman.

"Was he," asked Usermare, "the Hittite with the crazy eye?"

"I do not know of whom You speak," She said, "but I would ask:

Is his eye like the cast in the eye of Amen-khep-shu-ef?" Usermare gave a low moan. "They are alike," He said, "but never in my meditations have I seen them together."

She nodded.

"Now, I will never see them apart," He said. He must have squeezed Her hand for She gave a small cry of pain. When He apologized, She said in the sweetest voice, "I had forgotten how Your people feel much enthusiasm for the fingers of the slain." My Pharaoh laughed uneasily as if He did not know whether to approve of what She said, but then She added, "Our Hittite men are vain and very fierce. They say that what the Egyptians did on the night after the battle was effeminate."

"Effeminate?"

"I used to hear them say that if Metella had been with them, and they won the battle, they would not have collected hands, but heads. They would have cut off the head and neck of the little man who lives between the legs. Egyptians treated in such manner make a good soup, they used to say."

Usermare sighed. "I do not know the Hittites," He told Her. "I would not wish to sit in My garden with the head of My enemy on a tree."

"But You do not have to live with the evil fortunes of My people," She said. "Metella's headache was gone by the following night, and he wished to come out from the gates and destroy You. Yet, he could not. The night that came after the day of battle had a full moon. So the next day was Sappattu."

Gloom came to Usermare. As I listened to Her words, I knew they were like vines that would grow into His pride.

"When You left in the morning," She said, "My people watched from our parapets. We saw great disorder but could not move. We were in the Day of Sappattu. Our only consolation was that the Egyptians were so ignorant of our weakness on this day that they did not know enough to attack our walls. So we watched You march away. I was not to be born for seven more years, but I heard the story many times. In My sleep, I still watch the Egyptians leave.

"When You were all gone, My people came out and hunted through the fields for our dead and we brought them back. That night, we wailed inside our city. We gave voice to great laments in the hope that would enable us to reach into the true darkness of the night. The moon was still full, so we could see the terrible fields on the other side of the river, and because of that sight, we had to descend, each of us, into the deepest caves of our heart where no moonlight can ever reach. There we wept for the despair of all the Gods who are imprisoned in each mountain. If even one of Them as great as Marduk could hear our sorrow, He would no longer feel bound by the indifference of the other Gods. He would know our pity was for Him. So the wailing of the people who walked through the streets of Kadesh on this night was full of suffering in order that the stone hearts of the Gods might be touched.

"Yet to weep with such force called for more lamentation than can be known from a day of battle. We cried, therefore, for those ills which continue through the years. We wailed for those who were far away, and for gardens that were barren. We wailed for empty furrows and for all our children who had died too young, and for dead wives and husbands. We wailed for the suffering of the old, and for the dry rivers and the scorched fields, for the marshes that choke the fish, and the forests that never saw the sun, the desert that knows no shade. We wept for the shame of the vineyard whose grapes are bitter, and we wailed out of all those hours that are heavy with oppression because of all the ills that are near to us, but unknown.

"Here, in this land," She said, "you Egyptians do not wail. You celebrate. You feast with your Gods. We cry for ours. We know how They suffer. We wail at how They are blasphemed by us, and we wail for the wives whose husbands know other women, and the mothers who give birth to monsters. Sometimes we wail for those who do not know how to weep." She began to sing to Herself, but in a dirge of such misery, so strange to Usermare that He did not know how to reply, and He put on His Double-Crown and went out silently. Nor did He give me a sign to follow.

Being left without a word, I was reduced to the ranks of those menials whose most serious duty is to wait. I lay, therefore, on a couch in the anteroom while She paced about and, at last, lay down, and after a time, was asleep. That, I discovered, was more than I could ask for myself. The woes of Usermare weighed heavily on my own until I began to question the value of the powers Honey-Ball had bestowed, for now I lived in the same dread as my Pharaoh. I even knew that He was alone and stood in water up to His knees in the great wading pool that was the Eye of Maat. Small insects hovered about Him in the dark as He brooded on what Rama-Nefru had said, and tears came to His eyes. Her hair had fallen out. He did not know if the loss had come from shifting the stones of Seti and Thutmose, but He had prayed for the return of Her hair, and it did not return. He thought of the convulsions that had been loosed in Her while She slept and how, as He held Her, She snored in much fury, a desperate sound to come from a young throat. It was like the grunt of wild boars in the mountains of Syria. She had snored again last night, and He had found Himself longing for the perfumes of Nefertiri. Now, He did not know how to make amends. Rama-Nefru had said that Egyptians do not wail.

He thought of the ceremonies in the Temple of Osiris at Abydos. Thirty-five years gone by, back in the year of His ascension to the throne, He had attended such ceremonies, and no one had ever heard sounds to compare to the terrible wails that came out of the men and women who stood outside the gates of the Temple at Abydos. Their cries could have come from the earth itself, out of the rocks and roots and uncut stones of temples not yet built. And so He sighed, and stepped out of the water of the Eye of Maat and returned at last to Her room and lay beside Her through the night. But She did not stir, and in the darkness He had many thoughts of the Temple of Osiris at Abydos for when He was a young man in the first months of the year He was awaiting His coronation while the body of His Father, Seti, was being prepared for burial and lay its seventy days in a sacred bath of natron, He thought often of the God Osiris even as the flesh of His own Father turned to stone, and having traveled up and down the Nile to visit the sacred cities at Ombos and On, and the Temple of

Ptah at Memphi, He had come at last with fear and expectation to Abydos, the most sacred of all cities, the first, in truth, of the sacred places for the head of Osiris had been buried here by Isis.

"I know of this," said my Father most suddenly, and I could see how ready He was to speak, for His thoughts had stirred as suddenly as we catch a stick that is thrown to us in a dream. "Yes," said my Father. "When He came back to the bed of Rama-Nefru indeed He listened again to the wails of the multitude at Abydos, but, in the darkness, I think He ceased to brood on Her and remembered instead His visit to His Father's small temple at Abydos. Is that true?"

"It is exact," said Menenhetet.

"Yes, I know His thoughts," said Ptah-nem-hotep. "The temple to His Father was not finished, but abandoned by the river, and User-mare brooded upon the last years of His Father's illness, for Seti had been too weak to supervise His works, and died in gloom. Seti may have been a strong man, but He died in great fear of the ignorance of His Father, the first Ramses, Who would not know how to welcome Seti when He came to join the body of Osiris in the Land of the Dead. So, Seti knew a terrible fear of His own death, and when He spoke of Osiris it was always with the greatest veneration, indeed, no one was more devoted to the Temple of Osiris than Seti. Before so great a God, Seti even hesitated to say His own name. He was afraid that its likeness to the name of Set would prove offensive. When He began the new Temple at Abydos (that Usermare now found unfinished) those priests who would serve as His architects had informed Seti with much trembling that a house of worship dedicated to Osiris could not allow Set to have a place among the Gods inscribed on the walls. These priests could hardly speak after this for they were next obliged to tell Seti that His Name could only be written here as Osiris the First. Seti did not raise His sword, His club, nor His flail. Instead, He gave assent. Just so great was His fear. Usermare, sitting in His Father's unfinished temple, was moved by the death of His Father and made a vow to finish the temple.

"Now, thinking of that vow He had never fulfilled (and later so abused as to transport some of these stones upriver from Abydos to

His own Festival Hall of King Unas) He rose from the bed of Rama-Nefru in much uneasiness, and returned to the wading pool to greet the rising of the sun on this, the Fourth Day. After which He made His way to the Throne Room. There, while in the Seat, He hoped to meditate upon the ceremony that would greet the Day of Osiris to be celebrated here this morning in Thebes, instead of at Abydos, this year of the Godly Triumph.

"Yet, even as He sat in the embrace of Isis and knew Her as His Seat, so did the name of Set come into His meditation, and disturb His calm, and He could not contemplate the ceremonies He must perform today. He thought instead of the first year of His marriage to Nefertiri when, to please His father, He named Their first son Set-khep-shu-ef, and spoke the name of this son often to Seti. Yet so little had He fulfilled His vows to His Father, that even as Seti had been obliged to honor the name of Osiris more than His own, so did User-mare, after His Father's death, change the name of Set-khep-shu-ef to Amen-khep-shu-ef. Now, He shivered in the embrace of Isis and His thoughts were unsettled. Even when the High Priest said: 'You are upon Your Throne, Great King, and Her name is Isis: The body and blood of Your Throne is Isis,' the incantation did not compose Him. He grew mournful on the Throne of Isis. With His death, Horus would no longer live in Him, nor would He live in Horus. He would enter the Land of the Dead and dwell in the Lord Osiris. But would the love of Isis belong to Him? Who could say that His own women loved Him like Isis?

"Full of the unhappiness of these thoughts, He left the Throne Room and mounted His palanquin. On this day, Rama-Nefru would ride with Him. Even as He saw the pallor of Her skin in the sunlight against the brilliance of Her golden wig, He knew that She was ill. When She sat beside Him and did not offer Her hand, but only looked with no smile on the cheers of those who had been invited this morning into the Court of the Great Ones, so did He shiver, and was most morose as He stepped down from the Golden Belly and knelt before the shrine of Osiris. He tried to think of the grain that would come from the earth, but He could only brood upon the God Osiris trapped beneath.

"Yet, as the priests sang, He remembered how the women used to call forth the name of Isis in the fields before the first ear of corn was cut. They would thresh the corn and in the winnowing, Isis would rise to heaven.

"Before the shrine of Osiris, He listened to the priests sing:

> " 'Osiris is Unas in the chaff.
> " 'He has loathing of the earth.
> " 'Oh, dry His wounds.
> " 'Cleanse Him with the Eye of Horus
> " 'For Unas is up and away
> " 'To heaven!
> " 'To heaven!'

"Now, Usermare saw the Pharaoh Unas rising to heaven and in His heart, He tried to remember how in His dreams, He and Unas used to eat the flesh of the Gods."

It was here my Father ceased to speak. "I would go on," He said, "but now there are too many ceremonies to follow and much din before Me, and I do not want to risk the headache of Metella. Tell Me, therefore, of what you did on that day, and if you were with Nefertiri. That is what I cannot see."

Again, my great-grandfather nodded. "It is so," he said. "I was with Nefertiri."

Eleven

"In truth," said Menenhetet, and his tone was measured (as if, by the balance of Maat, it was proper that now he should speak and Ptah-nem-hotep rest) "I felt close in my thoughts to Nefertiri all the while I stood in the retinue of Usermare as He knelt before the shrine of Osiris, but it was only after He returned to the palanquin and was carried with Rama-Nefru back to the Throne Room to dress for another ceremony that I began to feel Nefertiri was not only thinking of me—and for the first time in these four days!—but that She wanted me. So, I left my place in the retinue, which, by now, offered no difficulty. Visiting Notables were everywhere eager to slip in. I slipped out, therefore, and left the gate of the Palace to wander through the crowds of Thebes, drunk already this morning from the night before, and again I could feel Nefertiri as if She were about, such certainty, however, much bespattered in the din, the dust and smoke, not to speak of the fearful number of interruptions from all too many of the crowd, who, seeing my fine dress, knew I belonged in the Court of the Great Ones, and therefore wished to be of service, or merely wished to talk to me—if only to be able to say they had spoken to a Notable. I returned to the Court of the Great Ones swearing to myself that I would never go out in fine dress again without a chariot to separate me from the people! So soon as I was back in the Columns of the White Goddess, therefore, I rummaged in the room of a carpenter and took up his oldest rags to leave again by the servants' gate wearing no more than a breechcloth and a headband.

"You would think from the way I rushed forth into the alleys, working my way through the fountains of every dirty little square and filthy gutter, in and under the sluices of each worn-out creaking shaduf, the breath of drunks in my face and the breasts of women rustling against me in many a crowd, that I, with freedom to act like a servant loose in a crowd, would know how to look, but I was in such a panic that Nefertiri was near and I did not see Her—my sense of Her as near to me most compelling—that the more I walked, the less certain I became of finding Her. Then the crowd became a panic for me as well. I was not used to being jostled aside by men whose clothes were whiter than mine, and was soon in such a rage that their drunkenness left me with vertigo. But then I was full of many desires that went in different directions. At each brush with a strange body, I was ready to throw the man to the ground, yet my longing for Nefertiri must also have been in my eyes because no whore failed to smile at me, and some wore balls of wax so powerful with perfume—and such foul stuff!—that I felt surrounded by molderings of honey and old sweat. Yet, when I pushed into a beer-house jammed with louts and soldiers, as well as every kind of poor bewildered stranger from every little river-town who had come along with his God from up or down the river, I commanded so little attention that I had to grab the waitress by the arm to get a beer and that almost brought on a fight. Then, the air stank. Drunks were throwing up on the dirt floor, and this crowd, forever ignorant of palace etiquette, were kneading their pastes into the earth without a pause. You could have let a few pigs wander in—no one would have known."

As my great-grandfather spoke, I could see him in my thoughts no longer, not his face at least, for he had begun to look to me like Bone-Smasher as I had followed our boatman on his wanderings through Memphi this afternoon, and lying there between my mother and Fa-

ther, the closer I fell back into the tender lips of sleep, the more did I
see the boatman, until I could even feel him making love to Eyaseyab,
and in my thoughts and dreams, he and my great-grandfather were
now passing each other. So did I even think I saw Bone-Smasher and
Eyaseyab in a hut in some servants' courtyard of one of the alleys
down which my great-grandfather was wandering, until I realized
with the languorous shift of pleasure that simple discoveries provide
when one is on this side of the swells of slumber, that they were in no
back street of Thebes but must be making love now in whichever
little room had been given to Eyaseyab for our stay in the Palace tonight, yes, I was out of my own dear cushions, and lolling on the rise
and rush of their bodies in the air of the night, yes, they were making
love in the servants' quarters of the Palace, my dear Eyaseyab who
kissed Sweet Finger and drew forth all that was sweet, yes, I had deserted my great-grandfather to live in her heart and now knew nothing of him, but was rich instead with her, and fine in my limbs. Then,
Bone-Smasher broke in like the lightning of Set and I heard a cracking of rock, and felt much throbbing, and maybe I even heard her cry
out, for on this patio, through the light breeze of the night came
many a moan, and much pleasure and woe there with the grunts and
scratching and roars and cackles of the beasts in all the pens and stables
far away, yet in the night, like the Gods, all sounds are near, and with
her cry, if I heard it, I must have passed from Eyaseyab's warm pleasure back into the longing of my great-grandfather for Nefertiri,
since now I could hear his story better, which is to say, see it more
clearly, and his voice no longer intervened in my ear so much as the
breath of his thoughts.

I was alone, he told us. I could have been, he murmured, living still
on the river of my childhood, no older than the boy who went forth
from my village to the army just so alone did I feel myself in the din
of this beer-house in the back-quarters of Thebes. Nor could I cease
to feel that Nefertiri was near, yet I would not see Her. But, then, did
I truly wish to see Her? I could measure the terror. Finding Her, I
could lose all I had gained in my life.

With that thought, a weight came down upon me (in the midst of all these sour half-fermented bodies) that was like the stones of a tomb, and for the first time I saw my life without pride. I did not think of my achievements (which were the blood and bone of my good esteem each morning) but saw instead all I had not done, the friends I had never made (for I trusted no man) the family I would never have (for I had trusted no woman enough to keep a family— how criminal had been the desertion of Renpu-Rept within my heart!) and at that instant, my nostrils full of the puke of others, just as atrocious seemed the contents of my own heart. I saw then the hopelessness of growing into an old man—for me, at least! I would not like to lie in my bed and clutch the medals my Pharaoh might yet give me, nor hear my titles repeated by old servants who would listen to my cough in the middle of the night and curse me for a miser. Such a death was hideous—to cough once in this life and once again in the Land of the Dead. "I do not want to die again in Khert-Neter," one of the drunks in the bar was singing, but then that song is the dirge of all drunks.

I thought of the gold mines at Eshuranib and the wisdom of Nefesh-Besher, and wondered if I had the power to be reborn in the belly of a great woman. Then it was as if the Gods came down in assembly about me, and I felt the balance of heaven waiting for what I would next decide, as if the timid poisons of my blood and the bravery of my heart stood arrayed before one another like legions in the hour when the horn is blown. I did not dare to breathe and yet no breath was more pure than all that quivered in my nose above the mash of this jeering puke, for I knew then—I, who had prayed like any other soldier to a hundred Gods and heard the voice of none, trusted none—I heard one God then. Whom, I do not know, but He was in my heartbeat, waiting for me to decide. And I said to myself, "I am not afraid of death. I will dare it," and knew that what I said was heard, oh, more than that, I would swear the light of the candles lowered in that bar as if the fires of Ra were quiet before the enormity of what I had said. It was then I left the place. I would look for Nefer-tiri.

So I was out in the street again, my arms like shields against the elbows of others, and a calm came to me of a sort I had never felt before. It had no peace in it, but for the quiet that comes when you know that no matter how many tortures lie in wait, at least you will never suffer impatience again. My life was before me, I felt. Whatever of it was left, was at last before me. I would not die in the grinding exasperation of the aged turned to stone by their fear of the stone that will lie on them, no, I would find Nefertiri and I would fuck Her. The thought of my cock in Her, my agony in Her honey, my fatigue in Her wealth, my pride in Her royal privacy, my beating heart in Her sweet quiver, my peasant meat in the sauce of a Queen, my sword in Usermare's skin!—every high and low passion I ever felt came together, and my life was simple. I would fuck Her or die in the attempt; or I would be with Her and no one would know; or was it that I would be with Her and we would love each other so well that I would dare what no one would dare: if She wished me to kill the Pharaoh, I would. I took a great breath then. Having said it to myself, I knew that I was like no Egyptian of common blood in the Two-Lands. A few might be found to kill a Pharaoh for their lord, the next Pharaoh. But none would do it for themselves, except me. I would dare to be Pharaoh if She were my Queen. His blood was no finer than mine. Descendant of the Superintendent of the River Mouths!

So I knew the peace of understanding. Never again would I protect myself for too little, nor fear catastrophe too much. Let it come. Let it come down upon me. I would be the Pharaoh, or no more than Her lover, or dead, or in Her belly, or none of these. But I would fear no man or thought any longer. In that moment, I felt as young and as strong as in my day at Kadesh and decided that if I were not the Pharaoh in this life, it would be in another.

Ptah-nem-hotep now spoke so quickly that I was lifted from the fine place between my great-grandfather's voice and my own sleep. "You made that day," said my Father, "a most curious promise to yourself. I must ask: Dear Menenhetet, how can I ever trust Myself to sleep if you are Vizier?"

"Good and Great God," said Menenhetet, "I have given to You a respect I offered no other Pharaoh. You ask me to tell all that I know and I honor Your need and the wisdom of Your mind. I tell myself that Your mind and mine can trust one another more closely than brothers since neither of us can abide stupidity. So I tell the truth. Not because I love You—I love no creature on earth but my great-grandson who is now Your son"—and here I felt a love come from him to me that was as rich in the good marrow of its feeling as all that passed between Bone-Smasher and Eyaseyab—"but because I honor You, You of the Divine Two-Houses, and believe that no Pharaoh ever had Your subtlety of mind nor Your rare power to honor the truth. I speak then to Your face, and say: Because Egypt is not strong today, there is no Vizier You can trust. I, at least, will never bore You."

"I am delighted by Your candor," said Ptah-nem-hotep, "if not altogether happy with the truth of what you say." He sighed, but then He laughed. "Go on with your story," He said, "I trust you in spite of Myself," and He laughed a little more as He said this and an astonishing kindliness went out from His body until I could feel it touch my great-grandfather, who, in turn, was so pleased by this warmth that he tapped his forehead with two fingers in an old chari-oteer's salute, a gesture he might not have used in a hundred and fifty years or more. I, however, could not continue to share what passed between them because I saw my mother's mouth and it revealed what her thoughts kept hidden. Some pain must have gripped her in this moment. I felt a malevolence on us, yet so faint only my mother and I could detect it. Then, I knew that if Nef-khep-aukhem were by now on the other side of Memphi, his curse was not. So I understood how an animal can stir when one hair in the million and infinity of his fur is askew.

Therefore, I did not listen to my great-grandfather as easily as be-fore, and many moments must have gone by before I could settle back into the embrace of my near-sleep and follow how he searched for Nefertiri by way of Her limp. It was that, my great-grandfather said, he was looking for, that is, looking for a woman of great beauty who, no matter how disguised, would show a small limp.

That, he told us, had become touching to him. It was the only indication in my Queen, he said, of Her true age—She still had the pain in Her hip. Yes, could be heard in my great-grandfather's thought, one was searching for a woman with a limp, yet with such single-mindedness that it took a while on leaving the bar to realize that what was needed were not eyes that could see farther ahead but a neck clever enough to know when to look back. It was only when my spine began to tingle that I began to feel how someone was following me. Yet whenever I turned around, I could not see who was there, only what had just been there. Then, as I whirled on the instant into an alley, I saw behind me a female servant in an old dark cloak, and so I climbed with one vault onto a roof to observe her as she passed. It was the face of a severe and middle-aged servant, so dark that she must be Nubian as much as Egyptian, or could it be a very dark Syrian? But, as she passed, I knew by Her walk it was Nefertiri. There was that tiny hitch in Her step, so bottomless in its rousing of pity in me. I slipped down from the roof and followed Her, but She could sense what was to the back of Her better than me, for in the next alley She came to a hut, opened the door, and turned around between its posts to give me a smile of welcome, and I, with the simple happiness of meeting Her in this deserted alley, gave Her both my arms in an embrace and felt Her divine mouth again, at last, on mine. Yet all the while we kissed—if not for the noble sophistication of that kiss—we could have been two peasants from my village. She wore no perfume, and I could sniff the odor that came from under Her arms, healthy and simple and full of the work of walking through Thebes.

Inside, was one dark room but there was light enough to see a few pots hung on the dirt-brick walls, and some stones in the corner for an oven, a hole in the roof for the smoke, that was all, an old woman's hut with a cot. She was the mother of one of Nefertiri's servants, and at the Festival, said my Queen. She would not be back until late this night. I could see it was true. There was not one person left in this alley—all were away at the Festival, mothers, infants, old people—a robber could have gone through these houses and walked off with two handfuls of grain; there was no more to steal.

I cannot say if it was the poverty, or the sheer, simple dirt of the place, but I knew pure gusto for Her. My cock was up like a bull. Without fine cosmetic, with no more than the dark dye She put on Her face, with no attention to Her hair nor Her clothing, She was like a middle-aged woman of the servant class, good-looking but with no remarkable beauty, and much covered up, Her breasts concealed in a woolen cloak. I desired Her all the more. It gave me strength in approaching, as if we were in my palace now, not Hers. I knew I would need no fine stories to bring forth my appetite, nor any touch of Her fingertips nor Her tongue, not even the sight of Her open thighs, no, I grasped at Her and grabbed Her, hugged Her and would have lifted Her onto the cot with room for me only on top, but She was acting like a true servant girl. Not a servant woman, a girl. She was strong as She resisted me, and I may say that She did not make a sound, as servant girls never will, or so near to never will if the mistress might be listening, and She fought me off, muscular and modest, allowing no more than the sight of that full bush of hair between Her legs which I obtained by raising Her skirt one push at a time, but like a servant girl She would not remove anything else nor show Herself in any nakedness, and now after the first kiss, She would not give me Her mouth again, no, She would not let me near. I could feel her intentions, and they were as heavy as all the leaden secrets of a servant, so much stolen here, so much bad done there. Now She pushed me off and said, "Wait. I am not ready. I am not ready at all," and to my great surprise, for I had never known any woman but a servant to act like this, began to scratch Her calves and continued to do this until Her legs were covered with white streaks, but no, She could not stop, as if this were the only way to calm Herself from the harassments of the day, and it was then I remembered how my mother and other women of my village used to do the same.

My groin could not have ached more if I had been thrust through by a spear, but when I gripped Her knee, She pushed away my hand. "Wait," She said, "I want to ask you about Rama-Nefru," and there, pressing against Her, I still had to stop and tell of all that was most intimate I had learned about Usermare and the Hittite, and it was not until I was done that She kissed me like a good boy, and sighed, and when I pressed forward again, said, "Wait, I want to tell you something." Then, still scratching with the most rhythmical movement of Her wrist as if every word heard about Usermare and His Hittite had first to be digested in Her blood, She began, much to my distraction, to relate a tale I had not heard since childhood, and in no way a story you would think to hear from a Queen. In truth, I had even heard it in my village, but so long ago, I could not remember what came next, yet She insisted on telling it, and there was a determination in Her voice that made me know I must listen. Perhaps it was that She spoke with a servant's accent. She certainly knew how people from the country between Memphi and Thebes will speak.

"This is a tale of two brothers," She said, "and I heard it from the old woman who lives in this place. She heard it from her mother. So this is the story of the hut where we are. You listen to it.

"There were two brothers, Anup, the older, and Bati, the younger. Anup had a large house and a good-looking wife, and Bati worked for him. But the younger brother was stronger and more handsome.

"One day when both brothers were in the field, Bati was sent back for seed, and Anup's wife saw him put the load of three men on his back, so she was much impressed. She stopped dressing her hair, and said, 'Come, let us lie together for an hour. If you please me, I will make you a shirt.' Bati became as wild as a cheetah of the South, and he said, 'Do not say that to me again,' and took up his load of seed and went back to the fields and worked beside Anup so hard that the older brother became tired and thought of his wife. So he left the field to be with her. But when Anup came back to his house, her jaw was covered with a rag. She told him Bati had beaten her because she refused to lie with him. 'If you permit your younger brother to live,' she said, 'I will kill myself.'

"Then the older brother also became like a cheetah of the South, and he put an edge on his knife, and he waited for Bati behind the stable door. Yet when his younger brother came toward the shed, the heifer who led the cows began to moo, and her voice told Bati that he was in danger. So he fled, and Anup ran after him, and Bati did not escape until he crossed the river in a skiff of papyrus at a steep place where Anup could not follow because there was no other boat. Besides, there were many crocodiles. Safe on the other side of the river, Bati now shouted, 'Why do you believe her? I will prove to you that I am innocent.' Then, he took out his knife and cut off the part of himself that was most valuable to him, and he threw it into the river. Then Anup wept and would have been ready to cross, even if he drowned, but he had too much fear of the crocodiles.

"Now, the younger brother said, 'I will take out my heart as well,' and he did, and he laid it on a young acacia tree. 'After this tree is cut down,' he said, 'look for my heart, and lay it in fresh water. Then I will live again.'

" 'How do I know if the tree is cut?' asked Anup.

" 'When the beer froths in your mug, come at once, even if it is seven years from now,' the younger brother said. And he died."

Nefertiri looked at me with all the severity a stranger places in his eye when he is telling an important story. "Anup went home," She said, "and he drove his wife away, and he waited. It was seven years to the day before a Queen came riding through the woods, saw the acacia, and found it so beautiful that it disturbed Her pleasure in Her own beauty. So She ordered the tree cut down. Then the beer frothed in the mug of Anup. The older brother went out to search for the heart of Bati, and found it in the topmost seed of the fallen acacia, and Anup put this seed in water until it came to life, and grew into a bull with the markings of Apis. The animal, so soon as it was full-size—which took a day and a night—even had the picture of a scarab on its tongue. This bull now told Anup to lead him to the Egyptian Court, and the Pharaoh was so pleased with the beast that He gave presents to Anup and sent him away. But, in the morning, the Pharaoh's Queen was alone with the bull. He dared to say to Her, 'You cut me down when I was a tree. Now I live again and am a bull.' The Queen went to the Pharaoh. 'Give Me the liver of that animal to eat,' She said, and the King loved Her so much that He sent His butchers. Yet so soon as they cut the bull's throat, two drops of blood fell by the steps of the Pharaoh's pavilion, and grew up overnight into twin cedars like the ones much beloved by Osiris when the Lord of the Dead rested in His coffin on the shores of Byblos.

"When the King saw this miracle, He invited the Queen to sit with Him beneath these trees. She was much disturbed. From the branches of Her cedar came a whisper: 'I am the one You tried to kill.' That night, when the Pharaoh was taking much pleasure with Her, She said, 'Grant Me what I want.'

" 'It is done,' He said.

"She said: 'Chop down Your trees. Make them into chests for Me.'

"The Pharaoh was not happy, but He sent for His best carpenters, and, while He watched, and She watched, they cut down the twin cedars. Both fell at once, and as they did, a chip flew from each tree and one entered the heart of the Pharaoh. It killed Him."

Nefertiri was silent. "What of the other chip?" I asked.

"It leaped," She said, "from the second cedar into the mouth of the Queen, and She swallowed it. Nine months later, a new Pharaoh was born." She looked into my eye, but no longer was She like a stranger. I knew that all the thoughts I had had about my life in the stench of the beer-house were not far from the thoughts She had known in the clothing of a servant. She, too, was ready to die.

So She stopped scratching and lifted the skirt Herself. Yet She still carried on as if She were a servant and would offer no more than Her buttocks. On this poor cot, full of the rustling of dried reeds under the stale cloth, it was like making love in old straw with all the odors of the farm, and there was no other way She would allow me into Her but by Her third mouth. In the middle of all the vigor this took, I could not pass the gates, yet with every push upon such a door, the expression on Her face would change until I saw another Ka of Her Fourteen. Great changes truly appeared in the contortions of Her face until even by the light of this hut, I could see the prodigious ugliness of Heqat, and Nefertiri was so excited and so beside Herself, that I wondered if Her powers were confused, especially if

Heqat could enter Her. Then, as if Her thoughts had certainly heard mine, there came into the cruel twist of Her mouth all the evil I used to see in the face of Honey-Ball when the most malignant of her curses were cast, and both of us gripped each other in the onset of appetites so low that, whether by Heqat or Honey-Ball, I felt as if we were both ugly, and I hated the Gods, and wished to despise Them.

It can only have been by the balance of Maat that I was now given in the midst of these stubborn efforts a sight of Usermare on Rama-Nefru's purple bed, and Their love, in contrast to ours, was as radiant and as narrow as a beam of light, nothing, I may say, of the deep measure, no matter how ugly, that we could know here, no thunder of delights for His mighty phallus, but the string of a harp in the moment it is plucked, and Usermare quivered in Rama-Nefru's finest light. Maybe it was finer than I could bear, for so little of me was as yet in Nefertiri, not much at all by the dry hinge She offered, that I withdrew, and tried to enter Her other mouth there between Her legs, but She would not allow me. "No," She murmured, "not when you are made of bronze," and forced me off by presenting Her buttocks once more. This time, I obeyed what I saw in Her face and turned around to kissing Her there, my tongue plunging like a second sword so that I must have stabbed Her many times and this brought forth so many royal groans that like a servant girl She kissed me back, and in the same place—I knew heaven then!—we were a two-headed beast for a while. She knew much of this kind of magic.

Then I could enter Her at last, although for the use of Her royal buttocks, Amen-khep-shu-ef would have done better I think as the lover. Back of the first gate was the lock of another, and She was like a siege with many walls. Still, I traveled up Her third mouth, push by push, equal to equal, and if it was Her vagina I wanted, my desire had hardly disappeared. Honey-Ball once told me how women entered by the third mouth feel the anger of Set stir in themselves, and cannot respect the man. Of course, we must respect most those who can kill us, and no woman is ever going to die trying to give birth when the cream of the man has been left in her bowels.

"I want the other," I said to Her, and She replied, "You will not enter that place again until the beer froths in your mug."

So I fucked Her by the ass, and saw all the faces of Heqat and Honey-Ball. Her nostrils were much contorted and She grunted like a beast, maybe this one of Her Fourteen Ka had never known such pleasure before! I beat upon Her stubborn throne while the incense of every perfume I had sniffed at every ceremony of the last four days passed through my head like birds, full flights of birds, and then I was left again with all the smells of sweat and swamp true to us now. We knew each other by all the odors of this hot twilight in this dark hut. I do not know if so much of Her own true odor had ever come forth before. She was much excited, more excited this time by Her asshole than by Her cunt the last, and again She began to speak but only at the end, as it all came nearer, so did She speak. Now, it did not matter that I was in Her by this low mouth, She was no longer a servant but my Queen, and "Oh," She said, "you are so wicked, you are in My *sha*. You are on My field, you are on My estate, oh, you swim in My swamp. *Sesh* and *sesh*. Write on Me, inscribe Me, *sesh* and *sesh*, You are My mud and My *maher*, My canal, My ooze, you are a devil of a man, sweet *kheru*, My swamp, My robber, My enemy, oh, go deep into the rot, stick it deep, touch the dead, oh, *khat, khat, khat,* put it in My quarry, put it up My tomb, give it to My ancestors, fuck Them all, give it to My ass, My ass," and She came forth with a shriek as loud as the cry She gave on the field dedicated to Amon when Usermare plunged into Her—She came forth, but it was like torture, and, by half, extorted. She was shaking beneath. I felt Her pain in my belly and thighs, and the relief She knew from releasing the pain. Then She slapped me across the face for daring to feel so close. I do not know if love of such a squalid nature would ever be known in my family again until . . . And here Menenhetet came most abruptly to a halt.

Our thoughts also stopped, then staggered forward and came into our heads again. For by the expression on my mother's face and on my Father's, it was clear that they had seen what I had seen—which was Hathfertiti and Nef-khep-aukhem making love in this manner. Was that a payment on my first father's curse? I know that Menenhetet, with all his wisdom, had nonetheless come near to saying what must never be said—how intimate my mother and first father had been! I know my mother now gave Menenhetet one long look, not empty of enmity, to say how much she felt that he had just betrayed her.

But Ptah-nem-hotep, as if stepping back from a wave by the riverbank lifted by the passing of a barge, only said, "Please go on."

Twelve

Menenhetet took his breath, and continued. But, now, I listened instead to his voice, as if my thoughts were no longer so certain they wished to see into his thoughts. "Yes," he said, "we were done, and She did not wait long to leave. At my offer to accompany Her, She refused, even said I must not follow, and in truth, we had the reek of each other that makes the heart cry out to be alone. So I did not mourn Her departure, and on leaving the hut was in so peculiar a state I did not wish to return to the gates of the Palace, but wandered instead through the city, its crowded alleys like a thicket. I kept breathing all of Her that was left on me until there was little to smell. She was truly gone, and I missed Her, even lusted after the odor of us both, like the lair of that beast which had been the two of us, yes, so exceptional was my condition (for again I felt death come near each time I used my elbows to beat a way through the crowd) that such danger was tender in my nose and offered a sweet fear to my chest, like the night on New Tyre when I stepped out of my window onto the bed of the secret whore of the King of Kadesh. Now I did not want the night nor that seductive presence still in my nostrils to cease being with me, and so I mourned the crudity of my acts with Nefertiri. For I loved Her again, loved all the sensuousness and delicacy of Her lovely appearance on that day I first came to serve when She had greeted me with the quiet but splendid sympathies of a Queen, and yet yearned for Her more after today, as if Set and Geb and all the eight Gods of the slime also held us together, and so I would know Her again, and more powerfully, and I felt once again the marriage of Her desire and mine.

"In truth, I was like a madman without Her. The fires on every street corner, and the smells of burning meat made me think again of the taste of human flesh. Near to thirty years came back to me from the face of one of our Nubian soldiers who said on the night of Kadesh, 'The meat of a man gives a strong heart for fighting. It is good to eat meat that has talked to us.' And now, as if not one of those thirty years had passed, I nodded in agreement with him, but it was death with whom I was ready to agree, death—more black and powerful than any Nubian—and I wondered if it were not like the gate to a great city. You did not have to travel up the Nile when you died looking for caverns that would take you into the Land of the Dead. On the contrary, you might march through a gate and horns be blown, many drums struck. Death might be like the streets of our markets. I had seen the first hours of death in many a dream when I wandered through the marketplaces of sleep. It must look like these alleys and the lights of the fire on the faces of the vendors selling meat. Trinkets were waved in my face from the hands of merchants and a whore was always whispering in my ear.

"I spent the rest of the night passing through brothels. If one speck of the meanest waste of the lowest Ka of my Great Queen had been left on my member, be sure I was now inflamed with every strength of the ram and the bull, and had not felt so much like a young soldier since I became First Charioteer. The prow of the Boat of Amon might as well have been moored between my legs for I was like my Pharaoh that night in the whorehouses and did not come back until dawn to sleep in the Steam of the Duad—for such was what we called our own Palace baths! The thousand lice who had invaded my body on this night—what with foul huts, coarse throngs, and whores' sheets—

soon fled in the vapors. I went back to my chamber, clean and drunk,
to sleep at last."

My mother most certainly interrupted here. "I could bear every
description you have given," she said, "because a woman in love will
offer herself without stint. And make no mistake, Nefertiri, no matter how She might despise it, had a most uncontrollable longing for
you. Yet, I cannot endure the hut She chose." Now my mother began
to tremble. "To lie down in a bed so filthy! What could She say to Her
own head of hair?"

Yet it was not Menenhetet who answered, but Ptah-nem-hotep.
His arm about her shoulders, as if she were already His Consort, He
said: "For those five days, the people, on proper occasions, could
come into the Court of the Great Ones, or mingle at the riverbank
with nobles. If the Festival of Festivals was to award the Pharaoh new
strength, then not only the Gods, but the beasts and people of Egypt,
the plants, and the workings of the trades must pass before Him, even
the pests. Is this not true, Menenhetet?"

"It is. On an ordinary day, one could not feel oneself a Notable if
a single louse was in one's nest, but, of course, no place was so clean as
the Palace. Even the quarters of our servants had couches on which a
Princess might sit. But for the Festival, it was different. I tell you,
Hathfertiti, you have never known a Godly Triumph, so you cannot
comprehend. For those few days, it was a mark of virtue to be, if even
for an hour, infested with strange creatures. It showed you were deep
in the judgments of Maat, and had mingled with the people. Even
you, on so great an event, would suffer your pests with pride."

"Never," said my mother, and held the Pharaoh's hand. "Never, I
promise you. I could not lie down, not even with my dearly beloved,
on a bed of vermin."

"We need only wait twenty-three years to see if you are still unchanged," my Father laughed, but she shuddered. "Never," she said.
"Why, until you spoke of that, I thought Nefertiri was much like
me."

"She was, and She was not," said Menenhetet. "It is the mark, after
all, of a Queen to be superior to Herself." When my mother glared at

him—which I never saw her do before—he looked back, but, a silence continuing, was the first to speak.

"By the time I awoke, we were well into the morning of the last day of the Triumph. I was weak from drink, excess, hot baths, and not enough sleep, but I was sober, and therefore felt apart from the others who were commencing to get drunk again. Like the surf of the Very Green, the air of this last morning may have been exalted with excitement, but even the priests were besotted. In the Court of the Great Ones, everyone mingled, and sounds of celebration came up from the city, together with rumors of fights in many quarters. Amen-khep-shu-ef, riding ahead, had arrived this morning with His Guard and the first legions of His army, bringing news of one more successful siege raised against the Libyans—one more town whose walls were gone!—and the people received Him like a Pharaoh. So I heard from every side, and you could see His men coming in to the booths of the Great Ones, some even praying before the shrine of their own nome Gods, or before Syrian altars or Nubian huts with who knows what rubbish inside? Some of His dirtiest troops were praying the most, while His Guard was everywhere with the ladies—I would not have wanted to be a rich merchant with a beautiful wife that morning.

"How the populace liked this Prince! As if my intimacy with His mother would be discerned by Him so soon as He saw my face, I took care to keep the people and the plazas of the Court of the Great Ones between us, and never had to be concerned with where He was. The happiness of the cheers told me. Indeed, in my much-used state, I even began to wonder if He had spoken again to His officers about me, for the passing looks in my direction from His Guard appeared even more evil to me than before.

"At midday, the Coronation of Usermare at His Godly Triumph began, although I do not know that I was able to follow all of that. It seemed to go on for much of the day and into the Collation that night when we finally celebrated the end of the Triumph with serious ceremonies and much entertainment following the contests and games of the afternoon. I remember there was a lot of betting over a race between four herds of oxen (who were called the Canopic Jars) and their herdsmen (the Four Sons of Horus)! We cheered them on to cries of 'Go, Hep! Faster, Tuamutef!' I do not know if it was the knowledge that Amen-khep-shu-ef's troops would be entering the city all day, but sacrilege—'The whip, Amset!'—was also in the air. Watching them race four times around the outer wall of the Horizon of Ra, I also roared with laughter. I was beginning to get drunk again. Everywhere, musicians were playing horns in your ear, a lovely plucking of strings, a frenzy of sistrums, and dancers performed by the river and at the meeting of every large avenue. In the fountain squares, and even in the Court of the Great Ones, wrestlers and jugglers were entertaining.

"Yet in the middle of all this, Usermare, as I say, was being crowned, and that I do not understand, for He had His Coronation in many a ceremony, over and over, and had had it already on the days before this."

"Tell Me," said Ptah-nem-hotep, "of the one you saw, and I will speak of its purpose."

"If I attempt to describe a ceremony that You and Your ancestor know better than I, it must have been, as You can understand, most moving to me. For when Usermare came out of the Throne Room on this day, those who were watching, and I was among them, gasped. 'He is shining like the sun,' I heard the man next to me whisper to his wife. As He seated Himself in the palanquin, a company of His Princes and Princesses came after Him, many carrying the standard of a God on high poles. Off they went. Priests walked before them burning incense. It was then that Amen-khep-shu-ef came marching up with cheers, and when He reached the Golden Belly, moved to the front of the right pole and supported it. His face was, therefore, the first to be seen, and ovations greeted both of Them, Pharaoh and Son, as Usermare was carried from plaza to plaza through the Court of the Great Ones to meet the God Min.

"Now this Min had been taken from His sanctuary and was also carried on a palanquin by many priests on each pole. Others fanned the God and threw bouquets and flowers before Him. The God Min, and the Good and Great God Ramses the Second, approached one another on a platform raised above the Court, and perfume was thrown before Them and incense was burned, while a cheer came up from all of us as the Gate of the Apis Bull opened. The animal came out looking like the Bull of Heaven. His horns were gilded and he was as beautiful as Usermare. He stood alone and defied approach. I do not know if it is a scent that bulls carry with them, but in my nose was the clear odor of cut grass lying on a field in the early morning. There were tears in my eyes. I was thinking of the forty women who opened their skirts to the Apis bull before Nefertiri opened Her thighs to me, and I wanted Her again with such desire that I feared my longing would enter the beast and agitate him. But on this morning as I soon could see, the animal had been given herbs to calm his fury, and after the first clatter upon his sight of all these people proved to be not fierce but tame, he joined the procession of priests who led him forth to Usermare. Now both the bull and our Good and Great God were introduced to Min, Who was presented in the opening of the cabin doors of His palanquin by His priests. From there Min was placed most tenderly on a small throne where He might be visible to all, but the sun shone so brightly on Him that you could see neither His features nor His form, only the molten ball of His light. All gasped, and Usermare covered His eyes with an arm. The bull moaned at the sight of Min Who was like a ball of golden fire.

"Now, I could see the God through the glare, and He had the body of Kheper the beetle, and lion's legs, but a man's face and a Pharaoh's crown upon which were two ram's horns, eight cobras, two discs for the sun and the moon, and two great feathers of gold as high as Himself. He also had a phallus of gold that came straight out from the side of His body, but so far that He had to hold it erect with one hand, indeed, it was as large as the phallus of Usermare, which says much, since the God in His height would not have come up to our Pharaoh's knees if not for being placed so high on His throne. I can say that at the sight of this God and His phallus, so did Usermare also show an erection, and the bull, if he had not been drugged, might have joined Them. Everyone who carried a lotus flower on a stick turned the blossom toward Them, and I felt the earth swell with love and heard

muted groans of desire beneath my feet. Many in the crowd felt the
same, for one could see erections beneath the skirt of many a man,
and more than a few women fainted. Indeed, in this sun, feeling such
desire, I was near to the most agreeable incontinence myself. No matter what I had done the night before, I could feel my share of the Nile
rising.

" 'All praise to Amon-Ra,' said the priest, thereby informing us
that this God Min, Lord of our Festival, and the most splendid divinity of our harvest, was Min-Amon, and so one more manifestation of
the million and one of Amon the Hidden and Ra the Light, and now
as the God and Pharaoh looked upon one another, Usermare into the
eyes of Min-Amon and Min-Amon into the eyes of Usermare, so the
presence of Amon-Ra was over all, and the bull, despite his herbs,
gave forth a bellow full of the echoes of a field beneath the sun and of
many caverns in the hills, while the priest began a long hymn to
Amon-Ra.

"I still hear it—every word. If Usermare had never ceased to be
our Pharaoh, not for one of these five days, still a hand was on our
heart and on the heart of all of Lower and Upper Egypt. In the Two-
Lands we knew with every breath that a catastrophe could come upon
us in any of these five days when Usermare was our Pharaoh, yet was
not. We knew He must be crowned again in order that His strength
be doubled for His years to come. Yet how could He be crowned at
His Godly Triumph, unless, for these five days, He had relinquished
the Throne?

"So, the true return of the Double-Crown to the head of Usermare came nearer as we heard the hymn of the High Priest to
Amon-Ra, and we cheered in assent and knew a high holiness in our
chests, our navels and our loins. The High Priest said: 'Praise be to
Amon-Ra, chief of all Gods, the beautiful One, the giver of life and
warmth to all beautiful cattle. You are the Bull of the Gods, the Lord
of Maat, the Father of Gods, the Creator of men and women, and
You are the Maker of animals. You are the Lord of all things that
exist, producer of wheat and barley, and You make the herb of the
field which gives life to cattle. The Gods acclaim You, for You have

made what is below and all things that are above. You illumine the
Two-Lands and You sail over the sky in peace. You make the color of
the skin of one race to be different from that of another, until there is
all the varieties of mankind, but You make them all to live. You hear
the prayer of he who is oppressed, and You are kind of heart to all
who call upon You. You deliver those who are afraid from those who
are violent, and You judge between the strong and the weak. You are
Lord of the mind. Knowledge comes out of Your mouth. The Nile
comes forth at Your will. You are the Governor of the Ancestors of
the Underworld. Your Name is Hidden.' "

I could feel an unrest in my Father that increased with every word
from Menenhetet's voice. "Can it be," asked Ptah-nem-hotep, "that
these were the words spoken to Usermare?"

"I remember them so."

"Please resume your hymn," said Ptah-nem-hotep.

"These were the words of the High Priest," repeated Menenhetet,
" 'Hail, Only One,' he said. 'Men came out of Your eyes, and the
Gods from Your mouth. You made the fish to live in the rivers and
gave the breath of life to the egg and to the reptiles that crawl. You
allow the rat to dwell in its hole and the bird to sit on the green tree.
Your might has many forms. You have spread the sky and founded the
earth. You are the Lord of grain and bring the cattle to graze in the
hills. Hail, Amon, Bull Who is beautiful of face, Judge of Horus and
Set! You have created the mountain and the silver and the lapis-lazuli.

" 'O Amon, Your rays shine on all faces. No tongue can declare
what You are. You steer the way through untold spaces over millions
of years and hundreds of thousands of years, You travel across the
watery abyss to the place You love, and all this You do in one little
moment of time before You rest, sink down, and make an end of the
hours.' "

"I have read only the last of these words," said Ptah-nem-hotep. "I
do not know of the other portions, although they are most powerful
and curious to Me."

"It leaves me much confused," said Menenhetet, "that my words
are unfamiliar. I have only my memory to trust, and our Khaibit, as

we know, lies in wait to deceive our Ka. Can it be that what I remember hearing on this day might be instead a hymn celebrated by a few High Priests of Amon among themselves, which is to say that I am now not remembering these words from my first life but from my second?"

"It is most remarkable," said Ptah-nem-hotep. "I know of such secret hymns—more even than Khem-Usha who is busy with government—yet I know nothing in the temple literature that would describe Amon as the Lord of the Mind or the Governor of the Ancestors of the Underworld." He shook His head and sighed. "No matter."

"What I tell," said Menenhetet, "is the truth I remember. I would never wish to be Your navigator and mishandle the oar."

"I call the error—if it is an error—most curious and would never think it evil, unless the Gods wish evil between us."

"You have more faith in the Gods at this hour than this afternoon," said my mother, but with such simplicity and recognition of what she had truly discerned that neither my Father nor my great-grandfather smiled, and Ptah-nem-hotep said at last, "It is true. Tonight the presence of My Double-Crown is felt in a manner I did not know before. Let Us honor both you and Menenhetet," whereupon He kissed me.

"No Pharaoh is more wise than Yourself," said Menenhetet.

"I am honored," said Ptah-nem-hotep.

Yet, even as the air is bruised when a bird is hit by a throwing-stick and falls to earth, so the echo of the hymn of the High Priest to Amon-Ra hovered between them, and I felt suspicion within my Father. I cannot say that He now trusted Menenhetet as well. If the first blow to my happiness had been the curse of Nef-khep-aukhem, this was the second. Despite their kind words to each other, I now felt a separation between my Father and great-grandfather, as if they no longer pulled upon the same burden together, but searched in different caves for separate treasures, and I, seeking to hold them together, felt at last a child's fatigue, and wished to weep.

"Go on," said my Father after a silence. "I would not care to interrupt you further."

"As I remember," said Menenhetet after another silence, "the High Priest was no sooner done with his words than another priest opened a gold cage out of which flew four geese in panic that their wings would not lift them quickly enough. Once up, however, they circled about the Court of the Great Ones, and flew away together to the South, later, as we were told, to separate so that they could carry the word to the four quarters of heaven. Now, as they disappeared, the High Priest said in full Authority-of-Voice, 'Horus receives the White Crown and the Red Crown. Ramses receives the White Crown and the Red Crown.' Yet I did not see how He had received either, since He was already wearing both. Only the words had been given to Him. Then another priest made Him an offering of a golden sickle and a sheaf of corn. A eunuch blessed by the priests came forward, kissed Usermare's feet, and lay on the ground with the root of the sheaf in his black hands. The Pharaoh held it by the top, and cut the stalk in the middle. Then ears of corn were strewn before the bull, and the animal was taken off to sacrifice.

"Now all of us who served in the Court came forward one by one to kiss His hand, embrace His knees, or bow to the ground depending on our nearness to Him, and when it was my turn, He gave me a splendid greeting and told me to go to the Throne Room and wait, and there, indeed, He followed me and a few others when He was done receiving homage.

"Now He was alone with eight of us, and said that in honor of our efforts, our devotion to Him, our loyalty, our courage and our discretion—whereupon I thought He looked distinctly at me—He had brought us together for the most special pleasure. He would now bestow on each of us, for this last night of the Triumph, a title. Tonight, we would serve as Masters of the Ceremonies of the Collation, and, He said, we would also hold this title in perpetuity and thereby arouse the awe of others for the rest of our lives. We would be known as His Eight Masters (upon which I immediately thought of the eight Gods of the slime—although I could tell by a look at the faces about me that the others most certainly did not). Now, to His Vizier, His Treasurer, His Chief Scribe, His Majordomo, and to a few of His Generals including myself, the awards were bestowed. We now possessed, we were told, titles that went back to the first Pharaoh, 'Old titles and great ones,' said Usermare. As each of us came forward, we were handed a golden scarab and Usermare intoned our new name. The Vizier became the Unique Companion of Usermare, and the Treasurer was called the Master of All that Grows for the King, while Pepti—who this day to my small surprise had been appointed Chief Scribe—was now honored again as the King's First Acquaintance in the Morning. Another, a General, who had gone on many successful mining expeditions (and had a skin as leathery as Sebek the crocodile) became Master of the Gold that Comes from the Earth, and the other three went forward—I cannot now think of their titles—but I, who was last, was told as I seized His hand, 'What would I ever do without My noble driver?' and He not only held my fingers with an emotion as fine as any offered to me by Rama-Nefru, but looked at me with eyes of love I had not seen Him show to me in many a year. 'Much depends on you,' He whispered—to my full ignorance of what He was talking about—and then He turned to the others and said that after much consideration, I would be called 'Master of the Secrets,' which when said in full, as in ancient times, would go: 'Master of the Secrets of the Things that Only One Man Knows.' This would be my title tonight, He said, and for the rest of my days, and I do not know if I had a glimpse then of other lives to come, but I nearly wept, and did later, so soon as I was alone—which was not for near to another hour, since we celebrated with our Pharaoh over a cup of kolobi, and looked at each other's scarabs and spoke among ourselves as Masters with the names of our new titles. No, it was not until I was back in the Columns, alone in my empty chamber, that I burst into tears, but then I did not cease sobbing for so long I could have been the Nile in flood. I had not cried once since leaving my village, but now I even cried for the hour I was taken into the army. For this, today, was the only gift Usermare had ever given me. So I wept from each of the Two-Lands in my heart. I do not believe we can ever know a great emotion until the noblest and commonest impulses in ourself are present at once. Even as Horus with His weak legs is a fool among

Gods, yet the feathers of His breast cover the sky, so I wept because I did not love my King well enough any longer to be loyal to this great gift He had given, and on the other hand, wept because I hated His heart for stirring my old love of Him. Now, I felt no desire to take the dreadful revenge of which Nefertiri had hinted to me. So I wept out of both eyes each time I thought of the wondrous title I now owned, and such it was: 'Master of the Secrets of the Things that Only One Man Knows.'"

"Yes, it is beautiful, and most suitable for you," said Hathfertiti, but her voice was not as warm as her words.

"That afternoon," said Menenhetet, "should have been the conclusion of the Coronation, and yet I cannot say that it was any end at all. In the Collation that night, Usermare was crowned again, and many ceremonies, as I say, were mixed with entertainments. It was certain that by evening, everyone was celebrating already, yet we did not know the full peace that comes only with a true Coronation."

"No, you did not," said Ptah-nem-hotep, "but that is because a Coronation is not a ceremony, nor a sacrifice, and cannot be achieved within one prayer, but, like the life of the Pharaoh Himself, needs all the shrines and more than a few of the contests. Even the lice, as you have suggested, partake of this exceptional turn of the fortunes in the Two-Lands, inasmuch as the Pharaoh, after thirty or more years, is now so powerful as to crown His own Double-Crown. Not only is He being fortified, therefore, at such a time, but the Gods as well. So all the Gods must be included. If not by Their own name, then by the body of another God who will share the name, yes, and the spirits must rise, not all at once, no more than the earth in all its valleys and terraces can be turned at once, but clod by clod. So is all of Egypt lifted here and replaced, ceremony by ceremony, so, at least, have I concluded from the depths of My studies. The hymn in the Court of the Great Ones on this last afternoon was only the largest event in a number of events as great as the number of the nomes, the people, the beasts, and all the Gods."

"Even as a High Priest," said Menenhetet, "I would not have been able to say it so well."

"I agree," said my mother to Ptah-nem-hotep, "*You* are the Master of the Secrets," but my Father for the first time since they had returned to the patio was annoyed by a remark of hers, and slapped her thigh for such giddiness of speech, pleasing Hathfertiti even more. "May I call myself the Unique Companion of Ptah-nem-hotep?" she asked with all the sauce in her voice of a favorite who would never be replaced, and I heard her next thought, I alone, for only I was nimble enough to know my mother's quickest moments. "I," she told herself, "am the true Master of the Secrets."

Thirteen

My mother was so pleased with this honor she had bestowed on herself that a sweetness rose from her tired arms and passed over my Father and me. The three of us sat on the couch, feeling the same balm, and I hovered once more near the pleasures of my sleep. The recollections of my great-grandfather were now less disturbing than before, and so I did not need to listen to his words, and allowed his thoughts to unfold as they would.

The Night of the Collation, he began, did not take place in the Festival Hall of King Unas but on a plaza in the Court of the Great Ones about which walls of reeds had been put up to enclose us. There was no roof. Still, it was called the Pavilion of King Unas, and we were sheltered overhead by trellises of vines and flowers supported only by narrow posts in order that all should have a fine view of the Pharaoh (which would not be true in the great Festival Hall with its heavy stone columns) no, the evening took place as if we were neither within a palace nor wholly open to the sky, but like the Gods, living between.

Much else was different on this night. The Pharaoh did not enter last, but first, took up His Seat on a raised wooden terrace with a heavy carpet upon which had been placed a gold throne with four painted wooden pillars for the canopy. Each of His guests bowed to Usermare as they entered, and to each woman He sent a necklace and a wreath of flowers, for each man, a gold goblet, and these were set on stands already full of fruit and flowers. Servants would pass the best wines from the finest vineyards of Khara, Dhakla, Fayum, from Tanis and Mareotis and Peluseum, and Hittite beer, darker than our Egyptian drink, was even served at Rama-Nefru's table, a strange beer with a smell of caves and roots, its malt molted more than ours, and made of the sprouts as well, a warlike beer, I think.

I can say that all the guests including the Princes and Princesses were in their seats when the three Queens appeared. Esonefret was first with Her seven sons and daughters, but, as usual, was so seldom considered or talked about in the daily life of the Court that She created no excitement once again, and indeed, Her children were as plain as Herself. Rama-Nefru was next and came forward into the Hall wearing two high feathers on Her crown, and in a robe of woven-air so transparent that the sight of Her superb little belly was less dazzling than the gleam of the small pale forest above Her thighs. Then came Nefertiri. She presented Herself in a splendor no other woman could equal. If much of Her body was not visible beneath Her heavy pale-gold raiment (the color to remind all of Rama-Nefru's lost hair) still Her gown ended not a hand's width above Her navel, and She wore no more than a collar to cover Her neck and a circlet of gold for Her hair. Thereby, one could not look at any sight but the Queen's breasts. They were equal to a young woman's. Their valley had the shadows of a temple, and the air in my nostrils quivered with desire. I had had Her last night but for the breasts. As if to prepare for this evening, She had refused to expose them. Still, their beauty lived in my palms from our first night when my fingers had leavened all of Her flesh. So I had to believe that the immanence of these breasts was in part from the fine work of my hands. This thought, however, had a short life, for Her entrance nearly produced a disturbance. Nefertiri smiled at all of us, the People of the Royal Circle seated near the Pharaoh, and the People of the Royal Court in the corners, then extended Her arm to the table where Her sons were seated, and Amen-khep-shu-ef stood up, came forward, and led Her to a place beside Him. At that, all who were in the Pavilion also stood up, and there were tumultuous cheers for the hero and His mother, indeed, such a demonstration with such lifting of goblets and such a casting of flowers before Her path, that a mighty desire spoke forth from this assemblage as if to say, "She is ours, not a Hittite." Even from where I sat beside Rama-Nefru, which was at a distance from Usermare (for He had put Her on His left and Nefertiri on His right, each on a dais equally apart from His own elevation—Esonefret was also on a dais but in the rear of the Hall!) I could discern that He had not been expecting this ovation. When it did not cease but continued so forcefully that lords and ladies renowned for their decorum were nonetheless clapping hands in the Royal Circle, and from the corners of the room came whistles, Usermare stood up with His Sceptre and His Crook raised high, thereby arousing greater applause, though not so much as I would have thought. Then all sat down. Beside me, I could feel Rama-Nefru, and when She took my fingers beneath the table, Her skin had the cold of Northern lands. "I told Him this would happen," She whispered. I, however, had had no warning myself other than the enthusiasm in Thebes for the return of Amen-khep-shu-ef all of this day, but after the nature of Nefertiri's entrance and Her son's greeting, and the number of nobles who were in no doubt about standing and cheering, I realized that Her appearance had been much planned. It was obvious that when Her son was by Her side, I was near neither to the Queen's thoughts nor to Her strength in our city. That left me overcome by how far I had drifted away from such concerns. I looked back upon the soldier I used to be and thought of his great skill in knowing the ambitions of all around him, indeed knowing them so well that he had become General-of-all-the-Armies. I was no longer that man. I might as well have died already. For what was I like now but some poor devotee of the perils and sweet meats of love, Master of the Secrets, indeed. I had been working so closely with women that I now knew too little about the strength of men. And I wondered at my own vanity to suppose that he who killed the

Pharaoh, meaning myself, could then be Pharaoh, I, who no longer had a soldier loyal to me, while out there were all the legions of Amen-khep-shu-ef.

At that moment, He looked in my direction across all the festivities of this room, and it was not the eyes of Amen-khep-shu-ef I stared into, but the door to the Land of the Dead. Those eyes were the gates through which I would pass. I thought, "Yes, this is the night on which I will die. It is at least a great and memorable night." I felt again those sentiments I had known in the beer-house, but now the tenderness of my fear came even closer, and every breath was fine with awe for me, for the air offered the simple happiness that no danger could approach until the party was done. I had these hours of celebration to enjoy.

Now, the Apis bull sacrificed this morning was served, the meats delectable, dripping with the juice of the Gods, and a rare fish, seldom taken from the Nile, was also served, and—being ready to count every taste of what might be the last of all the meals I would know this side of the Land of the Dead—I can tell You that there were nine different kinds of meat and six of poultry set before us, four kinds of bread and eight cakes, many sweets and more fruits than I could count. All the while, a countless group of musicians played reed pipes, a harp, drums, tambourines, cymbals, and at times, every last one would pick up a sistrum until it sounded like all the snakes of the Delta were among us, and you could feel how this party was taking place everywhere in Thebes, and, for all I knew, through all of the Two-Lands. So it felt to me, and I might as well have held the heartbeat of every married man and woman outside the Palace walls, since out of these five days just passed, as in no other time of their lives, what a number of faithful wives had been unfaithful! I could hear all that had been wild in the freedom of this Festival by the whirring of the sistrum and the hilarity of the voices, heard it everywhere but at our own table where Rama-Nefru sat in thoughtful gloom, barely able to give a passing smile to each passing noble eager for a sight of how She felt after the greeting Nefertiri received.

The entertainments began. We were offered a surprise. Pepti, honored this day by his release from the Gardens of the Secluded and promotion to the rank of Chief Scribe, was now given the additional honor of serving as the first diversion. So soon as he began, many were ready to laugh. For, as I explained to Rama-Nefru, he was reciting a story all had heard in their childhood, a sermon from a tutor whose pupil could not learn to write. I, who had never seen even one crude accounting on a shard of pottery until I was in the army, had to remain apart as I listened. I had other memories. When I was young, nobody I knew could write.

Pepti, in the best of moods for the best reasons, showed, however, much of his cleverness, and soon added new words to the story. He began, "My father, who was also a scribe, said to me, 'I shall make you love writing more than your own mother.' My father was wise, for I came to love it even more than my own wife." Here Pepti did not actually lift his kilt, but he did put his hands over all he no longer possessed, and the crowd—for there was no one in this audience who did not know of his daring surgery—roared with approval.

Having coaxed forth this happy if shameless beginning, Pepti now recited the sermon. His voice, which was as high in pitch as a child's, reedy as a pipe, and humorous in its quick and nasty shifts, entertained them greatly. Laughter roared up in everyone. He had the ability to suggest that he might mock himself, but laughed even more at others who thought they were laughing at him. Since his size was small and his plump and pompous manners most ridiculous, it was also comic. He was so arrogant. This, too, he knew, and besides, whenever they were ready to stop laughing at him, he began, in his easy fashion, to weep. Since the story he told was sad, his tears made it funny, and many nobles were slapping their thighs and pounding the tables, while a few of Amen-khep-shu-ef's officers, coarse as wild goats, fell to the ground and pounded the carpets. Just so funny to some did he seem. "Oh, what does it mean," Pepti cried out in scolding tones, "to say that an army man has a better life than a scribe? It is not so. Let me tell of one poor fellow whose life is full of trouble. As a child, his parents brought him to the barracks and he was shut up there."

"Shut up," yelled a few soldiers in delight at their humor and the wisdom of drink, but Pepti gave a smile to the Pharaoh with all his teeth—they were as white as the teeth of any eunuch!—and proceeded. "Poor boy," he said. "The army is so cruel to him. Each time he speaks, he receives a blow in the belly. When he is slow in responding to an order, they kick his feet. If he smiles, his mouth is split by a slap. Officers beat on him until he is too sore to sit. Anything he learns is taught by the art of flogging. If he is ugly, they ignore him. But if he is a pretty boy, they abuse him. 'I would die,' he cries out, 'but what help can the Seat-Maker be to me, if all are stealing my seat?'" There was wild laughter at this addition. "'Take heart,' said Pepti in a stern voice, imitating an officer, "'the way to become a man is by way of learning first how to be a woman.'" Truly, the Chief Scribe commanded the gates of laughter among these nobles. I felt my own annoyance that I would never know how to make others laugh so well.

"Hear further," said Pepti, "of these adventures. This boy, at last a grown man, and a good soldier, is obliged to travel to Syria over the mountains, but has to carry his food and water on his back. He is like a donkey. His bones are ready to break, and the water he drinks is filthy. When he faces the enemy and sees the anger in their eyes, he feels no better than a bird in a snare. Yet should he come back to Egypt alive, he will be treated like the wood that the worms eat. His clothes will be stolen and his servants will run away."

"Why do they roar at it so?" asked Rama-Nefru of me. "It is wearisome." She was watching Usermare bellow with enjoyment, while Nefertiri and Amen-khep-shu-ef laughed heartily. Many of the soldiers now began to show themselves in the fullness of their young muscles and smiled at the most beautiful women, daring already to flirt with them.

"I tell you, little scribe," said Pepti, "change your opinion that soldiers are happy and writers are miserable. It is not true. The scribe goes where he wishes in the Court and is fed and honored, while the soldier is so hungry he cannot sleep at night." Pepti bowed, and the guests roared at him, and gave their applause.

The musicians played again, and jugglers came out and acrobats and dancers, but I did not watch them. My eyes were on Nefertiri. Not once in this evening had She looked toward me. I could not come near Her thoughts and felt new animosity toward Amen-khep-shu-ef as I watched the adoration with which They fed each other and passed a goblet back and forth. If I was the Master of one Secret, it was the heat in the blood of Usermare: I felt His fear of Amen-khep-shu-ef, and the weight it put upon His pleasure that on this night He must control His wrath before wife and son.

Now a handsome young man came forward to be joined by a beautiful girl who wore no more than a small chain below her waist. Hand in hand, they approached the Pharaoh, knelt, and when his head touched the ground, the young man asked permission to offer a song.

"What is it about?" asked Usermare.

"O Beloved of Amon, in my song I will speak as a wild fig tree who begs a flower to enter the shade of his leaves so that he may talk to her."

"Well, tell her what you know, Wild Fig Tree," said Usermare to the happy uproar of the court.

The young man sang to the girl in a loud rich voice, full of great confidence in his ways with women:

> "Your leaves are drops of dew,
> "Your bower is green,
> "Greener than the papyrus
> "And more red than the ruby.
> "Your petals are honey
> "And your skin is opal,
> "Oh, come to me!"

He paused. The girl came forward until he could put his arm around her waist and he did this with skill, moving his wrist and elbow like the limb of a tree. Then he gave a wicked smile to the ladies, and sang the last two phrases:

"Oh, I do not tell what I see,
"No, I do not tell what I see!"

The Wild Fig Tree embraced the girl, lifted her up and carried her off, taking his way between the tables in the midst of great laughter while the Notables touched the girl's breasts and patted her buttocks.

The singer was followed by a group of dancers who, like the girl, wore nothing but a thin chain about their hips, and they danced not only before the Pharaoh but went their way between the guests, removing wreaths from the wine jars, filling the goblets, then setting back the wreaths. All the while, whenever they did not serve nor dance, they stood among us tapping their hands in concert with the music, their hips meandering through such undulations that I saw the serpentine of the white-walls at Memphi.

Pepti came forward again, but now he carried a palette as large as a shield, and a stick in the shape of a stylus that was longer than his arm. Holding these huge instruments, he pretended to write, while an immense charioteer, the largest I had ever seen, dressed like a twelve-year-old boy in a loincloth, sandals, and a pigtail thrown in front of one shoulder, stood in front of Pepti and rolled his head in shame.

"You have forsaken books," said Pepti. "You have given yourself up to pleasure. You wander through the streets. Every evening you smell of beer."

When I saw with what merriment Usermare was laughing, I knew much about Pepti's success in the Gardens. How he must have entertained the little queens and the Pharaoh! How much happier that abode must have been without my gloomy face. I felt the hot curse of envy and wondered how ready I could be to see my end, if my heart was still so jealous.

"The smell of your beer," said Pepti to the charioteer, "scares everyone away. You are a broken oar and cannot guide your boat to either side. You are a temple without its God, a house without bread." As he uttered these words in a voice which to everyone's amusement could not have been more pious, he made a great show of writing down all this wisdom he uttered. The stylus and palette were too un-gainly, however, and he was forever dropping one, or smearing the other, until he became so amusing that even Rama-Nefru began to laugh a little.

Soon enough, the giant charioteer put out his tongue at Pepti and walked away. Pretending to be very drunk, he blundered through the crowd and almost fell on various dignitaries, even, to the horror of many, had the high audacity, given the license of this entertainment, to weave and wander around the dais of the Pharaoh Himself. But then, before the charioteer went so far as to touch the posts of the canopy, he staggered over instead to a table of high Officials, and there came close to knocking them over. Then he rumbled up behind the Vizier and made the most convincing sounds of distress. So pow-erful were the groans of his insides that the Vizier could not keep himself from turning around with panic that he might be vomited upon, at which I began to laugh for the first time, and went on as if it were my last. Then the charioteer fell on his face in front of a Syrian waiter and began to kiss the servant's feet and caress his calves until he looked up, saw it was only a flunky, spat on the ground, leaped to his feet, started to run away, and fell again. Pepti kept following with the palette large as a shield and the pen longer than his arm, all the while trying to write, and not once did he cease scolding. "Here," said Pepti, "are your instructions. Do not forget them. Learn how to sing to the flute, recite to the sound of the pipe, intone your voice to the lyre, and give a good pluck to the harp," but the drunk fell instead among the naked dancing girls who embraced him, sat beside his prostrate body, played with his hair, and when he pretended not to revive, poured oil over him until he was sopping, then laid a wreath of dried leaves over his body. Nearly everyone was shrieking with greedy pleasure as if with each of their spasms of laughter, they could seat the Pharaoh more firmly in His Triumph and bring these days of uncertainty to an end, whereas I, deep in the gloom of Rama-Nefru, could not laugh anymore, and therefore brooded on the nature of merriment, and wondered if we did not laugh because we had seen the face of a God we never saw before, and so, we immediately looked away. One laughed in order to see no more. Thereby, the Gods were undisturbed. Of course, I could not laugh.

As I say, Rama-Nefru and I were the only ones. The charioteer, now patting himself with oil, tried to get up, slipped in his own pool, rose again, staggered, roused screams from the ladies at the thought of his wet body sliding over them, and landed at last on top of Pepti, crushing his palette and pen. All the while, reed pipes, drums, tambourines and sistrums played at a great rate as if the musicians were chasing demons. Then Pepti and the charioteer ran off to much applause while the floor was mopped of oil. A silence came. Usermare held up His Flail and flashed it through the air.

Now a sledge, making a great clatter, was pulled through the Pavilion by two oxen. On it was a mummy. Screams came forth.

"A real one?" asked Rama-Nefru of me.

"False," I said, and it was gone, and two sweepers came behind to clean up what the oxen had left. There was silence again. The entertainment was completed. The ceremonies would commence.

The Vizier came forward. A few nobles even groaned aloud. I do not remember the name of this Vizier, but then Usermare had had so many. Once I heard Him say, "A long-living Pharaoh is the strength of the Two-Lands, and a good Vizier is good for kissing His feet. There are many good Viziers."

This one, like most, was old, and he, too, was drunk tonight in happiness at being chosen one of the eight Masters. He gave a great many words where he could have offered a few, and spoke of Usermare as the rising sun who chased all that was dark out of Egypt. "When You rest in Your Palace," he said, "the words of all countries come to You, for Your ears are multitudinous and mighty. Your eye is clearer than the stars and You see farther than the sun." Here he paused, meditated on what he had said, and added, "To all who are assembled here, I say that the ear of the One is thus mighty that I need only utter a word in a far-off place but He hears it and summons me before Him. I cannot do a deed hidden from Him who sees with the eye of the Hidden One. I dare not even think of His virtues in the fear that I will not name them all, for He also knows my thoughts."

"I can't bear this," Rama-Nefru whispered. "I must leave."

"You cannot," I said.

"I am ill."

Heqat, seated nearby, was attempting to soothe Her. "You do not wish to leave," said Heqat. "In the end, He will choose You."

"My child needs Me," said Rama-Nefru.

I could feel Her fear. It came over me like the eight Gods of the slime, and all that She saw in Her mind was also in mine. I knew the Prince Peht-a-Ra was screaming. "I must go to Him," said Rama-Nefru. Yet Heqat's fear of the wrath of Usermare was greater than the terrors of Rama-Nefru, and Heqat calmed Her by saying, "I will bring His weeping to an end." Whereupon she looked across the Pavilion of King Unas all the way into a far corner where I could see Honey-Ball sitting with her family—Nefertiri had kept Her promise by half: Honey-Ball was here but most certainly not sitting with *Her*—and now I realized that Heqat stared with no small force into Honey-Ball's eyes. It was then I felt Rama-Nefru move more easily beside me, and She said, "He is crying no longer." I saw the face of Peht-a-Ra once more in Her thoughts, but did not wish to look further for fear His dark hair might turn to fire as I watched. The Vizier talked on and on. Honey-Ball now looked at me, and there was love in her eye like the love I had seen in the eyes of Usermare when He had given me the award, but her love I trusted more, and as if she asked a question, although I did not know what it might be, I nodded, and the tenderness I knew at the nearness of the pale presence of death itself came back.

The Vizier was reaching the summit of what he would say. "While we eat, and know the taste of the riches of our Two-Lands, while we drink, let us also tell each other that these ceremonies over the past five days have been the happy ties to draw the Entire Land, which is to say—the Two-Lands and the Pharaoh—together. Know then that in this hour, food is being passed forth from the breweries and bakeries of the Palace. Free bread and free beer go out to the people. May they have two new eyes for all the years to come. May Egypt be wealthy."

He sat down to a loud beating of applause from a few, and much polite tapping of hands, and then with a whoop, two wrestlers came forward. Behind each was a priest. One carried the standard of Horus, the other of Set, and these wrestlers—although their bodies were enormous—entered only into a mock contest, and that was just as well. For Set soon had his thumb on the eye of Horus, while Horus, in turn, had his hand on the testicles of Set. The two priests approached, however, each to pacify his wrestler, the priest for Horus not only lifting the hand of his man from the other's testicles, but wiping his own before leading him off. Then the priest returned at once with two sceptres to give to Usermare. Another priest, wearing the headdress of Thoth, came forward, knelt, and said aloud, "May You, the Bull of Heaven, hold these two sceptres. Thereby, may the testicles of Set be returned to the God, and the eyes of Horus be returned to the God, and may Your power, by this gift, increase in measure." I may say that despite my gloom, I could feel much power pass through all of us in the room, and I now knew twice the strength I could muster just before, even as Usermare now held two sceptres.

Our Pharaoh stood up. He said: "In My city, the people are eating. On the East Bank and West Bank of Thebes, they are eating loaves of bread and drinking beer. For on this, the last of the five days, they have been given two new eyes. From the grain of the sun and the spirits of the moon, they have been given two new eyes."

He put His two sceptres in a stand, and raised His arm to touch the Cobra on His Double-Crown. "Here is the eye of My Crown, which is the Eye of Horus."

At these words, many in the Court before Him murmured, "It is the Cobra. He embraces the Cobra." There were few who did not turn to stare at Nefertiri. Heqat, so soon as she sensed what Usermare would do next, whispered to Rama-Nefru, "Two years ago, at the last Godly Triumph, He saluted Her. Tonight, He will not." She was right. A murmur came out of the audience when He never looked at Nefertiri. This murmur increased as Amen-khep-shu-ef raised high His goblet and drank to Her, indeed, a few gasped.

The priest who stood before Usermare intoned most solemnly, "May Your eye never sadden," and took a censer of perfume from a golden case, and handed it to Him. Then the priest said, "Take into Yourself the fragrance of the Gods. All that cleanses us, comes from You. Your face is our fragrance."

Usermare waved the censer, and all tried to breathe the scent, for this was perfume that could be used only by the Pharaoh, and only on this night. A hush lay upon us. The perfume came from the herbs of the garden on whose door was painted the black pig of Set. We could smell it now—powerful was the scent—and the odor of Usermare was not like any that we had known before, but sublime and bestial at once, like the winding sheet of Osiris and the spoor of Hera-Ra.

The scent of the perfume had not dissipated, however, when twenty servants brought in a pillar twice the height of a man, and laid it carefully on the floor before the Throne. I had seen the backbone of Osiris raised in many a ceremony, but never one so high as this, and here made of marble, where before they were of papyrus stems. Moreover, the eyes and body of Osiris were carved into the middle of the pillar to speak of how the tree had grown around Him at Byblos.

Usermare stepped down from His Throne, removed His Double-Crown, set it within a golden shrine on a golden stand, and picked up a rope of papyrus attached to the head of the pillar. Amen-khep-shu-ef joined Him, and one by one, twenty of His sons came forward to stand at twenty ropes, while sixteen of His daughters also came forward from many a table, each to be handed a sistrum and necklace by the priests. When Rama-Nefru whispered to me, "Those necklaces are ugly," I made an unhappy face and told Her, "They are supposed to be an umbilical cord and placenta," which added to Her confusion (and mine) so soon as each of the Princesses, receiving the gift, was quick to say: "May Hathor give life to My nostrils." But then I understood the prayer, and it was simple. What else would an infant just parted from its navel cord wish to request, but air?

The Pharaoh and His sons began to pull on the ropes. As They did, the sons recited:

"O, Blood of Isis,
"O, Splendor of Isis,
"O, Magic Power of Isis,
"Protect our Great Pharaoh."

So soon as the pillar began to lift at one end, priests came forward
again and began to beat each other with sticks. "They are merciless to
each other," exclaimed Rama-Nefru with real interest, and before it
was over, half the combatants were on the ground. All the while, one
side kept crying out, "I fight for Horus," the other, "I will capture
Horus," but when the battle was done, the forces of Set fled from the
room, dragging their bruised and bleeding friends behind them, and
the pillar was quickly raised to the vertical. That drew another great
cheer.

The sixteen daughters of Usermare sang:

"Isis is faint on the water.
"Isis rises on the water.
"Her tears fall on the water.
"See, Horus enters His mother."

At that moment—was it that no one should fail to understand
what had just been sung?—Nefertiri took the hand of Amen-khep-
shu-ef and gave it a lingering kiss.

I do not know if She was certain that She would next be called, but
indeed Her share of the entertainment was upon us. Usermare rose,
and said in a voice to silence all things, "Let the Chief Concubines of
the God fill the Palace with love," and Nefertiri came forward and
was joined by six blind singers, and indeed they were called such
names as the Pleasure of the God, for their voices were beautiful beyond compare. If they were blind, then by the wisdom of Maat their
voices had become more beautiful. As they sang, Nefertiri kept time
with a sistrum, shaking it most lightly in the beginning when their
voices were more delicate than the zephyrs of this night, but soon
their song grew louder and caressed the breath of all of us.

Nefertiri stood with Her arm around one of the blind girls. I supposed it was the daughter of the servant that the guards of Usermare had beaten to death in the house of Nefertiri. For the Queen now looked with contempt at Her Pharaoh. This was Her hour in the Festival, and no one would usurp it. I saw Usermare grow pale, which I had never seen before, and all the nobles were weeping as they listened to these blind Concubines of the God. For nothing could be more moving to any of us than blindness, that scourge from the sands of Egypt itself. That is our affliction and the worst fate to fall on us, so we all wept for the beauty in the voices of these blind girls and, as they sang, I could feel Usermare's shame that the servant of Nefertiri had been killed.

> "O, yonder milk cows,
> "Weep for Him,
> "Do not fail to see Osiris
> "As He goes up,
> "For He ascends to heaven among the Gods."

I cannot say if Nefertiri was ever more beautiful. Her breasts were like the eyes of the sun and moon, and Her face was the noblest in the Two-Lands. It was then I saw that She was looking at me, and I felt a happiness like none I had known this night, and took a vow, "Oh, that She is looking at me in the hour I die."

> "Osiris is above Him,
> "His terror is in each limb,
> "Their arms give support to You,
> "And You will climb to heaven
> "By the way of His Ladder."

For so long as the Concubines continued to sing, Nefertiri would be mistress of the harem of Amon, of all the Secluded of the Hidden One. She would be equal to the Goddess Mut. Her power was great. Even Rama-Nefru was sobbing. So, desire passed through the Pavilion. Let Nefertiri return to the power She had lost! She was the Queen of all who were in this place, and I saw that Rama-Nefru's lips were bleeding where She had bitten them.

The singers were done. Of all the silences that had come on the Collation, none was so profound as the one in which we waited while the Throne of Amon that was kept in the Temple of Karnak, the ancient, holy throne in which the God used to sit when He was no more than the God of the nome of Thebes a thousand years ago, and not known yet as the Hidden One, was brought out with reverence by the priests and placed next to Usermare. The First Consort of the King would be invited to sit in the Throne of Amon. But Who would Usermare now consider to be the First Consort of the King?

Before such a choice could be made, the last Coronation had to be performed. Bak-ne-khon-su, having become the oldest High Priest in the Two-Lands, came forward, and accompanying him were two young priests carrying the golden shrine. Bak-ne-khon-su opened the doors and removed the White Crown and the Red Crown, but he was so old it took all his strength to hold them. Usermare bowed before the sight with such devotion that I knew His love of the Double-Crown was like the love of another man for his mate when the love is happy and never fades and so is always pleasing and strange.

Usermare said aloud:

> "Let there be terror of Me,
>   "like the terror of Thee,
> "Let there be fear of Me,
>   "like the fear of Thee,
> "Let there be awe of Me,
>   "like the awe of Thee,
> "Let there be love of Me,
>   "like the love of Thee."

Bak-ne-khon-su lifted the Red Crown of Lower Egypt and the White Crown of Upper Egypt and placed them on His head.

Usermare touched His Sceptre, His Flail, and His Double-Crown.

"You have come forth from Me," He said, "and I have come forth from Thee." Now He stood in silence, and looked about the room staring at many of us, one by one, until the silence was equal to a great commotion, and His heart was beating like a stallion. Then, I knew myself at last, and I was indeed "Master of the Secrets of the Things Only One Man Knows," for I knew His heart, and the terrible fear in it, and the great pride, and when He looked at me, I also knew for the first time that He loved me and valued me. For with His eyes, He asked, "What shall I do?" I felt His fear again. There is no magic whose terror is more powerful than the fear of a Pharaoh before the strength of His Son. To choose Nefertiri would calm every force that might rise against Him. With Rama-Nefru, He would only possess the radiance that is in the light of far-off lands. Yet His pride that He was the One was great, and He hated to bow before His fear of Amen-khep-shu-ef. In that uncertainty, as He stood there, Rama-Nefru was thinking of Her child. I saw the ringlets of Prince Peht-a-Ra, the black curly Hittite hair, and felt Her great fear. She whispered to me, "Tell Sesusi to take the other—I fear everything if He chooses Me." It was good that She spoke in Egyptian, for Her own head was a Hittite babble of sounds I did not know, and then I felt the heart of Nefertiri with its two hearts: one like a rose in the petals of its love, and the other a flame, and I did not know whether to send the thoughts of Rama-Nefru to Usermare, for if the Pharaoh were to choose Nefertiri, I would be like a finch, picking worms out of the crocodile's lazy jaws. No, I could not suffer that again.

In this moment I did not understand why He decided to do what He did, but I know now. In the embrace of Your mind, Great Ninth of the Ramses, I see Him, and understand that He could never make His choice from fear, or He would be no longer divine. The Gods could bless His power, or withdraw Their blessing, but no Pharaoh would ever decide a matter by the cheers or groans of His people—no, He must be true to the honor of Kadesh!—and so He looked away at last from Nefertiri, and extended His arm to Rama-Nefru. She stood up with a small sob and walked across the floor. Heqat was weeping openly, and I did not need to look in the direction of Amen-khep-shu-ef. Temple walls, I was certain, could crumble before His eyes.

The musicians played, and Rama-Nefru was seated in the Ancient Throne of Amon. Even as Her buttocks came to rest, much as if She had disturbed a small pool, so did the beer in my mug begin to froth. I do not know what songs were sung, nor how soon it was that the nobles began to leave, I do not even remember whether Honey-Ball passed before my table with her family, or did not, for I sat like stone, and was certain all the light in the room had altered. I could no longer see the golden illumination of each candle in the million and infinity of candles that decorated the Pavilion, but rather witnessed all before me through a red haze that was like the darker fires on a battlefield at night, and it was in this hour, although no one at the Collation would learn until later, that Peht-a-Ra, much disturbed by the unspoken excitements of the night, ran from His bed into the garden, there to step into the covered coals of a fire and screamed so piteously that Rama-Nefru writhed on the Throne of Amon. All who saw it said that the ancient gold of the God sent forth tortures to Her skin, but it was the flesh of Her child She felt, and I did not learn for many years, not until well into the middle of my next life, that these burns so crippled the legs of the child that the young Prince walked like Horus and had no strength in His feet, and died before He was three years old.

But I knew none of this. I sat in the light of the red haze that had come down upon me, and in my heart was the greatest panic, and the largest determination I had ever known. So I knew what Usermare felt. At last I took a breath and told myself again that I would guard against my death no longer, but like Nefesh-Besher would be ready to enter it, and would not turn back, no, I would not turn back. Yet my decision had no more conviction than the weight of a feather. But then I may have been close to my next life already, and, like a priest, was telling myself that the difference between a great truth and a dreadful lie might in the moment of greatest anguish weigh no more than a feather upon one's thoughts, and so I conceived of a feather and watched the flutter of its fall and knew a stirring of beauty in my heart. Was that the knowledge of truth?

I left the Pavilion of the Collation. Even as the Pharaoh had come in first, so would He be the last to leave, and I did not take farewell of Him nor of Rama-Nefru, but walked past the pool of the Eye of Maat whose surface now reflected the full moon tonight, and thought of the Hittite Sappattu. The white of my linen looked as brilliant to me as the pale wealth of the moon, and I could see the lands across the Very Green. For the first time in my life I thought of those lands much to the North where it must be as cold as the moon, and I do not know if it was the silence in which I traveled, or whether like a man already dead, I passed between Nefertiri's soldiers like a ghost, but I slipped into Her chambers, and the beer had not frothed in my mug for too little—She was waiting for me.

"Not here," She said. "I do not know how soon Amen-khep-shu-ef will be back from talking to His men," and before I could think of what this meant, She led me into Her gardens and we stopped in a bower by a small fountain with the leaves of a tree overhead. There was a marble bench cool to our skin in the moonlight, but Her body was warm and most passionate and tender, for She was also weeping. When I bent to kiss the first of Her magnificent breasts, She hugged my head with both hands, and whispered, "I will make love to you tonight by all three of My mouths," and began to laugh, the echoes of Her laughter sounding through the gardens, "Yes, I may as well," She said, "for you are the third of three men I love, and the only one on whom I may count, is that not so?"

I grasped Her with all my strength, with too much strength. The truth is that I was weakened by love for Usermare again. I could hate Him no longer, and if, last night, I had known the strength of a bull, now I had no more than the loins of a hare, but She was washed by pain on one hand, fury in the other, and never had I known Her more passionate. If She made love to me by all three mouths, She also called on many a God to wake my limbs, and my toes, my bowels and my lips, my belly and my heart, yes, even my mind and the long bow of my back, but the more passionate She became, the colder became my own heart, for in my fear I also had my pride, and would feel no fear, so I was very cold and much like a priest, indeed, I was a priest in the embrace of a lion, and as She spoke all those words so much alike upon which She loved to play, spoke of my lips and the banks of the river, of my heart and Her thirst, of the door of my mouth and the palanquin of my belly (for now She was above me), of the limbs of my legs and the little limbs of the mouth between Her legs, She also cried out as I entered, oh, so suddenly cried out, and with harsh words of fucking and theft and murder. *"Nek, nek, nek,"* She muttered, "fuck you, kill you, murder you, *nek, nek, nek,* you are My bowels and My grave, My eyes and My mind, My death, My tomb, oh, give Me your phallus, give Me your seed, come to Me for the slaughter. Die!" She said, "See, behold, oh, die," and we turned over, and She lay on Her back, the gates opening within Her. The Bull of Apis was in Her womb and the wings of the Divine Falcon, but in a quiet voice She asked, "Will you kill Him? Will you kill Him for Me?" and when I nodded, She began to come forth, and with such force that I, trapped like a climber in a fall of rocks, was swept along with Her, and in the fall, saw the islands of Her womb rising from the sea, and my seed rode forward in the channel between.

Yet in all the ways I could have met Her on all the great days of my life, I came forth instead in one small spurt, and my seed would never have reached Her home for I was not in it, no, it merely came out of me, and then I felt the hand of heaven on my back, a tongue of flame, a spear of anguish, seven times I felt such fire reach into each of my seven souls and spirits and the force of those blows drove me forward into my seed. Then I was beneath some water and swimming. I felt my heart divide. The Two-Lands sundered.

I rose up into the air and looked down on my body. It lay on Her body, and Amen-khep-shu-ef was above us both, wiping His dagger on my back, and there were seven founts of blood spurting forth from me. She was screaming, I think it was so, although in all my four lives I cannot swear to that, but I believe She said, "You fool, he would have done it for us," but then the part of me that had floated upward now sank back again into my seed, and I have some memory, dim at best, of many travels taken. Sometimes I seemed to dwell in a tent with many soft winds without, and sometimes lived by the banks of a shore and crocodiles went by. But as I died, I believe I entered the life of my own seed, and was reborn again in the proper season from the belly of Nefertiri, and as a cause of all the fears with which I made love the last time, yet by virtue of the audacity of the venture, my second life became the highest compromise of my ambitions, and I ended as a High Priest. But that is another story, and has nothing to do with Kadesh.

Fourteen

ꓔ꒰ "What happened to Amen-khep-shu-ef?" asked my mother. I knew then, if I did not know before, that by her refusal to honor the end of Menenhetet's story with a proper silence, her feelings toward him were now void of mercy.

This rudeness inflicted upon the pain of his recollections, he only sighed, and said, "For the act of killing me, no punishment would have come. But Amen-khep-shu-ef was in a rage at His mother, and, so, with two slices of His knife, He cut away Her navel, thereby severing Her connection to Her royal ancestors. At once, in remorse for this act, He cut off His own navel. Since He was even more savage with Himself than with His mother, He collapsed in Her gardens from loss of blood.

"Now, Usermare was still in the Pavilion, yet His vision saw what had happened, and having no one at His side whom He could better trust, He sent Pepti to dispatch His Son. The Chief Scribe, finding Amen-khep-shu-ef prone from loss of blood, lost not a moment severing the spinal cord at the back of His neck. For this unhesitating deed, Pepti was made Vizier, and served Usermare well. I never estimated the man nor his abilities with proper measure."

"And Nefertiri?"

My great-grandfather was silent. "Since She was my mother, I cannot speak of Her in this fashion. You would do better to respect my silence, for you are still no more than my granddaughter."

VII

The Book of Secrets

One

My mother, however, showed no sign of fear. Indeed, her manner was near to frivolous, and this displeased my Father. The end of Menenhetet's recital lay heavily upon Him. He sighed with no small sound, the sorrows of these events passing through His lips, and even looked upon His fingers in curious contemplation, as though to measure how much His hand could hold.

Then, He and my great-grandfather began to gaze at one another with something shamefaced in their expressions. Neither man seemed pleased in this hour, nor yet ready to confess it. My great-grandfather certainly looked twice weary, once from the exhaustion of his story, and again from the doubt that the sum of all he had had to say on this long night would achieve his ends.

Nor was my Father satisfied. The last taste had failed to bring contentment. On the contrary, He was wishing for more. "I asked," He said, "to be told of the Battle of Kadesh, and when that was done, I requested you to go on. You have been gracious, and have done so, and I believe you held nothing from Me."

"It may be," said Menenhetet, "that I told too much."

"Only when you spoke," remarked my mother with a mean and lively spite, "of your largest intentions."

"No, you gave us all that must be told," said Ptah-nem-hotep, "and I respect you for it."

Menenhetet bowed his head gently.

"I would even meet your honesty. Your thoughts, revealed in their true shape, have taught Me much about My Kingdom. Yet now I long for you to make Me a little more familiar with your other lives."

My great-grandfather looked most uneasy. "It would not be worth Your patience," he said. "By the measure of my first life, they do not offer as much knowledge."

"Oh, I will have none of this," said my Father. "My ancestor, Usermare, left you Master of the Secrets of the Things that Only One Man Sees. That is a fine enough title for Me. I speak to you without concealment: In times of weakness, a Pharaoh must search for understanding that no one else can have. Otherwise how would His Reign survive?"

"I did not deserve the title. Others knew more."

"You are tiresome," said Hathfertiti. "Why do you not please the Pharaoh?"

"I would," said Menenhetet, "if I knew how. I do not comprehend my second life, however, with the clarity of the first. My first mother saw Amon as I was conceived. But what was in the heart of Nefertiri? Sometimes I think the most powerful passion that a beautiful woman can feel, when she is proud and very spoiled, is to watch her lover die."

His words were sent as directly to my mother as an arrow, and would, at another time, have agitated her, but she was keen in this hour. The evening had served her well. "What a cruel remark," she said. "I think Nefertiri felt more love for you than was proper. And the consequences were dear for Her. To lose one's navel and one's oldest son . . ." She shuddered with no small effect.

"Yes," said Menenhetet, and gave his own sigh. Again, I felt his fatigue. "I have spent many years," he said, "pondering a matter I cannot comprehend. Who can say whether Nefertiri saw me on that last night with love, or merely paid too great a price for some curse from Honey-Ball, who, I promise you, had to feel most murderously betrayed by her poor seats on the Night of the Collation. I think such thoughts when there is little to cheer me. Yet I also know hours when I tell myself that the Gods thought well enough of Menenhetet to let him be carried in the womb of a Queen."

"Oh, yes," said Hathfertiti. "Your true wish is still to become a Pharaoh, even if you have always failed."

My great-grandfather looked back at her carefully and shook his head. "You make too much of an hour when I saw that as my hope."

"Why, you delight in such a thought," said Ptah-nem-hotep. "Dear Menenhetet, do not deny your desire. Even now, I saw the light leap into your eye when Hathfertiti spoke of such a wish."

"It would be sacrilegious," replied my great-grandfather, but I do not know if he had the strength to dispute his granddaughter and the Pharaoh at once.

In any case, Hathfertiti mocked him. "Sacrilegious?" she said. "How can you be this pious? Has the taste of bat shit left your mouth altogether?"

"At every moment," replied Menenhetet, "you act more like a Queen."

Yet when Ptah-nem-hotep only laughed with pleasure at this remark, as though to suggest it was not impossible, Menenhetet must have decided to retreat. "I would," he said, "attempt to tell You of these other lives, for it is my pride to remain tireless in Your service, but the effort to bring back such memories has already proved exhausting. As soon shift the stones of one's tomb! Indeed, I aspire to less than You think. To look backward is to weary oneself, and the task of remembering my former lives has become my true craft. I would even say that much of my fourth existence has been spent in debilitating trances."

Here, my mother gave a passionate and furious laugh. "Not all of it was learned in misery," she cried out.

"There were," Menenhetet admitted, "other routes to my recollections. But they do not exist any longer."

"No," she said, "they do not."

My Father's annoyance was increasing. "It is near to dawn," He said, "and we have stayed up for so long that we may as well wait for morning. I do not have an Eye of Maat in which to bathe and greet the appearance of Ra, nor is the Palace, I fear, nearly so grand as it must have been in Thebes before Usermare moved His Court here, but nonetheless, we have our baths. There we can relax from the agreeable labors of this night. Shall we move now, or wait a little longer?"

"I would prefer to stay," said my mother, "on this patio. I love sitting with our son between us."

"Well, then," said Ptah-nem-hotep to Menenhetet, "I will say again that I appreciate the prodigious effort of your honesty, and can promise that it counts for much."

"Indeed," said Menenhetet, "for how much?"

"Oh, shame!" said my mother, except that she did not speak aloud. I only heard her thought.

"It would count for all," said Ptah-nem-hotep, "if one question did not remain. When a man as capable as yourself becomes a Vizier, he also comes so near to the Double-Crown that he can capture it. Especially in times like these. How can I trust that is not your desire? I tell you I would be happier if I knew more of your second life, and your third. You are still a stranger, you see?"

"The echo of what I say," said Menenhetet, "begins to weigh more than all I can say."

"You are an old and stubborn man," said Hathfertiti.

"Moreover," said Ptah-nem-hotep, "you have no choice."

"I have, as You say, no choice. So I must do my best," said my great-grandfather, but his shame was not absent at how his pride had been snatched piece by piece, and his lips were thin with anger when he began to speak.

Two

Yet, if they would steal his pride so would he play with their patience. While he related matters of interest and gave some observations on what he had learned, all the same, he managed to speak of his second existence, and of his third, in hardly more time than it took to tell of Tyre and New Tyre, and, in every bend of his manner, was ready to suggest that he would seek to finish before the rise of the sun.

I cannot say why, but there was much in my great-grandfather's reluctance that brought back my uneasy thoughts of Nef-khep-aukhem, and although I had never spent a night in the desert, now I felt as if we were gathered about the embers of a fire, while outside the circle of our light, beasts were gathering.

"In my second life," said Menenhetet, "I grew up in the Gardens of the Secluded as the son of Honey-Ball, and slept in her bed every night. Yet I also had dreams of my true mother and saw Her poor face in many of these dreams and would wake up in terror for She had no nose. The revenge of Usermare was terrible. Before He banished Nefertiri, He cut off Her nostrils, and She lived the rest of Her life behind a veil and never came back to Thebes."

"Aiiigh," said Hathfertiti.

"Aiiigh," said my great-grandfather, and observed a silence. "Since my dreams were not only frightful but true, Honey-Ball decided to tell the story of how I came to her, and I learned of these matters when I was six and much like our own Menenhetet the Second, a beautiful little boy, and wiser in my ways than most young men, for wisdom like perfume rises out of its own essence. So I understood, even before she told me, that Honey-Ball was not my mother, not at least by the cord that leads from one life to the next, although I always felt she was of the nearest flesh to myself. Indeed, after I was told the name of my true mother, I came to think that in the eyes of the Gods, Honey-Ball and Nefertiri must be like Great Sisters, even as Isis and Nephthys, and each with her own fearful scar."

"Can you tell us," asked Ptah-nem-hotep, "how you were sent from one to the other?"

"I was told that Nefertiri stayed in seclusion all the while She was pregnant, and so no one knew of this state but Her nearest servant. I would wish to think that She honored our hour or two of love sufficiently to take these many precautions and thereby keep me in Her belly. Afterward, but a few days old, I was sent to Honey-Ball by way of a eunuch and a wet-nurse. Stupefied by three drops of kolobi so that I would neither fret nor bawl, I was delivered by Pepti in a hamper of fruit through the Gates of the Secluded and passed under the eyes of Senedj. Pepti, after taking a prodigious bribe twice, once from Nefertiri, and again from Honey-Ball, stayed in the Gardens long enough on that day to make an addition to the records. So in the Ledger of the Coming-Forth of Usermare there was now an entry that He had known Honey-Ball on a day to confirm that it was His infant she now held in her arms. She was, of course, so heavy that no one could claim she was or was not pregnant in the time between."

"I am amazed," said Ptah-nem-hotep, "that Pepti would take such a chance for any amount of gold. He was the Vizier, after all."

"He was nothing if not audacious," said Menenhetet. "But then, to make up for his own loss by surgery, he ate the testicles of bulls every day to gain valor. Besides, he had an advantage he could count upon with the two women. If they wished to destroy him, they must destroy themselves as well. Given their concern for me, he could keep a grip on them. In truth, I think he saw them as most useful instruments for his future purposes. But he never had the opportunity. Given the excitements of his high office, he gorged too much on rich meat and drank volumes of spiced wine until he grew an ulcer. Long before I was old enough to hear the story, he was already gone, bled to death inside, and died in large fear of Khert-Neter despite the knowledge that Usermare was bound to give him a great funeral. It is my observation that none fear death more than the most clever of the scribes."

He sighed. "Having been told this much about my true mother, I can say that I thought of Her often. There was a statue of Nefertiri in the Gardens of the Secluded. There She stood, naked, and without a navel. It was only when I was old enough to leave the Gardens that I came to understand how fine, in this situation, was the humor of Usermare. For now, I saw many statues of Her, all with the same blank belly, and all with Her name in a cartouche on the back to inform you that She was the Great Consort of the King, yes, He had statues made of Her after She was, for all purposes, His Consort no more, and lived alone in solitude in a small place in a foreign land, some said as far away as Byblos. That was the mother of whom I dreamed and I always saw Her face behind a veil. But that was all I saw of Her. I grew up in the Gardens as a Rameside, as the son of Usermare by a little queen who was neither a favorite, nor young."

"Did she teach her magic again?" asked my Father.

"Honey-Ball now practiced it less. The Invocation to Isis may have swallowed some of her gifts, and her exchange of curses with Heqat, Usermare, and Nefertiri must have consumed more. Besides, who can say what Rama-Nefru took from her? I still hear the body of Mermer crash into the wall. Say it was kindness enough for Honey-Ball to tell me about the Master of the Secrets who had been my father. Yet with all she knew, many recollections came to me more clearly than to her. I did not know why, not then, but when I was still very young, I was able to correct her about the color of the gown Nefertiri wore to the Collation, and when Honey-Ball recollected that she was wrong, and the linen had indeed been pale-gold, she did not say a word for three days but conducted many rites of purification.

"That, however, was a rare occasion, and she performed her ceremonies less, and began to enjoy gossip more. Since I was not only her child but her confidant, I heard a great deal about Usermare and Rama-Nefru. Be certain, I listened to all I could hear. After all, He had preferred Rama-Nefru over my mother. Honey-Ball, like a true gossip, was wicked in what she told, yet curiously impartial, as if the story was worth more than any affection or animus for the person. So I learned that Rama-Nefru, after grieving for the death of Peht-a-Ra, had other children and put on a great deal of weight, and Her hair returned, although now it was darker.

"Listening to Honey-Ball and, indeed, to the stories of other little queens when they stopped by, I learned of the visits Usermare and Rama-Nefru began to make to the harem at Miwer in the Fayum, which was where She had been sent when first She came to Egypt. It was much remarked among our little queens in Thebes that Rama-Nefru had finally learned to enjoy a good deal more of Usermare than His five fingertips and began to participate with Him in parties for the little queens of Miwer until it was said that Rama-Nefru not only loved women more than She loved Him, but became the only woman who could chastise Usermare. They said He loved to bellow like a bull on those occasions when She used a flail. How can I know if this is so?

"Then a change came into the lives of all of us in Thebes. I do not understand why it was done, unless the presence of Nefertiri and Amen-khep-shu-ef would not leave His thoughts, but there came a year when Usermare decided to move His Palace, His Vizier, His Governor, His Superintendents and Officers from Thebes to Memphi. Of course, most of His new temples and nearly all of His wars and trading were to the North. Besides, Rama-Nefru desired the change. As He did all things, so did He move entirely, and Memphi became His new capital.

"That was a great loss to the Gardens of the Secluded. They would never be the same, not under any Pharaoh. Usermare brought a few of the youngest little queens to Miwer, which is, after all, close to Memphi, and took care of those who remained behind. But He never visited the Secluded any longer, not even when in Thebes. Since I, at the age of ten, gave every proof of being a sickly boy who would never make a warrior, I had already been sent to the School of the Temple of Amon at Karnak to be instructed in the disciplines of priests, and a year later, Honey-Ball was given permission to leave the Gardens, as many an older little queen was now doing. Immediately, she took a house near my school in order to visit me often.

"That, however, was only one of many changes. While the wealth and the power of Amon still belonged to Thebes, most of the Notables soon deserted their mansions to move to the Court at Memphi. Thebes continued to live as a great city, but only by way of its priests who began to carry themselves like men of great wealth so soon as they came to occupy the empty villas. There came a day when you could not know where the Temple ended and the town began.

"Yet, as the years went by, Usermare also tired of Rama-Nefru, and finally married one of His own daughters by the third Queen, Esonefret, the plain and ugly woman who had never been given His fair attention. Her daughter, Bint-Anath, also plain as a young girl, grew more agreeable later, and was always with Usermare in the last years of His Reign. He even gave Her the title of King's Great Wife which made Bint-Anath equal to Her mother, to Rama-Nefru, and to Nefertiri. Usermare lived closely with this daughter in His old age, and also gave many favors to the only one of His sons by Nefertiri who was not dead, the same fourth son, Kham-Uese, who used to carry the Golden Bowl. Yes, Kham-Uese became renowned not only as a High Priest of Ptah in Memphi, but as a great magician, and later was sent to foreign lands to show his skills."

"I have heard of him," said Ptah-nem-hotep. "He is the ancestor of our Khem-Usha. I also share that name, Kham-Uese. It is one of My favorite names. I am curious. Can you tell Me? Is it true that this son of Ramses the Second, Kham-Uese, was truly the last of our great magicians who could chop off the neck of a goose, lay the head on one side of a temple, the body on the other, then coax the two halves to come together, whereupon the goose would cackle?"

"It is all but true. I saw him do it once, and both parts of the goose did not move, only the body. Moreover, it was not half around the temple, but for the distance of the long side, sixty paces I would say, and then the body did turn the corner to meet the head. While the goose never cackled, still its wings flapped once. It is not a true magic, however. By great effort, I used to be able, when I was a young priest, to direct my thoughts into the body of a just-beheaded goose in such a manner that instead of flopping all about, I could send it forward in a straight line for as much as twenty paces. This, however, was my best effort, and while I was considered good at the practice in my time, I never became so skilled as to take the bird around the corner, nor could I prevail upon it to flap its wings when it met the head. Back in the time of Khufu, more magicians, doubtless, were adept at such matters. I am sure the four sides of the temple were traversed then, and the goose would cackle. But I would say the skills of Kham-Uese were only impressive to me before I learned a few of them myself. Still, I can tell You that if Usermare kept any noble sentiments for Nefertiri, it could be seen in His devotion to this son who certainly turned out well after a most unpromising youth. Even so, He died many years before His Father. Of course, that was not unusual for the sons of Ramses the Second. Usermare became very old, and most of His sons were gone before Him, indeed, He lived for so long that I, in my second life, even became High Priest of Amon in Thebes before He was gone. Toward the end, after Kham-Uese died, He drew close to me, and although the trip up the river grew difficult for Him, the old Pharaoh would visit Thebes, or summon me to Memphi. Having no idea that He might have known me before, He treated me, nonetheless, like the son of a true Queen, not a little queen. I remember Him saying in His old man's voice, 'I want you to do your best to speak to the Lord Osiris for Me.'

" 'It will be done,' I would say.

" 'Tell Him to pay attention to the temples I have built. There, He will see how I wish all matters to continue. The inscriptions on the stones will tell Him what He needs to know.'

" 'It will be done.'

" 'The Lord Osiris is a very intelligent and noble God,' Usermare would say in the last of His voice, and He sounded like two shards of pottery being rubbed together. He had added chambers, pylons, obelisks, colonnades and halls to many a great temple in Egypt, and a myriad of statues had His name, but by His last year, He was void, I can tell You, of the sense of smell, the clear sight of His eyes, the hearing of His ear and the pitch of His voice—I was one of the few who could distinguish any of His words—and He had very little memory. All the same, it took Him one full season of flood, and one of sowing, to die. For the last month, He hardly breathed. So faint was the wind from His heart that over the final three days many of us disputed whether or not He was still alive since no hair in His nose would stir and His skin was almost as cold as the stone that would receive Him. Yet His eyes, after many an interval, would blink.

"Near His mortuary temple in Western Thebes, one pillar of rose granite is carved: 'I am Usermare, King of Kings. He who would know who I am, and where I rest, must first surpass one of My deeds.'

"Who could replace Him? It was Merenptah, His thirteenth son, the brother of Bint-Anath. What a pity I never knew Esonefret. That plain and stupid Queen may have had virtues no one saw if Her children did so well. Yes, Merenptah was the thirteenth of Ramses' sons by all His Queens, and the twelve before were dead. So He was old when He became Pharaoh, bald and fat, and He had waited long. The enemies of Egypt took new courage when Sesusi was no more. If His reputation had lived among them like a lion, so for forty years there had been no true struggle. Now, all were ready to march against Merenptah. Yet, He treated the Libyans and Syrians as if He were a Hittite. Woe to those tribes He conquered! He did not make trophies of hands, but had His soldiers cast the genitals of the dead into a pile. He would attempt more than His Father! Of course, it was long since we had known a war or a victory.

"Of little use was it to Him. Merenptah died five years later in the Tenth Year of His Reign and His tomb was built in a great hurry. Stones were taken from the sanctuary of Amenhotep the Third, and Merenptah even dared to cut His name on some of the monuments of His Father. Of course, I knew little of this Pharaoh, for my second life came to an end only a few years after Usermare's death, and my third life was spent under many a reign. There was one who was Seti the Second, and then a Siptah, and a woman named Tiwoseret, while in between was even a Merenptah-Siptah. For a time, there were no Kings at all. Just so confused were the Two-Lands by the loss of Usermare, and for many years the river was low."

"You tell us nothing of yourself," my Father complained at last.

"He will not," said Hathfertiti.

It was then I felt anger. My great-grandfather had been like a Pharaoh to me and I trembled constantly in his presence, yet now, I felt pity for his exhaustion. "Can't you see," I cried out, "that he is tired! Even as I am weary." My voice must have carried the echo of a grown man, for Ptah-nem-hotep began to laugh, and then my mother, and Menenhetet last of all.

Now, Ptah-nem-hotep said more gently, "I will not insist. It is just that I am familiar with much of what you tell Me, and so would be more interested to hear of your life as a High Priest."

My great-grandfather nodded. I do not know if it was my defense of him, but he looked revived. Or, was it, sly? "There is justice," he said, "in rebuking me for what I have not done. Let me attempt to be a stranger to You no more."

Three

"Great authority belongs to the High Priest," said Menenhe-tet, "and yet, by the balance of Maat, such authority becomes savorless over the years. Only as a young man was I content to be a priest, but, by then, it was evident that I would rise in the Temple. No one in school could read or write so well as me, and—due, perhaps, to my physical delicacy—I showed great respect for the order and grace of each ceremony. Since nothing was prized so much as the power of memory, I did not chafe like other students at the onerous requirements of our exercises, but would repeat one prayer for the four or forty-two times entailed, or paint the same sacred words through all of a day. I was at peace as a student, and when still a young priest had the manner of an old one, and knew our devotions well. In a temple, the Gods do not act out of whim, but by law. That is why the Temple is there. We must never forget that one of our names for a priest is 'slave-of-the-God.' The law is so detailed that only the drudgery of a priest could comprehend it, and then only by his cere-mony. That was how I desired to be. I was happy such laws could not easily be told to others, but depended on the movements of one's hands, the posture of one's prayer, and the authority of one's voice within each word. Only in that way could one feel the presence of the Gods and Their true force. No surprise then, if I rose in the offices from Reader to Third Priest to Second Priest, but it was not often that one became High Priest in the Temple of Amon at Karnak much before forty. When you consider that only the son of a High Priest was expected to become a High Priest, and this was even true for the smallest temple and the least-respected God, to rise so high when you did not belong to a family of such men was rare. But then, while no longer a warrior in body, I still had the spirit of such a man in my heart.

"I also had Honey-Ball. She was no mean advantage. She knew how to use the resources of her family! Whatever influence could pass from the Temple of Amon at Sais to ours in Thebes was invoked for me as well as the most useful precepts for advancement, all inspired by Honey-Ball. If I wished to become High Priest at Karnak, she reasoned, I must bring new splendor to the Temple. I, sharing her thought, exclaimed that Usermare must give His promise to be buried in Thebes. That would do much for us. With His withdrawal to Memphi, so, too, had passed our belief that He would ever rest in His tomb here.

" 'You can succeed in making Him think,' she said, 'that Amon will never forgive Him unless He comes back.'

"I was His son—at least so far as He knew—but I had a hundred half brothers like myself. In those days, He did not yet know me. Honey-Ball's family could do much for me in the Temple, but could hardly assist my pale claims as a little Prince. So an interview with Usermare would not be easy. Yet, Honey-Ball arranged it. Not only, I am certain, did she conduct a ceremony (she was careful to conceal that from me!—I was most censorious as a young priest) but she also wrote to Him and spoke of how she felt Him walk within her heart each time she beheld me.

"On His next visit to Thebes, Honey-Ball and I were invited, therefore, to His Court, and He took a liking to me and loved the cleverness of my answers—even as You, Great Ninth of the Ramses, were delighted with the replies of this boy, my great-grandson. Thereby, I became one of the few of His many sons who might feel able to visit with his Father when He came to Thebes. It took five years, however, before I could feel so close to Him as to speak of His burial but, there, Honey-Ball was not wrong. His fear of Amon had hardly been lost. To my surprise, He welcomed my suggestion. I think no one else had dared to propose that a Pharaoh great as Usermare rest near other Pharaohs.

"Next I had the foresight to see that once our great Pharaoh was buried among us, a rich source of revenue would be ready for the Temple. We could emulate the City of the Dead in Abydos. I was even the priest who drew up the plans for the funerary plots of our own Necropolis. I can hardly tell You how successful they were. No wealthy man, no matter how remote his nome, could fail to understand that the eminence of his Ka in the Land of the Dead would be judged by the placement of his tomb in Thebes. I soon learned that any site so fortunate as to look out upon the mortuary temple of Ramses the Second was worth many times the price of a fine plot without such a view.

"By such enterprise, I was most successful in multiplying our revenues, and had the satisfaction of becoming High Priest at Karnak before the death of Honey-Ball. Be certain I had reserved for her the most splendid plot in the Necropolis at Thebes, but she made me promise that so soon as she was embalmed, I would take her down the river to her family tomb at Sais. It was then I understood how much she longed to go back to her swamps during all those years she remained in Thebes in order to be of aid to me. The nicest aspect of her death was the gentleness of it. She passed away in all her massive majesty like a ship drifting out cleanly on the rise of the tide.

"Without her, I was for the first time lost in the solitude that gives such fear of our tomb. The Temple was never wealthier, and my renown as a High Priest was not small, yet I knew terrible boredom. There was so much power, yet only small satisfaction in the exercise of it. The restlessness of the high Temple official came to me, and little matters became more important than large ones. I scolded the

cooks for spoiling a meal as fiercely as I upbraided the priests for an
error in prayer. To serve as the instrument of the Gods is a powerful
vocation for a timid youth with a weak body and a fine mind, but it is
not intoxicating for a grown man.

"Echoes of my past life, moreover, were returning. Now that
Usermare and Honey-Ball were gone, those walls of the mind that
kept me enclosed in the duties of my second life gave way. I had
known from the time I was six how I had been conceived, yet for so
long as Honey-Ball and Sesusi were alive, I did not seek to know any
more of my first life—it was enough that I was different from others.

"Now, to alleviate my boredom, came intimations of the other
man I had been. In the midst of conducting a high ceremony, I would
see Honey-Ball before me, and she was young and her skin was red
from the fires of her altar, and the excitement of her magic. Those
great breasts swung before me.

"It was known among us that Set could disturb a prayer by sending
lewd images, but these pictures came, I knew, from my memory, not
my dreams. For they seemed natural to me, and that could not have
been true if an unhappy God were attacking my ritual. Then I remembered how I used to feel in my young days when learning to
write. At such times, a strong man seemed to stir within me and stare
with yearning at symbols he could hardly decipher. Yet I could read
them with ease. One day, fully awake, I felt as if I were in a dream for
I found myself fighting at Kadesh, and knew the arms of Nefertiri.
While I cannot say that my first life returned with clarity, still enough
came to mind to leave me most unsatisfied. I felt superior to others.
Now a High Priest, and in command of more wealth than any man
could amass, I still did not have a gold cup I could call my own.
Wealthy men became interesting to me, therefore. To have our Pharaoh reigning in one city but our great temples in another, was to
open the gates to great wealth. Why, I cannot say, unless it is that
rich men do not dare to show their gains so openly when they must
remain in awe of the nearness of the Pharaoh. Now, however, in
Thebes it was easier for the wealthy to purchase indulgences. It can be
said that a thousand rich men near the Temple, while not equal to the

Pharaoh, are a substitute. I became absorbed in their pleasures, and was a most improper High Priest, indeed, I could not sleep at night for thought of the wealth being buried every day in the Necropolis of Western Thebes. I not only knew of the protections taken for these tombs of the wealthiest men, but had a list in the most beautiful hand—the writing of our best Temple scribes was elegant!—of just which jewels and pieces of gilded furniture had been sealed in their crypts.

"I also knew some of the chief brigands of these parts. I had not forgotten the description of the thieves of Kurna that Usermare gave me and, when one of those fellows would be captured from time to time, I would send messages to his family before he was punished. There came a night when I rose from my sleepless bed and crossed the river on our Temple ferry, much to the amazement of our ferryman. That night, I walked all the way to Kurna by myself to make arrangements. Before these thieves would trust me, I had to arrange for one of their brothers, just captured, to be released from his shackles and made my servant. More than a few tombs were broken into, and some fine objects were brought forth. The courage of these thieves was increased by the exorcisms I could offer against the curses of each vault. What a scandal it would have been if I were discovered!

"Still, the hand of Pepti had not been on me for too little when I was an infant, and I grew more audacious. I remember one splendid gold chair plucked from the tomb of an old merchant that I sold through agents to a Nomarch from Abydos. When this fellow died, his mummy was sent to Thebes—from Abydos!—and he was entombed with his wealth, and soon robbed. Lo, I sold the same chair again!

"I can tell You that by the end of my second life, I had become an immensely wealthy man, and took care to conceal these treasures in the cliffs of the Eastern Desert. Since trips to my cave would often take me away from the Temple for all of a day, there was grumbling at my laziness in high office. Be assured I never worked so hard."

"But what," asked Ptah-nem-hotep, "was the reason for burying such wealth?"

"I had every intention," said Menenhetet, "of enjoying this treasure in my third life."

"You were thinking in such a manner? You have not told us."

"There is more to tell, after all. You see, I had fallen in love—as
only a priest can—with one of the leading whores of Thebes, a
woman whose beauty was considerably greater than her charm, but
then I hardly knew how to look for a woman. On the other hand,
much had come back to me of my last hour with Nefertiri. The more
I pondered this event, the more I became convinced (from what I
could remember of the carnal knowledge of my first life) that my first
rebirth should not have taken place. I began to think I had been most
fortunate. If I had not been stabbed in that fear-filled instant when I
came weakly forth, nothing would have happened. Without such a
shock, I could never have conceived myself, not in such lustless fashion! So if I was going to live again, and enjoy my third life—which
was now my aim—then I must not only learn the arts of making love,
but penetrate these rigors of the coming-forth. Until now, as a priest,
I knew them in no better way than by my hand, or in the confusion
of priestly frolics. So I went to this most beautiful and expensive
whore for my study. Nub-Utchat was how she was called, and if, by
one meaning of her name, she was the golden eye of the Gods, she
was the golden outcast by the other, and both names belonged to her
just as much as the Two-Lands belong to Egypt, for she soon found
out where I kept my wealth even if I never told her. Perhaps I gave the
place away while talking in my sleep, or she may have known enough
to spy upon my trips to the desert, but, by whichever route, my wager
that I, in my third life, would remember where my treasures had been
buried came to nothing, for so soon as I was dead she found the cave.
By the time I was old enough to look about in my third life, be certain
Nub-Utchat had spent it all."

"One does not have to be told," said Ptah-nem-hotep, "how a
whore spends money, but is it clear how you performed your feat a
second time?"

"I may lack the power to explain."

"You will make the effort," said Ptah-nem-hotep in a gentle voice.

"I will try." Menenhetet closed his eyes in contemplation. "If I was conceived on the night my father knew he would be killed, be assured the same fear was present in every ceremony I performed as a priest. Indeed it was the essence of my piety. That may be why my ceremonies were so well ordered and so grave. I was sensitive to the tender presence of death in all I did. When I began to feel this greed in myself, therefore, for all that is carnal, do not be surprised if I could soon overcome my ignorance of the arts of love since that is also a ceremony calling for fine respect. So I learned again, as I had with Renpu-Rept, how to dally for hours and wander at the edge. I could draw into myself all that was rich and foul, splendid and nasty, groaning and glorious in Nub-Utchat, and yet not go spilling forth in misery at all the thefts and corruptions her blood would ask of me, could, yes, still absorb her seven souls and spirits far up into my loins and my heart until my life became not only faint, but more and more like a fine thread. All of me which was not in her grew ready to voyage out of my body and enter my Ka. At such moments I knew I had only to tear a thread between my body and my Ka, that silver thread—or so I saw it when my eyes were closed—and I would die. My heart would burst even as I came forth. I cannot tell you how many nights I hovered on such a brink. Yet, I always returned. I enjoyed these pleasures too much to give them up. So I never plucked the silver thread that connected my body to my seven souls and spirits, no, not until the night she betrayed me.

"I can say that this manner of making love, while most delicate, and steeped in many sweet turns, may have lacked the vigor that was more to her taste. For, be certain, this slow penetration, not only of our flesh but of our thoughts and spirits, depended on much gentleness in our movements during certain feats of balance I would perform on the very edge."

"No way of making love is more divine," said Hathfertiti, caressing Ptah-nem-hotep with a look to say how well she had known just such a pleasure tonight. Menenhetet, however, after a pause for the interruption, continued to speak.

"On this one night when all of me was much divided, my Ka exploring the very gates of the Duad, even as the head of my member must have been deep within her womb, so must she have seen at last that cave where my wealth was buried, for she gave an inescapable pull, and I was in the fall. I just had time to say goodbye to all of me, thread, Ka, and the rest of my souls—I knew I would never have a coming-forth again so tumultuous as this, and I went: No priest ever saw the Gods in more brilliance than myself. My longings and my greed flew out of me like a rainbow. Again, I knew the great pain in my upper back, just once this time, not seven strokes, and heard her last scream, although it was mine, and no knife I felt but the bursting of my heart in that whore's arms. While we rested, I thought of the child I had just made in her, and only later, on awakening, as I stood to urinate, did I see myself on the ground.

"The eyes with which I saw my dead body belonged, of course, to my Ka, and he, poor fellow, was able to return into the belly of Nub-Utchat only on the next night while she was tremendously distracted with the ardors of making love to one of her favorite clients, a most powerful brigand from Kurna. But as, in the months to come, I grew in her belly, my Ka could not rest with the calm that is so essential for the term we live in the womb. On the contrary, my Ka and the rest of me came forth much wrenched and poked by the grossness of strangers who pounded upon my head for all the while I was in my new mother's belly, and I think that many of the memories of my first and second existence were so nearly beaten out of me that it has taken all of my fourth life to recover them."

Four

"I was raised by Nub-Utchat, and once again grew up in a harem, although here was no Pharaoh. Any male of Thebes was free to enter. Nor had I chosen my mother with good sense. While she had seized my wealth in the Eastern Desert and quickly gave up the brothel to purchase a great mansion for herself, she had the appetite of a Queen, and the itch to gamble of a charioteer, so the money was soon gone and she was a whore again. Before I was eighteen, she died of high fevers. Black water passed in her urine. I was then a big strong fellow with much congealed in my heart. I had few good sentiments, but I knew how to talk to people: I could, as our saying goes, 'Sell a feather to a Pharaoh and charge Him for gold.' I understood women as well as you could from living in a brothel, and men I appreciated by their manners or lack of them. Rude manners, after all, had belabored my unborn head.

"Let us say I knew how to find my way. I was making a living at the time in my mother's trade: I had become a brothel-keeper and a good one. We were more than ever a city of priests, so by the balance of Maat, we had roistering brothels, and mine, I could say, was the best. With two lives in preparation for such a trade, why not?

"All the same, even in the pots of Thebes, I was aware of the chaos at the Court in Memphi. There was a new Pharaoh every few years and not one but two famines in that era. I may even have suffered some hunger myself. Still, I had the good fortune to trust my dreams, and they told me to go north to the Delta where the papyrus plant grows most profusely. There I must start a papyrus workshop and export the product to Syria and other lands. If I did so, why then this dream told me, I would recover the treasure my mother had spent.

"I was still no more than a fat fellow with a merry disposition and a good tongue, but I succeeded while passing through Memphi to talk to the Chief Scribe of the Vizier of the Pharaoh Setnakht (which Chief Scribe had visited my brothel often when in Thebes—for he liked not only the women, but the food I served, and the baths I kept). Now, I convinced him that my venture in papyrus was worthy of consideration. To speed my way, he gave me a charter (with a special tax to be paid directly to him) and I could now begin a Royal Workshop. I spent much of the rest of my third life in Sais, and before it was over, amassed a fortune. How my papyrus was in demand throughout Syria!

"They were eager in the East to replace their heavy clay tablets and so be able to send more messages on the same donkey. Before, you could put fifty clay tablets on the beast's back and half would arrive in a broken state; now you could pack five hundred rolls of papyrus, and all would be as you sent them unless harm came to the caravan itself. These people of Syria and Lebanon, and even the Hittites, began to use our papyrus so much that before all was done, they succeeded in improving their chariots as well. For so soon as they could copy our drawings of chariots, so they also learned how to make them. If no piece of papyrus could show them how to turn a horse by the reins around one's waist, still they may yet learn that as well, and then it will be said that I, in my third life, was one of those Egyptians who helped to hasten the downfall of Egypt. Too many secrets have been revealed to the Syrians by the gift of papyrus. They have begun to copy our sacred letters and, in so doing, have polluted them. One can no longer discern at a glance whether it is the flowing style of the old Secluded, the legible presentations of the bookkeeper, or the mysterious curves we added to our drawings in the Inner Temple. In former days, one did not always have to take the same meaning from the same mark, and that was a security. Now, because of the Syrians, everyone can read each other, and even a common scribe will look upon the finest writing without awe. He does not have to suppose that the words contain more than one message. It means that the wise and the foolish, the generous and the greedy, are all informed equally well. So, we have fewer secrets from other lands. Indeed, we used to have another saying in those years: 'He who has our handwriting, knows our Ka.'"

"You find nothing good to say of yourself," observed my Father.

"It was not an era when one could approve of much. I have lived in greater times. I remember that I hired many Libyans and Syrians to work for me. More product came forth from their hands than from my fellow Egyptians who, having almost as many holidays as workdays, did not seem determined to offer their best labor, and were always ready to strike. It was certainly not as it had been under Usermare. Now, the Libyans and Syrians worked harder, made more papyrus, and took their arts back to their lands, yet I was content to employ them for they made me a rich man in a few years."

"Surely the papyrus was not the only source of your fortune?"

"I also speculated on the purchase and sale of Necropolis plots. The wisdom of my second life was with me in that manner. Thereby, I built another fortune on the first. It is the only road to wealth. One needs a small fortune to fertilize a greater one. You see, the removal of the capital to Memphi, which seemed, at that time, equal to the downfall of Thebes, ended by enriching the old city. For, now, only the Temple of Amon could hold together the Two-Lands. Pharaohs might be weak, but the Temple grew strong. So did the price of land increase in each alley of the City of the Dead, and, for that matter, through all of Thebes. The same mansion my mother purchased for little was now worth more than the palace of an Eastern King, and it could be said that men of substance like myself either congregated in the Delta, or at Thebes, and often spent no more than a night in Memphi on the trip back and forth."

"What you tell Me is of value, although not remarkable," Ptah-nem-hotep now said. "From your remarks I learn that rich men act much like one another. I prefer to ask instead: What of the woman you picked to be your mother for a fourth life? Can it be said that you had more wisdom by now?"

"Hopefully, it can be said," replied Menenhetet, but I could feel how his voice had lost the power to protect himself well. "The times were troubled," he repeated, "and married life was full of scandal. I had a friend who married a Princess from the sturdy line of Esonefret. But he was soon murdered by his wife's lover. Then my friend's child by this same Princess was sent to a peasant village. There the boy died of fever. That was not a story to inspire me with faith in noble mothers. It made a most powerful impression on me."

"Given what you had learned from your first life, and your second, surely there was no surprise for you in such a story?" my Father now said.

"In each life, I had to develop the power to recollect what happened before. In my third life, good natural judgment may have lived in my flesh even when it did not rise to my thoughts, but I can only say that the ill fortune of my friend shocked me greatly. So I looked in the other direction and chose a woman of the people who was strong and loyal. She had grown up in a peasant village and in childhood lived through our two famines. That gave me the confidence she could survive in troubled times. I wanted a woman to protect my wealth. That is exactly what my third wife, soon to be my fourth mother, was able to do for me.

"I can say that I was not in good health. I had succeeded in satisfying the buried appetites of my second life, but paid the cost. Conceived by Nub-Utchat with much disturbance to my seven souls and spirits, I had hardly cleansed myself by a life spent in commerce and pleasure. I drank a great deal and took many spices to stimulate my blood and was sick before I was thirty. I had all the ailments one could

reasonably acquire: gout, obesity, inflammation of my eyes, and cur-
vature of the spine. If there had been earlier years when I made love
with all the force of a fat young bull, I was, by now, much used up.
Invariably, I needed the ministrations of my wife to arouse me. But
then, I may as well confess that she was not my true choice—I would,
indeed, have preferred a Princess (just like the one who did my dead
friend in) yet, given my squalid beginnings, none would have me. I
admit that was the true bruise upon my feelings in those years. To
have wealth unleavened by distinction is to know the plenitudes and
miseries of a sow. Still, I took what I could get, and was resigned. For
the first time in three lives, death would come at an appropriate time.
I was older at thirty-three than at any age I had known before, and
lived in profound gloom. For by the end of my third life I had become
interested in all the matters I scorned when young. I wished devoutly
to recapture my first and second lives but no longer had the strength
to pursue those well-buried memories. Then I made my poor condition worse by taking, to the horror of my good wife, many herbs and
poisons to encourage the distant recollections for which I searched,
and thereby purchased many fevers that sent my mind on far-off journeys. I conceived myself for the last time out of the depths of a trance
I entered through no more skill than my choice of poison—whores
and their pimps know as much about herbs as any doctor or witch. So
I came forth for a last time even as I collapsed. It was what I desired.
All that was gross in me fell back into the ruins of my body, but my
seed was sent across the bridge, and that seed, I hope, was not like me,
but finer. I believe we have the power, when unhappy with ourselves,
to prepare a few virtues we do not possess and pass them to our seed.
I looked, therefore, to find a new life that would put much emphasis
on wisdom, understanding, and the best use of many subtle arts.

"My plans were well formulated. If, in my first life, I was born as
Meni, the son of a peasant woman, I was still the son of a peasant
woman when I entered my fourth existence. My wealth, however,
was preserved this time. That enabled me to live as I wished. So I have
been a General again (although of no consequence in comparison to
my first life), a doctor, a nobleman by my marriage to a Princess (de-

scended from no one less than Kham-Uese!) and because of my wealth, I was also a Notable, a true pillar of our society. Or so," he said mockingly, "so, hopefully, I would be described."

"But you know perfectly well. You have been a figure of constant interest among us for years," my Father replied, and added, "Yes, even when I was a young priest in the Temple of Ptah, I used, behind our white walls, to hear of you. They said that all the hundred and sixty years—it was one hundred and sixty years then—of your four lives were equally alive for you." He smiled. He could not resist the unkind words. "They said that when you were drunk you bragged of it."

"Oh, it is not true," said Menenhetet. "I was merely indiscreet. I made the mistake of telling a few close friends. Word could not have passed more quickly. I learned that a close friend is not the equal of a great secret."

"But how do you awake these sleeping powers? It seems to be different in every life, is it not?" My Father spoke, however, in a voice to betray as little interest as possible.

"Even," replied Menenhetet, "as Amenhotep the Second had the determination to slay more lions than any Pharaoh, so do You pursue the secrets that live in the root of the tongue."

"Is it not," asked my Father, and I could see He was displeased, "that you refuse to tell Me?"

"Or do You give me credit for knowledge I may not possess?"

"Your last remark is a subtle discourtesy, and by it, you sully the light that has shone upon us this evening."

"Tell Him how you awake these powers," said Hathfertiti.

My great-grandfather pretended she had not spoken. "In my fourth life, unlike the others, I was born with more sense of what had gone before. I do not know why. But, as a child, many a piece of papyrus with which I played was soon inscribed by me with sacred marks familiar only to the Inner Temple of Thebes during the last years of Usermare. My skills with sword and chariot were also brilliant when I was young, and for the first time it could be said that I was wise enough to have an early marriage with an attractive young woman of my own class. Not only had my mother not remained a widow, but she proved sensible enough to better our social position by marrying an illegitimate descendant of Amen-khep-shu-ef. Since my old rival (now my ancestor!) had always been too busy at sieges to have more than a few children, the line, while not in the channel of Succession, had grown more elevated with every new Pharaoh. So the new family I entered by my mother's second marriage was as well regarded as the line of my bride, and many entertainments were given for us. I can only say that the early years of my fourth life were so agreeable, and my daughter, the mother of Your own Hathfertiti, Ast-en-Ra, was so beautiful and charming, that if my wife had not died while I was away in Libya campaigning (where I was the youngest General to reach such rank) I might have spent my life in prominent office and have had many other children. The death of my wife, however, taught one frightful lesson. I did not mourn her as I expected to. The memory of my first three lives hovered in my mind like three ghosts standing before my door. I understood that I could hardly rush into a public life when the multitudinous desires of other lives lay unfulfilled behind me, or half-fulfilled, or much unremembered. So I resigned from the army and took up the learning of medicine as a way, I now suspect, of slowly approaching my true interest which was magic. I spent years studying such intricate matters as how to press the oil for the easement of gout in the evening when the air is soft, or in discerning which of our three seasons is most efficacious for the use of each herb on our pharmacological lists. I kept records of the curative properties of the roe of fish against sterility, and made studies of which substances were best taken by each of the three mouths, or by application to the flesh itself. Also which powders could be inhaled as steam through a reed. A gentleman of luxury, I preferred to be comprehensive, and inscribed on papyrus all that I did, and noted the results, even when it was a question of listing prescriptions compounded from twenty-five or thirty substances, indeed, I could not ignore how many cures depended on the judicious use of all that is revolting. I soon discovered that the most dependable ingredients were varieties of dung, and pondering this, ceremonies practiced

with Honey-Ball came back to me, and I embarked on the study of
magic that has been the consolation of my fourth life. I do not know
that it has been the happiest study. For I have come to see that Amon
may have visited my first mother, but I, as yet, have not honored the
gift with any great deed. If I failed in my first life, and betrayed much
in my second, fouled every nest with my third, so I must see my
fourth life as the one where I sought to use what I learned in order to
learn much more. Why else would I offer secrets on this night that I
have told to no one else?"

"Still," said Ptah-nem-hotep, "I cannot begin to think of high service for you next to Me when I do not even have an explanation for
your use of bats."

In a tone of much resignation, Menenhetet said, "They are filthy
creatures, hysterical as monkeys, restless as vermin. They are shrill
and cling to one another. But their leavings contain all they cannot
use. They are endowed, therefore, with the power to endure loneliness."

"I begin to understand your curious habit," said my Father in a
voice of surprising sympathy. "That vile paste must offer strength to
bear the loneliness of your hundred and eighty years."

Menenhetet bowed his head at the understanding of the Pharaoh.
But I was aware of another wisdom in my Father, and it was not one
I had felt before. At this instant, I knew He had come to a grave decision. Menenhetet would not be His Vizier. He did not wish to gaze
upon one hundred and eighty years of loneliness each day.

My great-grandfather shifted in his seat. I do not know if he, too,
was now alert to the difference in the air, but he only nodded mo-
rosely when Ptah-nem-hotep, as if to conceal where His thoughts
had taken Him, went on: "Neither do you tell Me of your trances."

"Tell Him," said Hathfertiti.

"Yes," said our Pharaoh, "I would like to know more of your
trances."

"If you do not tell Him, I will," my mother declared.

When Menenhetet did not reply, my mother startled us. "It is
dreadful," she said to Menenhetet. "I have regarded you as greater

than all but the greatest Gods. Now, I cannot believe how you are silent. I think you are stupid."

"No, how can he be stupid?" exclaimed Ptah-nem-hotep.

"He is. He does not know what is true at this moment for me. I, who have always had two hearts, one to love a man, and the other to despise him, am now devoted to one man with both my hearts." What she said next was most powerful for she did not utter the words, but allowed us to hear them in her thoughts, "I loved to tell a lie to every lover, but now I know the virtue of the truth."

"Only a Pharaoh can reach the depths of your Two-Lands," Menenhetet said to her, and bowed.

"Why don't you tell the Ninth how I was used? Do you know," she said to Ptah-nem-hotep, "that I became the inspiration for his magic? Tell Him," she said again to Menenhetet. "Tell Him how I entered your ceremonies when I was twelve. Tell how you seduced me."

"You were not a virgin."

"No," said Hathfertiti, "I was not. But no one ever seduced me in such a fashion before. Tell Him."

"I cannot speak of this matter," said Menenhetet.

Nor could I look at him. I had never seen a wounded man. I did not know how a soldier would hold himself after a spear had entered his chest, but Menenhetet was gray and most exhausted. In the course of this night, he had risen many times from his fatigue and come upon new vigor in each uncoiling of his knowledge, but now he looked as if his blood were gone.

"The first time Menenhetet came to me," said Hathfertiti, "I do not know what was used. But he seduced me with a drink, and I became inert. He took his pleasure—which was then his greatest pleasure—to make love to me as if I were a dead woman beneath. A dead woman brought him nearer to his purpose, I suppose, than a live one."

"It was not like that," said Menenhetet.

"No," said Hathfertiti, "it wasn't. It was a ceremony. When I grew up, you did not need to seduce me with a drink. I had come to like

what we did. You taught me to accompany you into your *caverns*."
She said this last word in so thick a voice, and so full of anger that I
did not know if she were speaking of a buried shrine or a deep pit, but
she was furious. "That is where his trances would take me—into the
deep part of the stream. Into caverns. I never learned anything better
than the fear of what crawls in the dark." Now she turned to Ptah-
nem-hotep and said, "I do not wish to conceal these matters. While in
my trances, I would hear my grandfather speak to Honey-Ball and to
Usermare and Nefertiri, and that was well, but then he was also in
communion with the eight Gods of the slime. I was the filth between
his fingers, and he made a mockery of my poor marriage to Nef-
khep-aukhem. Let me tell you the worst. They were not caverns we
entered, but tombs. I know what it is to make love in caverns that are
filled with the reveries of the dead." How startling was the wisdom of
my mother! She knew that this must repel our Pharaoh less than it
would bind Him to her.

"I cannot endure another minute of this conversation," said Menenhetet, "my hopes are extinct," and he stood up and without bowing left the room, although, like an old man, one could hear him falter
down the stairs of the patio in the darkness before the dawn. That was
the last time I saw my great-grandfather among us.

Five

So soon as he was gone, however, I could no longer see very well. My mother and Father still sat on either side of me, but they had become as shapeless as smoke, and the pillars of the patio were not visible. I felt as if I were on my knees before a man in some vault of stone, and could choose—by no more than the inclination of my heart—to rest in the damp of this tomb as easily as I could go back to my parents.

Yet, almost at once, the force of their presence commenced to quiver through every turn I took in the folds of my spell. Now, I could see their faces near me in the night, and then I knew that my thoughts were close again to my mother's thoughts. Silently, she was speaking to Ptah-nem-hotep—I heard the anguish in each silence! "Do You love me?" she asked. "Why have You chosen me?" And these questions burst forth to be followed at once by her unvoiced lament: "I have lost my husband on this night, and now I have lost the man who was my father, my lover, my God, my dearest enemy, the friend I feared the most, my guide to the Gods. He was all of this to me. Yet I love You, and have so adored You for seven years that I am ready to give him up. In truth, I drove him away. Yet You are a cold man. Do You love me? Can I trust You?"

Ptah-nem-hotep now replied with His thoughts. They passed through my body as if each of these unvoiced words were hands to lift and carry me. "On the day, seven years ago, that we went out on My skiff to hunt, My stick hit more birds than ever before. With you beside Me, I needed only to cast up the throwing-stick and no flight could escape untouched. No woman had ever done as much for Me before. None did again until this night. So I love you. You will be My Queen."

"It is true," thought my mother, but now her thoughts were so secret that only I could hear them. "He is a weak man who would be strong. There is no ardor like the devotion of such men when you can satisfy them." Aloud, she said, "Let us go. Let us lie down together." What she did not say even to herself, yet I heard her better than herself, was that He would never lose His desire for her since His taste, as she could see, was for secrets, and the more He learned of the worst things she had done, the more would He be delighted.

They stood up then and embraced, and my Father picked up my body. I do not know if it was the loss of the couch, but I felt a vertigo. Much disorder was in the air, and I felt the heavens stir in my stomach and wondered if there would be convulsions in the sky.

Then I knew the cause for such disturbance. It passed into me directly from my Father's arms. Khem-Usha had come onto the patio. I saw him through one half-opened eye which I closed on the spot, not wishing to see him at all, and near asleep, drifted through voices that came upon me like crocodiles thrashing in water too deep for my feet to reach. Maybe they would swim off and I would know no more.

But I heard (no matter how far away I might be from all these voices) that there were troops outside the Palace. "They belong to Nes-Amon," I listened to Khem-Usha say, and then, "You can use my militia. I have called them out tonight." There was much discussion, and my mother was in all of it, full of harsh but decisive opinions. I could hear her tell my Father, "If Your Household Guard is not supported by Khem-Usha's men, You will have no Royal Troops. They will go over to Nes-Amon." Much more argument came here, and quick voices—I heard my Father say, "No, that is intolerable, I cannot grant you such powers"—and they argued, and my mother said, "You have no choice, You have no choice," no, He had no choice, "You do not," said Khem-Usha, and they talked more. "No," I heard my Father say most clearly, "No, Menenhetet will not be the Vizier, no, I do not have such an intention." Then, there was less disturbance and more peace in the air. I could feel myself being handed over to my mother and carried by her in the first light of the dawn that glistened like a thread of silver across my closed eyes whenever I attempted to open them, and in the distance, I heard shouts commencing, and the din that comes from much purpose and much confusion meeting quickly with one another. I knew by the smell of goat dung and old charcoal fires that we were now in the servants' quarters where Eyaseyab was sleeping, and then I heard my mother say to her, "Take care, take the greatest care. There may be trouble." Now I was in the plump arms of Eyaseyab, and knew her like the pit of my own arm if not for her odor which was as strange and strong as a man's, yes, a man had been on her tonight, that I knew by *his* odor. He smelled like a beast who lived on a rock by the sea, and then I thought about such odors no more for I was set down on a mat, and her finger, out of old habit, teased the hair behind my ear. I wondered if she would lie down beside me and take Sweet Finger into her lips again, but even as such warmth began to stroll through my thighs, I heard a curse from the next room and a man came in. It was Bone-Smasher. By the way he walked, I knew that Eyaseyab belonged to him, and would no longer think of those two slaves, the Hebrew and the Nubian, who used to fight for her in the servant quarters of my home—was it now the home of Nef-khep-aukhem?

I do not know if it was my sweet feelings that had inspired Bone-Smasher, or whether his strong feelings left me feeling sweet, but now I could hear them making love, and that was different from all I had learned tonight. Here they did not speak, but growled often, and then he roared and she gave cries so shrill only a bird of the brightest feathers could have uttered them. I felt as if I were home again for I

was back with the sounds of the servants' quarters, indeed all the animals were waking up in the dawn, and other servants were making
love in their huts. You could feel everything stirring over the earth,
water being lapped, seed gobbled, the animals crying out to the bay-
ing of other beasts across the stalls. I remember thinking that servants
made love without the presence of the Gods, and thereby it was
warmer here, and for all I knew more satisfying than the love of those
I knew, although there might be less light when they came forth. Yet
I wondered if it was not like tasting the most wonderful soup. You
could feel it enter the domain of your belly, one fine territory after
another. Immersed in the crooning voice of Eyaseyab after all was
done, listening to her soothe the man and herself by the caress of her
hand on his back, I fell asleep, yes, fell asleep after all this night without a true sleep, and had no dreams, although there seemed to be
many shouts in the air and men running.

When I awakened, my mother was by my side to inform me my
great-grandfather was dead. "Come," she said, "let us take a walk."
There were now soldiers on every path of the Palace and in every
courtyard, and I saw the disorder of a day that would not be like other
days when every soldier you passed looked away. Now they stared at
everybody twice and were never on one foot longer than it took them
to shift to the other.

My mother did not weep as she told me, but there was a look of
great solemnity on her face and her eyes were empty so that when she
paused and did not speak, it was like looking at the head of a statue.
"Your great-grandfather," she said, "would certainly want you to
know how he died and with what courage."

He had been apprehended, she told me, by the troops of Khem-
Usha. They had found an old and distinguished man sitting on the
same gold chair that served for Ptah-nem-hotep's seat when we first
came before the Pharaoh on His balcony. Now, pinioned, and under
guard, Menenhetet had been led into a chamber where Ptah-nem-
hotep and Khem-Usha sat together with Hathfertiti. Our Pharaoh,
however, had had him unbound, and said: "For this night, you were
My substitute. You were the heart of the Two-Lands, and the Gods

listened to you. That will be Your glory. For You were a Pharaoh, indeed, on this night, and this is as it should be, and satisfies Maat, since as I look upon it, I know that You could never have become My Vizier. I could not trust Your ambition. I can, however, honor Your genius."

Saying this, my Father had handed over to Menenhetet His own short knife.

My mother said: "I was terrified. By the look on your great-grandfather's mouth, I believed he would bury the knife in Ptah-nem-hotep's chest. Khem-Usha certainly thought so. I saw fear on his face. Do you know, to offer that knife was one of the bravest acts I have ever seen. But it was wise as well."

Menenhetet had bowed, and touched his forehead to the ground seven times. Then he went into the next room to perform the last ceremony of the substitute. He took the knife and cut off his ears and his lips and his loins, and then, in great suffering, he began to pray. There was much loss of blood. Before he fainted from the ferocity of the pain, he cut his throat.

My mother shuddered, but her eyes were full of light. "No man but Menenhetet could have endured such a death," she said.

As I heard the story, the gold of the midday sun darkened into purple, and I felt as if I, too, were dying. The eyes of my mother continued to gaze at me, yet the longer I looked into them, the more her eyes came together until it was only one eye I saw, and then one light, and that was like a star in a dark sky. All that I had seen before me was gone. I was on my knees in the depths of a pyramid and down a long shaft came the light of a star reflected in a bowl of water.

Now, I could no longer see the star. Only a navel before my eyes. It was the withered navel of the Ka of Menenhetet and I was back in all the stink and fury of the old man's phallus in my mouth.

Six

I was a young man of twenty on my knees, and all I knew of the boy I once had been, receded from my heart. I was here in my Ka, and no more than my Ka, and for the second time this night the old man began to come forth. Or was I merely enduring the first time over again? Could this be the suffering of the Ka?

Then all of him came forth, and in great bitterness. His seed was like a purge, foul and bitter, and I would have liked to vomit but could not. I had to take into me the misery he felt, and all of his urge for revenge upon my mother.

So, with his phallus still in my mouth, I knew the shame of Menenhetet. Now, the Ka of my great-grandfather weighed upon my Ka as Usermare must have weighed on him.

I also knew his exhaustion. It came down upon me like a cataract. In none of his four lives had he found what he desired. That much I knew, and then I swallowed, and all the venom of his Khaibit came into me—from my great-grandfather's seed came the pure venom of his Khaibit. That would now be my knowledge of the past.

I would live by the guidance of his shadow. My Ka would have to choose its way in the Land of the Dead by the light of his Khaibit. If his stories were untrue, I would not know what was before me. To recollect one's past was the need of one's Ka, but such wisdom must be evil when owned by another.

So I did not know whether to trust what I would see, and yet, not knowing, I began, nonetheless, to recall what happened to my parents and to me after the last night of my great-grandfather's life. Of course, I had no choice. How could I not follow what came to me? It concerned nothing less than the events of my life after Menenhetet was gone—was it fifteen years from the day of his death to mine? That is what I seemed to remember (had death come upon me when I was twenty or twenty-one?) yes, my life had certainly continued into an early death—witness the land where I was now. And I even felt one pang of sympathy for the modest fashion in which Menenhetet had told us of his second life and his third life. For I could not see any more of my own.

But my great-grandfather, exhausted by the fury of his coming-forth, now placed himself beside me gently, and sat back against a wall of this alcove in the massive tomb of Khufu (with its empty sarcophagus—yes, that, too, I now recalled!). Side by side, our buttocks on the floor, we began to stare into the darkness until the wall across, not five paces away, began to shimmer. I saw sights that were like colored paintings on a temple wall. Yet each time such an image became clear, it was as if I looked into the bowl of water where I had seen the star and stirred it with my hand, for many waves spread out from each light. The pictures moved as if they lived within my head just so much as on the wall, and finally I could not know how I saw it—everything moved so often. Then I decided that to look at the living from these tombs of the dead was even more confusing than to see what happened through the memory of another. In truth, it was like reaching for a fish. One's hand would never go where one's eye could see, and the water bent one's arm and darted away.

To show how little I could trust what was offered to me, the first sight proved disgusting, and I did not wish to believe it. The face of Ptah-nem-hotep came before me slyly eating a very small piece of flesh from the mutilated body of Menenhetet. That was what I saw, and as if the wall could speak, or at least give resonance to the feelings of those who moved upon its surface, I knew the Pharaoh's passion for wisdom was more desperate now that Menenhetet was dead. As His teeth chewed on the fearful meat, it was all believable to me. It certainly explained why He changed so greatly over the remaining years of His life, and why I could not remember Him now as a good parent. Eating that morsel of my great-grandfather must have altered Ptah-nem-hotep gravely, left Him mean. Lacking the courage of Menenhetet, He could only acquire ruthlessness.

My mother spoke then within my ear and said, "You are wrong to think harshly of your Father. Taking your great-grandfather into Himself has bound the Pharaoh to our family." She had no more than to say such words, and much came before me: I saw Them together often, my Mother, now indeed the Queen, and beside Him on His throne. Then I recalled that not one year passed from the Night of the Pig before She gave Him a son, my half brother, yes, She was much His Queen and there at every great ceremony He conducted. He was present now at many more festivals than before, and whenever the Concubines of the Gods offered a song to the Pharaoh, my Mother, like Nefertiri, shook a sistrum. They were not unhappy in Their first year.

I also began to remember, however, that They often quarreled. While it could never be said that They ceased to delight in each other's flesh (and indeed were a court scandal for the length of the hours They spent with one another) still, They were never content with one another's little manners, and like most married people fought invariably over the same matter. For years I could hear Them quarrel about the shop of Nef-khep-aukhem in Memphi.

Indeed, so often must these quarrels have taken place that my memory revived sufficiently for the pictures to cease for a time. Thoughts of Nef-khep-aukhem came back to me instead, and I recalled the outrage he aroused in Ptah-nem-hotep on that morning when Khem-Usha's troops occupied the Palace. For in the course of bargaining with the High Priest on that dawn, Ptah-nem-hotep learned that Nef-khep-aukhem, so soon as he had left the patio, hastened directly to Khem-Usha's chambers in Memphi, and there gave much information to the High Priest about my great-grandfather's ambitions as well as the Pharaoh's increasing sympathy for them.

This story having come back to me from the outraged lips of my Mother, She thought it likely that neither the troops of Khem-Usha nor of Nes-Amon would have moved that night if not for Nef-khep-aukhem. The truth, as my Mother would have it, was that Nes-Amon did not assemble his men until he heard the sounds of Khem-Usha's militia getting ready in the dark.

This treachery put my new Father into a greater rage than any other event of that dawn. Then, Nef-khep-aukhem, thinking it wise to collect his reward from the High Priest so soon as possible, made the error of appearing at the Palace too early. Ptah-nem-hotep declared to Khem-Usha that the way to commence a true equality between Pharaoh and High Priest was not to begin by taunting Him with the presence of his treacherous Overseer. Indeed, my Father resented such arrogance so much that Khem-Usha, comprehending how dear was this point, pretended for a time to be obdurate in his loyalty to Nef-khep-aukhem. Thereby, he gained many concessions in the exchange before agreeing that the former Overseer of the Cosmetic Box be banished from the Palace. Indeed, my Mother declared that if not for Her intervention, Nef-khep-aukhem would have been killed.

Now, I recalled that Her feelings soon altered. My former father, alert, as ever, to the needs of others, soon opened a shop in Memphi for the care of ladies. As far as anyone knew, this was the first enterprise of its sort ever in the Two-Lands. Which lady, until that hour, did not have her own servant to care for her hair? Since the hands of Nef-khep-aukhem, however, were known by all to have touched the head of the Pharaoh Himself, the shop was successful at once. My first father soon became prosperous. But there was not a day at the Palace when Hathfertiti did not quarrel with Her second husband about the presence in Memphi of Her first. She was hideously humiliated, She kept telling Him. Yet She could not convince Ptah-nem-hotep to put such commerce out of existence by an edict, or, at the least, buy Nef

off with an estate in some provincial nome. Ptah-nem-hotep's old affection for His Overseer had revived. I would hear Him tell Her that
unfaithfulness for one night was forgivable. Consider the provoca-
tion!

This, of course, left the onus on my Mother. For that, She never
had any patience. Like many beautiful women, She could not bear to
be blamed. So She took pains to prove that the unfaithfulness of His
old Cosmetic Box was considerably more serious. Nef-khep-aukhem,
She declared, had not served as a spy for Khem-Usha just on this one
night, but, to the contrary, had been his informant for years. Her ev-
idence was slender, however, and Ptah-nem-hotep refused to accept
it. I think the nearness of Nef-khep-aukhem was a way to remind
Hathfertiti of how much She owed to Her second marriage. I expect
He needed such a cudgel to keep Her in place. I could always hear
Their quarrels. "You do not see how it demeans You," She would tell
Him. "People say You live with the woman of a wig-maker."

"On the contrary," He would reply, "there is not a lady in Memphi who does not admire him most prodigiously." So forth. Over the
years, it soured Hathfertiti. She could never forgive Him for not
yielding to Her. Then, there were other matters to take away more of
Her respect. I do not know which rights were given to Khem-Usha
on the first morning, as opposed to those ceded later, but my Mother
remained Queen of the Two-Lands for only three years before Her
powers as well as my Father's were reduced by half. In the Tenth Year
of the Reign of Ramses the Ninth, it was promulgated that Amenhotep (the new appellation chosen by Khem-Usha—and equal to four
Pharaohs!) was now raised in godliness equal to Ramses the Ninth. At
a great festival, confirmed by many ceremonies, Amenhotep, High
Priest of the Temple of Amon in Thebes, was given full sanction to
govern all of Upper Egypt. A vast array of gold and silver vessels was
presented to Him, and it was declared that all revenues in Upper
Egypt from all sources would now go to the treasury of Amon directly and need not pass through the vaults of the Pharaoh. Amenhotep's figure was also inscribed on many temple walls. He stood next to
Ramses the Ninth, and both Gods were equal in height—four times

higher They stood on such walls than all servants and officials next to Them.

I do not know whether my Mother kept any great love for Ptah-nem-hotep after this, but by what I now saw in my mind, I supposed that She did not. To my singular surprise, I saw Menenhetet again in my thoughts. He looked five, or might it be ten years older, and my Mother was heavier than She had been while he was still alive. So I was obliged to wonder if the story She had told me of his dismemberment had no truth. Was it a tale of horror chosen to make me wish never to think of Menenhetet again? For now, if my memory were not being fed by the eight Gods of the slime—just so slippery did it all become!—the truth seemed to be that Menenhetet had not killed himself, although doubtless given such an invitation by the Pharaoh. And I saw the intolerable agitation that my great-grandfather's refusal caused in Ptah-nem-hotep. If He had most clearly deceived Menenhetet by offering no reward for the incalculable gifts presented to His mind on that long night, yet, like a true Monarch, He still felt betrayed. Menenhetet would not endow Him with the final gift of devotion—he chose not to serve as a substitute and kill himself.

Not to do so left Menenhetet, however, at Khem-Usha's mercy. The High Priest soon succeeded in stripping my great-grandfather's wealth. His estates in Upper Egypt were purchased for ridiculously low prices by the Temple, indeed, Khem-Usha set the prices, and if Menenhetet had not agreed, the Temple would most certainly have taken his lands. Then the rest of his holdings in Lower Egypt, including the great mansion (from whose rooftop I had watched him make love to my mother) were, at Hathfertiti's insistence, acquired with equally low reimbursement by the Pharaoh. My Mother most certainly did not wish to have my great-grandfather near, and on this occasion, succeeded in Her desires. Menenhetet was obliged to live on a poor estate on the West Bank of Thebes purchased with what little he had been left.

So fixed was I at gazing into these images that I was startled by a movement from the Ka of Menenhetet beside me. His thigh began to shake against the side of my thigh, and I could hear his agitation in the sound of his breath. It offered the conviction that we shared this memory, that it was his, and he did not lie. For this, incontestably, would be the way he recalled it, that is, with much disquiet. Then these events became so extraordinary that I could not cease watching.

For Menenhetet did not live on his one poor estate in some solemn ingathering of the last years, no, he managed to join the thieves of Kurna, and thereby acquired another fortune while robbing the tombs of the Pharaohs. If he could not in any of his four lives wear the Double-Crown himself, and thereby enter the Land of the Dead as a God, then at least he could plunder Their crypts, and most skillfully he did, tunneling from one tomb to the next with no sign showing on the surface. Then, in the year Menenhetet felt himself close again to his death—which was late in my fifteenth year, and thereby the Sixteenth Year of the Reign of Ramses the Ninth—he slipped back into Memphi and succeeded in visiting my Mother.

Now, upon the wall, I saw him making love to Her. It was the last time. Even as he sat beside me, he gave an oath of expiration, yet I saw him die in Her arms, and knew, from the resonance of Her profound weeping, that he had been successful, and for the fourth time, in impregnating a woman with the ardors of his last act. His force upon Her must still have been great, for my Mother, despite every objection by Ptah-nem-hotep, took all the necessary steps to see that his body was most carefully embalmed.

In the second month of Her pregnancy, however, before my Father could be aware that She was carrying (although He would certainly have assumed it was His child, since no matter how much unpleasantness now lived between Them, one could count on the pleasure They took together) Hathfertiti, nonetheless, wrought a last revenge on Menenhetet. She took purges until She aborted the child. There would be no fifth life for my great-grandfather. He did not become my infant brother.

His Ka was left, therefore, most cruelly evicted. If it decided to return to the embalmed body of the old man, and took up abode there—which it must have done, or how else could he now sit beside me?—still I am not certain what escaped, and what was lost. Part of him, like a ghost, knowing no dwelling, may have attached itself to me. For at the age of sixteen, I certainly became ungovernable in the eyes of my parents.

My younger brother, Amen-khep-shu-ef the Second, an expression, I expect, of my Father's desire that one of His Sons, at least, be a great warrior, was soon seen as He-Who-would-become-Ramses-the-Tenth. This never plagued me until my sixteenth year when Amen-Ka was nine. Then I grew defiant. Not only did I gamble and carouse, behave, in short, like a Prince, but I became impolite to Ptah-nem-hotep and was excruciatingly rude to my Mother on the subject of the chapel She built for the four mummies who made up the remains of my great-grandfather. After a good deal of expense and a long search by Her agents, She had finally been able to locate the first Menenhetet, and the second. If the third was not difficult to find—he was there in the same tomb his widow had built for him, and no thieves had yet broken in—the crypt of the High Priest was pillaged. It could not even be certain that the mummy who remained, stripped of amulets and gems, was Menenhetet until much study was given to the prayers written on the linen wrappings, but they, fortunately, proved sufficiently recondite to belong to a High Priest. However, the Menenhetet of the first life, the Master of the Secrets, was only found because Hathfertiti, despite a separation of near to ten years, was still able to live in the mind of my great-grandfather. On his last visit, as they made love, She journeyed with him into the depths of a trance. Thereby, She saw the place of his first death, and even watched the servants of Honey-Ball rescue his body from the pile of offal on which it had been thrown. Saved from decomposition by an immediate embalming, Honey-Ball, after the seventy days, commissioned a traveling merchant from the Delta to take the coffin downriver to Sais where she had him put in a modest tomb near her family vault. It was there that Queen Hathfertiti found the mummy of this first Menenhetet (with the mummy of Honey-Ball lying beside him) and now finding Herself at last in full possession of the remains, She prevailed upon Ptah-nem-hotep to permit each of these four well-wrapped eminences, each in its own heavy coffin, to be pulled around the Palace walls by teams of oxen. Afterward She kept the mummies in a chapel surrounded by a moat, and it had, for protection, a crocodile in the water. Just so prodigious, I believe, was Her fear of the Ka of Menenhetet.

Of course, it was never wise to attempt to comprehend my Mother. She was faithful at maintaining the chapel, even to keeping Ptah-nem-hotep amused about it and thereby tolerant—She would make dreadful jokes to the effect that She could feel well protected by Her four Canopic jars!—and while She certainly kept up the care of it after His death, She decided, so soon as I died, even, indeed, while I lay in my bath of natron, that Menenhetet-of-the-fourth-life, which is to say, his mummy, sarcophagus and jars, was to be moved by some peculiar logic of Her heart to the same mean tomb to which I would be sent. But, then, much had changed in Her life after Ptah-nem-hotep's death.

Toward the end, He aged grievously. As my royal Father grew older, so did He lose that handsomeness of feature which had set Him apart from other men, and His cheeks grew heavy and His neck thickened. He was forever dejected. In the Sixteenth (and next to last) year of His Reign, it was discovered that several tombs of old Pharaohs in Western Thebes had been despoiled. The boldness of the brigands was demeaning to Him. The thieves seemed all too ready for the wrath of any Pharaoh, living or dead. The mummy of Sebekemsef, hundreds of years old, had been stripped of its gems and His Queen violated as well. When the culprits were captured (and proved to be workmen in the Necropolis) Ptah-nem-hotep discovered that many of His officials were implicated as well. The mayors of West Thebes and East Thebes accused each other. There was no end to the inquiries. Nes-Amon (who survived as Chief Scribe after his dreams of higher office were ended by Khem-Usha) was even sent to Thebes to keep a record of the commission.

That was the year Ptah-nem-hotep began to age so noticeably. And I began to feel a desire for my Mother which proved so difficult to restrain I know it could only have risen from the Ka of Menenhetet's unborn child. When my Mother also proved affected by these passions, we began to feel as blessed by the Gods—or, was it despised?—as Nefertiri and Amen-khep-shu-ef.

It was then, in the six months before His death, that my Father raised Amen-Ka to be a co-regent with Himself. He even gave my brother the title of Ramses the Tenth, Kheper-Maat-Ra, Setpenere Amen-khep-shu-ef Meri-Amon. Thus was I deprived of my birthright, if my weak claim can so be called, considering how I was conceived. Yet even in that year, so soon as Ptah-nem-hotep died (and how my Mother wept at His funeral) so did my brother, not ten years old, have to contend with a greater scandal than the plundered vault of the Pharaoh Sebekemsef.

It was discovered that the long-hidden tomb of Ramses the Second high in the hills (that place most difficult of access to which Usermare had once led His First Charioteer) had been violated. The tomb of the Father, Seti the First, was also pillaged. Was there a Pharaoh left Whose tomb had not been entered? My poor brother! In the midst of great public bewilderment, with unrest everywhere, He celebrated His tenth birthday in Memphi even as word came from Thebes that barbarians out of the Western Desert had captured the city. Khem-Usha (whom I could not think of in any way as Amenhotep) was held captive for six months and tortured. When released at last, he was no better than a frail old man. Amen-Ka had two more years on the throne and died. When He was gone, so, too, ended all royal prerogatives for Hathfertiti and me. A great-nephew of Ramses the Third became Ramses the Eleventh, and shortly thereafter, I was dead. How, I do not know. No picture chose to form in my mind. I could not even rely on the treacherous memory of Menenhetet. Other images, however, appeared on the wall. Now I could witness a most peculiar phenomenon. I began to watch the reign of those who came after me. That passed before us. The first of these strange rulers was a new High Priest named Hrihor. He ruled in Thebes, and the Two-Lands were more divided. Then came a Syrian, or some such fellow, named Nesubenedded, and he ruled Lower Egypt from Memphi to Tanis on the Very Green.

During these years, violent entries into Pharaohs' tombs were as common as a plague, and officials came to feel so helpless that in much desperation, they shifted the royal bodies until Usermare was even placed in the tomb of Seti the First. But when Their outer rooms were again broken into, both Pharaohs, with Their wives, were now transferred to the tomb of Amenhotep the First and before long, the priests had to hide a good many of these royal bodies in an unmarked grave west of Thebes. In such a dark pit, among the cliffs, rested Ahmose, and Amenhotep the First, and Thutmose the Second, and Thutmose the Great, Who was the Third, and Seti the First and Ramses the Second and many others, packed side by side like a litter of stillborn beasts. I could not believe what I saw. The wall spoke of sights not even my great-grandfather could dare to conceive. Indeed, my Ka felt like a bottomless pit before the weight of these Pharaohs disrupted from Their tombs, and I had to wonder if the Two-Lands were now lost and without a foundation.

All this while, the Ka of Menenhetet had not said another word to me. Yet I saw him smile at all that was before us, and wondered how many of these pictures might have come from his mind. Then, I remembered my own mummy badly wrapped, the cloth at my feet open to maggots, and gloom came to me. I still could not remember how I died. The more I pondered, the less I saw on the wall, and wondered why I seemed to be so certain that I was killed one night in a drunken brawl.

As I brooded on this, I saw the same beer-house I had glimpsed in the hour I lay in the wondrous room where the fish were painted on the floor, and I had a glimpse of Bone-Smasher again as he came close to his own drunken fight. Much as I wished to learn about my own dying, I was obliged instead to follow my own fortunes no more, but had to witness many changes in the lives of Bone-Smasher and Eyaseyab. While I thought I would not care to watch, I soon became curious. For much passed before me rapidly. Their faces began to age soon after Bone-Smasher was made Captain of the Royal Barge as a reward for having protected me through the morning when Khem-Usha's troops occupied the Palace.

The helm of the Royal Barge was not, however, an office to which he was suited. Bone-Smasher was uncouth to work for a King. So he was soon moved to other tasks. Before long, he slipped further, and ended at last as he had begun—a man who drank too much and turned violent when sodden, even to Eyaseyab who had become his wife.

Eyaseyab loved him, however; so well, and so much for every day of their life together, that she may even have been rewarded by Maat. A second prosperity began for Bone-Smasher. He went to visit Menenhetet in order to seek work, and found it. My great-grandfather had been looking for a man savage enough to serve as runner between the thieves of Kurna and himself.

Bone-Smasher became so useful at this task that Eyaseyab was soon able to leave my mother's service and bought a home on the Western Bank of Thebes with the good riches his labors provided. They had children, and my former nurse might have become a respectable matron with her own family tomb in the City of the Dead, but Bone-Smasher grew careless after Menenhetet's death, and was one of the brigands arrested for plundering the tomb of Usermare. Soon executed, he was thrown away in an unmarked grave.

Eyaseyab never found his body. She came back to Memphi and worked once more for my mother as Mistress of All Maids. One night, however, in order to fulfill a vow to her husband, she slipped out to the Necropolis. By the illumination of the pictures on the wall, I saw her dare the ghost, that same fellow with the unbelievably evil breath I had encountered on the walk back to my tomb. It proved a fearful meeting for Eyaseyab, but she did not flee, and waited until the ghost, with all his imprecations, moved farther down the alley on his nightly watch. Then she buried a little statue which she had had made of Bone-Smasher, there, right in front of the door to my tomb. For the vow to Bone-Smasher, whispered into his ear, had promised that if he were thrown into an unmarked grave, she would have a likeness made of him, and find the tomb of Menenhetet, and bury it near. I came near to weeping as I thought of the loyalty of my old nurse, and thereby discovered that my Ka had kept Sweet Finger, for he, too, remembered her.

Why I saw the story, I do not know, but I can say that after these tears, my sorrow began to move from concern for Eyaseyab to the misery of contemplating my own death. Now I could see my old nurse working for my mother on the last day I could remember, there, dressed in the clothes of a widow and still mourning Bone-Smasher. Yet the sight of Eyaseyab was now equal to a sight of myself in my mother's bed. I was no longer a child, but a man, and my mother and I were lovers.

What passed between us, I could not bring myself to recollect—except I knew there was no other woman I desired more. Yet, in that bed, even as we held each other, was the weight of our shame. For if love between brother and sister was commonplace to all our lives, the same could not be said of a passion for one's mother. Now I remembered Hathfertiti's fear before the gossip of Memphi, indeed it had been so great, and whispered so about us, that she had joined with Nef-khep-aukhem once more, and for a second time, became his wife.

There, sitting beside my great-grandfather, my poor Ka bewildered once more by these poor fragments of recollection, I found the place, at last, where two shards joined. For now I remembered how I used to make love to the priest and his sister, that one who had buttocks like a plump panther. Her brother had been no priest, not a priest at all, but Nef-khep-aukhem—who, for sanitary reasons had shaved off all hair—and his sister was my mother.

In misery, in this tomb of Khufu, I was obliged to contemplate the perfumed squalor and prodigious animosity of the most fearful jealousy, the most dreadful quarrels between Nef-khep-aukhem, Hathfertiti and myself. The outcome—did I now remember it, or merely think I did?—was that three brutes were hired by my uncle (who once supposed he was my father, and was now certainly my rival) yes, were chosen by him to waylay me in a bar. Before it was done—what a damnable waste, what a shattering of expectations—I was dead. All that had lived in the little boy who was six, all of his tenderness, his wisdom, his pleasure, all that spoke of his days to come, and the promise of it, was gone. There had been no more purpose than in the squashing of a beetle. I could have wept for myself as if lamenting another. In all the debauchery of these last few years, I had never thought that I would not emerge with some—at least—of the expectations of my earliest years redeemed. Now I would not. He was gone. Menenhetet the Second was dead—a young life and a wasted one! Yes, tears came to my eyes, as powerful as the purity of mourning for a stranger, and I shook within. And as I trembled in this anguish, the walls began to stir, and in our darkness, before I could even feel a great fear, the presence of the Duad was on the wall. We were in the Duad.

Seven

I had always supposed that the Land of the Dead could not be reached without a journey of great difficulty. One would march for days under a sun as hot as the desert of Eshuranib, and then be faced with a descent down a precipitous drop into caverns where you could not see. The mist from the hot baths would render every handhold treacherous. Yet, now, sitting beside the Ka of my great-grandfather, his hip touching mine, these visions moved about in so natural a manner that I no longer knew if what I witnessed was in my mind, in my great-grandfather's, or would prove to be a property of the wall. Some creatures I saw drew near and gave every threat of swarming over me, yet, always, before I could feel too much oppressed, they went away, as if at my command. So it was. So be it. I was in the Duad. Although I had never entered a jungle but had only heard about such places from Nubian eunuchs who served in the Palace, there was now much rustle in my ear and many honking sounds and all the din and turmoil one might expect from a great thicket of a forest. Everywhere I could hear gates fly open, and sounds of weeping from the distraught as well as the cries of Gods Who spoke like animals. The shriek of a hawk came to me and the cries of waterfowl in their nest, the whirring of bees and terrible great groans of the bull-Gods, even male cats in heat. I saw the Ka of all who were so unfortunate as to be the enemies of Ra, and witnessed the destruction of their bodies at the First Gate, and the loss of their shadows as they fell into pits of fire. Flames flowed forth from the mouths of Goddesses. And all these wonders were without fear for me. Soon, I could separate the keepers of the gate from the wretches waiting to be judged, inasmuch as the Gods had the bodies of men or women, but walked about with the heads of hawks and herons and jackals and rams upon Their necks, and one great fellow of a God had the head of a beetle. While I did not speak to the Ka of my great-grandfather, I was tempted to remark that many of these Gods looked the same as the drawings of Them on the temple walls.

Then, with the safety of the blessed—yet how could I be blessed when my tomb was spoiled?—we saw the First Gate pass before us, no, we did not walk through it, but upon the wall it drifted by, and I wondered if we were in the sacred Boat of Ra and so could pass and feel no fire. I do not know how I knew (for I saw no other passengers but my great-grandfather and myself) yet I can say that now we were in the Second Bend of the Duad, and here we watched a few wretches stoop to drink cold water from the springs, and we saw how all who told too many lies in their life began to scream. For the water boiled so soon as it touched their tongue. I saw the rich man, Fekh-futi, and he was now in garments soiled with the mud of the riverbank. He had carried the toe of Honey-Ball through many a gate, but was still here at the beginning because his misdeeds had proved more numerous than his virtues. Now he lay upon his back while the Third Gate showed the pivot of its hinge implanted in his eye, and each time the great door opened or closed, he uttered the piteous cry of a man who has spent his life seeking his advantage too directly. Beside him, writhed others in their bonds.

Then we passed through a long tunnel with a bull's mouth at the end, and in it, I saw twelve victims who lived in a lake of boiling waters. The stench of the lake was so powerful that birds flew away in panic so soon as they passed over, yet I could not smell the stench of the sulphur, although I saw many dragging their shadow behind them, and one lake was so crowded that it had two rows of forty-two cobras within, and they had no need to spit fire since the word they uttered was sufficiently terrible that the shadows of the dead withered before them.

In the Fifth Bend of the Duad, were twelve mummies. Even as I watched, a God with the head of a jackal came near and told them to cast off their wrappings, remove their wigs, collect their bones and flesh, and open their eyes. For now they could desert the caverns of Seker and rise to the great estate to which He would lead them. But farther on was only a pool of boiling water and so they were without an abode in the caverns of the dead. In the Sixth Bend of the Duad, I saw a God with the head of a fish, and He could pacify monsters of the sea by shaking out a net to His own powerful incantation. He knew the genius of the net and how to tie knots that would confound monsters and I saw the beetle Khepera and His bulk was very great, even the size of eight lions, and He moved through every fire without being scorched. I saw Khepera navigate the gold and silver Boat of Ra through the body of a great serpent, and indeed, He entered by a hole in the tail, and emerged from the mouth, and in the Seventh and Last Bend we even passed by the monster who is named Ammit, and He is the Eater of the Dead and usually rests at the side of the scales while Anubis weighs the heart of him who will be judged. So soon as the heart is too heavy for the feather of truth, then Ammit will devour it. And He was a monster with the head of a crocodile, the legs of a lion, and the most hideous smell. Indeed, it was so awful that even through the wall, a whiff came to me, and in it was the stench of all the foul hearts he had devoured. I thought again of the first time I smelled the breath of the ghost of the Necropolis, and wondered if in the hour when I approached the scales, and the truth of my life appeared, would my heart also be part of this stink? But it must. When the heart was without evil, it weighed no more than a feather, and mine felt as heavy as a Canopic jar.

In our alcove within the Pyramid of Khufu, now that there was no vision on the wall, I did not suffer much fear. While these visions of the Duad had been as thick as mists, and I could hear the screams, still they did not shiver in my Ka, nor did I cringe before the flames, and there was no great heat. I began to wonder if what I had seen was the Land of the Dead or merely its Khaibit? Could it be that Khert-Neter had ceased to exist? Had what I witnessed been no more than its memory of itself? I thought of the outraged tombs of the Pharaohs, and how Their bodies had been brought together in one cave where they were so packed in on Themselves, mummy upon mummy, that perhaps the Duad could breathe no longer. Yes, the loss of the tombs of the Pharaohs might mean the end of the great river of the dead and all its territories. Was that why Khert-Neter had only appeared before me like an image on the wall, and I knew no fear? If so, my Ka would not know how to find Anubis, nor would my heart be weighed. There would be nothing, after all, for Ammit to eat.

Yet I did not feel relief. Through my life I had listened to descriptions of what could befall you in the Land of the Dead, but now I had to wonder if one's anguish might prove more simple. Because now I knew how I had died, and could count the waste of my life, and that was suffering enough. As if to answer my thought, I saw before me the face of Hathfertiti, and she was more disfigured than a leper. I could not say how she had perished, but by her flesh it was certain she had been allowed to decompose for many days. Before I could even wonder who had taken such revenge upon her Ka, I knew it was not revenge but simple precaution I beheld. Nef-khep-aukhem must have ordered that the body of his wife be left unattended after she expired. When a husband is jealous of a wife, there is no trust in the embalmers. To allay all fear that they will make love to the body of the deceased, the husband does not allow her to be preserved until she has begun to rot.

Or, had Ptah-nem-hotep been the one to leave such commands to treat her so? I could not even know whose heart was as hideous as this vision of her altered face. Oh, that was cause for agitation more than any sight in the Land of the Dead. My true suffering came up again. Did I have any memory? How could I prepare?

It was then that my great-grandfather put two fingers gently on my knee, as to squeeze forth the quietest attention, and began to speak.

Eight

"It is true," he said. "The Duad is no more than a ghost. But then you must understand that you have been dead for a thousand years. The Pharaohs are gone. Egypt belongs to others. We only know weak Princes, and they are the sons of men from far-off places. Even the nations have changed. One hears no more of the Hittites. There is one land on the other side of the Very Green that you would not have known in the years when you were alive. It is a country far to the north and west of Tyre and yet enough time has gone by for this people to grow great, then lose their strength. That is the length of the time that has passed. Now, another great nation lives even farther to the west across the Very Green, and the people of that nation were barbarians when you were born. Our Gods, if we speak of Ra and Isis, Horus and Set, are now in their possession. If you think of the story I told of our Gods at the beginning of our travels, I will now confess that I imparted it to you in the way that these Romans and Greeks tell it to each other. That is why my tale was familiar yet different from what you know. For our Land of the Dead now belongs to them, and the Greeks think no more of it than a picture that is seen on the wall of a cave. So you will do better in the trials

ahead if you comprehend the humors of their mind. In our day, Ra
was neither old nor decrepit but the source of all radiance, and Horus
may have been weak in the legs but He was the Lord of the sky and
His feathers were our clouds, His eyes were the sun and the moon.
Even Set had the power to shake the heavens with thunder. But the
Greeks know less of the differences between Gods and men, and the
Romans wish to despise such differences. So they tell the story in
their manner. Of course, their Gods are smaller than ours. In the true
account, which I did not relate, I could have described how in the
hour that Set brought His last accusations against Horus and lost, the
Gods most certainly did not laugh at Him, as the Greeks would have
it, but dragged Set into Their great hall and threw Him on the ground.
Then They demanded that Osiris sit upon the face of Set. That was
necessary to declare the victory of righteousness over evil, and is our
idea of a throne. Whereas the Greeks only see it as a chair for Kings so
noble as to love knowledge more than the Gods.

"Think, then," he added, "how fortunate you are that I am your
guide. I have been on so many travels through Khert-Neter that now
you are able to avoid the last of its fumes. Why, the worst you have
known of such matters is my coming-forth in your mouth, and that
was so horrible you could take no more. You are spoiled. You will
never know the suffering of a true death."

He said it, and I felt a peculiar woe. If I would never encounter the
trials of the Duad, then a void would dwell in the last of my seven
souls and spirits. My Ka would never encounter a true test of its courage. I might even live forever and never die a second time, but then
there is no loneliness, I decided then, that is worse than being ignorant of the worth of your soul.

I sat there in the pits of a new misery. Upon me came the weight
of the failure of my great-grandfather in his four lives. I could feel
how the magnitude of his desire remained as large as the pain of his
defeats. All he had wished to become, even his unbalanced appetite to
become a Pharaoh, could be measured by the adoration he knew for
Osiris. Because as I remembered from his descriptions of that Lord
(try as he would to confuse me with tales of the Greeks!) my great-

grandfather must live near to the sorrow that dwelt in the heart of the Lord of the Dead. Who but Osiris hoped to discover what would yet come forth from Gods unborn? Indeed how else could I comprehend the feelings of the Lord Osiris if I did not share them myself? He was the God Who longed to create the works and the marvels of the future. So He suffered the most from every high purpose that failed. He would know how bitter it had been for my great-grandfather to be so defeated that the taste of his seed was foul?

Yet I had no more than lived through the onset of such faint compassion for my great-grandfather and his Lord Osiris, when the most astonishing phenomenon began. I reached over to put my hand on Menenhetet—I was lonely indeed—and as I did so, he disappeared. Or, so I thought. It was too dark to see. Yet, where his body had been, was now a darkness deeper than the darkness that surrounded me, and I felt a faint odor in my nostrils, delightful as the perfume of the rose. Then the walls at my back ceased to feel like stone but turned soft and commenced to collapse like the muddy sides of a riverbank. I could hear water pouring into our chamber, and then all I breathed was overcome by one whole stench—no question whether I could smell it!—I was in the rush of the river. Across from me was now a sight of the Elysian Fields, and the grain was golden and the sky blue, but the current tore through my legs in a tumult of forces. The wall receded from me even as I took each step. The stench grew worse, the waters rose above my head and I did not know how to swim. By the horror of my limbs, I knew I was sinking into fecal waters. Down on me came the outrages and squalors of life. The furies of my shame were choking my breath. I had no strength to contest these waters, and was ready to give up my will. But my shame began to expire as well. A peace that was like death itself, as darkness comes to the sky in the evening, was on my heart. I was ready. I would die my second death and know no more. Even the abominable onslaught of the offal ceased to be loathsome. I could smell the odor of a rose once more, indeed it was like a rose at evening.

Then, I heard the voice of my great-grandfather. "You do not have to perish," he said in my ear.

I knew what he meant. His thought had come already to my mind—it came with the peace that was like death itself. One might drown in the bowels of this river and be washed into the fields. The last of oneself would pass into the plants of the field.

Or—could one have a bold and final choice?—could one enter another fundament? At the center of radiance was pain.

I felt the shadow of my great-grandfather embrace my Ka. The sweet smell of the rose was no longer here. The stinks were upon us again. I loathed them. I did not wish to die a second time. Yet I did not know if I dared to enter the fundament of pain. For I was worthless, and my great-grandfather was damned and worthless, and we were beset by mighty curses. I felt the sorrow of his heart, however, come into me, and with a thought as beautiful as radiance itself: If the souls of the dead would try to reach the heavens of highest endeavor then they must look to mate with one another. But since the soul was no longer a man nor a woman, or to know it better, now contained all the men and women among whom one had lived, it might not matter in the Land of the Dead whether the vow was taken between a man and a woman, two men or two women, no, no more was required than that they would dare to share the same fate. By that blessing, for I saw this thought in great radiance, so was I also given a vision again of the absurd old man full of farts whom I had met in my tomb. His body had reeked of the Land of the Dead (inasmuch as he had had the stubbornness to swim the Duad, but not the strength to leave it) and now I perceived that in his loneliness, he wished for me to join him. The tales he had told our Pharaoh, had been told for me as well. It was I whom he wanted to trust him. And I did. Here in the Duad, in this hour, I would trust him.

I felt the Ka of Menenhetet expire. With one convulsion, the power of his heart came into me, and I knew that my youth (my demonically thwarted youth!) would be strengthened by his will, strong as the will of four men, and he was strong indeed.

Many lights appeared above my head, and they were like a ladder of lights with many rungs. I seized the first, and began to ascend from the river. The ladder twisted and was not easy to climb, but, as it swayed, the fields of gold on the other bank receded from me, as did the waters, and I took the rungs of this ladder one by one, and each rung was as strong as the umbilical cord of each person I had known well, and I felt the embrace of their bodies. They came about me as I climbed and held my arms, and I could not move to the next rung until I lived with the honest thought of how I loved them or how I did not, and recalled all I loved most in each, and all I loved least. There was every loss in my limbs as I passed again through the early love of my mother, but I had to grapple up the rungs of her fear of me when I was no longer a child but her lover, and I wept for Ptah-nem-hotep that He had not become a greater man but a smaller one, and tasted His expiring love for Himself in the fatigues of my breath, yes, and I went up on the spirits of the dead until I was high above the Pyramid.

Now, Honey-Ball and Nefertiri were near, and I climbed as if the arms of Usermare were for my use, and the head of Hera-Ra was like my own. I saw again a vision of great cities to come, and knew the strength of the Ka must be great. For even as the tender force of the flower breaks through the stone, so would the strength of the Ka be immense if its true desire were opposed. And thereby, as I ascended the ladder, I could know the purpose of my Ka by the presence of our strength. So I mounted on this ladder of lights to that place in the heavens where one might gaze like Osiris upon the portents of all that is ahead, and try to turn the storm before it breaks. All the while I knew the fear that I was not pure enough for such a task, nor my great-grandfather, and neither of us could offer a feather to lie upon the heart as nicely as the sense of right and wrong. Then I saw my Ba, saw that small bird whose face was my own face, and I had not seen it since it flew away as my Ka approached its tomb. It was here above me now, the soul of my heart even as the Ka was my Double, and so the Ba could tell me that purity and goodness were worth less to Osiris than strength. Menenhetet would not be used because he was a good man, but because he was a strong one. Indeed, the Lord Osiris might be as desperate as ourselves when it came to choosing His troops. Such was the thought of the Ba, the purest part of my heart.

Yet, my Ka replied that nothing could be worth more to the Ka than to know its purpose, and that I felt by the presence of our strength as I went up the ladder. I think all magic was at my feet. As I climbed, I saw the moon, and Osiris was in it waiting for me, and by either arm was Horus and Set. I was near to the Boat of Ra. All that was in me shifted, even Time itself.

For, now, a comet approaches. I suffer the onslaught of a frightful wind. A pain is coming that will be like no pain felt before. I hear the scream of earth exploding. In this terror, vast as the abyss, I still know more than fear. Here, at the center of pain is radiance. May my hope of heaven now prove equal to my ignorance of where I go. Whether I am the Second or the First Menenhetet, or the creature of our twice seven separate souls and lights, I would hardly declare, and so I do not know if I will labor in greed forever among the demonic or serve some noble purpose I cannot name.

By this I am told that I must enter into the power of the word. For the first sound to come out of the will had to traverse the fundament of pain. So I cry out in the voice of the newly born at the mystery of my first breath, and enter the Boat of Ra.

We sail across dominions barely seen, washed by the swells of time. We plow through fields of magnetism. Past and future come together on thunderheads and our dead hearts live with lightning in the wounds of the Gods.

1972–1982

Born in 1923 in Long Branch, New Jersey, and raised in Brooklyn, NORMAN MAILER was one of the most influential writers of the second half of the twentieth century and a leading public intellectual for nearly sixty years. He is the author of more than forty books. *The Castle in the Forest,* his last novel, was his eleventh *New York Times* best-seller. His first novel, *The Naked and the Dead,* has never gone out of print. His 1968 nonfiction narrative, *The Armies of the Night,* won the Pulitzer Prize and the National Book Award. He won a second Pulitzer for *The Executioner's Song* and is the only person to date to have won Pulitzers in both fiction and nonfiction. Five of his books were nominated for National Book Awards, and he won a lifetime achievement award from the National Book Foundation in 2005. Mr. Mailer died in 2007 in New York City.